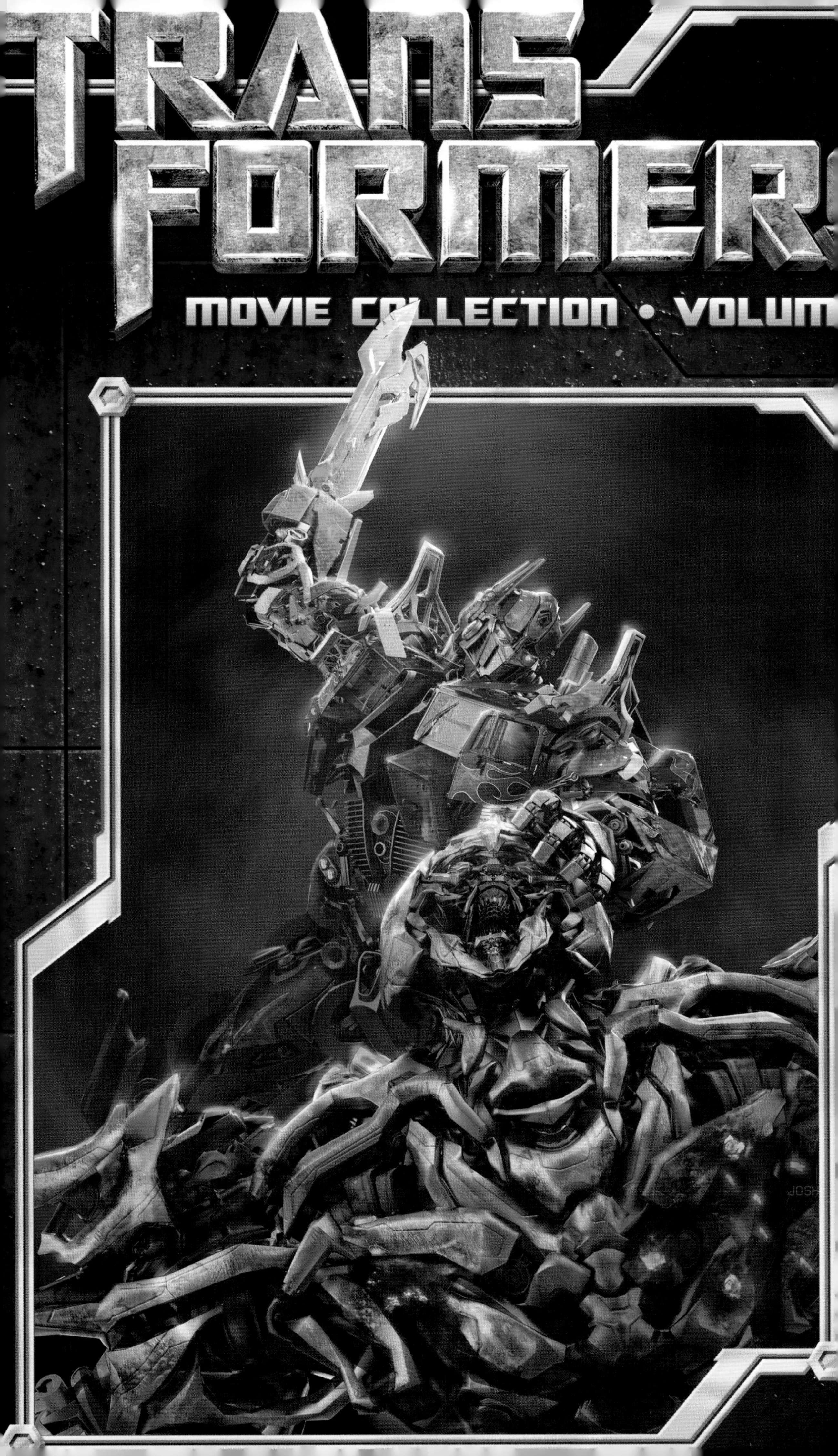
TRANS
FORMER
MOVIE COLLECTION • VOLUM

ISBN: 978-1-60010-643-9

13 12 11 10   1 2 3 4

Special thanks to Hasbro's Aaron Archer, Michael Kelly, Amie Lozanski, Ed Lane, Michael Provost, Val Roca, Erin Hillman, Jos Huxley, Samantha Lomow, and Michael Verrecchia for their invaluable assistance.

Licensed By:

IDW Publishing
Operations:
Ted Adams, Chief Executive Officer
Greg Goldstein, Chief Operating Officer
Matthew Ruzicka, CPA, Chief Financial Officer
Alan Payne, VP of Sales
Lorelei Bunjes, Dir. of Digital Services
AnnaMaria White, Marketing & PR Manager
Marci Hubbard, Executive Assistant
Alonzo Simon, Shipping Manager
Angela Loggins, Staff Accountant

Editorial:
Chris Ryall, Publisher/Editor-in-Chief
Scott Dunbier, Editor, Special Projects
Andy Schmidt, Senior Editor
Bob Schreck, Senior Editor
Justin Eisinger, Editor
Kris Oprisko, Editor/Foreign Lic.
Denton J. Tipton, Editor
Tom Waltz, Editor
Mariah Huehner, Associate Editor
Carlos Guzman, Editorial Assistant

Design:
Robbie Robbins, EVP/Sr. Graphic Artist
Neil Uyetake, Art Director
Chris Mowry, Graphic Artist
Amauri Osorio, Graphic Artist
Gilberto Lazcano, Production Assistant

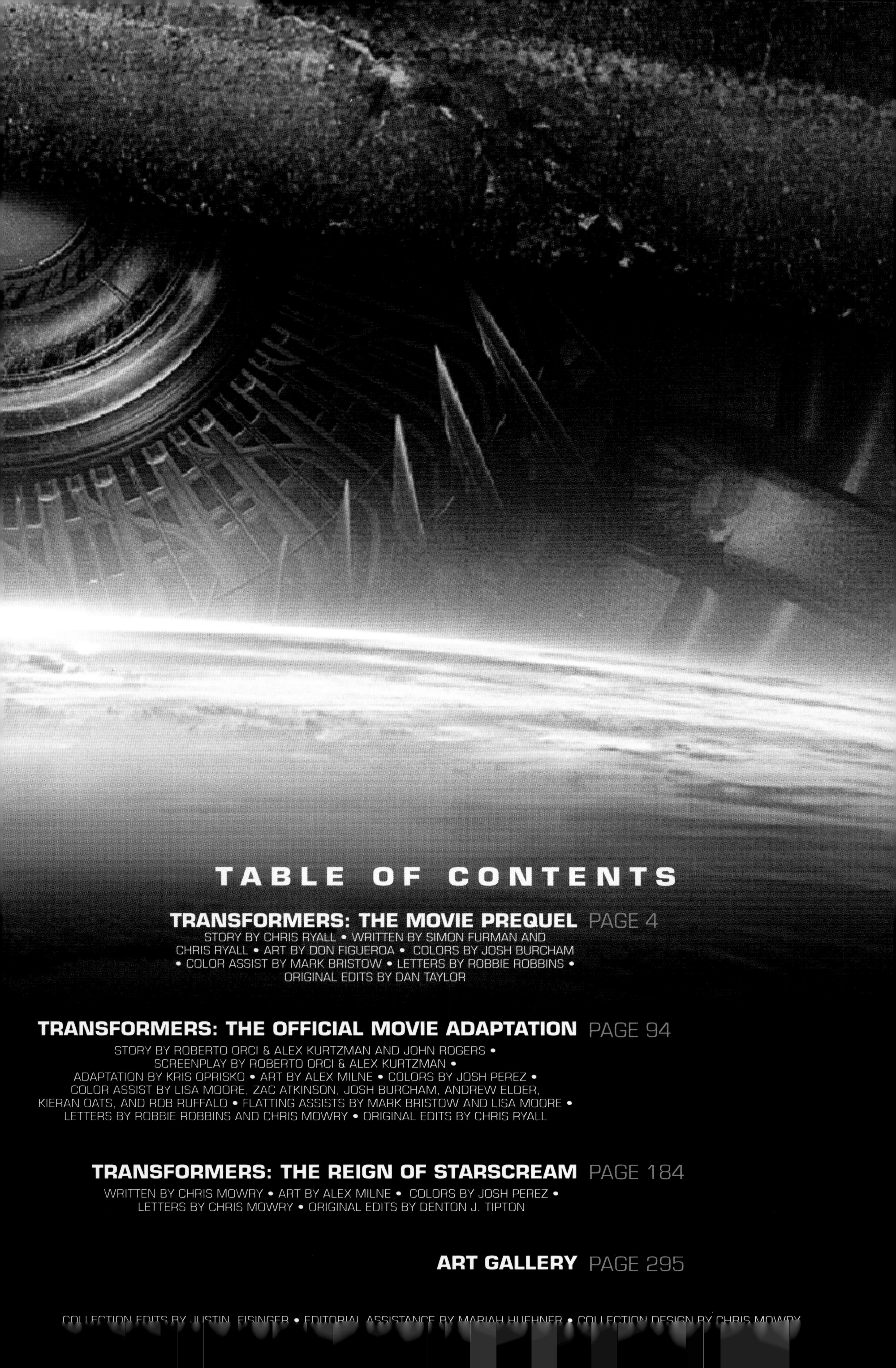

TABLE OF CONTENTS

COLLECTION EDITS BY JUSTIN EISINGER • EDITORIAL ASSISTANCE BY MARIAH HUEHNER • COLLECTION DESIGN BY CHRIS MOWRY

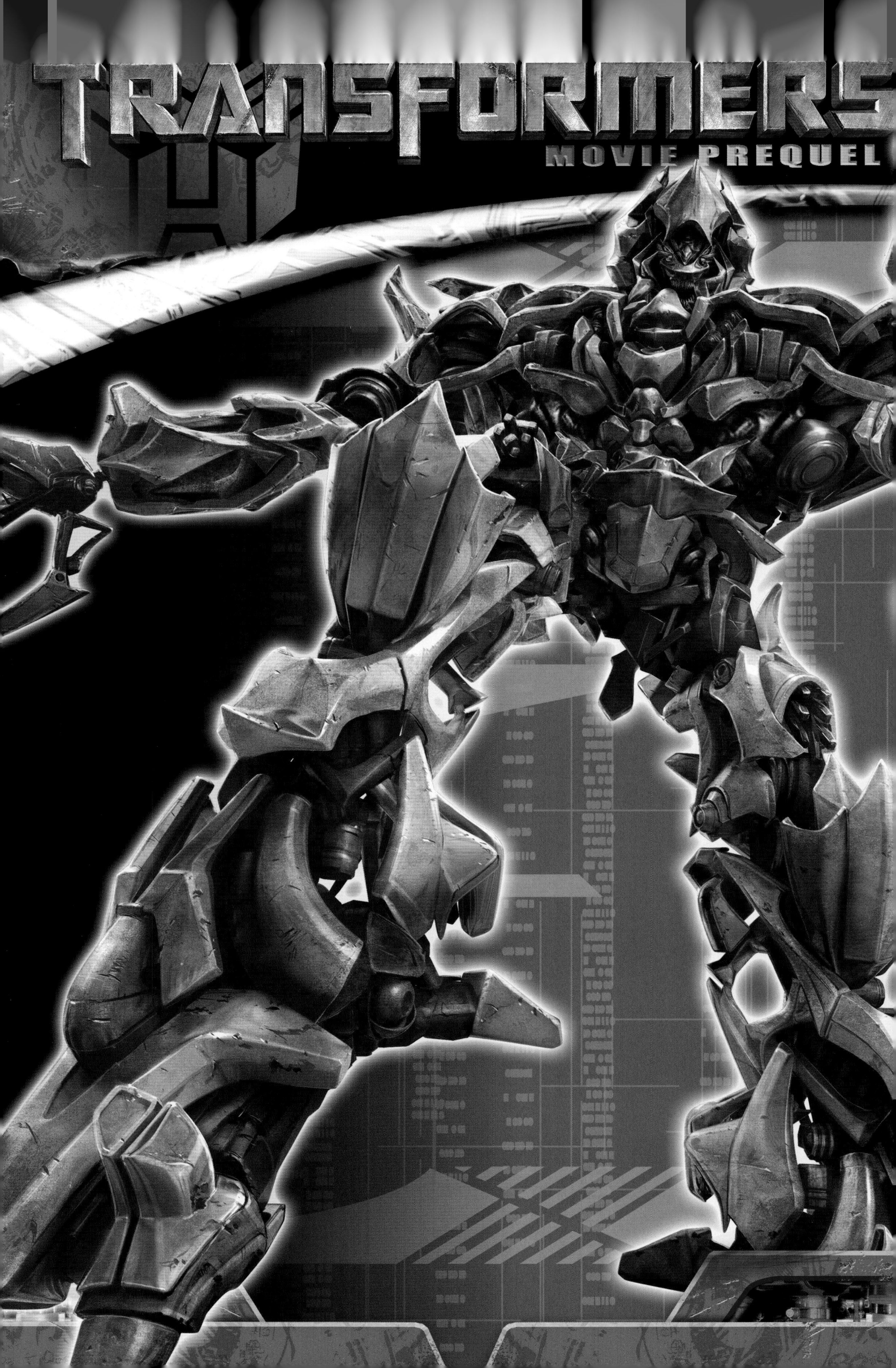
TRANSFORMERS
MOVIE PREQUEL

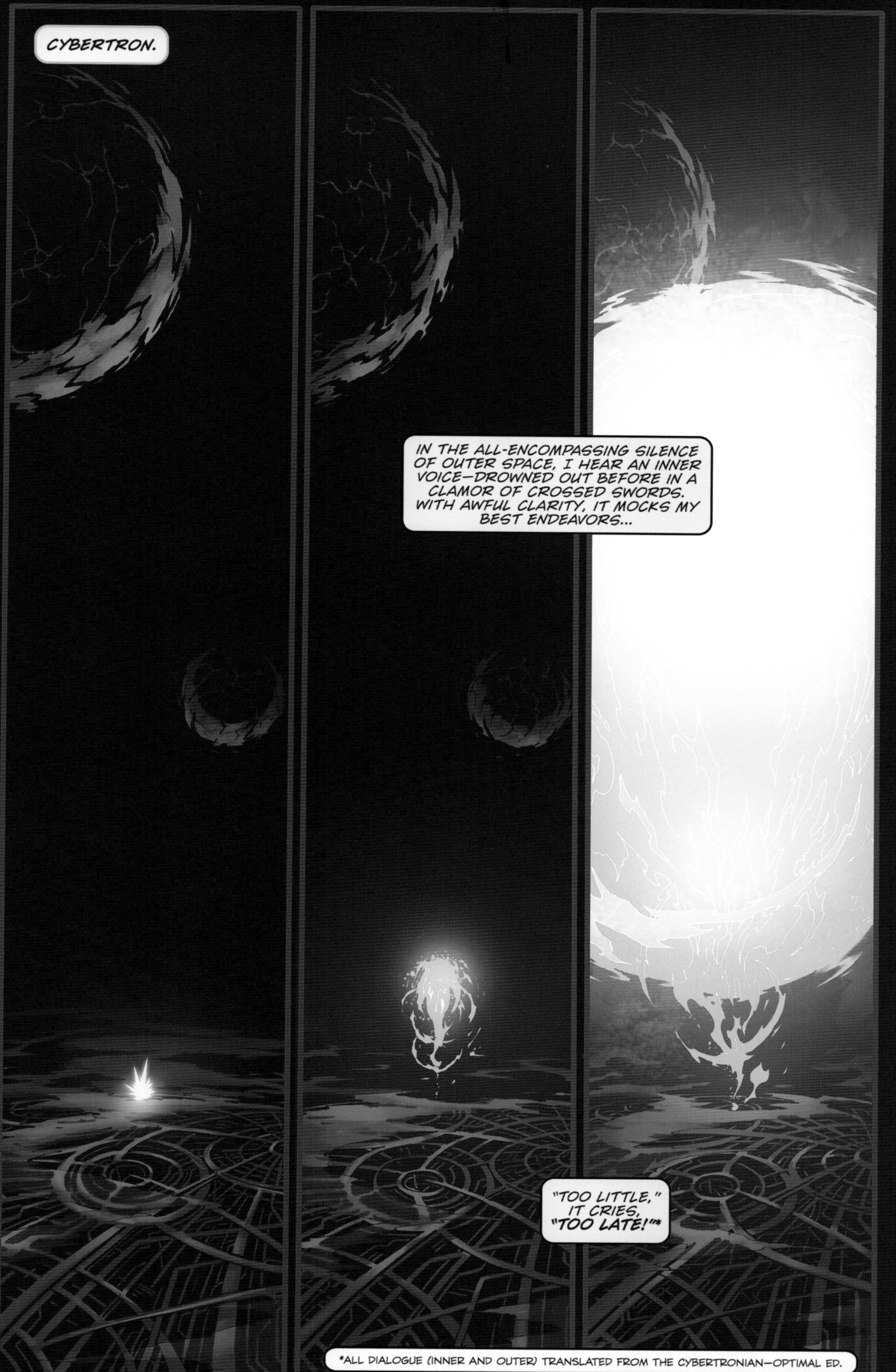
CYBERTRON.
IN THE ALL-ENCOMPASSING SILENCE OF OUTER SPACE, I HEAR AN INNER VOICE—DROWNED OUT BEFORE IN A CLAMOR OF CROSSED SWORDS. WITH AWFUL CLARITY, IT MOCKS MY BEST ENDEAVORS...
"TOO LITTLE," IT CRIES, "TOO LATE!"*
*ALL DIALOGUE (INNER AND OUTER) TRANSLATED FROM THE CYBERTRONIAN—OPTIMAL ED.

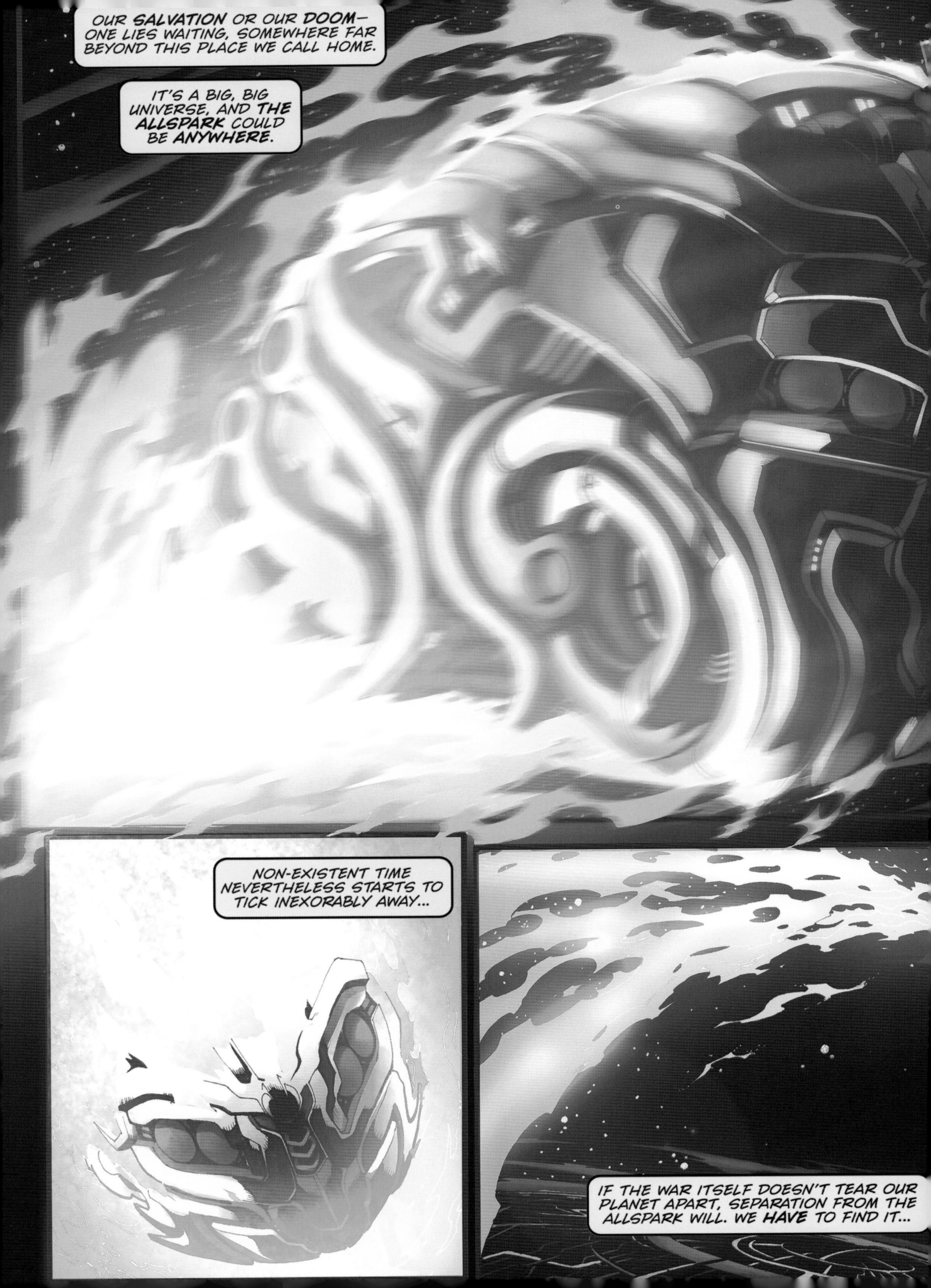
OUR SALVATION OR OUR DOOM—ONE LIES WAITING, SOMEWHERE FAR BEYOND THIS PLACE WE CALL HOME.
IT'S A BIG, BIG UNIVERSE, AND THE ALLSPARK COULD BE ANYWHERE.
NON-EXISTENT TIME NEVERTHELESS STARTS TO TICK INEXORABLY AWAY...
IF THE WAR ITSELF DOESN'T TEAR OUR PLANET APART, SEPARATION FROM THE ALLSPARK WILL. WE HAVE TO FIND IT...

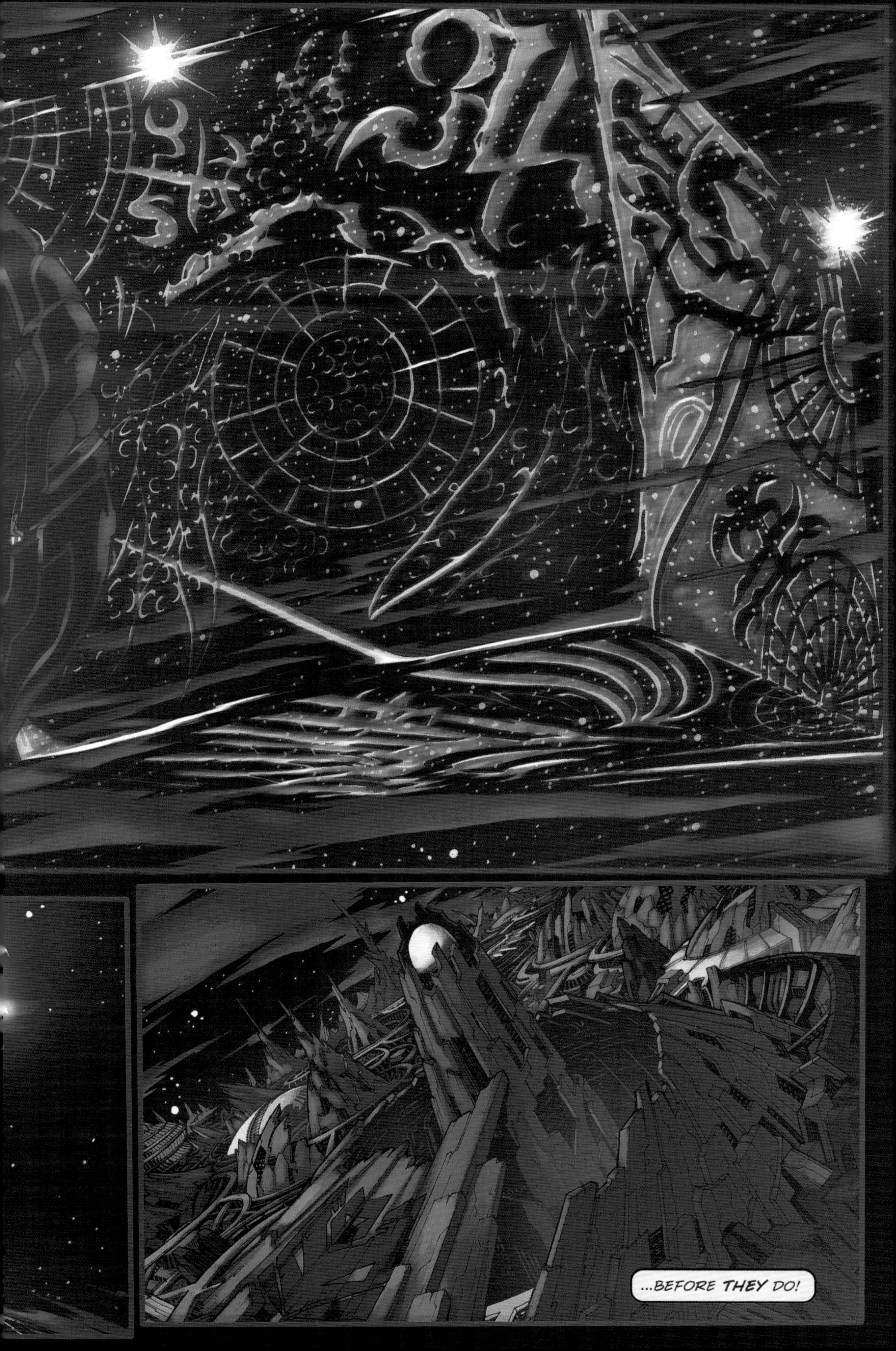
...BEFORE THEY DO!

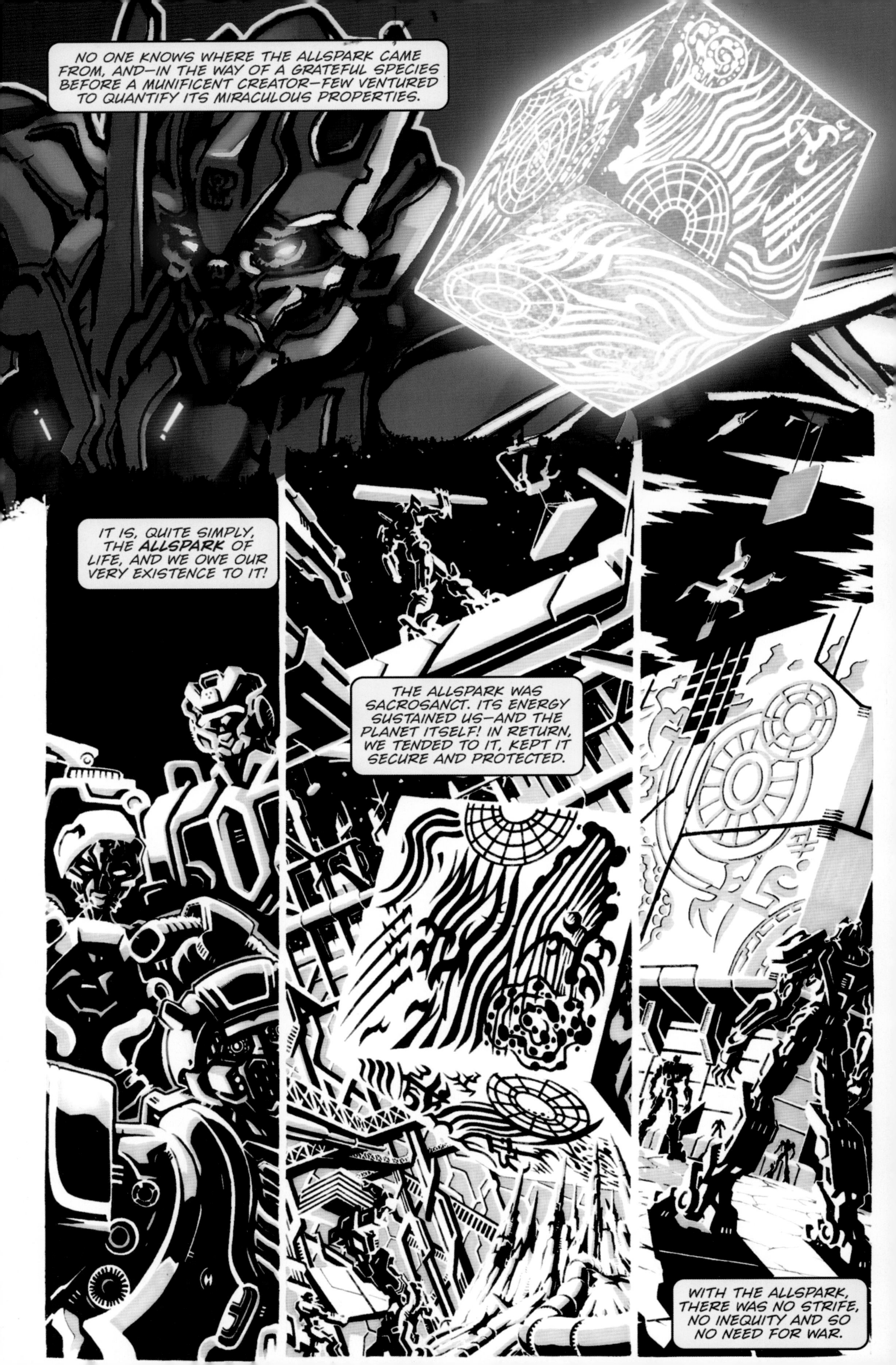
NO ONE KNOWS WHERE THE ALLSPARK CAME FROM, AND—IN THE WAY OF A GRATEFUL SPECIES BEFORE A MUNIFICENT CREATOR—FEW VENTURED TO QUANTIFY ITS MIRACULOUS PROPERTIES.
IT IS, QUITE SIMPLY, THE **ALLSPARK** OF LIFE, AND WE OWE OUR VERY EXISTENCE TO IT!
THE ALLSPARK WAS SACROSANCT. ITS ENERGY SUSTAINED US—AND THE PLANET ITSELF! IN RETURN, WE TENDED TO IT, KEPT IT SECURE AND PROTECTED.
WITH THE ALLSPARK, THERE WAS NO STRIFE, NO INEQUITY AND SO NO NEED FOR WAR.

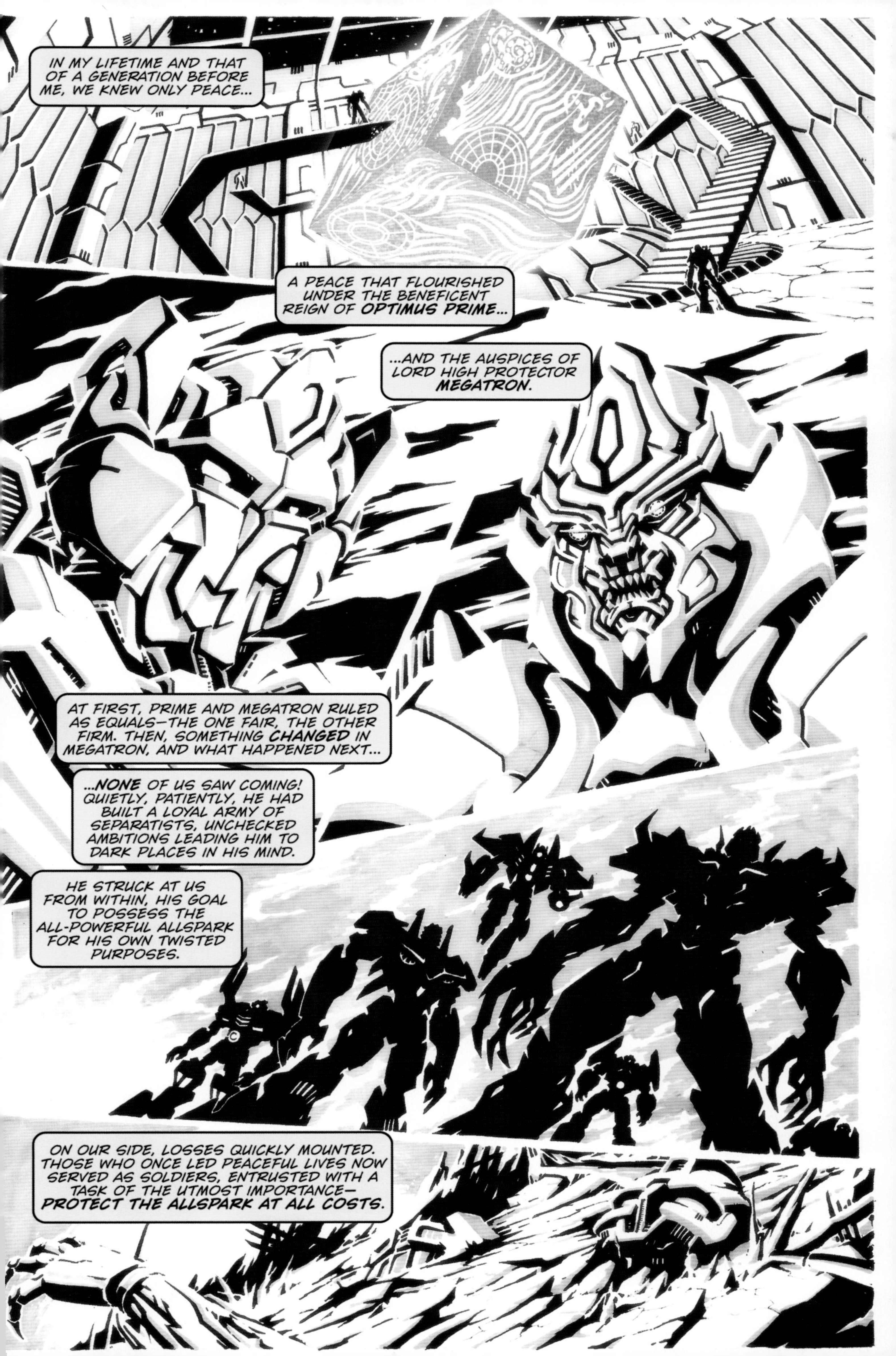

IN MY LIFETIME AND THAT OF A GENERATION BEFORE ME, WE KNEW ONLY PEACE...
A PEACE THAT FLOURISHED UNDER THE BENEFICENT REIGN OF **OPTIMUS PRIME**...
...AND THE AUSPICES OF LORD HIGH PROTECTOR **MEGATRON**.
AT FIRST, PRIME AND MEGATRON RULED AS EQUALS—THE ONE FAIR, THE OTHER FIRM. THEN, SOMETHING **CHANGED** IN MEGATRON, AND WHAT HAPPENED NEXT...
...**NONE** OF US SAW COMING! QUIETLY, PATIENTLY, HE HAD BUILT A LOYAL ARMY OF SEPARATISTS, UNCHECKED AMBITIONS LEADING HIM TO DARK PLACES IN HIS MIND.
HE STRUCK AT US FROM WITHIN, HIS GOAL TO POSSESS THE ALL-POWERFUL ALLSPARK FOR HIS OWN TWISTED PURPOSES.
ON OUR SIDE, LOSSES QUICKLY MOUNTED. THOSE WHO ONCE LED PEACEFUL LIVES NOW SERVED AS SOLDIERS, ENTRUSTED WITH A TASK OF THE UTMOST IMPORTANCE—**PROTECT THE ALLSPARK AT ALL COSTS**.

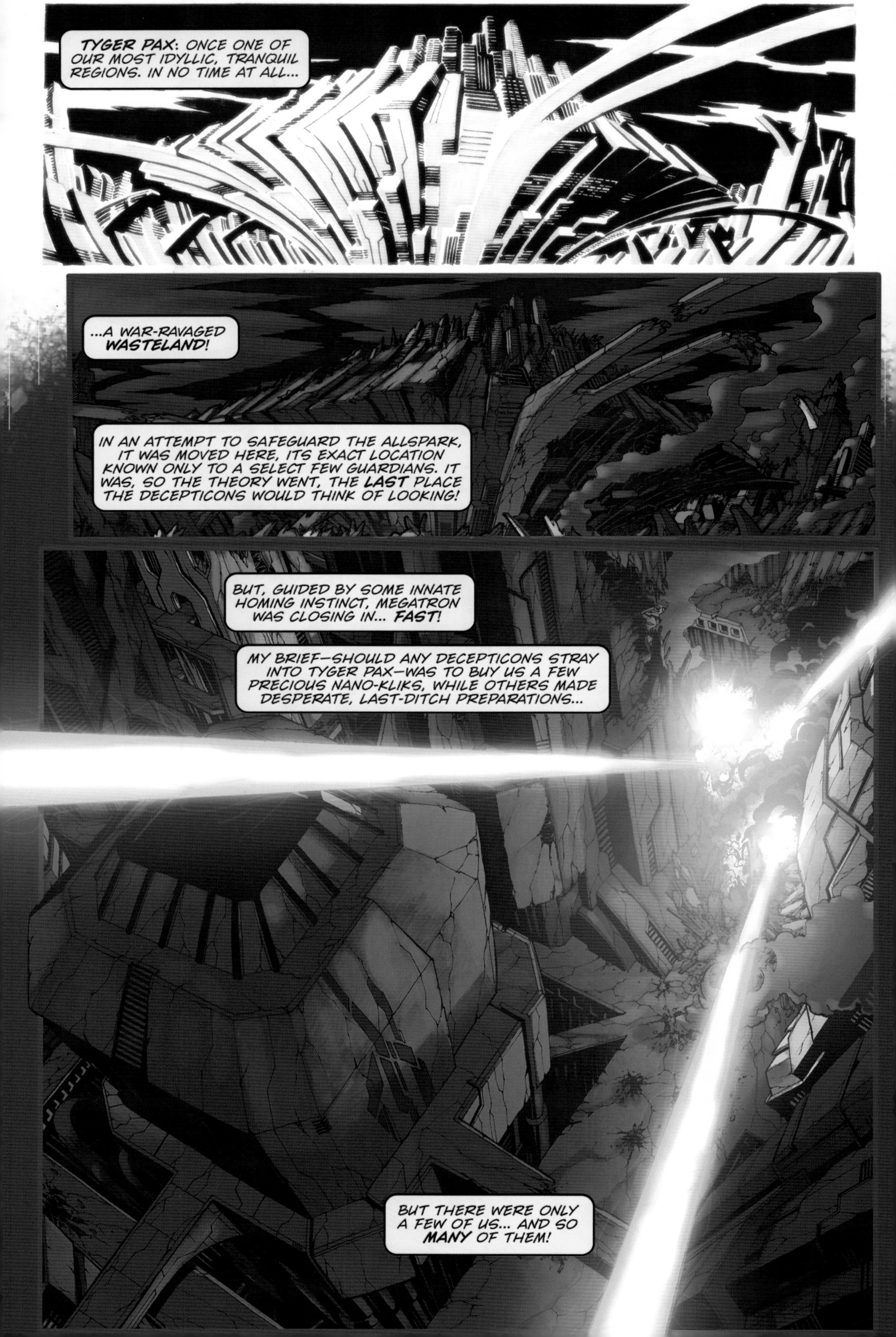

TYGER PAX: ONCE ONE OF OUR MOST IDYLLIC, TRANQUIL REGIONS. IN NO TIME AT ALL...
...A WAR-RAVAGED WASTELAND!
IN AN ATTEMPT TO SAFEGUARD THE ALLSPARK, IT WAS MOVED HERE, ITS EXACT LOCATION KNOWN ONLY TO A SELECT FEW GUARDIANS. IT WAS, SO THE THEORY WENT, THE LAST PLACE THE DECEPTICONS WOULD THINK OF LOOKING!
BUT, GUIDED BY SOME INNATE HOMING INSTINCT, MEGATRON WAS CLOSING IN... FAST!
MY BRIEF—SHOULD ANY DECEPTICONS STRAY INTO TYGER PAX—WAS TO BUY US A FEW PRECIOUS NANO-KLIKS, WHILE OTHERS MADE DESPERATE, LAST-DITCH PREPARATIONS...
BUT THERE WERE ONLY A FEW OF US... AND SO MANY OF THEM!

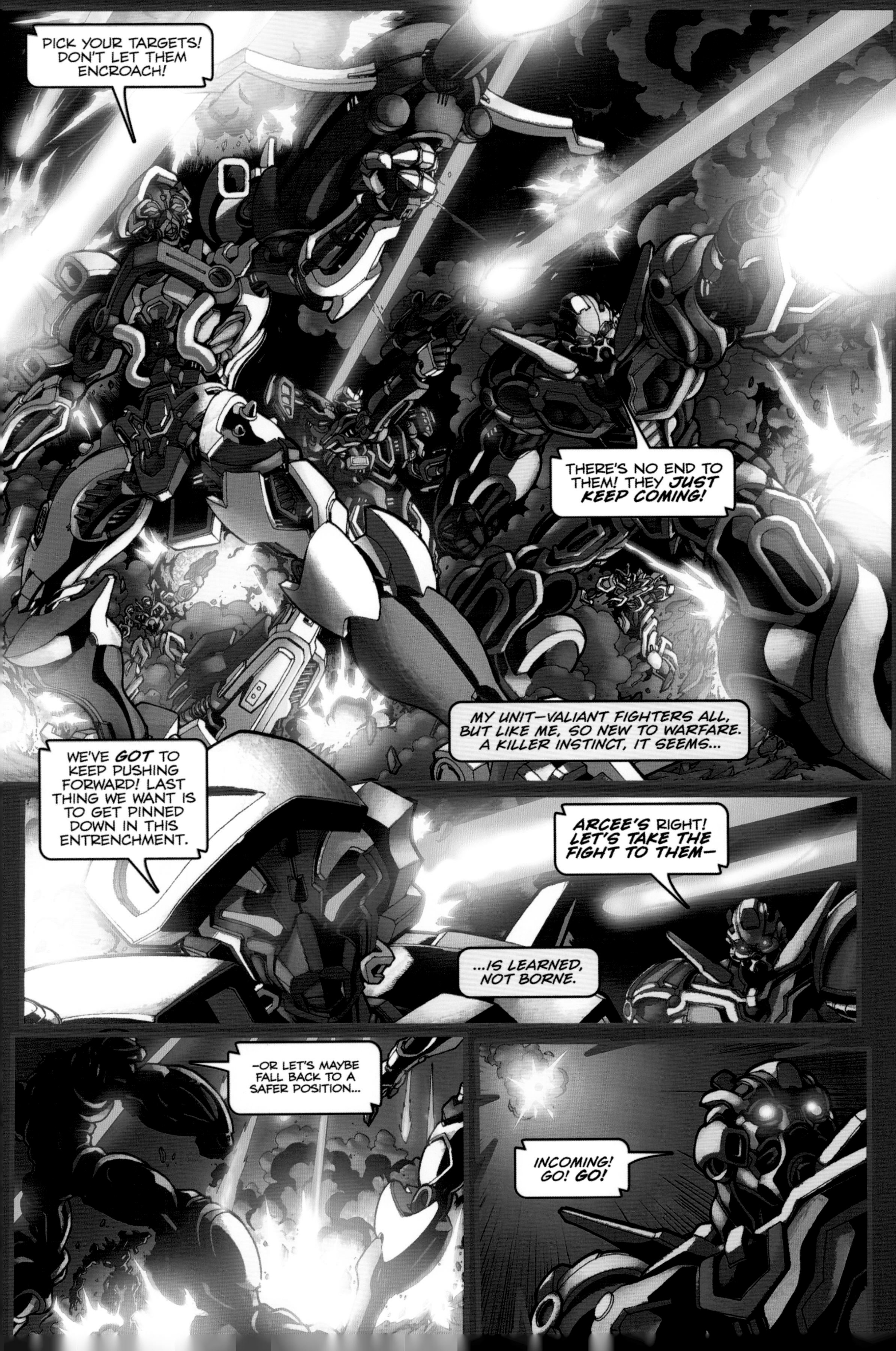
PICK YOUR TARGETS! DON'T LET THEM ENCROACH!
THERE'S NO END TO THEM! THEY **JUST KEEP COMING!**
MY UNIT—VALIANT FIGHTERS ALL, BUT LIKE ME, SO NEW TO WARFARE. A KILLER INSTINCT, IT SEEMS...
WE'VE **GOT** TO KEEP PUSHING FORWARD! LAST THING WE WANT IS TO GET PINNED DOWN IN THIS ENTRENCHMENT.
ARCEE'S RIGHT! **LET'S TAKE THE FIGHT TO THEM**—
...IS LEARNED, NOT BORNE.
—OR LET'S MAYBE FALL BACK TO A SAFER POSITION...
INCOMING! GO! **GO!**

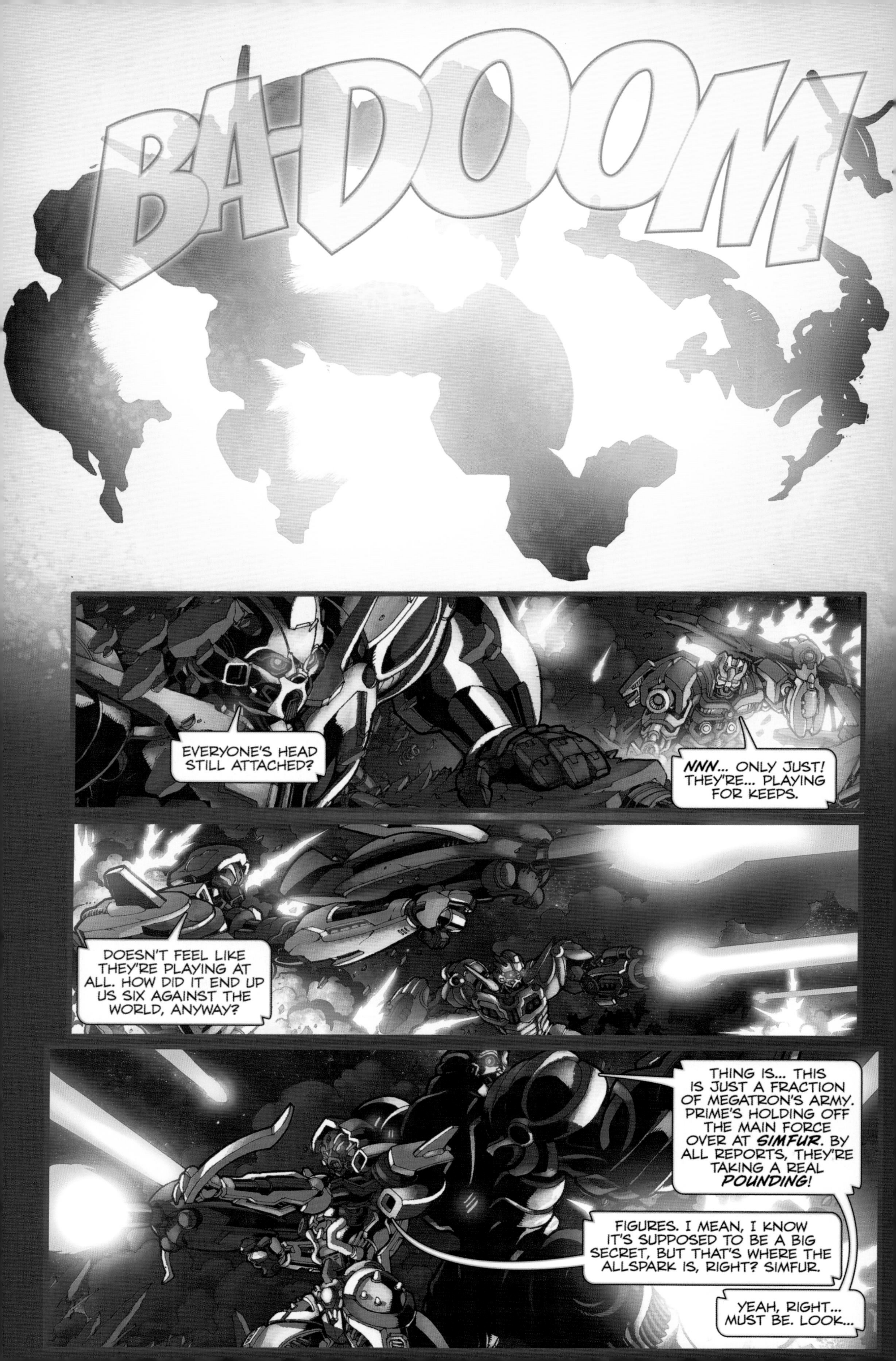
BA-DOOM
EVERYONE'S HEAD STILL ATTACHED?
NNN... ONLY JUST! THEY'RE... PLAYING FOR KEEPS.
DOESN'T FEEL LIKE THEY'RE PLAYING AT ALL. HOW DID IT END UP US SIX AGAINST THE WORLD, ANYWAY?
THING IS... THIS IS JUST A FRACTION OF MEGATRON'S ARMY. PRIME'S HOLDING OFF THE MAIN FORCE OVER AT SIMFUR. BY ALL REPORTS, THEY'RE TAKING A REAL POUNDING!
FIGURES. I MEAN, I KNOW IT'S SUPPOSED TO BE A BIG SECRET, BUT THAT'S WHERE THE ALLSPARK IS, RIGHT? SIMFUR.
YEAH, RIGHT... MUST BE. LOOK...

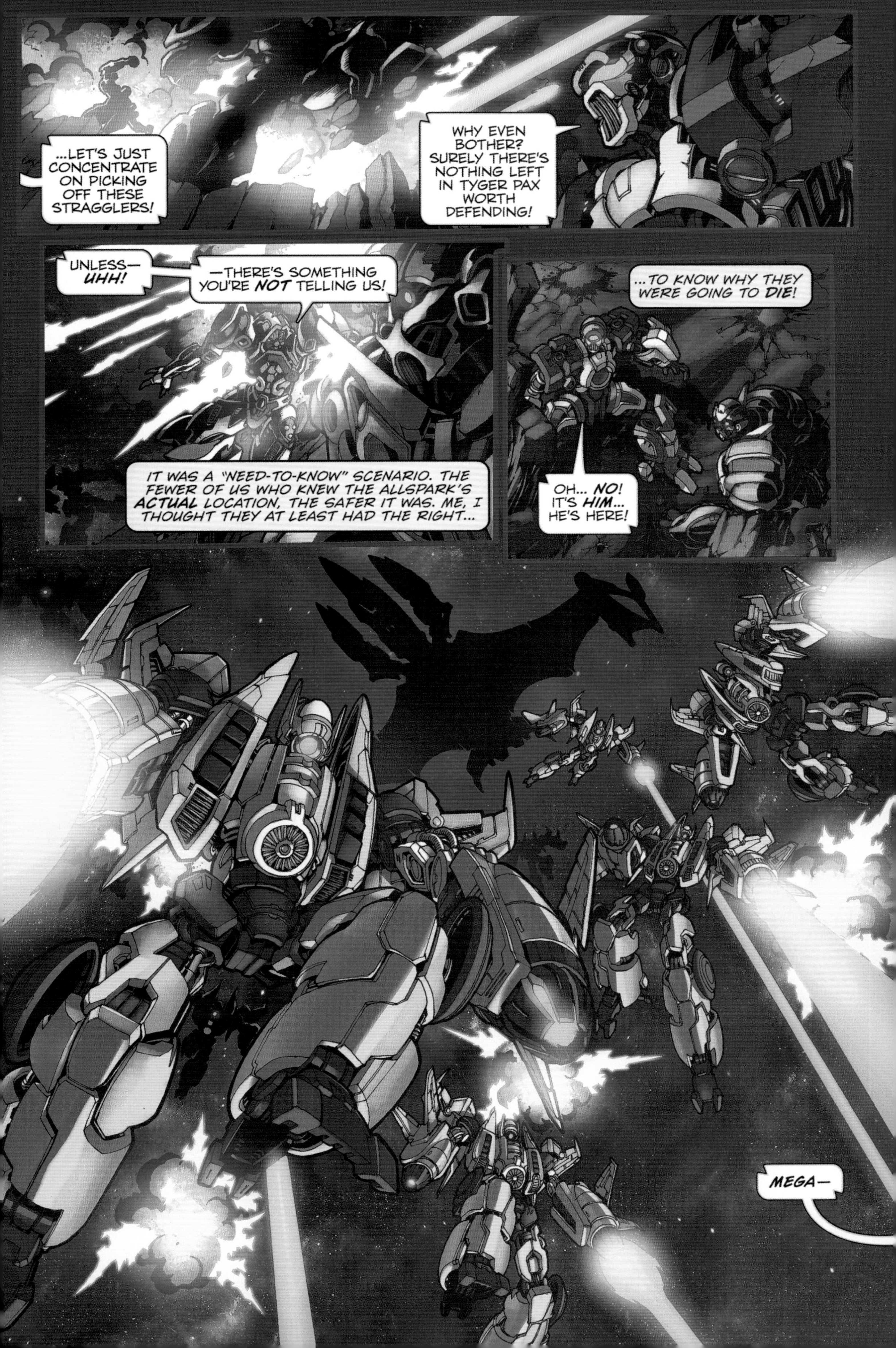
...LET'S JUST CONCENTRATE ON PICKING OFF THESE STRAGGLERS!
WHY EVEN BOTHER? SURELY THERE'S NOTHING LEFT IN TYGER PAX WORTH DEFENDING!
UNLESS— UHH!
—THERE'S SOMETHING YOU'RE NOT TELLING US!
IT WAS A "NEED-TO-KNOW" SCENARIO. THE FEWER OF US WHO KNEW THE ALLSPARK'S ACTUAL LOCATION, THE SAFER IT WAS. ME, I THOUGHT THEY AT LEAST HAD THE RIGHT...
...TO KNOW WHY THEY WERE GOING TO DIE!
OH... NO! IT'S HIM... HE'S HERE!
MEGA—

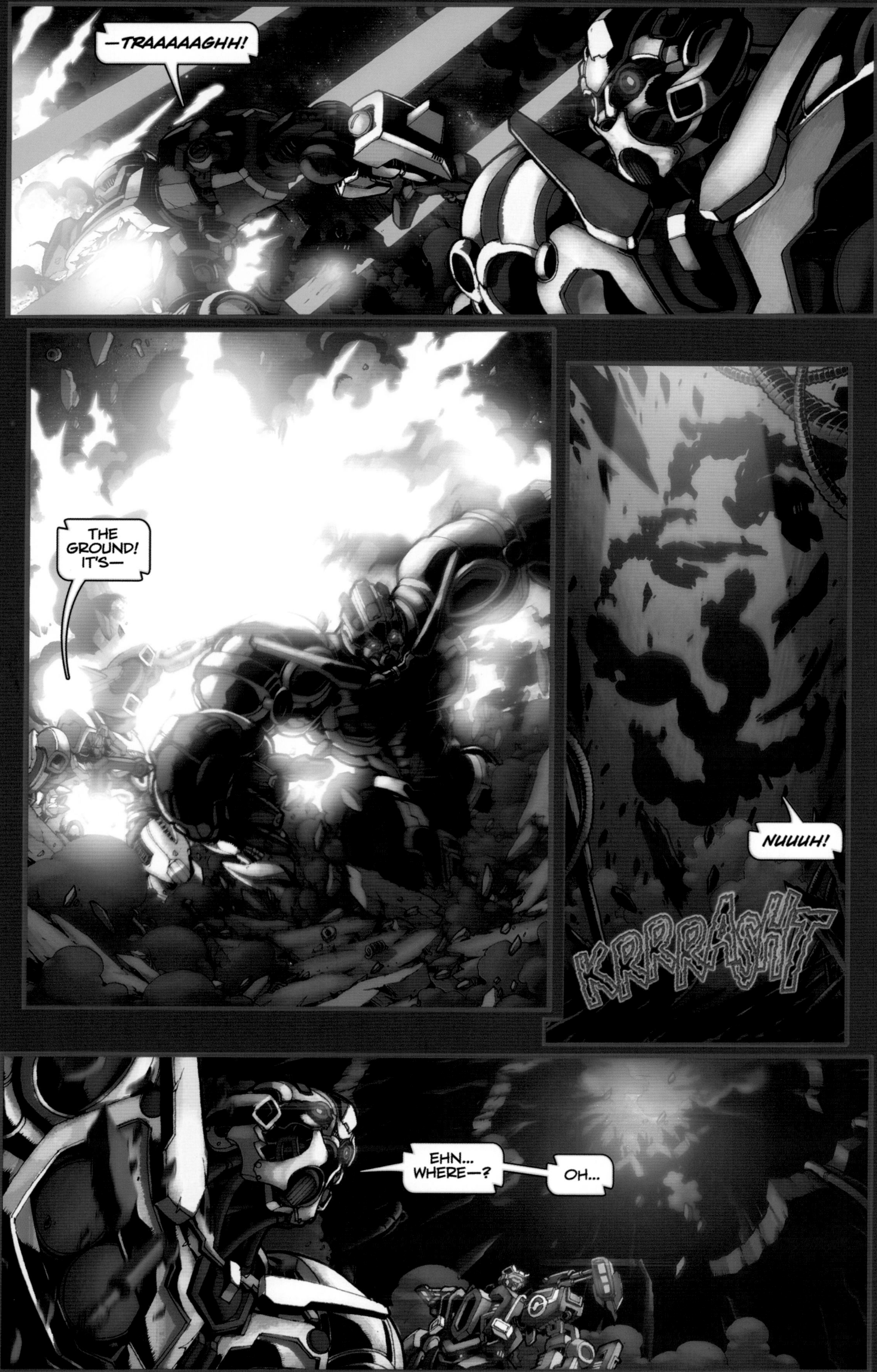
—TRAAAAAAGHH!
THE GROUND! IT'S—
NUUUH!
KRRRASHT
EHN... WHERE—?
OH...

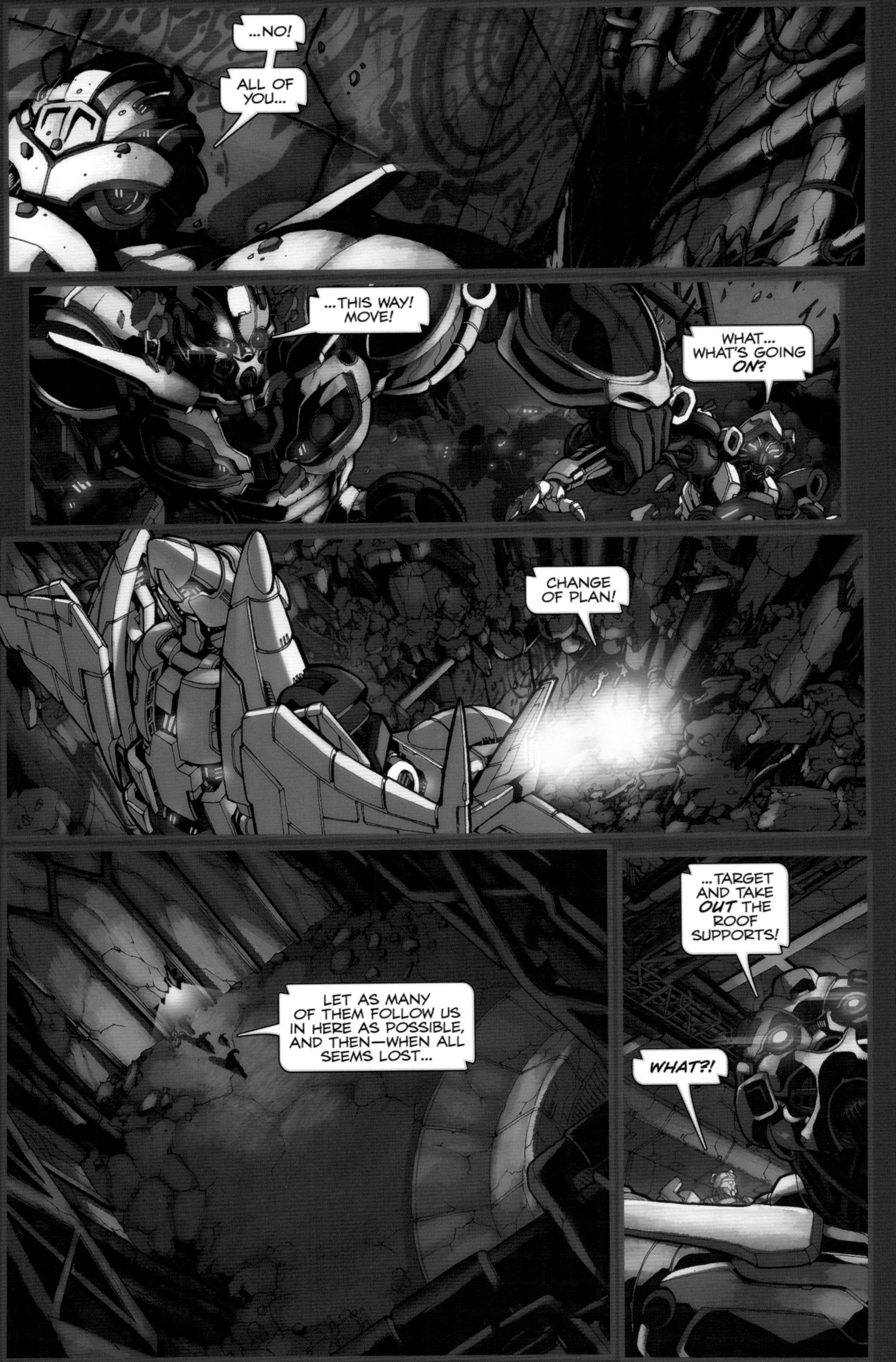
...NO!
ALL OF YOU...
...THIS WAY! MOVE!
WHAT... WHAT'S GOING ON?
CHANGE OF PLAN!
LET AS MANY OF THEM FOLLOW US IN HERE AS POSSIBLE, AND THEN—WHEN ALL SEEMS LOST...
...TARGET AND TAKE OUT THE ROOF SUPPORTS!
WHAT?!

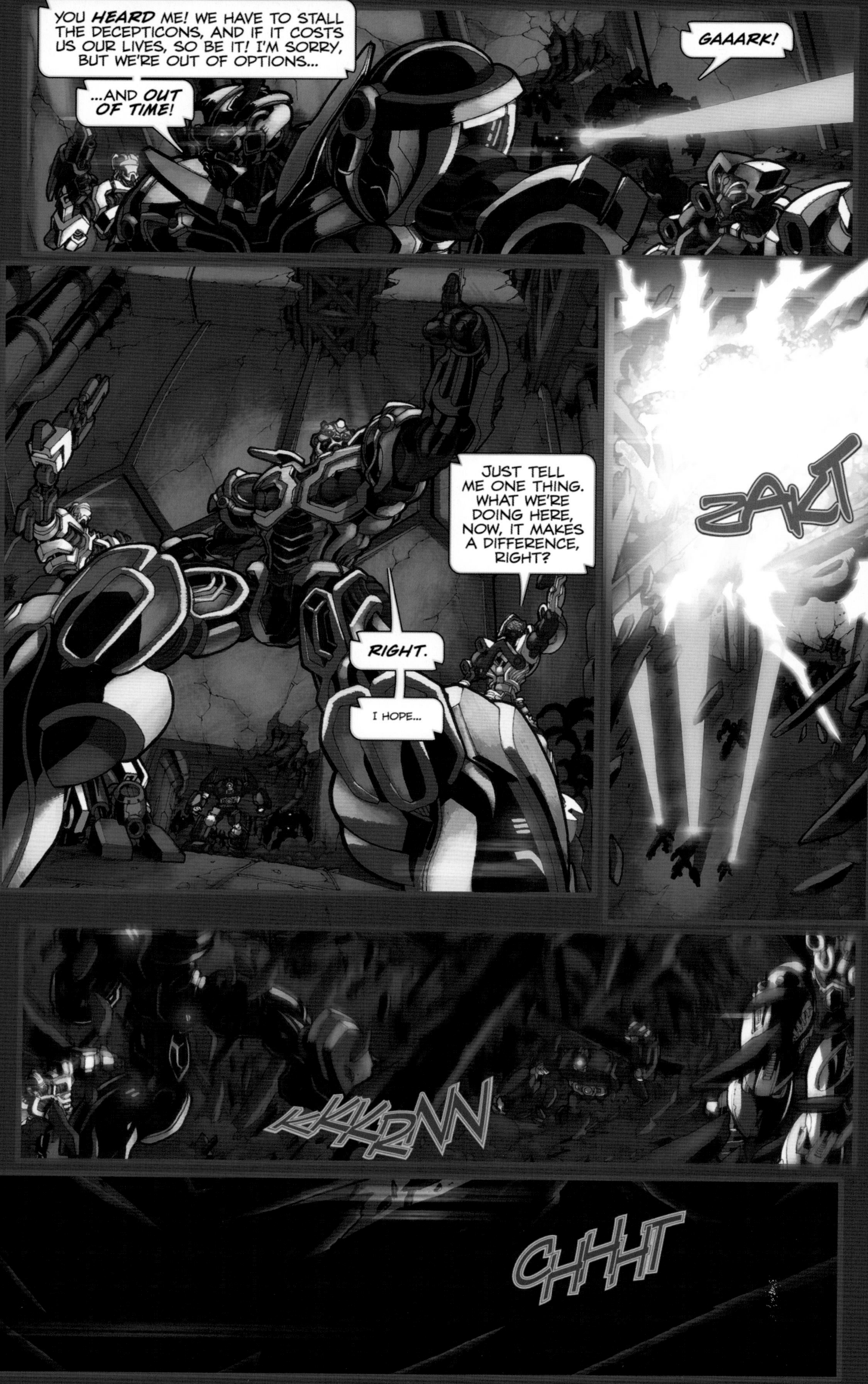
YOU HEARD ME! WE HAVE TO STALL THE DECEPTICONS, AND IF IT COSTS US OUR LIVES, SO BE IT! I'M SORRY, BUT WE'RE OUT OF OPTIONS...
...AND OUT OF TIME!
GAAARK!
JUST TELL ME ONE THING. WHAT WE'RE DOING HERE, NOW, IT MAKES A DIFFERENCE, RIGHT?
RIGHT.
I HOPE...
ZAKT
KKKKRNN
CHHHT

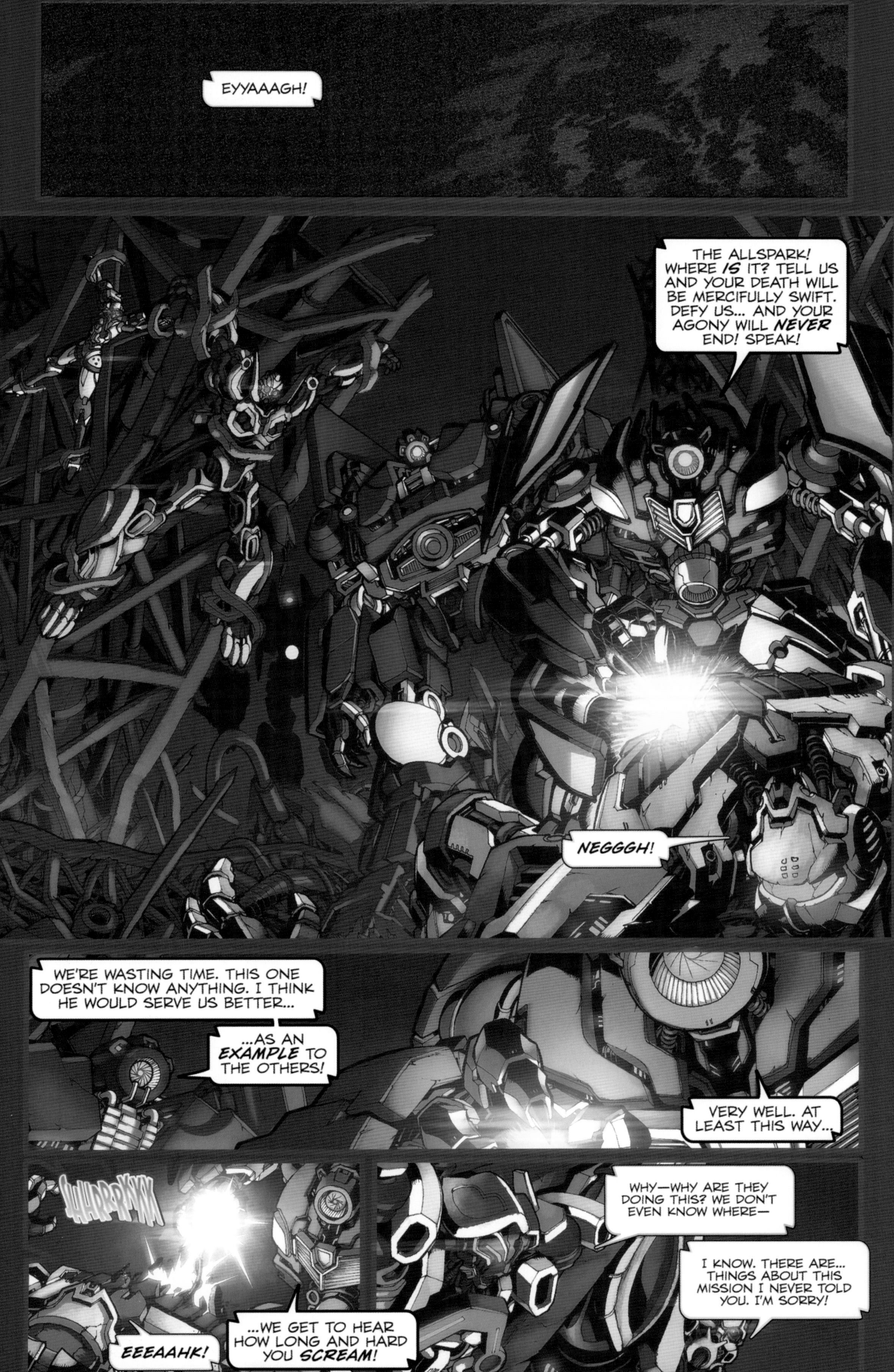
EYYAAAGH!
THE ALLSPARK! WHERE *IS* IT? TELL US AND YOUR DEATH WILL BE MERCIFULLY SWIFT. DEFY US... AND YOUR AGONY WILL ***NEVER*** END! SPEAK!
NEGGGH!
WE'RE WASTING TIME. THIS ONE DOESN'T KNOW ANYTHING. I THINK HE WOULD SERVE US BETTER...
...AS AN ***EXAMPLE*** TO THE OTHERS!
VERY WELL. AT LEAST THIS WAY...
EEEAAHK!
...WE GET TO HEAR HOW LONG AND HARD YOU ***SCREAM!***
WHY—WHY ARE THEY DOING THIS? WE DON'T EVEN KNOW WHERE—
I KNOW. THERE ARE... THINGS ABOUT THIS MISSION I NEVER TOLD YOU. I'M SORRY!

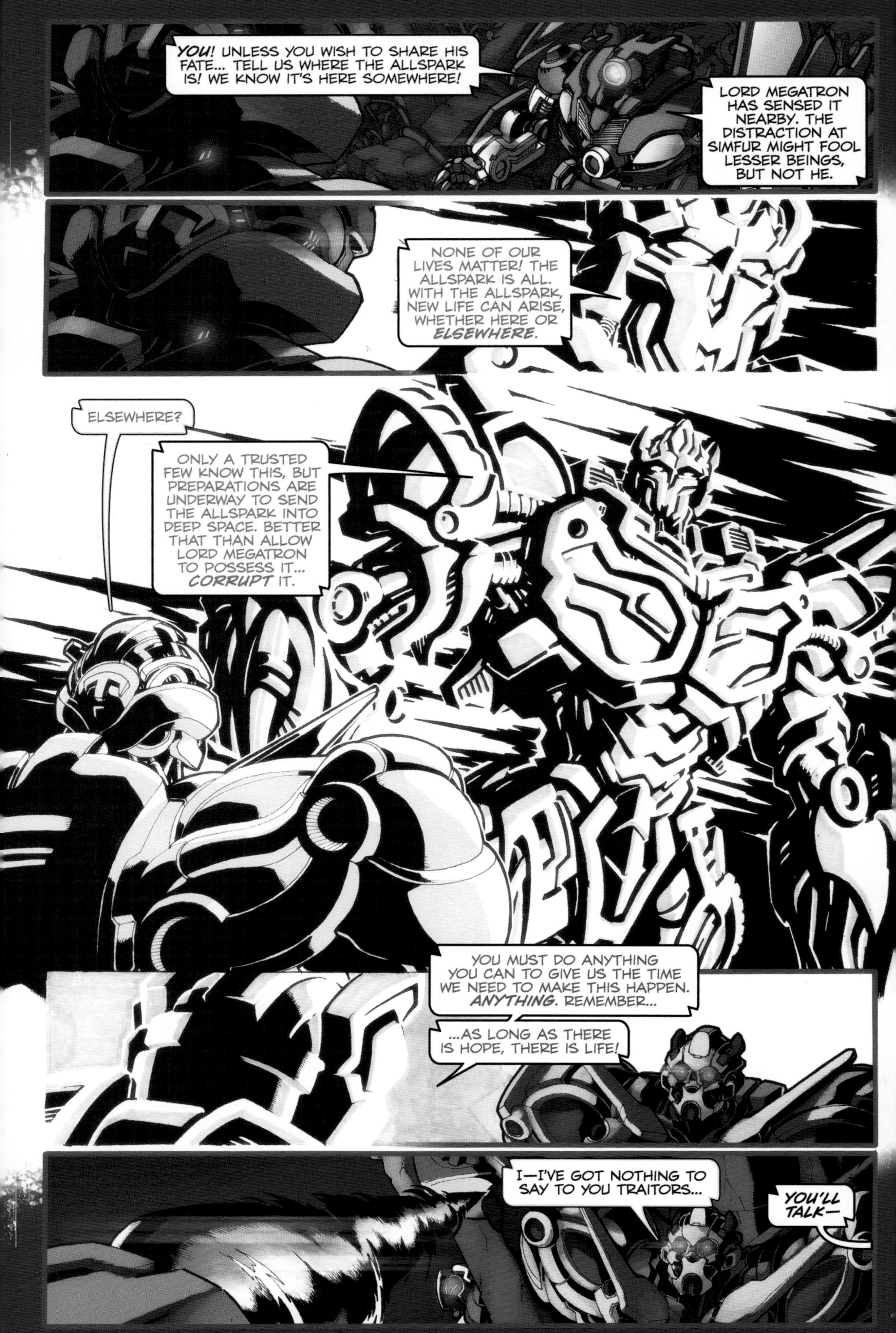

YOU! UNLESS YOU WISH TO SHARE HIS FATE... TELL US WHERE THE ALLSPARK IS! WE KNOW IT'S HERE SOMEWHERE!
LORD MEGATRON HAS SENSED IT NEARBY. THE DISTRACTION AT SIMFUR MIGHT FOOL LESSER BEINGS, BUT NOT HE.
NONE OF OUR LIVES MATTER! THE ALLSPARK IS ALL. WITH THE ALLSPARK, NEW LIFE CAN ARISE, WHETHER HERE OR ELSEWHERE.
ELSEWHERE?
ONLY A TRUSTED FEW KNOW THIS, BUT PREPARATIONS ARE UNDERWAY TO SEND THE ALLSPARK INTO DEEP SPACE. BETTER THAT THAN ALLOW LORD MEGATRON TO POSSESS IT... CORRUPT IT.
YOU MUST DO ANYTHING YOU CAN TO GIVE US THE TIME WE NEED TO MAKE THIS HAPPEN. ANYTHING. REMEMBER...
...AS LONG AS THERE IS HOPE, THERE IS LIFE!
I—I'VE GOT NOTHING TO SAY TO YOU TRAITORS...
YOU'LL TALK—

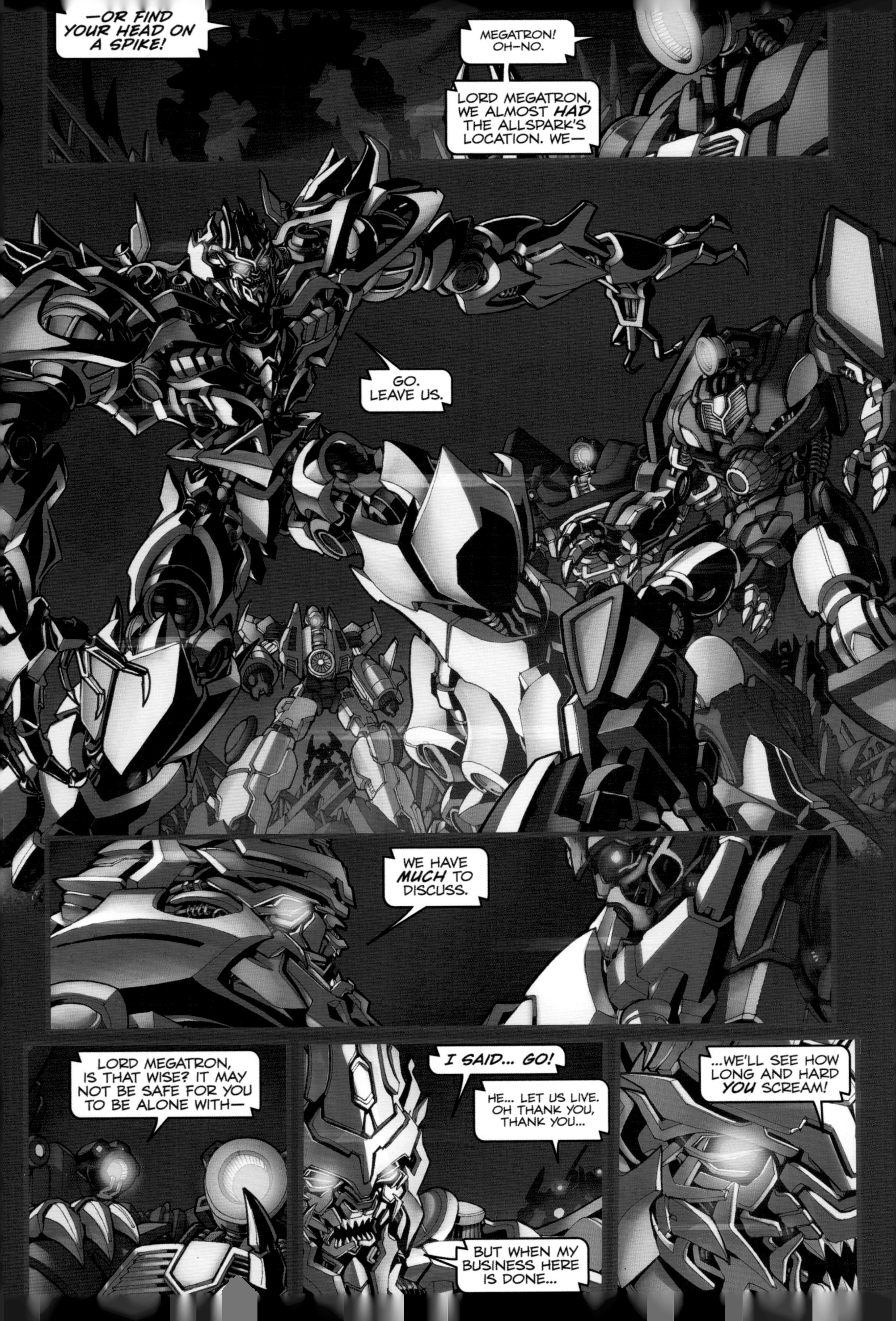
—OR FIND YOUR HEAD ON A SPIKE!
MEGATRON! OH—NO.
LORD MEGATRON, WE ALMOST HAD THE ALLSPARK'S LOCATION. WE—
GO. LEAVE US.
WE HAVE MUCH TO DISCUSS.
LORD MEGATRON, IS THAT WISE? IT MAY NOT BE SAFE FOR YOU TO BE ALONE WITH—
I SAID... GO!
HE... LET US LIVE. OH THANK YOU, THANK YOU...
BUT WHEN MY BUSINESS HERE IS DONE...
...WE'LL SEE HOW LONG AND HARD YOU SCREAM!

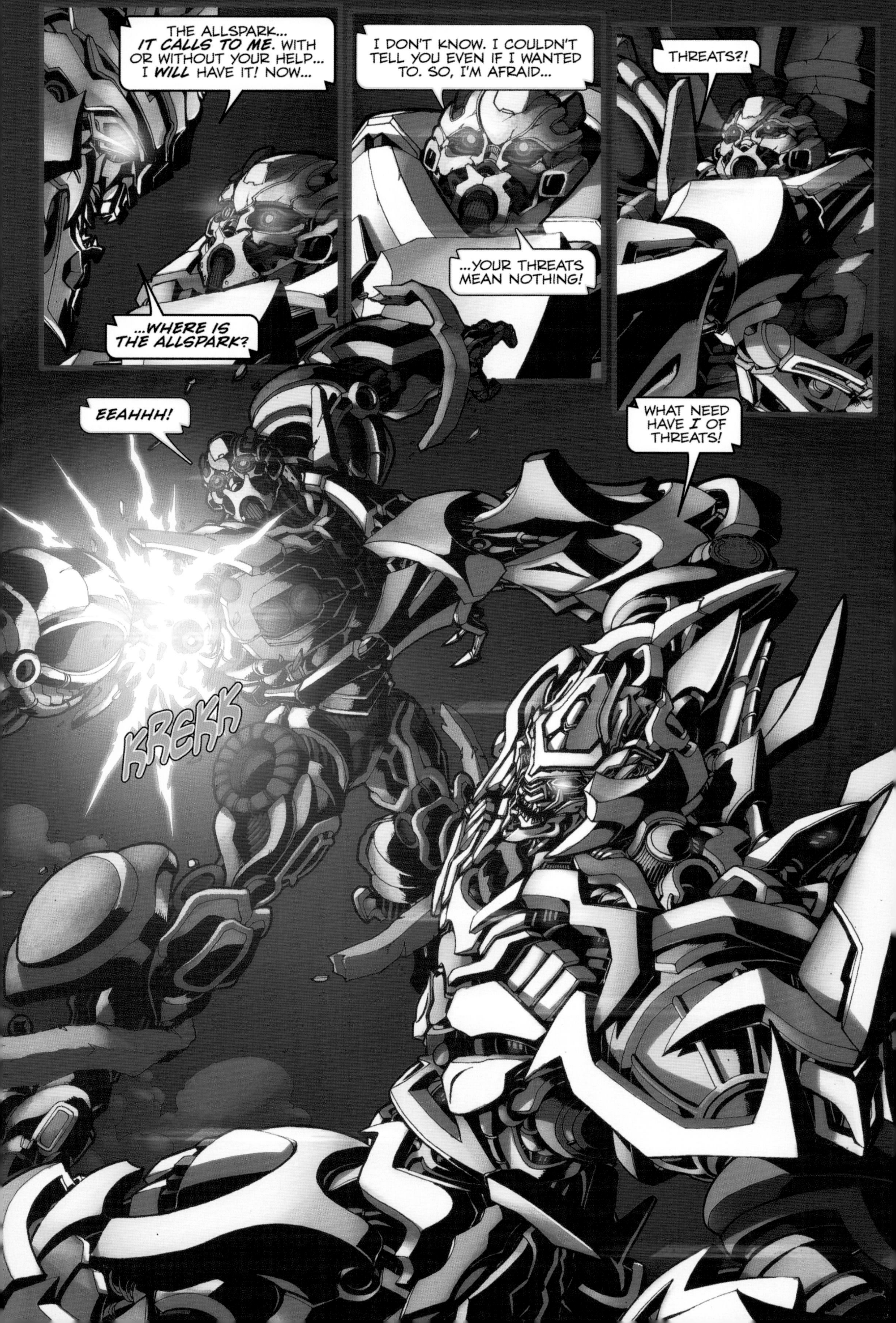
THE ALLSPARK... IT CALLS TO ME. WITH OR WITHOUT YOUR HELP... I WILL HAVE IT! NOW...
...WHERE IS THE ALLSPARK?
I DON'T KNOW. I COULDN'T TELL YOU EVEN IF I WANTED TO. SO, I'M AFRAID...
...YOUR THREATS MEAN NOTHING!
THREATS?!
WHAT NEED HAVE I OF THREATS!
EEAHHH!
KREKK

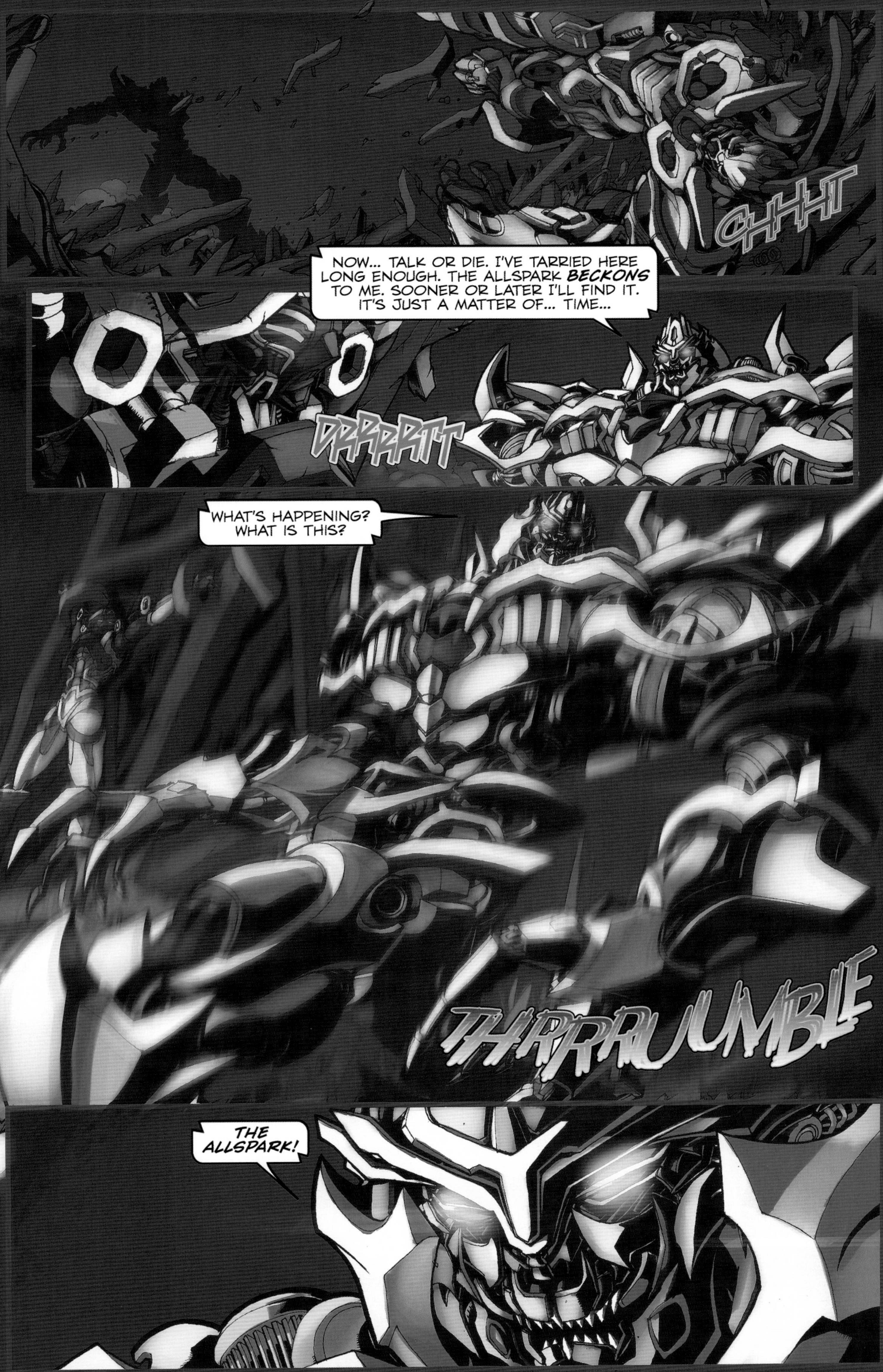
CHHHT
NOW... TALK OR DIE. I'VE TARRIED HERE LONG ENOUGH. THE ALLSPARK BECKONS TO ME. SOONER OR LATER I'LL FIND IT. IT'S JUST A MATTER OF... TIME...
DRRRRTT
WHAT'S HAPPENING? WHAT IS THIS?
THRRRUUMBLE
THE ALLSPARK!

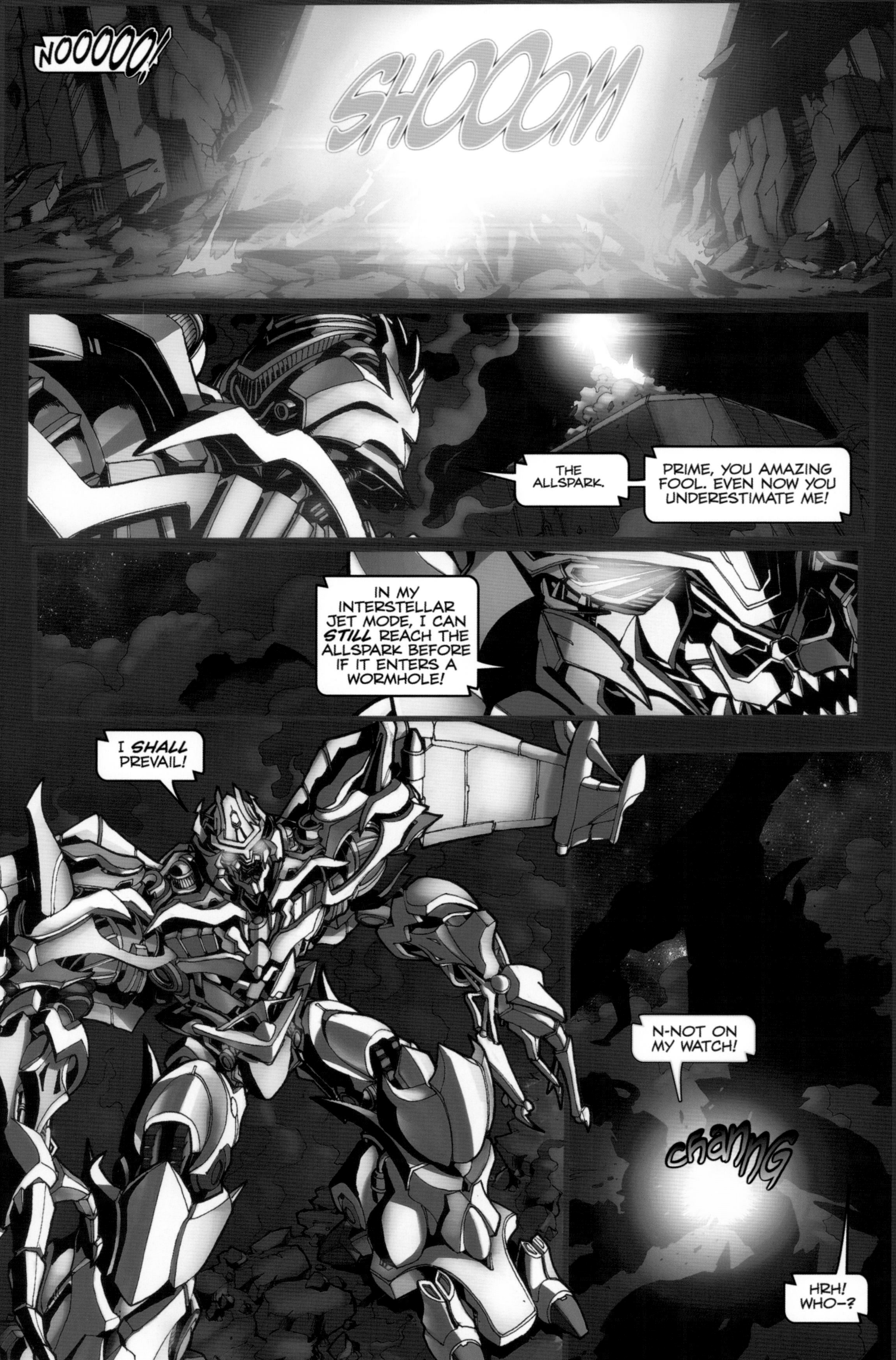
NOOOOO!
SHOOOM
THE ALLSPARK.
PRIME, YOU AMAZING FOOL. EVEN NOW YOU UNDERESTIMATE ME!
IN MY INTERSTELLAR JET MODE, I CAN STILL REACH THE ALLSPARK BEFORE IF IT ENTERS A WORMHOLE!
I SHALL PREVAIL!
N-NOT ON MY WATCH!
CHANNG
HRH! WHO-?

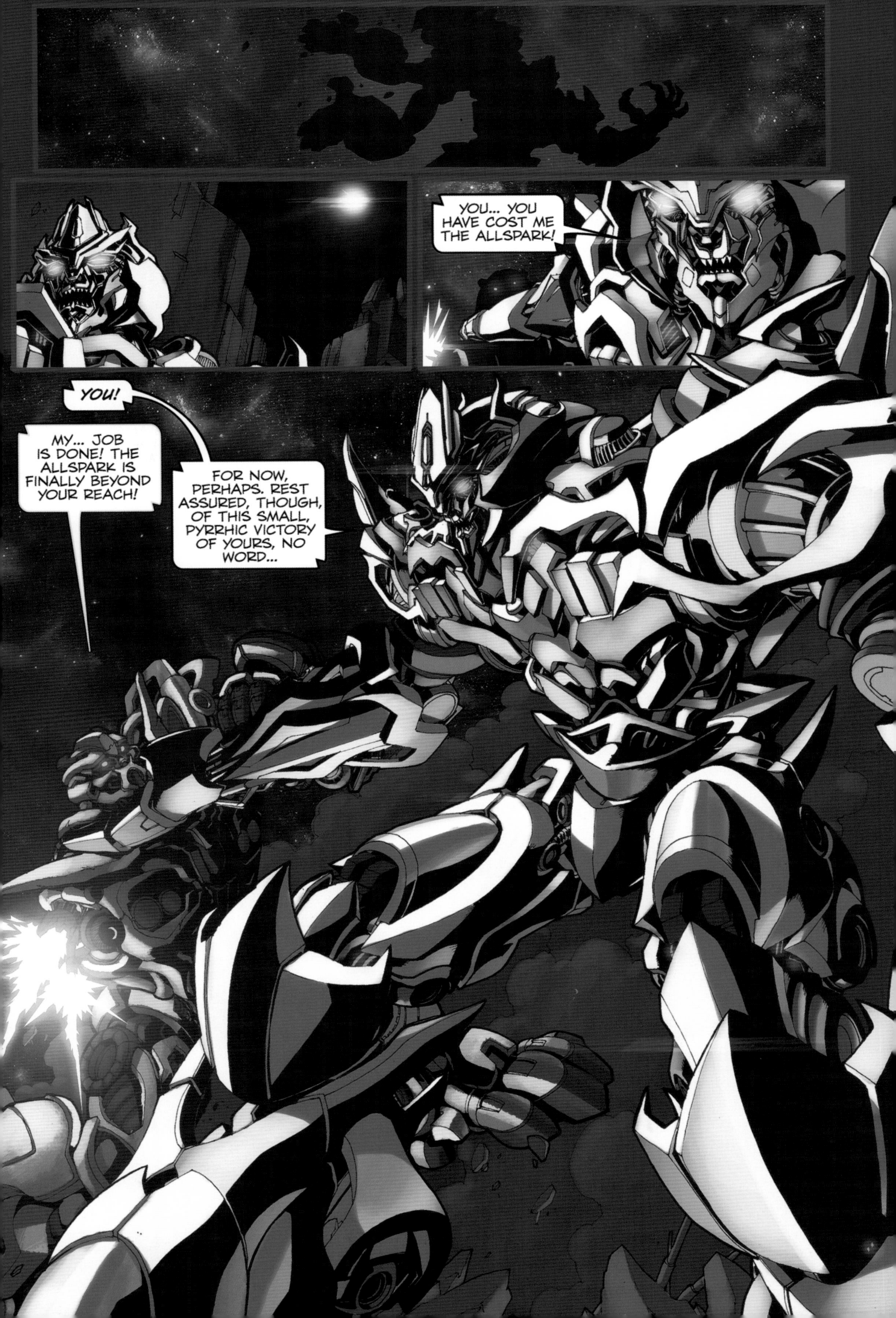
YOU... YOU HAVE COST ME THE ALLSPARK!
MY... JOB IS DONE! THE ALLSPARK IS FINALLY BEYOND YOUR REACH!
YOU!
FOR NOW, PERHAPS. REST ASSURED, THOUGH, OF THIS SMALL, PYRRHIC VICTORY OF YOURS, NO WORD...

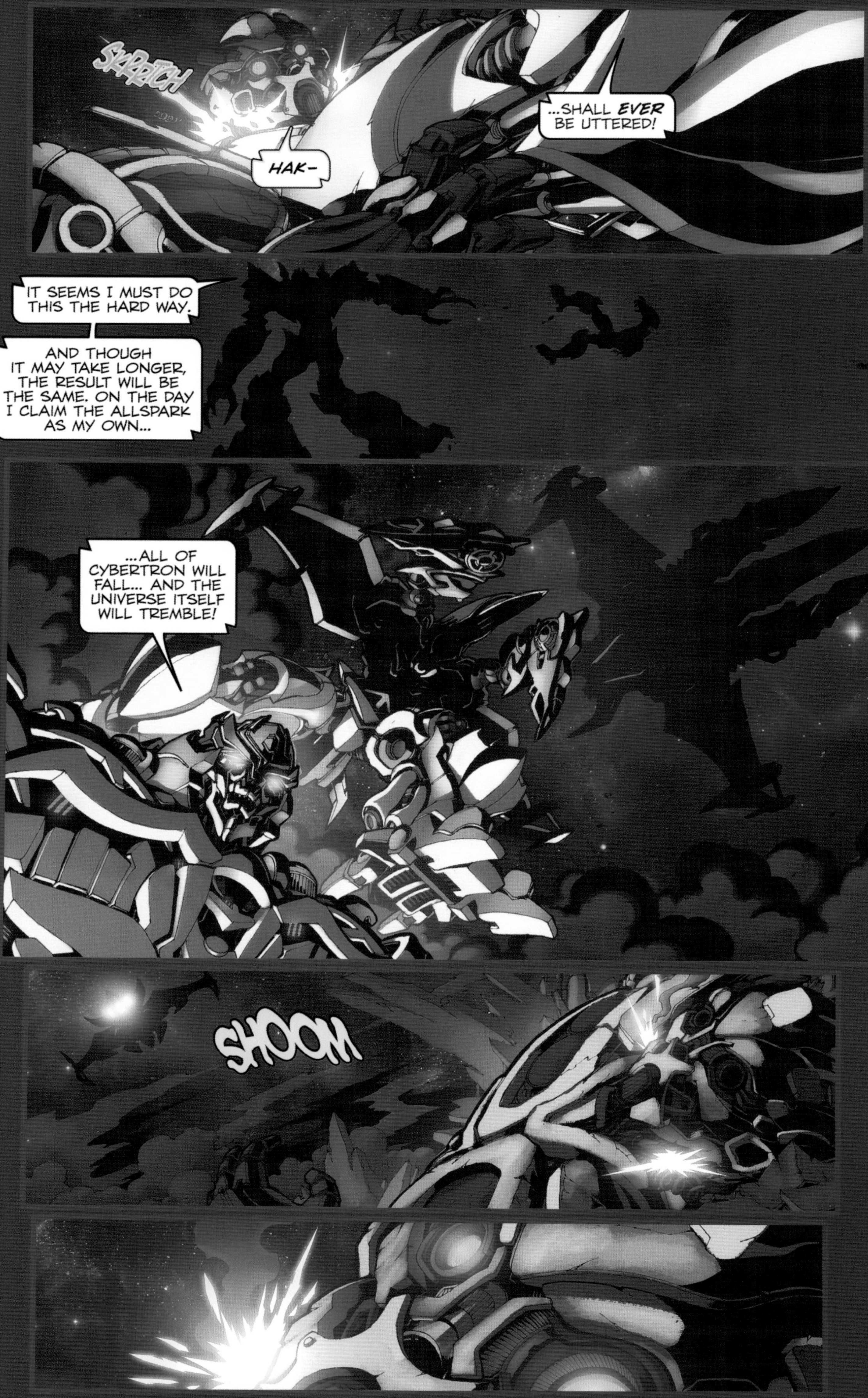
SKRRTCH
HAK-
...SHALL EVER BE UTTERED!
IT SEEMS I MUST DO THIS THE HARD WAY.
AND THOUGH IT MAY TAKE LONGER, THE RESULT WILL BE THE SAME. ON THE DAY I CLAIM THE ALLSPARK AS MY OWN...
...ALL OF CYBERTRON WILL FALL... AND THE UNIVERSE ITSELF WILL TREMBLE!
SHOOM

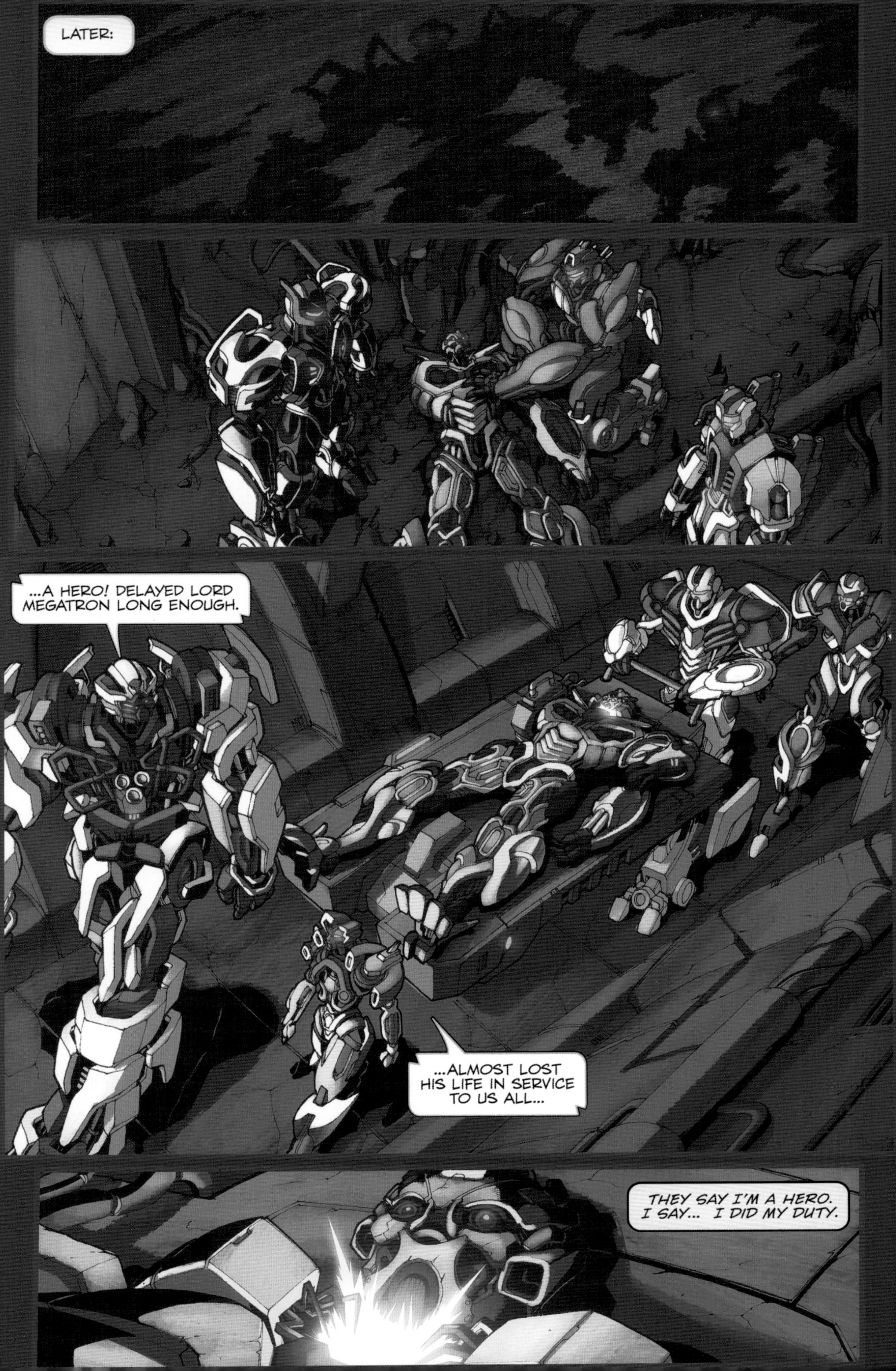
LATER:
...A HERO! DELAYED LORD MEGATRON LONG ENOUGH.
...ALMOST LOST HIS LIFE IN SERVICE TO US ALL...
THEY SAY I'M A HERO. I SAY... I DID MY DUTY.

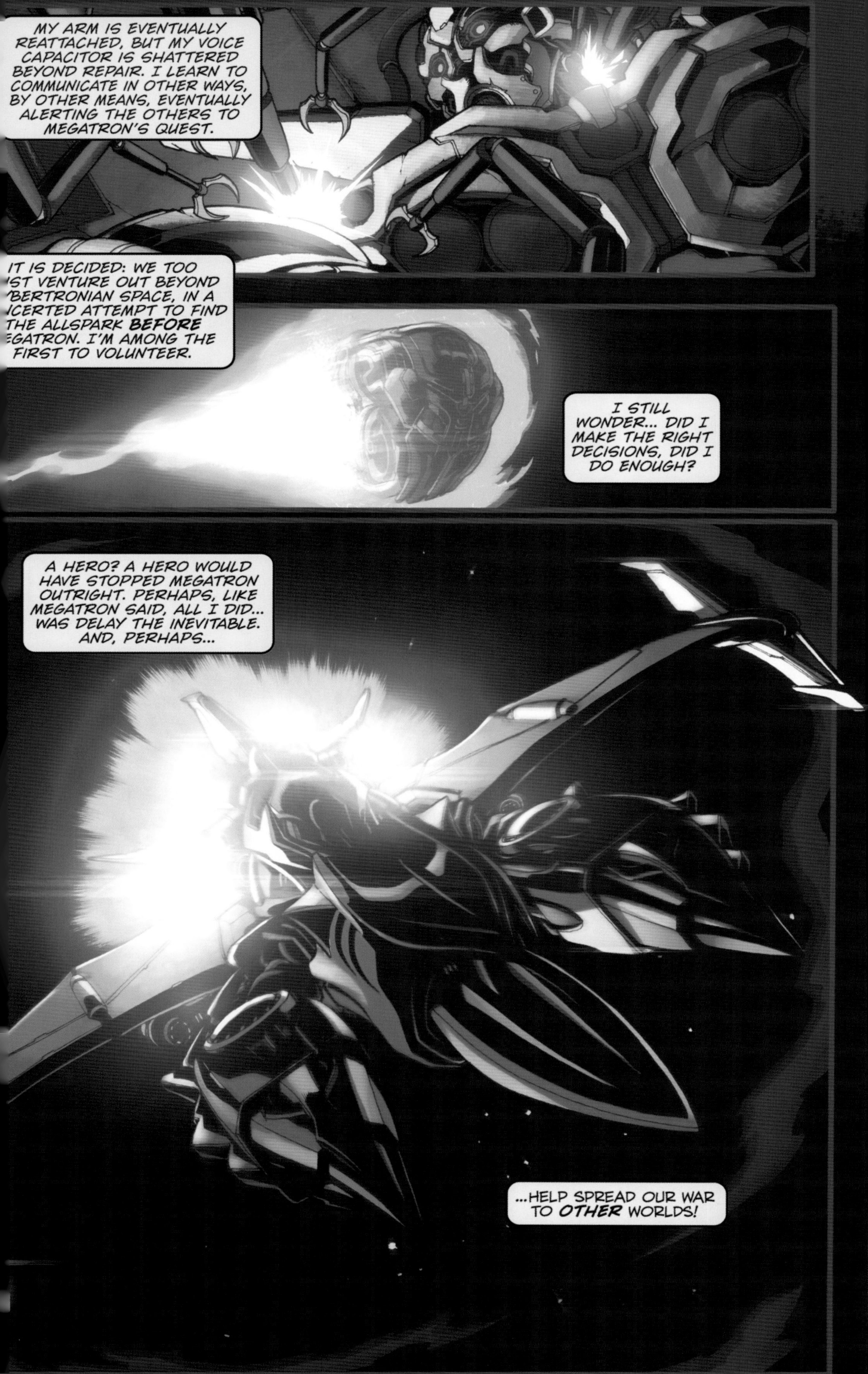
MY ARM IS EVENTUALLY REATTACHED, BUT MY VOICE CAPACITOR IS SHATTERED BEYOND REPAIR. I LEARN TO COMMUNICATE IN OTHER WAYS, BY OTHER MEANS, EVENTUALLY ALERTING THE OTHERS TO MEGATRON'S QUEST.
IT IS DECIDED: WE TOO
ST VENTURE OUT BEYOND
BERTRONIAN SPACE, IN A
CERTED ATTEMPT TO FIND
THE ALLSPARK **BEFORE**
EGATRON. I'M AMONG THE
FIRST TO VOLUNTEER.
I STILL WONDER... DID I MAKE THE RIGHT DECISIONS, DID I DO ENOUGH?
A HERO? A HERO WOULD HAVE STOPPED MEGATRON OUTRIGHT. PERHAPS, LIKE MEGATRON SAID, ALL I DID... WAS DELAY THE INEVITABLE. AND, PERHAPS...
...HELP SPREAD OUR WAR TO ***OTHER*** WORLDS!

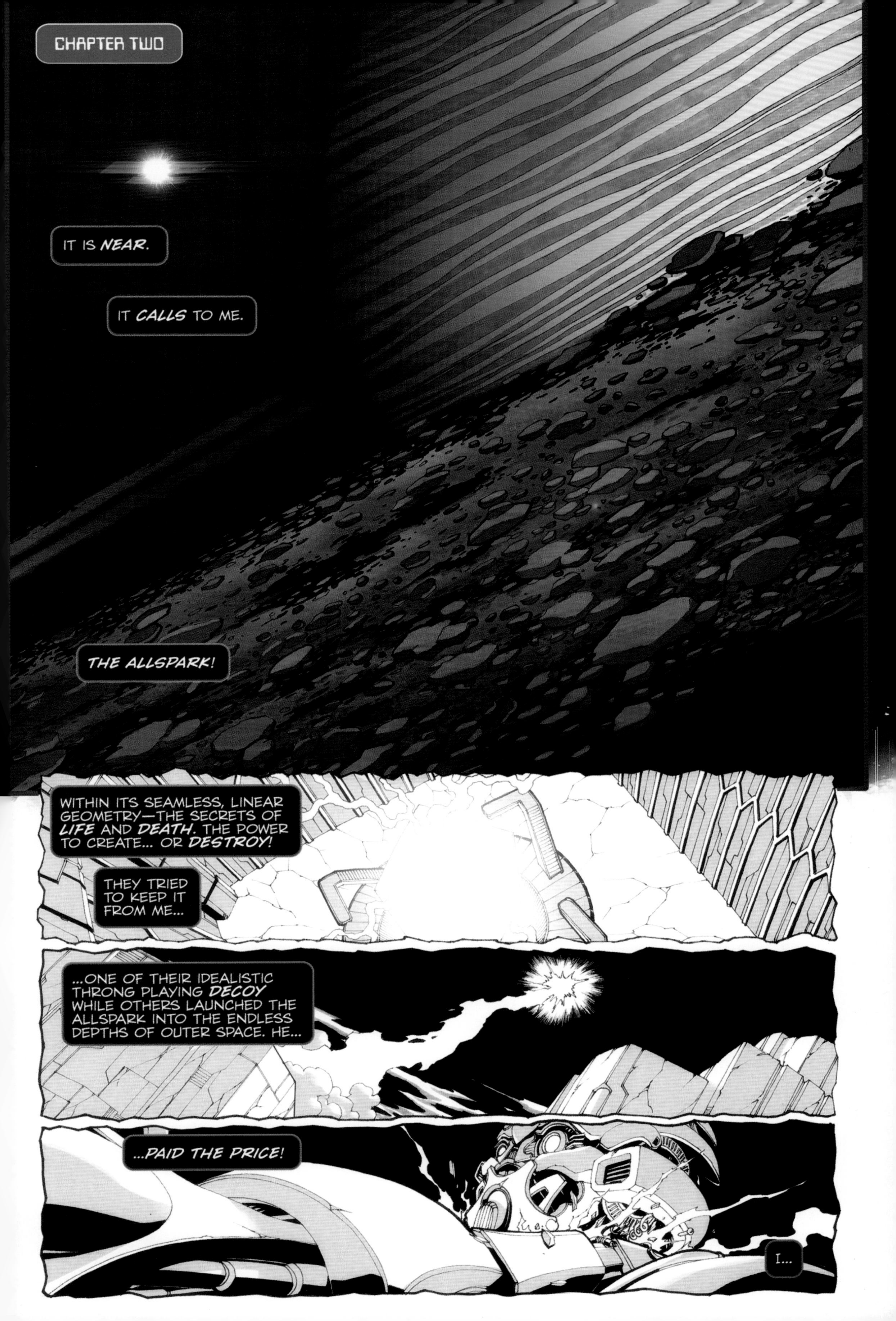
CHAPTER TWO
IT IS NEAR.
IT CALLS TO ME.
THE ALLSPARK!
WITHIN ITS SEAMLESS, LINEAR GEOMETRY—THE SECRETS OF LIFE AND DEATH. THE POWER TO CREATE... OR DESTROY!
THEY TRIED TO KEEP IT FROM ME...
...ONE OF THEIR IDEALISTIC THRONG PLAYING DECOY WHILE OTHERS LAUNCHED THE ALLSPARK INTO THE ENDLESS DEPTHS OF OUTER SPACE. HE...
...PAID THE PRICE!
I...

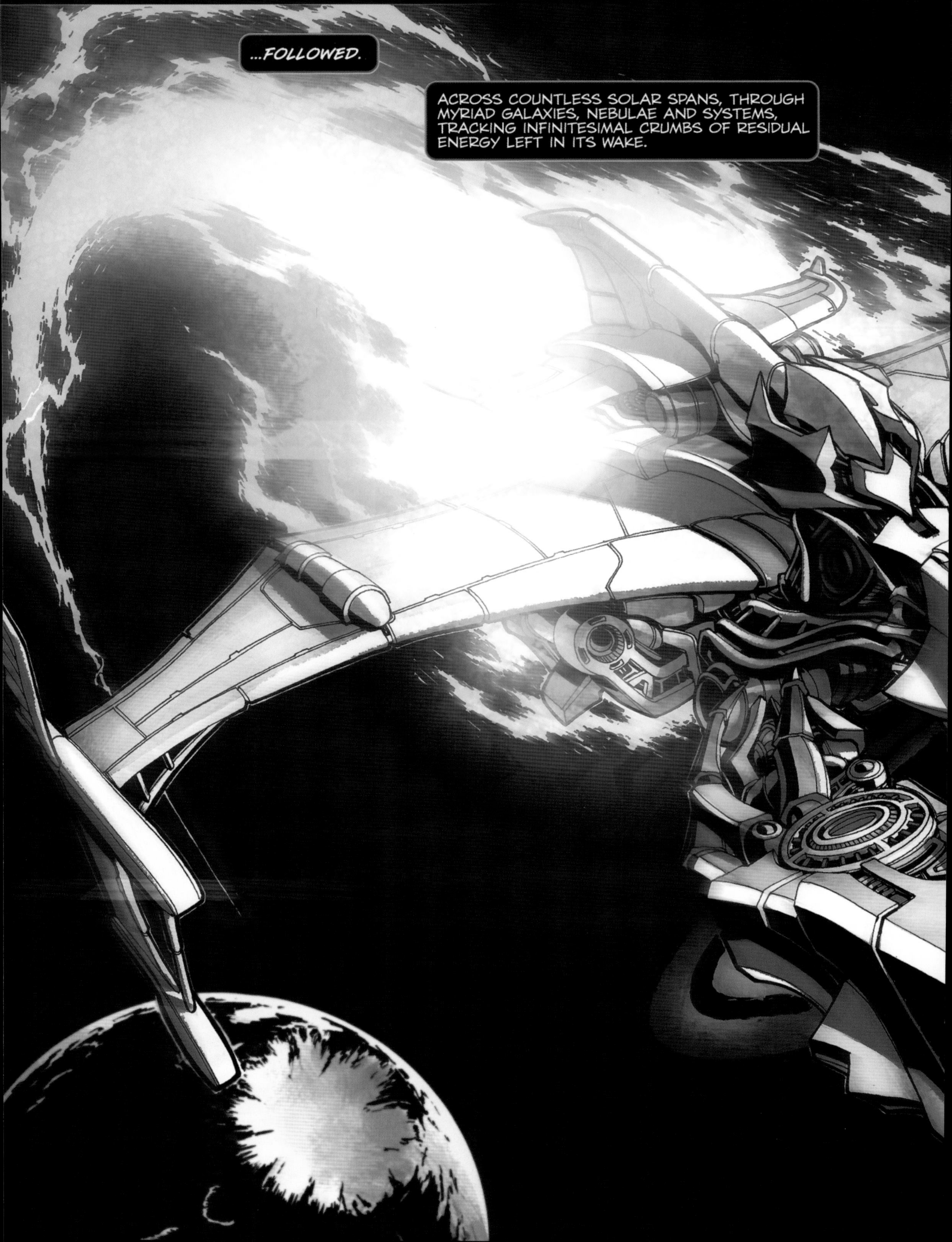
...FOLLOWED.
ACROSS COUNTLESS SOLAR SPANS, THROUGH MYRIAD GALAXIES, NEBULAE AND SYSTEMS, TRACKING INFINITESIMAL CRUMBS OF RESIDUAL ENERGY LEFT IN ITS WAKE.

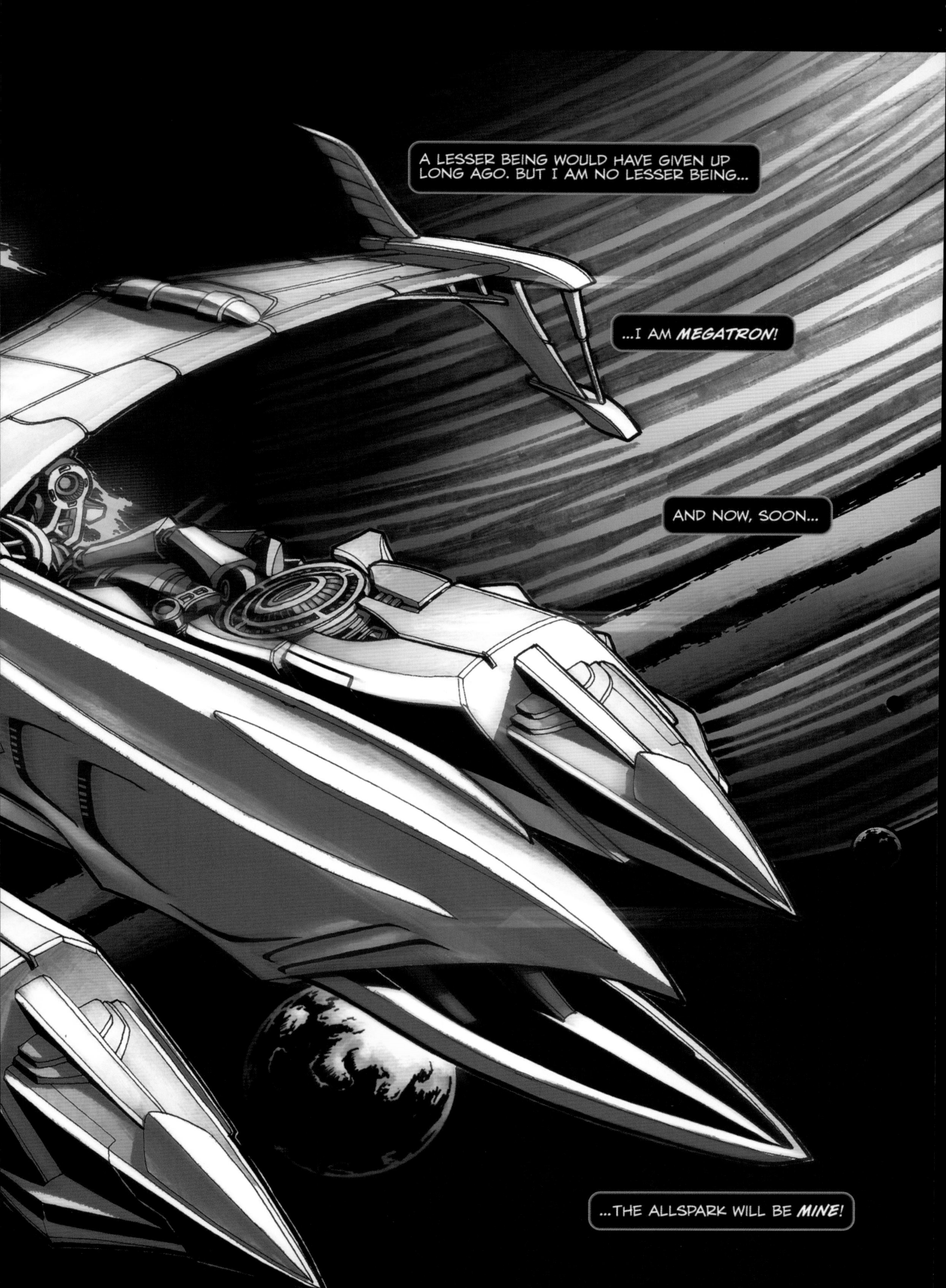
A LESSER BEING WOULD HAVE GIVEN UP LONG AGO. BUT I AM NO LESSER BEING...
...I AM *MEGATRON!*
AND NOW, SOON...
...THE ALLSPARK WILL BE *MINE!*

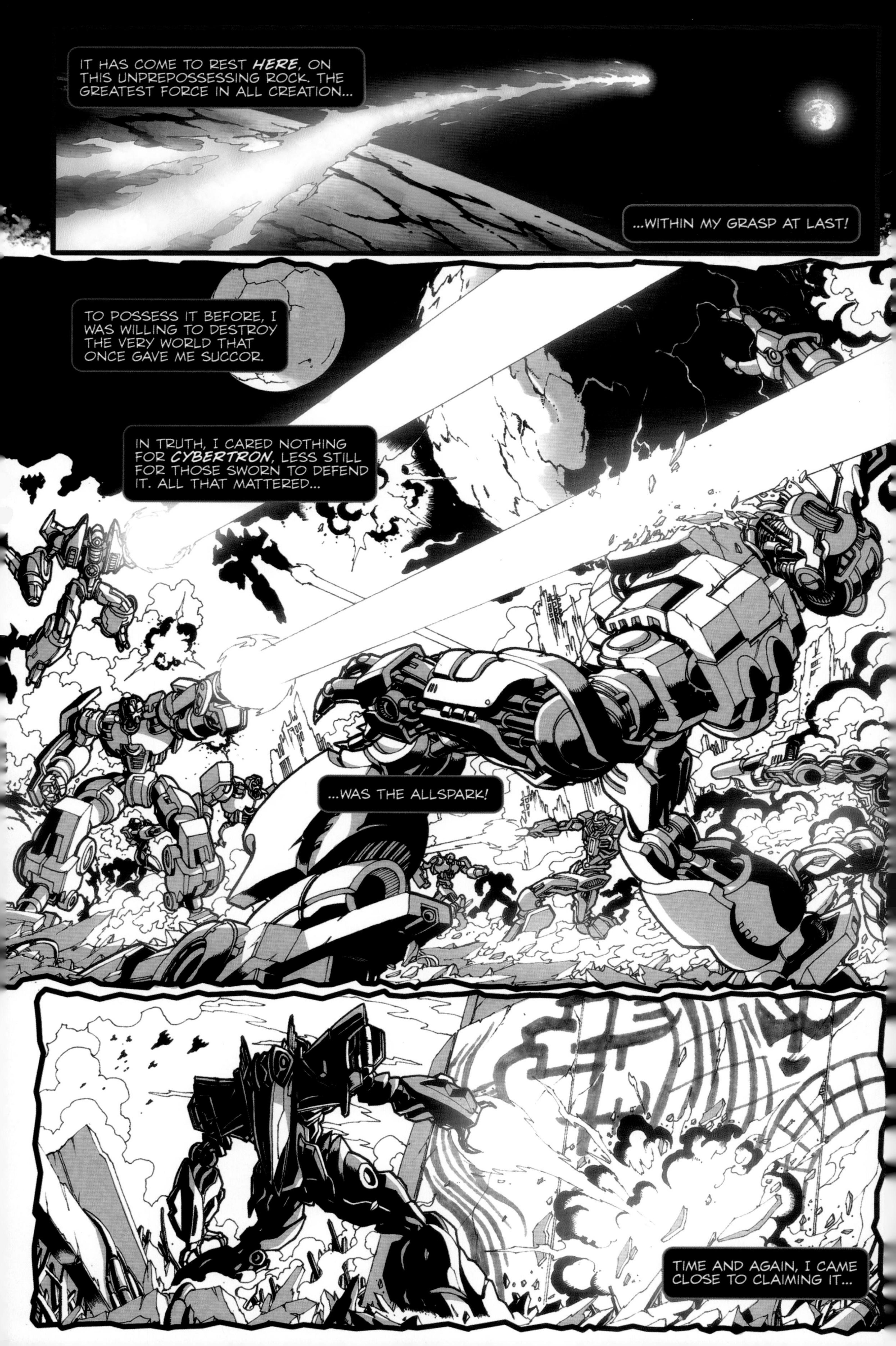
IT HAS COME TO REST *HERE*, ON THIS UNPREPOSSESSING ROCK. THE GREATEST FORCE IN ALL CREATION...
...WITHIN MY GRASP AT LAST!
TO POSSESS IT BEFORE, I WAS WILLING TO DESTROY THE VERY WORLD THAT ONCE GAVE ME SUCCOR.
IN TRUTH, I CARED NOTHING FOR *CYBERTRON*, LESS STILL FOR THOSE SWORN TO DEFEND IT. ALL THAT MATTERED...
...WAS THE ALLSPARK!
TIME AND AGAIN, I CAME CLOSE TO CLAIMING IT...

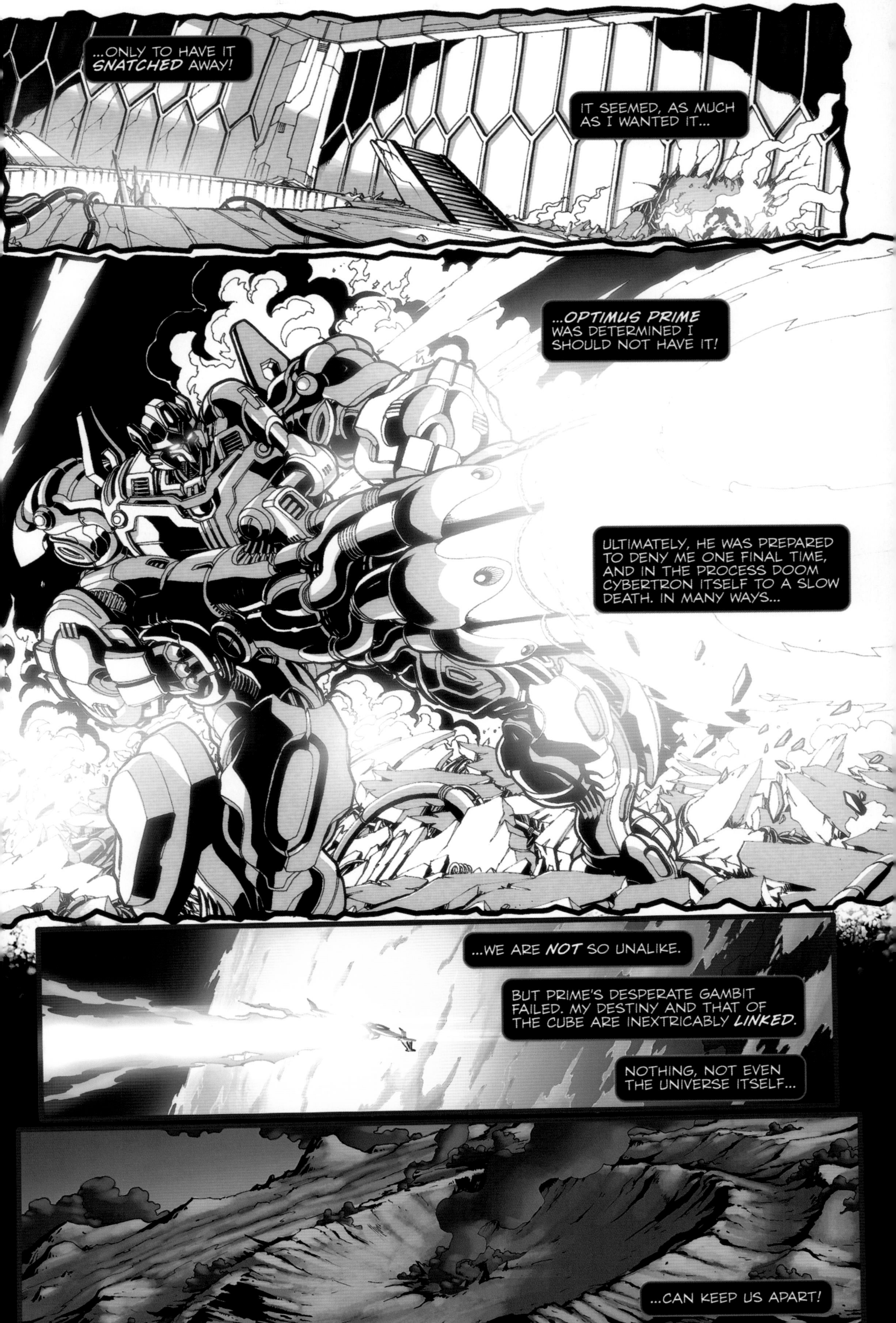
...ONLY TO HAVE IT SNATCHED AWAY!
IT SEEMED, AS MUCH AS I WANTED IT...
...OPTIMUS PRIME WAS DETERMINED I SHOULD NOT HAVE IT!
ULTIMATELY, HE WAS PREPARED TO DENY ME ONE FINAL TIME, AND IN THE PROCESS DOOM CYBERTRON ITSELF TO A SLOW DEATH. IN MANY WAYS...
...WE ARE NOT SO UNALIKE.
BUT PRIME'S DESPERATE GAMBIT FAILED. MY DESTINY AND THAT OF THE CUBE ARE INEXTRICABLY LINKED.
NOTHING, NOT EVEN THE UNIVERSE ITSELF...
...CAN KEEP US APART!

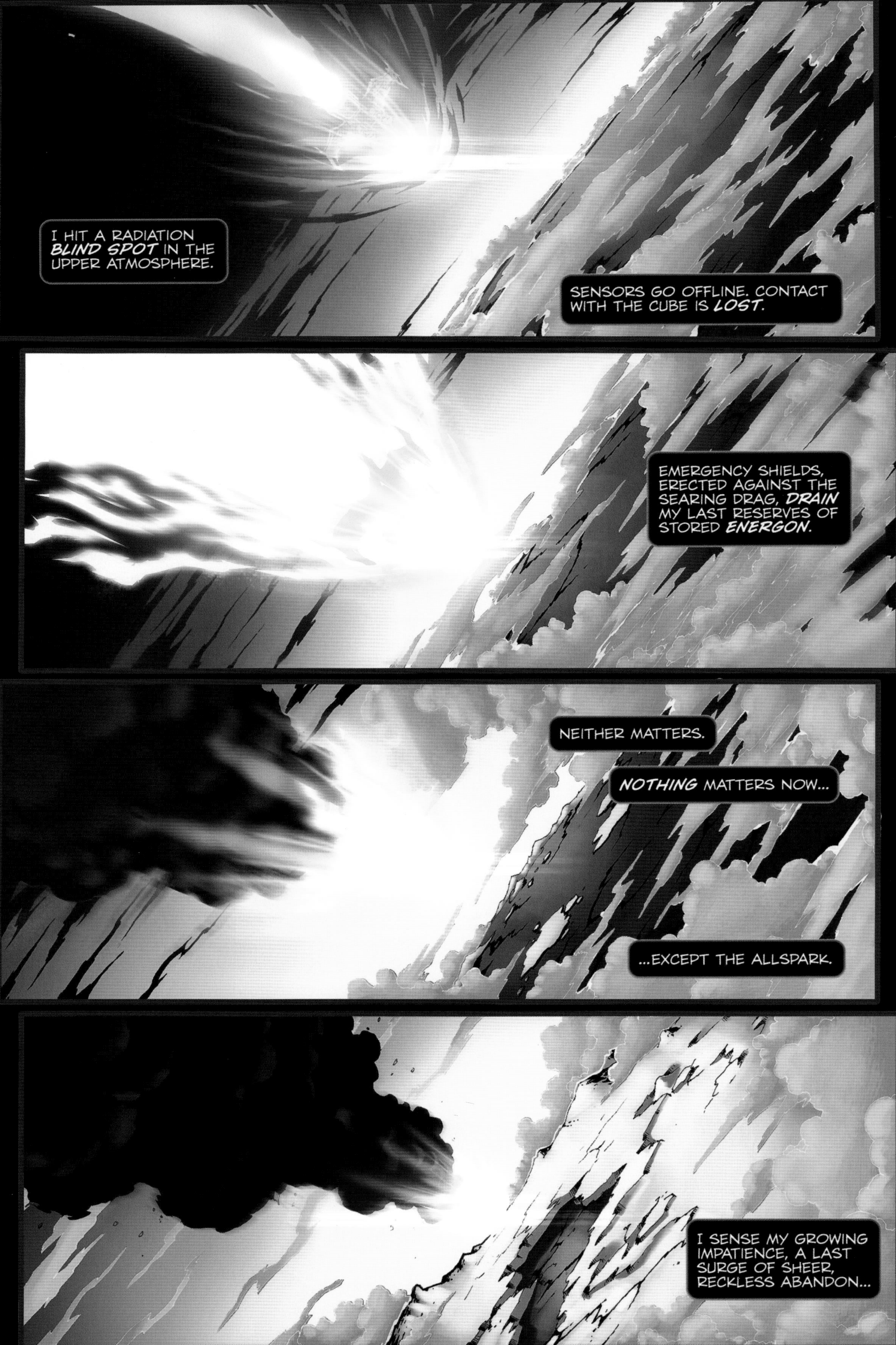
I HIT A RADIATION BLIND SPOT IN THE UPPER ATMOSPHERE.
SENSORS GO OFFLINE. CONTACT WITH THE CUBE IS LOST.
EMERGENCY SHIELDS, ERECTED AGAINST THE SEARING DRAG, DRAIN MY LAST RESERVES OF STORED ENERGON.
NEITHER MATTERS.
NOTHING MATTERS NOW...
...EXCEPT THE ALLSPARK.
I SENSE MY GROWING IMPATIENCE, A LAST SURGE OF SHEER, RECKLESS ABANDON...

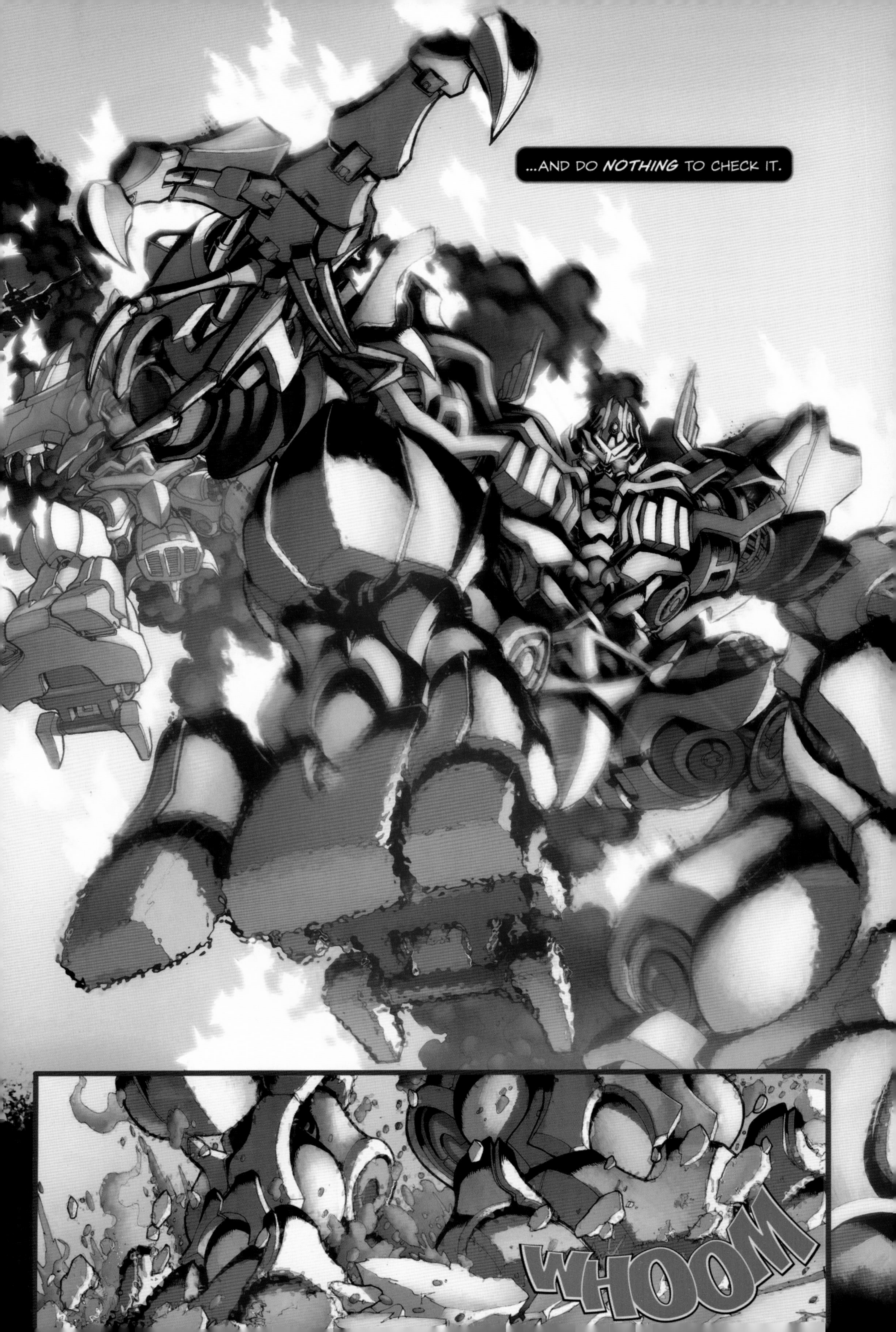

...AND DO NOTHING TO CHECK IT.
WHOOM

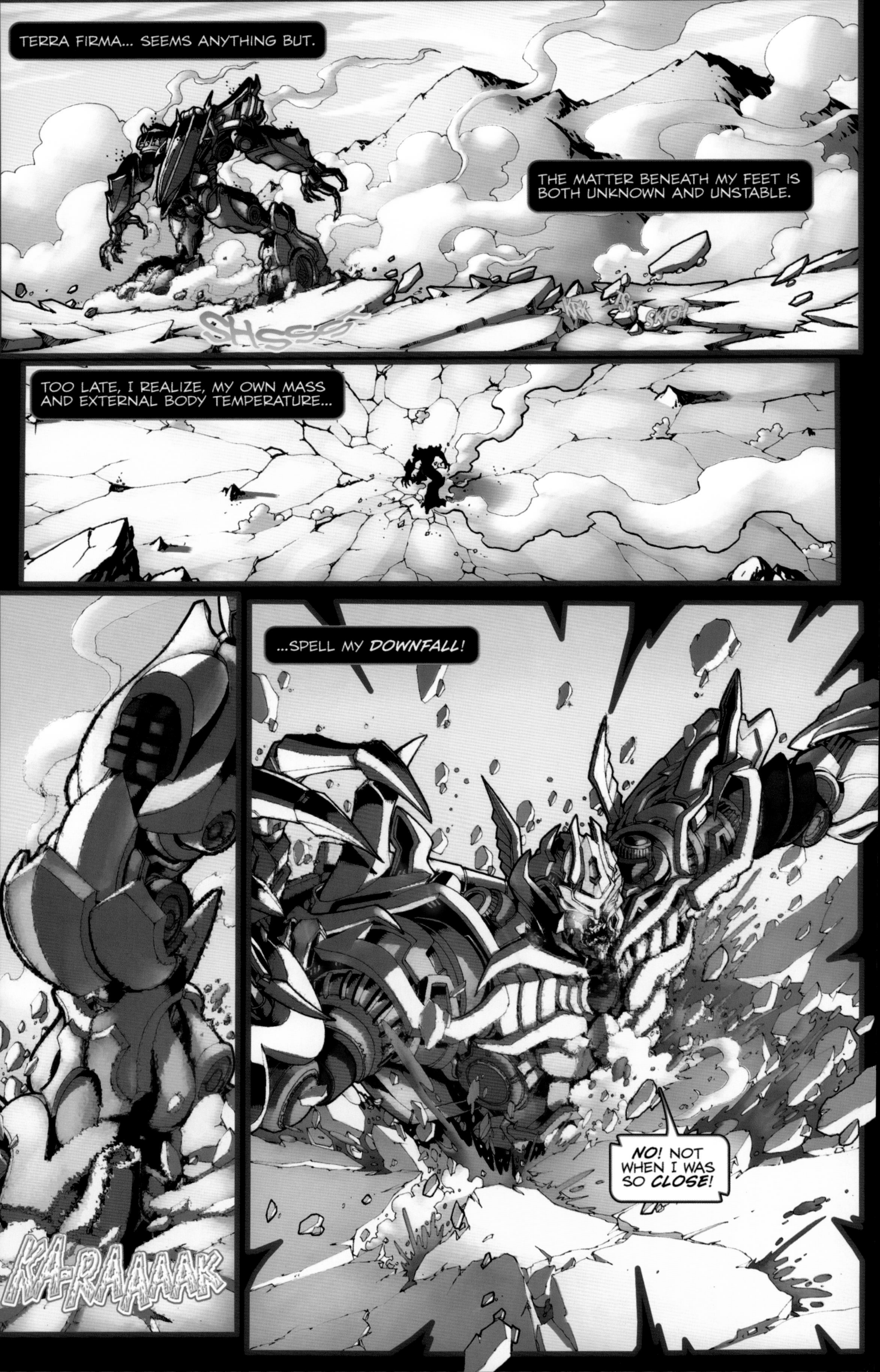
TERRA FIRMA... SEEMS ANYTHING BUT.
THE MATTER BENEATH MY FEET IS BOTH UNKNOWN AND UNSTABLE.
SHSSST
KRK
TSK
SKTCH
TOO LATE, I REALIZE, MY OWN MASS AND EXTERNAL BODY TEMPERATURE...
KA-RAAAAK
...SPELL MY *DOWNFALL*!
NO! NOT WHEN I WAS SO ***CLOSE!***

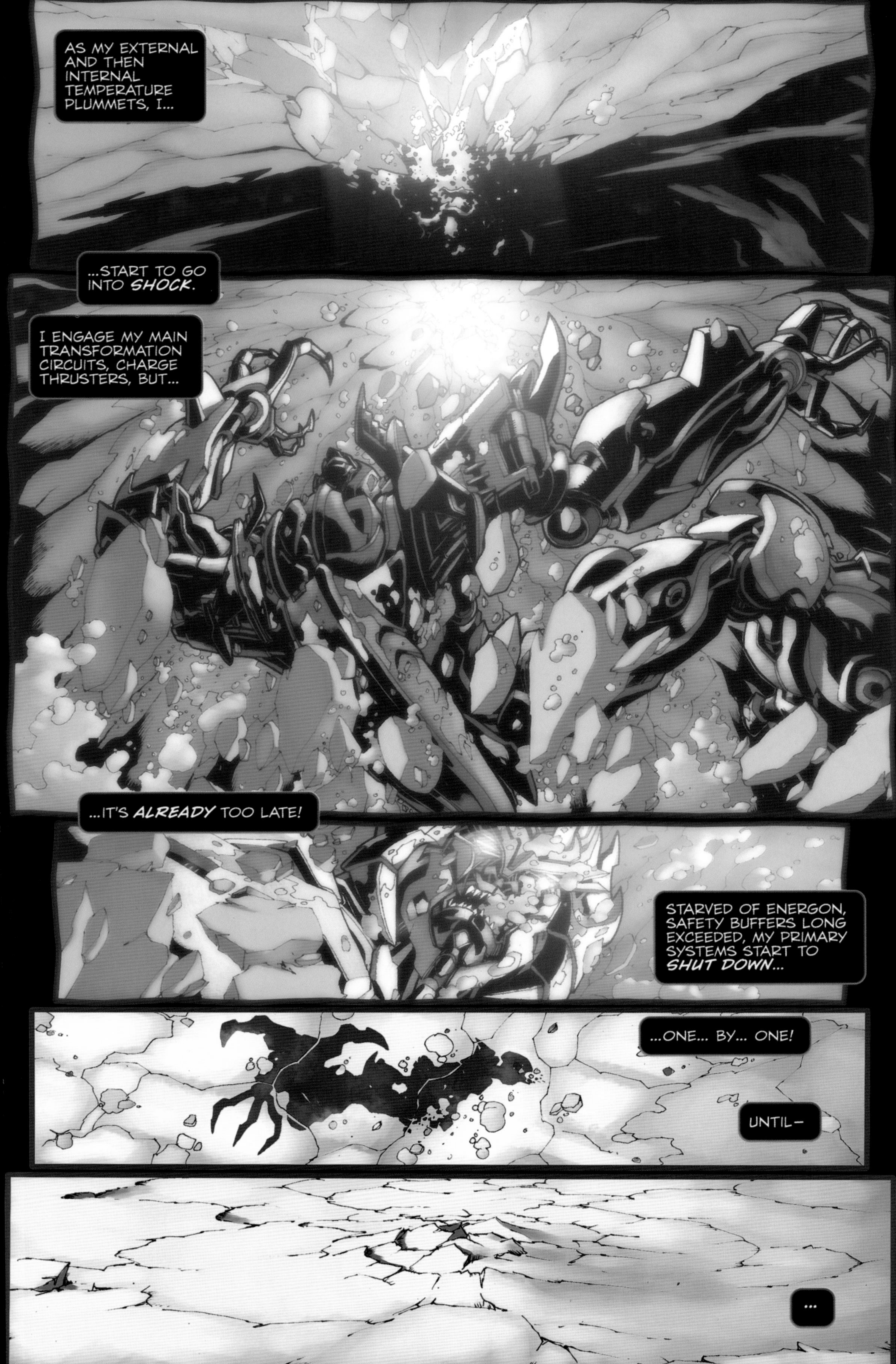

AS MY EXTERNAL AND THEN INTERNAL TEMPERATURE PLUMMETS, I...
...START TO GO INTO SHOCK.
I ENGAGE MY MAIN TRANSFORMATION CIRCUITS, CHARGE THRUSTERS, BUT...
...IT'S ALREADY TOO LATE!
STARVED OF ENERGON, SAFETY BUFFERS LONG EXCEEDED, MY PRIMARY SYSTEMS START TO SHUT DOWN...
...ONE... BY... ONE!
UNTIL–
...

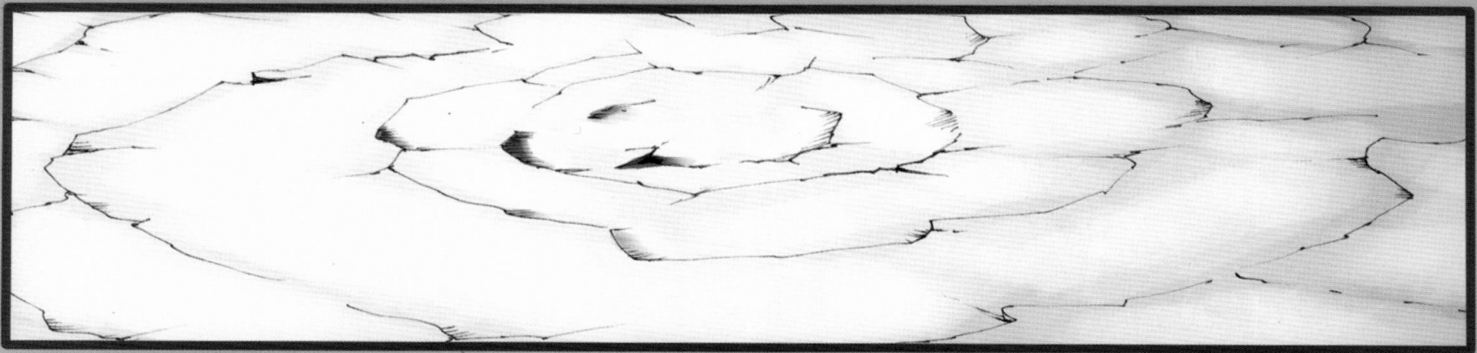

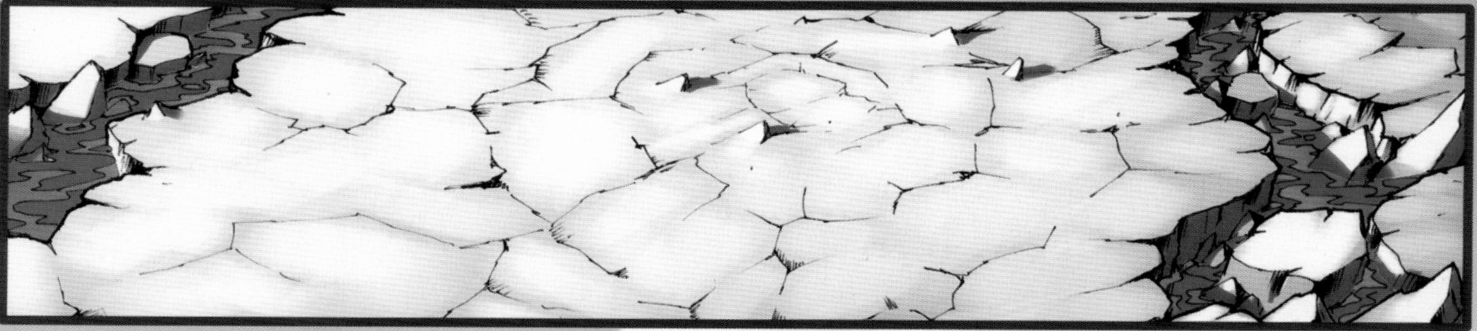

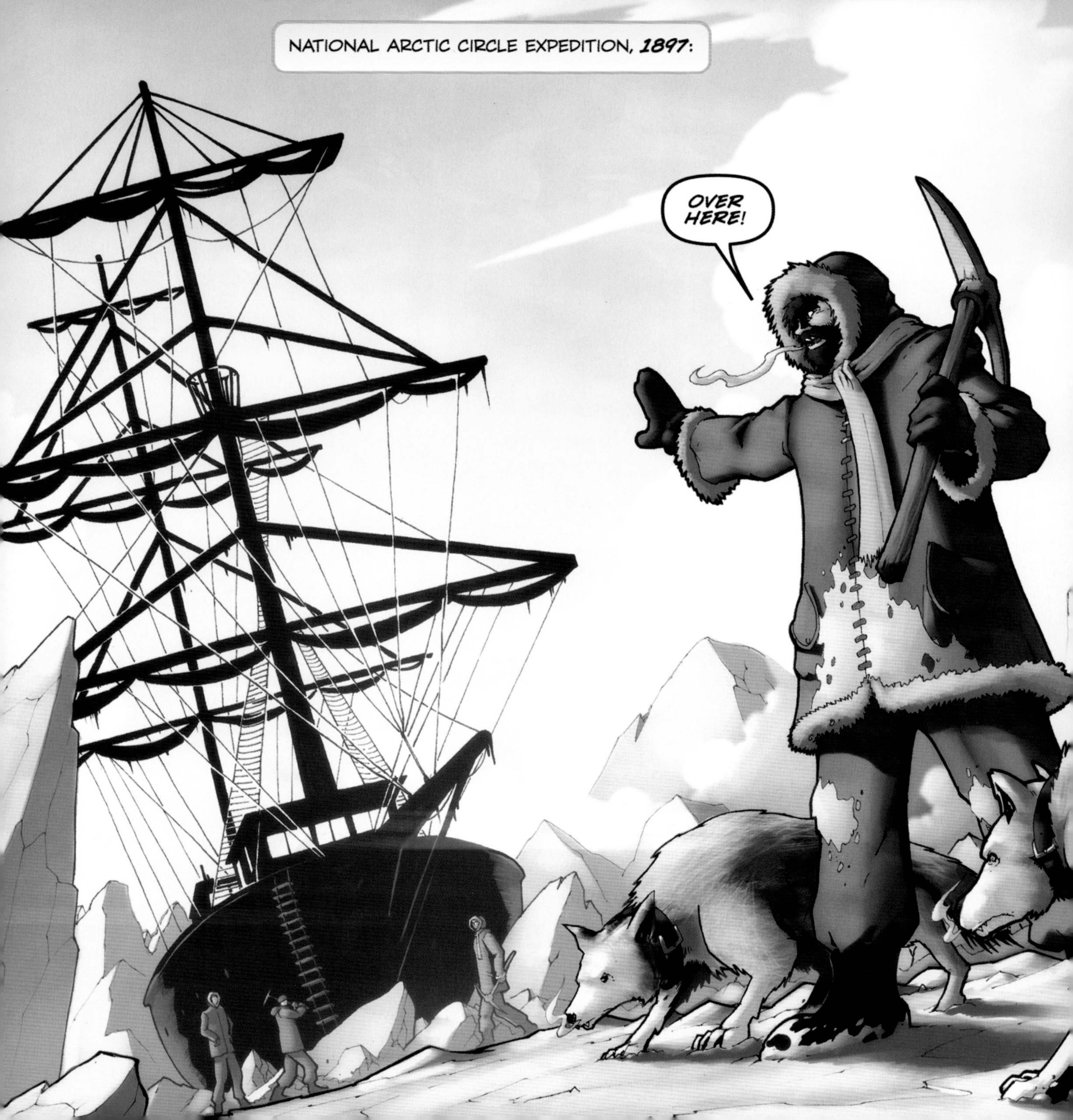
NATIONAL ARCTIC CIRCLE EXPEDITION, *1897*:
OVER HERE!

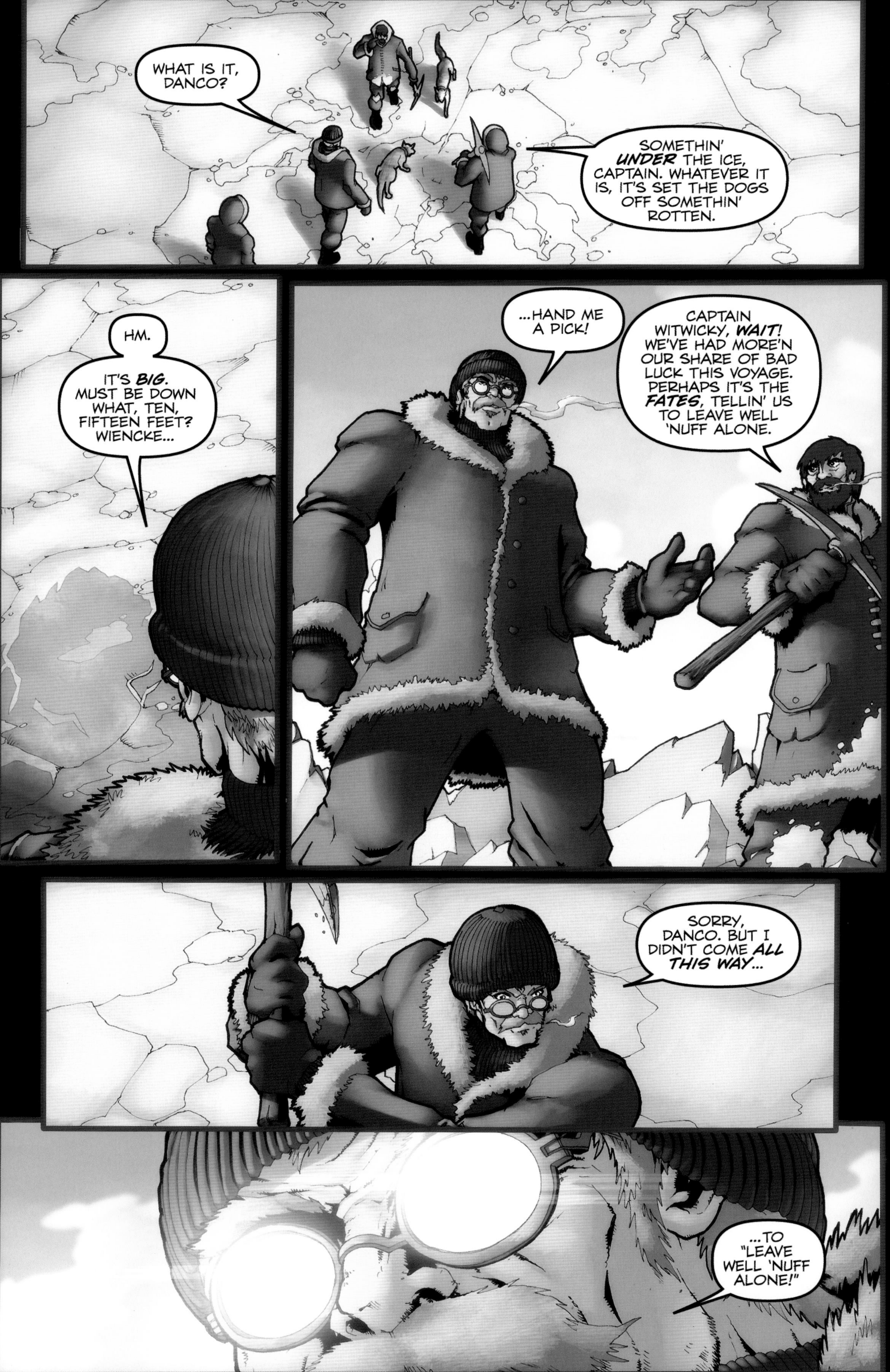
WHAT IS IT, DANCO?
SOMETHIN' UNDER THE ICE, CAPTAIN. WHATEVER IT IS, IT'S SET THE DOGS OFF SOMETHIN' ROTTEN.
HM.
IT'S BIG. MUST BE DOWN WHAT, TEN, FIFTEEN FEET? WIENCKE...
...HAND ME A PICK!
CAPTAIN WITWICKY, WAIT! WE'VE HAD MORE'N OUR SHARE OF BAD LUCK THIS VOYAGE. PERHAPS IT'S THE FATES, TELLIN' US TO LEAVE WELL 'NUFF ALONE.
SORRY, DANCO. BUT I DIDN'T COME ALL THIS WAY...
...TO "LEAVE WELL 'NUFF ALONE!"

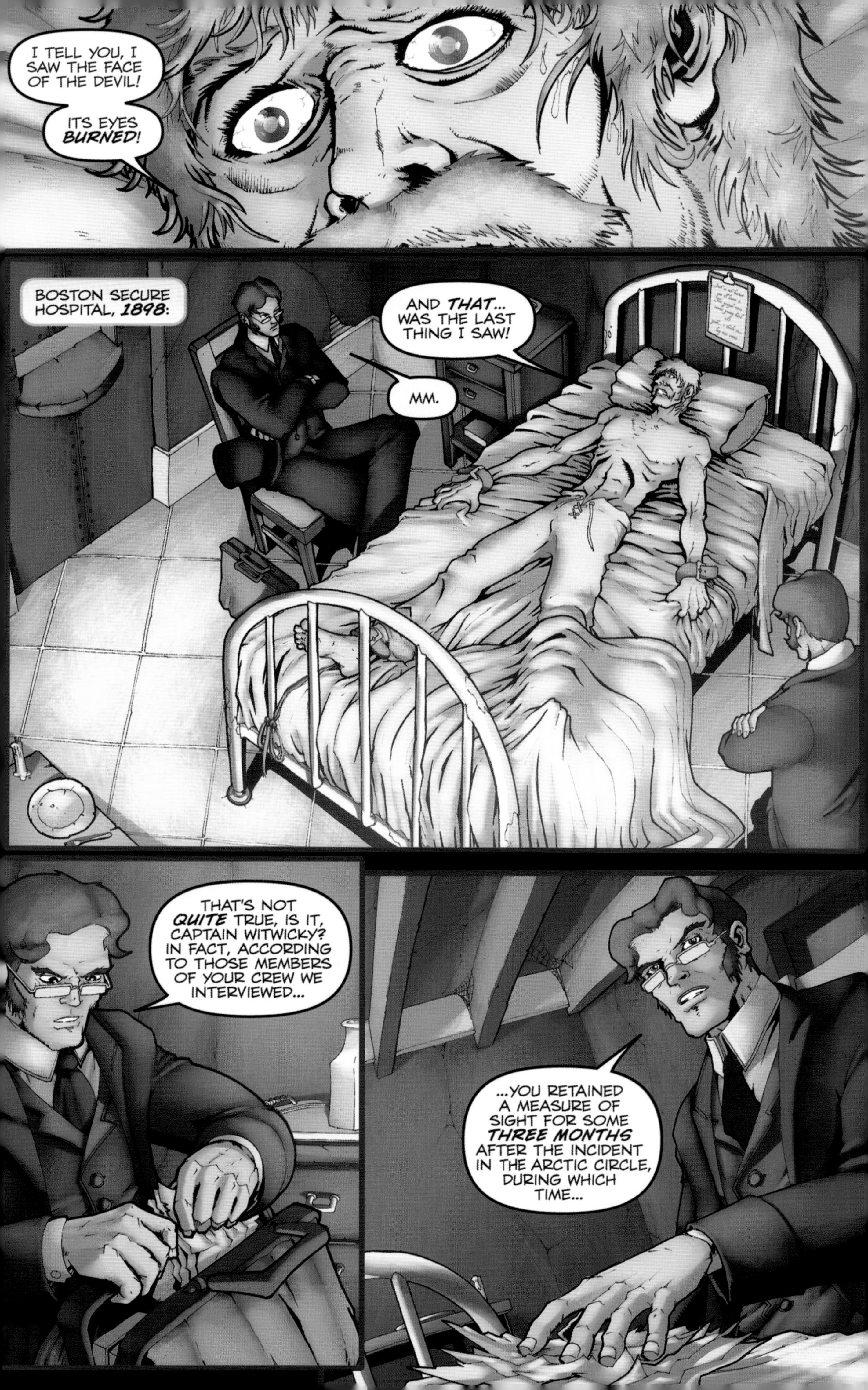
I TELL YOU, I SAW THE FACE OF THE DEVIL!
ITS EYES BURNED!
BOSTON SECURE HOSPITAL, 1898:
AND THAT... WAS THE LAST THING I SAW!
MM.
THAT'S NOT QUITE TRUE, IS IT, CAPTAIN WITWICKY? IN FACT, ACCORDING TO THOSE MEMBERS OF YOUR CREW WE INTERVIEWED...
...YOU RETAINED A MEASURE OF SIGHT FOR SOME THREE MONTHS AFTER THE INCIDENT IN THE ARCTIC CIRCLE, DURING WHICH TIME...

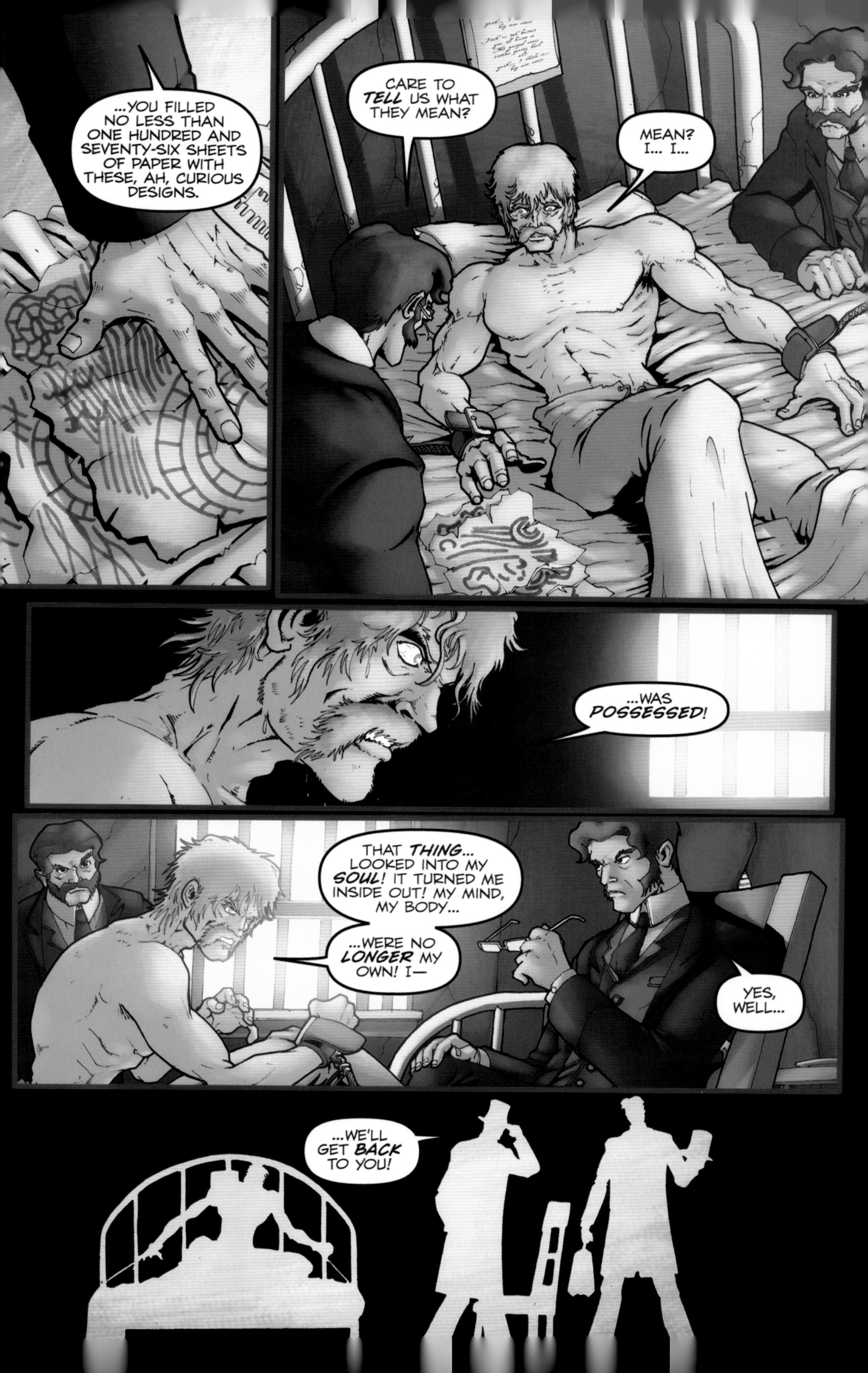
...YOU FILLED NO LESS THAN ONE HUNDRED AND SEVENTY-SIX SHEETS OF PAPER WITH THESE, AH, CURIOUS DESIGNS.
CARE TO TELL US WHAT THEY MEAN?
MEAN? I... I...
...WAS POSSESSED!
THAT THING... LOOKED INTO MY SOUL! IT TURNED ME INSIDE OUT! MY MIND, MY BODY...
...WERE NO LONGER MY OWN! I—
YES, WELL...
...WE'LL GET BACK TO YOU!

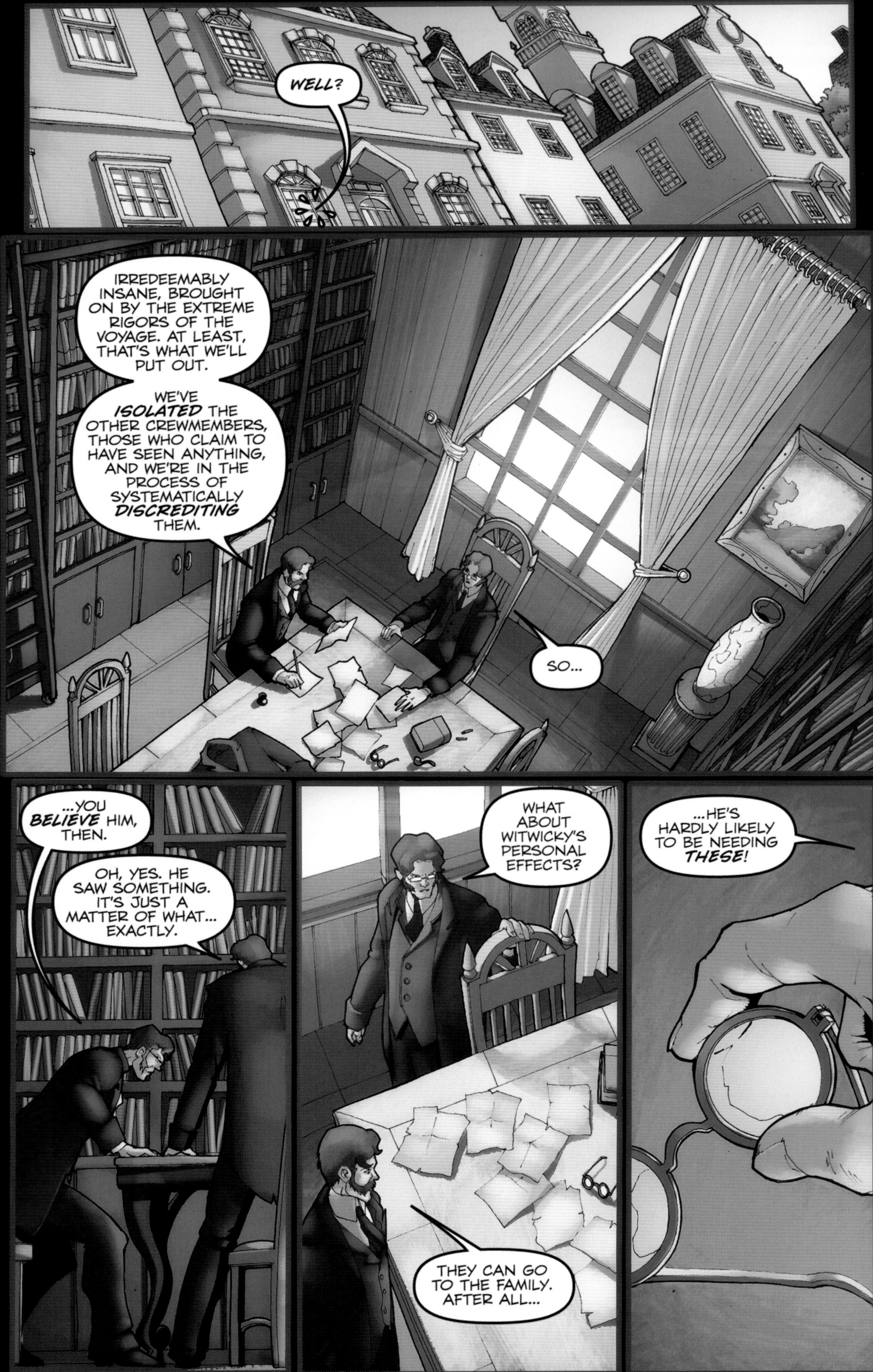
WELL?
IRREDEEMABLY INSANE, BROUGHT ON BY THE EXTREME RIGORS OF THE VOYAGE. AT LEAST, THAT'S WHAT WE'LL PUT OUT.
WE'VE ISOLATED THE OTHER CREWMEMBERS, THOSE WHO CLAIM TO HAVE SEEN ANYTHING, AND WE'RE IN THE PROCESS OF SYSTEMATICALLY DISCREDITING THEM.
SO...
...YOU BELIEVE HIM, THEN.
OH, YES. HE SAW SOMETHING. IT'S JUST A MATTER OF WHAT... EXACTLY.
WHAT ABOUT WITWICKY'S PERSONAL EFFECTS?
THEY CAN GO TO THE FAMILY. AFTER ALL...
...HE'S HARDLY LIKELY TO BE NEEDING THESE!

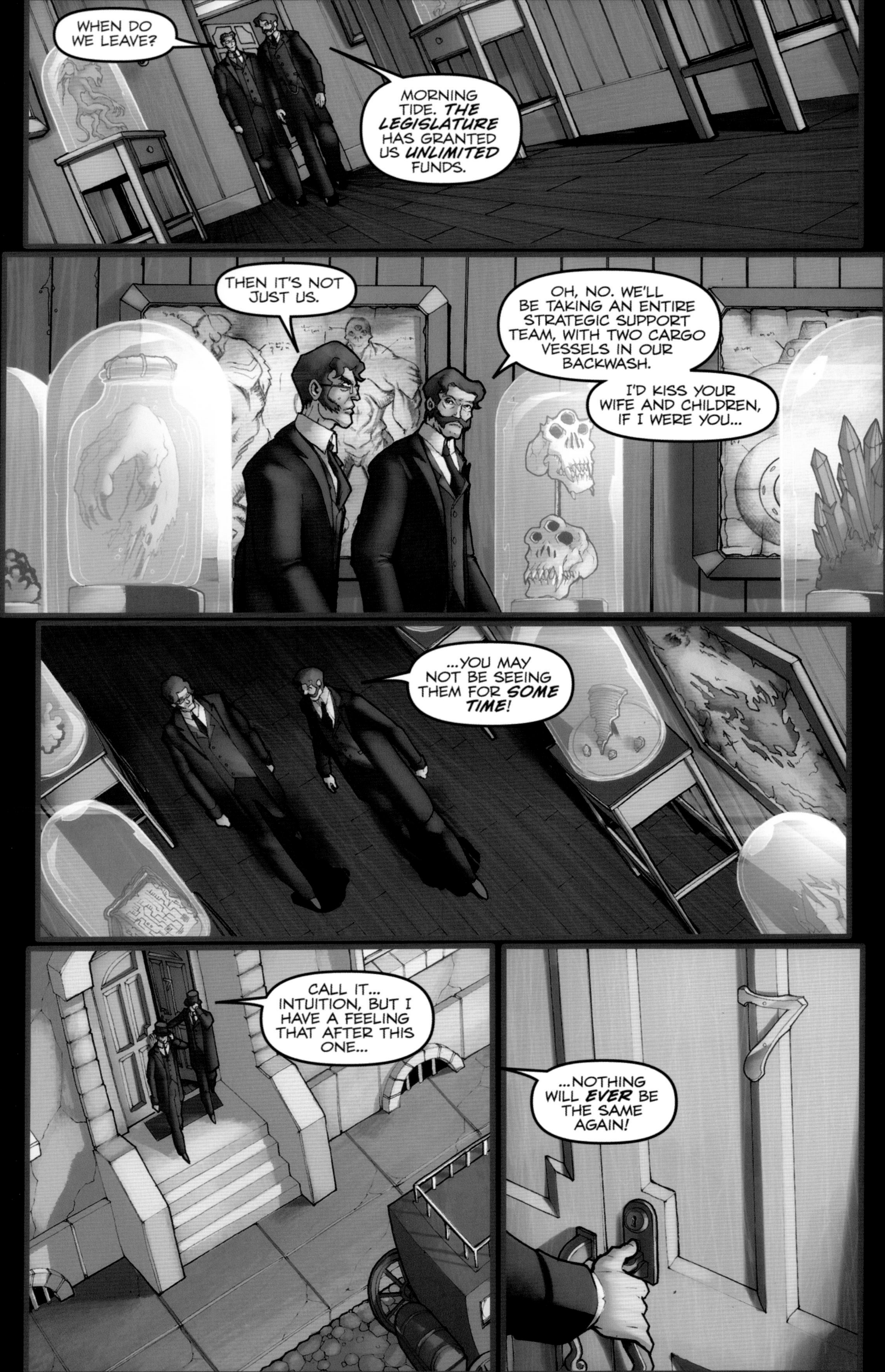
WHEN DO WE LEAVE?
MORNING TIDE. THE LEGISLATURE HAS GRANTED US UNLIMITED FUNDS.
THEN IT'S NOT JUST US.
OH, NO. WE'LL BE TAKING AN ENTIRE STRATEGIC SUPPORT TEAM, WITH TWO CARGO VESSELS IN OUR BACKWASH.
I'D KISS YOUR WIFE AND CHILDREN, IF I WERE YOU...
...YOU MAY NOT BE SEEING THEM FOR SOME TIME!
CALL IT... INTUITION, BUT I HAVE A FEELING THAT AFTER THIS ONE...
...NOTHING WILL EVER BE THE SAME AGAIN!

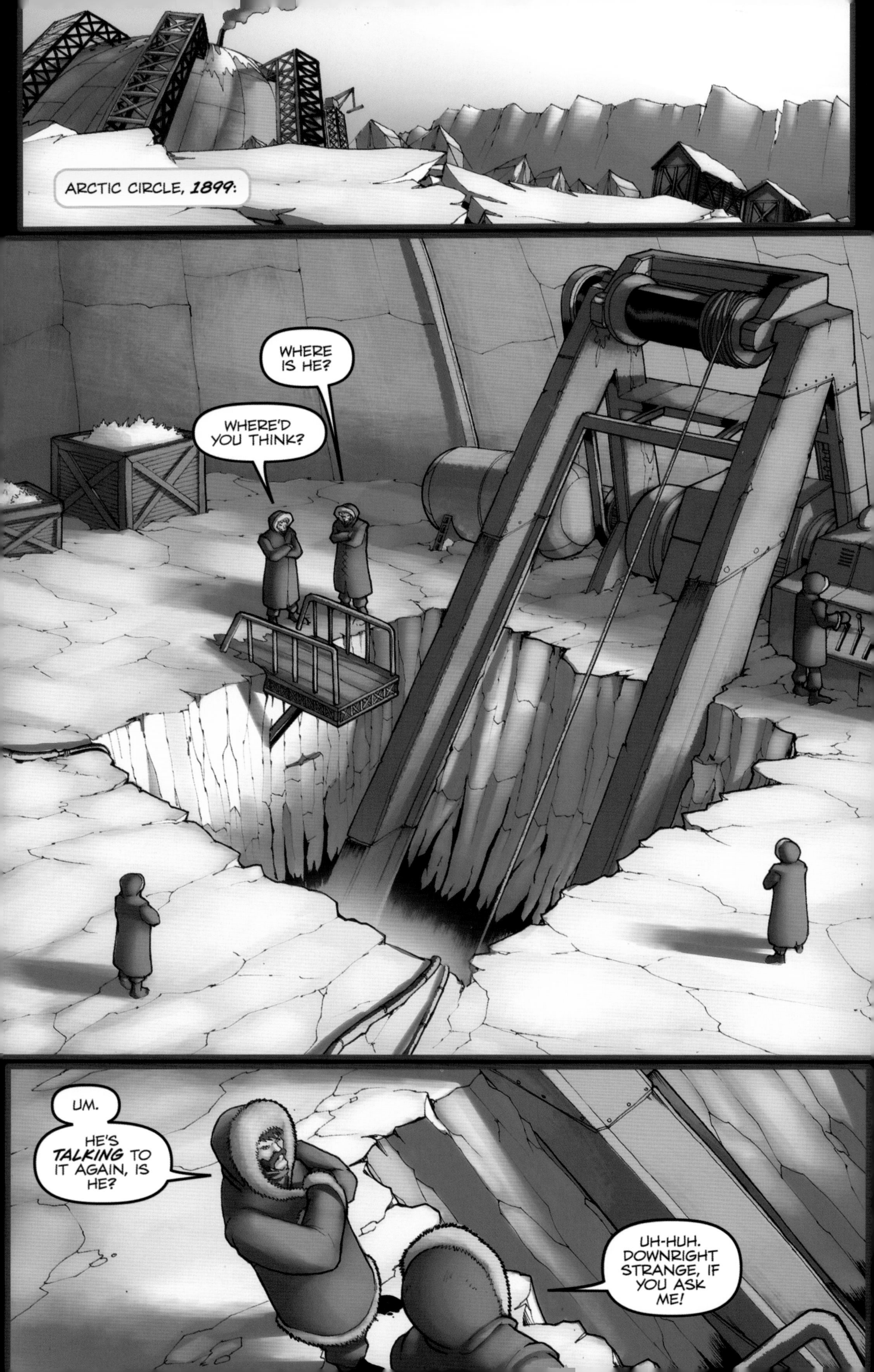
ARCTIC CIRCLE, **1899**:
WHERE IS HE?
WHERE'D YOU THINK?
UM.
HE'S ***TALKING*** TO IT AGAIN, IS HE?
UH-HUH. DOWNRIGHT STRANGE, IF YOU ASK ME!

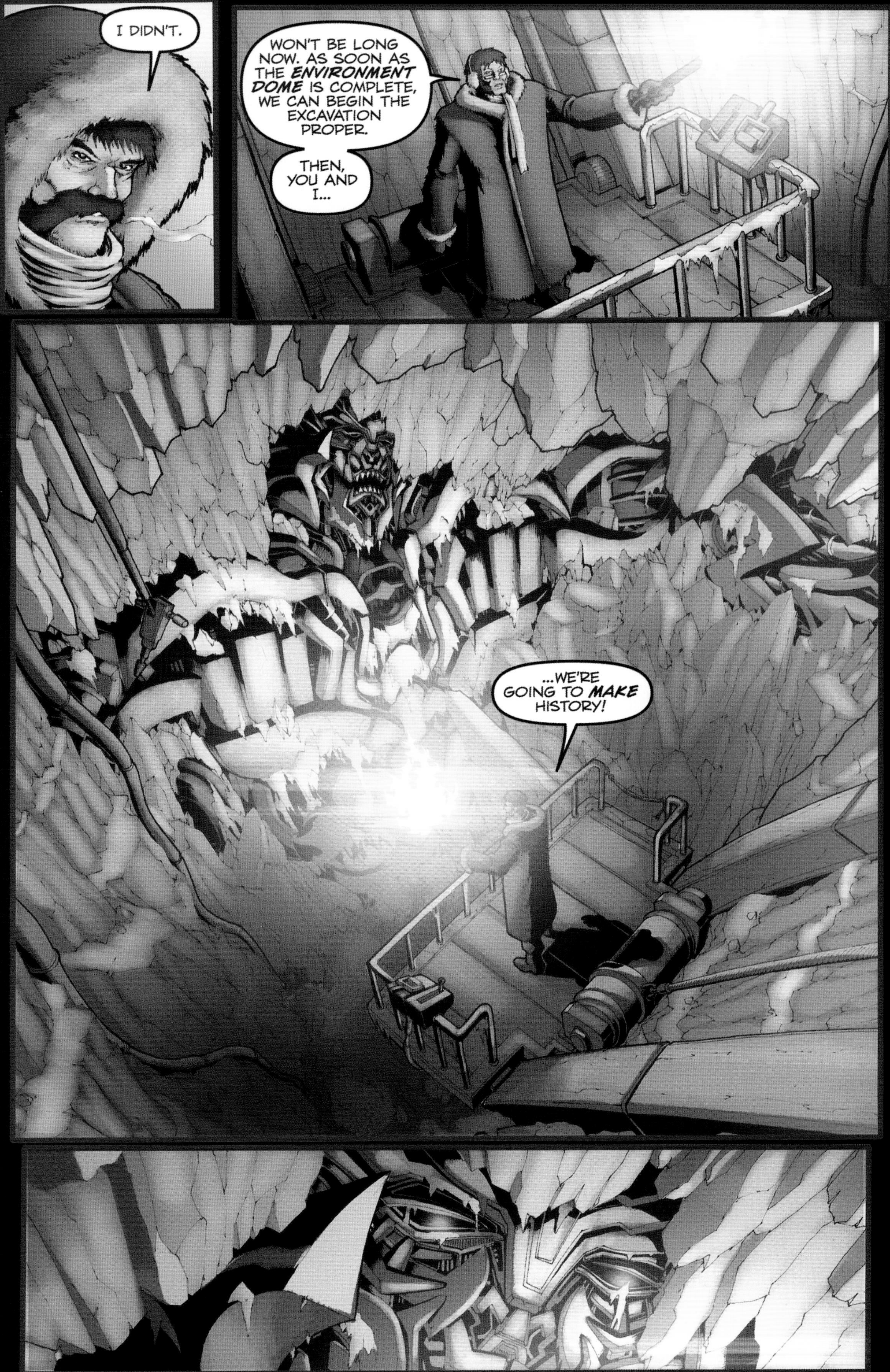
I DIDN'T.
WON'T BE LONG NOW. AS SOON AS THE ENVIRONMENT DOME IS COMPLETE, WE CAN BEGIN THE EXCAVATION PROPER.
THEN, YOU AND I...
...WE'RE GOING TO MAKE HISTORY!

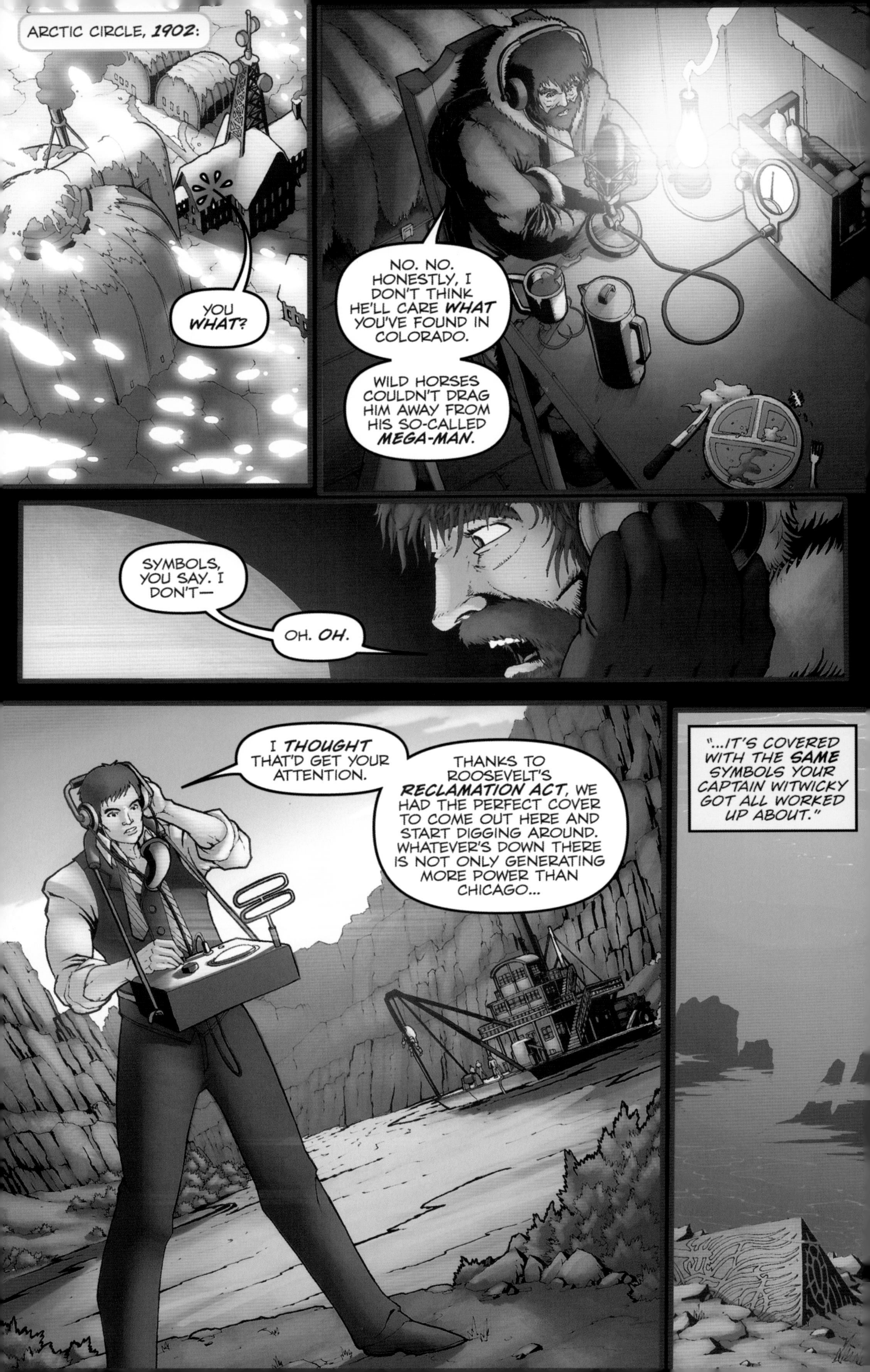

ARCTIC CIRCLE, 1902:
YOU WHAT?
NO. NO. HONESTLY, I DON'T THINK HE'LL CARE WHAT YOU'VE FOUND IN COLORADO.
WILD HORSES COULDN'T DRAG HIM AWAY FROM HIS SO-CALLED MEGA-MAN.
SYMBOLS, YOU SAY. I DON'T—
OH. OH.
I THOUGHT THAT'D GET YOUR ATTENTION.
THANKS TO ROOSEVELT'S RECLAMATION ACT, WE HAD THE PERFECT COVER TO COME OUT HERE AND START DIGGING AROUND. WHATEVER'S DOWN THERE IS NOT ONLY GENERATING MORE POWER THAN CHICAGO...
"...IT'S COVERED WITH THE SAME SYMBOLS YOUR CAPTAIN WITWICKY GOT ALL WORKED UP ABOUT."

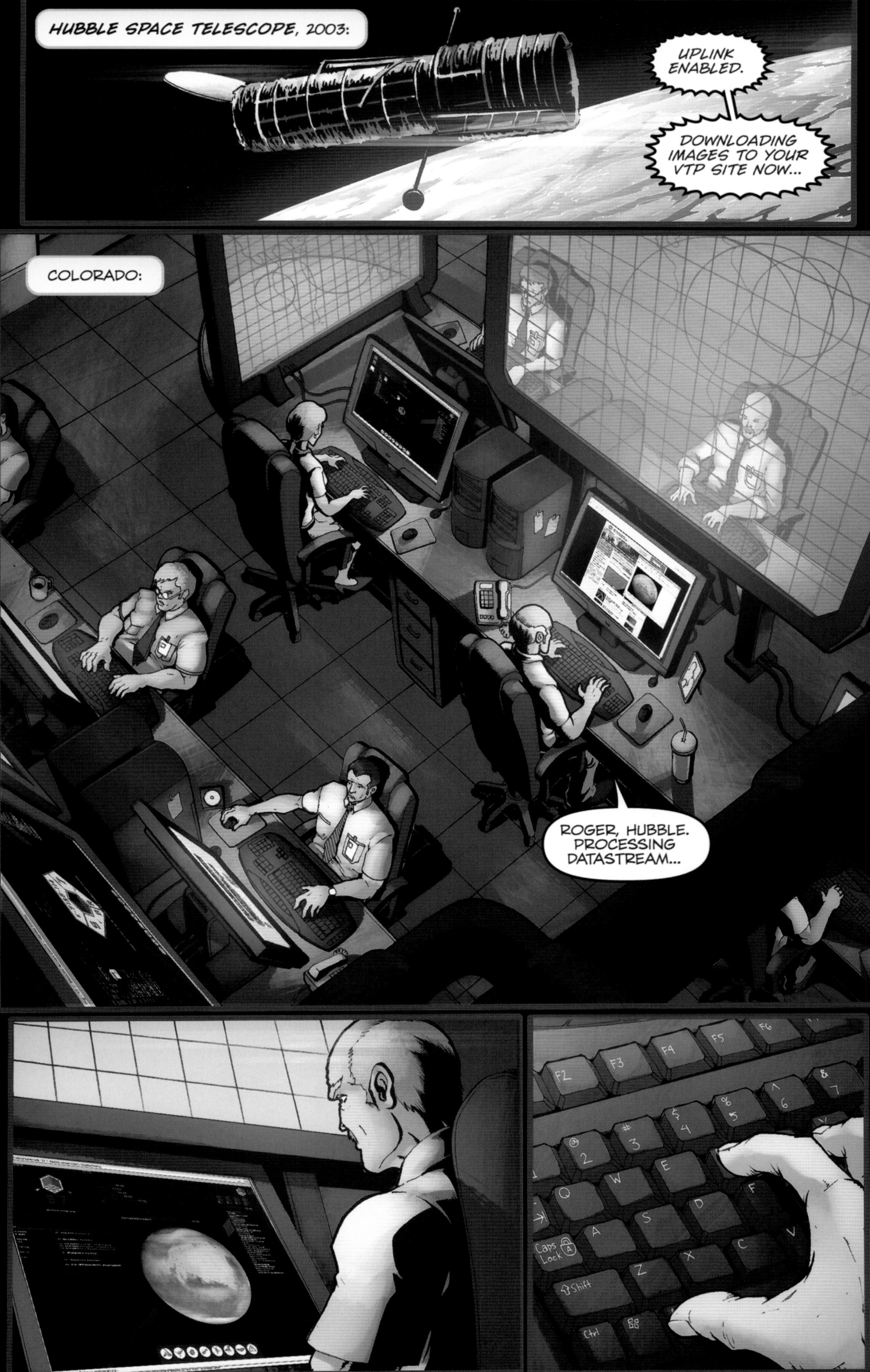
HUBBLE SPACE TELESCOPE, 2003:
UPLINK ENABLED.
DOWNLOADING IMAGES TO YOUR VTP SITE NOW...
COLORADO:
ROGER, HUBBLE. PROCESSING DATASTREAM...

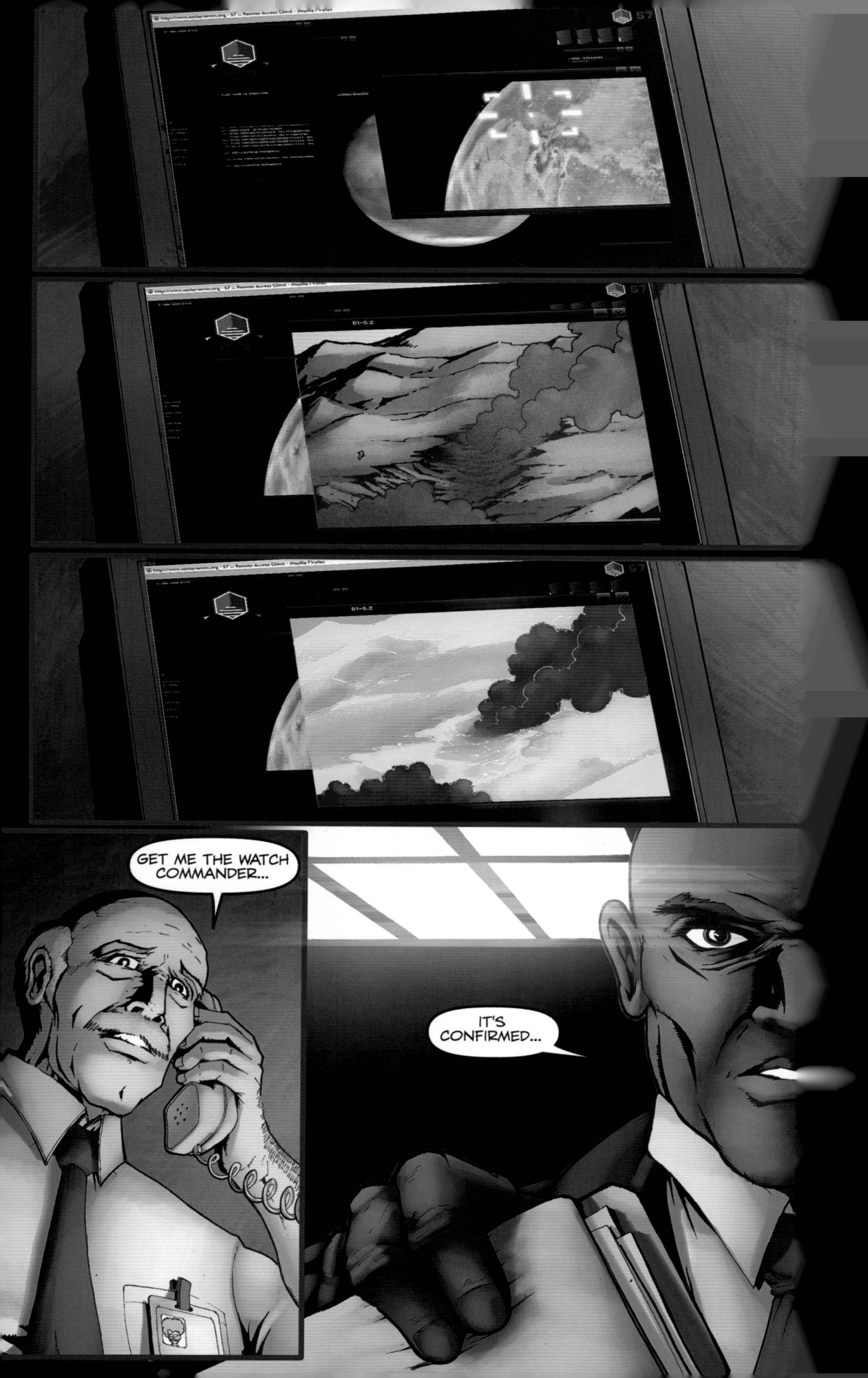
GET ME THE WATCH COMMANDER...
IT'S CONFIRMED...

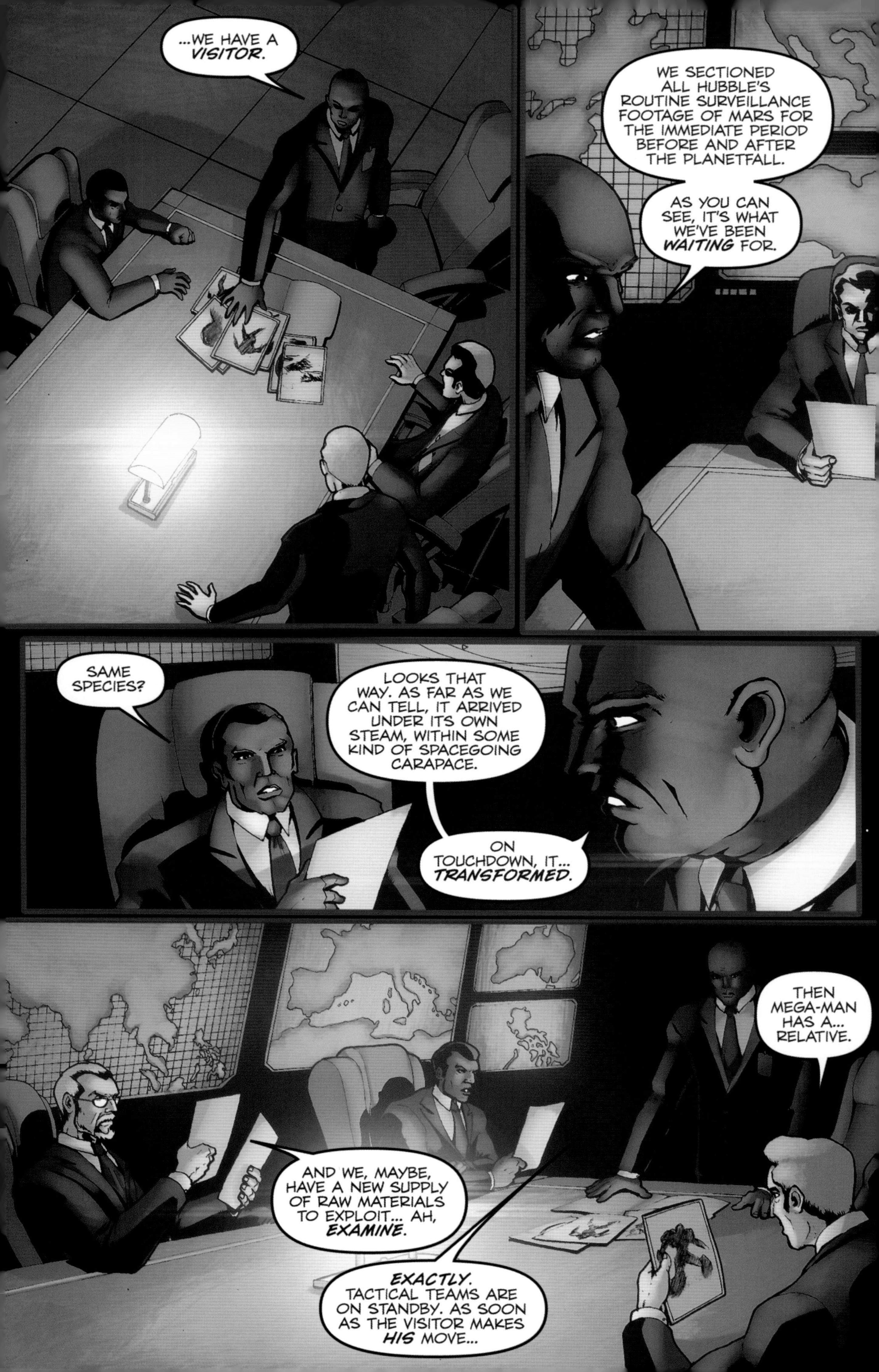
...WE HAVE A VISITOR.
WE SECTIONED ALL HUBBLE'S ROUTINE SURVEILLANCE FOOTAGE OF MARS FOR THE IMMEDIATE PERIOD BEFORE AND AFTER THE PLANETFALL.
AS YOU CAN SEE, IT'S WHAT WE'VE BEEN WAITING FOR.
SAME SPECIES?
LOOKS THAT WAY. AS FAR AS WE CAN TELL, IT ARRIVED UNDER ITS OWN STEAM, WITHIN SOME KIND OF SPACEGOING CARAPACE.
ON TOUCHDOWN, IT... TRANSFORMED.
THEN MEGA-MAN HAS A... RELATIVE.
AND WE, MAYBE, HAVE A NEW SUPPLY OF RAW MATERIALS TO EXPLOIT... AH, EXAMINE.
EXACTLY. TACTICAL TEAMS ARE ON STANDBY. AS SOON AS THE VISITOR MAKES HIS MOVE...

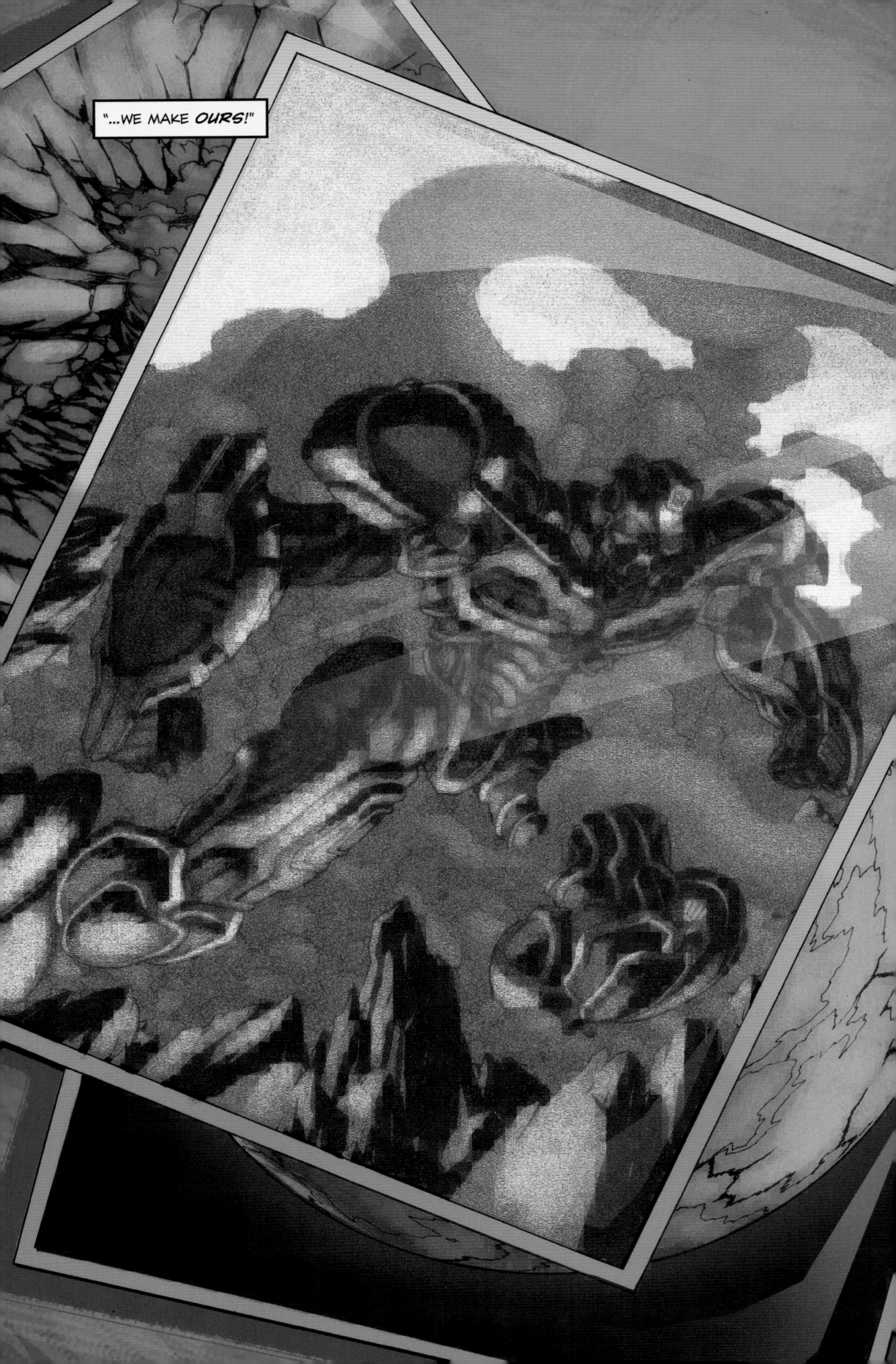
"...WE MAKE OURS!"

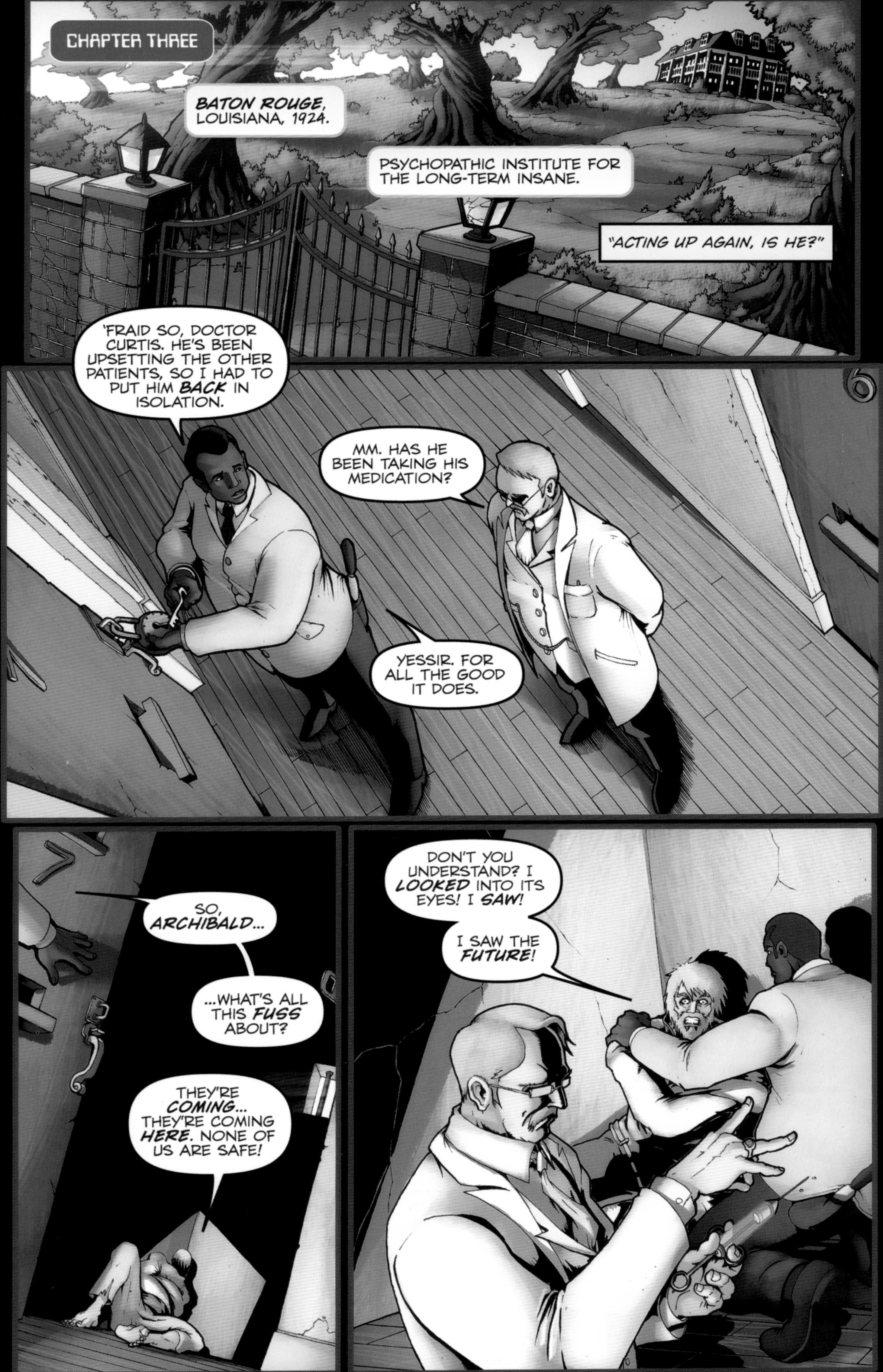
CHAPTER THREE
BATON ROUGE, LOUISIANA, 1924.
PSYCHOPATHIC INSTITUTE FOR THE LONG-TERM INSANE.
"ACTING UP AGAIN, IS HE?"
'FRAID SO, DOCTOR CURTIS. HE'S BEEN UPSETTING THE OTHER PATIENTS, SO I HAD TO PUT HIM BACK IN ISOLATION.
MM. HAS HE BEEN TAKING HIS MEDICATION?
YESSIR. FOR ALL THE GOOD IT DOES.
SO, ARCHIBALD...
...WHAT'S ALL THIS FUSS ABOUT?
THEY'RE COMING... THEY'RE COMING HERE. NONE OF US ARE SAFE!
DON'T YOU UNDERSTAND? I LOOKED INTO ITS EYES! I SAW!
I SAW THE FUTURE!

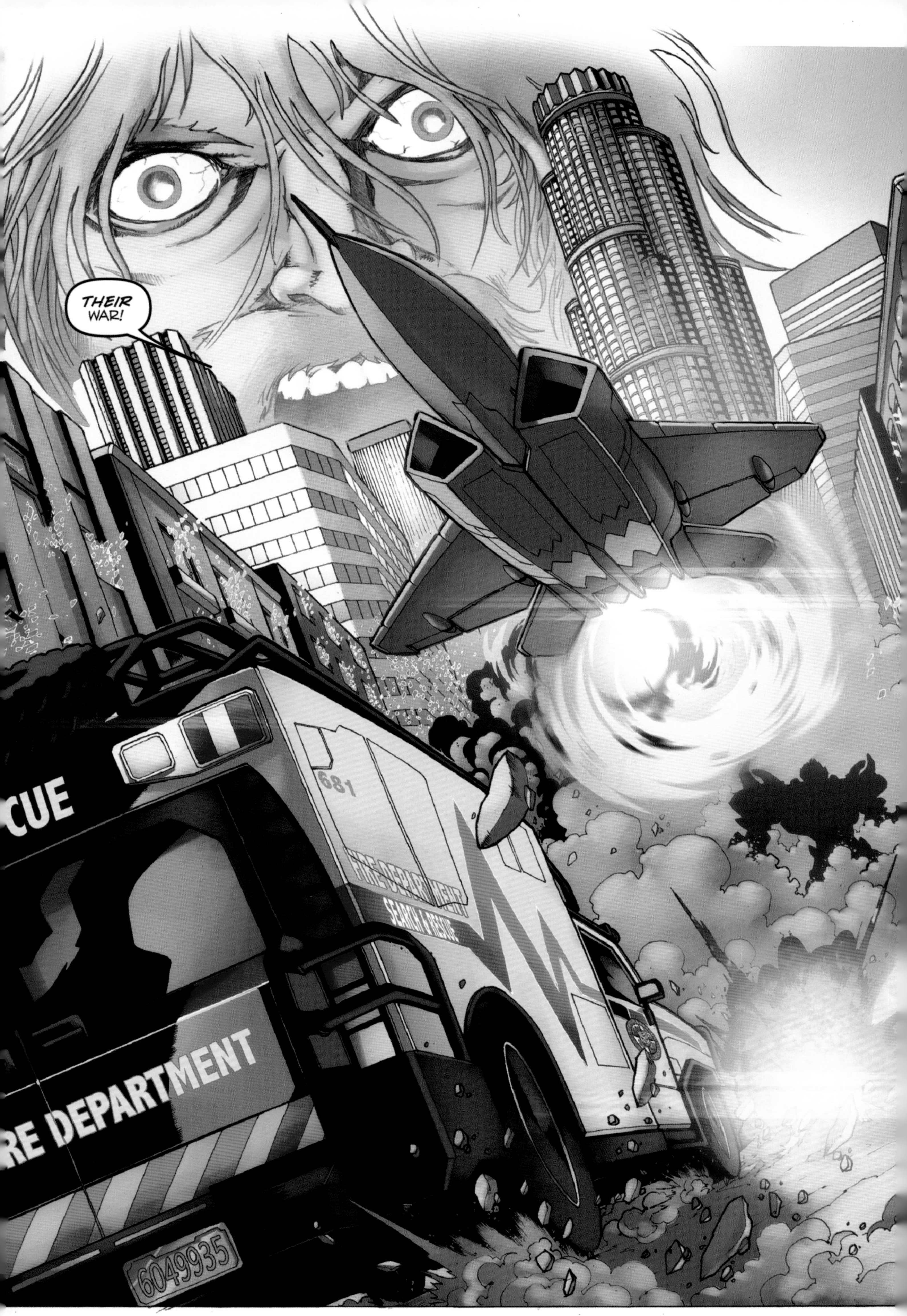
THEIR WAR!
CUE
RE DEPARTMENT
681
FIRE DEPARTMENT
SEARCH & RESCUE
6049935

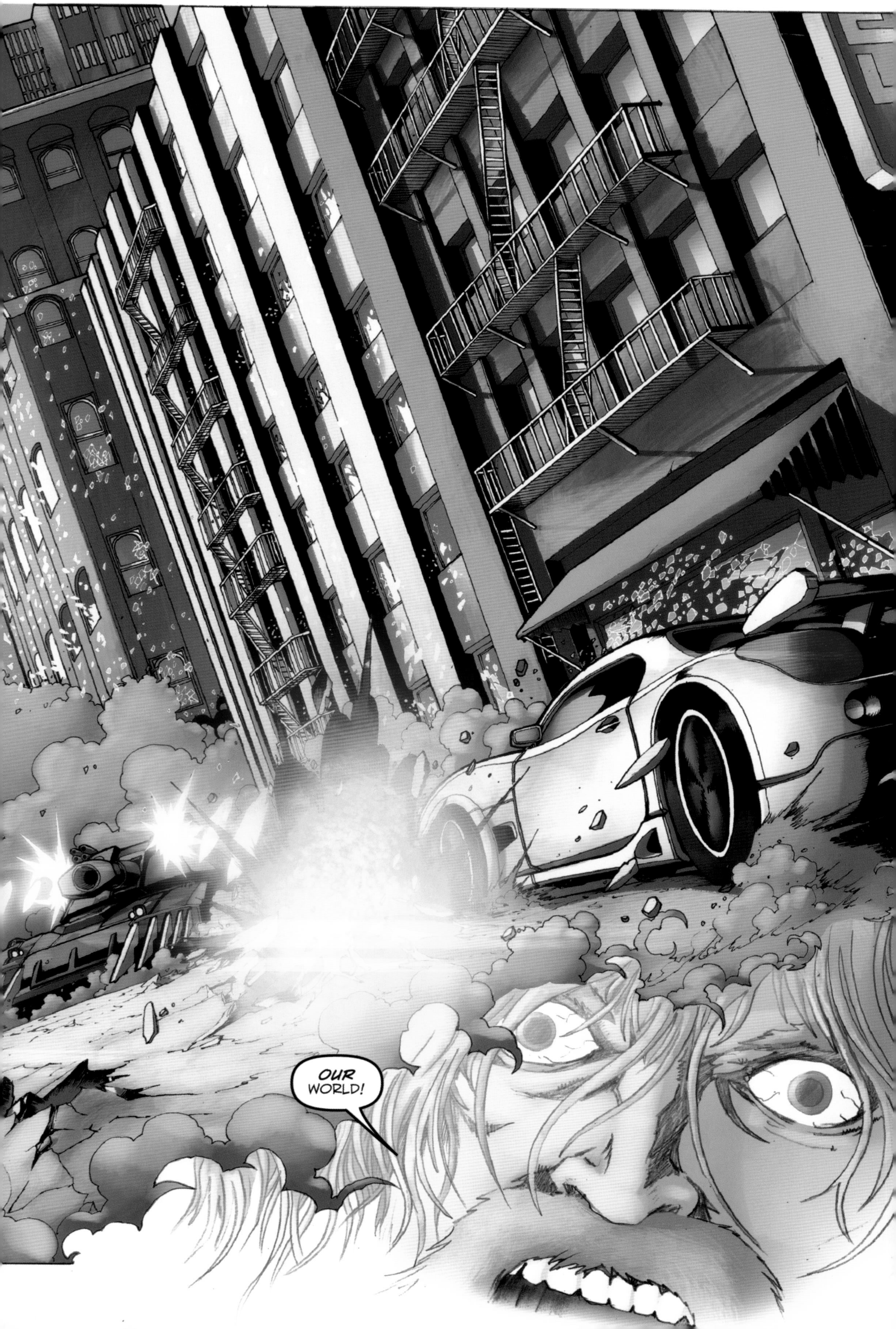
OUR WORLD!

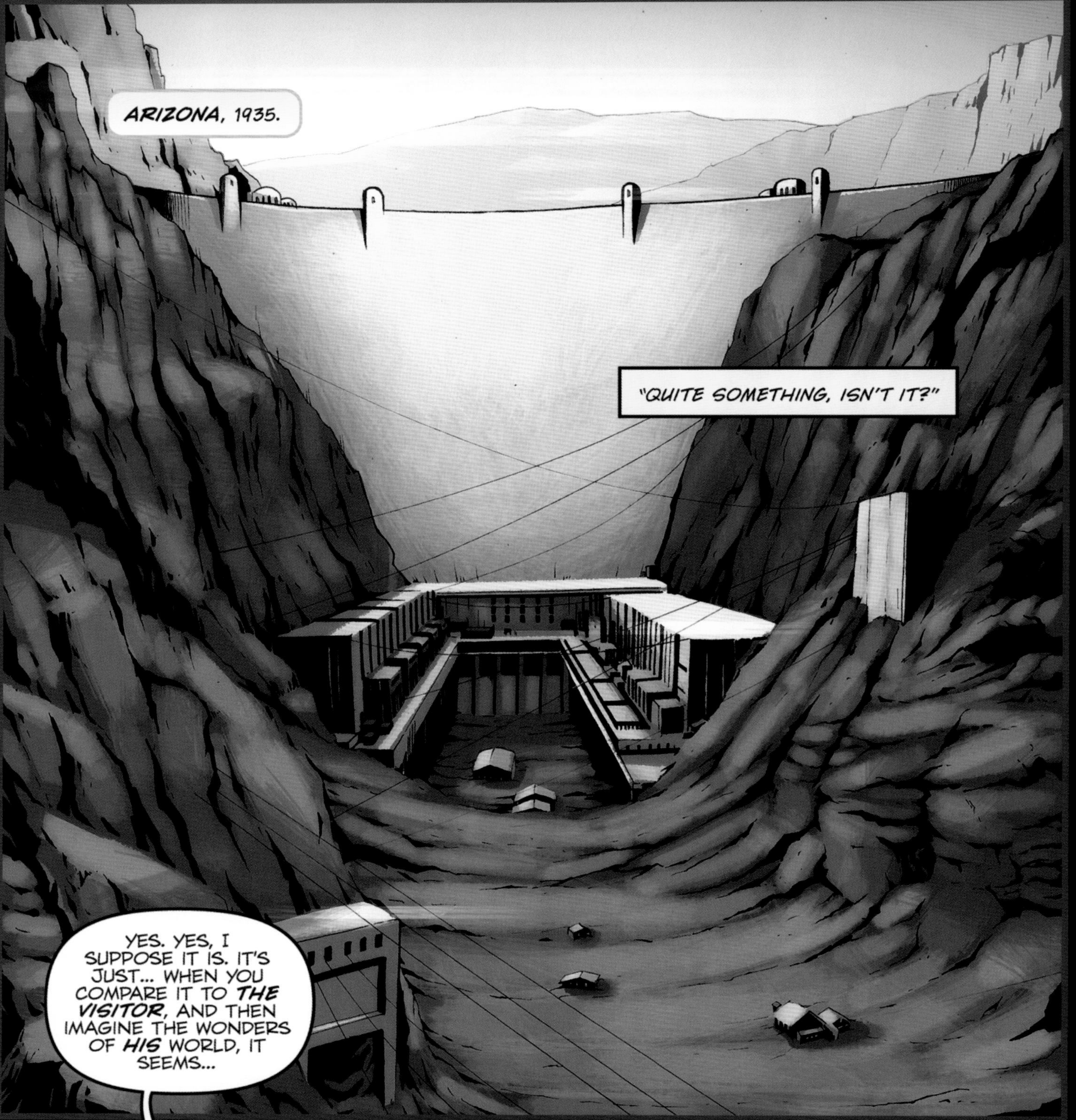
ARIZONA, 1935.
"QUITE SOMETHING, ISN'T IT?"
YES. YES, I SUPPOSE IT IS. IT'S JUST... WHEN YOU COMPARE IT TO THE VISITOR, AND THEN IMAGINE THE WONDERS OF HIS WORLD, IT SEEMS...
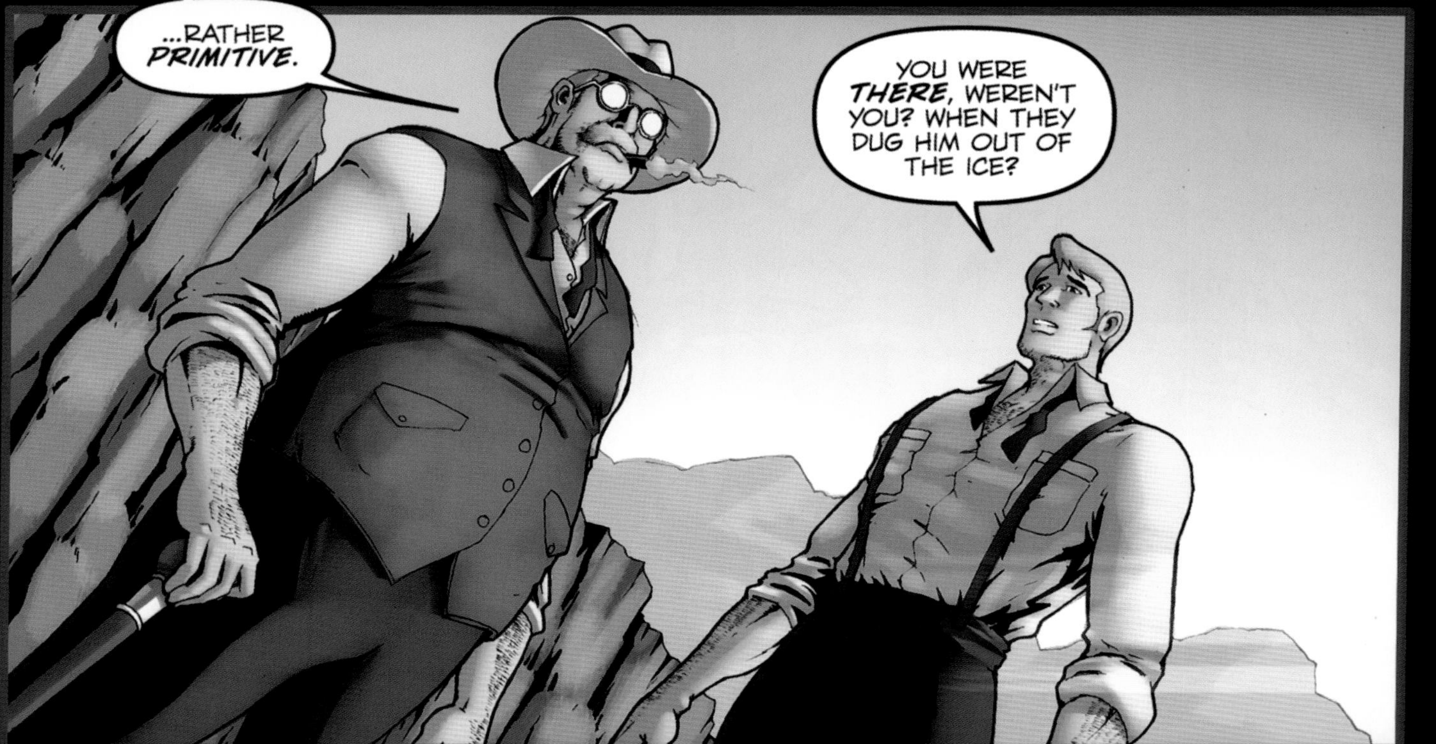
...RATHER PRIMITIVE.
YOU WERE THERE, WEREN'T YOU? WHEN THEY DUG HIM OUT OF THE ICE?

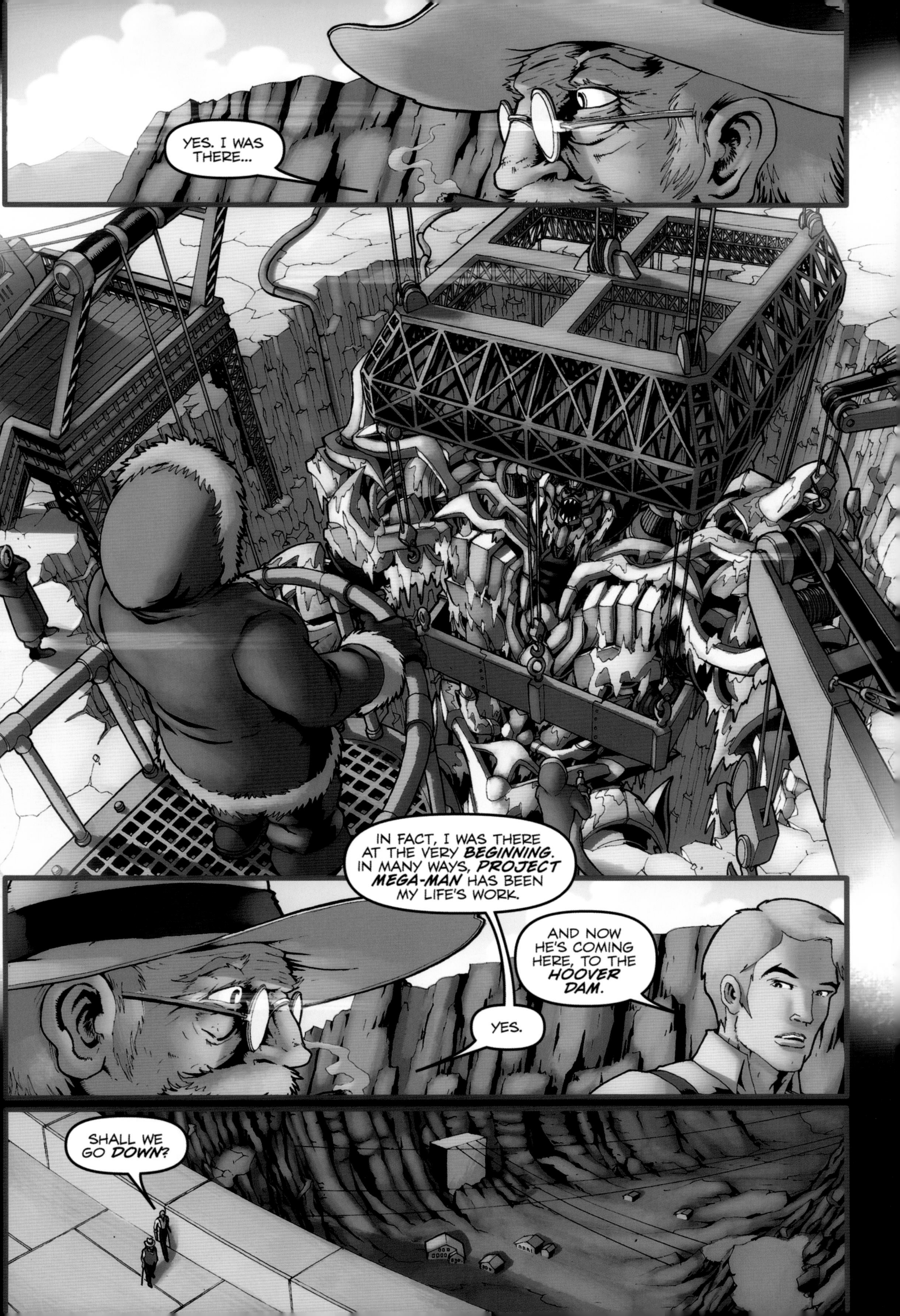

YES. I WAS THERE...
IN FACT, I WAS THERE AT THE VERY BEGINNING. IN MANY WAYS, PROJECT MEGA-MAN HAS BEEN MY LIFE'S WORK.
AND NOW HE'S COMING HERE, TO THE HOOVER DAM.
YES.
SHALL WE GO DOWN?

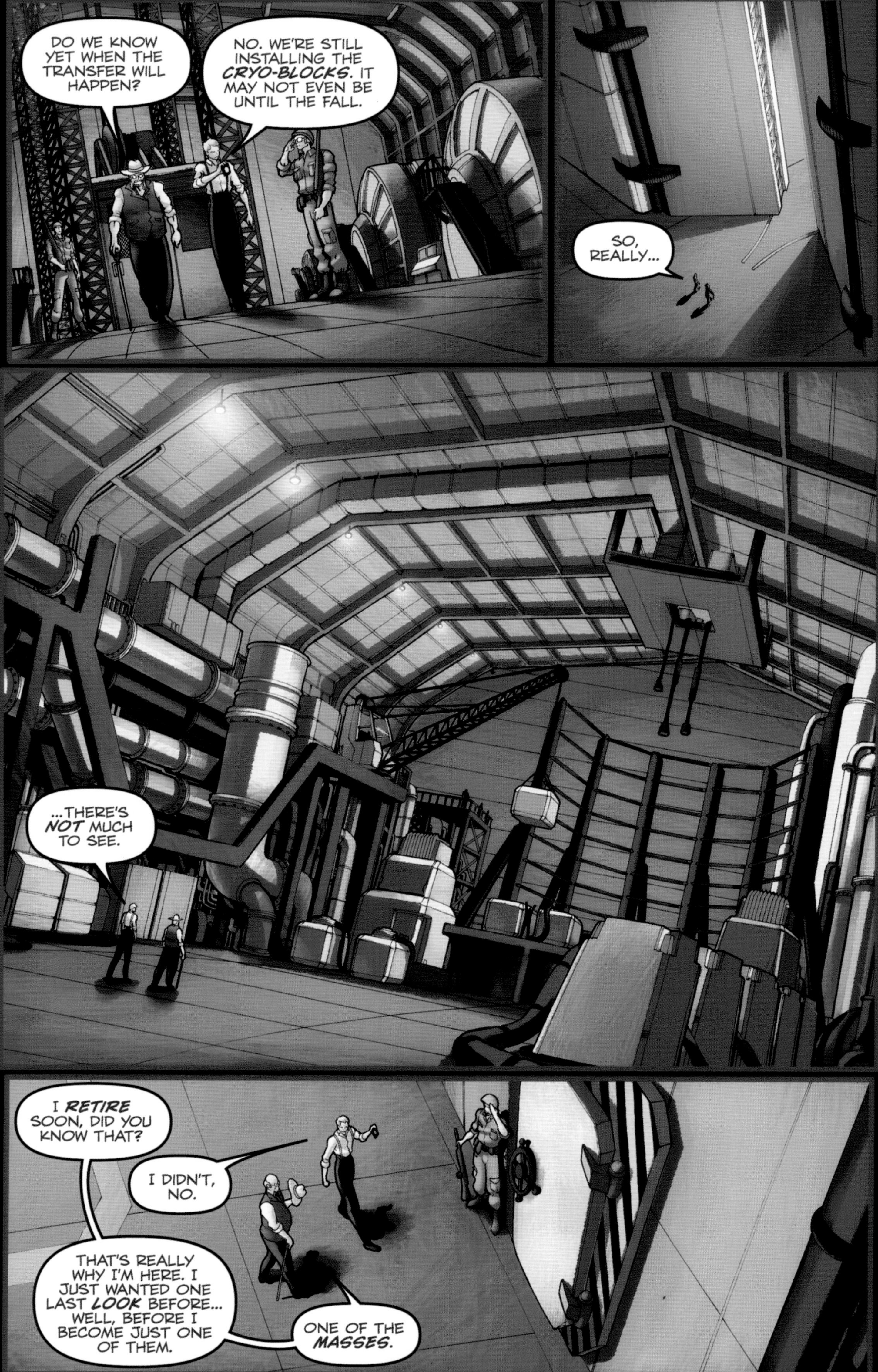

DO WE KNOW YET WHEN THE TRANSFER WILL HAPPEN?
NO. WE'RE STILL INSTALLING THE CRYO-BLOCKS. IT MAY NOT EVEN BE UNTIL THE FALL.
SO, REALLY...
...THERE'S NOT MUCH TO SEE.
I RETIRE SOON, DID YOU KNOW THAT?
I DIDN'T, NO.
THAT'S REALLY WHY I'M HERE. I JUST WANTED ONE LAST LOOK BEFORE... WELL, BEFORE I BECOME JUST ONE OF THEM.
ONE OF THE MASSES.

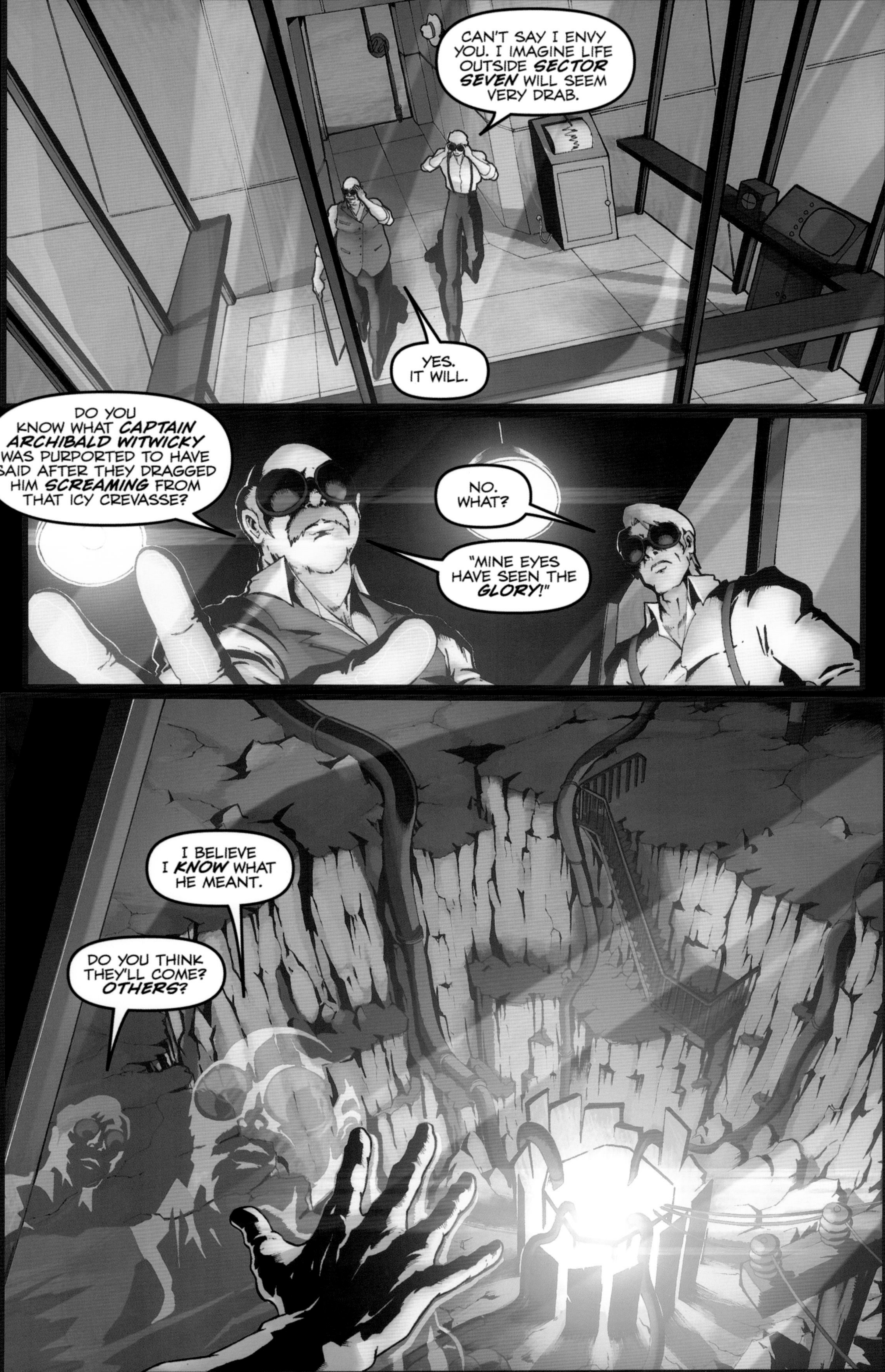

CAN'T SAY I ENVY YOU. I IMAGINE LIFE OUTSIDE SECTOR SEVEN WILL SEEM VERY DRAB.
YES. IT WILL.
DO YOU KNOW WHAT CAPTAIN ARCHIBALD WITWICKY WAS PURPORTED TO HAVE SAID AFTER THEY DRAGGED HIM SCREAMING FROM THAT ICY CREVASSE?
NO. WHAT?
"MINE EYES HAVE SEEN THE GLORY!"
I BELIEVE I KNOW WHAT HE MEANT.
DO YOU THINK THEY'LL COME? OTHERS?

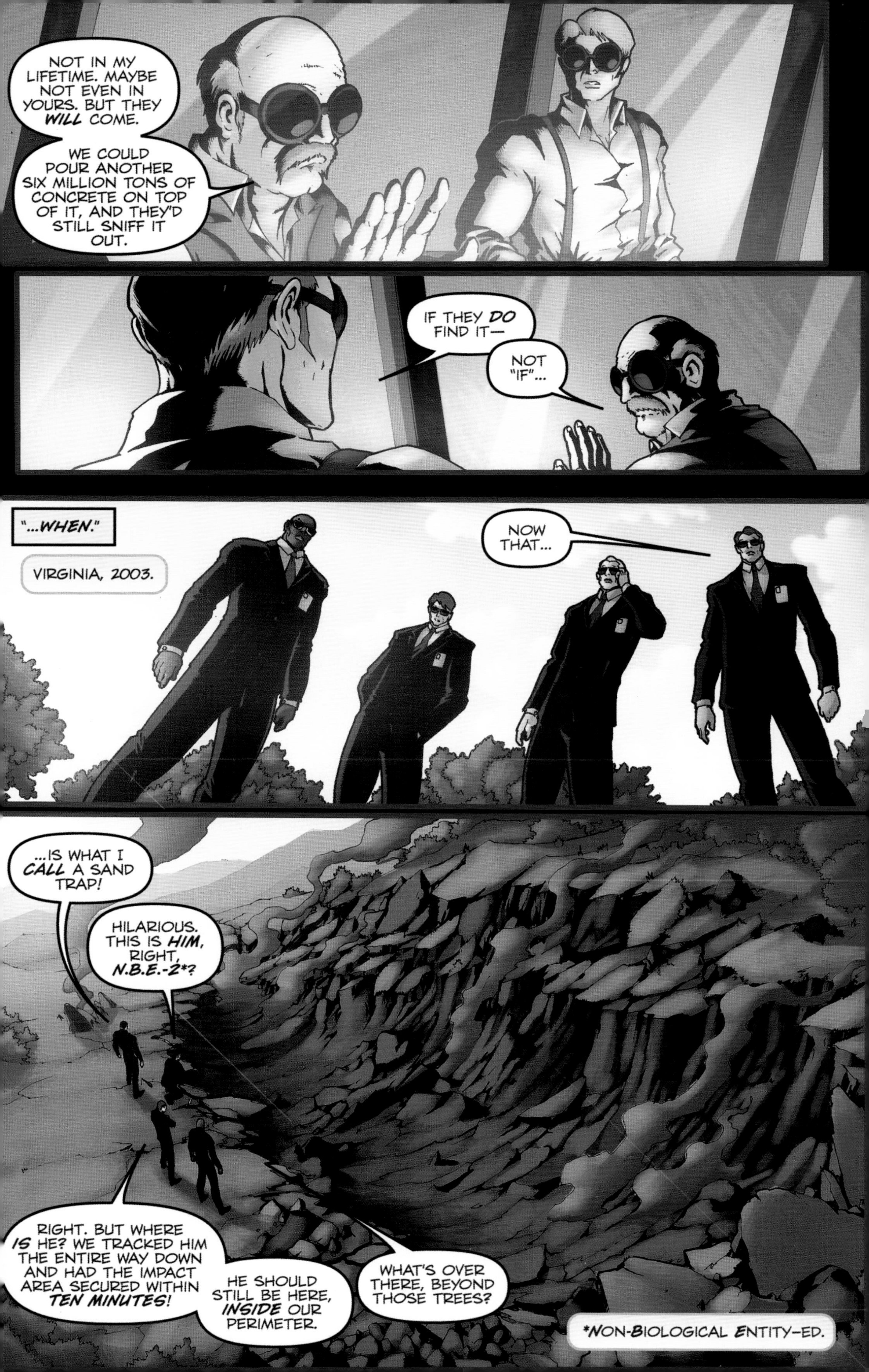
NOT IN MY LIFETIME. MAYBE NOT EVEN IN YOURS. BUT THEY WILL COME.
WE COULD POUR ANOTHER SIX MILLION TONS OF CONCRETE ON TOP OF IT, AND THEY'D STILL SNIFF IT OUT.
IF THEY DO FIND IT—
NOT "IF"...
"...WHEN."
VIRGINIA, 2003.
NOW THAT...
...IS WHAT I CALL A SAND TRAP!
HILARIOUS. THIS IS HIM, RIGHT, N.B.E.-2*?
RIGHT. BUT WHERE IS HE? WE TRACKED HIM THE ENTIRE WAY DOWN AND HAD THE IMPACT AREA SECURED WITHIN TEN MINUTES!
HE SHOULD STILL BE HERE, INSIDE OUR PERIMETER.
WHAT'S OVER THERE, BEYOND THOSE TREES?
*NON-BIOLOGICAL ENTITY—ED.

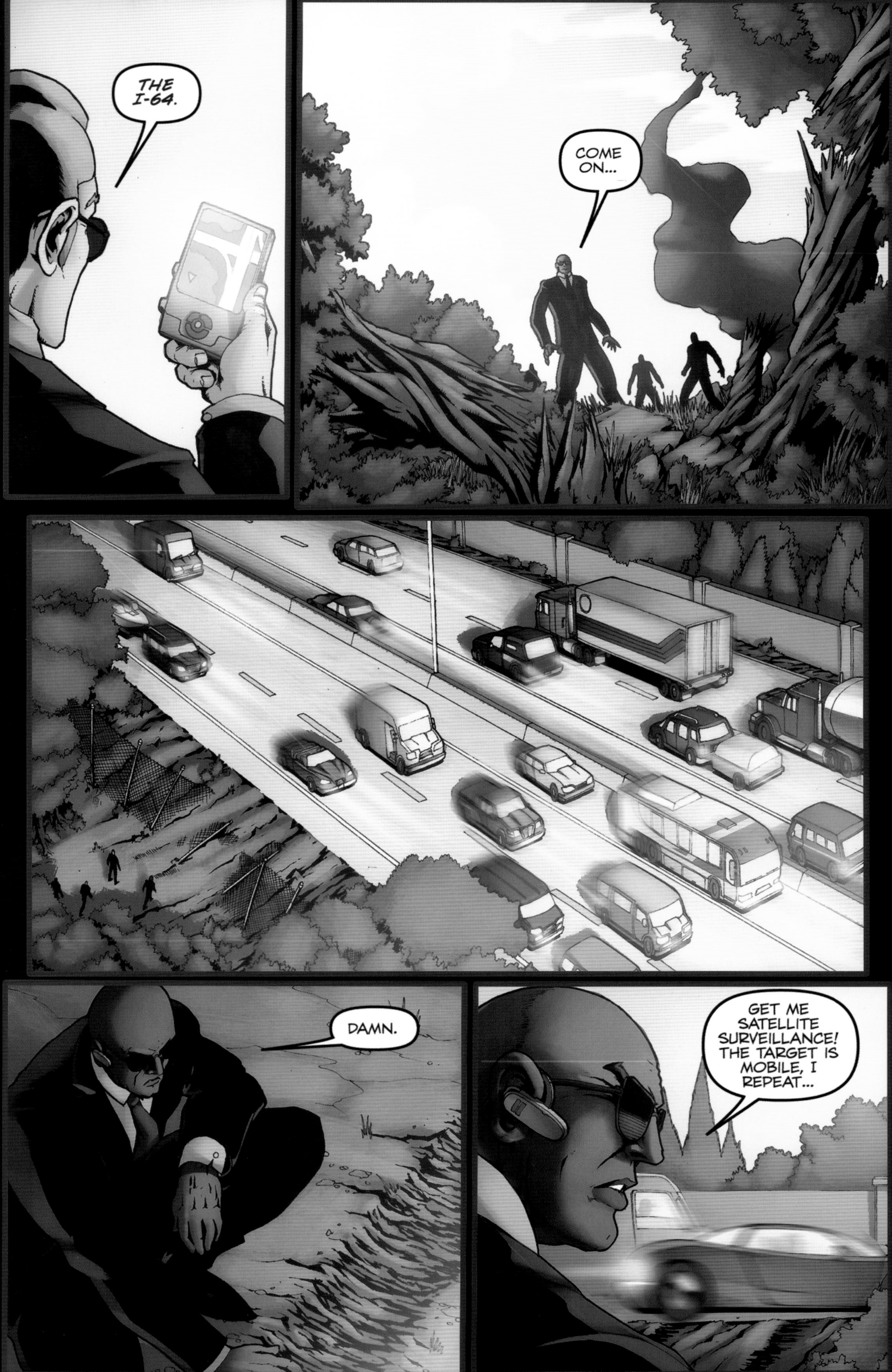
THE I-64.
COME ON...
DAMN.
GET ME SATELLITE SURVEILLANCE! THE TARGET IS MOBILE, I REPEAT...

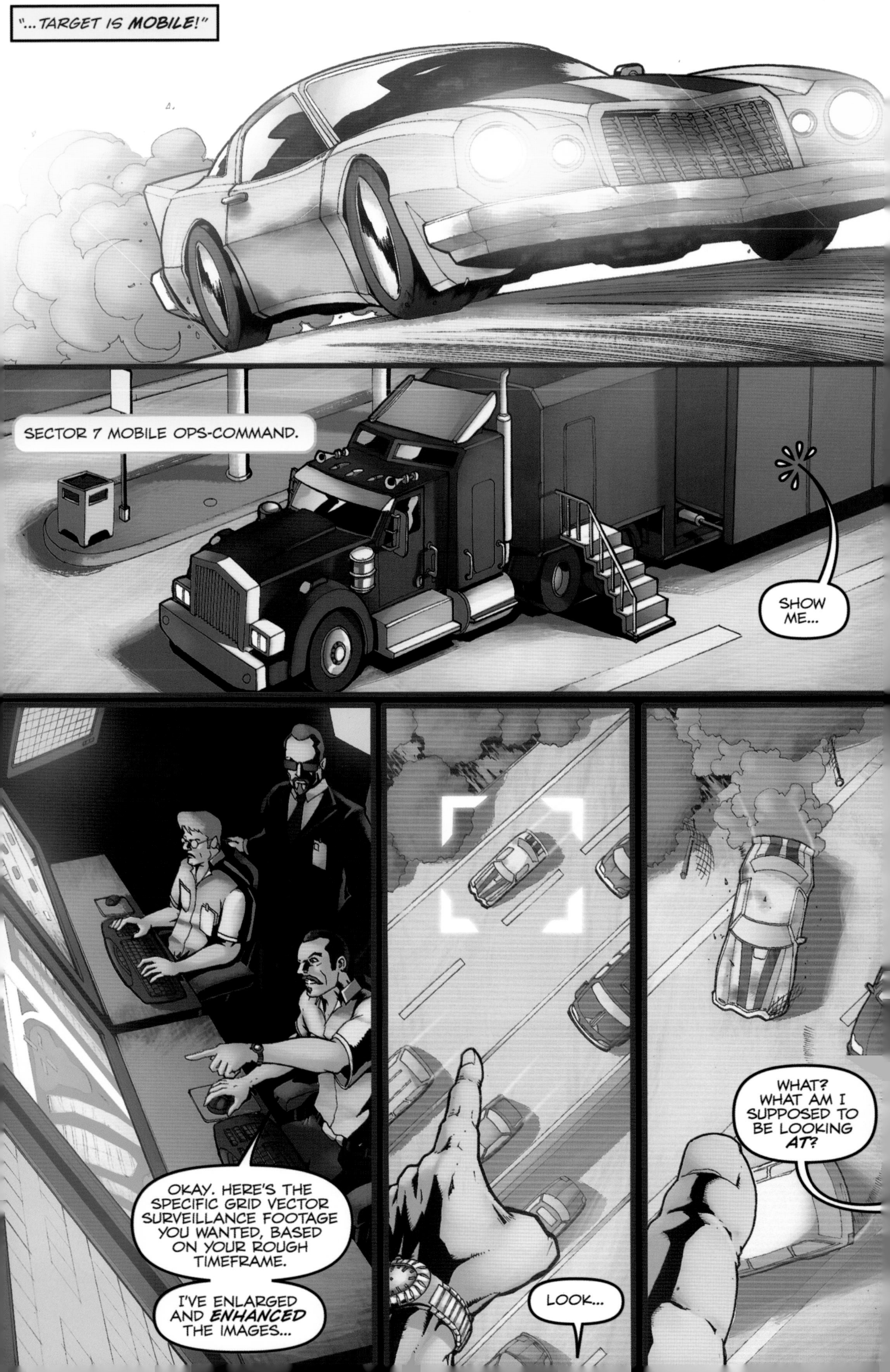
"...TARGET IS MOBILE!"
SECTOR 7 MOBILE OPS-COMMAND.
SHOW ME...
OKAY. HERE'S THE SPECIFIC GRID VECTOR SURVEILLANCE FOOTAGE YOU WANTED, BASED ON YOUR ROUGH TIMEFRAME.
I'VE ENLARGED AND ENHANCED THE IMAGES...
LOOK...
WHAT? WHAT AM I SUPPOSED TO BE LOOKING AT?

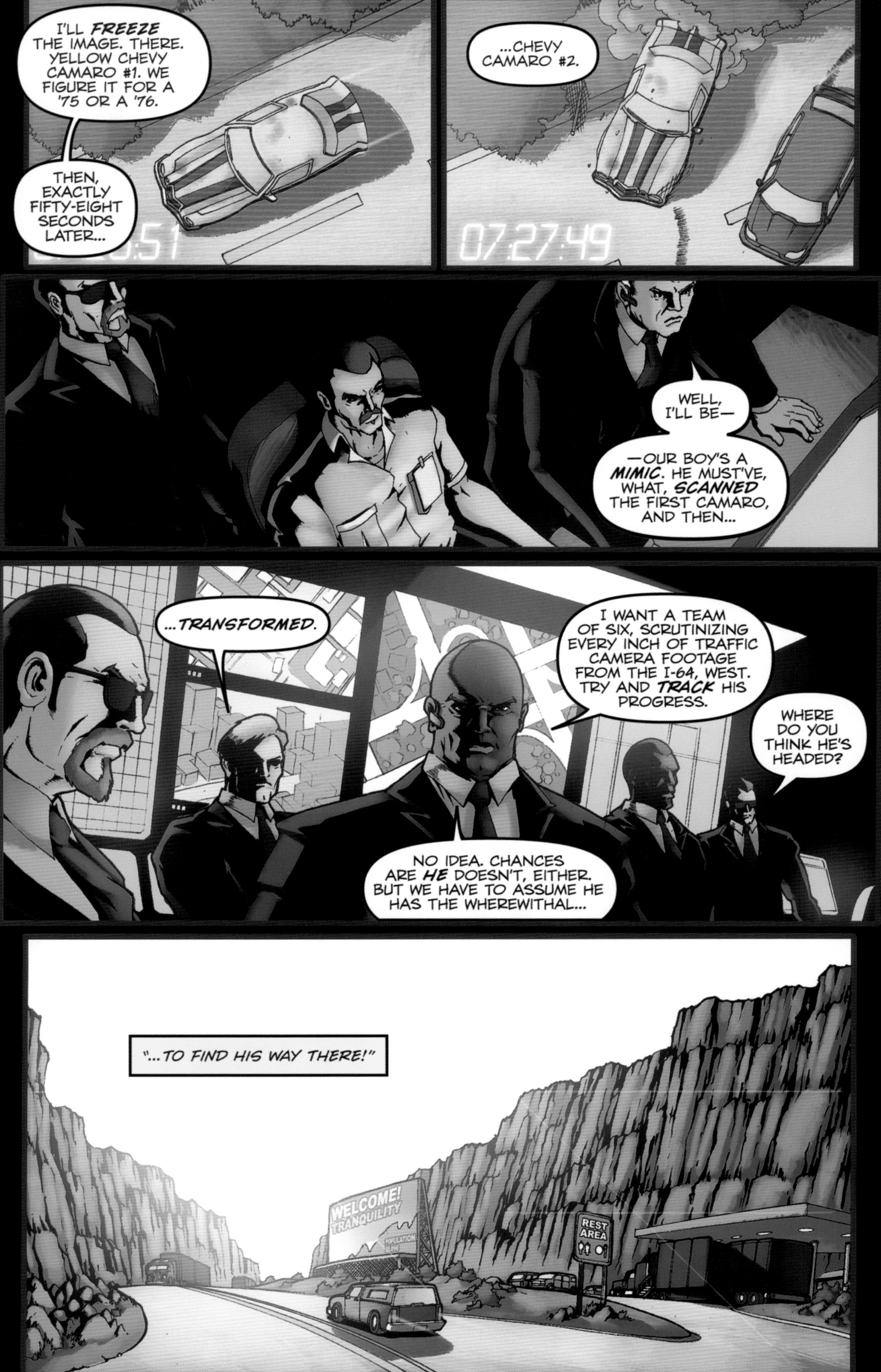
I'LL FREEZE THE IMAGE. THERE. YELLOW CHEVY CAMARO #1. WE FIGURE IT FOR A '75 OR A '76.
THEN, EXACTLY FIFTY-EIGHT SECONDS LATER...
...CHEVY CAMARO #2.
07:27:49
WELL, I'LL BE—
—OUR BOY'S A MIMIC. HE MUST'VE, WHAT, SCANNED THE FIRST CAMARO, AND THEN...
...TRANSFORMED.
I WANT A TEAM OF SIX, SCRUTINIZING EVERY INCH OF TRAFFIC CAMERA FOOTAGE FROM THE I-64, WEST. TRY AND TRACK HIS PROGRESS.
WHERE DO YOU THINK HE'S HEADED?
NO IDEA. CHANCES ARE HE DOESN'T, EITHER. BUT WE HAVE TO ASSUME HE HAS THE WHEREWITHAL...
"...TO FIND HIS WAY THERE!"
WELCOME! TRANQUILITY
REST AREA

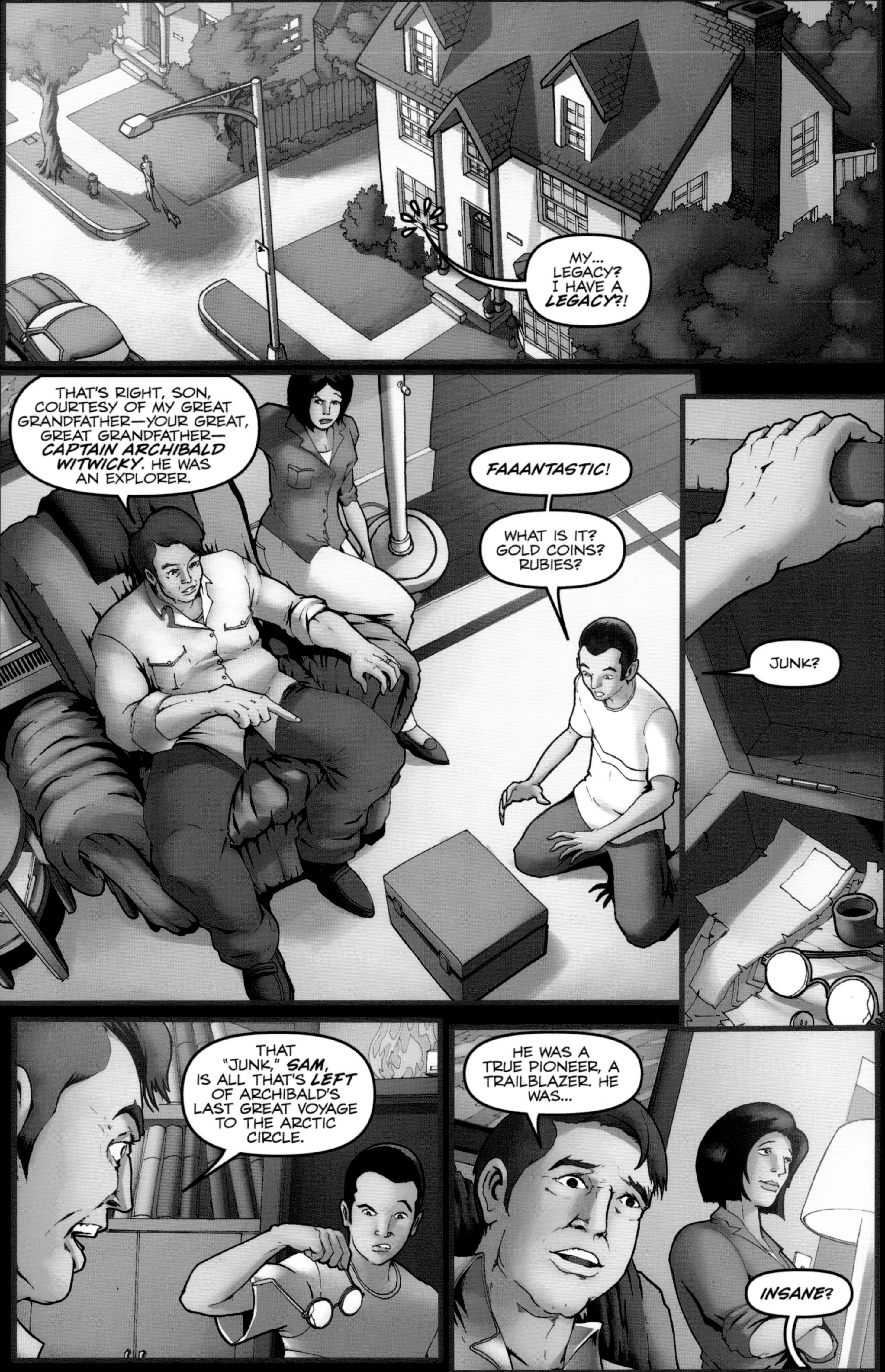
MY... LEGACY? I HAVE A LEGACY?!
THAT'S RIGHT, SON, COURTESY OF MY GREAT GRANDFATHER—YOUR GREAT, GREAT GRANDFATHER—CAPTAIN ARCHIBALD WITWICKY. HE WAS AN EXPLORER.
FAAANTASTIC!
WHAT IS IT? GOLD COINS? RUBIES?
JUNK?
THAT "JUNK," SAM, IS ALL THAT'S LEFT OF ARCHIBALD'S LAST GREAT VOYAGE TO THE ARCTIC CIRCLE.
HE WAS A TRUE PIONEER, A TRAILBLAZER. HE WAS...
INSANE?

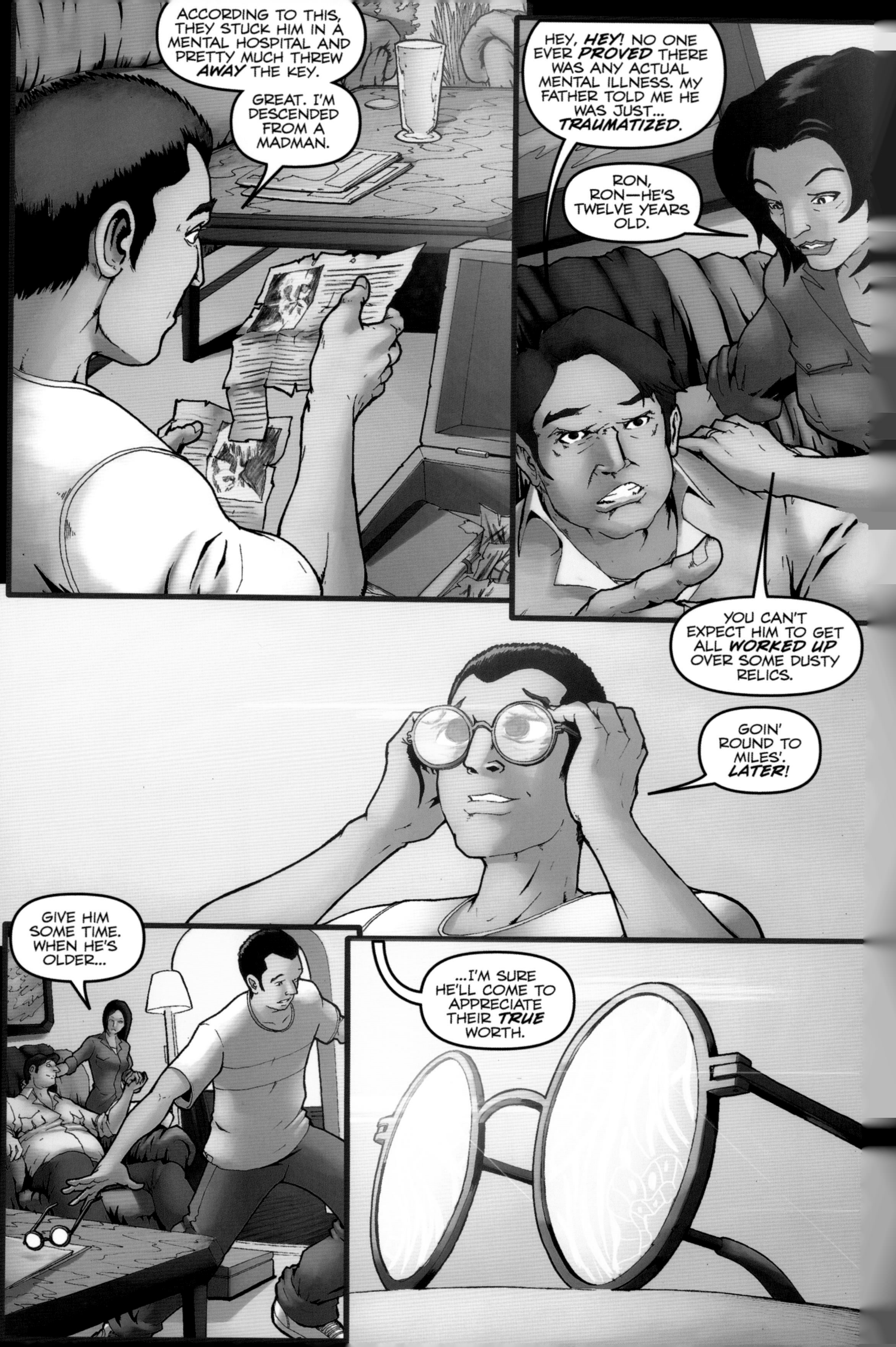
ACCORDING TO THIS, THEY STUCK HIM IN A MENTAL HOSPITAL AND PRETTY MUCH THREW AWAY THE KEY.
GREAT. I'M DESCENDED FROM A MADMAN.
HEY, HEY! NO ONE EVER PROVED THERE WAS ANY ACTUAL MENTAL ILLNESS. MY FATHER TOLD ME HE WAS JUST... TRAUMATIZED.
RON, RON—HE'S TWELVE YEARS OLD.
YOU CAN'T EXPECT HIM TO GET ALL WORKED UP OVER SOME DUSTY RELICS.
GOIN' ROUND TO MILES'. LATER!
GIVE HIM SOME TIME. WHEN HE'S OLDER...
...I'M SURE HE'LL COME TO APPRECIATE THEIR TRUE WORTH.

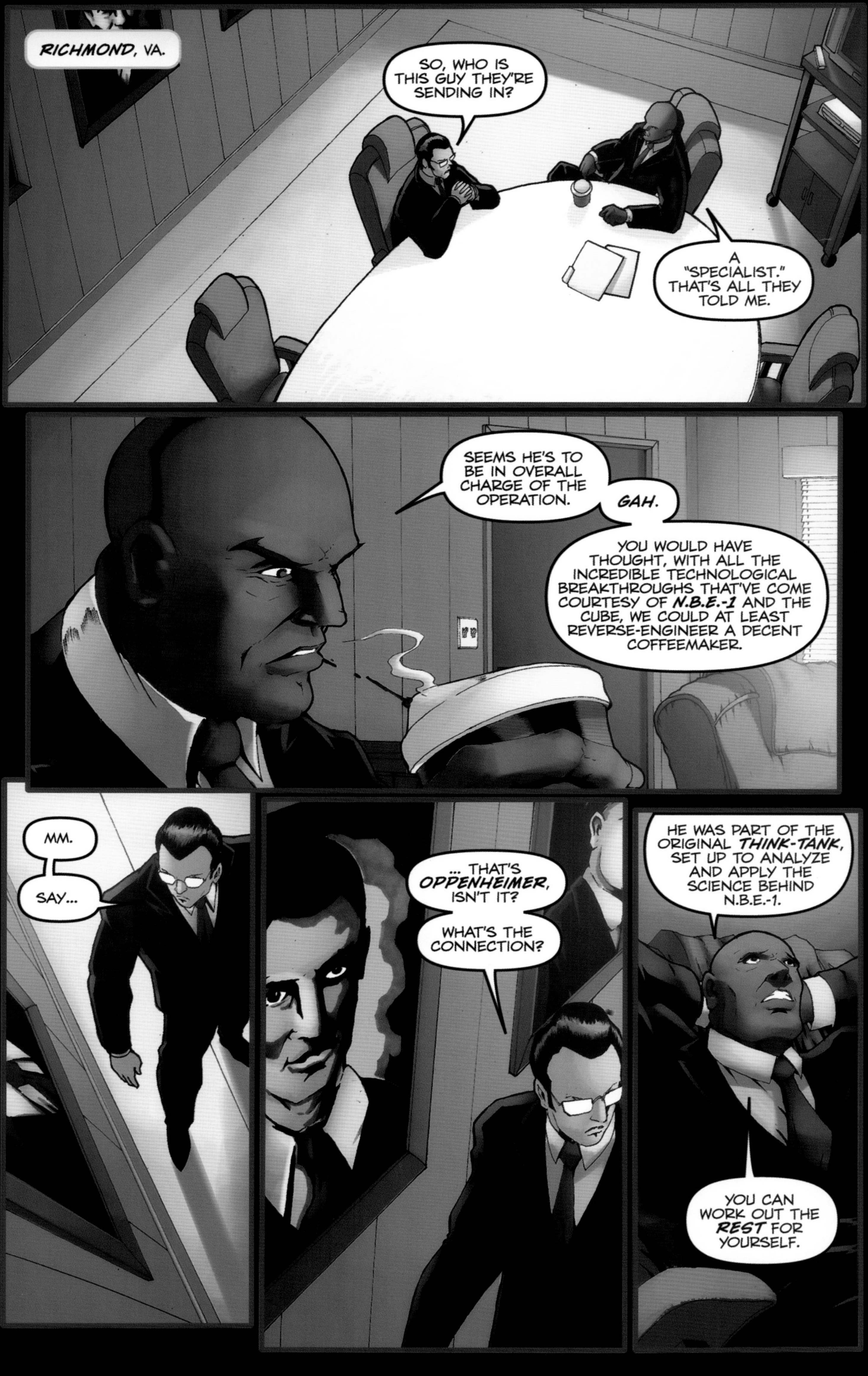
RICHMOND, VA.
SO, WHO IS THIS GUY THEY'RE SENDING IN?
A "SPECIALIST." THAT'S ALL THEY TOLD ME.
SEEMS HE'S TO BE IN OVERALL CHARGE OF THE OPERATION.
GAH.
YOU WOULD HAVE THOUGHT, WITH ALL THE INCREDIBLE TECHNOLOGICAL BREAKTHROUGHS THAT'VE COME COURTESY OF N.B.E.-1 AND THE CUBE, WE COULD AT LEAST REVERSE-ENGINEER A DECENT COFFEEMAKER.
MM.
SAY...
... THAT'S OPPENHEIMER, ISN'T IT?
WHAT'S THE CONNECTION?
HE WAS PART OF THE ORIGINAL THINK-TANK, SET UP TO ANALYZE AND APPLY THE SCIENCE BEHIND N.B.E.-1.
YOU CAN WORK OUT THE REST FOR YOURSELF.

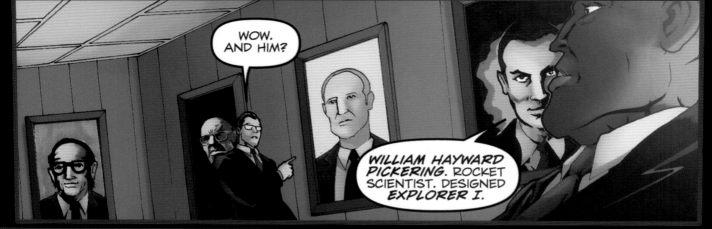

WOW. AND HIM?

WILLIAM HAYWARD PICKERING. ROCKET SCIENTIST. DESIGNED EXPLORER I.

N.B.E.-1?

YEP. HOW ELSE DO YOU THINK WE WON THE SPACE RACE?

SO... ALL THESE—

GENTLEMEN. SORRY TO KEEP YOU WAITING...

...I AM AGENT SIMMONS.

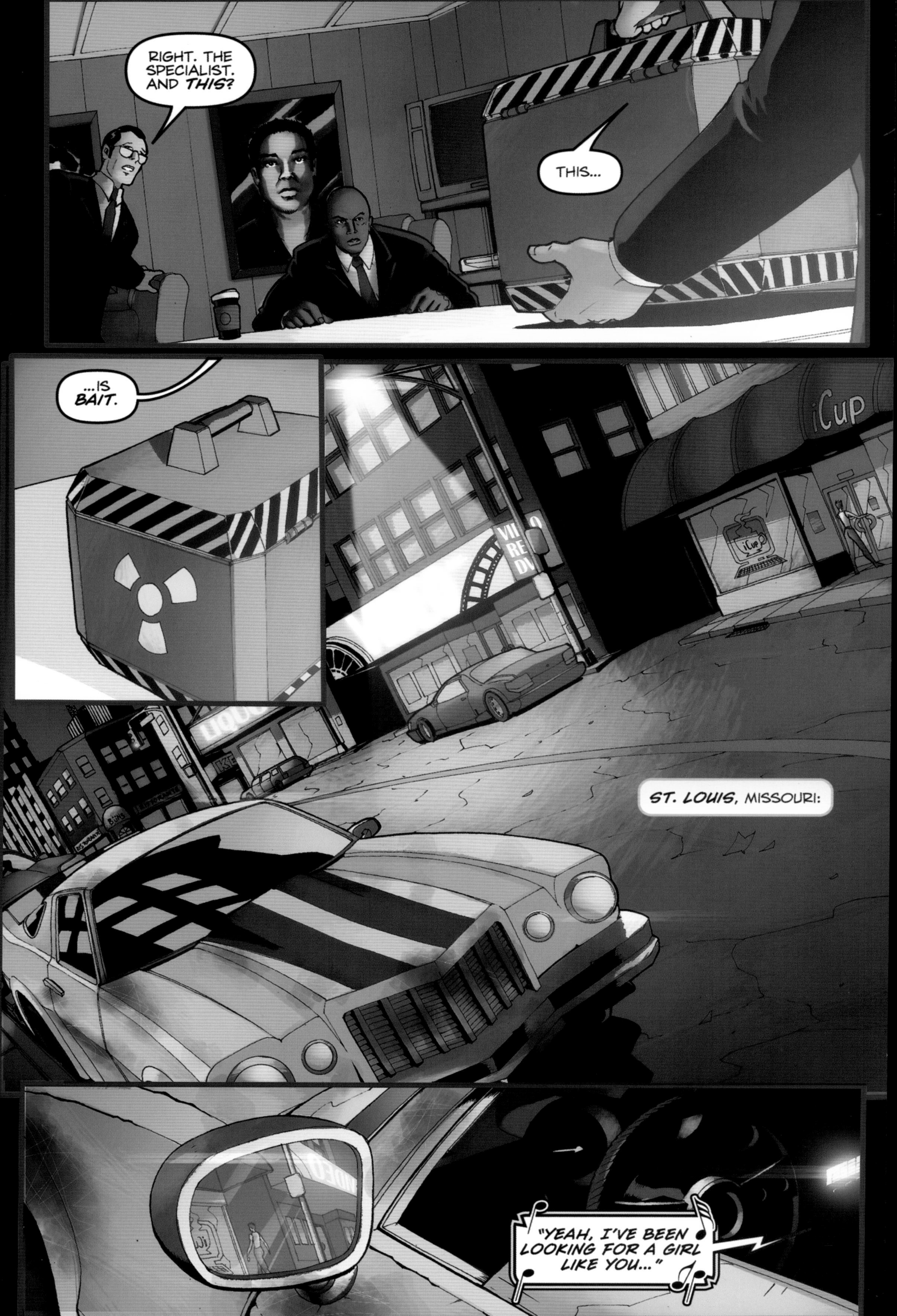
RIGHT. THE SPECIALIST. AND *THIS*?
THIS...
...IS *BAIT*.
iCup
LIQUO
ST. LOUIS, MISSOURI:
"YEAH, I'VE BEEN LOOKING FOR A GIRL LIKE YOU..."

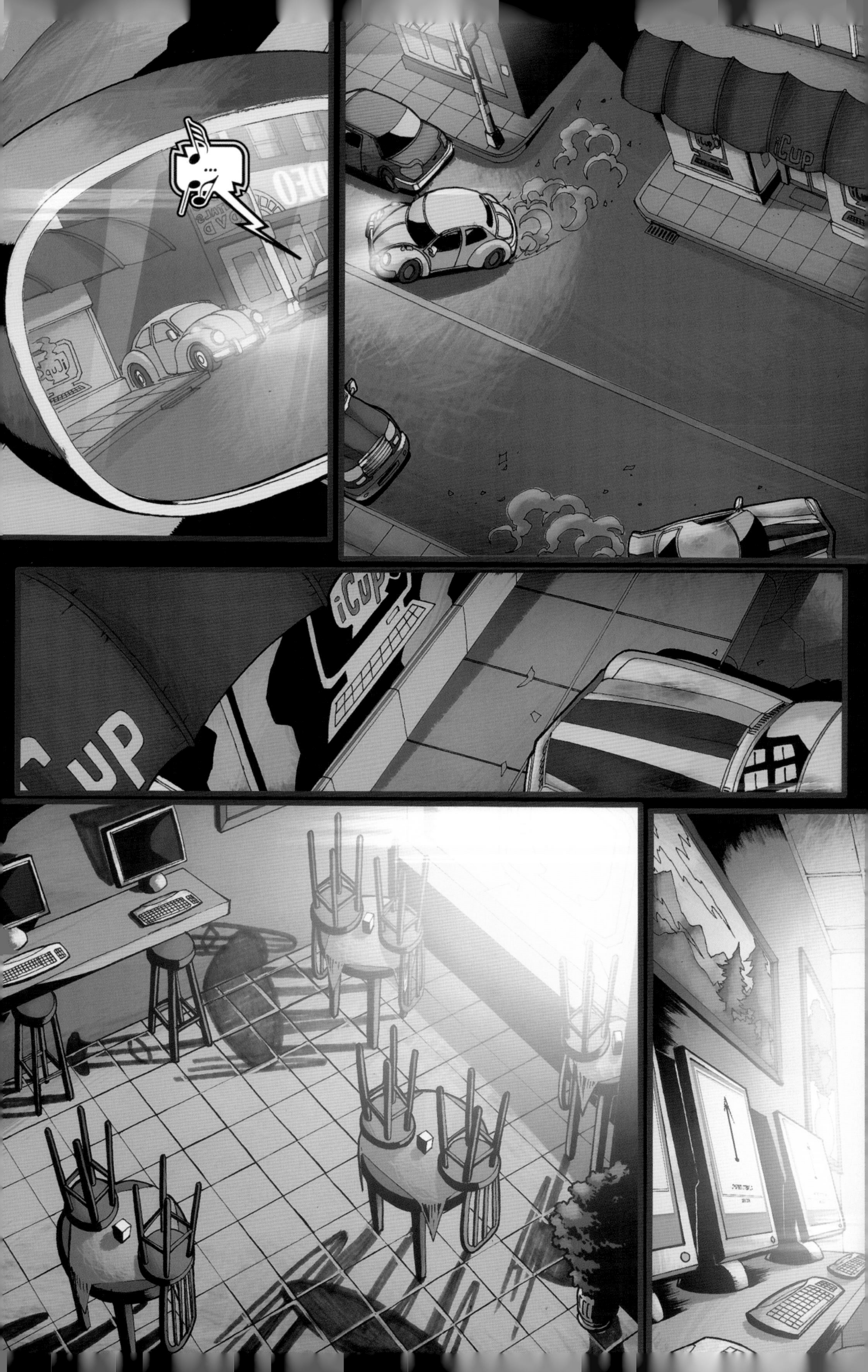
...
iCup
iCup
iCup

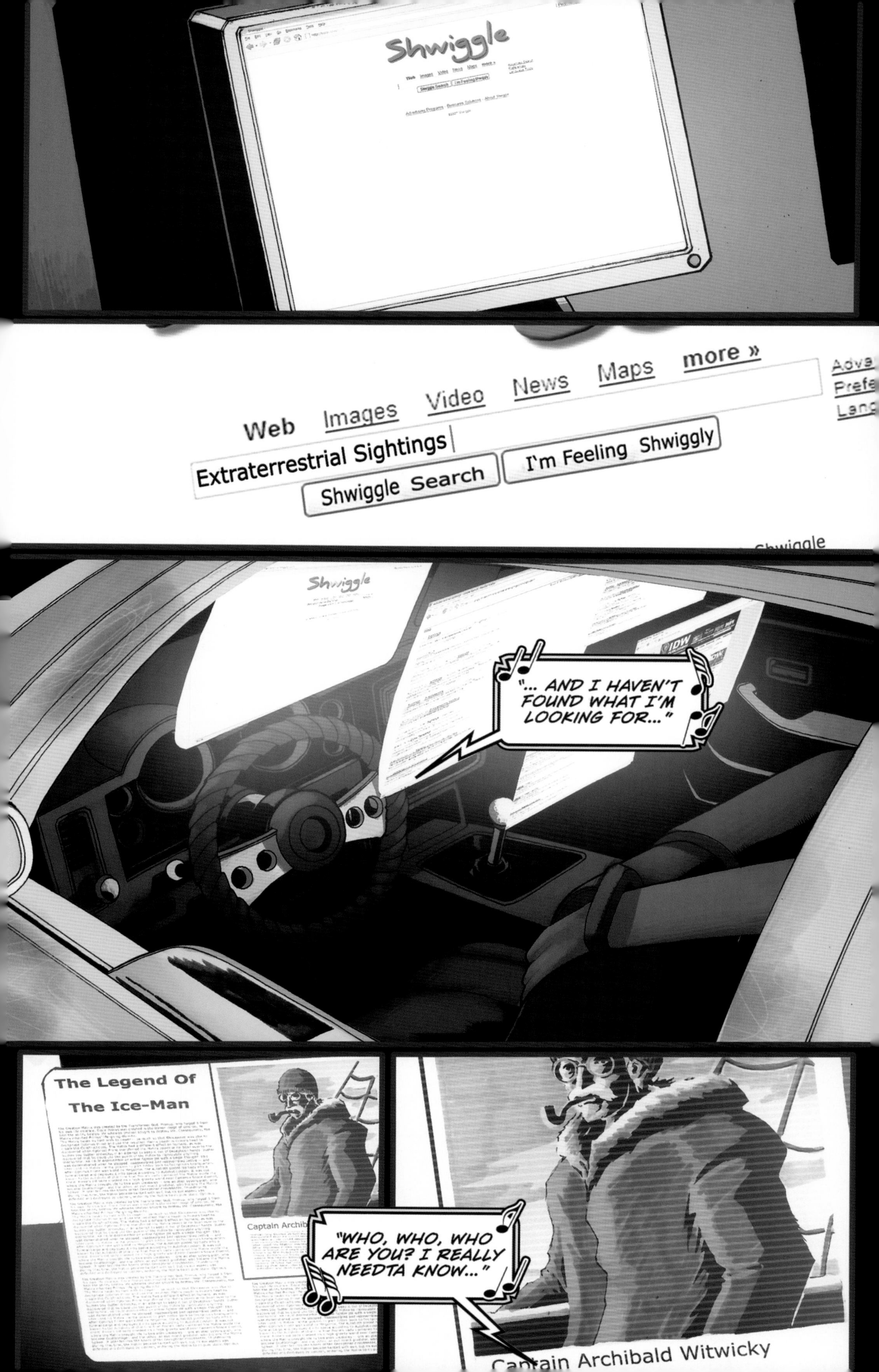
Shwiggle
Web Images Video News Maps more »
Extraterrestrial Sightings
Shwiggle Search
I'm Feeling Shwiggly
"... AND I HAVEN'T FOUND WHAT I'M LOOKING FOR..."
The Legend Of The Ice-Man
"WHO, WHO, WHO ARE YOU? I REALLY NEEDTA KNOW..."
Captain Archibald Witwicky

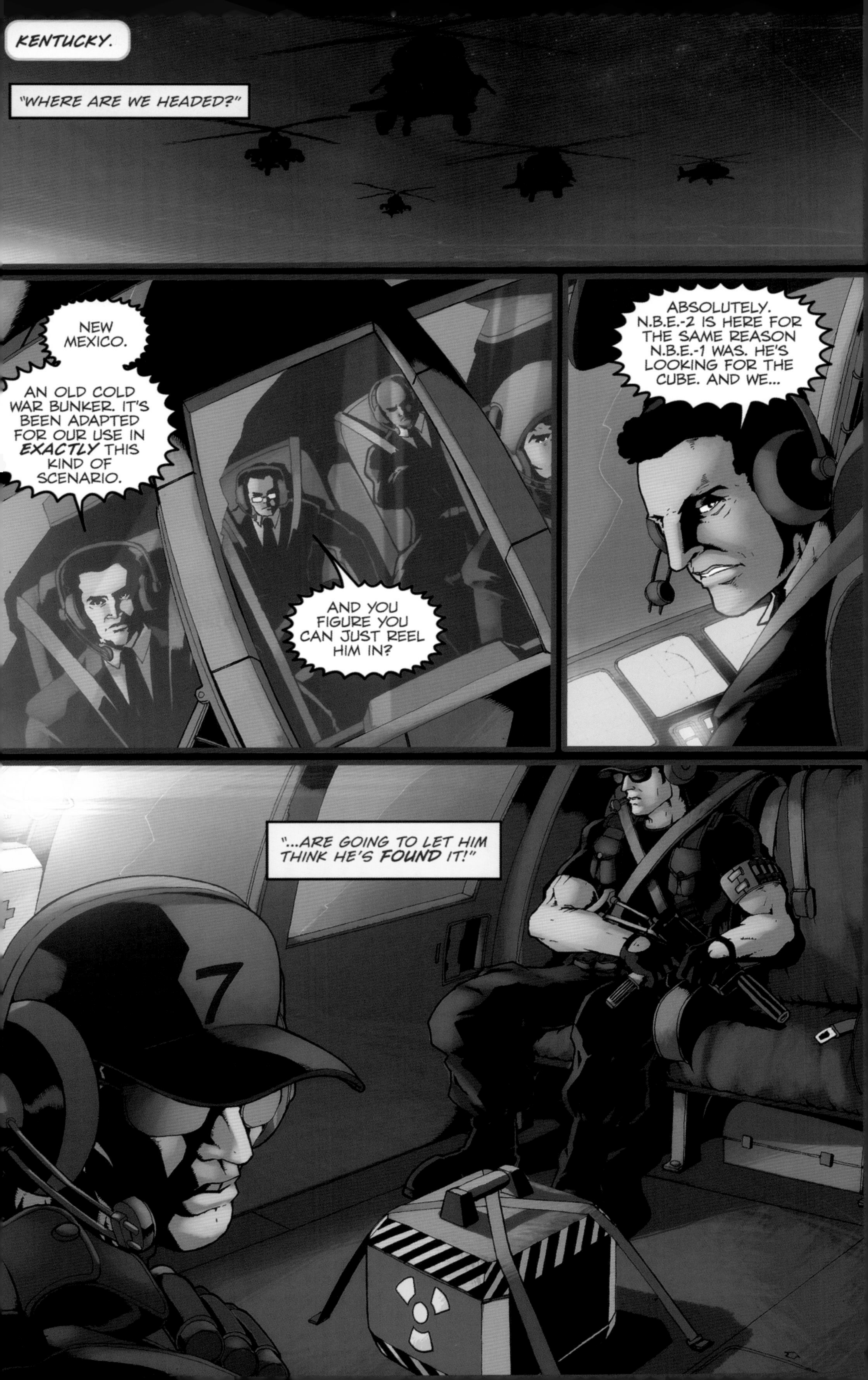
KENTUCKY.
"WHERE ARE WE HEADED?"
NEW MEXICO.
AN OLD COLD WAR BUNKER. IT'S BEEN ADAPTED FOR OUR USE IN EXACTLY THIS KIND OF SCENARIO.
AND YOU FIGURE YOU CAN JUST REEL HIM IN?
ABSOLUTELY. N.B.E.-2 IS HERE FOR THE SAME REASON N.B.E.-1 WAS. HE'S LOOKING FOR THE CUBE. AND WE...
"...ARE GOING TO LET HIM THINK HE'S FOUND IT!"

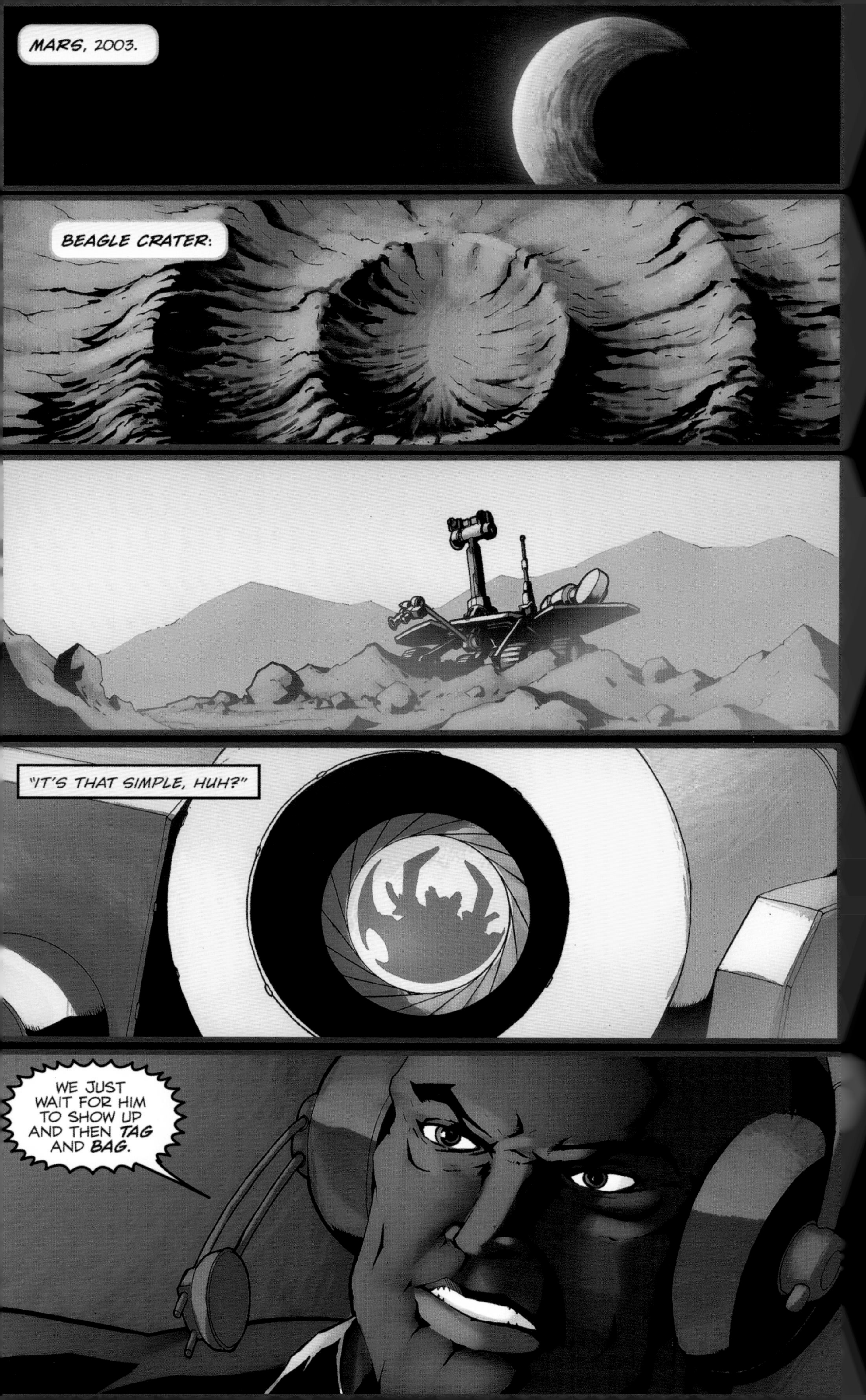
MARS, 2003.
BEAGLE CRATER:
"IT'S THAT SIMPLE, HUH?"
WE JUST WAIT FOR HIM TO SHOW UP AND THEN TAG AND BAG.

YEAH, IT'S *THAT* SIMPLE. LOOK, IT'S NOT LIKE WE DON'T KNOW WHAT WE'RE *DEALING* WITH HERE. WE'VE HAD OVER 100 YEARS TO PREPARE.

ALL WE NEED...

"...IS TO *NOT* TAKE OUR EYE OFF THE BALL!"

VRANNK

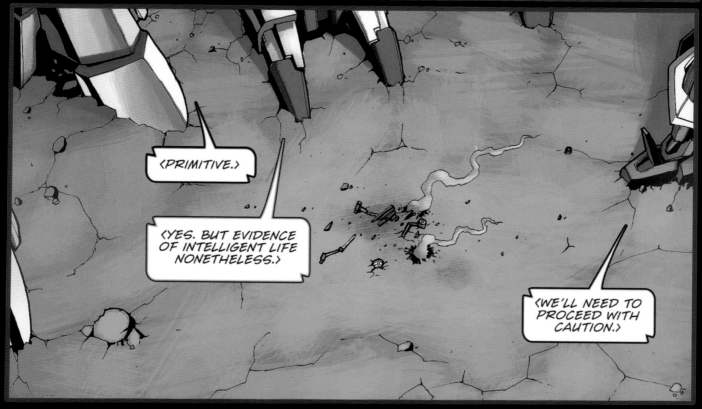

‹PRIMITIVE.›

‹YES. BUT EVIDENCE OF INTELLIGENT LIFE NONETHELESS.›

‹WE'LL NEED TO PROCEED WITH CAUTION.›

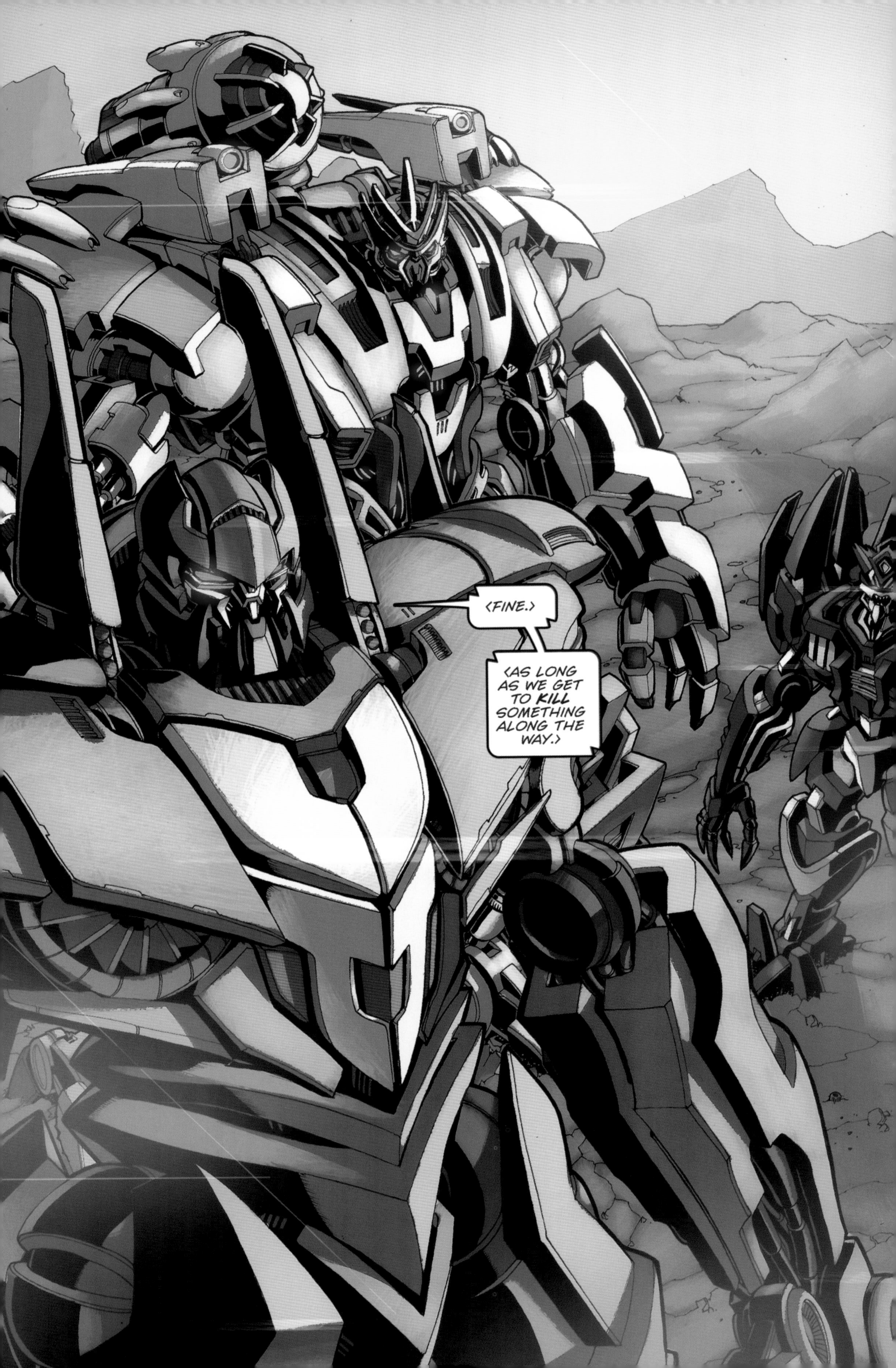
<FINE.>
<AS LONG AS WE GET TO **KILL** SOMETHING ALONG THE WAY.>

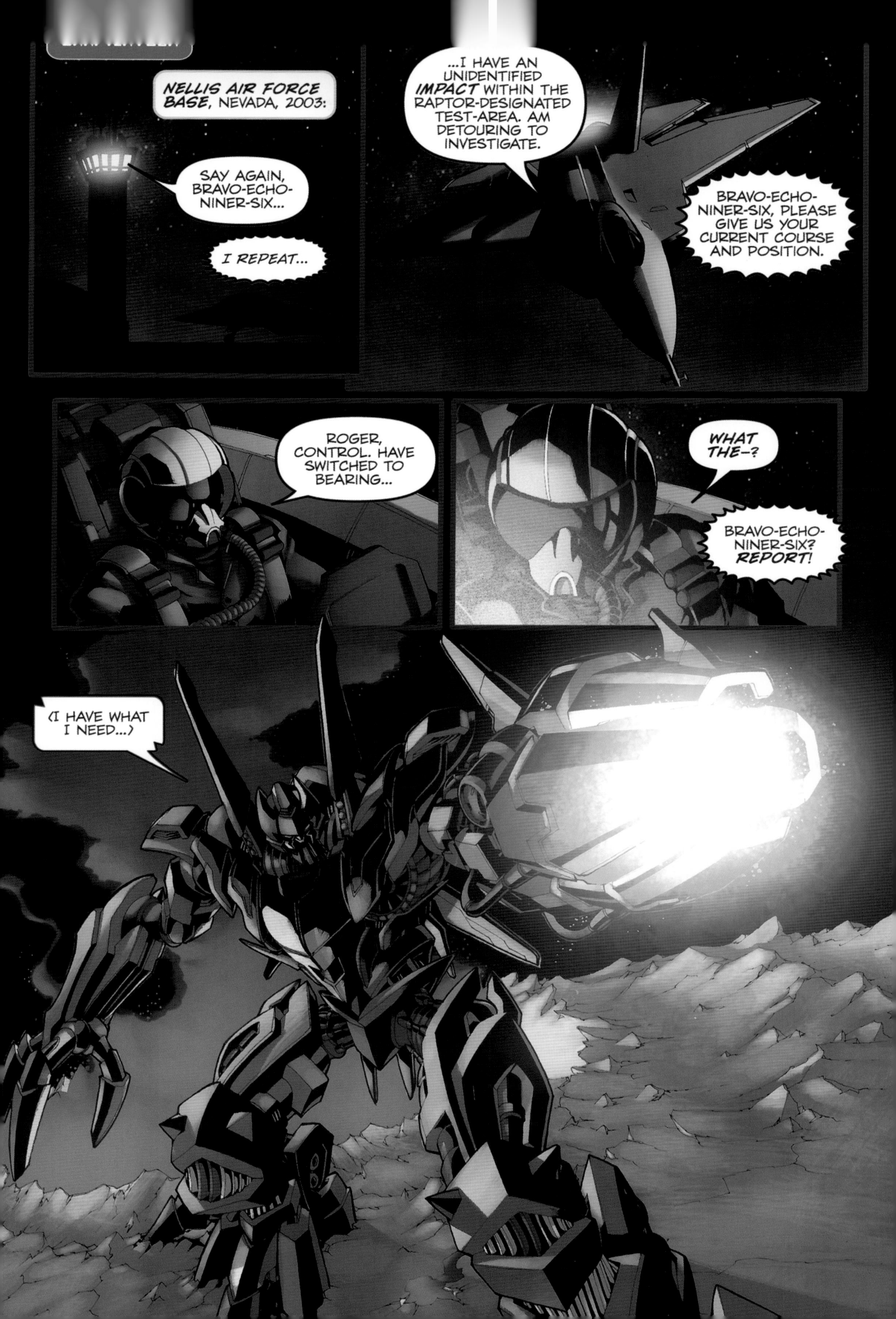
NELLIS AIR FORCE BASE, NEVADA, 2003:
SAY AGAIN, BRAVO-ECHO-NINER-SIX...
I REPEAT...
...I HAVE AN UNIDENTIFIED IMPACT WITHIN THE RAPTOR-DESIGNATED TEST-AREA. AM DETOURING TO INVESTIGATE.
BRAVO-ECHO-NINER-SIX, PLEASE GIVE US YOUR CURRENT COURSE AND POSITION.
ROGER, CONTROL. HAVE SWITCHED TO BEARING...
WHAT THE--?
BRAVO-ECHO-NINER-SIX? REPORT!
‹I HAVE WHAT I NEED...›

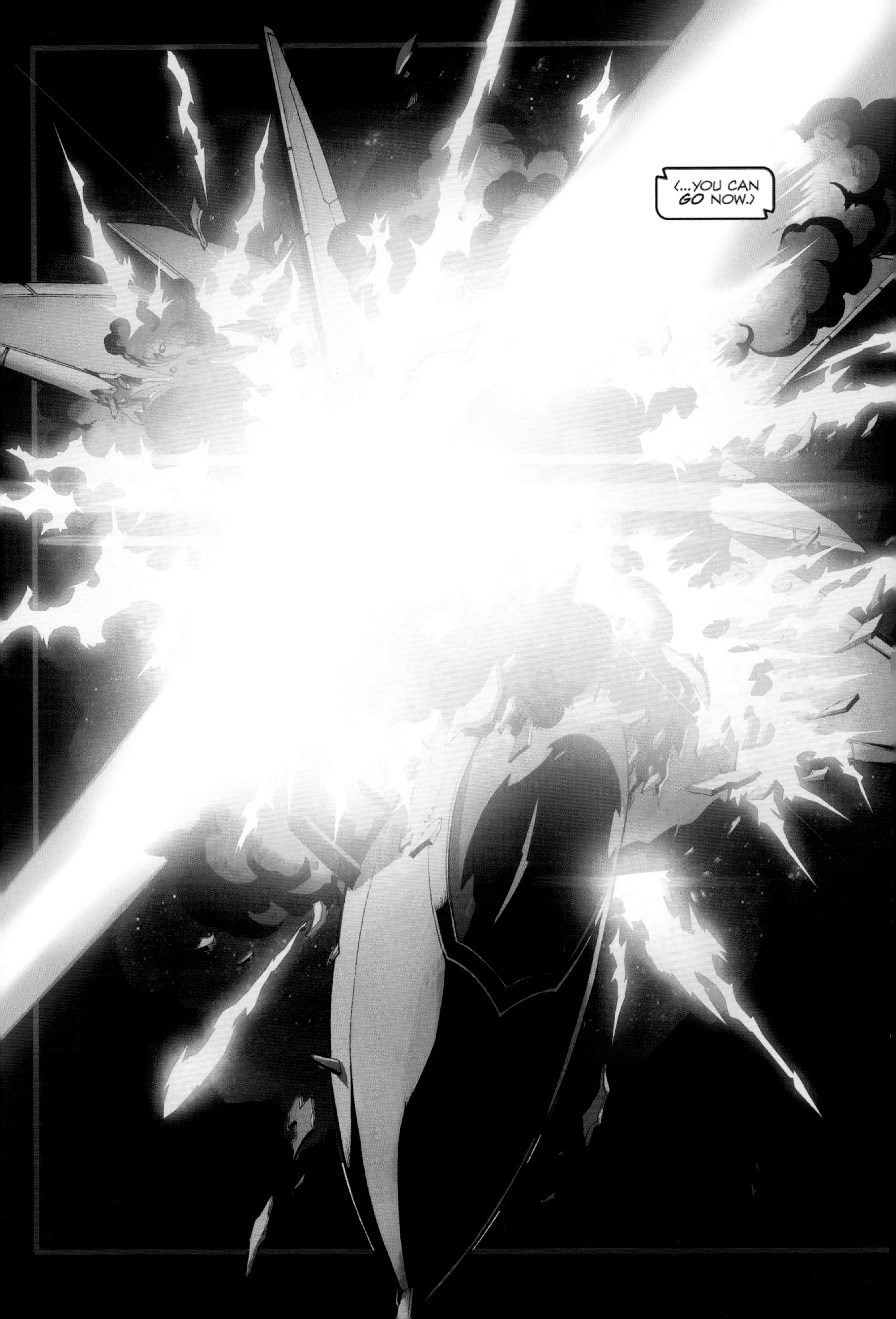
‹...YOU CAN GO NOW.›

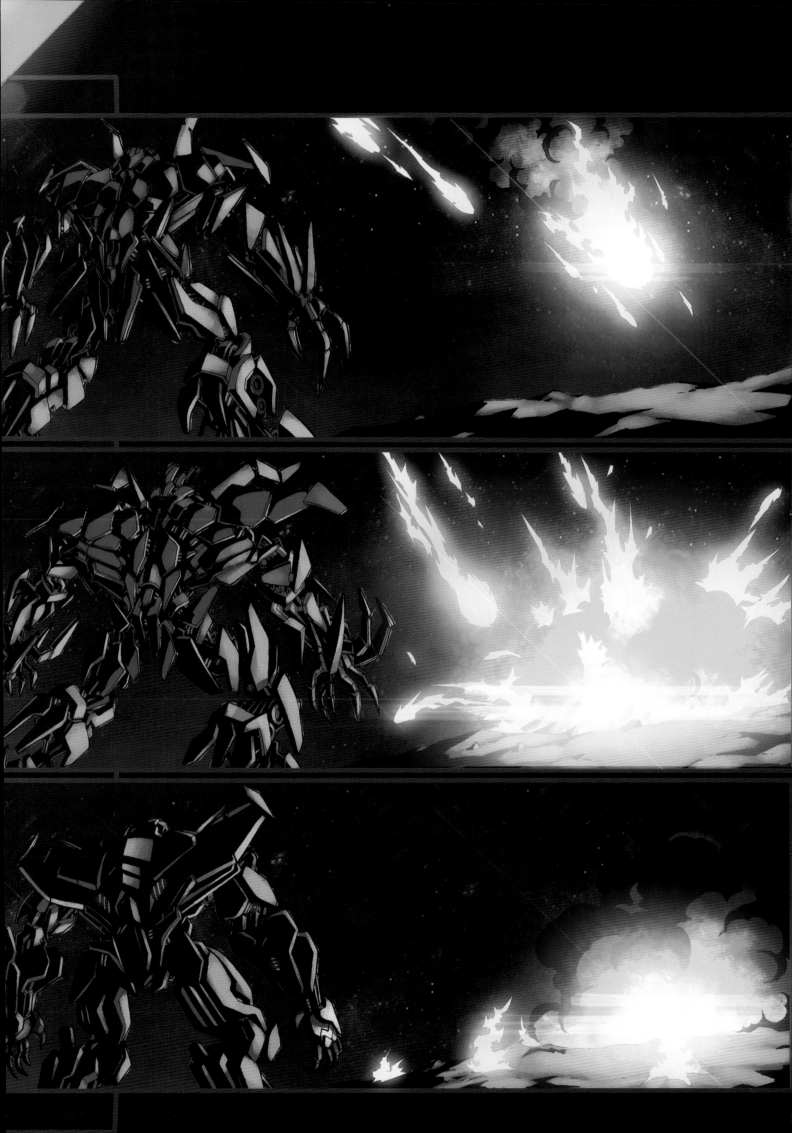

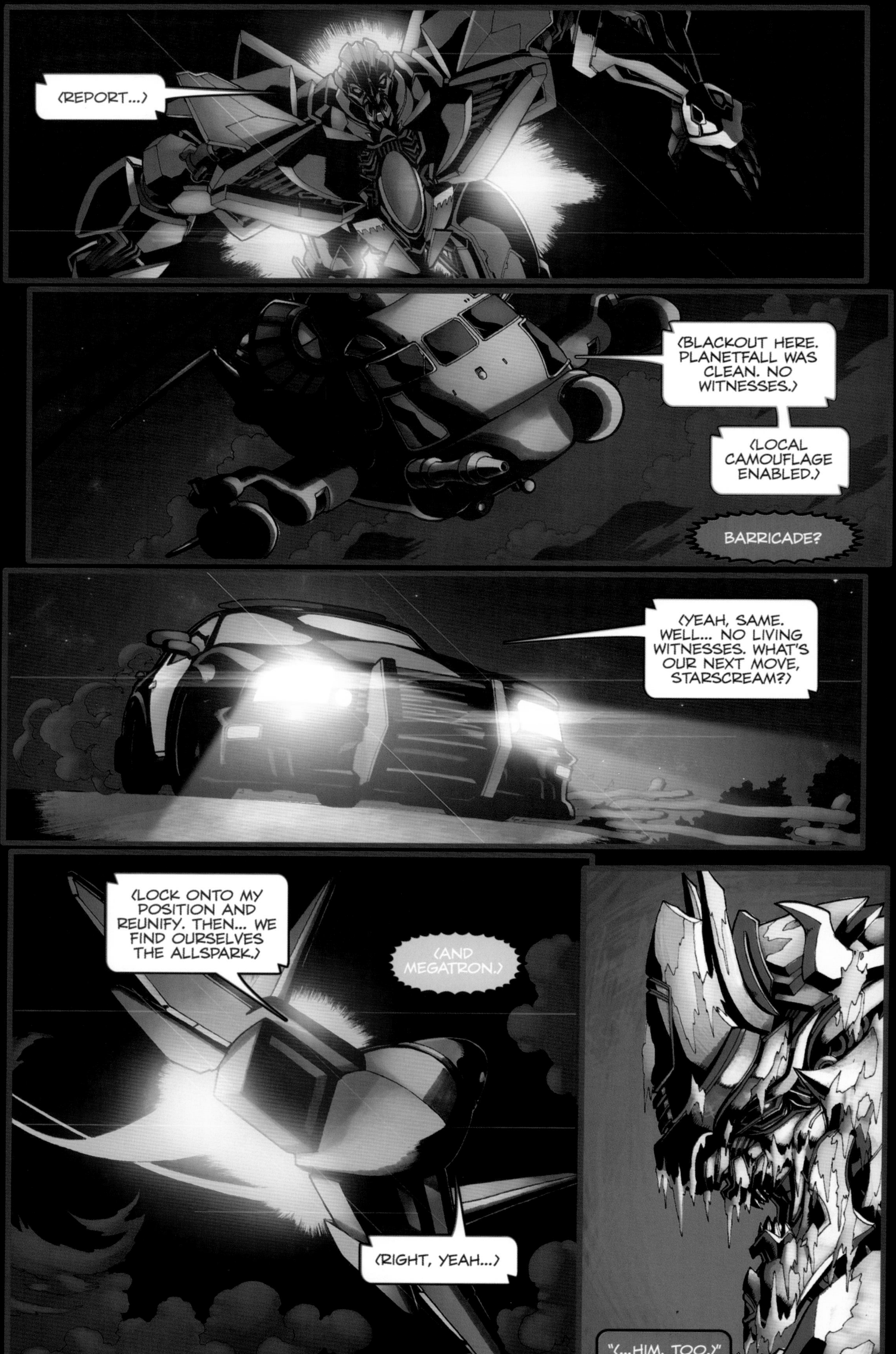
(REPORT...)
(BLACKOUT HERE. PLANETFALL WAS CLEAN. NO WITNESSES.)
(LOCAL CAMOUFLAGE ENABLED.)
BARRICADE?
(YEAH, SAME. WELL... NO LIVING WITNESSES. WHAT'S OUR NEXT MOVE, STARSCREAM?)
(LOCK ONTO MY POSITION AND REUNIFY. THEN... WE FIND OURSELVES THE ALLSPARK.)
(AND MEGATRON.)
(RIGHT, YEAH...)
"(...HIM, TOO.)"

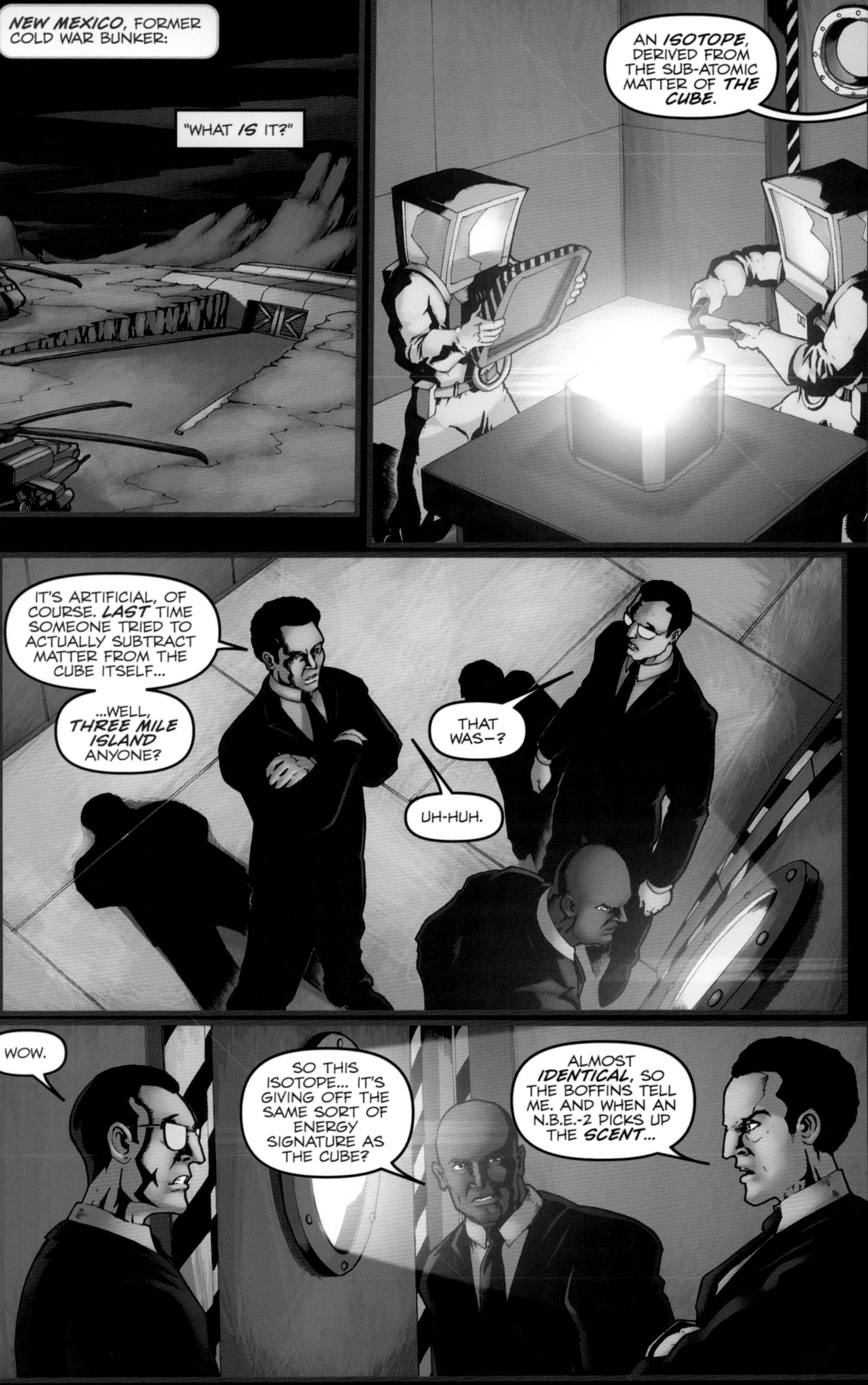
NEW MEXICO, FORMER COLD WAR BUNKER:
"WHAT IS IT?"
AN ISOTOPE, DERIVED FROM THE SUB-ATOMIC MATTER OF THE CUBE.
IT'S ARTIFICIAL, OF COURSE. LAST TIME SOMEONE TRIED TO ACTUALLY SUBTRACT MATTER FROM THE CUBE ITSELF...
...WELL, THREE MILE ISLAND ANYONE?
THAT WAS—?
UH-HUH.
WOW.
SO THIS ISOTOPE... IT'S GIVING OFF THE SAME SORT OF ENERGY SIGNATURE AS THE CUBE?
ALMOST IDENTICAL, SO THE BOFFINS TELL ME. AND WHEN AN N.B.E.-2 PICKS UP THE SCENT...

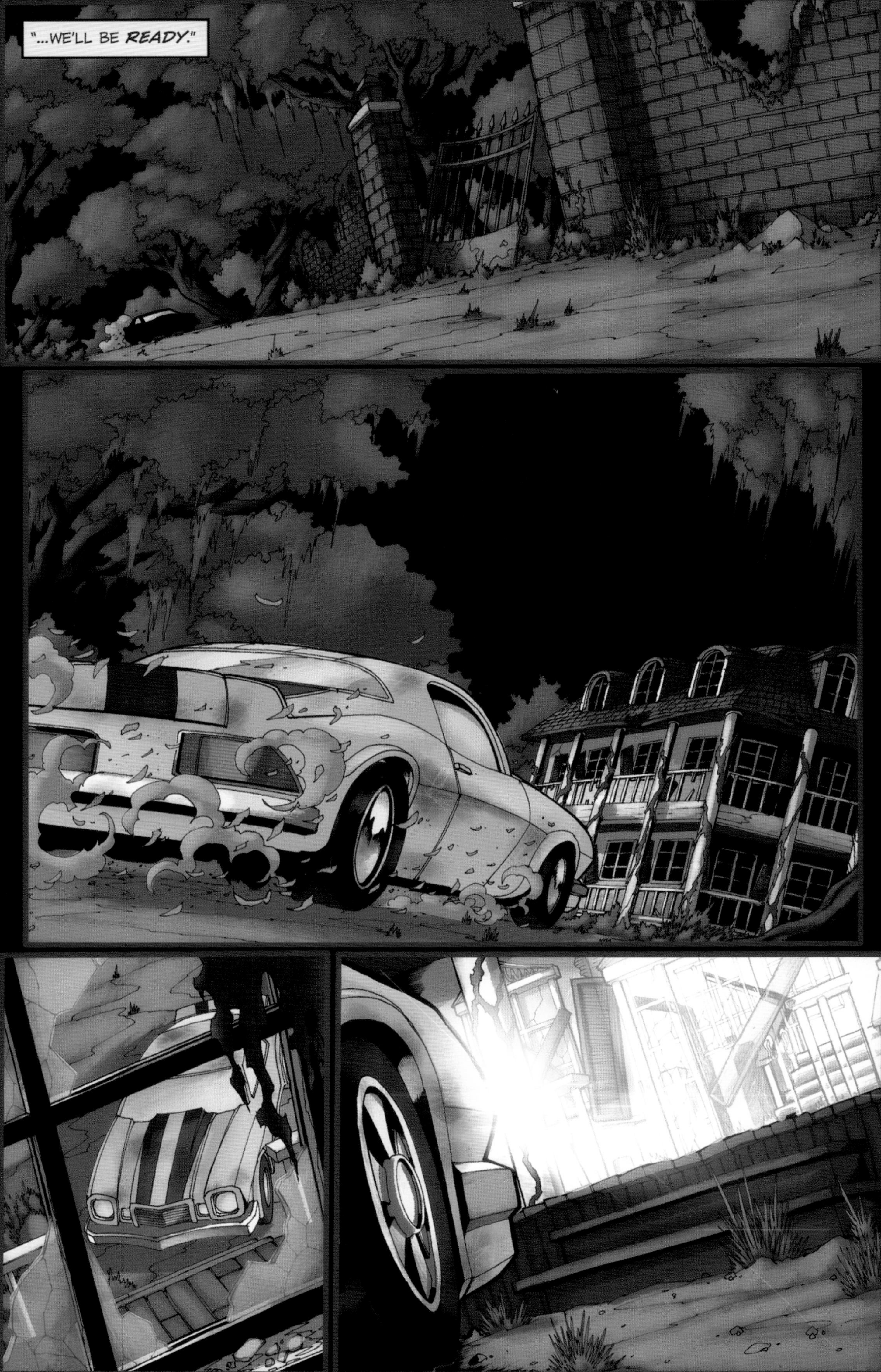
"...WE'LL BE READY."

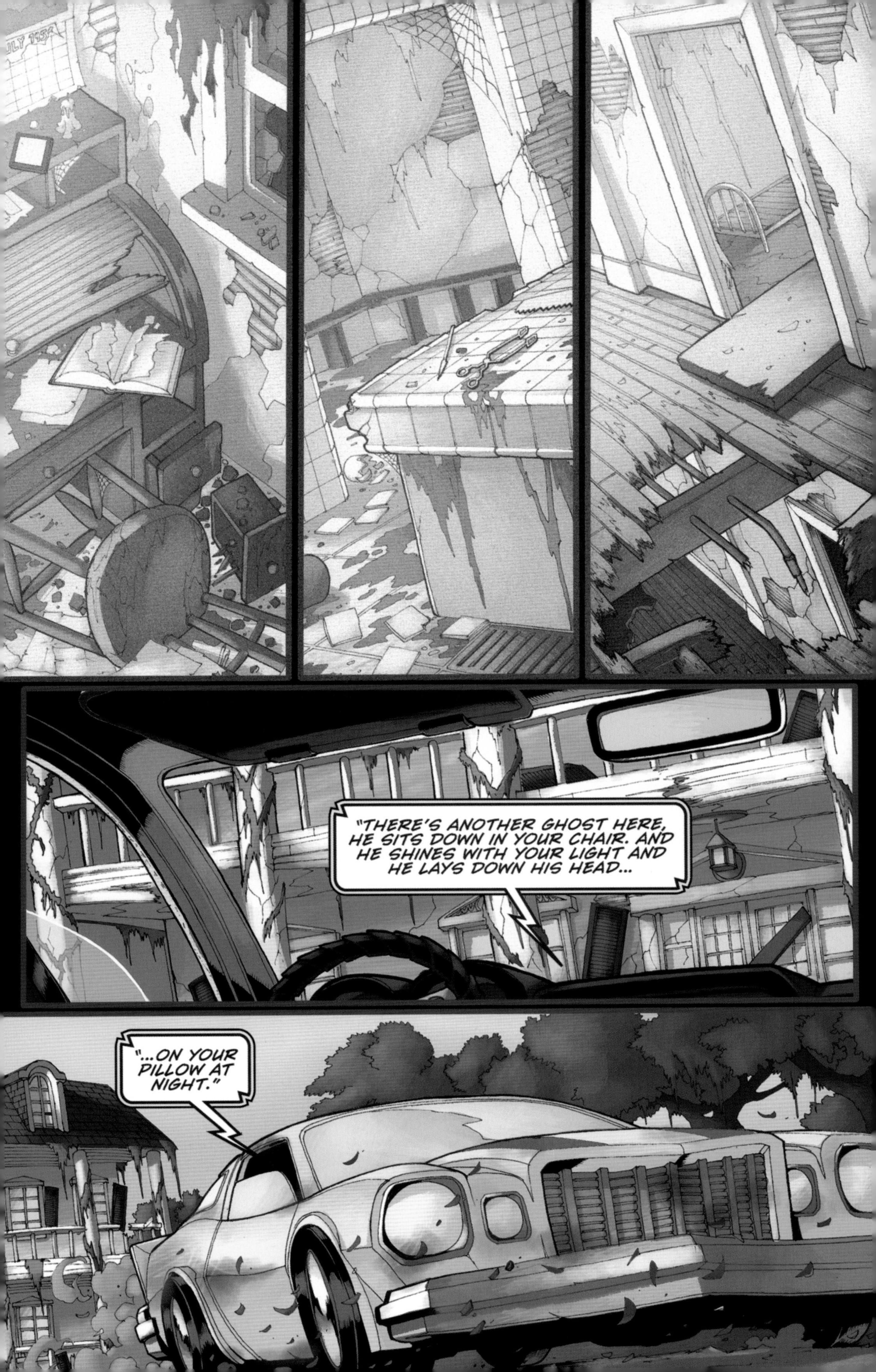

"THERE'S ANOTHER GHOST HERE, HE SITS DOWN IN YOUR CHAIR. AND HE SHINES WITH YOUR LIGHT AND HE LAYS DOWN HIS HEAD...
"...ON YOUR PILLOW AT NIGHT."

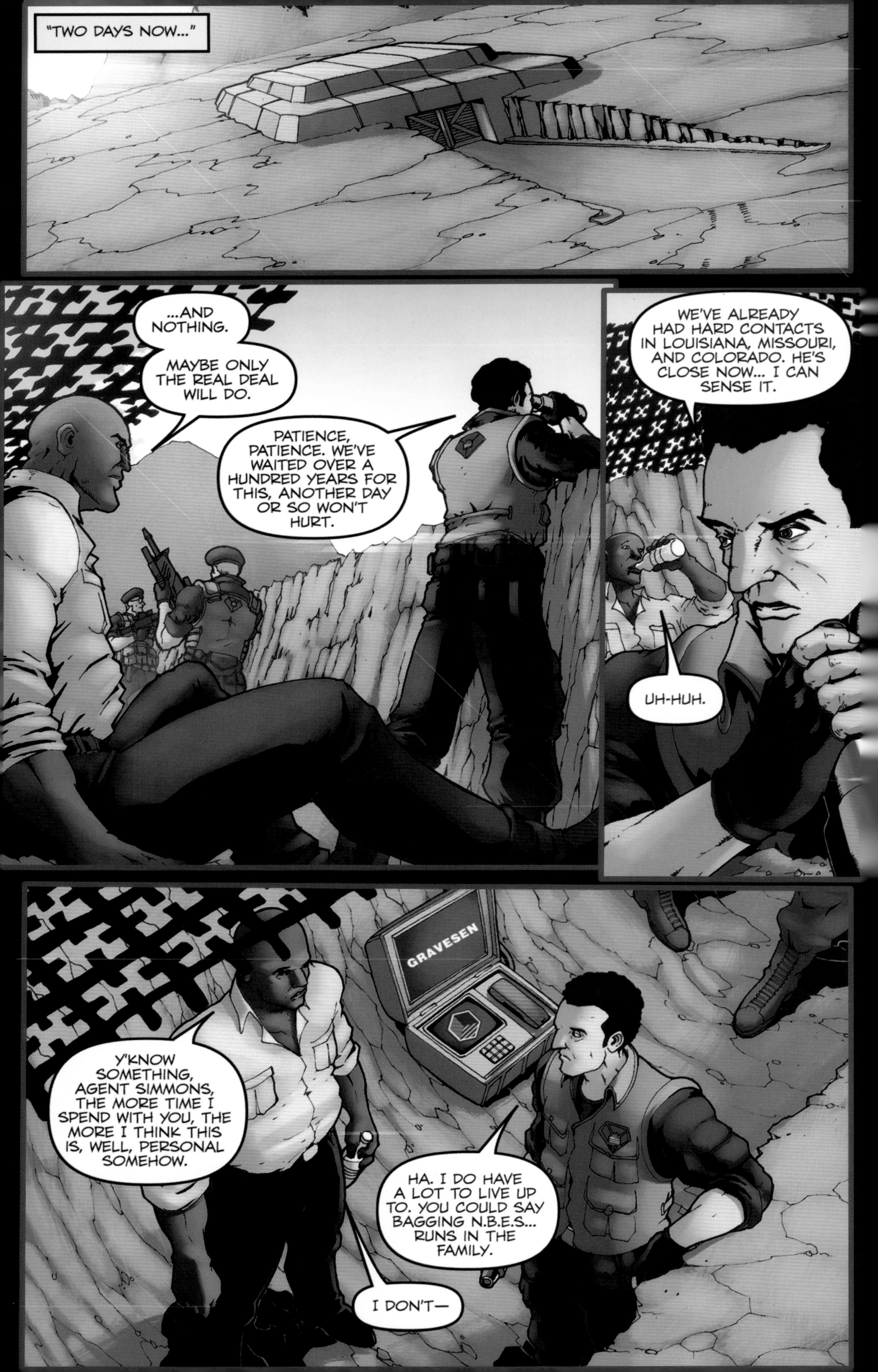
"TWO DAYS NOW..."
...AND NOTHING.
MAYBE ONLY THE REAL DEAL WILL DO.
PATIENCE, PATIENCE. WE'VE WAITED OVER A HUNDRED YEARS FOR THIS, ANOTHER DAY OR SO WON'T HURT.
WE'VE ALREADY HAD HARD CONTACTS IN LOUISIANA, MISSOURI, AND COLORADO. HE'S CLOSE NOW... I CAN SENSE IT.
UH-HUH.
GRAVESEN
Y'KNOW SOMETHING, AGENT SIMMONS, THE MORE TIME I SPEND WITH YOU, THE MORE I THINK THIS IS, WELL, PERSONAL SOMEHOW.
HA. I DO HAVE A LOT TO LIVE UP TO. YOU COULD SAY BAGGING N.B.E.S... RUNS IN THE FAMILY.
I DON'T—

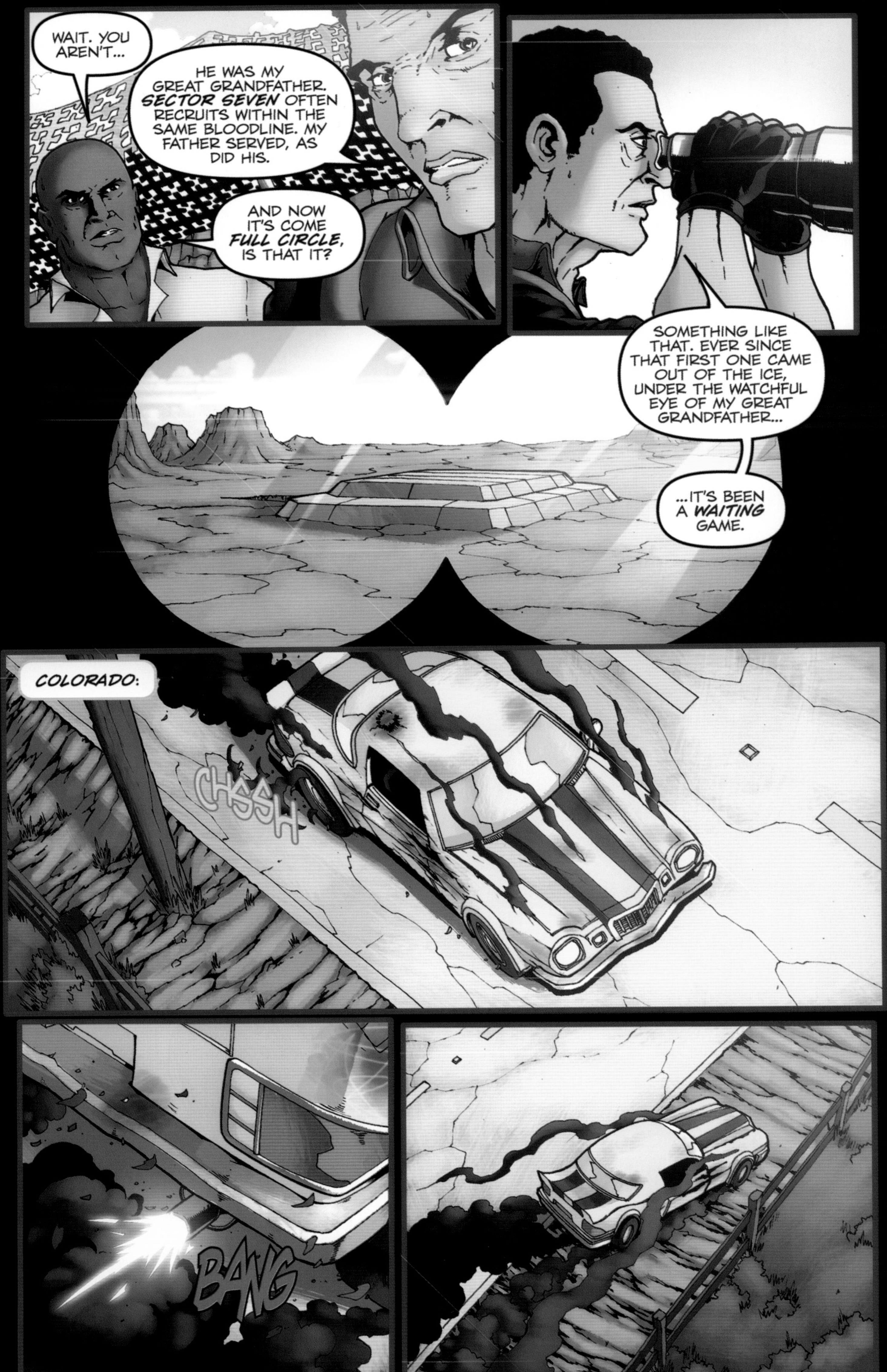
WAIT. YOU AREN'T...
HE WAS MY GREAT GRANDFATHER. SECTOR SEVEN OFTEN RECRUITS WITHIN THE SAME BLOODLINE. MY FATHER SERVED, AS DID HIS.
AND NOW IT'S COME FULL CIRCLE, IS THAT IT?
SOMETHING LIKE THAT. EVER SINCE THAT FIRST ONE CAME OUT OF THE ICE, UNDER THE WATCHFUL EYE OF MY GREAT GRANDFATHER...
...IT'S BEEN A WAITING GAME.
COLORADO:
CHSSH
BANG

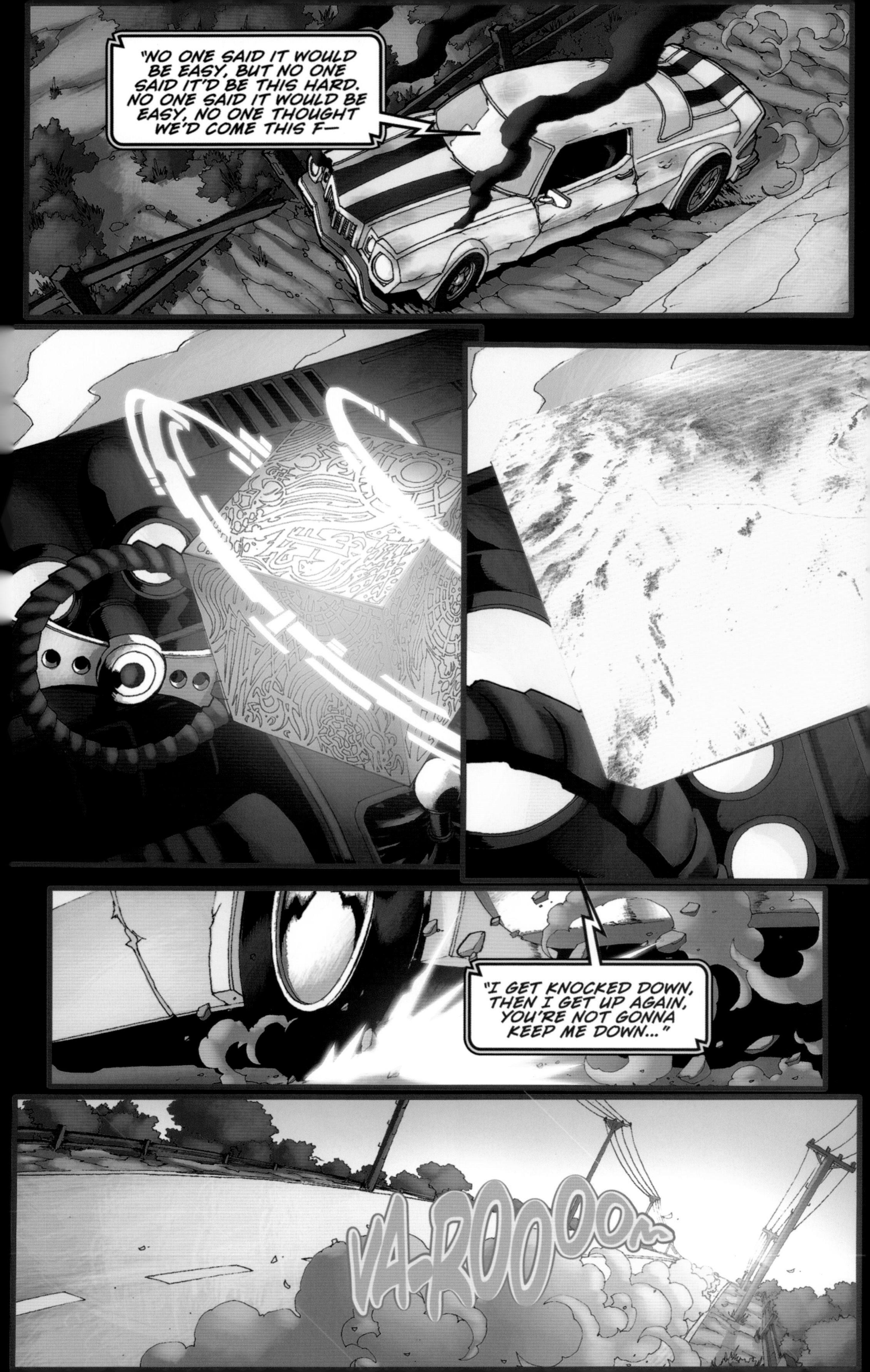
"NO ONE SAID IT WOULD BE EASY, BUT NO ONE SAID IT'D BE THIS HARD. NO ONE SAID IT WOULD BE EASY, NO ONE THOUGHT WE'D COME THIS F—
"I GET KNOCKED DOWN, THEN I GET UP AGAIN, YOU'RE NOT GONNA KEEP ME DOWN..."
VA-ROOOOOm

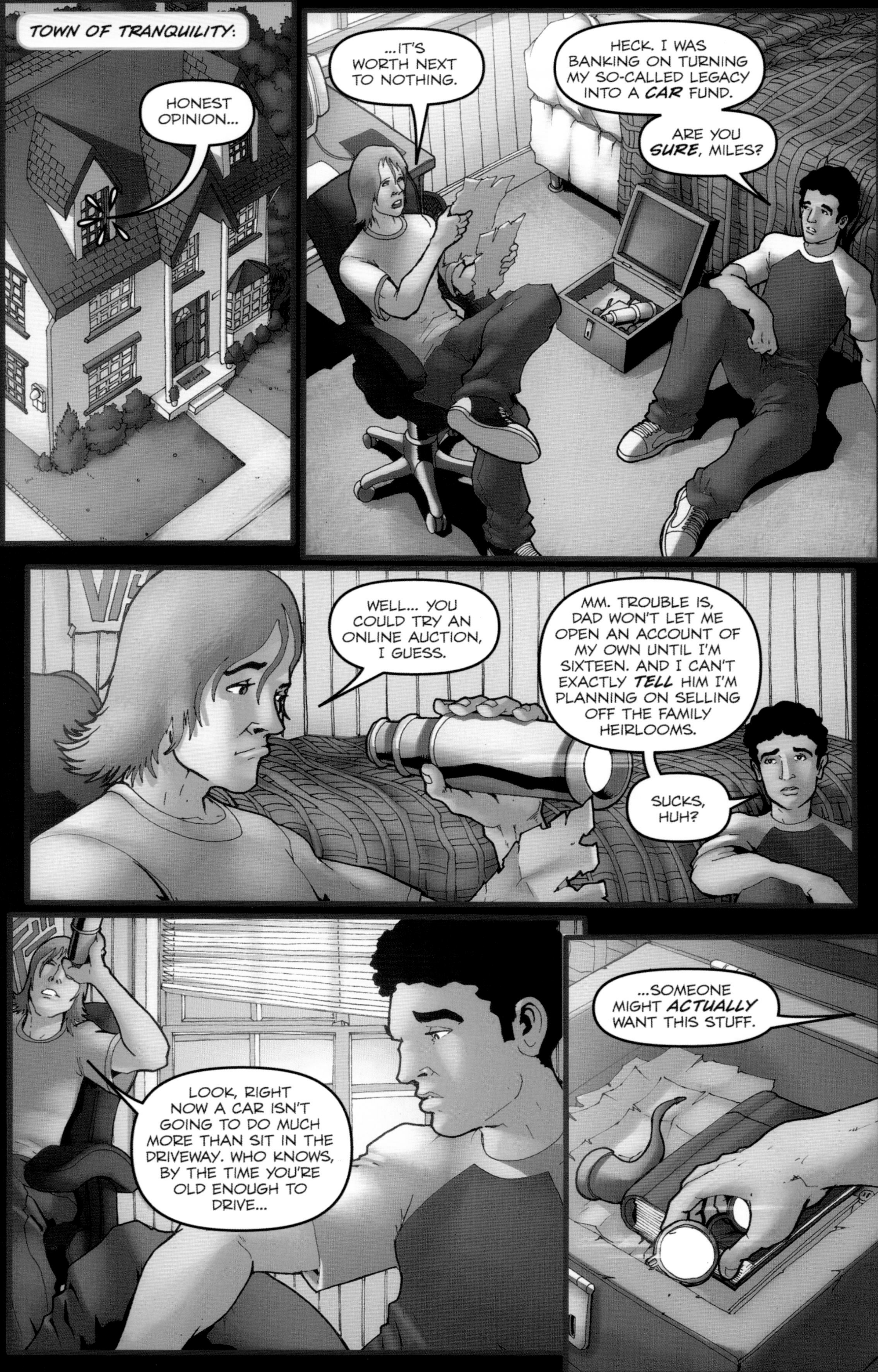
TOWN OF TRANQUILITY:
HONEST OPINION...
...IT'S WORTH NEXT TO NOTHING.
HECK. I WAS BANKING ON TURNING MY SO-CALLED LEGACY INTO A CAR FUND.
ARE YOU SURE, MILES?
WELL... YOU COULD TRY AN ONLINE AUCTION, I GUESS.
MM. TROUBLE IS, DAD WON'T LET ME OPEN AN ACCOUNT OF MY OWN UNTIL I'M SIXTEEN. AND I CAN'T EXACTLY TELL HIM I'M PLANNING ON SELLING OFF THE FAMILY HEIRLOOMS.
SUCKS, HUH?
LOOK, RIGHT NOW A CAR ISN'T GOING TO DO MUCH MORE THAN SIT IN THE DRIVEWAY. WHO KNOWS, BY THE TIME YOU'RE OLD ENOUGH TO DRIVE...
...SOMEONE MIGHT ACTUALLY WANT THIS STUFF.

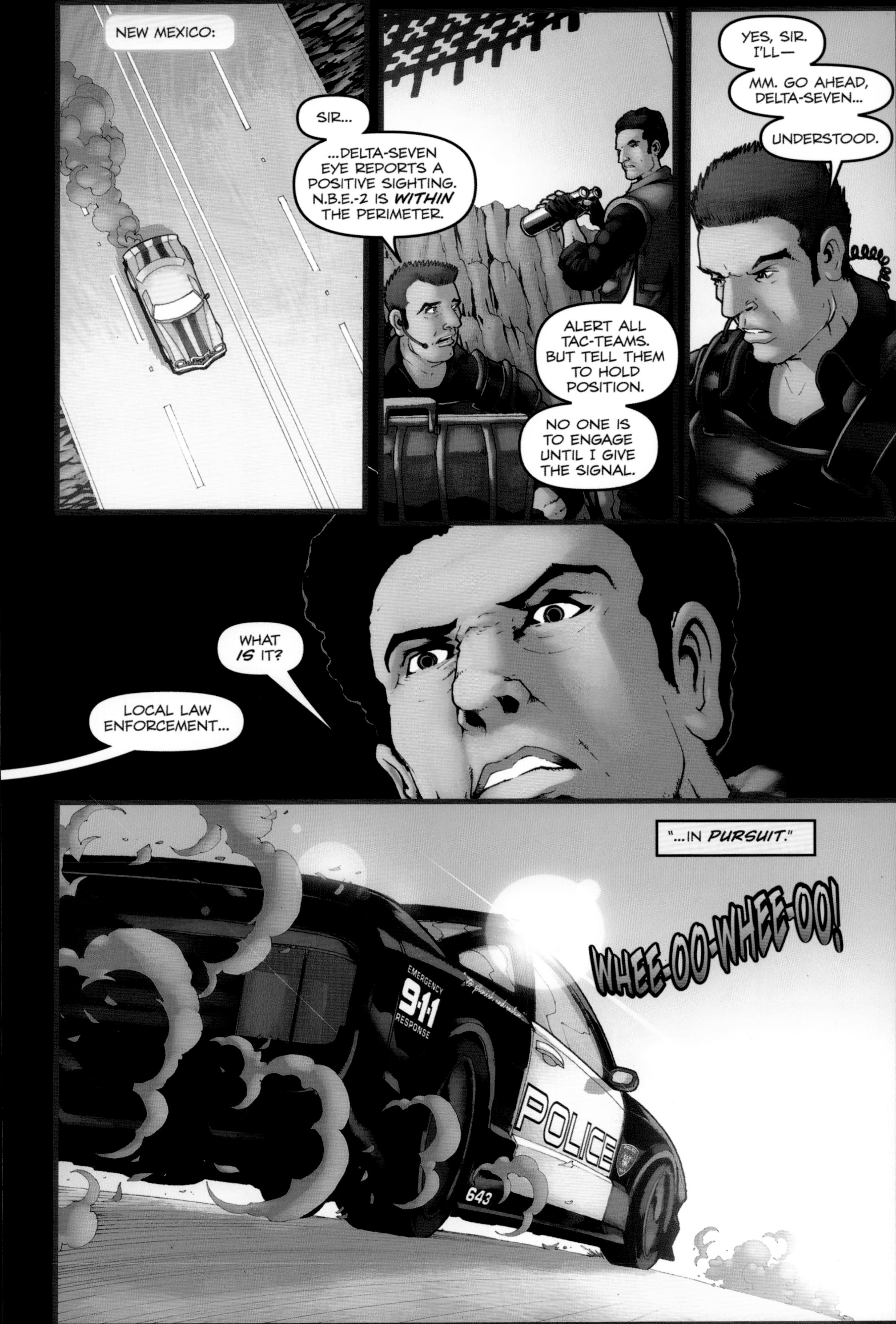
NEW MEXICO:
SIR...
...DELTA-SEVEN EYE REPORTS A POSITIVE SIGHTING. N.B.E.-2 IS *WITHIN* THE PERIMETER.
ALERT ALL TAC-TEAMS. BUT TELL THEM TO HOLD POSITION.
NO ONE IS TO ENGAGE UNTIL I GIVE THE SIGNAL.
YES, SIR. I'LL—
MM. GO AHEAD, DELTA-SEVEN...
UNDERSTOOD.
WHAT *IS* IT?
LOCAL LAW ENFORCEMENT...
"...IN *PURSUIT*."
WHEE-OO-WHEE-OO!
EMERGENCY 9·1·1 RESPONSE
POLICE
643

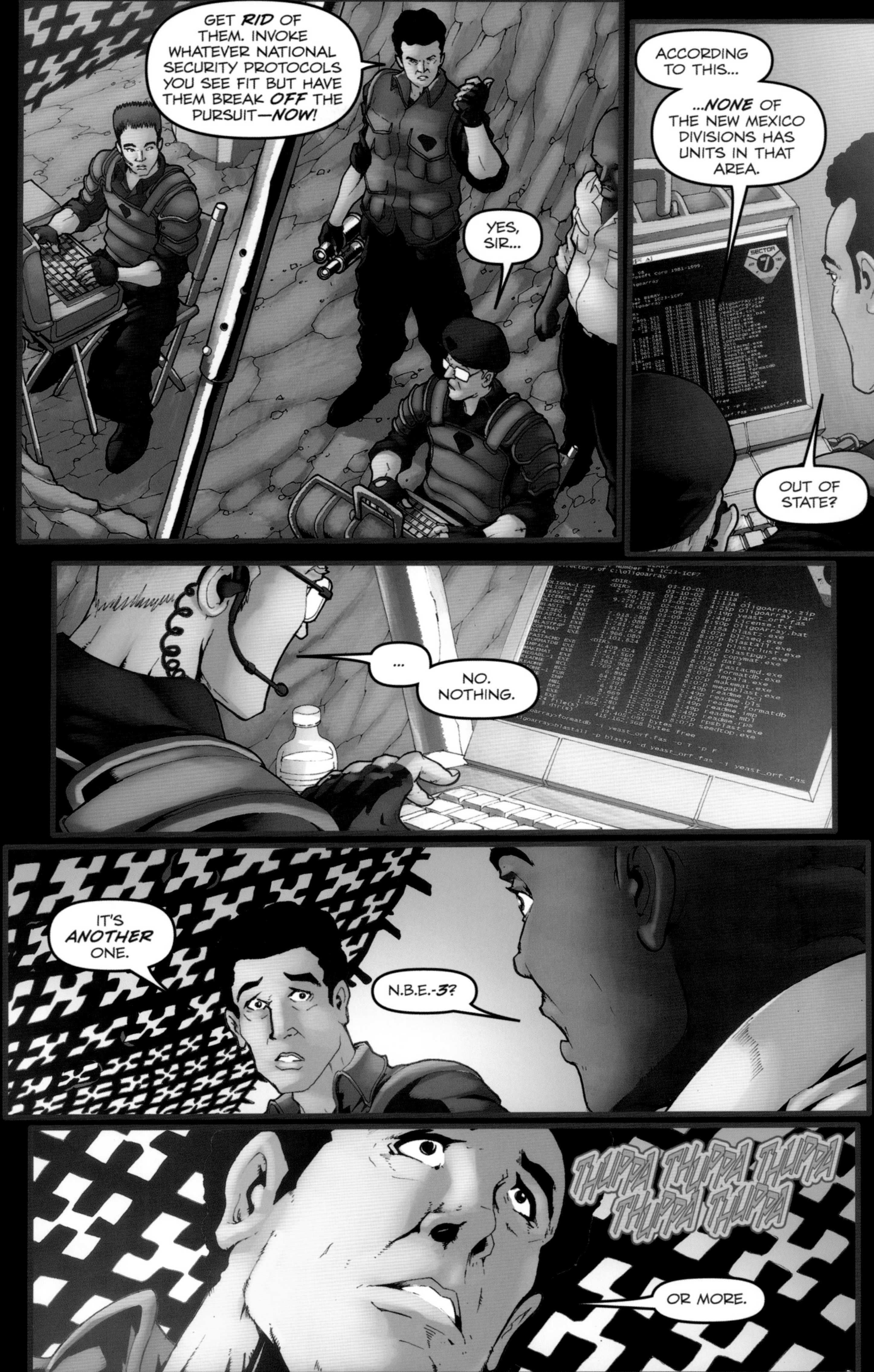
GET RID OF THEM. INVOKE WHATEVER NATIONAL SECURITY PROTOCOLS YOU SEE FIT BUT HAVE THEM BREAK OFF THE PURSUIT—NOW!
YES, SIR...
ACCORDING TO THIS...
...NONE OF THE NEW MEXICO DIVISIONS HAS UNITS IN THAT AREA.
OUT OF STATE?
...
NO. NOTHING.
IT'S ANOTHER ONE.
N.B.E.-3?
THUPPA THUPPA THUPPA THUPPA THUPPA
OR MORE.

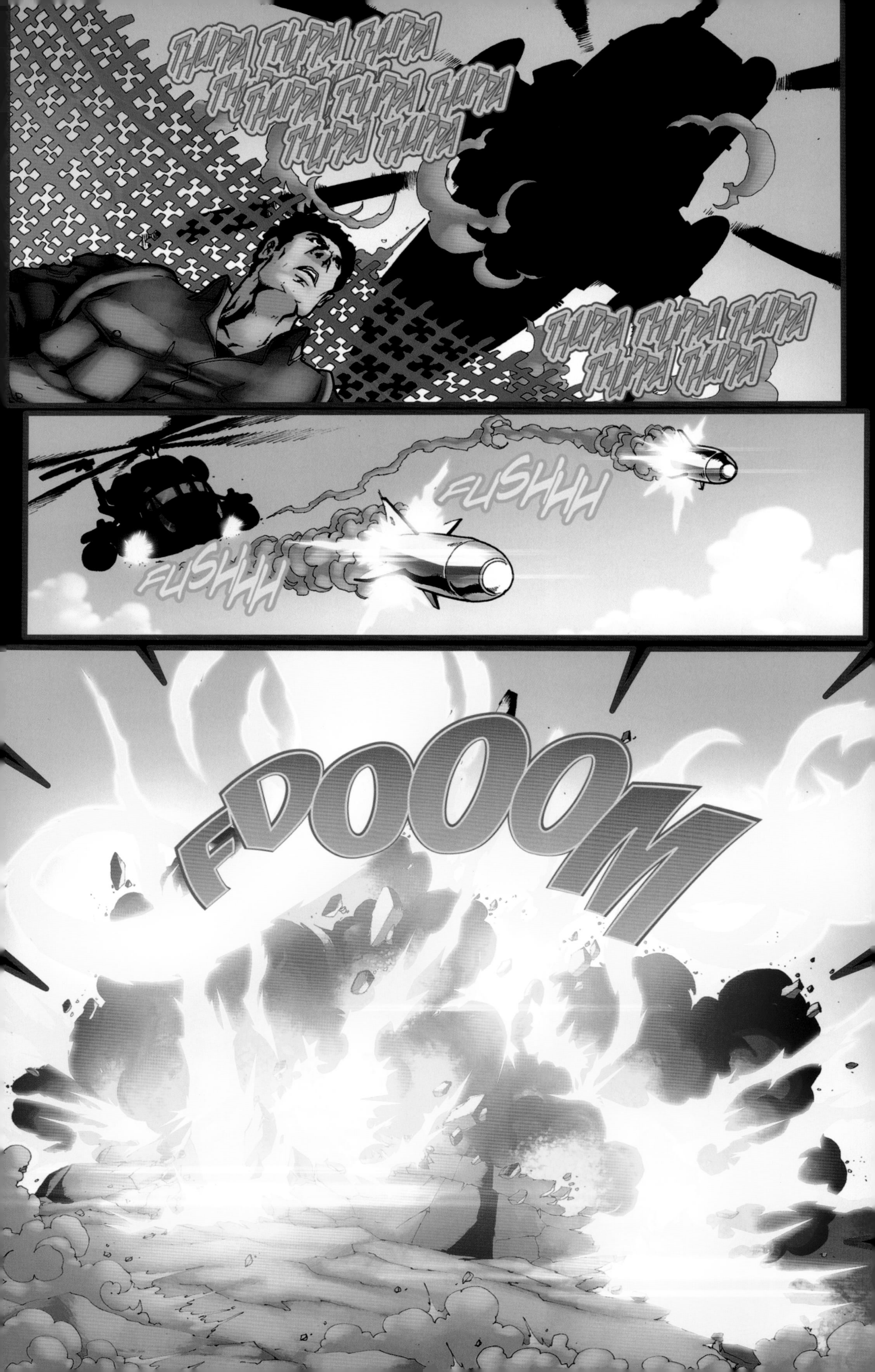

THUPPA THUPPA THUPPA
THUPPA THUPPA THUPPA
THUPPA THUPPA
THUPPA THUPPA THUPPA
THUPPA THUPPA
FUSHHH
FUSHHH
FDOOOM

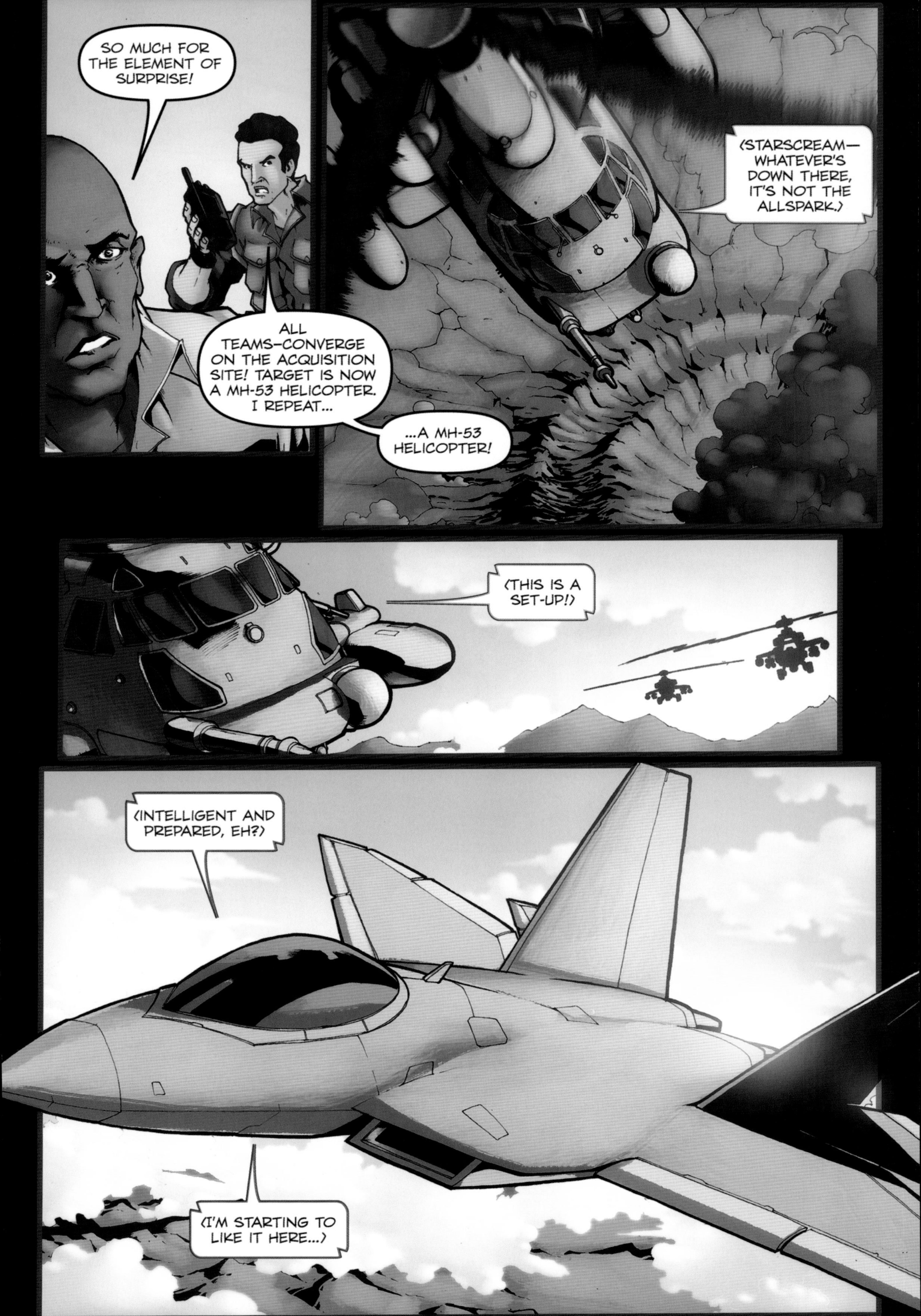
SO MUCH FOR THE ELEMENT OF SURPRISE!
ALL TEAMS–CONVERGE ON THE ACQUISITION SITE! TARGET IS NOW A MH-53 HELICOPTER. I REPEAT...
...A MH-53 HELICOPTER!
(STARSCREAM— WHATEVER'S DOWN THERE, IT'S NOT THE ALLSPARK.)
(THIS IS A SET-UP!)
(INTELLIGENT AND PREPARED, EH?)
(I'M STARTING TO LIKE IT HERE...)

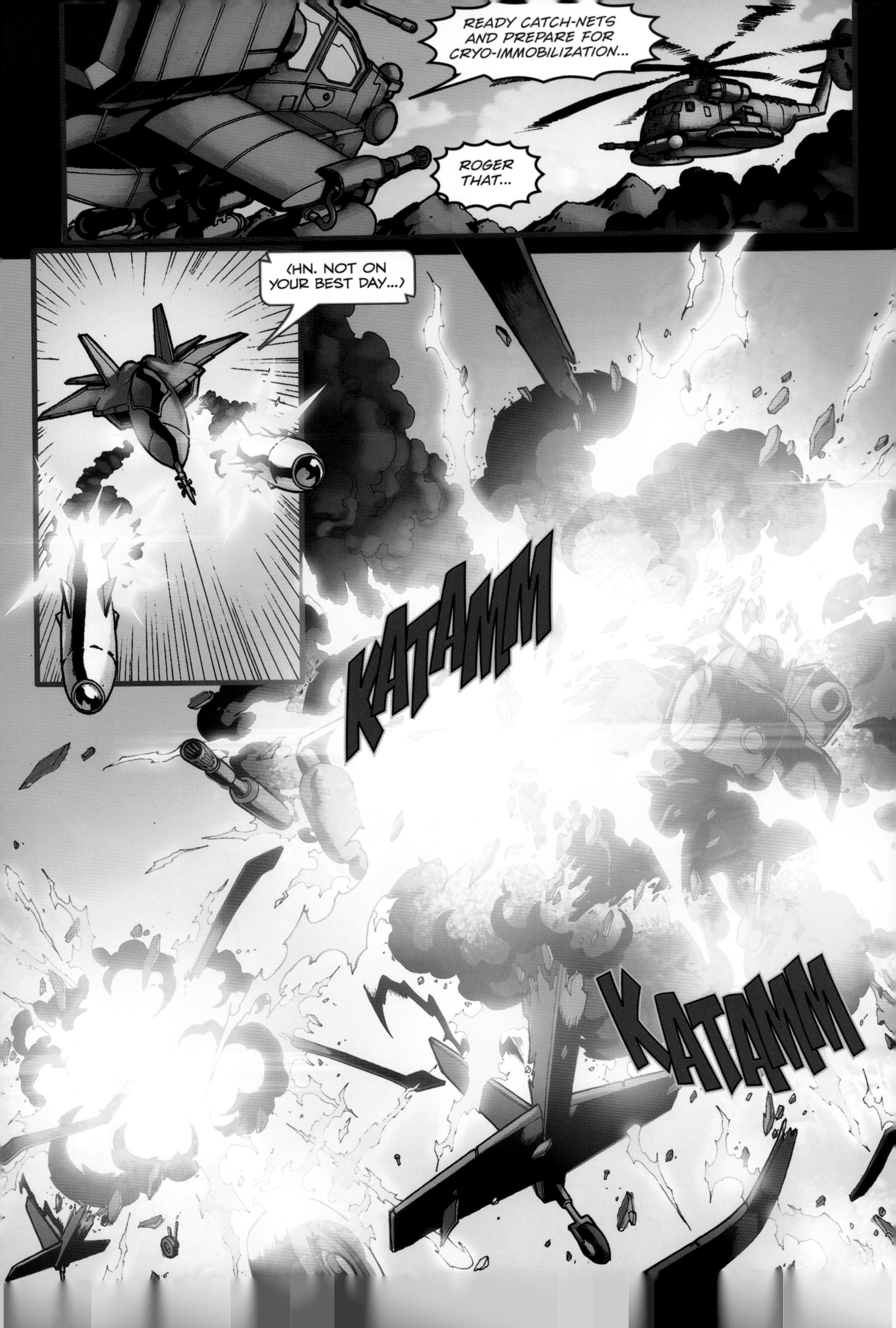

READY CATCH-NETS AND PREPARE FOR CRYO-IMMOBILIZATION...
ROGER THAT...
(HN. NOT ON YOUR BEST DAY...)
KATAMM
KATAMM

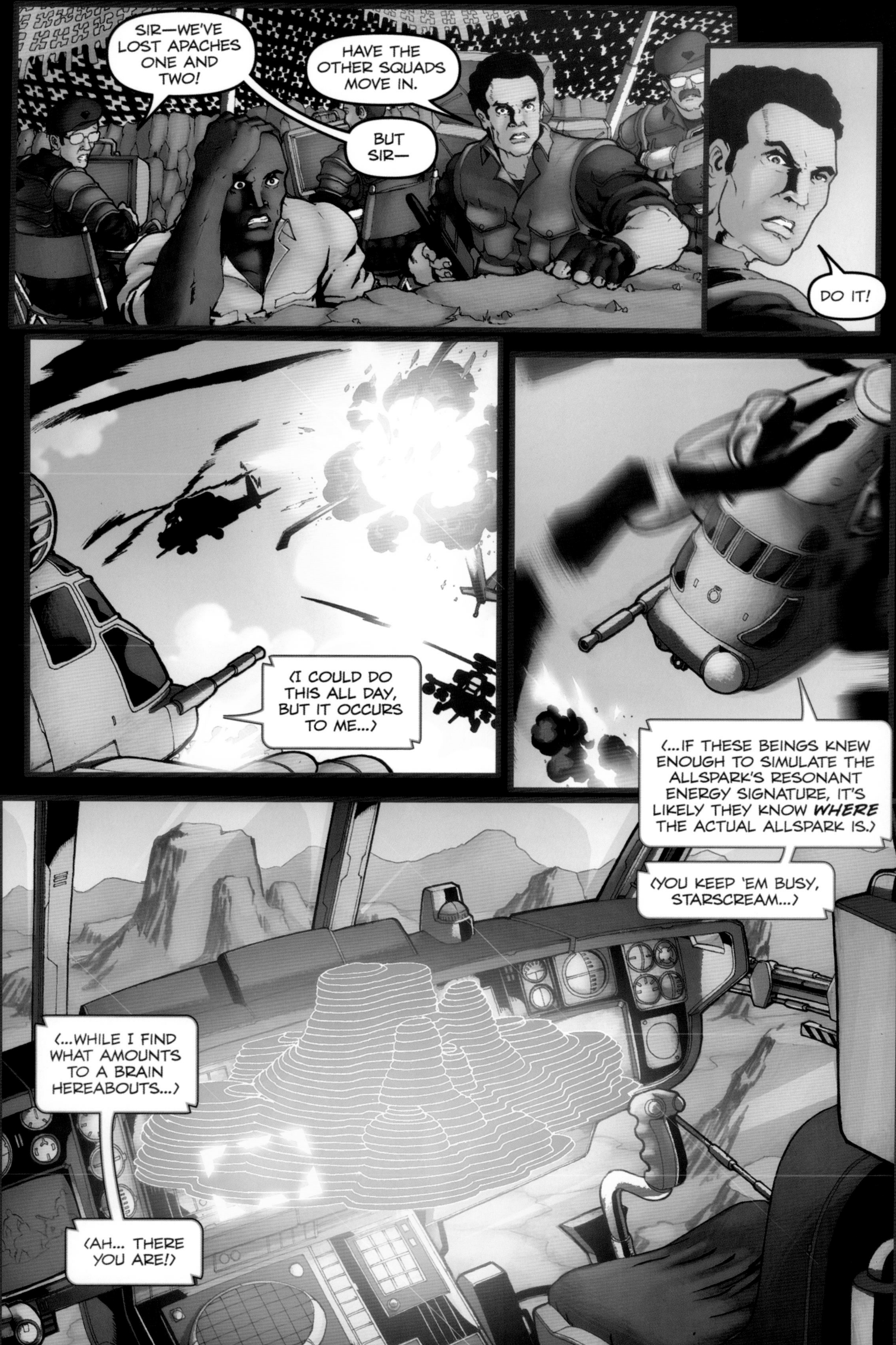
SIR—WE'VE LOST APACHES ONE AND TWO!
HAVE THE OTHER SQUADS MOVE IN.
BUT SIR—
DO IT!
‹I COULD DO THIS ALL DAY, BUT IT OCCURS TO ME...›
‹...IF THESE BEINGS KNEW ENOUGH TO SIMULATE THE ALLSPARK'S RESONANT ENERGY SIGNATURE, IT'S LIKELY THEY KNOW *WHERE* THE ACTUAL ALLSPARK IS.›
‹YOU KEEP 'EM BUSY, STARSCREAM...›
‹...WHILE I FIND WHAT AMOUNTS TO A BRAIN HEREABOUTS...›
‹AH... THERE YOU ARE!›

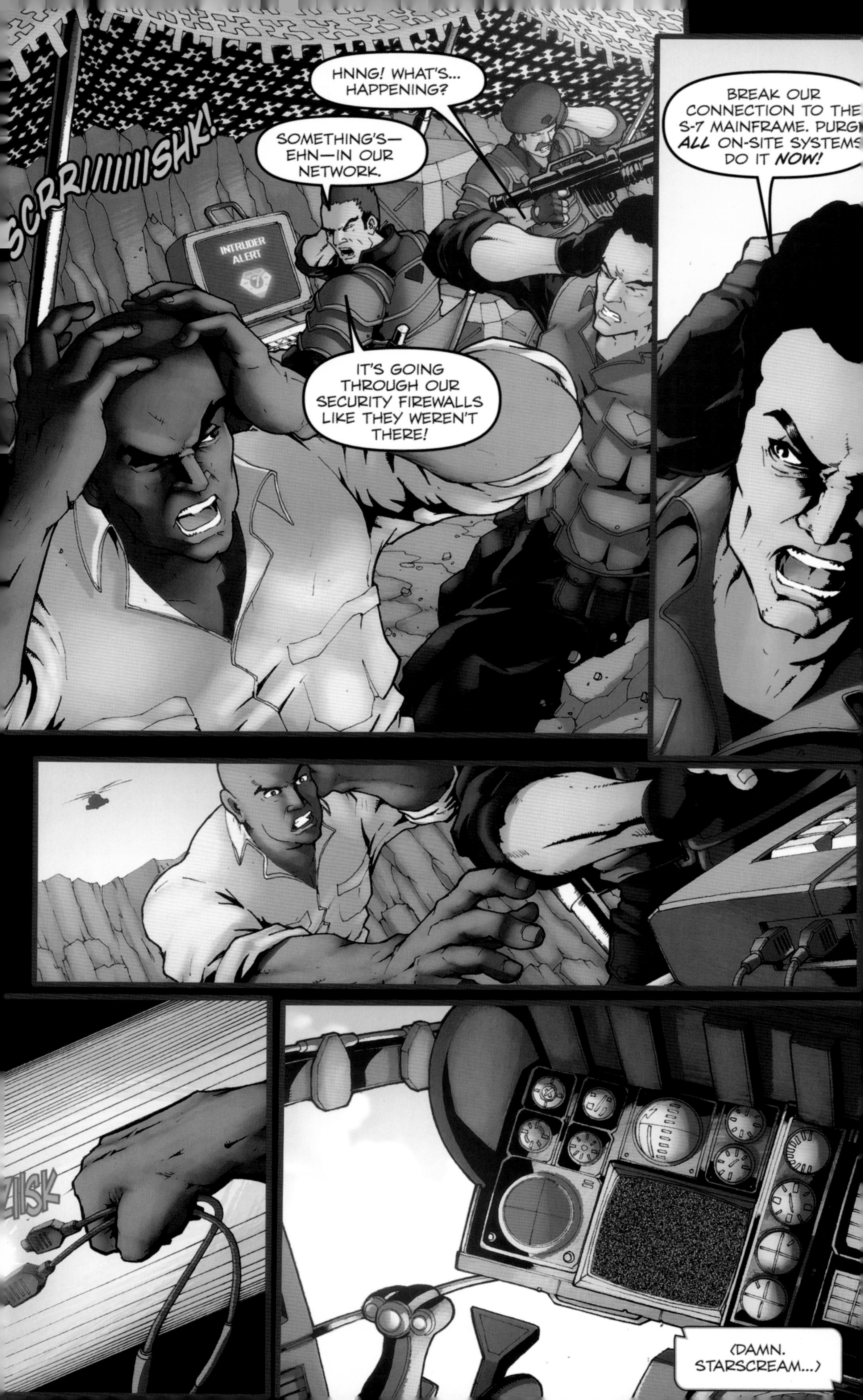
SCRRI!!!!!!!!SHK!
HNNG! WHAT'S... HAPPENING?
SOMETHING'S— EHN—IN OUR NETWORK.
INTRUDER ALERT
IT'S GOING THROUGH OUR SECURITY FIREWALLS LIKE THEY WEREN'T THERE!
BREAK OUR CONNECTION TO THE S-7 MAINFRAME. PURG ALL ON-SITE SYSTEMS DO IT NOW!
ZIISK
(DAMN. STARSCREAM...)

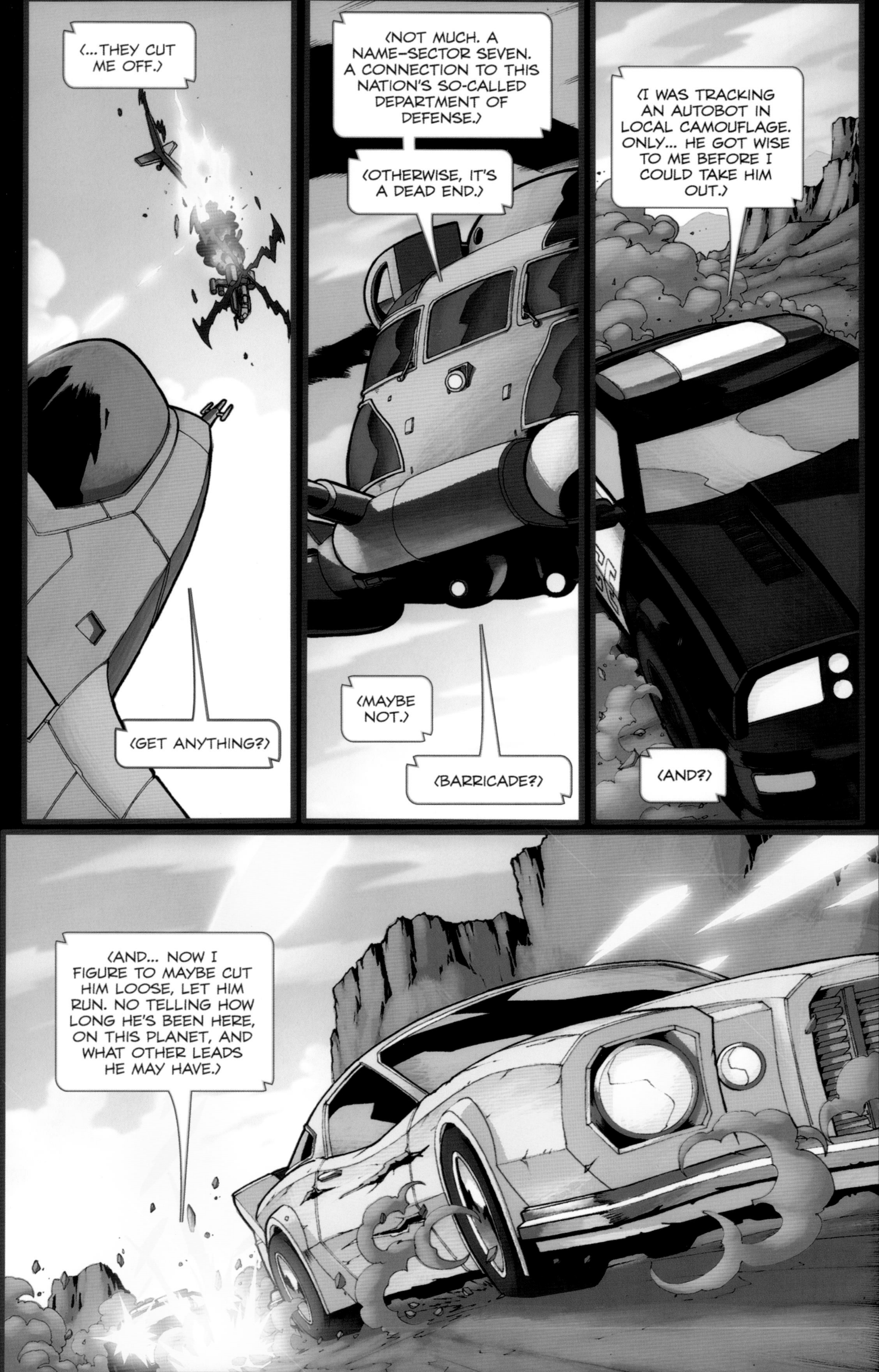

(...THEY CUT ME OFF.)
(GET ANYTHING?)
(NOT MUCH. A NAME--SECTOR SEVEN. A CONNECTION TO THIS NATION'S SO-CALLED DEPARTMENT OF DEFENSE.)
(OTHERWISE, IT'S A DEAD END.)
(MAYBE NOT.)
(BARRICADE?)
(I WAS TRACKING AN AUTOBOT IN LOCAL CAMOUFLAGE. ONLY... HE GOT WISE TO ME BEFORE I COULD TAKE HIM OUT.)
(AND?)
(AND... NOW I FIGURE TO MAYBE CUT HIM LOOSE, LET HIM RUN. NO TELLING HOW LONG HE'S BEEN HERE, ON THIS PLANET, AND WHAT OTHER LEADS HE MAY HAVE.)

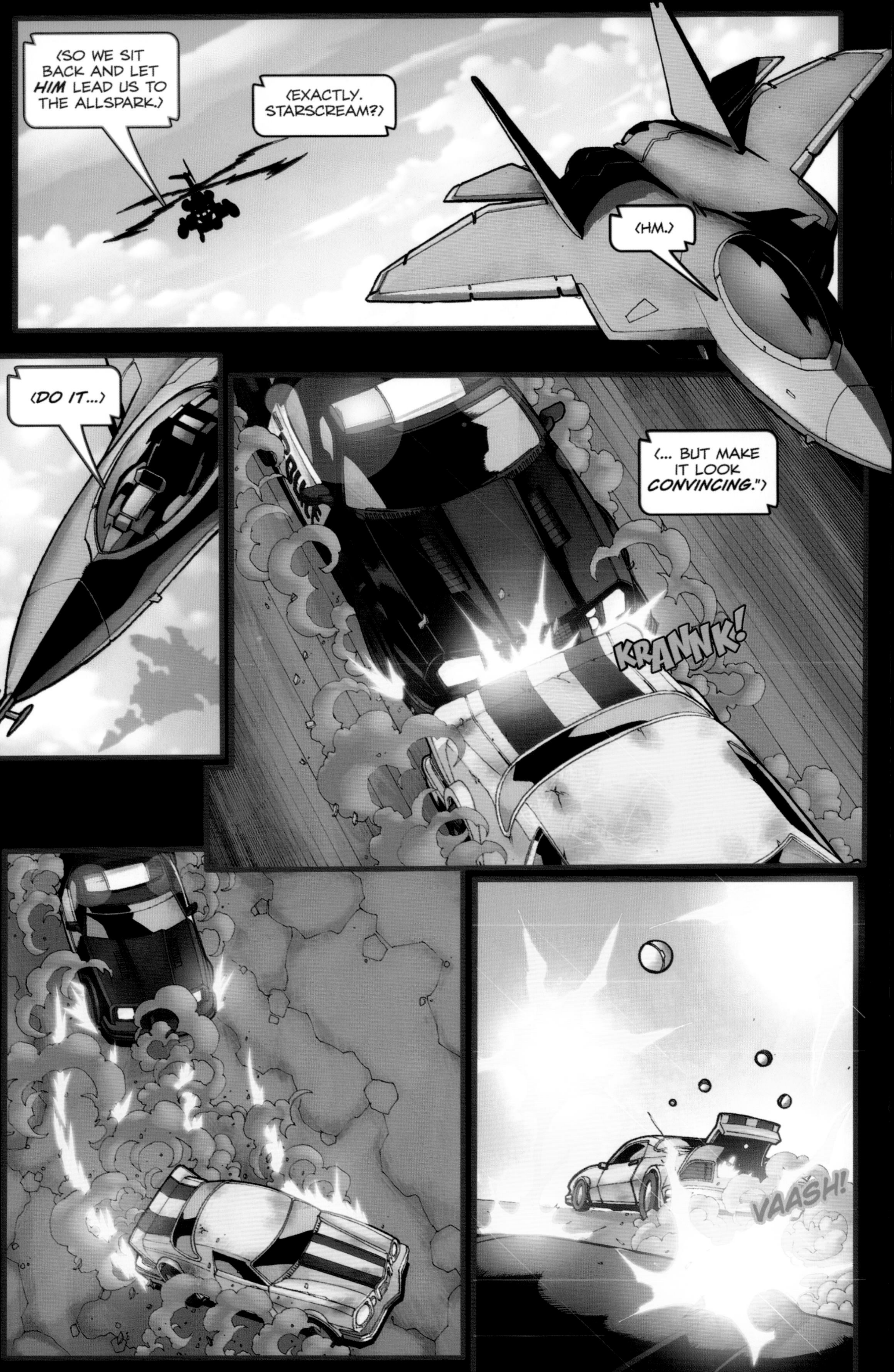

‹SO WE SIT BACK AND LET HIM LEAD US TO THE ALLSPARK.›
‹EXACTLY. STARSCREAM?›
‹HM.›
‹DO IT...›
‹... BUT MAKE IT LOOK CONVINCING."›
KRANNK!
VAASH!

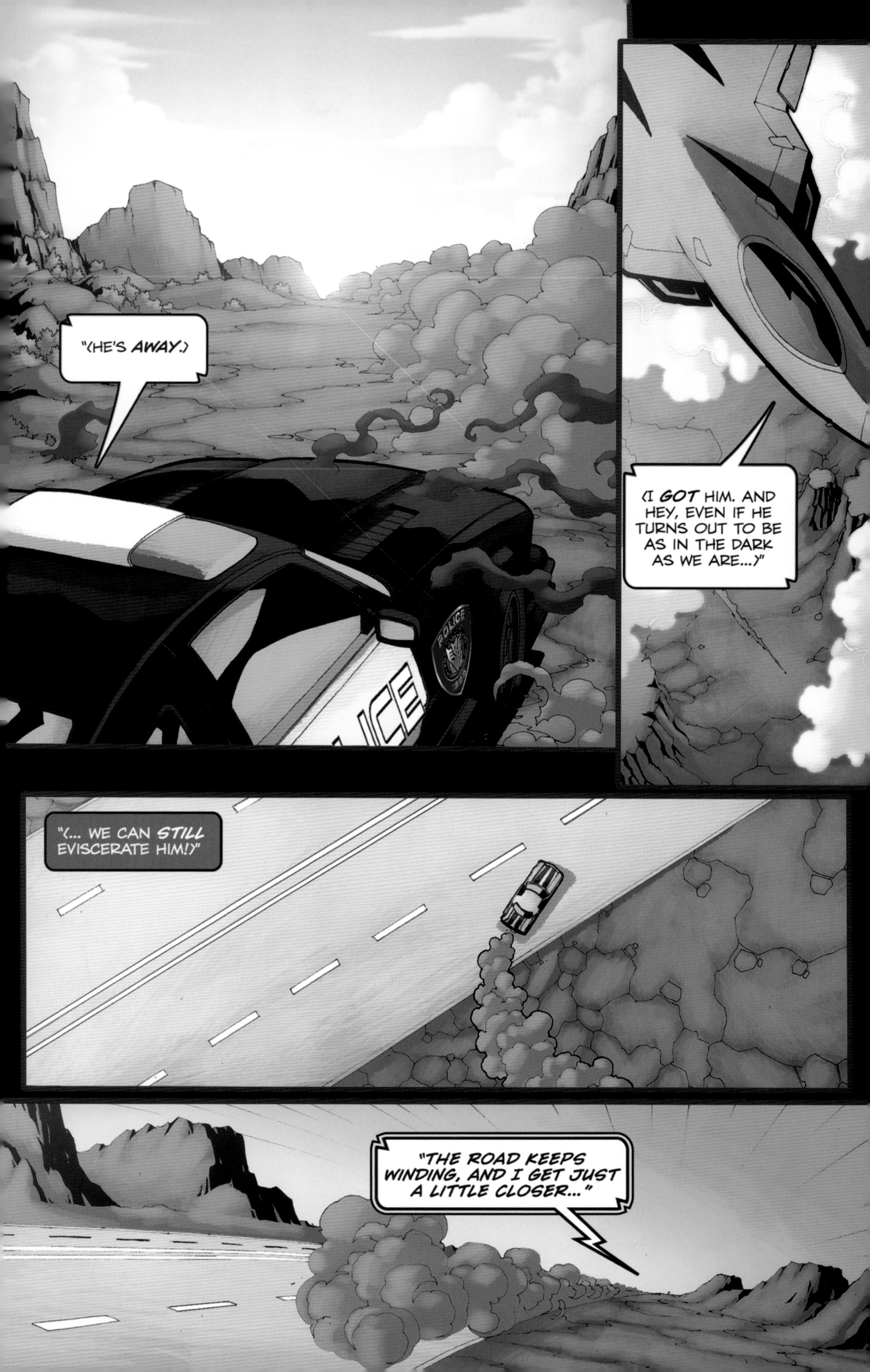
"‹HE'S **AWAY.**›
‹I **GOT** HIM. AND HEY, EVEN IF HE TURNS OUT TO BE AS IN THE DARK AS WE ARE...›"
"‹... WE CAN **STILL** EVISCERATE HIM!›"
"THE ROAD KEEPS WINDING, AND I GET JUST A LITTLE CLOSER..."

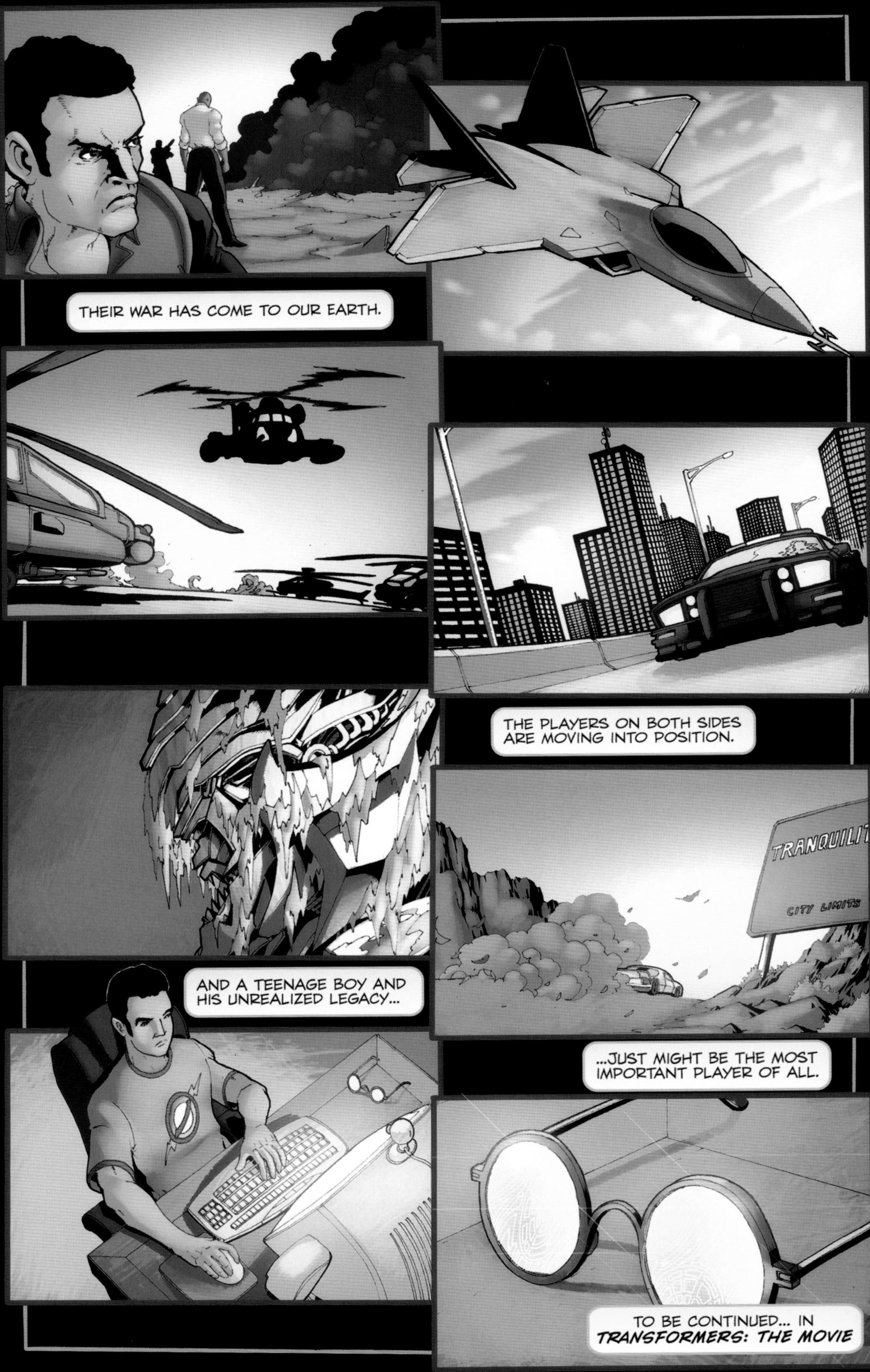
THEIR WAR HAS COME TO OUR EARTH.
THE PLAYERS ON BOTH SIDES ARE MOVING INTO POSITION.
TRANQUILIT
CITY LIMITS
AND A TEENAGE BOY AND HIS UNREALIZED LEGACY...
...JUST MIGHT BE THE MOST IMPORTANT PLAYER OF ALL.
TO BE CONTINUED... IN *TRANSFORMERS: THE MOVIE*

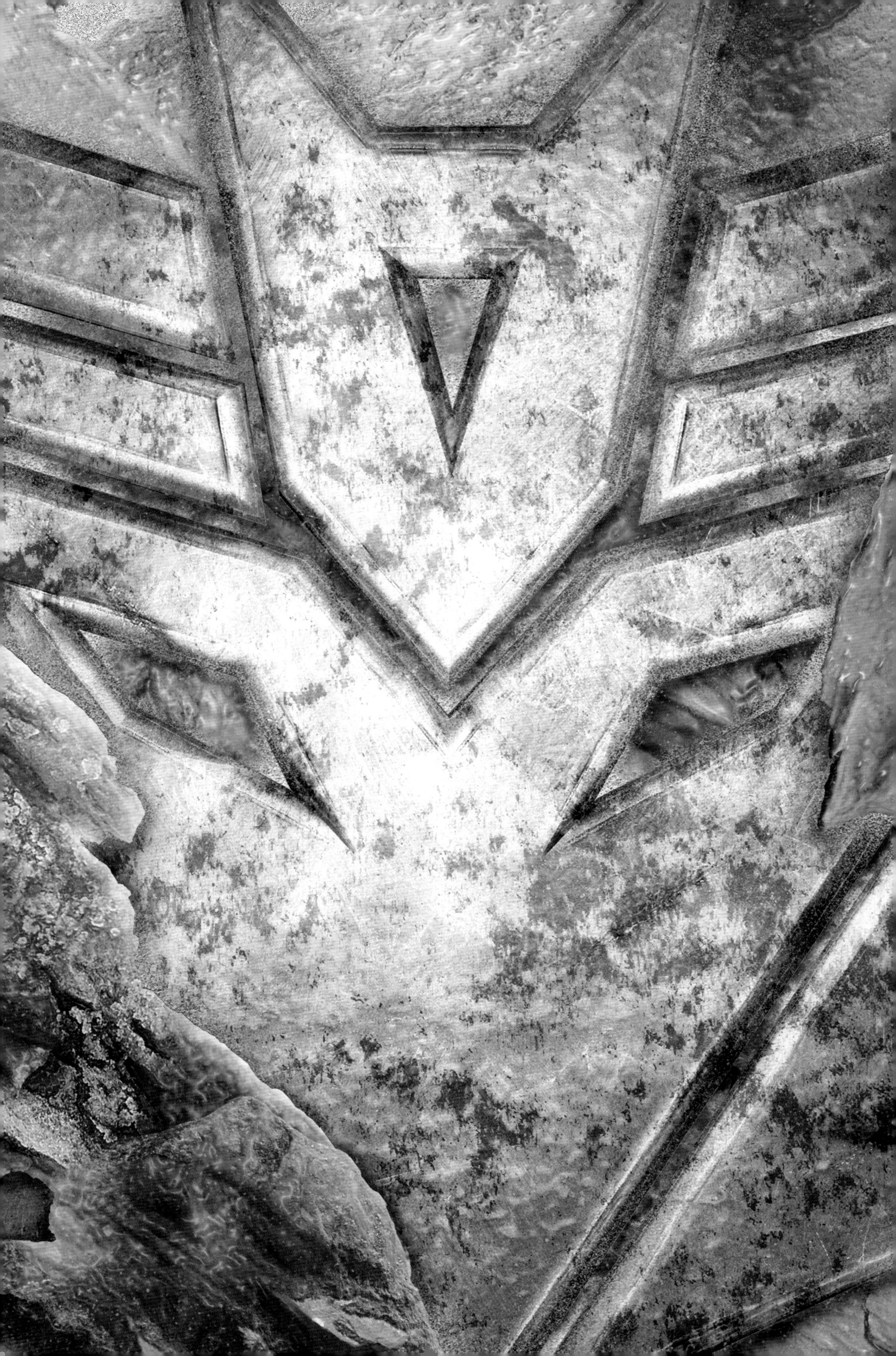

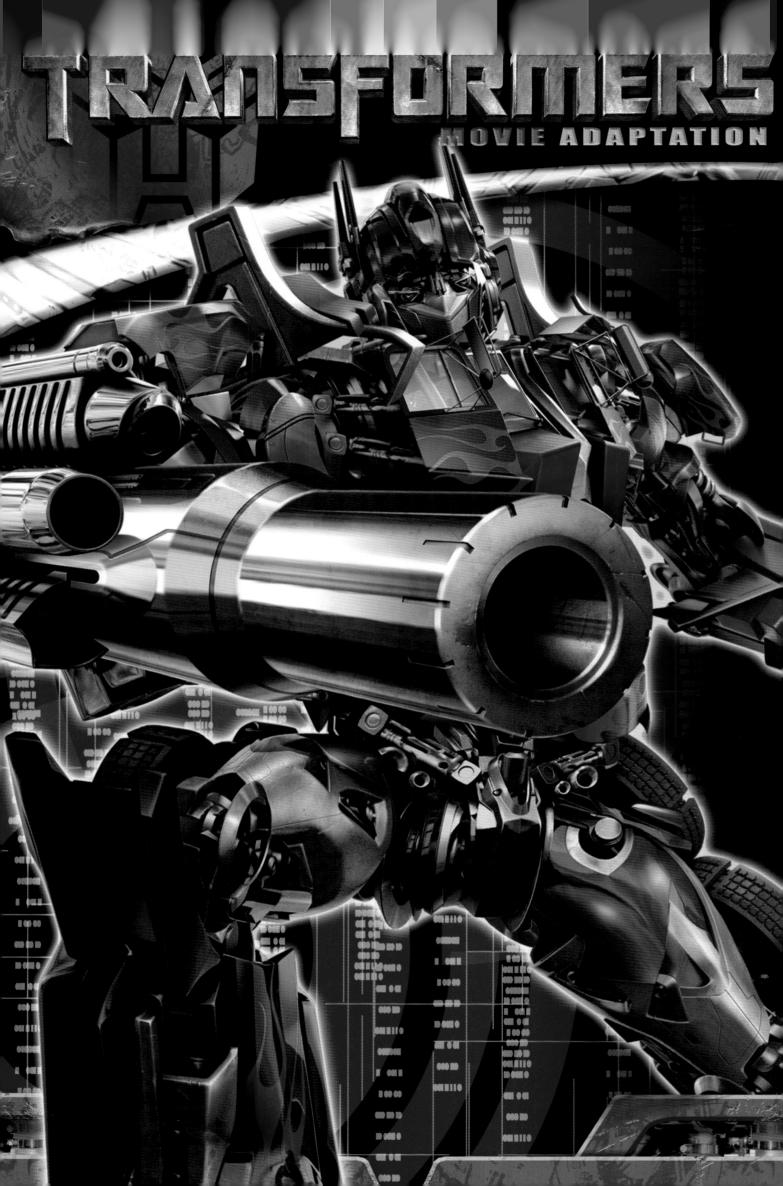

TRANSFORMERS
MOVIE ADAPTATION

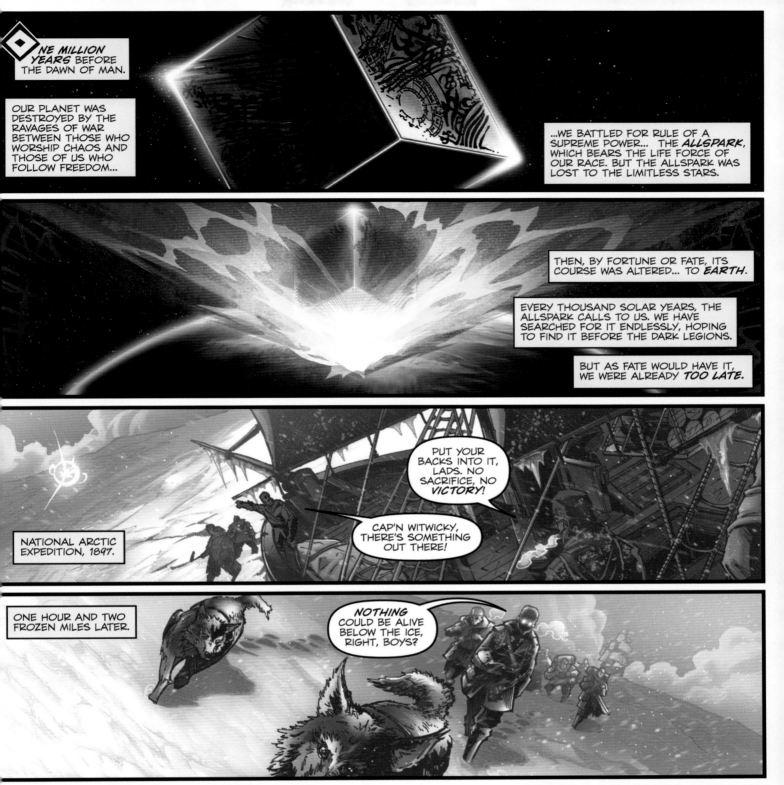

ONE MILLION YEARS BEFORE THE DAWN OF MAN.

OUR PLANET WAS DESTROYED BY THE RAVAGES OF WAR BETWEEN THOSE WHO WORSHIP CHAOS AND THOSE OF US WHO FOLLOW FREEDOM...

...WE BATTLED FOR RULE OF A SUPREME POWER... THE *ALLSPARK*, WHICH BEARS THE LIFE FORCE OF OUR RACE. BUT THE ALLSPARK WAS LOST TO THE LIMITLESS STARS.

THEN, BY FORTUNE OR FATE, ITS COURSE WAS ALTERED... TO *EARTH*.

EVERY THOUSAND SOLAR YEARS, THE ALLSPARK CALLS TO US. WE HAVE SEARCHED FOR IT ENDLESSLY, HOPING TO FIND IT BEFORE THE DARK LEGIONS.

BUT AS FATE WOULD HAVE IT, WE WERE ALREADY *TOO LATE*.

NATIONAL ARCTIC EXPEDITION, 1897.

PUT YOUR BACKS INTO IT, LADS. NO SACRIFICE, NO *VICTORY*!

CAP'N WITWICKY, THERE'S SOMETHING OUT THERE!

ONE HOUR AND TWO FROZEN MILES LATER.

NOTHING COULD BE ALIVE BELOW THE ICE, RIGHT, BOYS?

BOYS?

KRRCK

KERRACK

AAAAA!

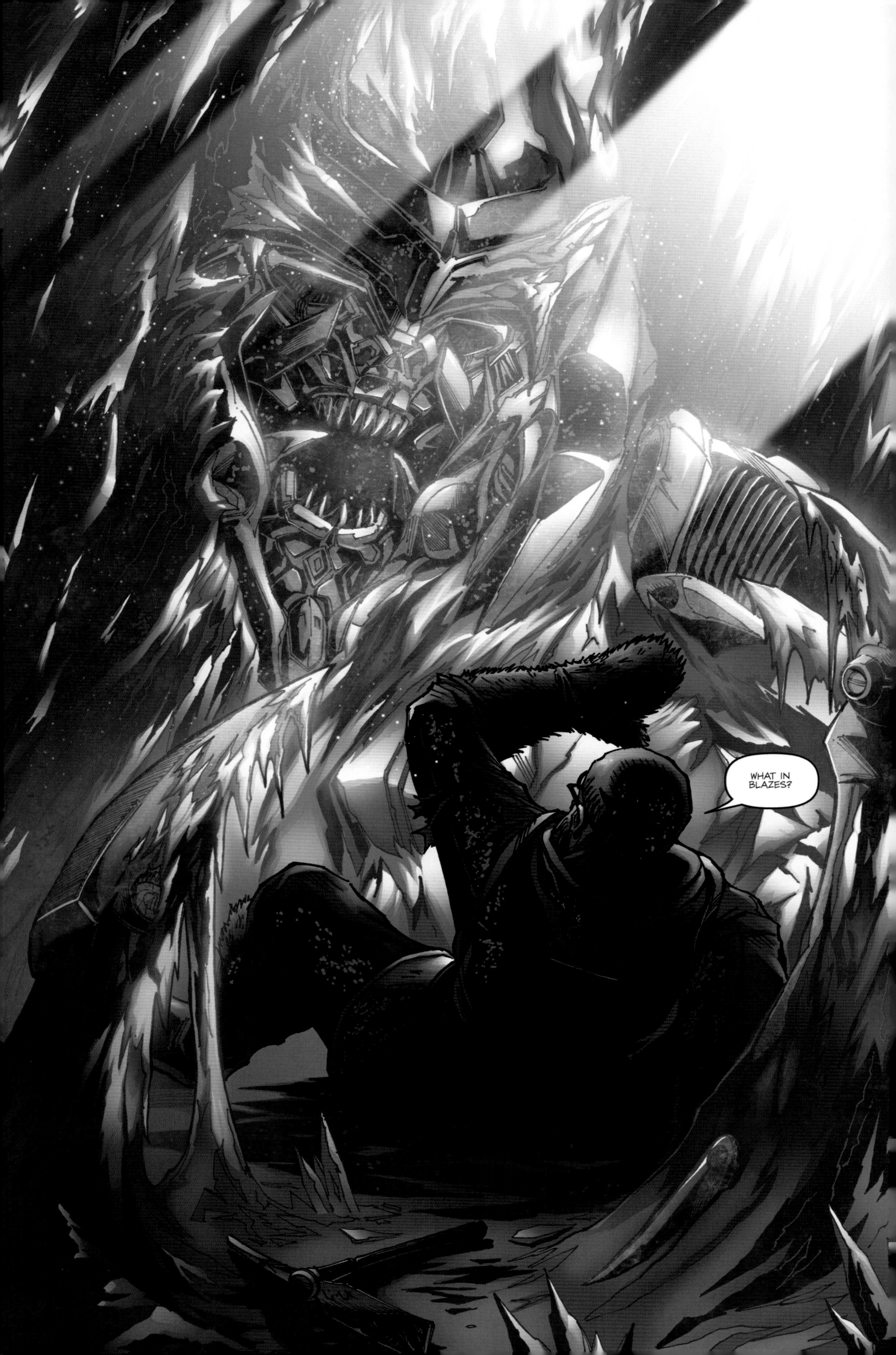
WHAT IN BLAZES?

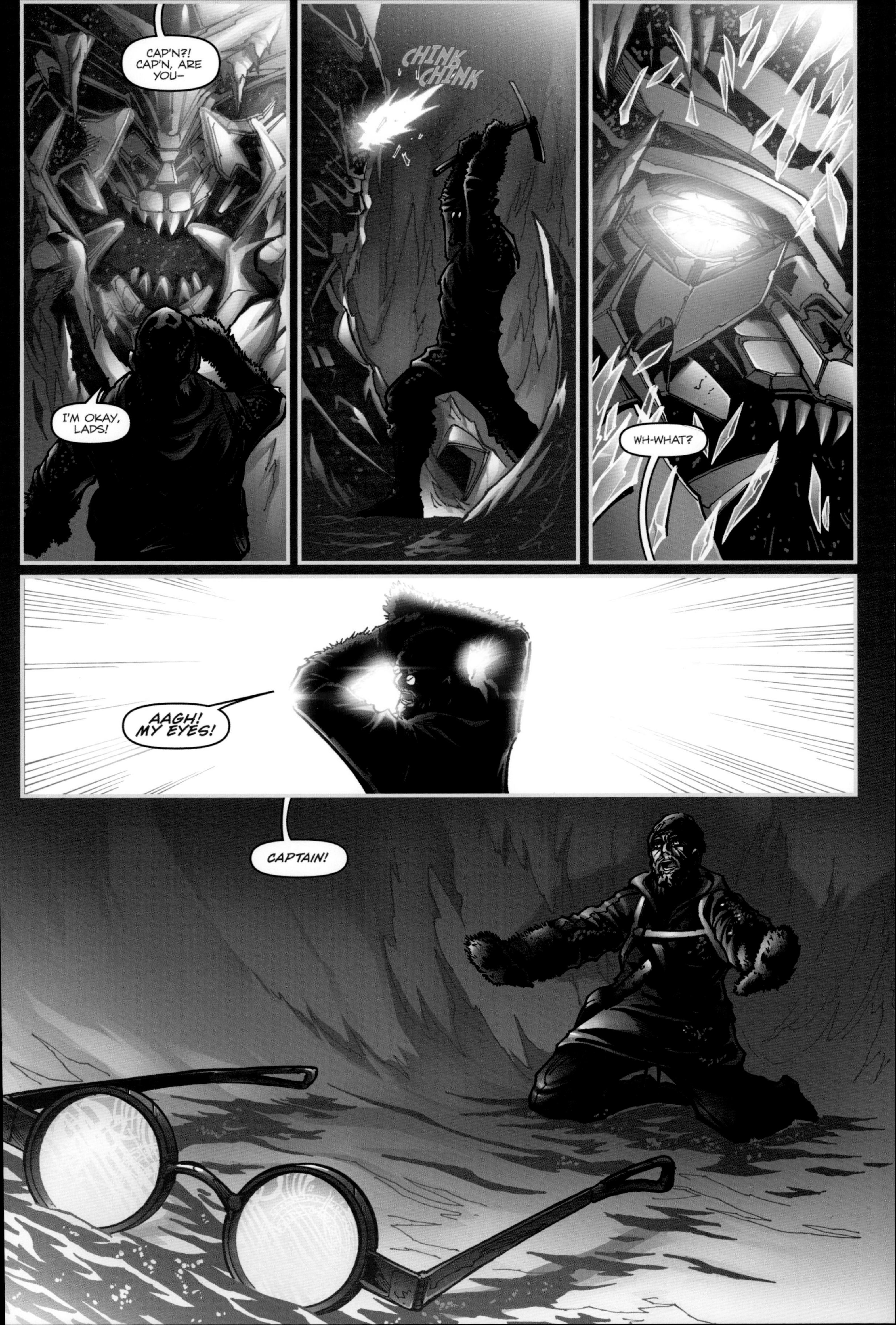
CAP'N?! CAP'N, ARE YOU–
I'M OKAY, LADS!
CHINK CHINK
WH-WHAT?
AAGH! MY EYES!
CAPTAIN!

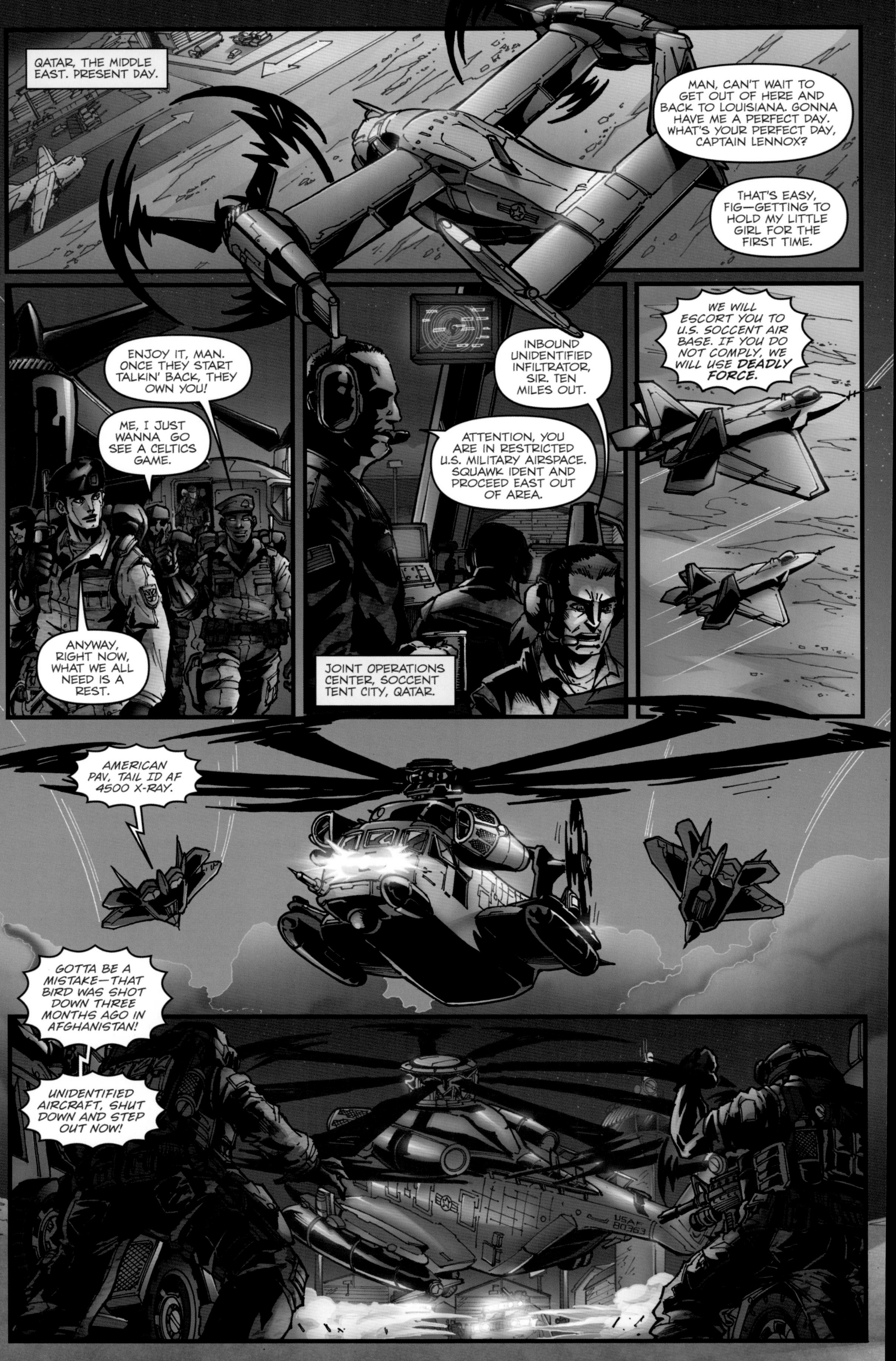
QATAR, THE MIDDLE EAST. PRESENT DAY.
MAN, CAN'T WAIT TO GET OUT OF HERE AND BACK TO LOUISIANA. GONNA HAVE ME A PERFECT DAY. WHAT'S YOUR PERFECT DAY, CAPTAIN LENNOX?
THAT'S EASY, FIG—GETTING TO HOLD MY LITTLE GIRL FOR THE FIRST TIME.
ENJOY IT, MAN. ONCE THEY START TALKIN' BACK, THEY OWN YOU!
ME, I JUST WANNA GO SEE A CELTICS GAME.
ANYWAY, RIGHT NOW, WHAT WE ALL NEED IS A REST.
INBOUND UNIDENTIFIED INFILTRATOR, SIR. TEN MILES OUT.
ATTENTION, YOU ARE IN RESTRICTED U.S. MILITARY AIRSPACE. SQUAWK IDENT AND PROCEED EAST OUT OF AREA.
JOINT OPERATIONS CENTER, SOCCENT TENT CITY, QATAR.
WE WILL ESCORT YOU TO U.S. SOCCENT AIR BASE. IF YOU DO NOT COMPLY, WE WILL USE DEADLY FORCE.
AMERICAN PAV, TAIL ID AF 4500 X-RAY.
GOTTA BE A MISTAKE—THAT BIRD WAS SHOT DOWN THREE MONTHS AGO IN AFGHANISTAN!
UNIDENTIFIED AIRCRAFT, SHUT DOWN AND STEP OUT NOW!
USAF 80363

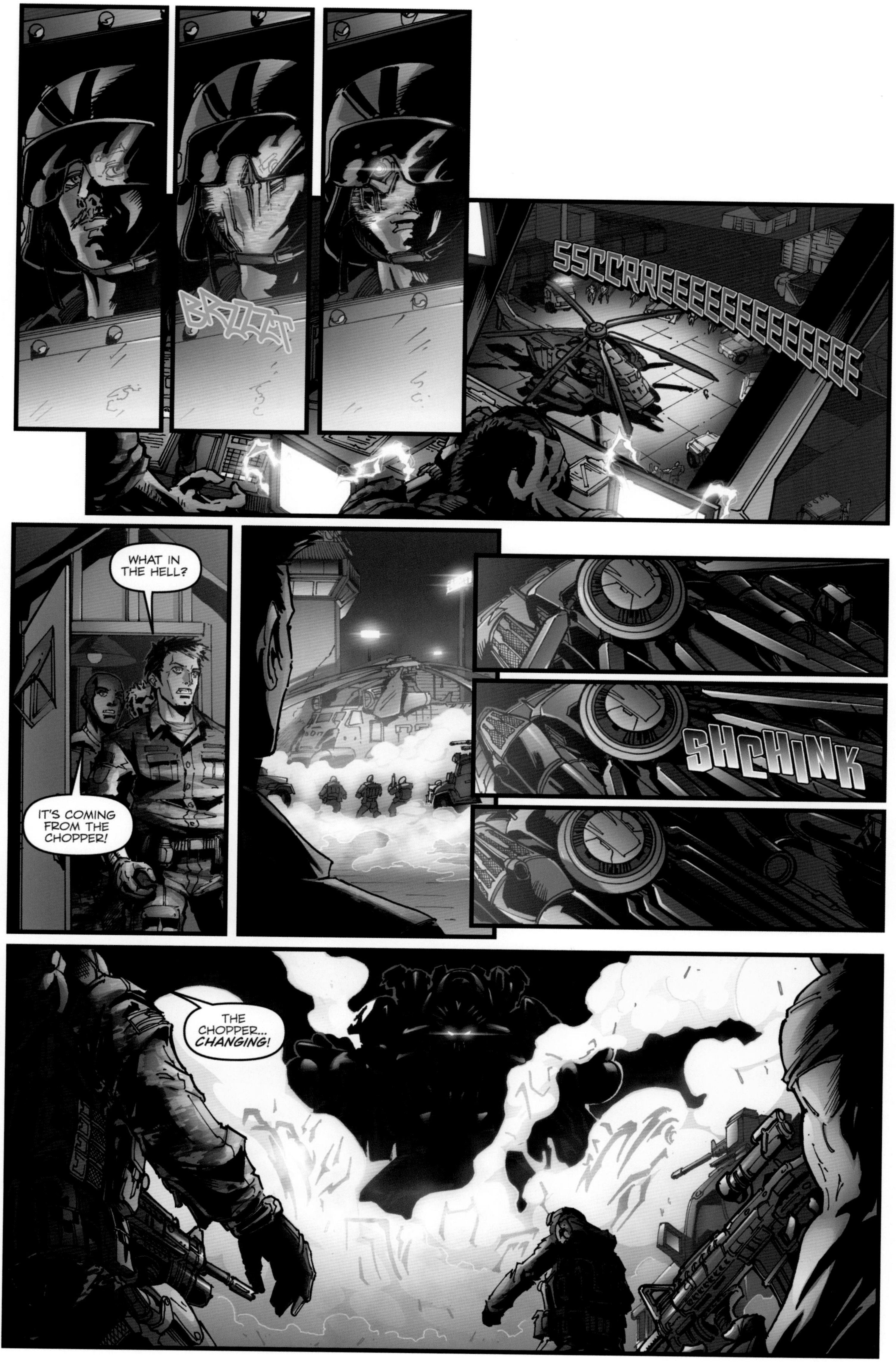
BRZZZT
SSCCRREEEEEEEEEEEEEE
WHAT IN THE HELL?
IT'S COMING FROM THE CHOPPER!
SHCHINK
THE CHOPPER... CHANGING!

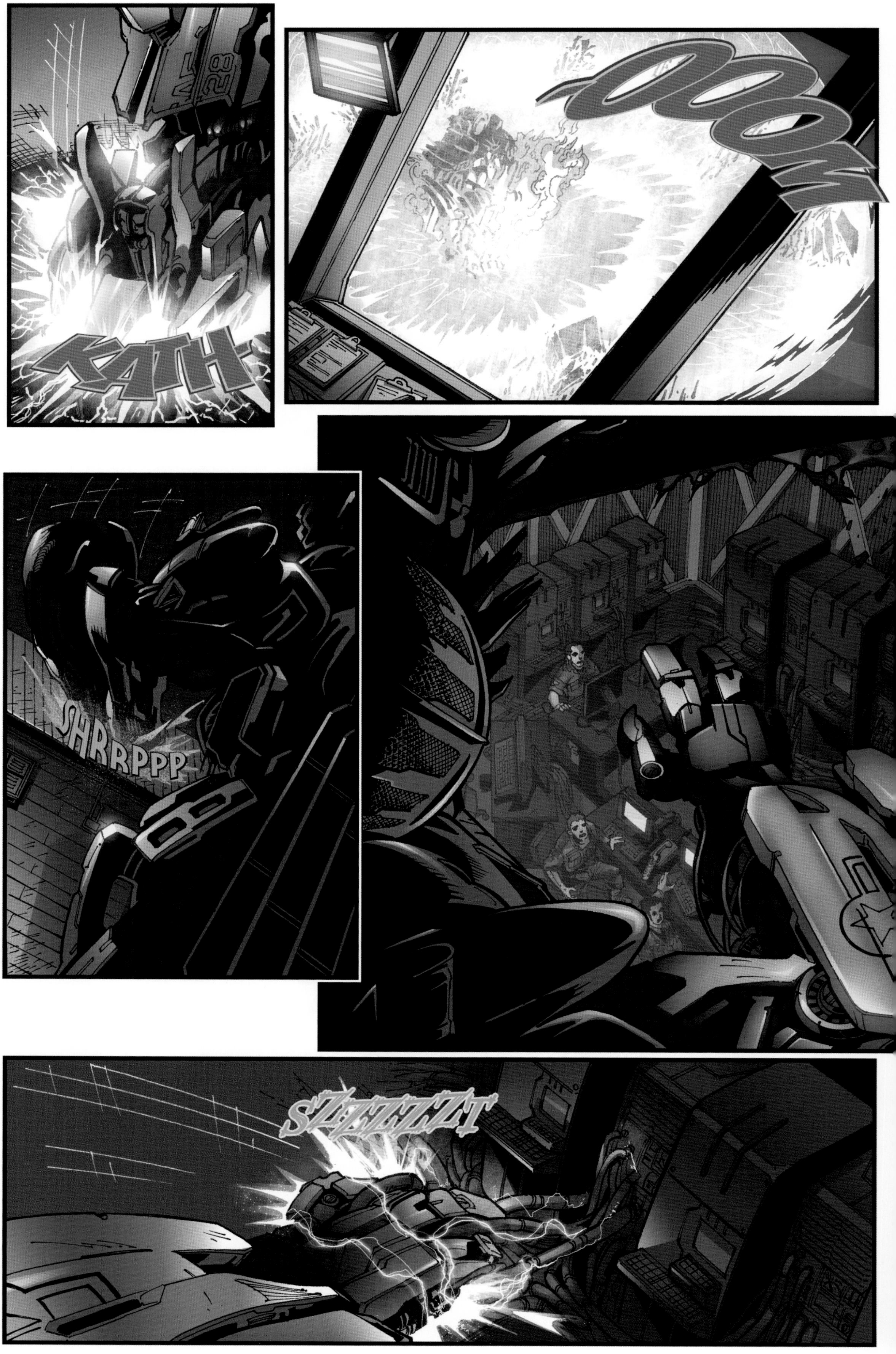
KATH
-OOOM
SHRRPPP
SZZZZZT

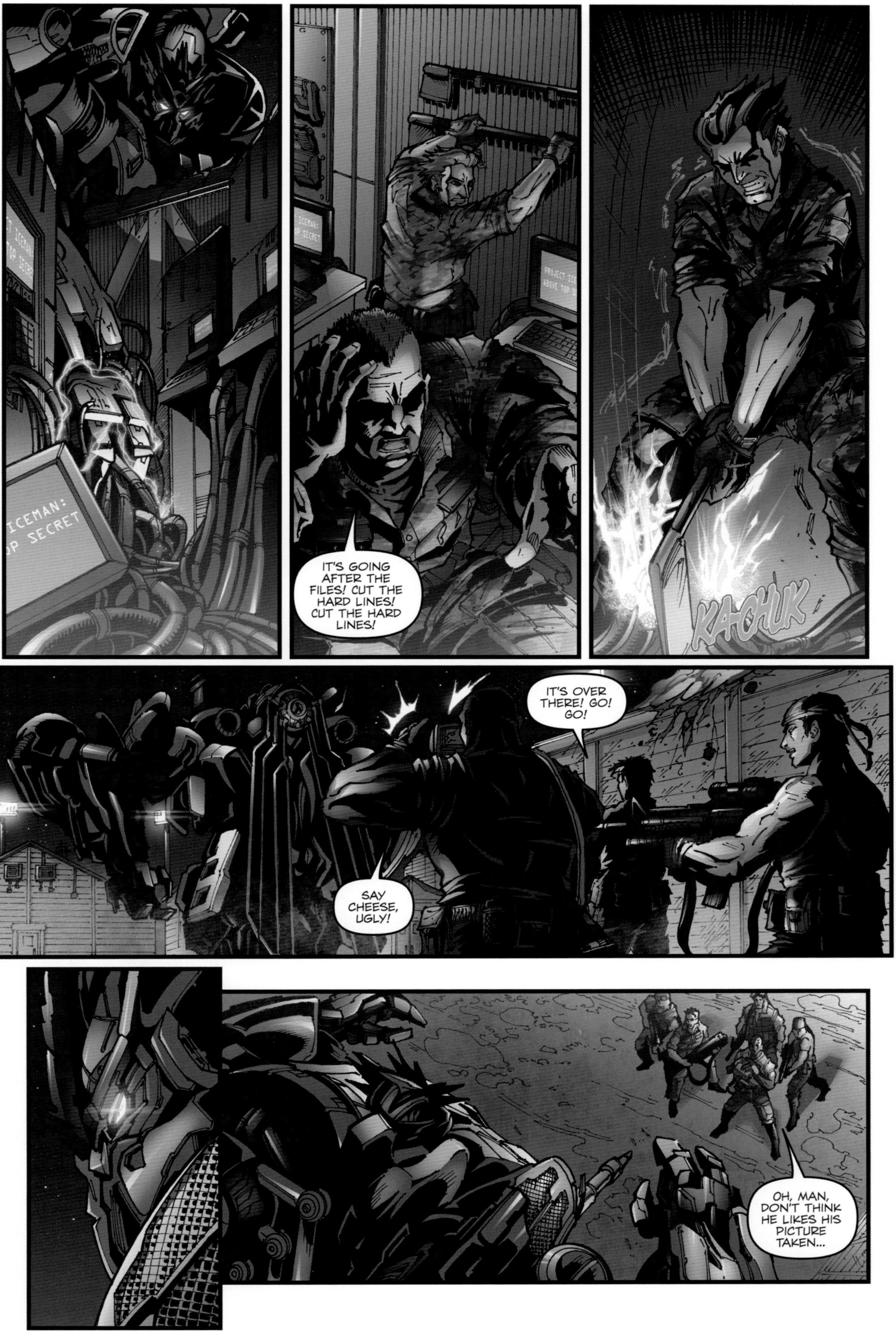
IT'S GOING AFTER THE FILES! CUT THE HARD LINES! CUT THE HARD LINES!
KA-CHUK
IT'S OVER THERE! GO! GO!
SAY CHEESE, UGLY!
OH, MAN, DON'T THINK HE LIKES HIS PICTURE TAKEN...

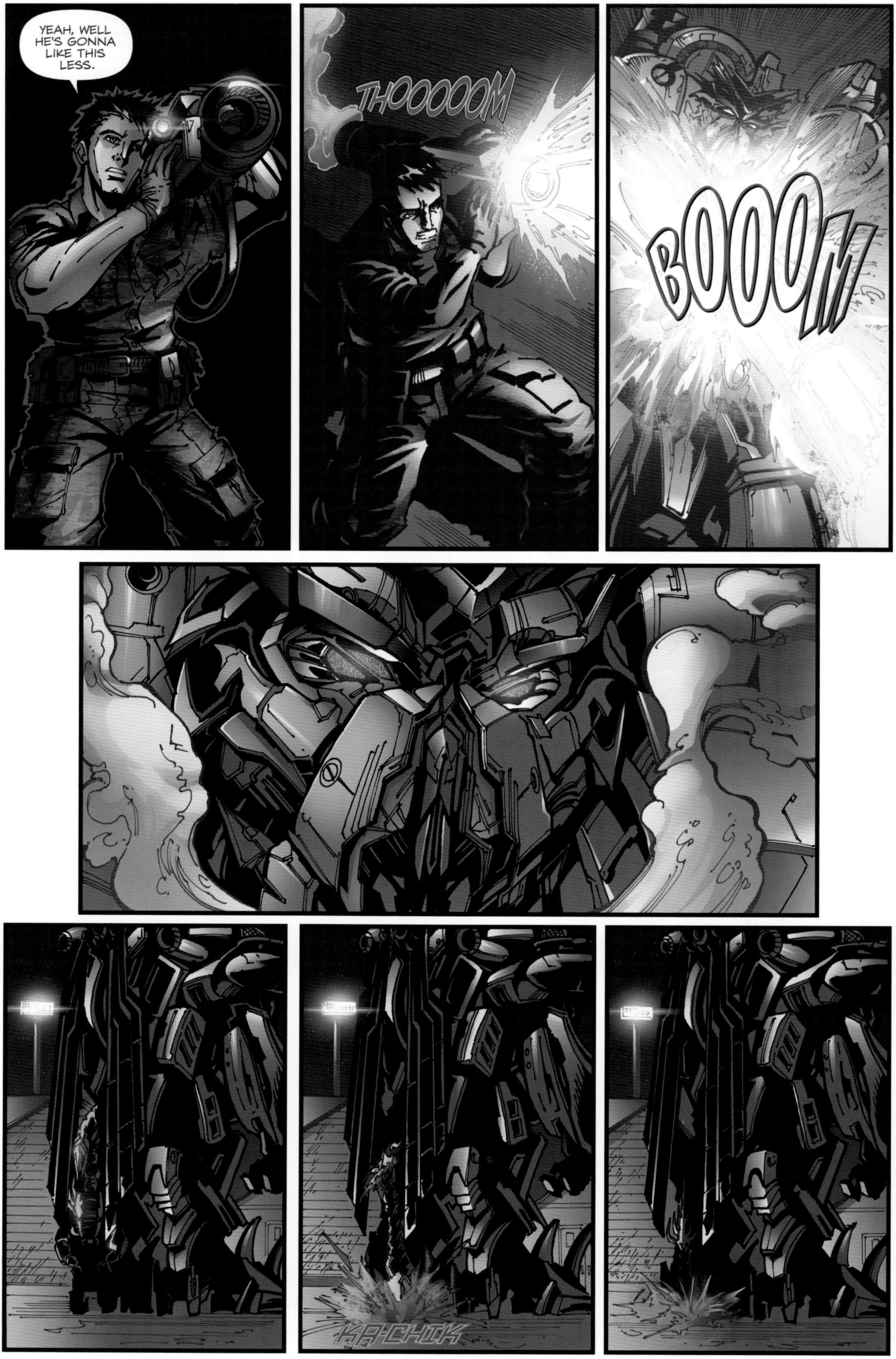
YEAH, WELL HE'S GONNA LIKE THIS LESS.
THOOOOOM
BOOOM
KA-CHIK

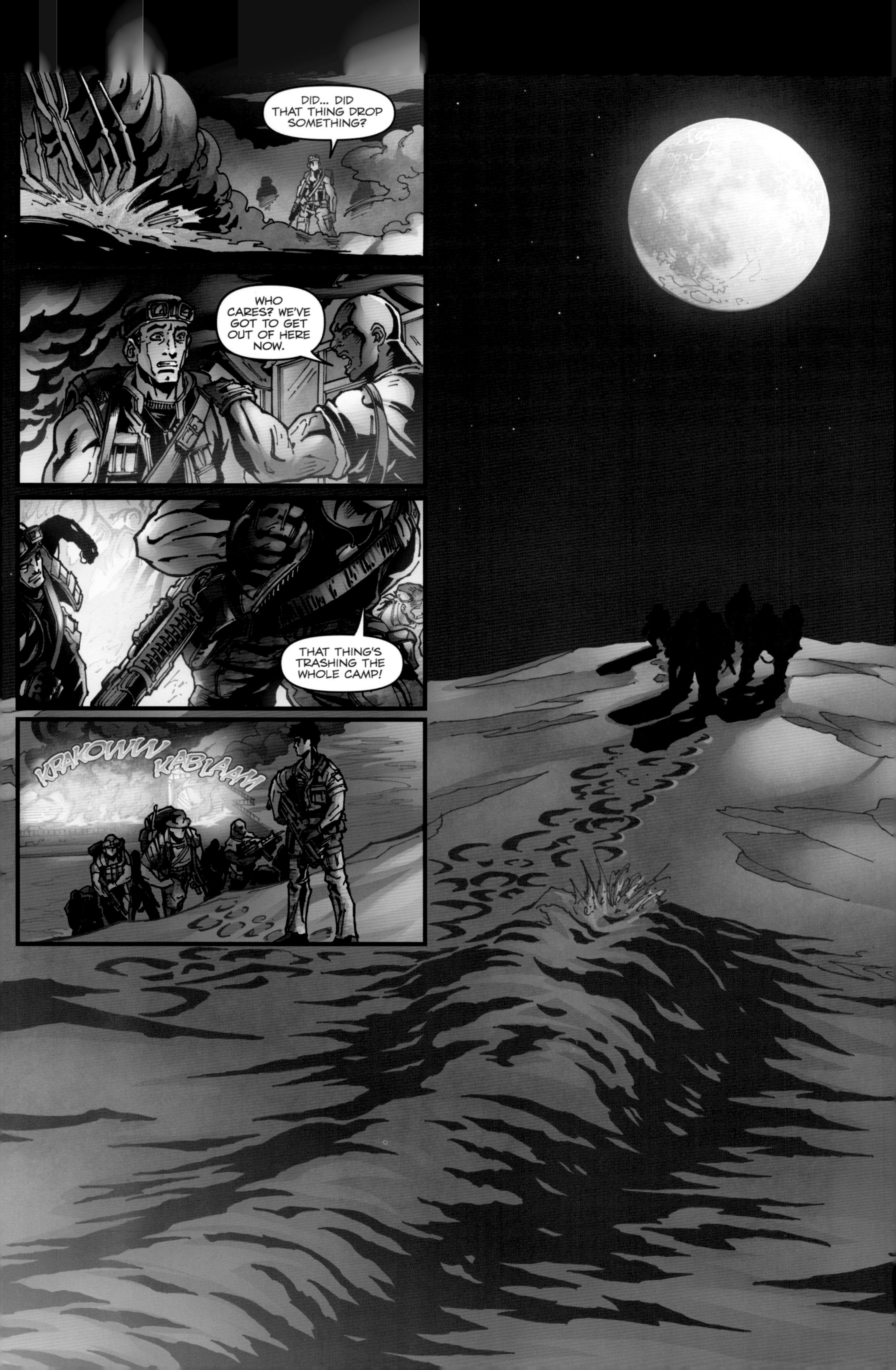

DID... DID THAT THING DROP SOMETHING?
WHO CARES? WE'VE GOT TO GET OUT OF HERE NOW.
THAT THING'S TRASHING THE WHOLE CAMP!
KRAKOWW
KABLAAM

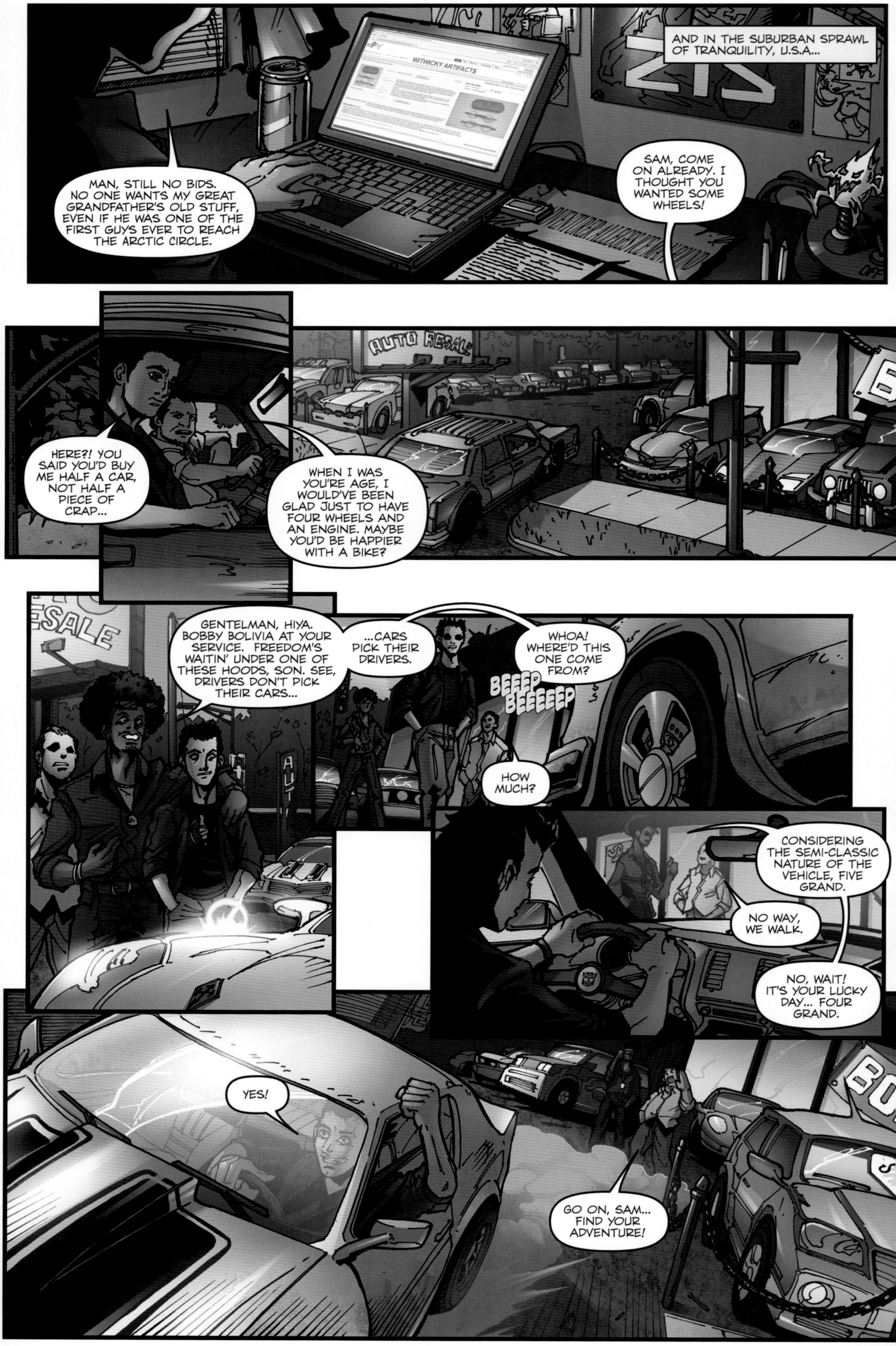
AND IN THE SUBURBAN SPRAWL OF TRANQUILITY, U.S.A...
WITWICKY ARTIFACTS
MAN, STILL NO BIDS. NO ONE WANTS MY GREAT GRANDFATHER'S OLD STUFF, EVEN IF HE WAS ONE OF THE FIRST GUYS EVER TO REACH THE ARCTIC CIRCLE.
SAM, COME ON ALREADY. I THOUGHT YOU WANTED SOME WHEELS!
AUTO RESALE
HERE?! YOU SAID YOU'D BUY ME HALF A CAR, NOT HALF A PIECE OF CRAP...
WHEN I WAS YOU'RE AGE, I WOULD'VE BEEN GLAD JUST TO HAVE FOUR WHEELS AND AN ENGINE. MAYBE YOU'D BE HAPPIER WITH A BIKE?
GENTELMAN, HIYA. BOBBY BOLIVIA AT YOUR SERVICE. FREEDOM'S WAITIN' UNDER ONE OF THESE HOODS, SON. SEE, DRIVERS DON'T PICK THEIR CARS...
...CARS PICK THEIR DRIVERS.
BEEEP BEEEEEP
WHOA! WHERE'D THIS ONE COME FROM?
HOW MUCH?
CONSIDERING THE SEMI-CLASSIC NATURE OF THE VEHICLE, FIVE GRAND.
NO WAY, WE WALK.
NO, WAIT! IT'S YOUR LUCKY DAY... FOUR GRAND.
YES!
GO ON, SAM... FIND YOUR ADVENTURE!

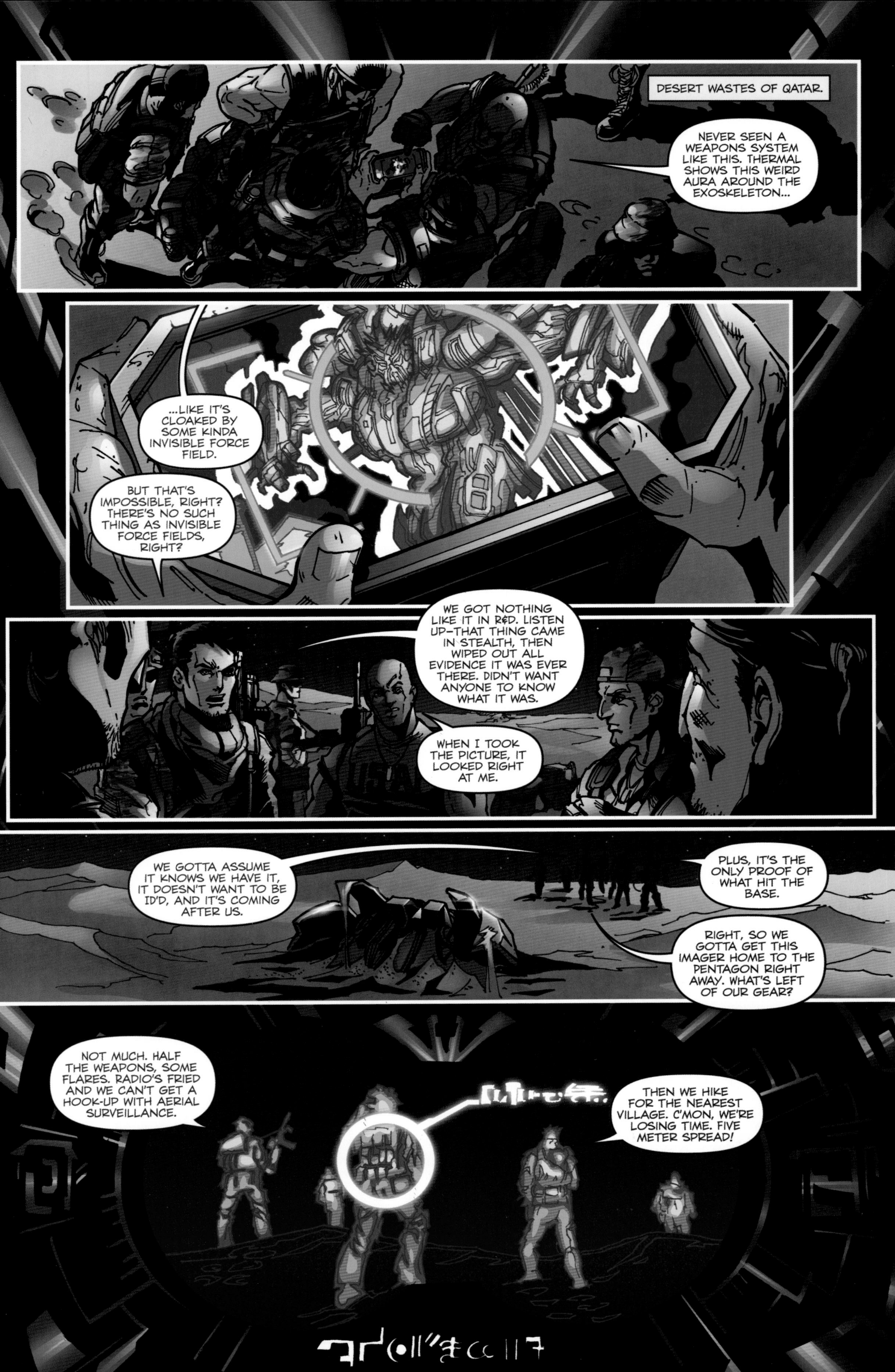

DESERT WASTES OF QATAR.
NEVER SEEN A WEAPONS SYSTEM LIKE THIS. THERMAL SHOWS THIS WEIRD AURA AROUND THE EXOSKELETON...
...LIKE IT'S CLOAKED BY SOME KINDA INVISIBLE FORCE FIELD.
BUT THAT'S IMPOSSIBLE, RIGHT? THERE'S NO SUCH THING AS INVISIBLE FORCE FIELDS, RIGHT?
WE GOT NOTHING LIKE IT IN R&D. LISTEN UP—THAT THING CAME IN STEALTH, THEN WIPED OUT ALL EVIDENCE IT WAS EVER THERE. DIDN'T WANT ANYONE TO KNOW WHAT IT WAS.
WHEN I TOOK THE PICTURE, IT LOOKED RIGHT AT ME.
USA
WE GOTTA ASSUME IT KNOWS WE HAVE IT, IT DOESN'T WANT TO BE ID'D, AND IT'S COMING AFTER US.
PLUS, IT'S THE ONLY PROOF OF WHAT HIT THE BASE.
RIGHT, SO WE GOTTA GET THIS IMAGER HOME TO THE PENTAGON RIGHT AWAY. WHAT'S LEFT OF OUR GEAR?
NOT MUCH. HALF THE WEAPONS, SOME FLARES. RADIO'S FRIED AND WE CAN'T GET A HOOK-UP WITH AERIAL SURVEILLANCE.
THEN WE HIKE FOR THE NEAREST VILLAGE. C'MON, WE'RE LOSING TIME. FIVE METER SPREAD!

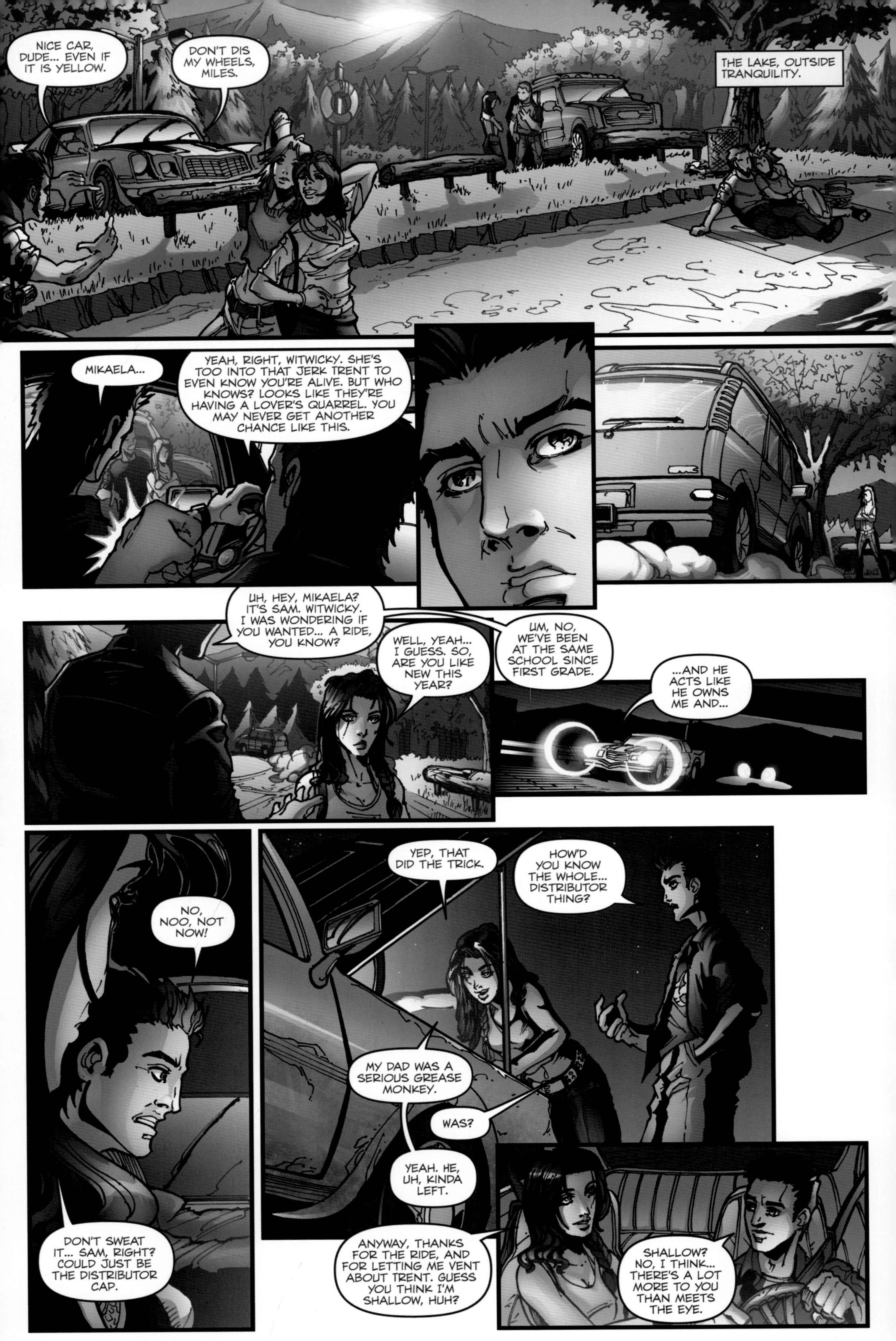
NICE CAR, DUDE... EVEN IF IT IS YELLOW.
DON'T DIS MY WHEELS, MILES.
THE LAKE, OUTSIDE TRANQUILITY.
MIKAELA...
YEAH, RIGHT, WITWICKY. SHE'S TOO INTO THAT JERK TRENT TO EVEN KNOW YOU'RE ALIVE. BUT WHO KNOWS? LOOKS LIKE THEY'RE HAVING A LOVER'S QUARREL. YOU MAY NEVER GET ANOTHER CHANCE LIKE THIS.
UH, HEY, MIKAELA? IT'S SAM. WITWICKY. I WAS WONDERING IF YOU WANTED... A RIDE, YOU KNOW?
WELL, YEAH... I GUESS. SO, ARE YOU LIKE NEW THIS YEAR?
UM, NO, WE'VE BEEN AT THE SAME SCHOOL SINCE FIRST GRADE.
...AND HE ACTS LIKE HE OWNS ME AND...
NO, NOO, NOT NOW!
DON'T SWEAT IT... SAM, RIGHT? COULD JUST BE THE DISTRIBUTOR CAP.
YEP, THAT DID THE TRICK.
HOW'D YOU KNOW THE WHOLE... DISTRIBUTOR THING?
MY DAD WAS A SERIOUS GREASE MONKEY.
WAS?
YEAH. HE, UH, KINDA LEFT.
ANYWAY, THANKS FOR THE RIDE, AND FOR LETTING ME VENT ABOUT TRENT. GUESS YOU THINK I'M SHALLOW, HUH?
SHALLOW? NO, I THINK... THERE'S A LOT MORE TO YOU THAN MEETS THE EYE.

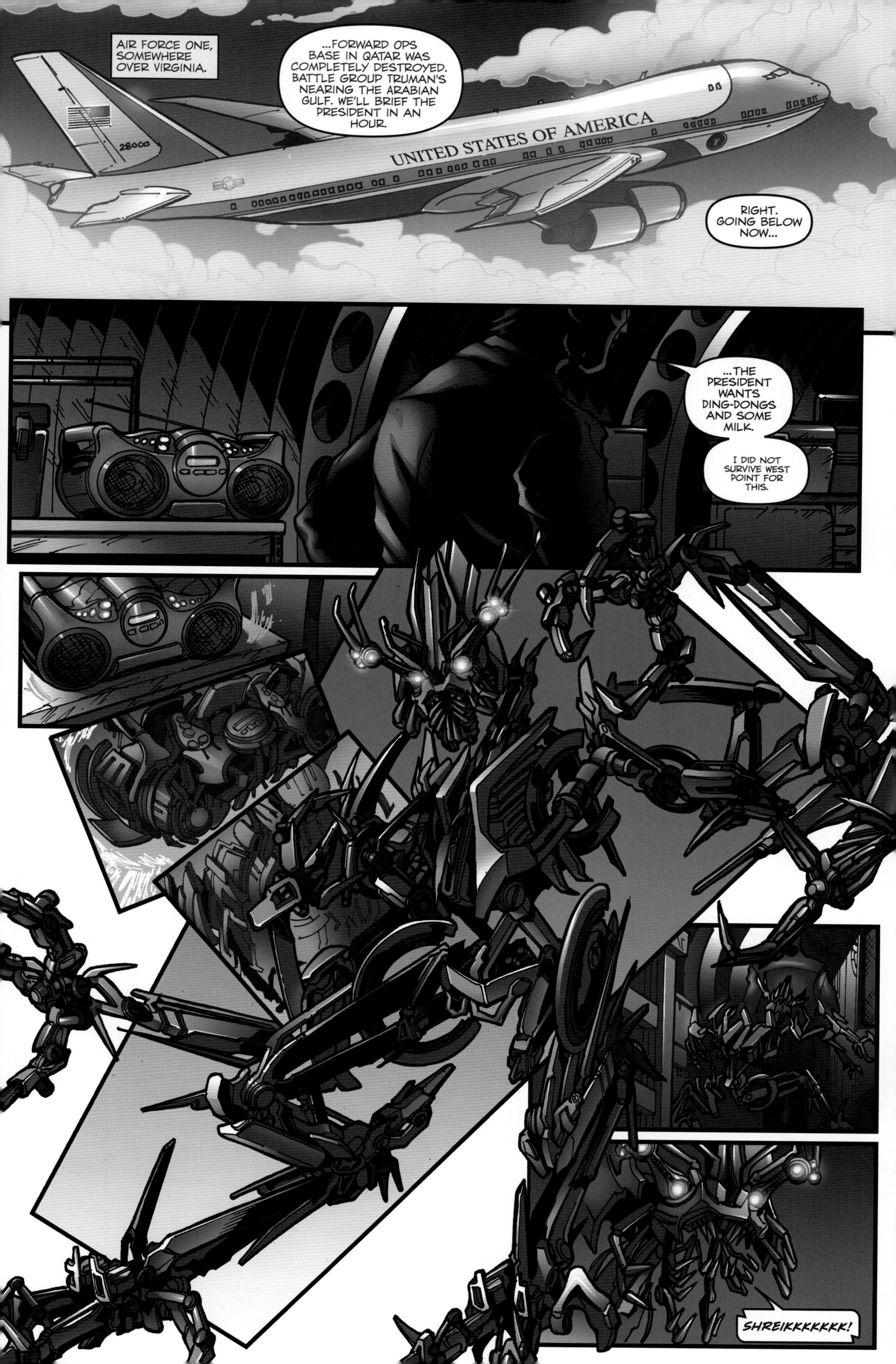
AIR FORCE ONE, SOMEWHERE OVER VIRGINIA.
...FORWARD OPS BASE IN QATAR WAS COMPLETELY DESTROYED. BATTLE GROUP TRUMAN'S NEARING THE ARABIAN GULF. WE'LL BRIEF THE PRESIDENT IN AN HOUR.
UNITED STATES OF AMERICA
28000
RIGHT. GOING BELOW NOW...
...THE PRESIDENT WANTS DING-DONGS AND SOME MILK.
I DID NOT SURVIVE WEST POINT FOR THIS.
SHREIKKKKKKK!

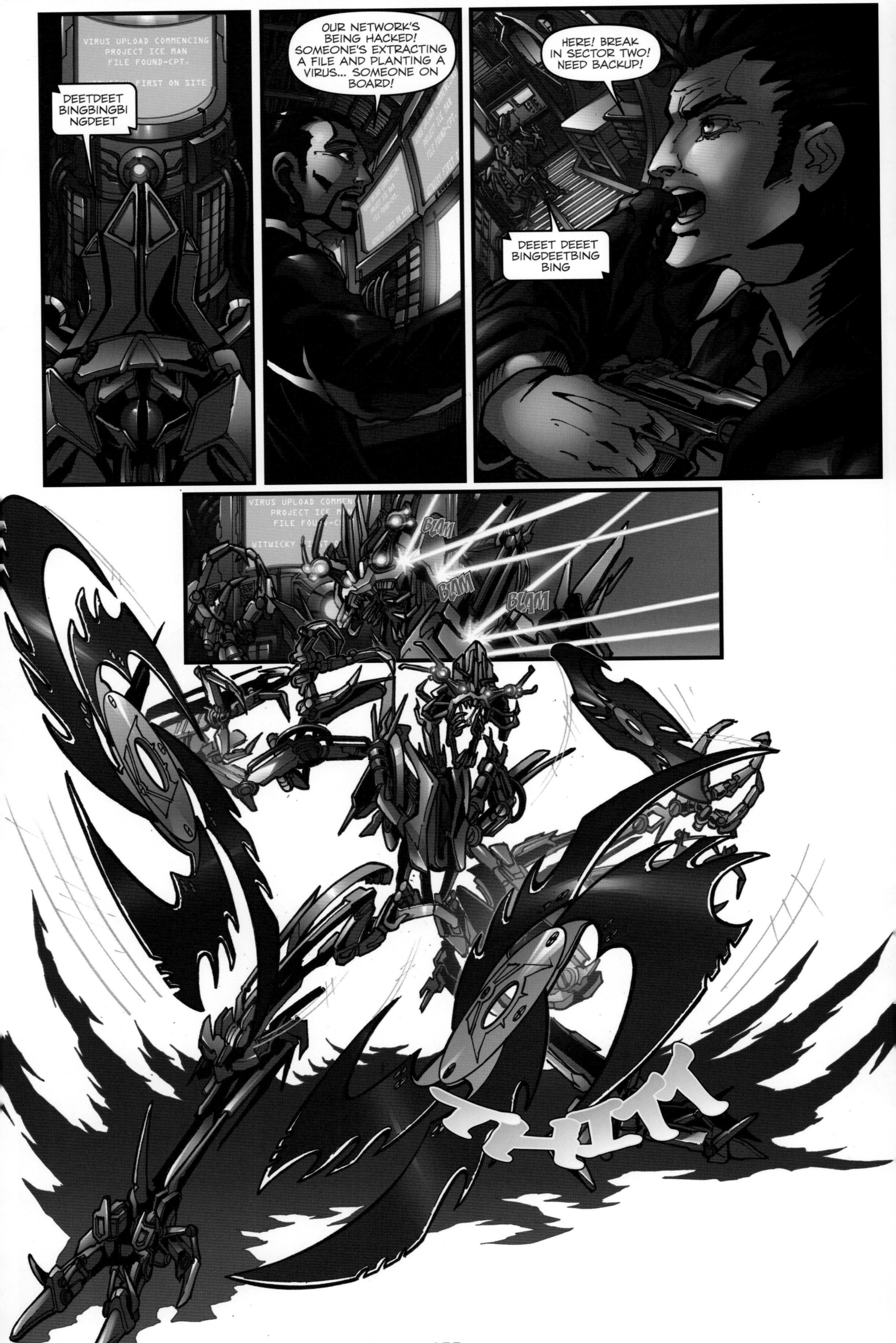
VIRUS UPLOAD COMMENCING
PROJECT ICE MAN
FILE FOUND-CPT.
DEETDEET BINGBINGBI NGDEET
OUR NETWORK'S BEING HACKED! SOMEONE'S EXTRACTING A FILE AND PLANTING A VIRUS... SOMEONE ON BOARD!
HERE! BREAK IN SECTOR TWO! NEED BACKUP!
DEEET DEEET BINGDEETBING BING
BLAM
BLAM
BLAM

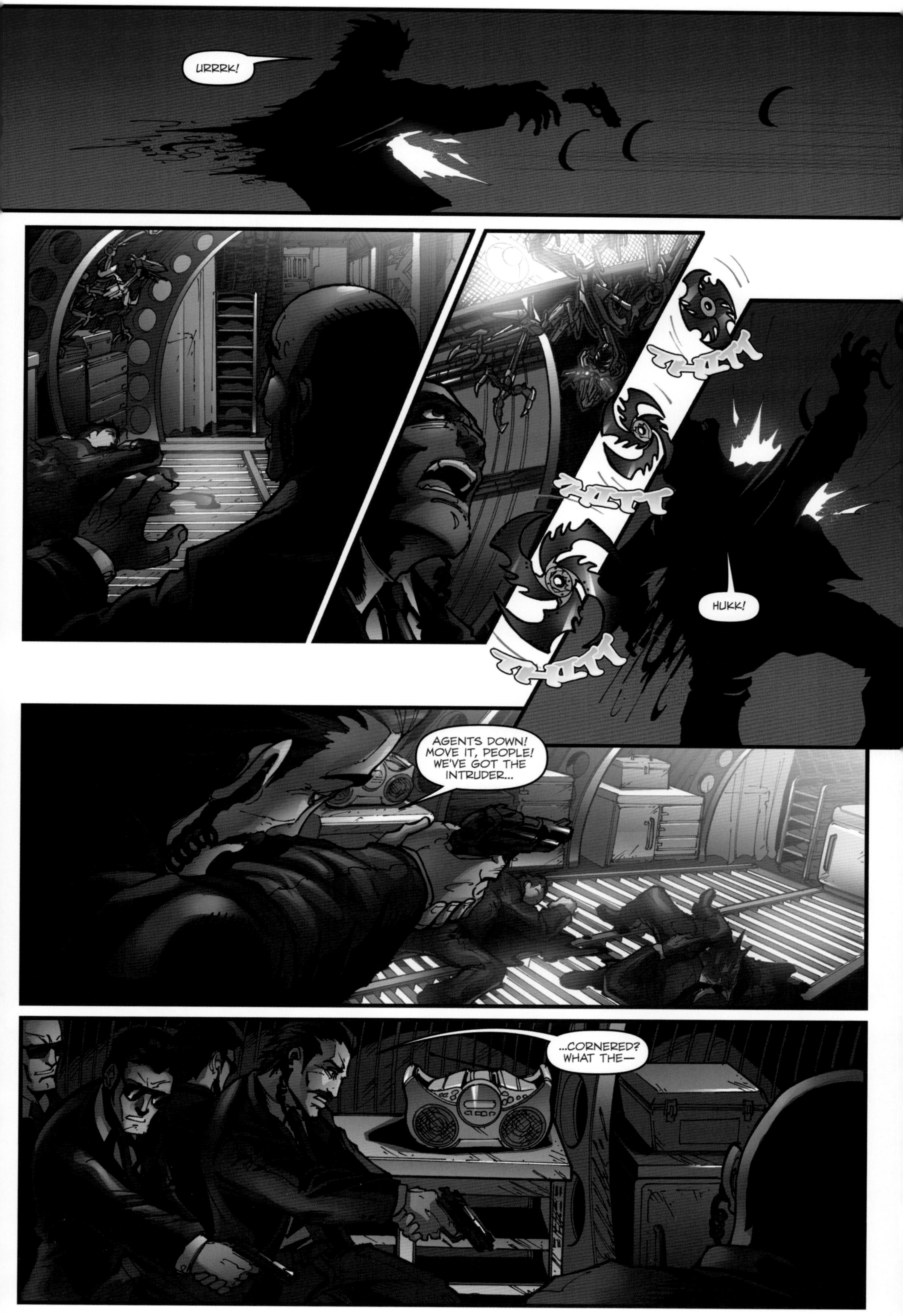
URRRK!
THTT
THTT
THTT
HUKK!
AGENTS DOWN! MOVE IT, PEOPLE! WE'VE GOT THE INTRUDER...
...CORNERED? WHAT THE—

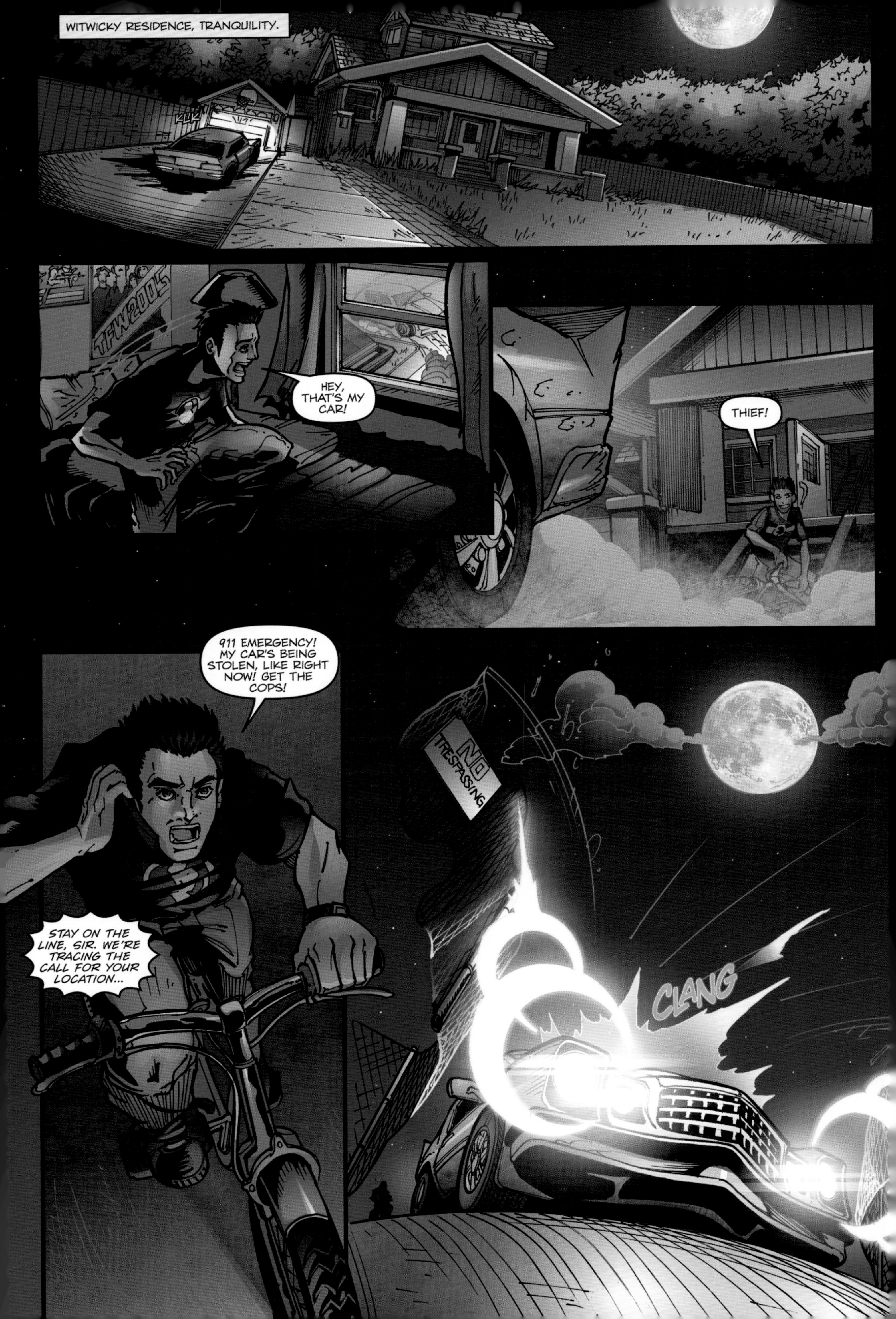
WITWICKY RESIDENCE, TRANQUILITY.
KLIK
HEY, THAT'S MY CAR!
THIEF!
911 EMERGENCY! MY CAR'S BEING STOLEN, LIKE RIGHT NOW! GET THE COPS!
STAY ON THE LINE, SIR. WE'RE TRACING THE CALL FOR YOUR LOCATION...
NO TRESPASSING
CLANG

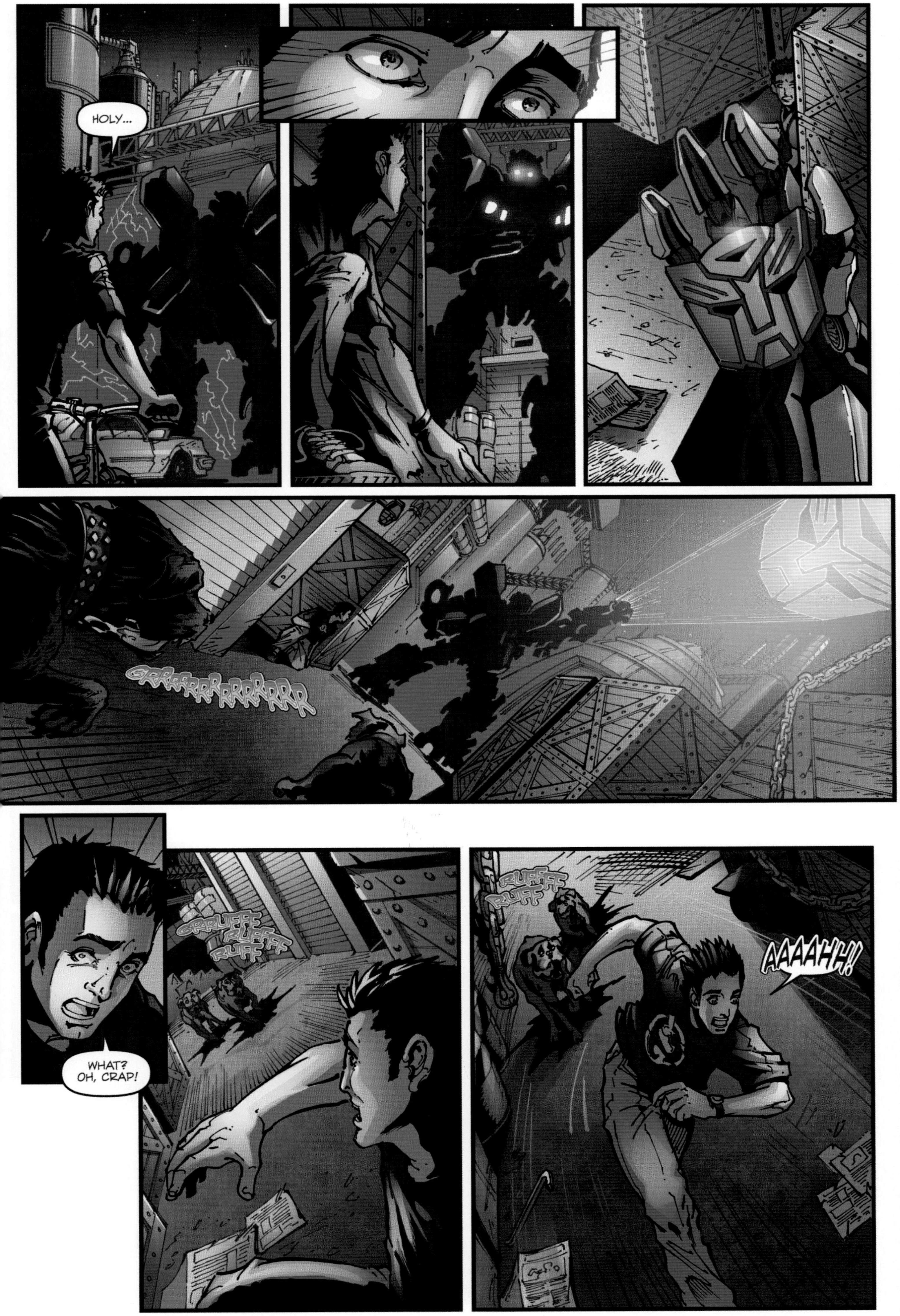
HOLY...
GRRRRRRRRRRRRRRR
WHAT? OH, CRAP!
GRRUFFF RUFFFF RUFF
RUFFFF RUFF
AAAAHH!

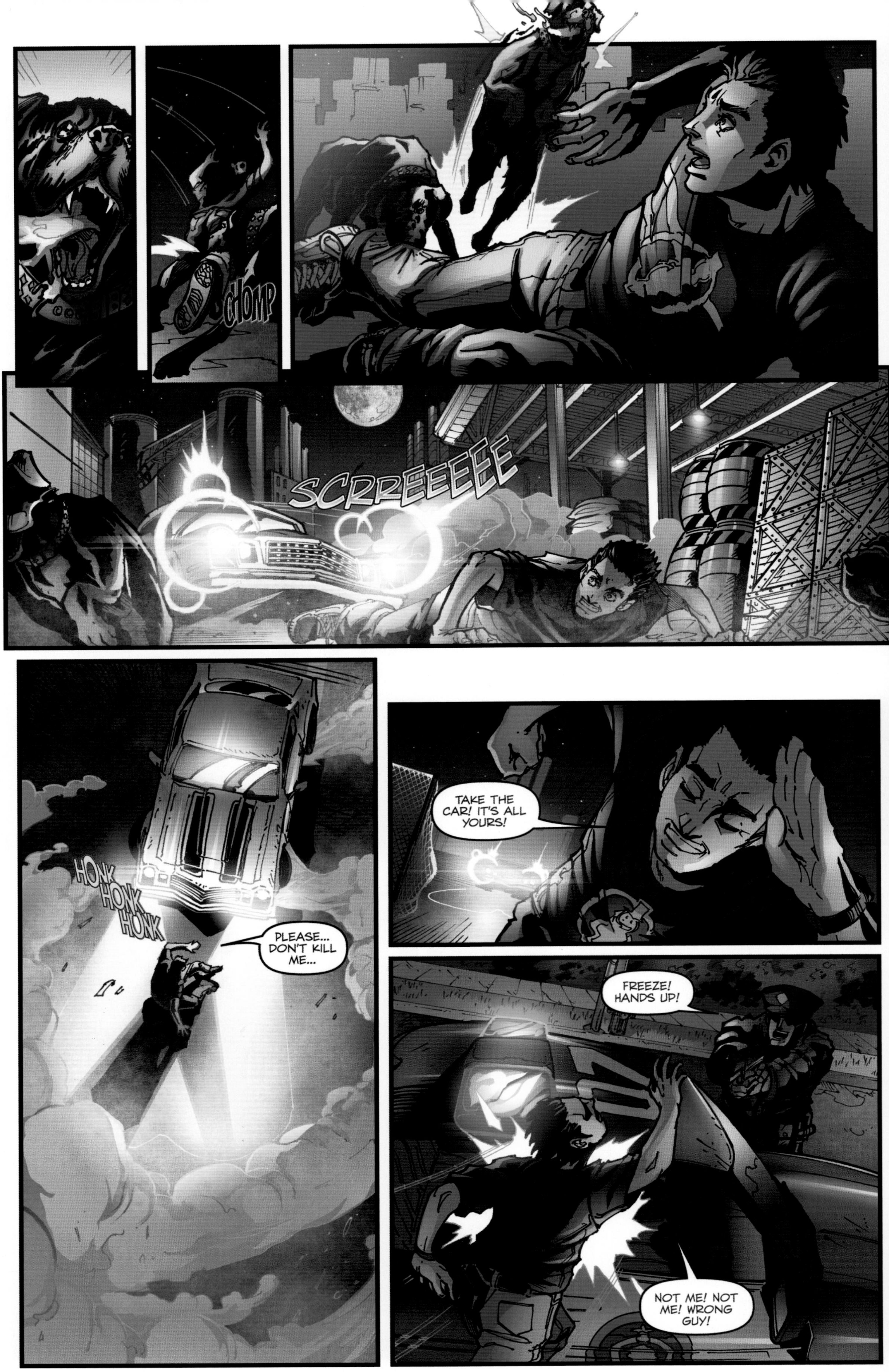
CHOMP
SCRREEEEEE
HONK HONK HONK
PLEASE... DON'T KILL ME...
TAKE THE CAR! IT'S ALL YOURS!
FREEZE! HANDS UP!
NOT ME! NOT ME! WRONG GUY!

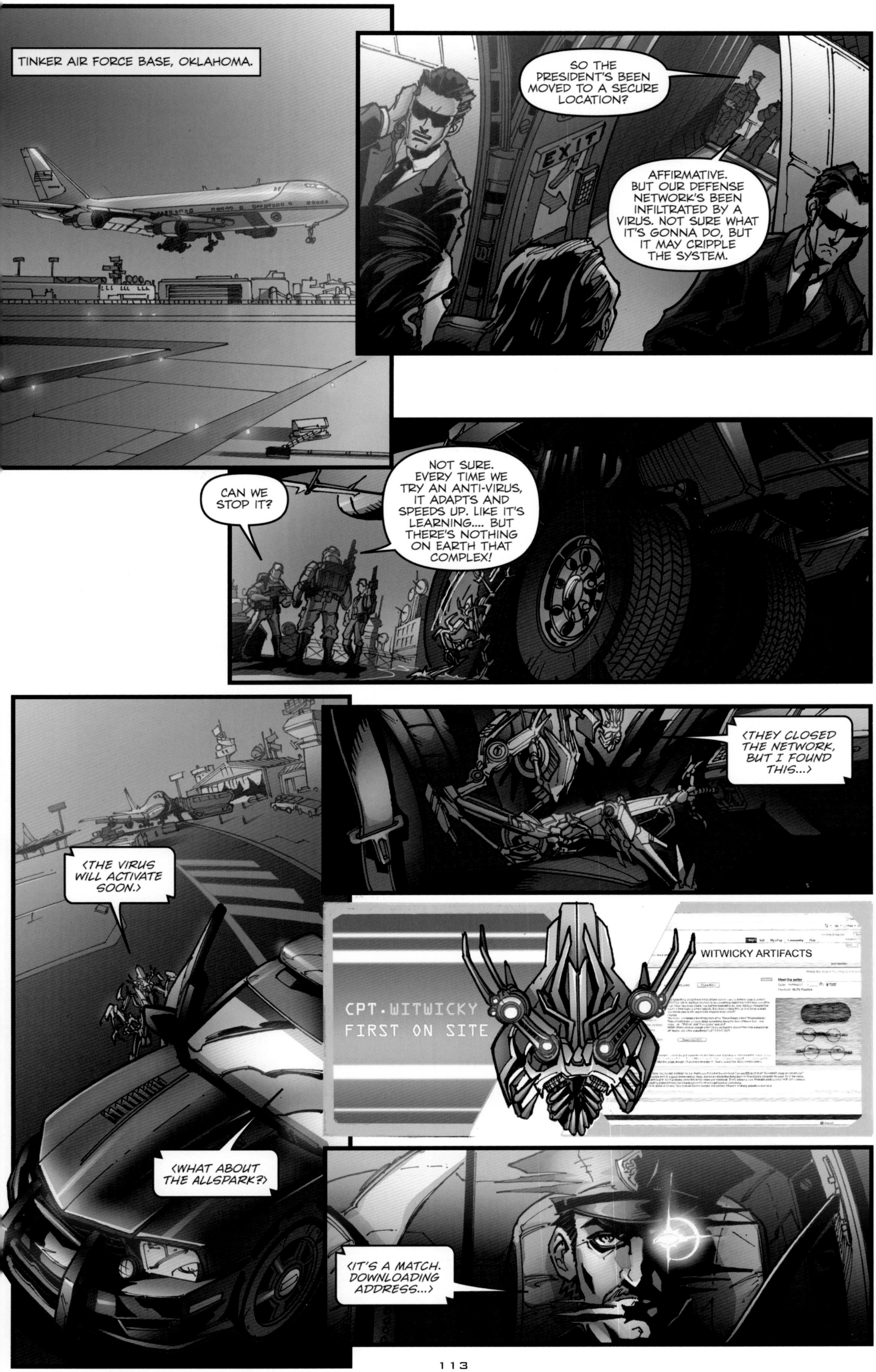
TINKER AIR FORCE BASE, OKLAHOMA.
SO THE PRESIDENT'S BEEN MOVED TO A SECURE LOCATION?
EXIT
AFFIRMATIVE. BUT OUR DEFENSE NETWORK'S BEEN INFILTRATED BY A VIRUS. NOT SURE WHAT IT'S GONNA DO, BUT IT MAY CRIPPLE THE SYSTEM.
CAN WE STOP IT?
NOT SURE. EVERY TIME WE TRY AN ANTI-VIRUS, IT ADAPTS AND SPEEDS UP. LIKE IT'S LEARNING.... BUT THERE'S NOTHING ON EARTH THAT COMPLEX!
‹THE VIRUS WILL ACTIVATE SOON.›
‹THEY CLOSED THE NETWORK, BUT I FOUND THIS...›
CPT.WITWICKY
FIRST ON SITE
WITWICKY ARTIFACTS
Meet the seller
‹WHAT ABOUT THE ALLSPARK?›
‹IT'S A MATCH. DOWNLOADING ADDRESS...›

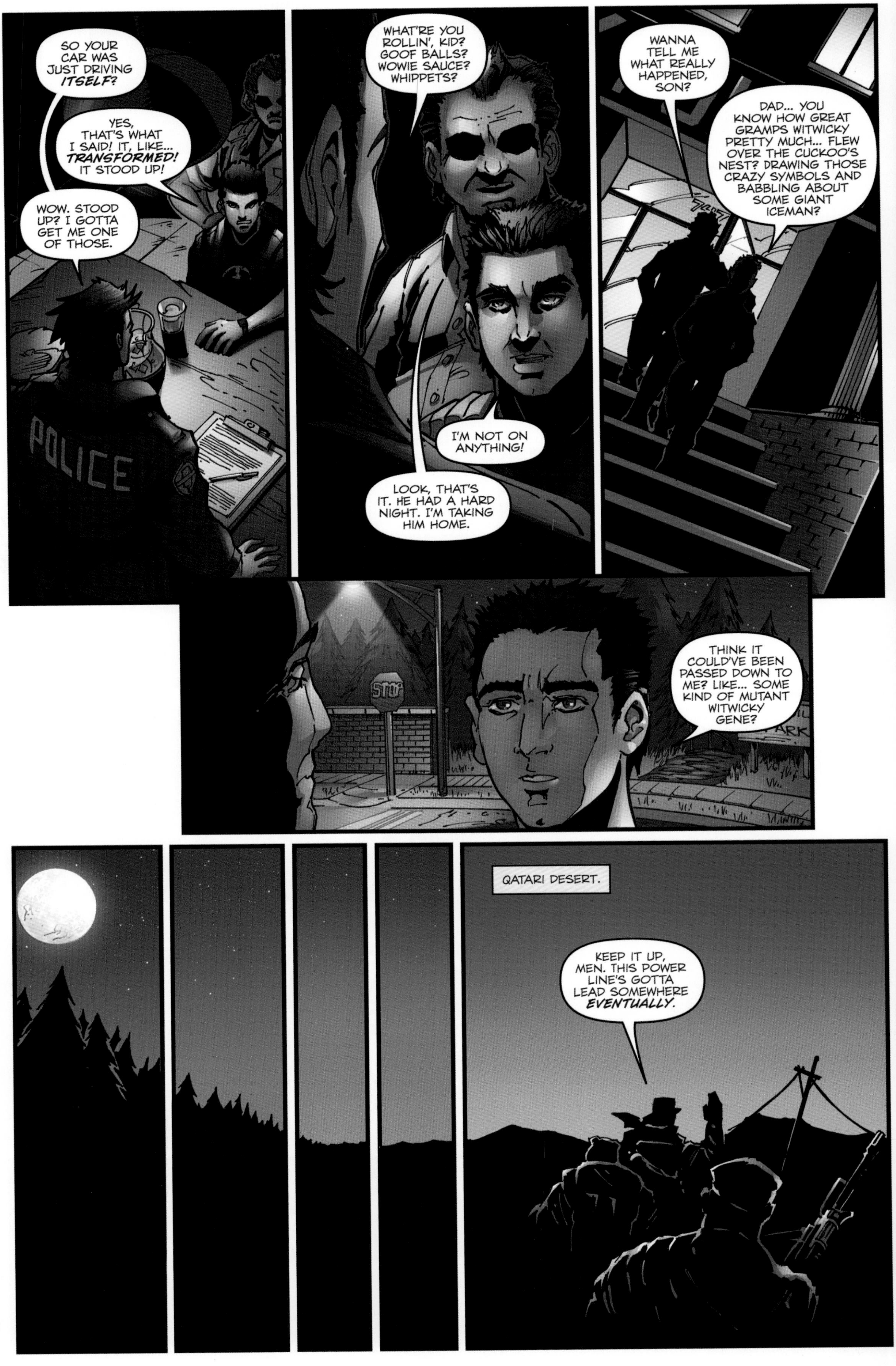

SO YOUR CAR WAS JUST DRIVING *ITSELF*?
YES, THAT'S WHAT I SAID! IT, LIKE... *TRANSFORMED!* IT STOOD UP!
WOW. STOOD UP? I GOTTA GET ME ONE OF THOSE.
POLICE
WHAT'RE YOU ROLLIN', KID? GOOF BALLS? WOWIE SAUCE? WHIPPETS?
I'M NOT ON ANYTHING!
LOOK, THAT'S IT. HE HAD A HARD NIGHT. I'M TAKING HIM HOME.
WANNA TELL ME WHAT REALLY HAPPENED, SON?
DAD... YOU KNOW HOW GREAT GRAMPS WITWICKY PRETTY MUCH... FLEW OVER THE CUCKOO'S NEST? DRAWING THOSE CRAZY SYMBOLS AND BABBLING ABOUT SOME GIANT ICEMAN?
STOP
THINK IT COULD'VE BEEN PASSED DOWN TO ME? LIKE... SOME KIND OF MUTANT WITWICKY GENE?
QATARI DESERT.
KEEP IT UP, MEN. THIS POWER LINE'S GOTTA LEAD SOMEWHERE *EVENTUALLY*.

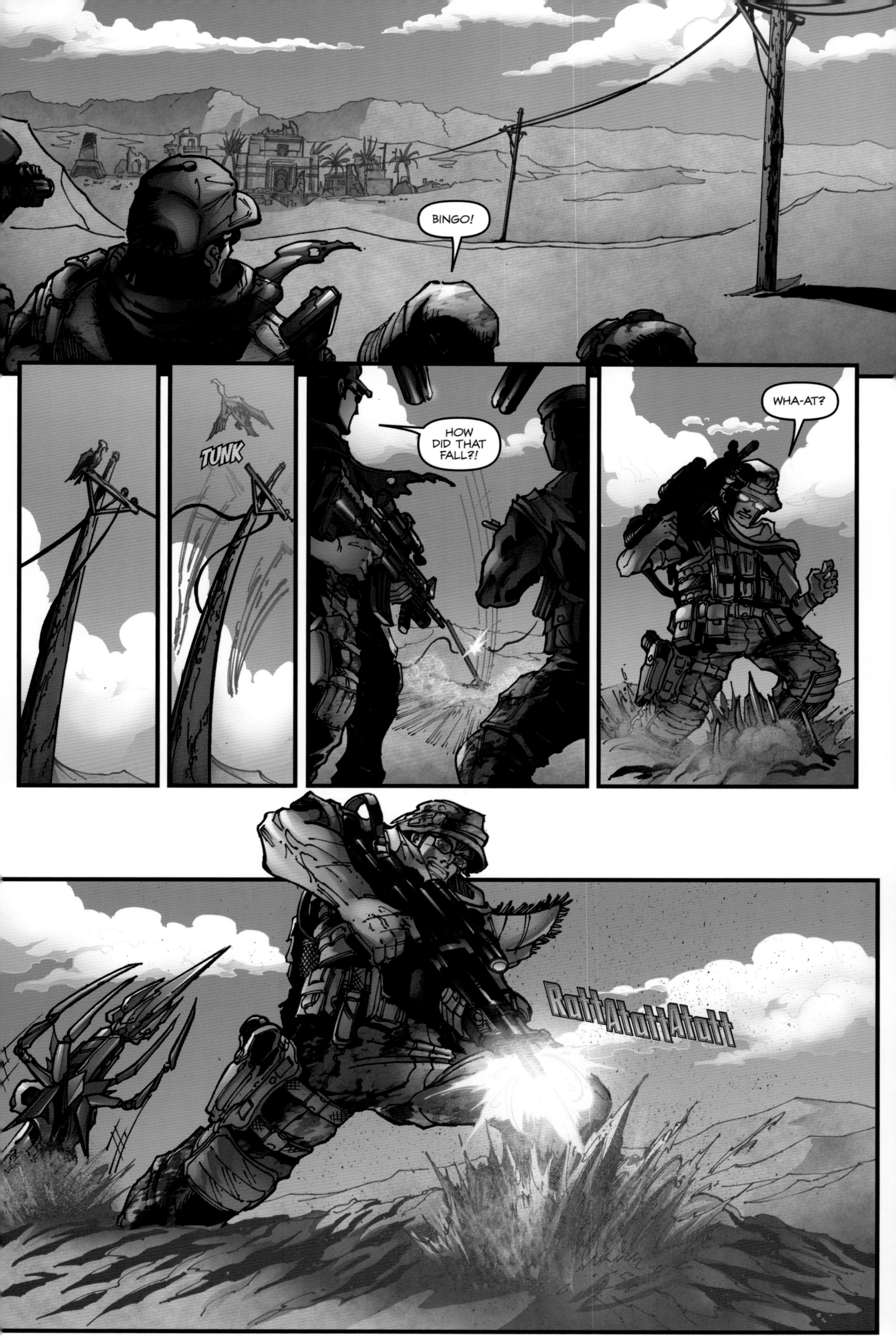

BINGO!
TUNK
HOW DID THAT FALL?!
WHA-AT?
RattAtattAtatt

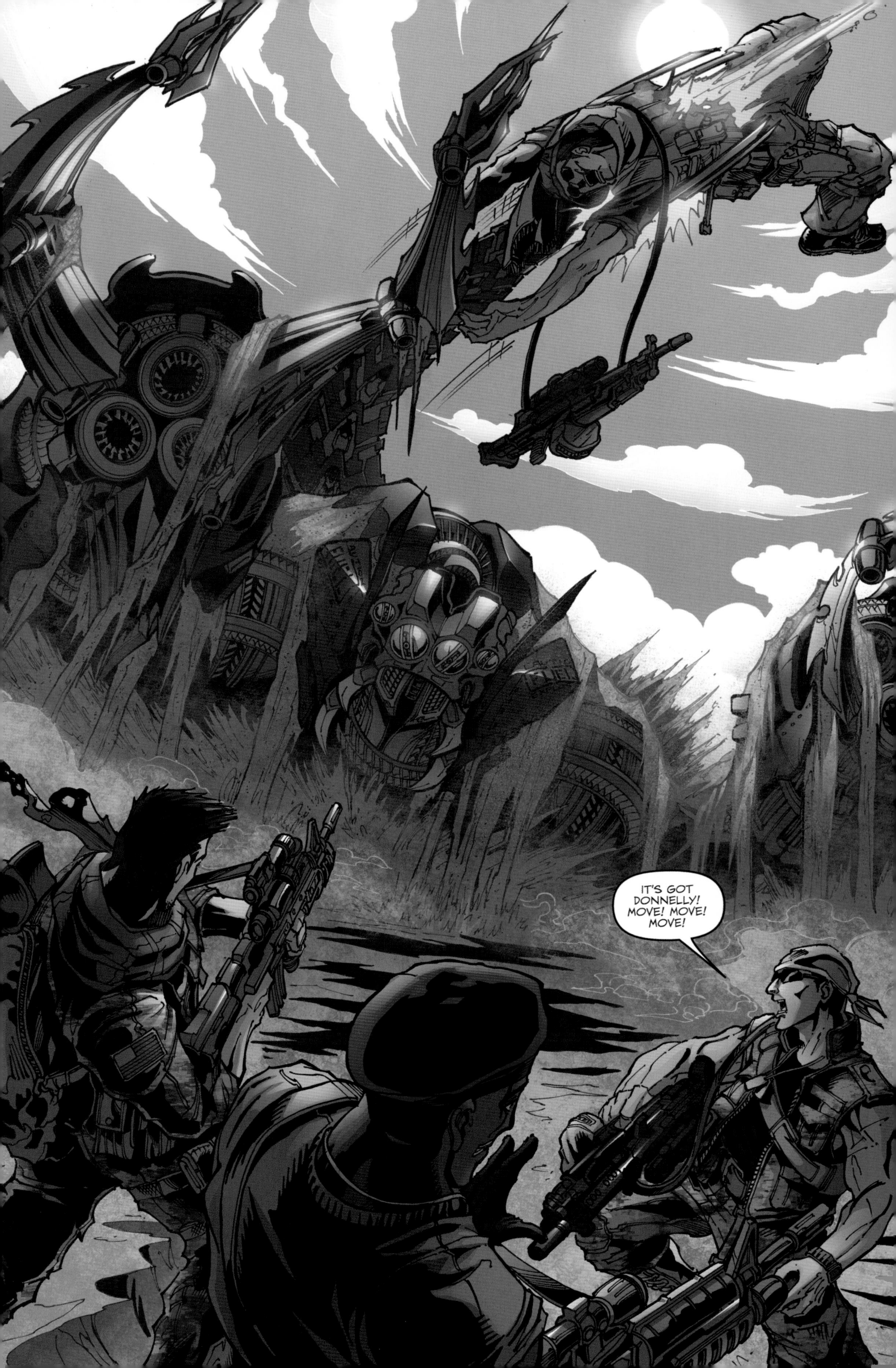
IT'S GOT DONNELLY! MOVE! MOVE! MOVE!

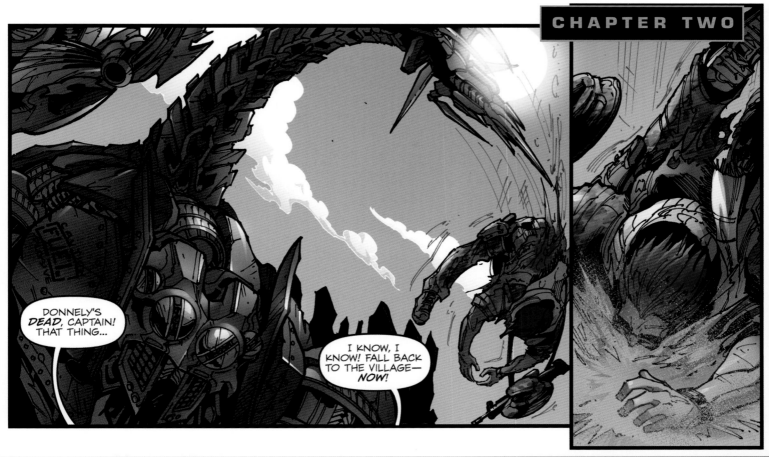

DONNELY'S *DEAD*, CAPTAIN! THAT THING...

I KNOW, I KNOW! FALL BACK TO THE VILLAGE— *NOW!*

YOU TWO, COVER THE ROAD! FIG, TAKE POINT! EPPS, IN THE BACK!

117

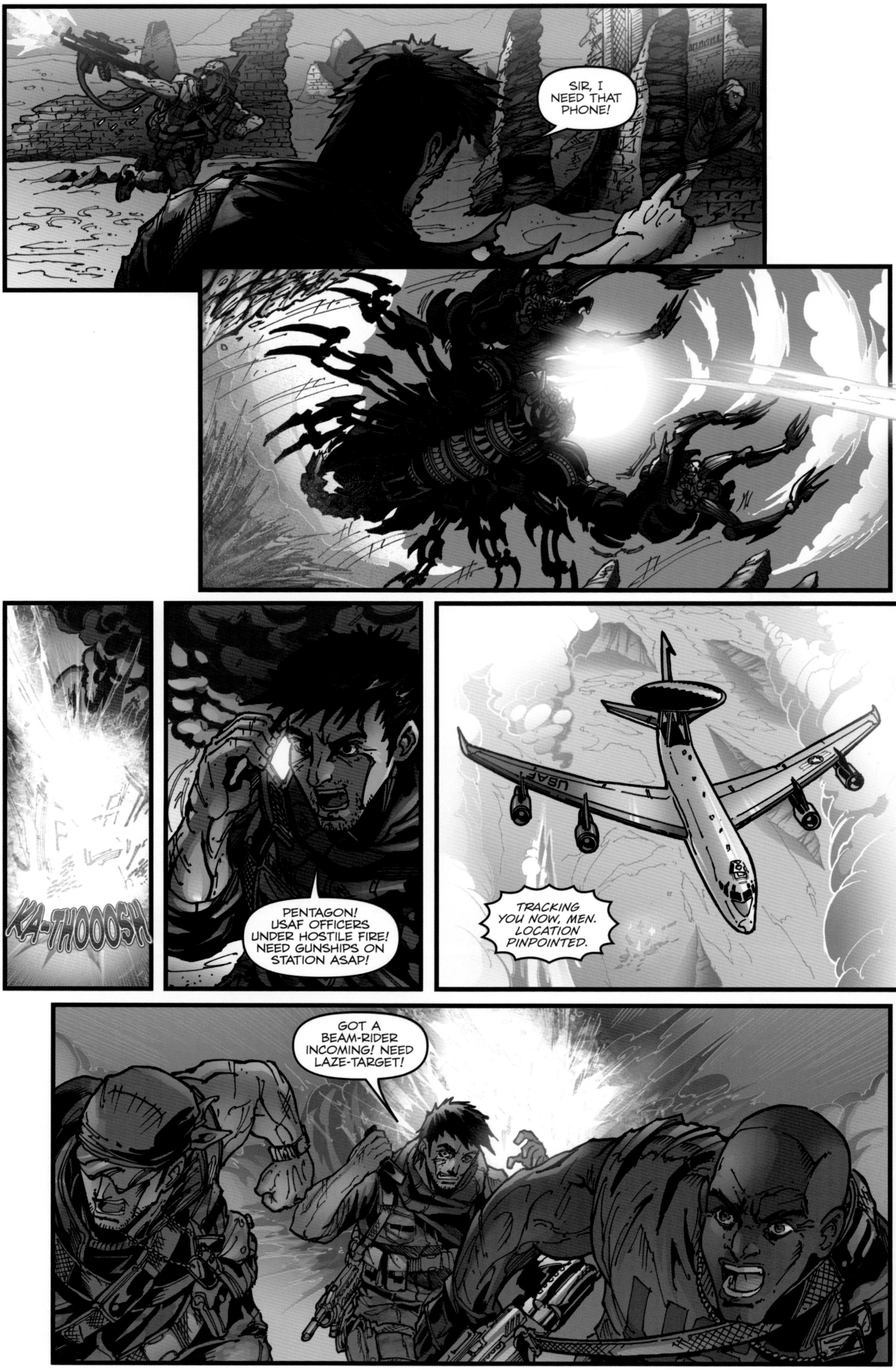
SIR, I NEED THAT PHONE!
KA-THOOOSH
PENTAGON! USAF OFFICERS UNDER HOSTILE FIRE! NEED GUNSHIPS ON STATION ASAP!
USAF
TRACKING YOU NOW, MEN. LOCATION PINPOINTED.
GOT A BEAM-RIDER INCOMING! NEED LAZE-TARGET!

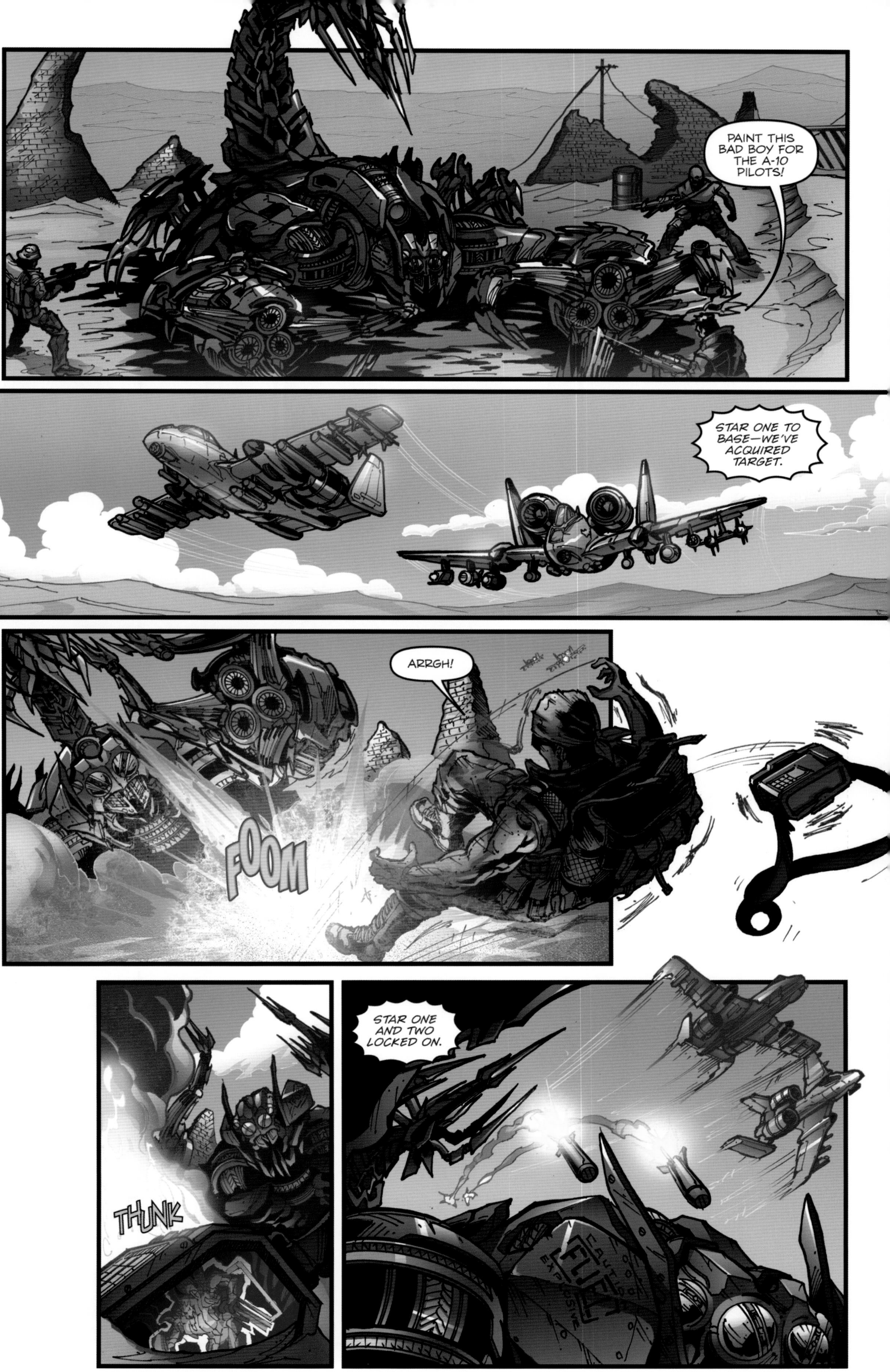
PAINT THIS BAD BOY FOR THE A-10 PILOTS!
STAR ONE TO BASE—WE'VE ACQUIRED TARGET.
ARRGH!
FOOM
THUNK
STAR ONE AND TWO LOCKED ON.

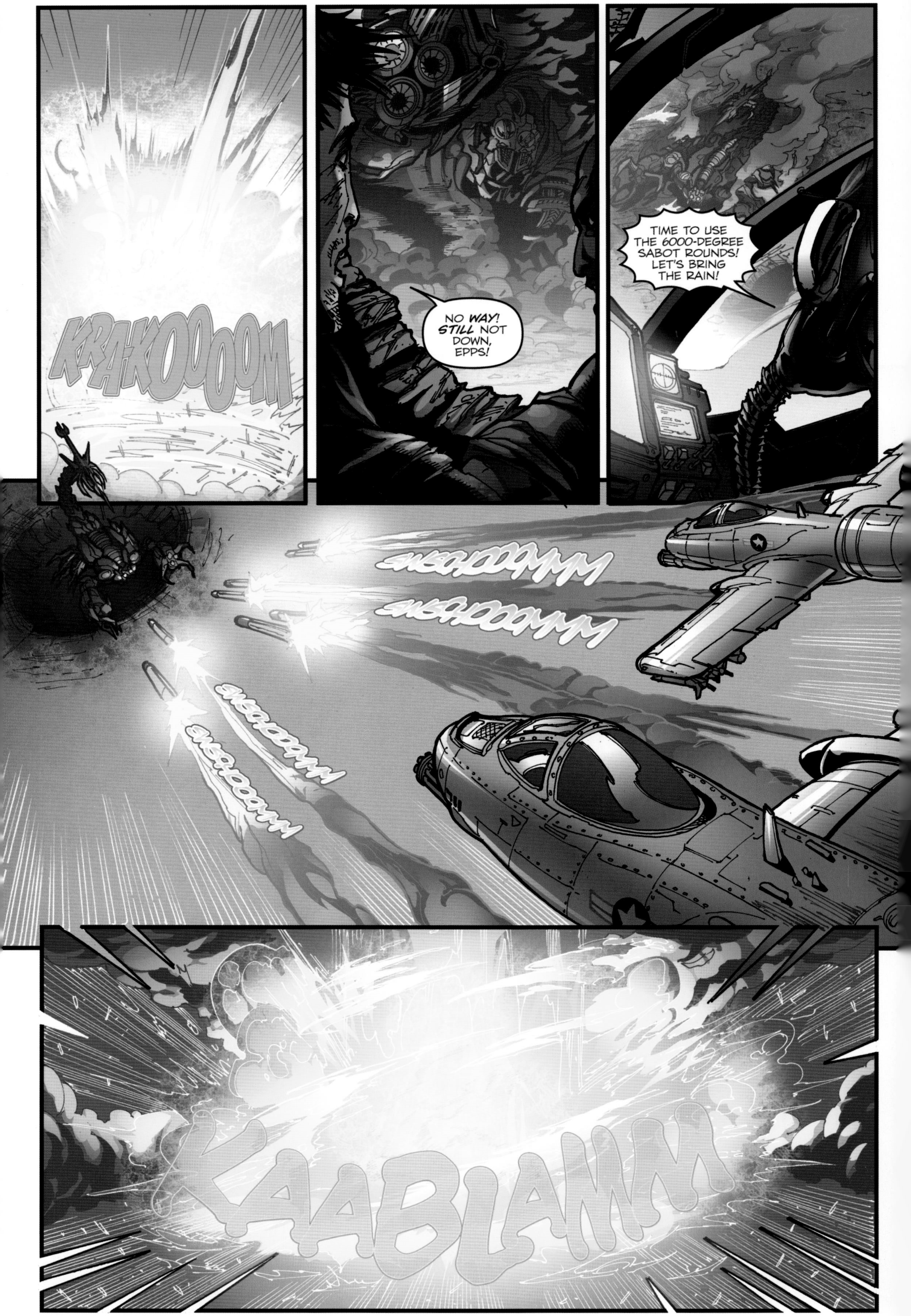
KRAKOOOOM
NO WAY! STILL NOT DOWN, EPPS!
TIME TO USE THE 6000-DEGREE SABOT ROUNDS! LET'S BRING THE RAIN!
KAABLAMM

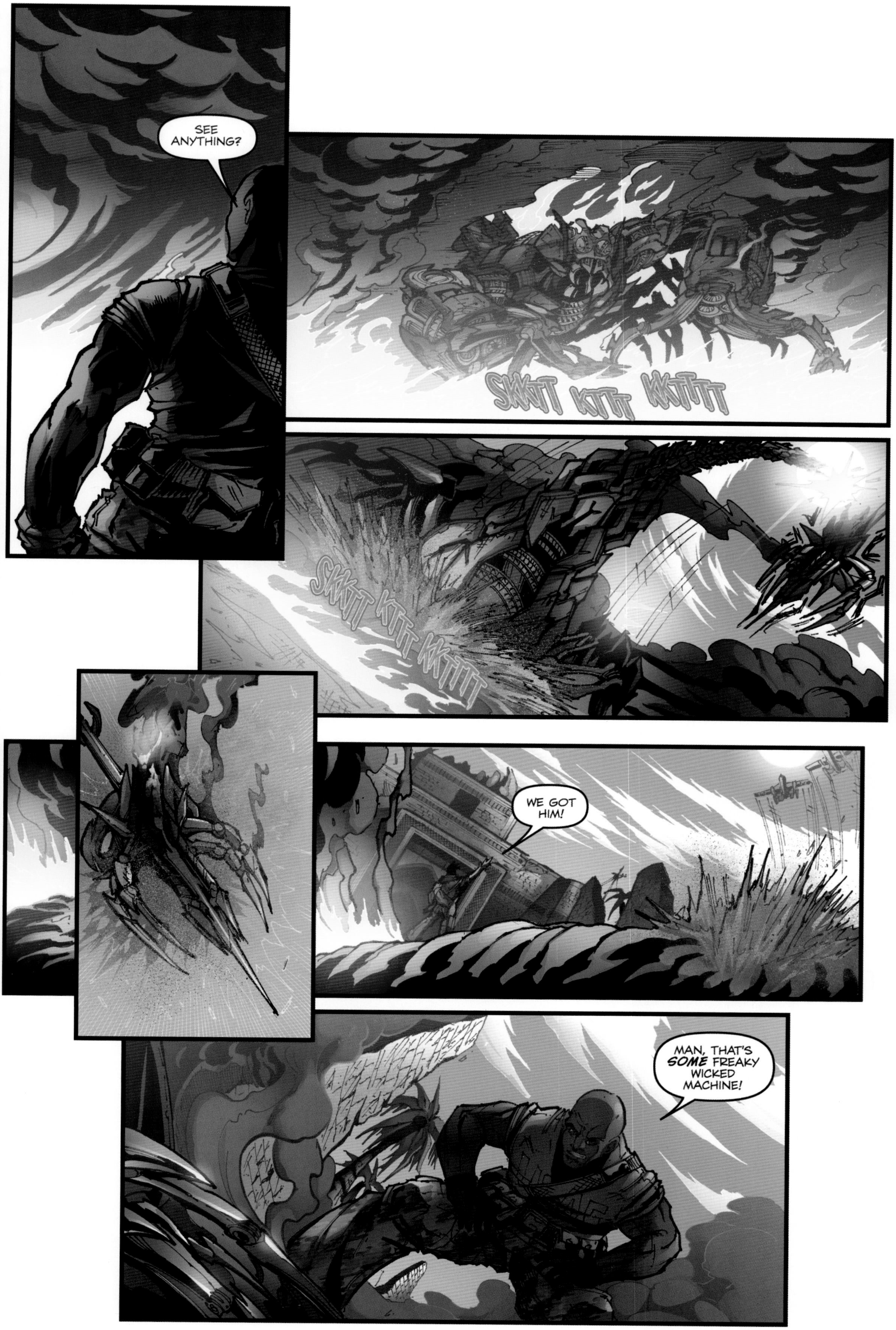
SEE ANYTHING?
SKKTT KTTT KKTTTTT
SKKTT KTTT KKTTTTT
WE GOT HIM!
MAN, THAT'S *SOME* FREAKY WICKED MACHINE!

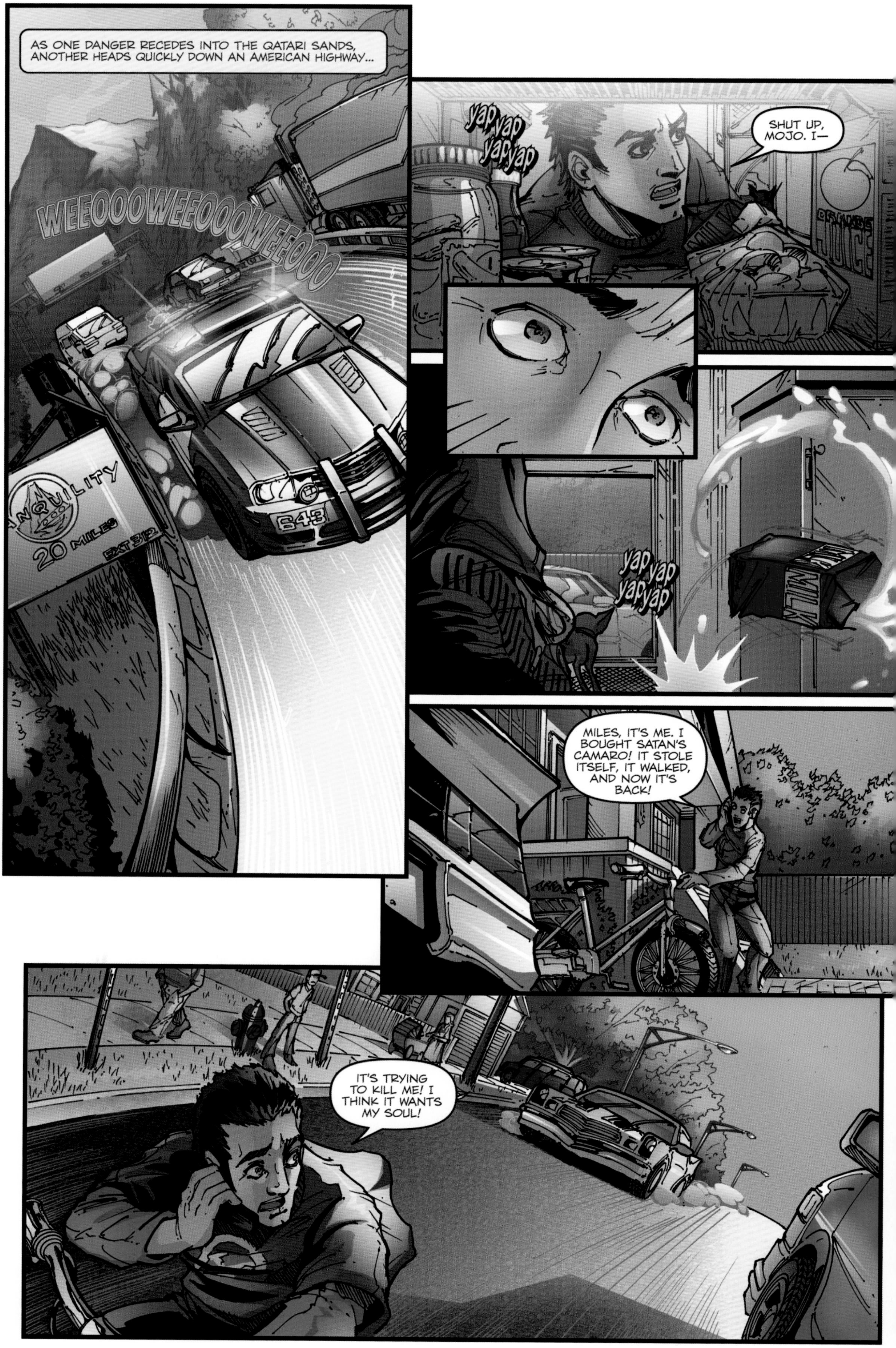

AS ONE DANGER RECEDES INTO THE QATARI SANDS, ANOTHER HEADS QUICKLY DOWN AN AMERICAN HIGHWAY...
WEEOOOWEEOOOWEEOOO
20 MILES
643
yapyap yapyap
SHUT UP, MOJO. I—
JUICE
yapyap yapyap
MILK
MILES, IT'S ME. I BOUGHT SATAN'S CAMARO! IT STOLE ITSELF, IT WALKED, AND NOW IT'S BACK!
IT'S TRYING TO KILL ME! I THINK IT WANTS MY SOUL!

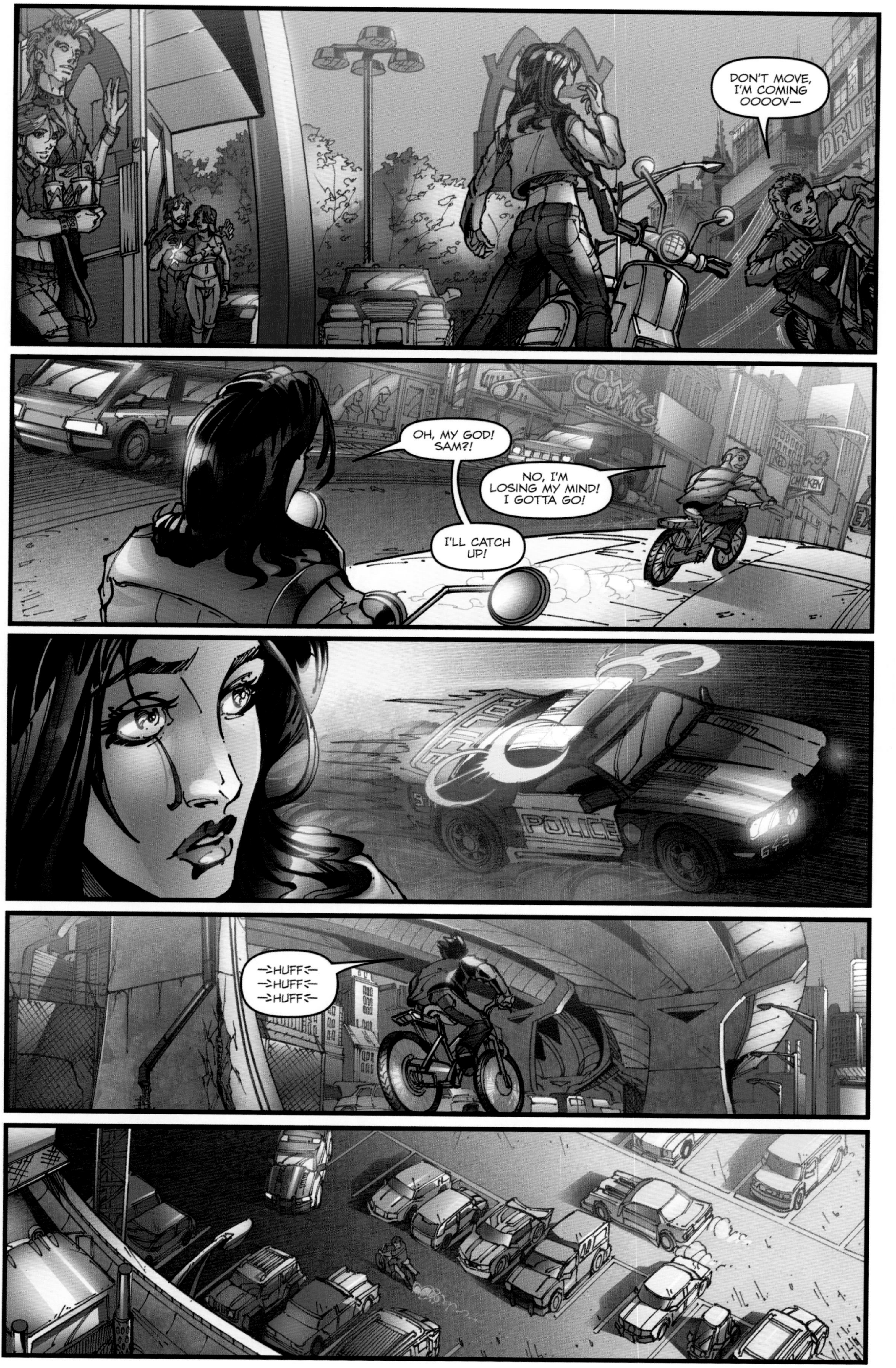
DON'T MOVE, I'M COMING OOOOV—
OH, MY GOD! SAM?!
NO, I'M LOSING MY MIND! I GOTTA GO!
I'LL CATCH UP!
POLICE
—HUFF— —HUFF— —HUFF—

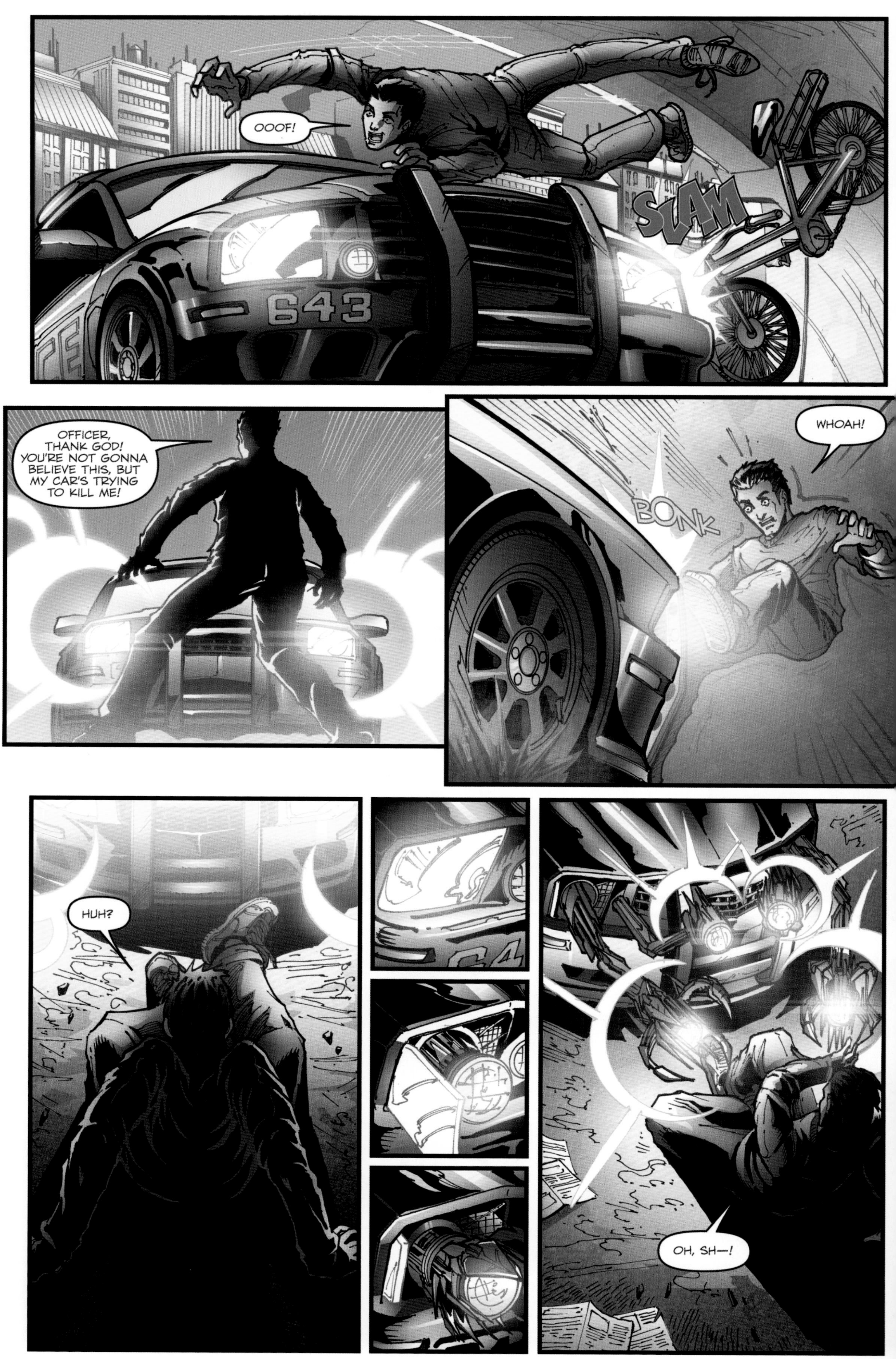
OOOF!
SLAM
643
OFFICER, THANK GOD! YOU'RE NOT GONNA BELIEVE THIS, BUT MY CAR'S TRYING TO KILL ME!
WHOAH!
BONK
HUH?
OH, SH—!

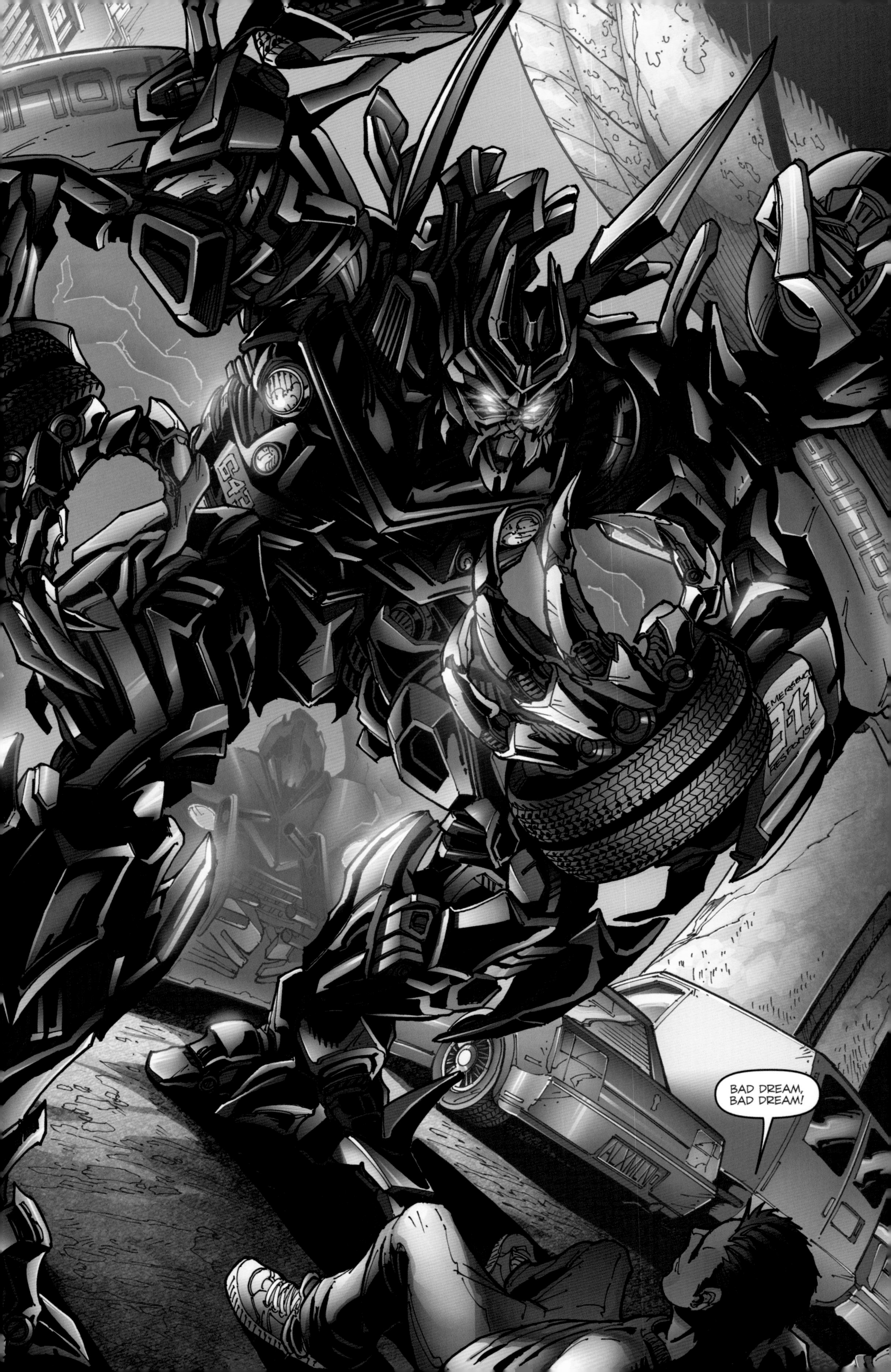
BAD DREAM, BAD DREAM!

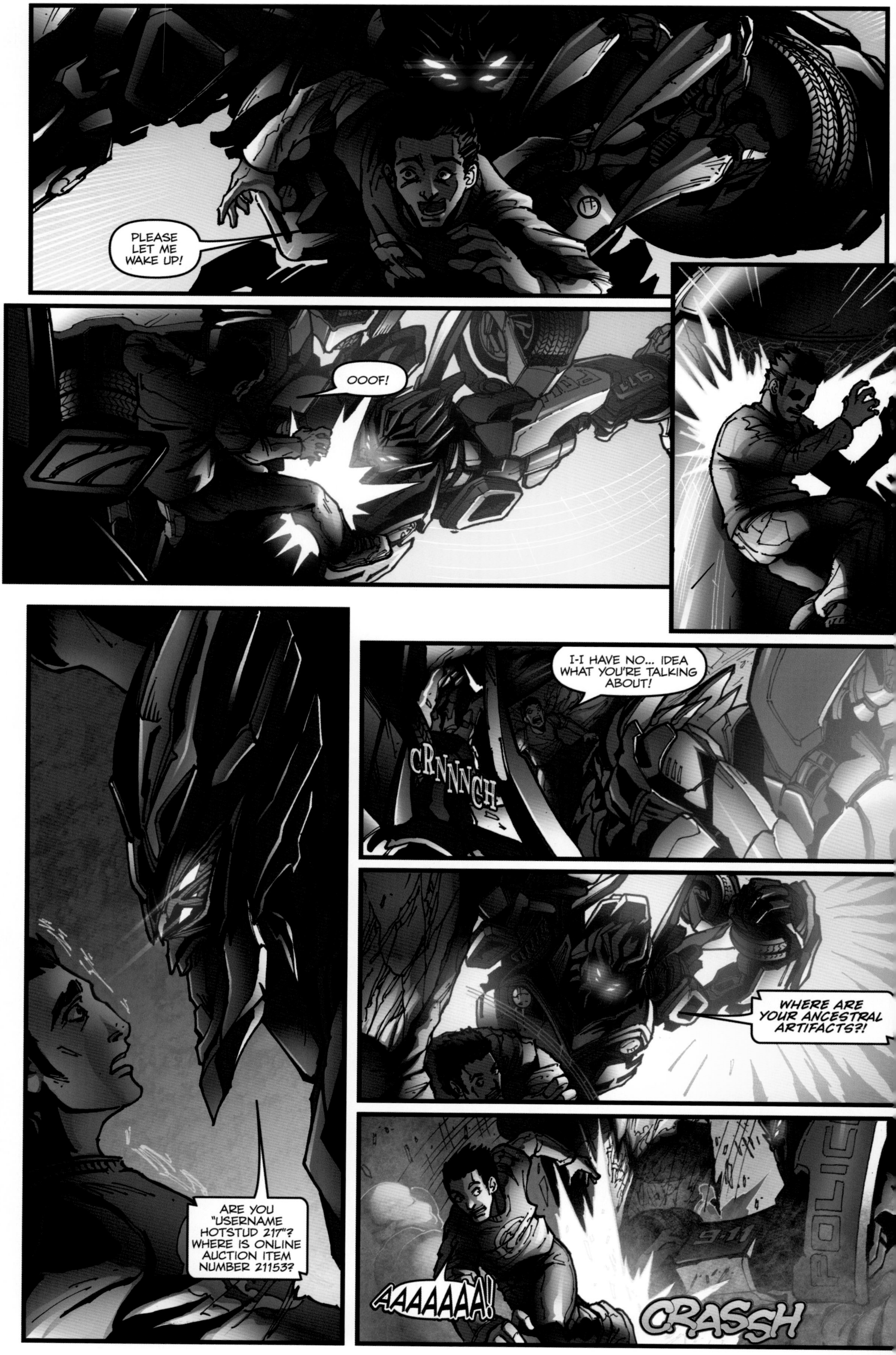
PLEASE LET ME WAKE UP!
OOOF!
I-I HAVE NO... IDEA WHAT YOU'RE TALKING ABOUT!
CRNNNCH
WHERE ARE YOUR ANCESTRAL ARTIFACTS?!
ARE YOU "USERNAME HOTSTUD 217"? WHERE IS ONLINE AUCTION ITEM NUMBER 21153?
AAAAAAA!
CRASSH

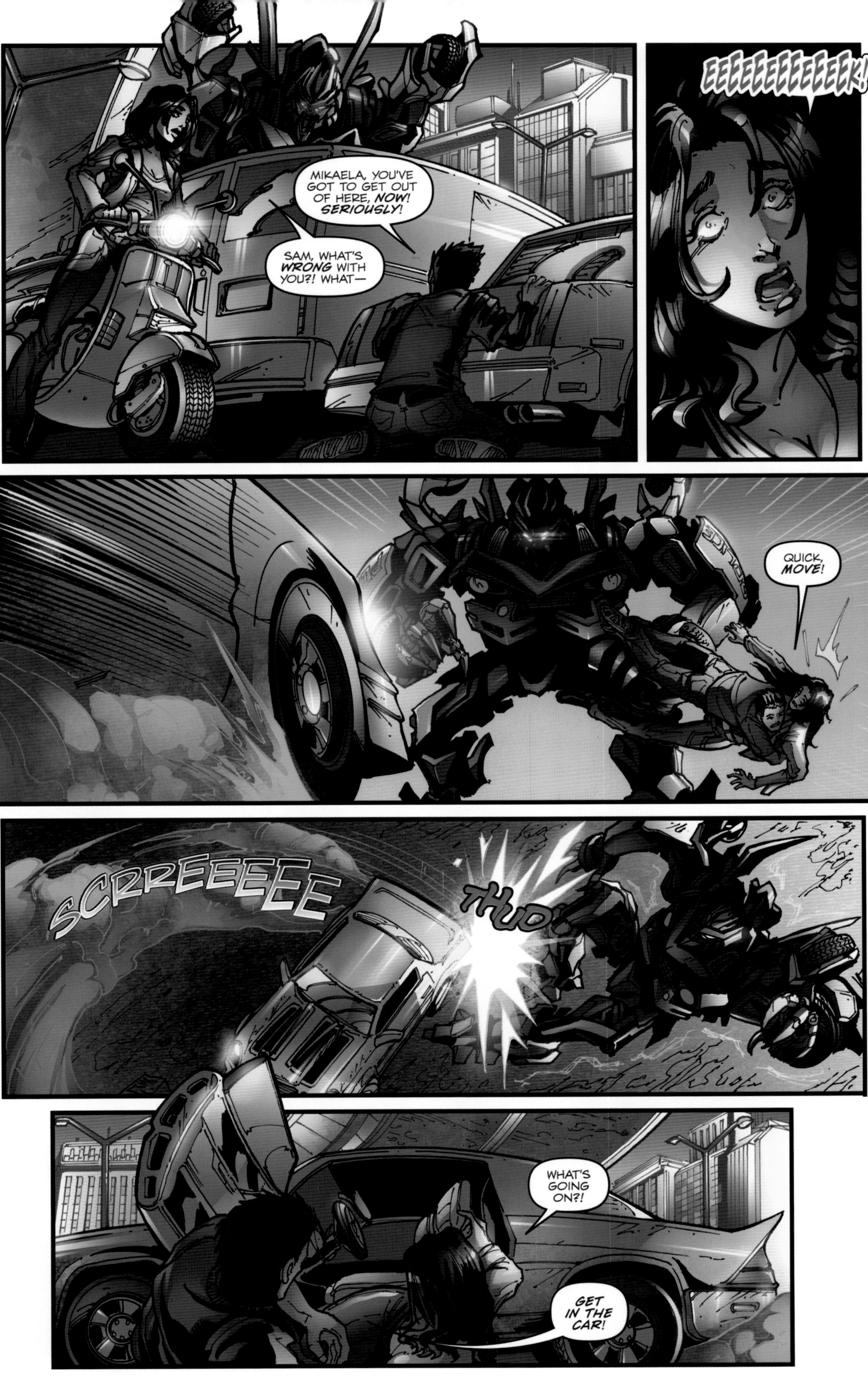
MIKAELA, YOU'VE GOT TO GET OUT OF HERE, **NOW**! **SERIOUSLY**!
SAM, WHAT'S **WRONG** WITH YOU?! WHAT—
EEEEEEEEEEEEK!
QUICK, **MOVE**!
SCRREEEEEE
THUD
WHAT'S GOING ON?!
GET IN THE CAR!

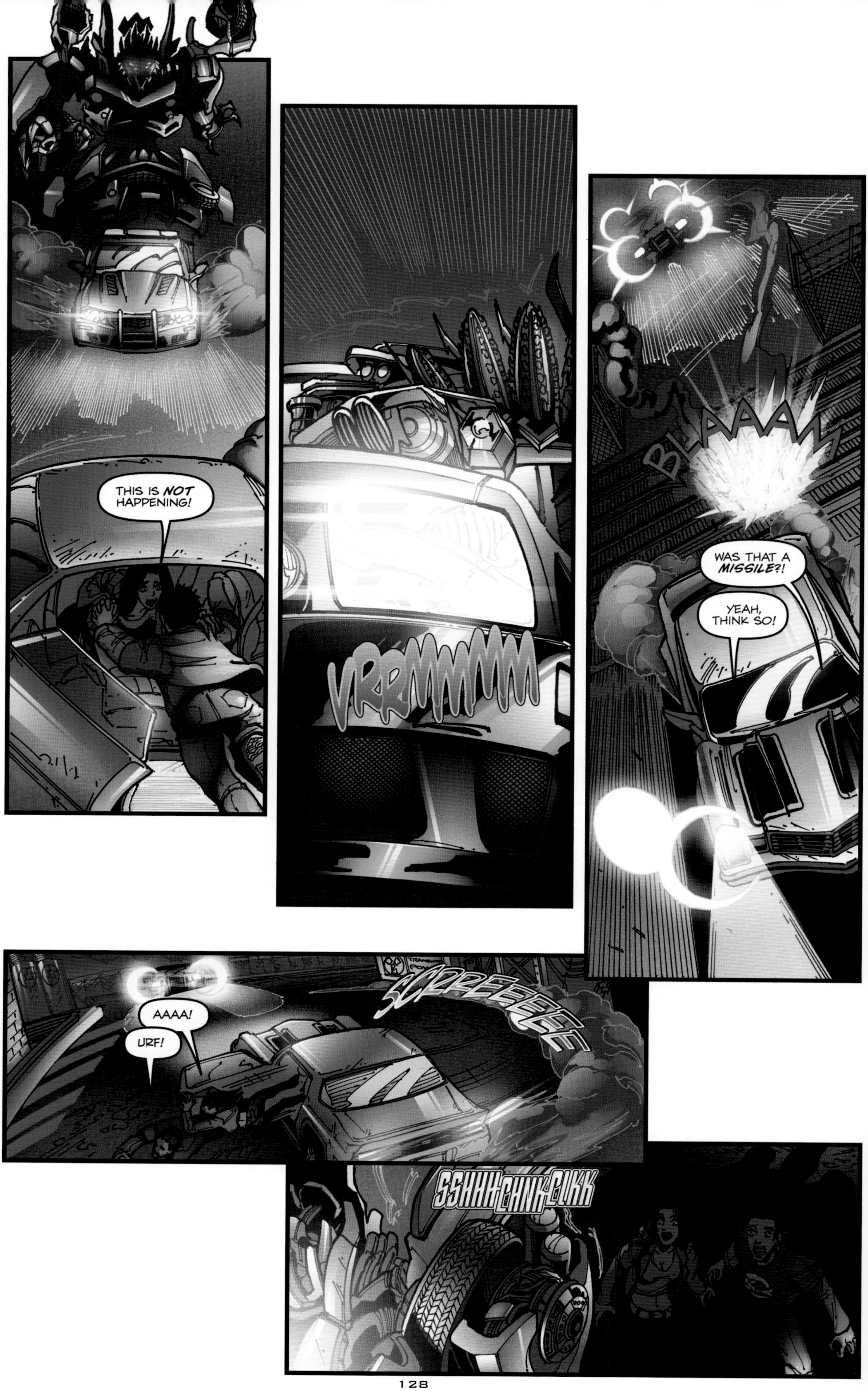
THIS IS *NOT* HAPPENING!
VRRMMMMM
BLAAAM
WAS THAT A *MISSILE?!*
YEAH, THINK SO!
SCREEEEEE
AAAA!
URF!
SSHKK CHNK CLIKK

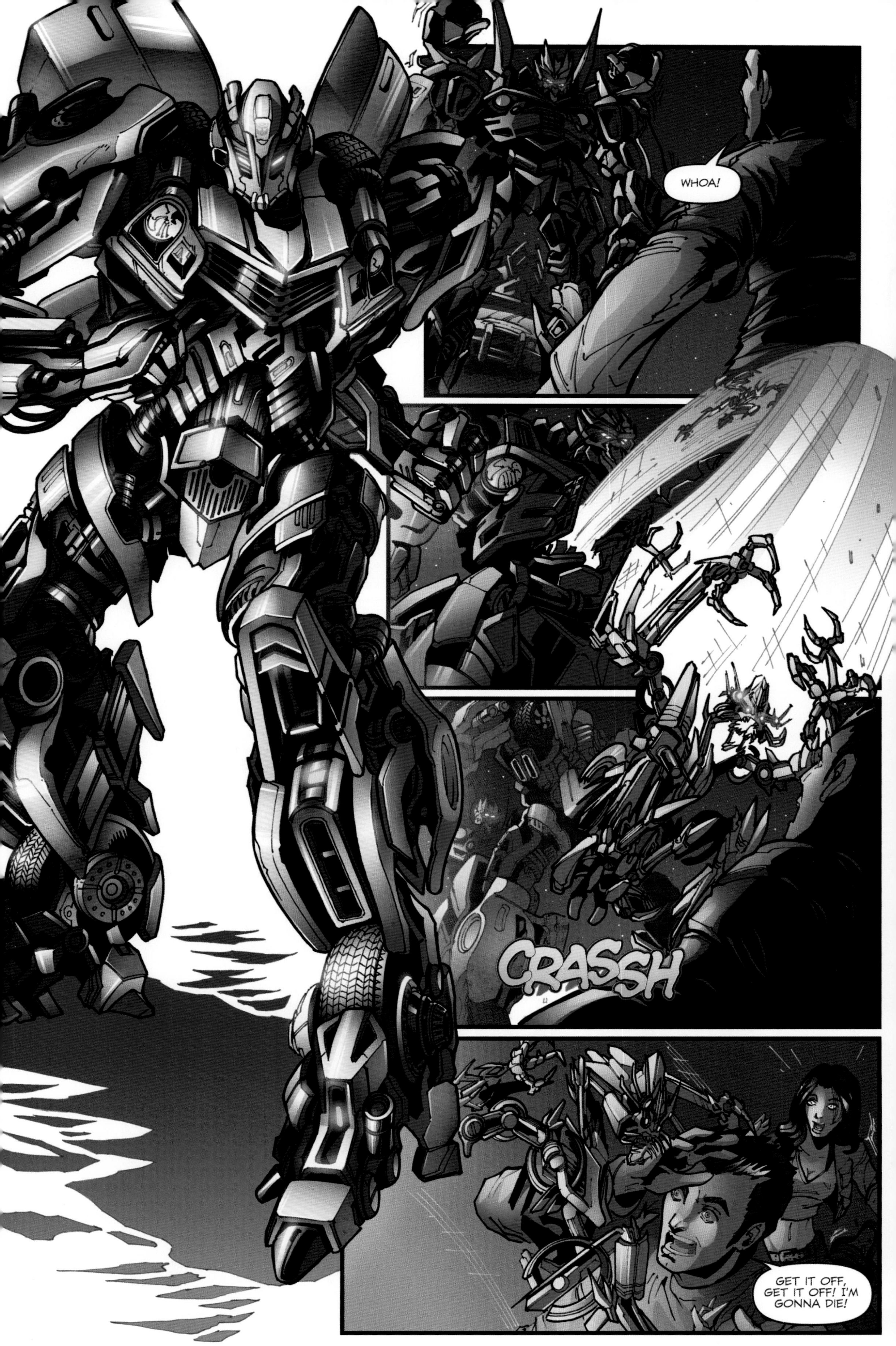
WHOA!
CRASSH
GET IT OFF, GET IT OFF! I'M GONNA DIE!

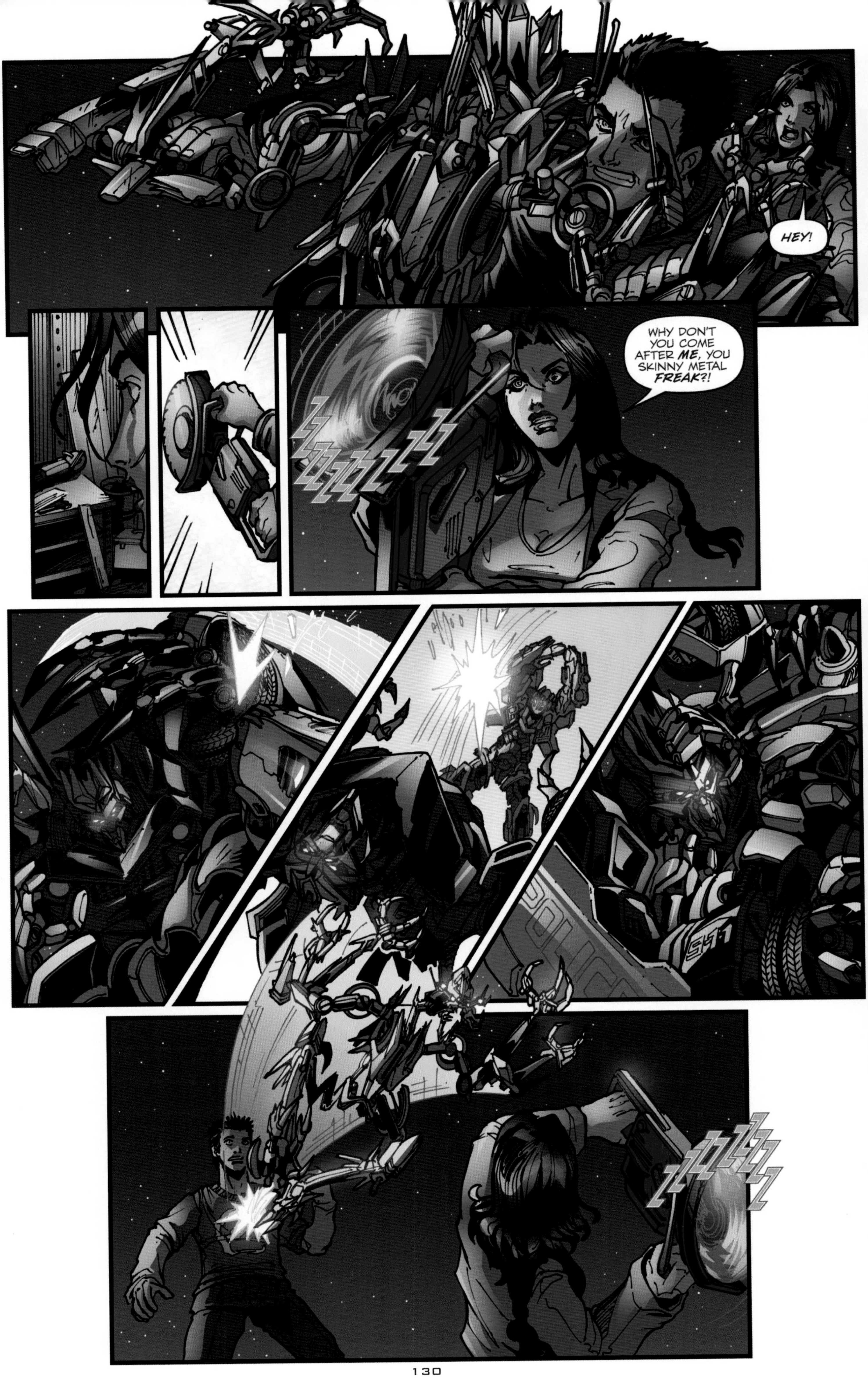
HEY!
WHY DON'T YOU COME AFTER *ME*, YOU SKINNY METAL *FREAK*?!

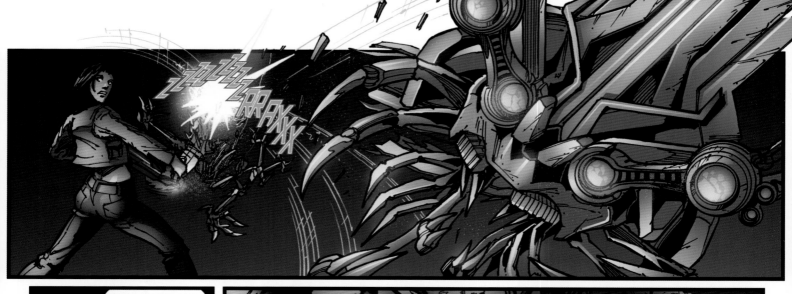

NOT SO TOUGH WITHOUT A BODY, ARE YA?

SAM, LOOK!

BOOOM

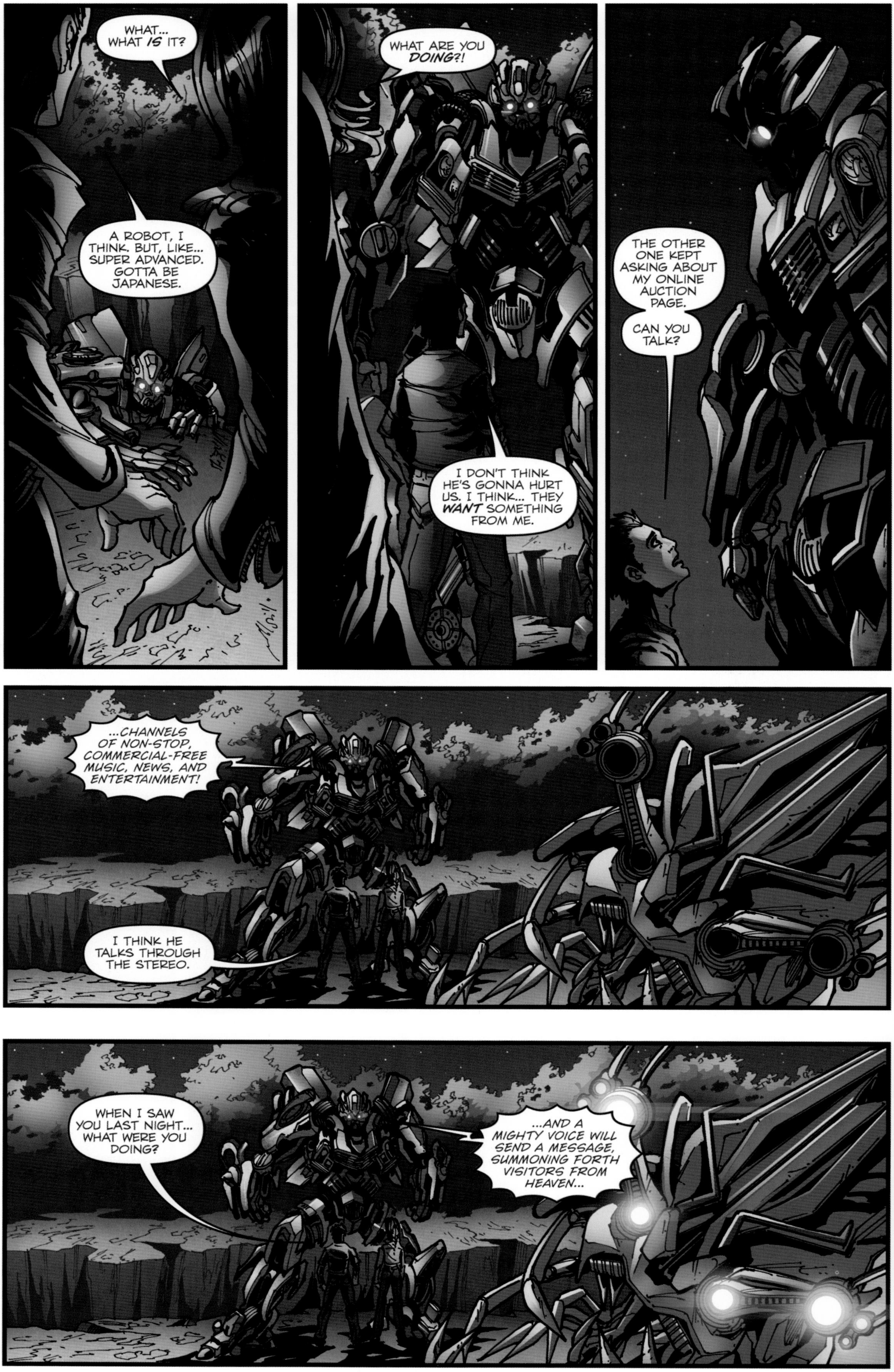
WHAT... WHAT IS IT?
A ROBOT, I THINK. BUT, LIKE... SUPER ADVANCED. GOTTA BE JAPANESE.
WHAT ARE YOU DOING?!
I DON'T THINK HE'S GONNA HURT US. I THINK... THEY WANT SOMETHING FROM ME.
THE OTHER ONE KEPT ASKING ABOUT MY ONLINE AUCTION PAGE.
CAN YOU TALK?
...CHANNELS OF NON-STOP, COMMERCIAL-FREE MUSIC, NEWS, AND ENTERTAINMENT!
I THINK HE TALKS THROUGH THE STEREO.
WHEN I SAW YOU LAST NIGHT... WHAT WERE YOU DOING?
...AND A MIGHTY VOICE WILL SEND A MESSAGE, SUMMONING FORTH VISITORS FROM HEAVEN...

SKRRRICK

YOU WERE CALLING SOMEONE?

VISITORS FROM HEAVEN? WHAT'RE YOU, LIKE, AN ALIEN?

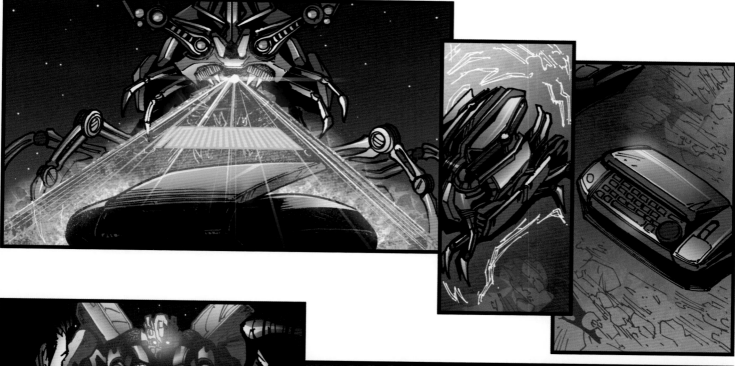

I THINK... IT WANTS US TO GET IN.

AND GO WHERE?

I DON'T KNOW, BUT THINK ABOUT IT... WHEN WE LOOK BACK ON THIS YEARS FROM NOW, DON'T YOU WANNA BE ABLE TO SAY WE HAD THE *GUTS* TO GET IN THE CAR?

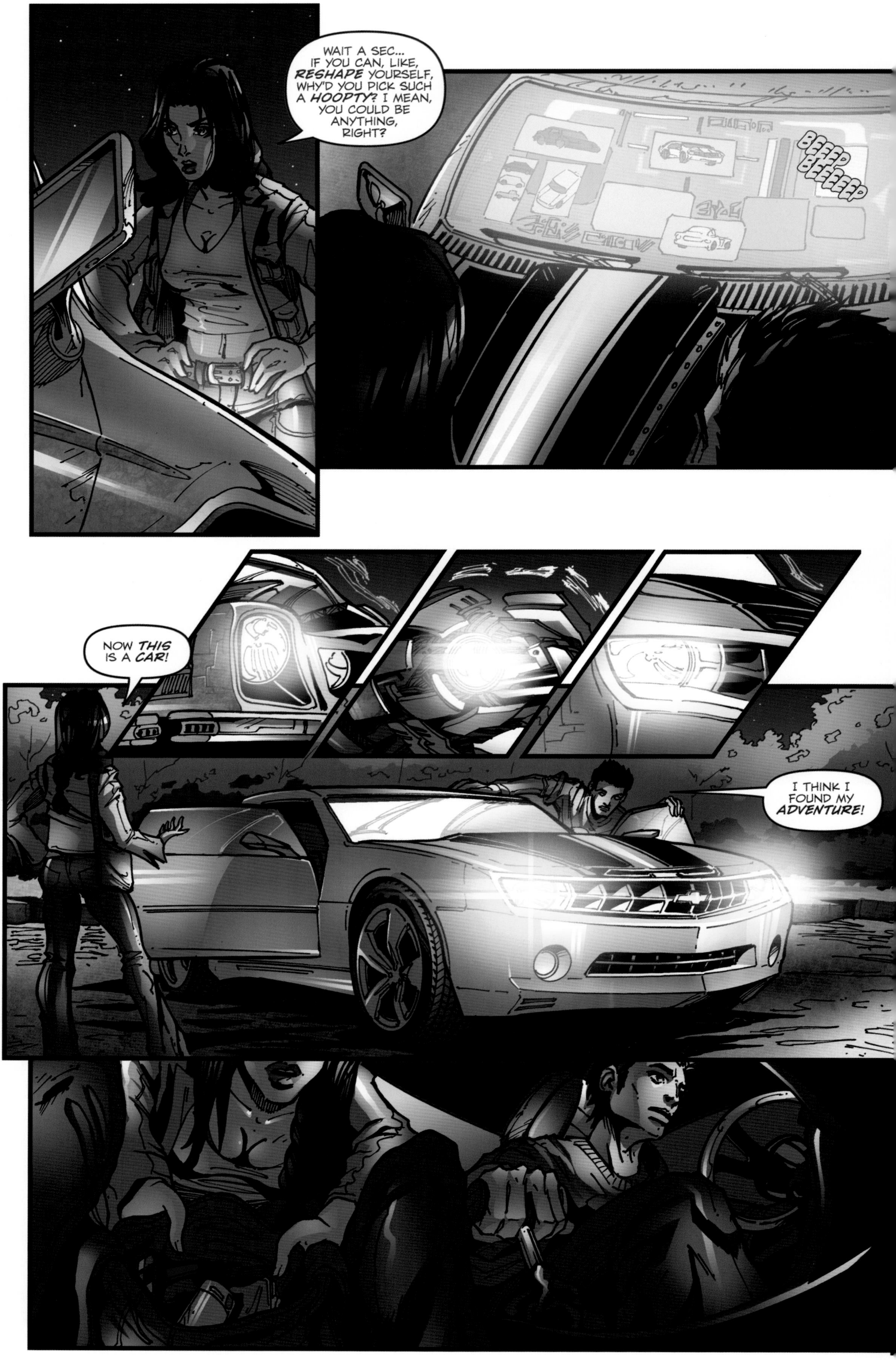

WAIT A SEC... IF YOU CAN, LIKE, **RESHAPE** YOURSELF, WHY'D YOU PICK SUCH A **HOOPTY?** I MEAN, YOU COULD BE ANYTHING, RIGHT?
BEEEP BEEEEEP
NOW *THIS* IS A *CAR*!
I THINK I FOUND MY **ADVENTURE**!

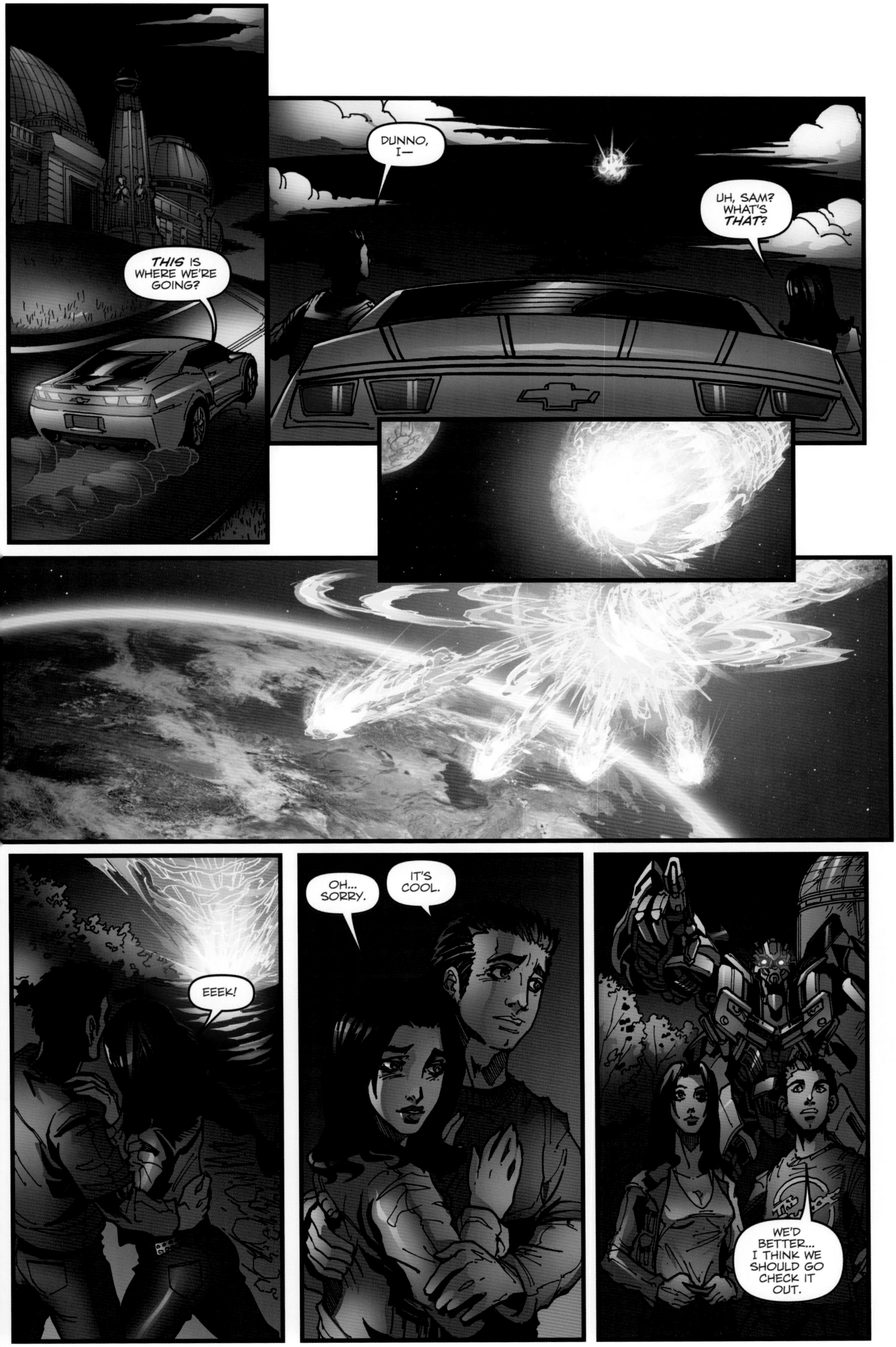
THIS IS WHERE WE'RE GOING?
DUNNO, I—
UH, SAM? WHAT'S THAT?
EEEK!
OH... SORRY.
IT'S COOL.
WE'D BETTER... I THINK WE SHOULD GO CHECK IT OUT.

ELSEWHERE IN AND AROUND THE CITY, FOUR MORE METEORS CRASH INTO THE EARTH...

...ALL BEARING AN *UNIMAGINABLE* CARGO.

WHAT... WHAT IS IT?

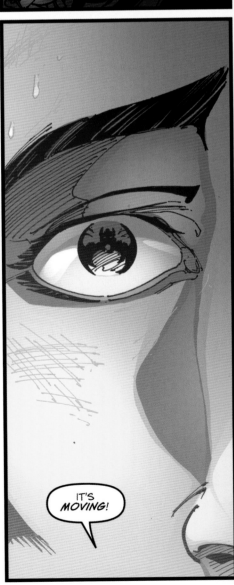

IT'S *MOVING!*

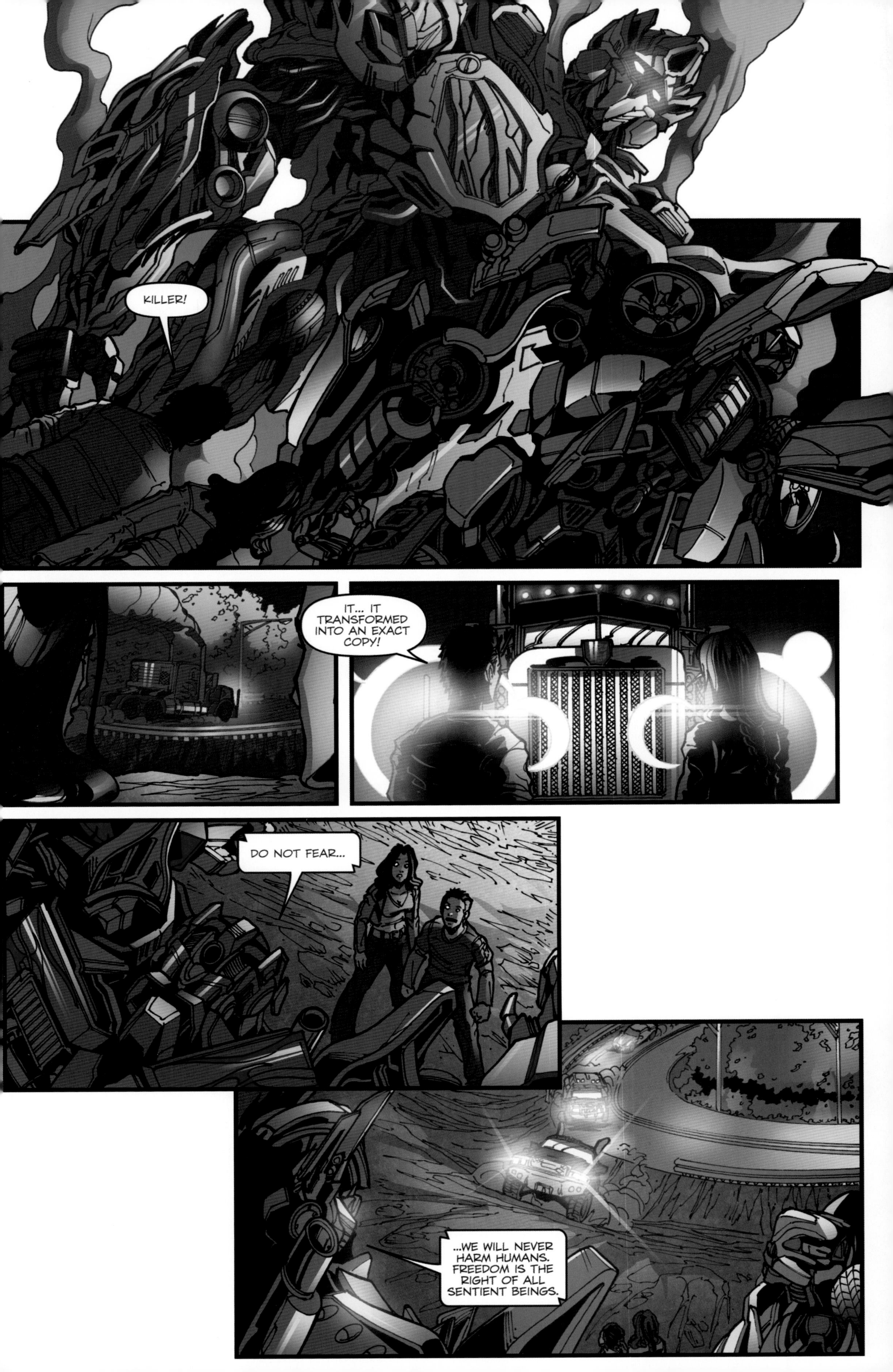
KILLER!
IT... IT TRANSFORMED INTO AN EXACT COPY!
DO NOT FEAR...
...WE WILL NEVER HARM HUMANS. FREEDOM IS THE RIGHT OF ALL SENTIENT BEINGS.

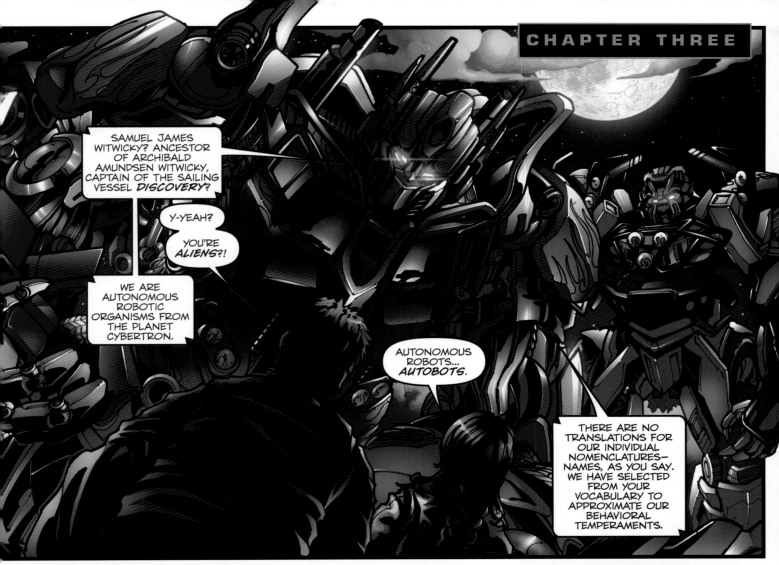

SAMUEL JAMES WITWICKY? ANCESTOR OF ARCHIBALD AMUNDSEN WITWICKY, CAPTAIN OF THE SAILING VESSEL *DISCOVERY*?

Y-YEAH?

YOU'RE *ALIENS*?!

WE ARE AUTONOMOUS ROBOTIC ORGANISMS FROM THE PLANET CYBERTRON.

AUTONOMOUS ROBOTS... *AUTOBOTS*.

THERE ARE NO TRANSLATIONS FOR OUR INDIVIDUAL NOMENCLATURES— NAMES, AS YOU SAY. WE HAVE SELECTED FROM YOUR VOCABULARY TO APPROXIMATE OUR BEHAVIORAL TEMPERAMENTS.

MY FIRST LIEUTENANT, *JAZZ*.

OUR WEAPONS SPECIALIST, *IRONHIDE*.

OUR MEDICAL OFFICER, *RATCHET*.

AND YOU ALREADY KNOW *BUMBLEBEE*, GUARDIAN OF SAM WITWICKY.

139

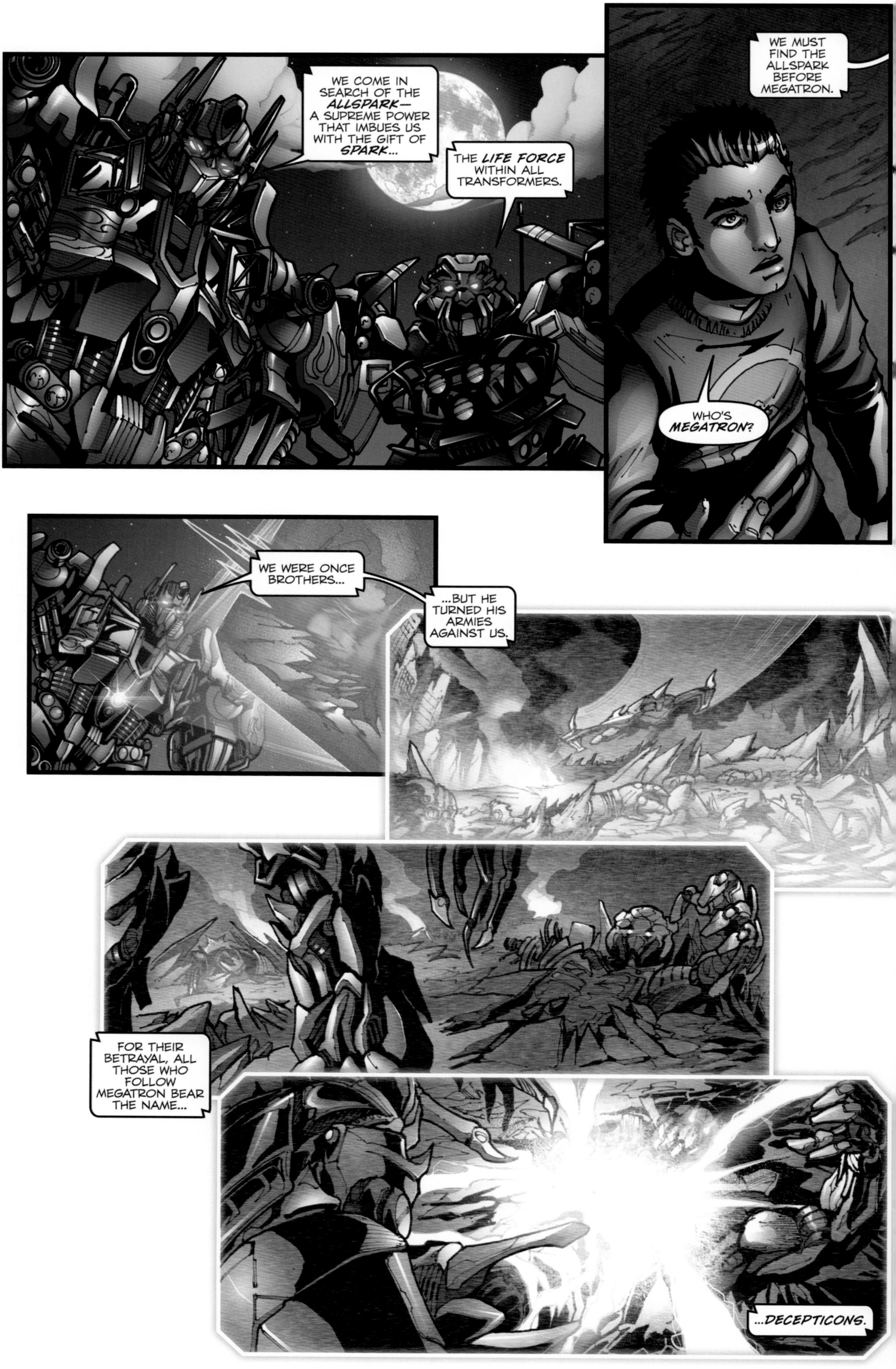
WE COME IN SEARCH OF THE ALLSPARK— A SUPREME POWER THAT IMBUES US WITH THE GIFT OF SPARK...
THE LIFE FORCE WITHIN ALL TRANSFORMERS.
WE MUST FIND THE ALLSPARK BEFORE MEGATRON.
WHO'S MEGATRON?
WE WERE ONCE BROTHERS...
...BUT HE TURNED HIS ARMIES AGAINST US.
FOR THEIR BETRAYAL, ALL THOSE WHO FOLLOW MEGATRON BEAR THE NAME...
...DECEPTICONS.

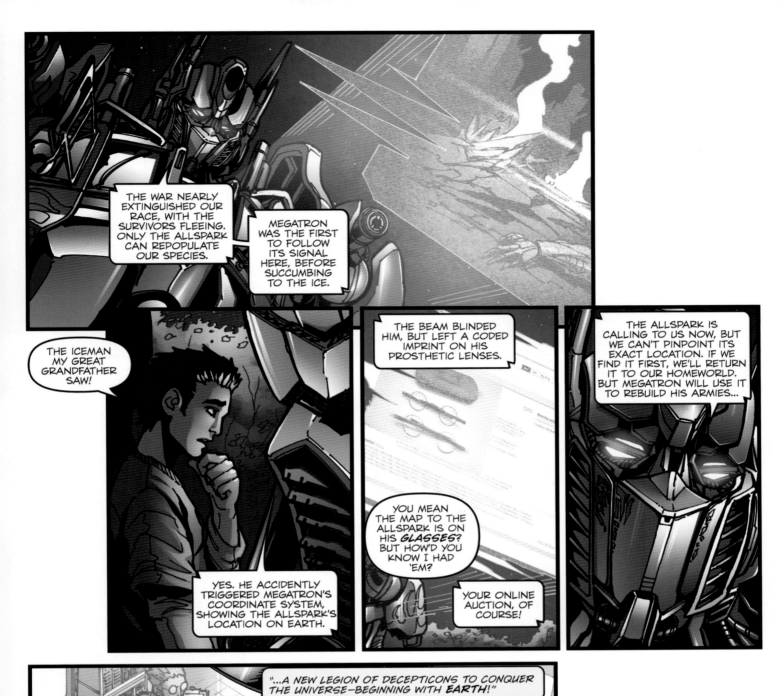

THE WAR NEARLY EXTINGUISHED OUR RACE, WITH THE SURVIVORS FLEEING. ONLY THE ALLSPARK CAN REPOPULATE OUR SPECIES.

MEGATRON WAS THE FIRST TO FOLLOW ITS SIGNAL HERE, BEFORE SUCCUMBING TO THE ICE.

THE ICEMAN MY GREAT GRANDFATHER SAW!

YES. HE ACCIDENTLY TRIGGERED MEGATRON'S COORDINATE SYSTEM, SHOWING THE ALLSPARK'S LOCATION ON EARTH.

THE BEAM BLINDED HIM, BUT LEFT A CODED IMPRINT ON HIS PROSTHETIC LENSES.

YOU MEAN THE MAP TO THE ALLSPARK IS ON HIS *GLASSES*? BUT HOW'D YOU KNOW I HAD 'EM?

YOUR ONLINE AUCTION, OF COURSE!

THE ALLSPARK IS CALLING TO US NOW, BUT WE CAN'T PINPOINT ITS EXACT LOCATION. IF WE FIND IT FIRST, WE'LL RETURN IT TO OUR HOMEWORLD. BUT MEGATRON WILL USE IT TO REBUILD HIS ARMIES...

"...A NEW LEGION OF DECEPTICONS TO CONQUER THE UNIVERSE—BEGINNING WITH *EARTH*!"

...SEEMS TO BE SOME KIND OF SELF-REGENERATING MOLECULAR ARMOR!

BUT LOOK HERE...

...NO REGENERATION WHERE THE SABOT ROUND HIT. MEANS THAT THESE THINGS MUST REACT TO *TEMPERATURE*.

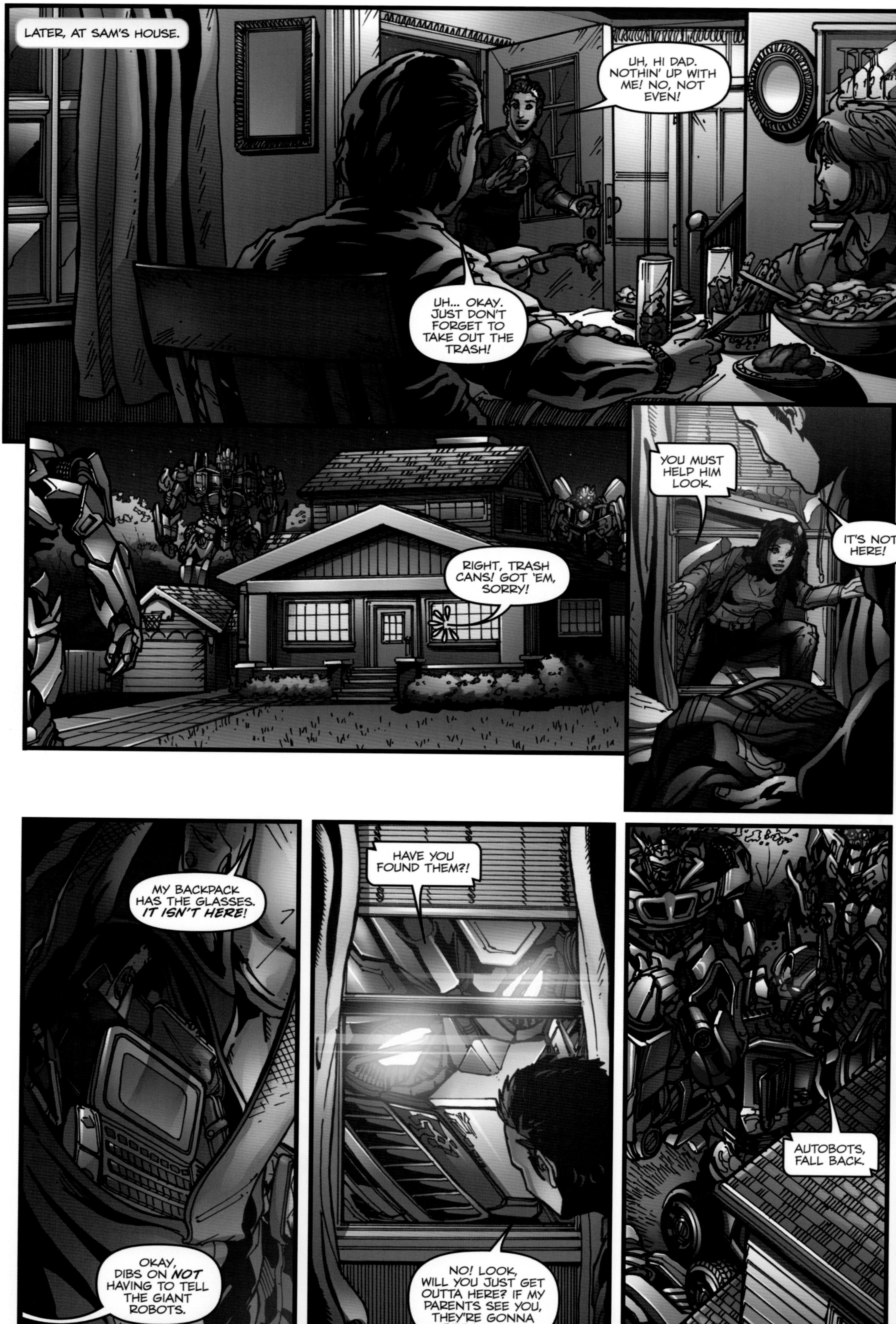
LATER, AT SAM'S HOUSE.
UH, HI DAD. NOTHIN' UP WITH ME! NO, NOT EVEN!
UH... OKAY. JUST DON'T FORGET TO TAKE OUT THE TRASH!
RIGHT, TRASH CANS! GOT 'EM, SORRY!
YOU MUST HELP HIM LOOK.
IT'S NOT HERE!
MY BACKPACK HAS THE GLASSES. IT ISN'T HERE!
OKAY, DIBS ON NOT HAVING TO TELL THE GIANT ROBOTS.
HAVE YOU FOUND THEM?!
NO! LOOK, WILL YOU JUST GET OUTTA HERE? IF MY PARENTS SEE YOU, THEY'RE GONNA FREAK! HIDE!
AUTOBOTS, FALL BACK.

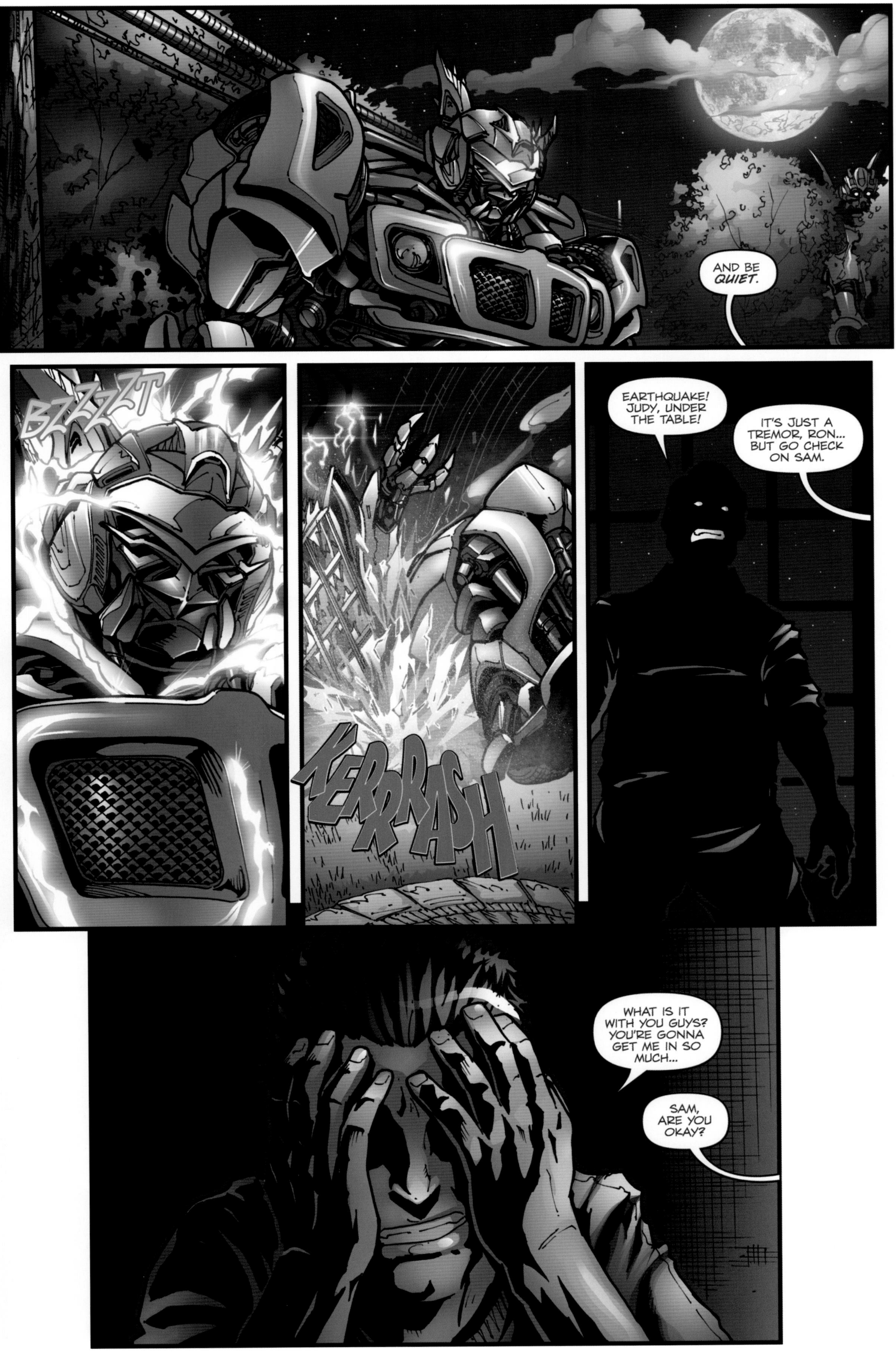
AND BE QUIET.
BZZZZT
KERRRASH
EARTHQUAKE! JUDY, UNDER THE TABLE!
IT'S JUST A TREMOR, RON... BUT GO CHECK ON SAM.
WHAT IS IT WITH YOU GUYS? YOU'RE GONNA GET ME IN SO MUCH...
SAM, ARE YOU OKAY?

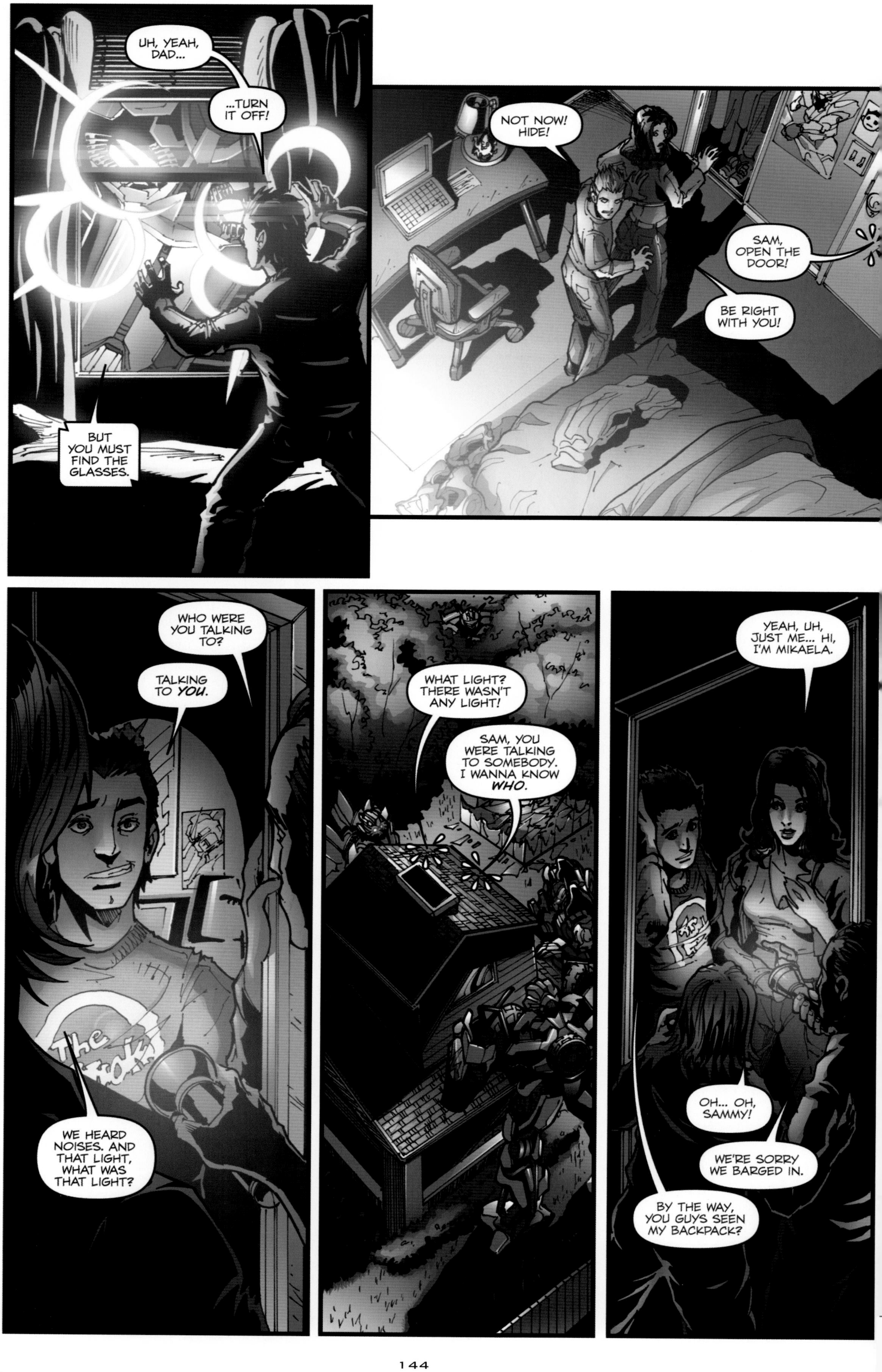
UH, YEAH, DAD...
...TURN IT OFF!
BUT YOU MUST FIND THE GLASSES.
NOT NOW! HIDE!
SAM, OPEN THE DOOR!
BE RIGHT WITH YOU!
WHO WERE YOU TALKING TO?
TALKING TO ***YOU***.
WE HEARD NOISES. AND THAT LIGHT, WHAT WAS THAT LIGHT?
WHAT LIGHT? THERE WASN'T ANY LIGHT!
SAM, YOU WERE TALKING TO SOMEBODY. I WANNA KNOW ***WHO***.
YEAH, UH, JUST ME... HI, I'M MIKAELA.
OH... OH, SAMMY!
WE'RE SORRY WE BARGED IN.
BY THE WAY, YOU GUYS SEEN MY BACKPACK?

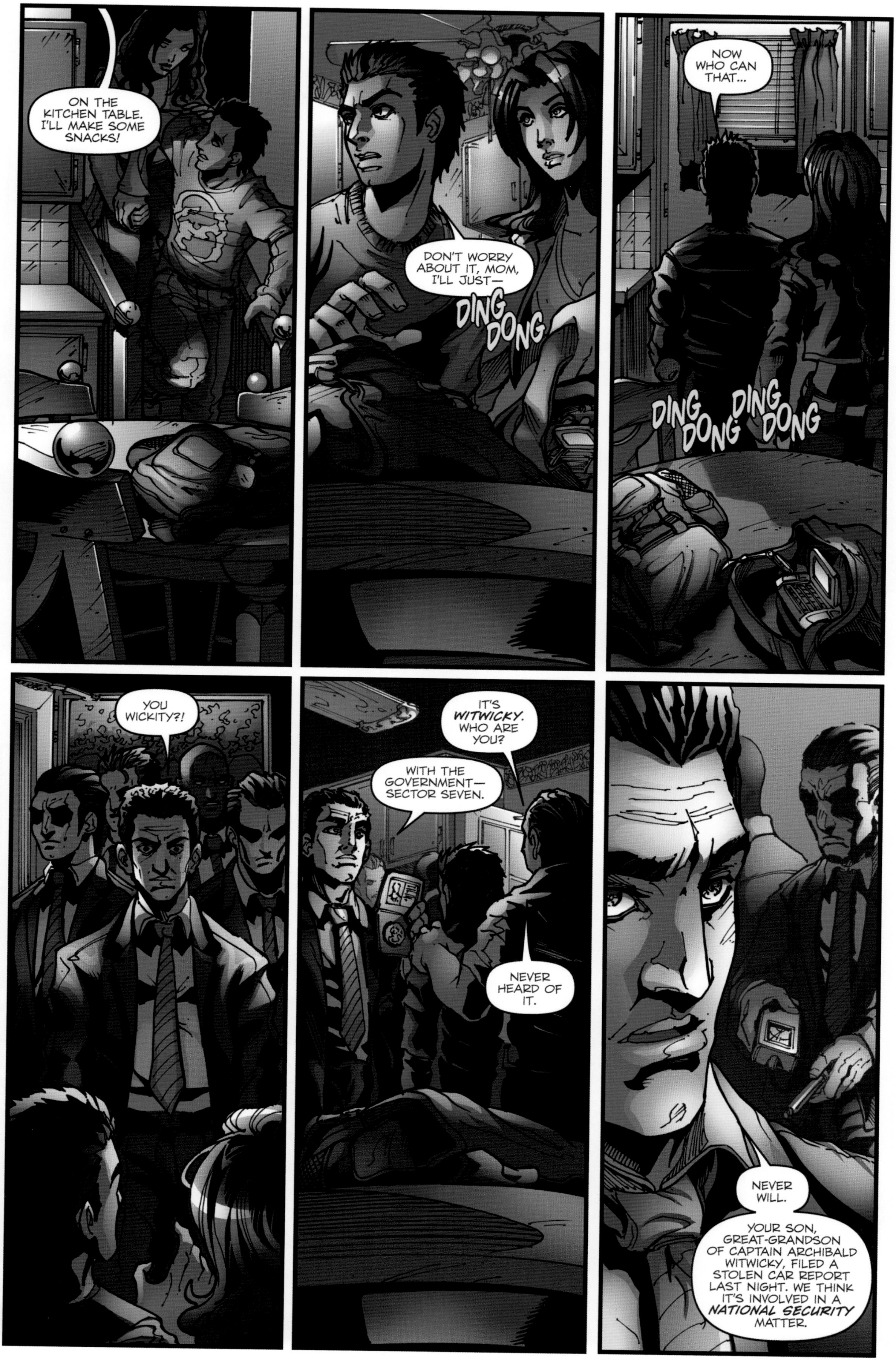
ON THE KITCHEN TABLE. I'LL MAKE SOME SNACKS!
DON'T WORRY ABOUT IT, MOM, I'LL JUST—
DING DONG
NOW WHO CAN THAT...
DING DONG DING DONG
YOU WICKITY?!
IT'S WITWICKY. WHO ARE YOU?
WITH THE GOVERNMENT— SECTOR SEVEN.
NEVER HEARD OF IT.
NEVER WILL.
YOUR SON, GREAT-GRANDSON OF CAPTAIN ARCHIBALD WITWICKY, FILED A STOLEN CAR REPORT LAST NIGHT. WE THINK IT'S INVOLVED IN A NATIONAL SECURITY MATTER.

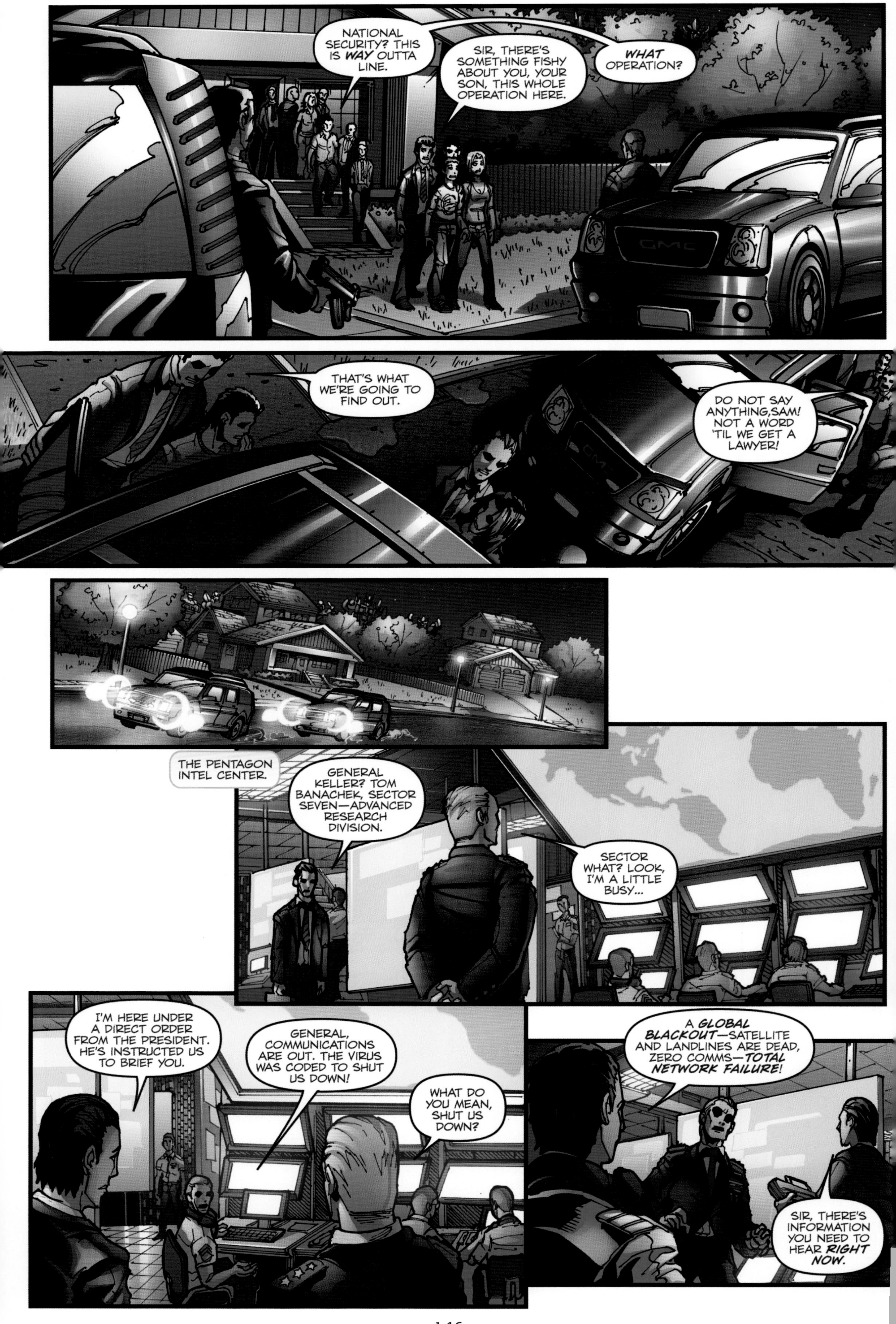

NATIONAL SECURITY? THIS IS WAY OUTTA LINE.
SIR, THERE'S SOMETHING FISHY ABOUT YOU, YOUR SON, THIS WHOLE OPERATION HERE.
WHAT OPERATION?
THAT'S WHAT WE'RE GOING TO FIND OUT.
DO NOT SAY ANYTHING,SAM! NOT A WORD 'TIL WE GET A LAWYER!
THE PENTAGON INTEL CENTER.
GENERAL KELLER? TOM BANACHEK, SECTOR SEVEN—ADVANCED RESEARCH DIVISION.
SECTOR WHAT? LOOK, I'M A LITTLE BUSY...
I'M HERE UNDER A DIRECT ORDER FROM THE PRESIDENT. HE'S INSTRUCTED US TO BRIEF YOU.
GENERAL, COMMUNICATIONS ARE OUT. THE VIRUS WAS CODED TO SHUT US DOWN!
WHAT DO YOU MEAN, SHUT US DOWN?
A GLOBAL BLACKOUT—SATELLITE AND LANDLINES ARE DEAD, ZERO COMMS—TOTAL NETWORK FAILURE!
SIR, THERE'S INFORMATION YOU NEED TO HEAR RIGHT NOW.

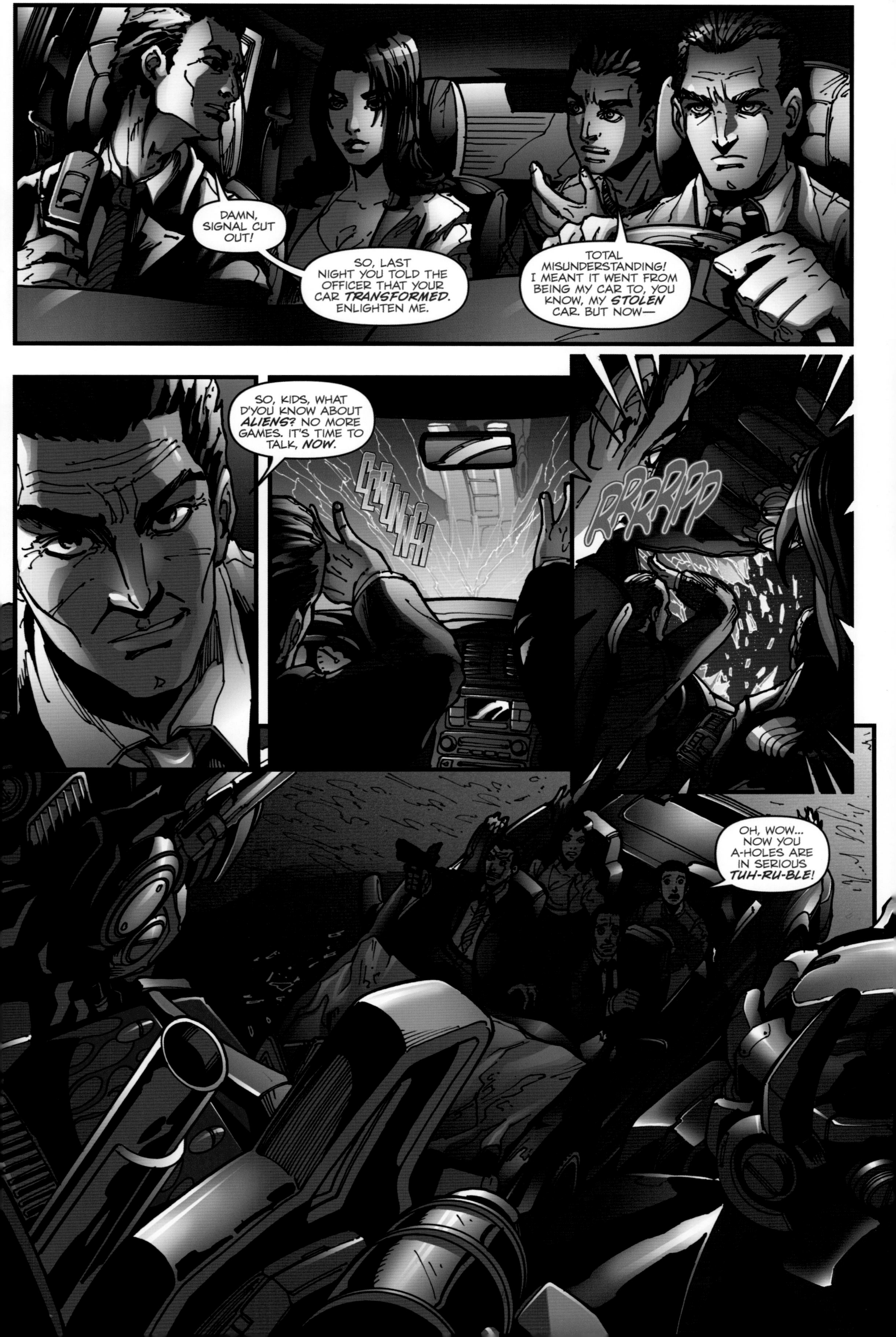
DAMN, SIGNAL CUT OUT!
SO, LAST NIGHT YOU TOLD THE OFFICER THAT YOUR CAR TRANSFORMED. ENLIGHTEN ME.
TOTAL MISUNDERSTANDING! I MEANT IT WENT FROM BEING MY CAR TO, YOU KNOW, MY STOLEN CAR. BUT NOW—
SO, KIDS, WHAT D'YOU KNOW ABOUT ALIENS? NO MORE GAMES. IT'S TIME TO TALK, NOW.
CCRUNCH
RRRRIPP
OH, WOW... NOW YOU A-HOLES ARE IN SERIOUS TUH-RU-BLE!

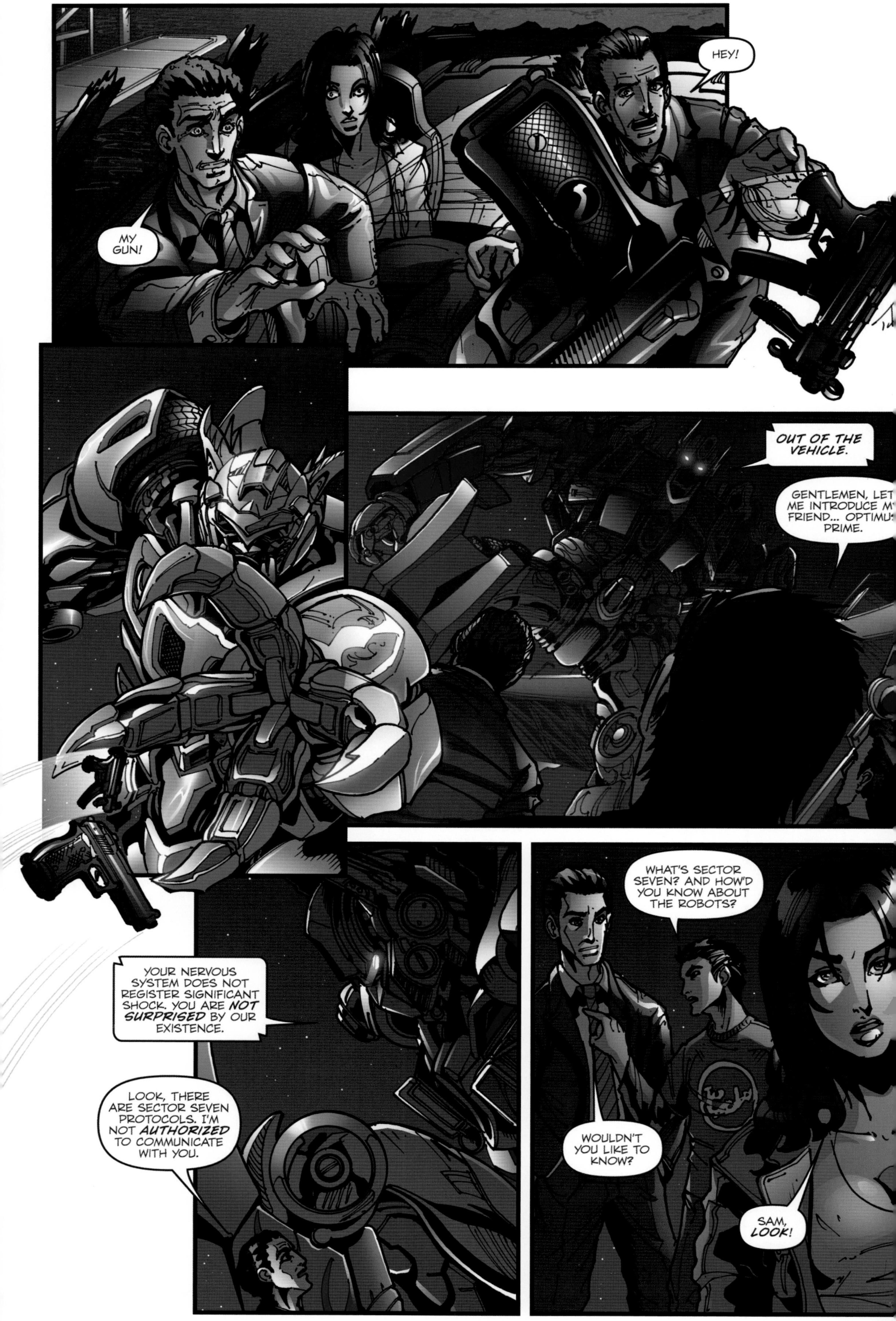

HEY!
MY GUN!
OUT OF THE VEHICLE.
GENTLEMEN, LET ME INTRODUCE M FRIEND... OPTIMU PRIME.
YOUR NERVOUS SYSTEM DOES NOT REGISTER SIGNIFICANT SHOCK. YOU ARE **NOT SURPRISED** BY OUR EXISTENCE.
LOOK, THERE ARE SECTOR SEVEN PROTOCOLS. I'M NOT **AUTHORIZED** TO COMMUNICATE WITH YOU.
WHAT'S SECTOR SEVEN? AND HOW'D YOU KNOW ABOUT THE ROBOTS?
WOULDN'T YOU LIKE TO KNOW?
SAM, **LOOK!**

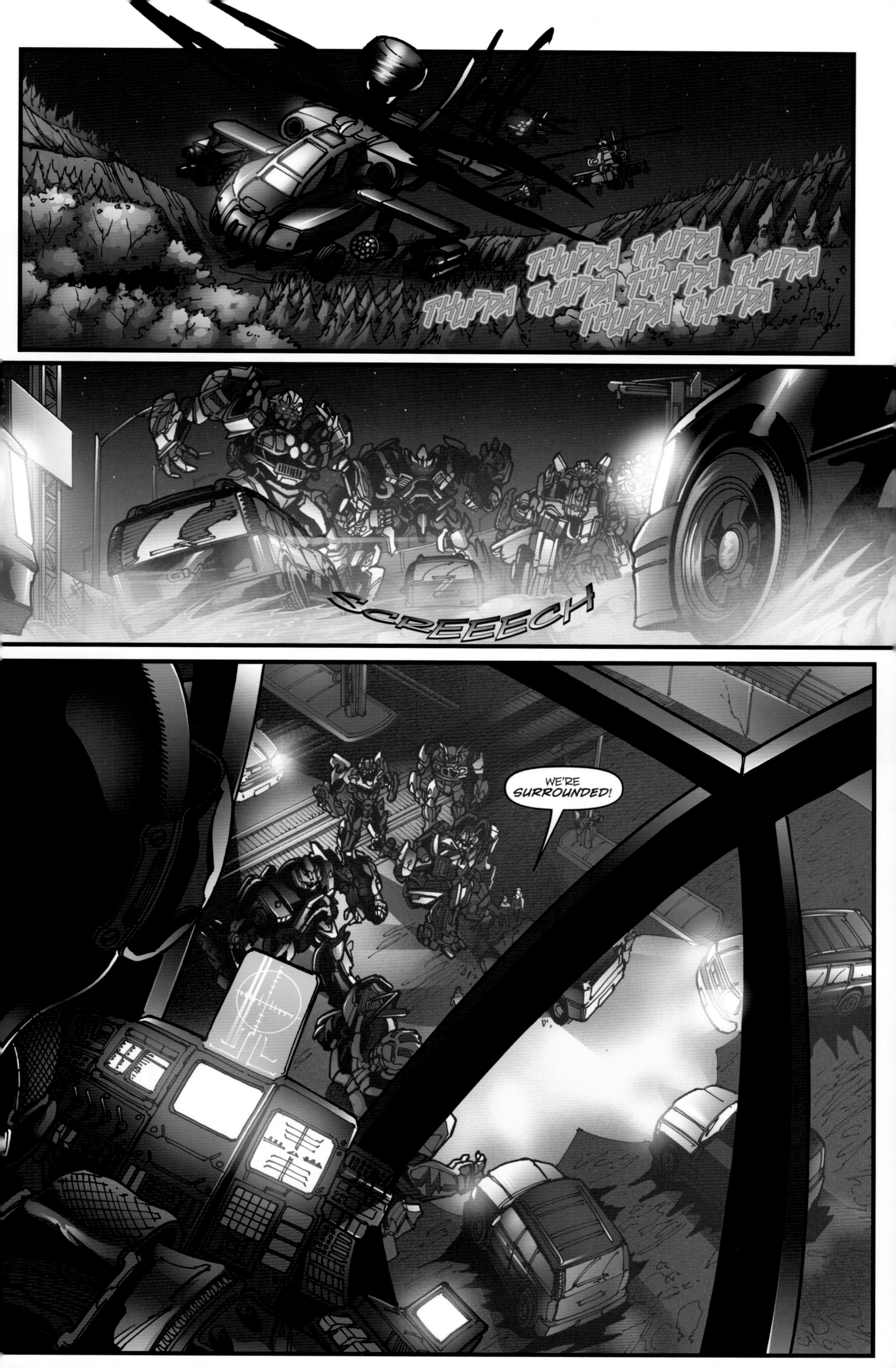
THUPPA THUPPA
THUPPA THUPPA THUPPA THUPPA
THUPPA THUPPA
SCREEEECH
WE'RE SURROUNDED!

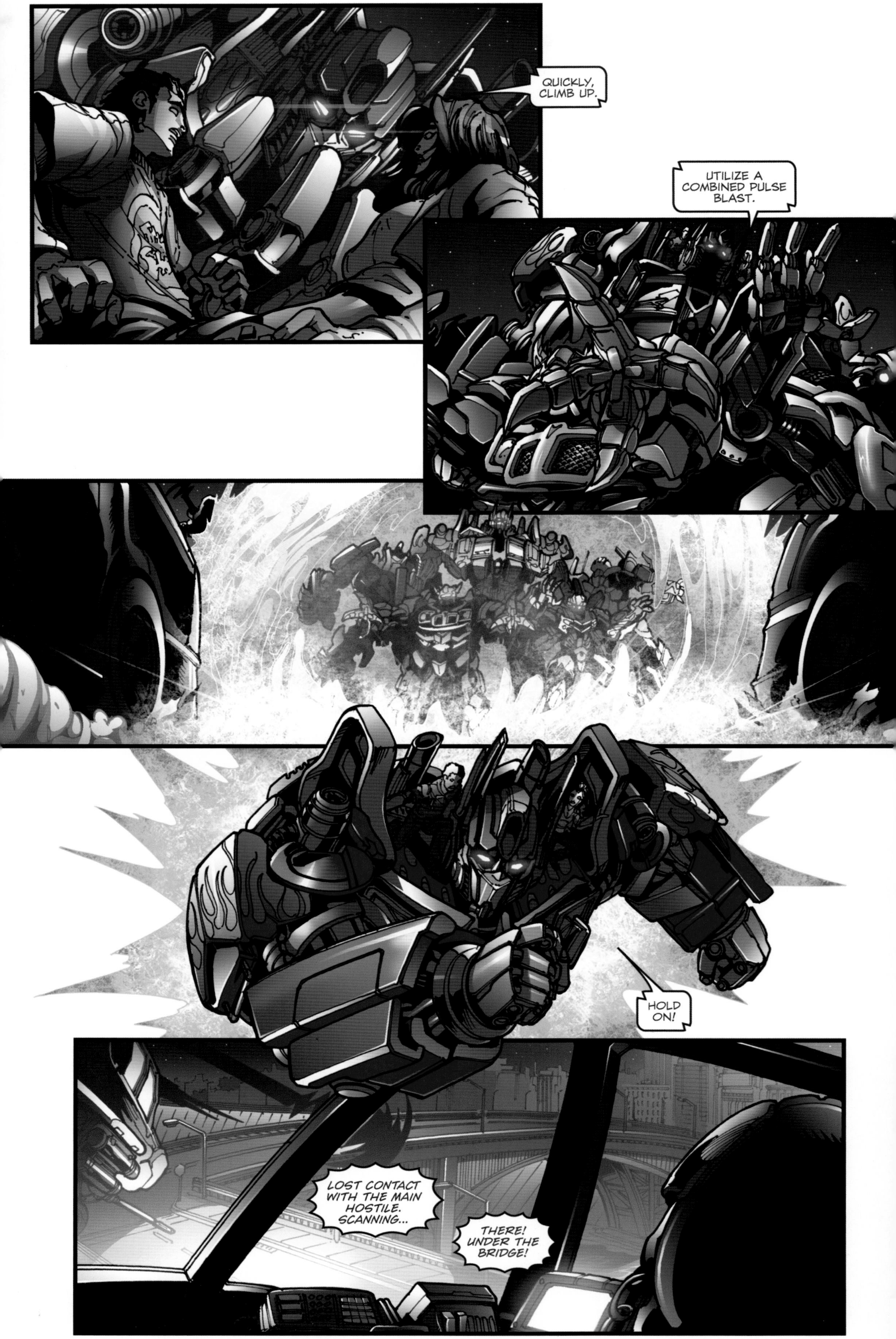
QUICKLY, CLIMB UP.
UTILIZE A COMBINED PULSE BLAST.
HOLD ON!
LOST CONTACT WITH THE MAIN HOSTILE. SCANNING...
THERE! UNDER THE BRIDGE!

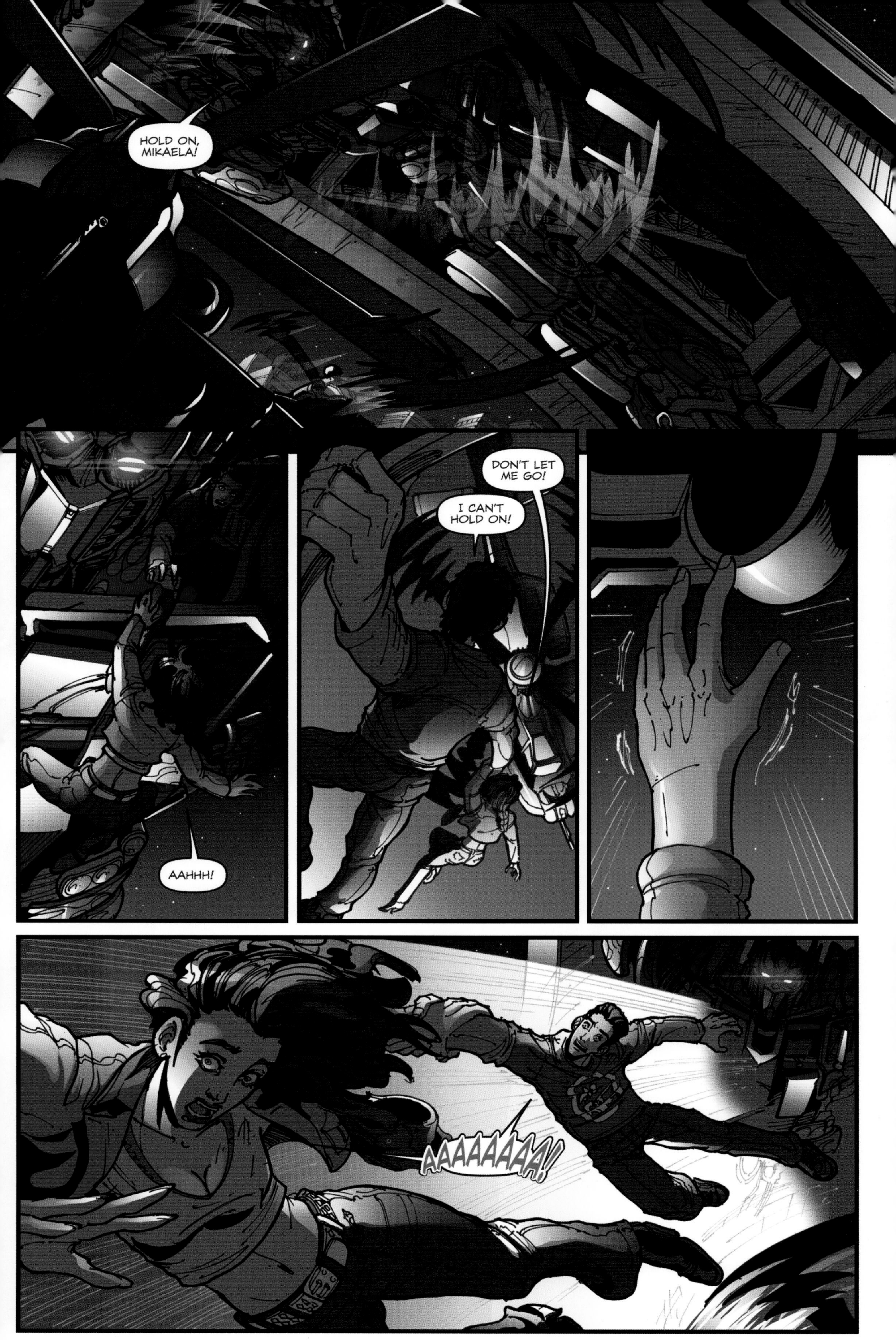
HOLD ON, MIKAELA!
AAHHH!
DON'T LET ME GO!
I CAN'T HOLD ON!
AAAAAAAA!

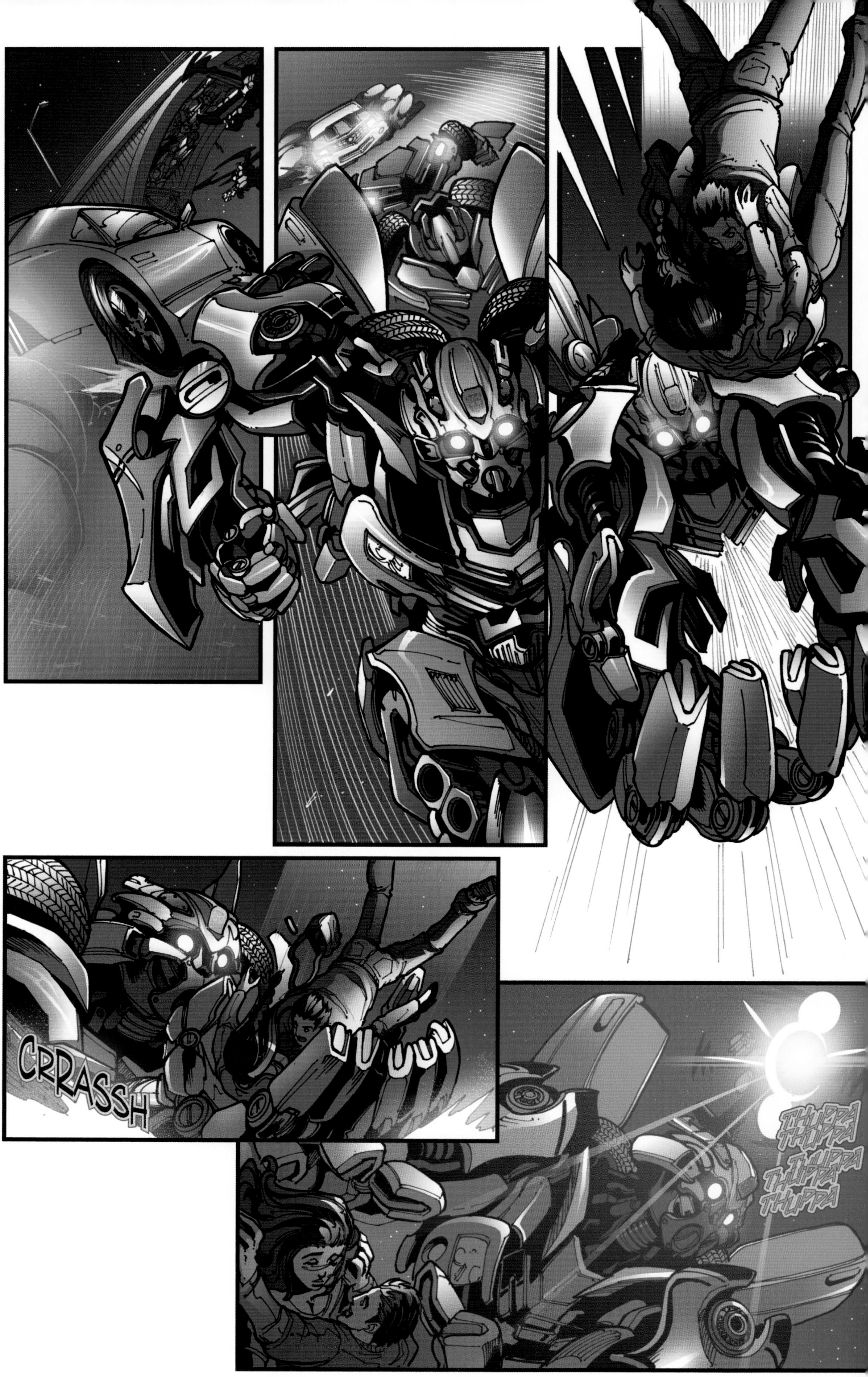
CRRASSH
THUPPA THUPPA THUPPA THUPPA THUPPA

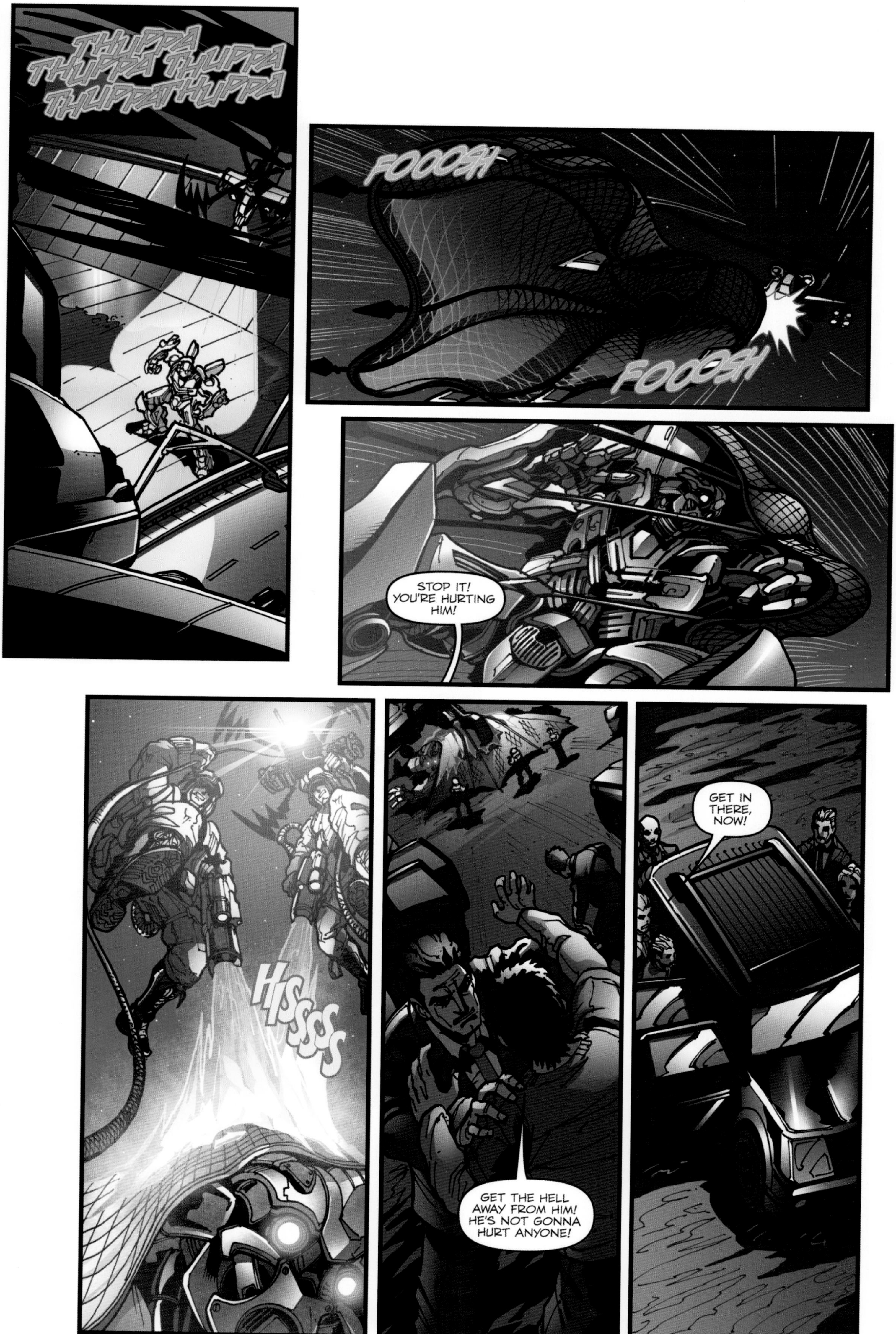
THUPPA THUPPA THUPPA THUPPA THUPPA
FOOOSH
FOOOSH
STOP IT! YOU'RE HURTING HIM!
HISSSSS
GET THE HELL AWAY FROM HIM! HE'S NOT GONNA HURT ANYONE!
GET IN THERE, NOW!

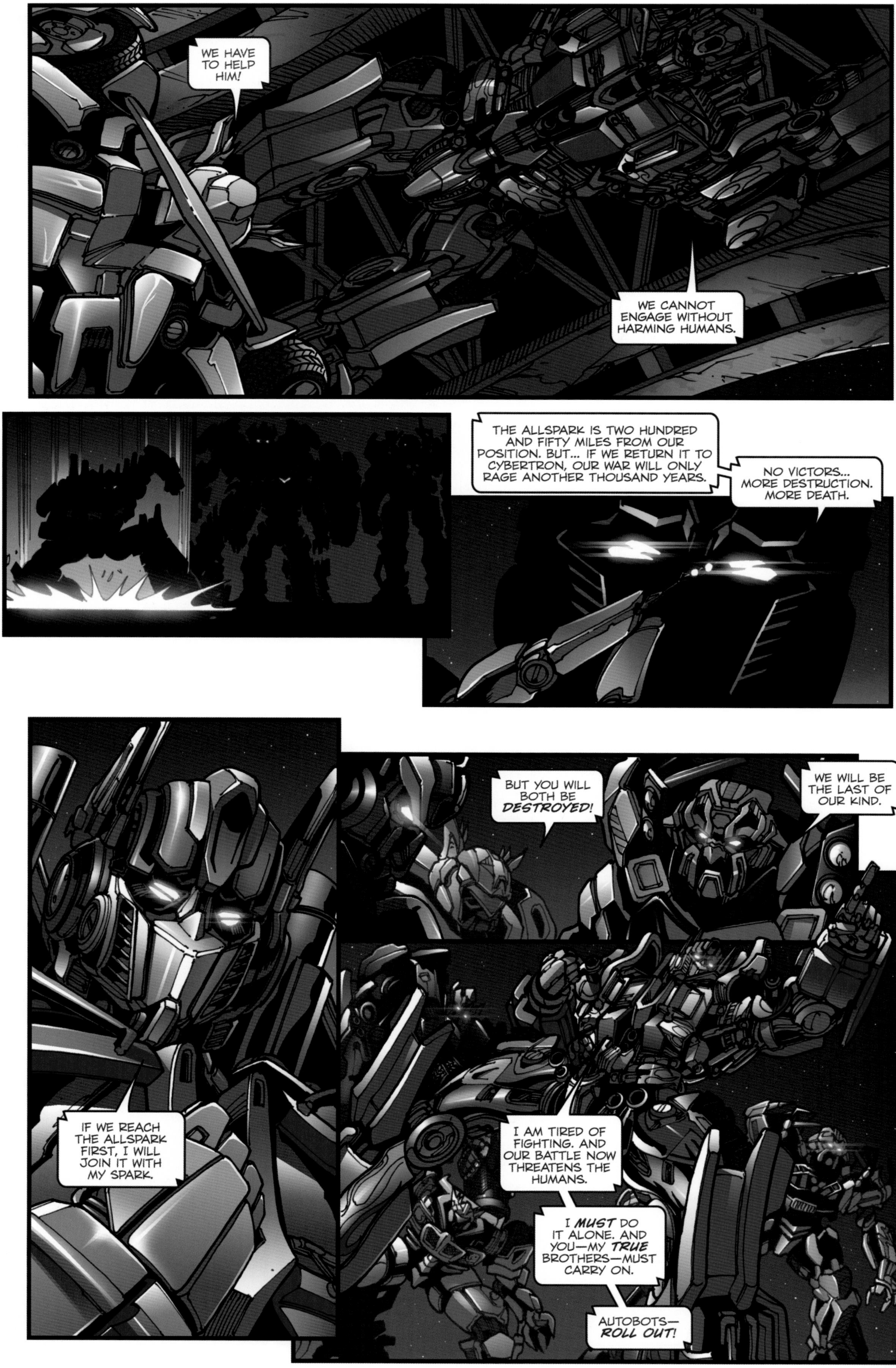
WE HAVE TO HELP HIM!
WE CANNOT ENGAGE WITHOUT HARMING HUMANS.
THE ALLSPARK IS TWO HUNDRED AND FIFTY MILES FROM OUR POSITION. BUT... IF WE RETURN IT TO CYBERTRON, OUR WAR WILL ONLY RAGE ANOTHER THOUSAND YEARS.
NO VICTORS... MORE DESTRUCTION. MORE DEATH.
IF WE REACH THE ALLSPARK FIRST, I WILL JOIN IT WITH MY SPARK.
BUT YOU WILL BOTH BE ***DESTROYED***!
WE WILL BE THE LAST OF OUR KIND.
I AM TIRED OF FIGHTING. AND OUR BATTLE NOW THREATENS THE HUMANS.
I ***MUST*** DO IT ALONE. AND YOU—MY ***TRUE*** BROTHERS—MUST CARRY ON.
AUTOBOTS— ***ROLL OUT***!

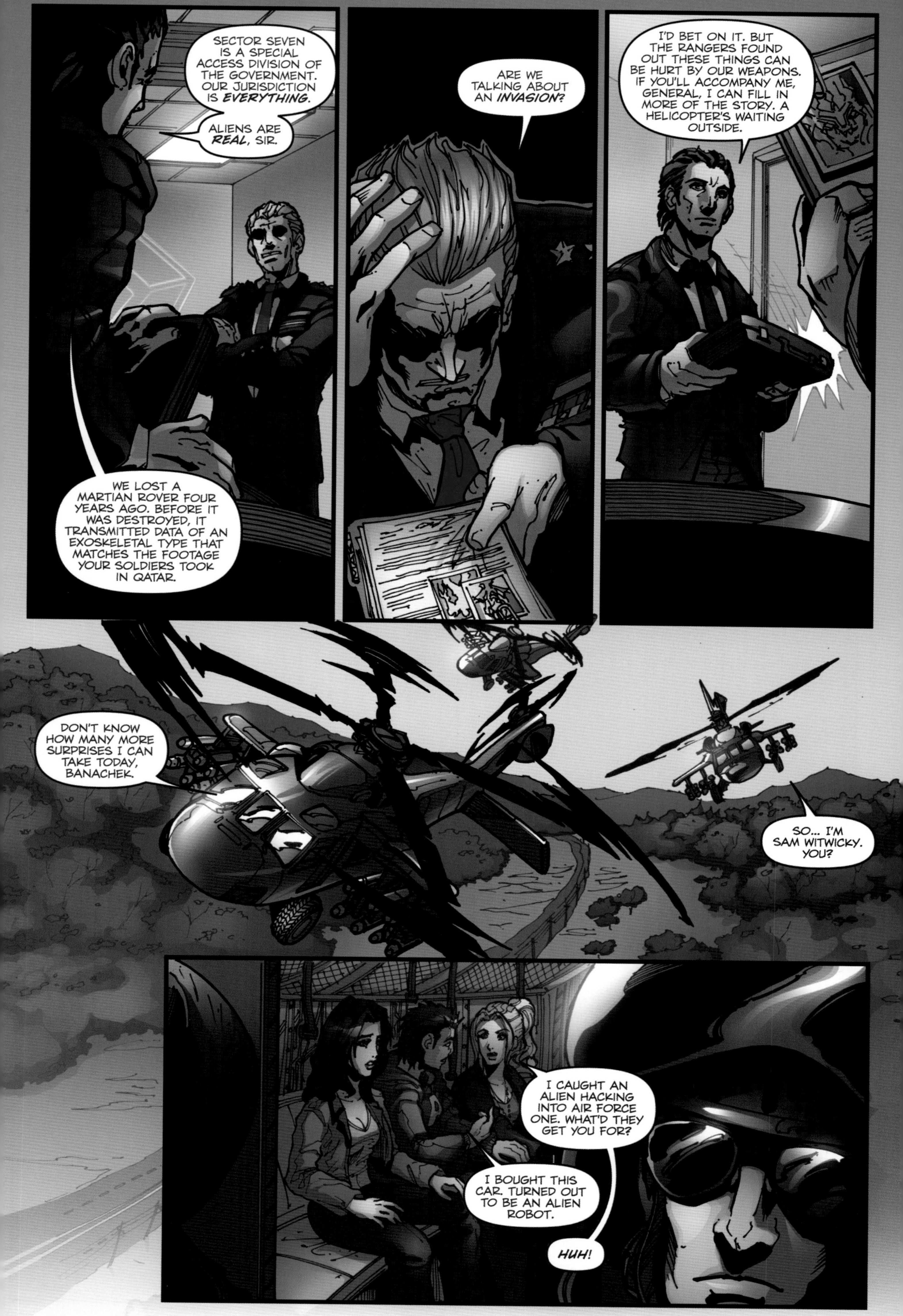
SECTOR SEVEN IS A SPECIAL ACCESS DIVISION OF THE GOVERNMENT. OUR JURISDICTION IS EVERYTHING.
ALIENS ARE REAL, SIR.
WE LOST A MARTIAN ROVER FOUR YEARS AGO. BEFORE IT WAS DESTROYED, IT TRANSMITTED DATA OF AN EXOSKELETAL TYPE THAT MATCHES THE FOOTAGE YOUR SOLDIERS TOOK IN QATAR.
ARE WE TALKING ABOUT AN INVASION?
I'D BET ON IT. BUT THE RANGERS FOUND OUT THESE THINGS CAN BE HURT BY OUR WEAPONS. IF YOU'LL ACCOMPANY ME, GENERAL, I CAN FILL IN MORE OF THE STORY. A HELICOPTER'S WAITING OUTSIDE.
DON'T KNOW HOW MANY MORE SURPRISES I CAN TAKE TODAY, BANACHEK.
SO... I'M SAM WITWICKY. YOU?
I CAUGHT AN ALIEN HACKING INTO AIR FORCE ONE. WHAT'D THEY GET YOU FOR?
I BOUGHT THIS CAR. TURNED OUT TO BE AN ALIEN ROBOT.
HUH!

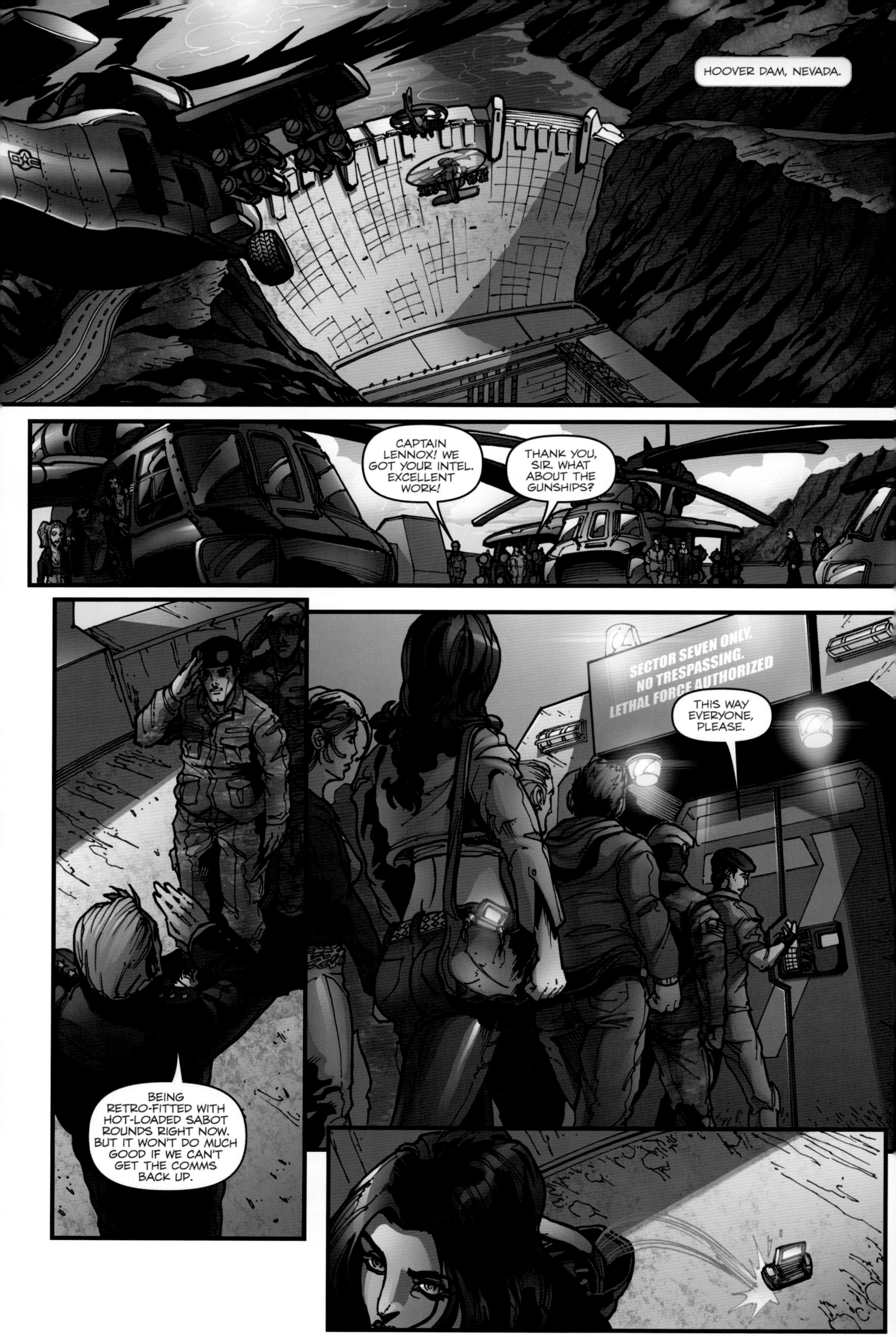
HOOVER DAM, NEVADA.
CAPTAIN LENNOX! WE GOT YOUR INTEL. EXCELLENT WORK!
THANK YOU, SIR. WHAT ABOUT THE GUNSHIPS?
BEING RETRO-FITTED WITH HOT-LOADED SABOT ROUNDS RIGHT NOW. BUT IT WON'T DO MUCH GOOD IF WE CAN'T GET THE COMMS BACK UP.
SECTOR SEVEN ONLY. NO TRESPASSING. LETHAL FORCE AUTHORIZED
THIS WAY EVERYONE, PLEASE.

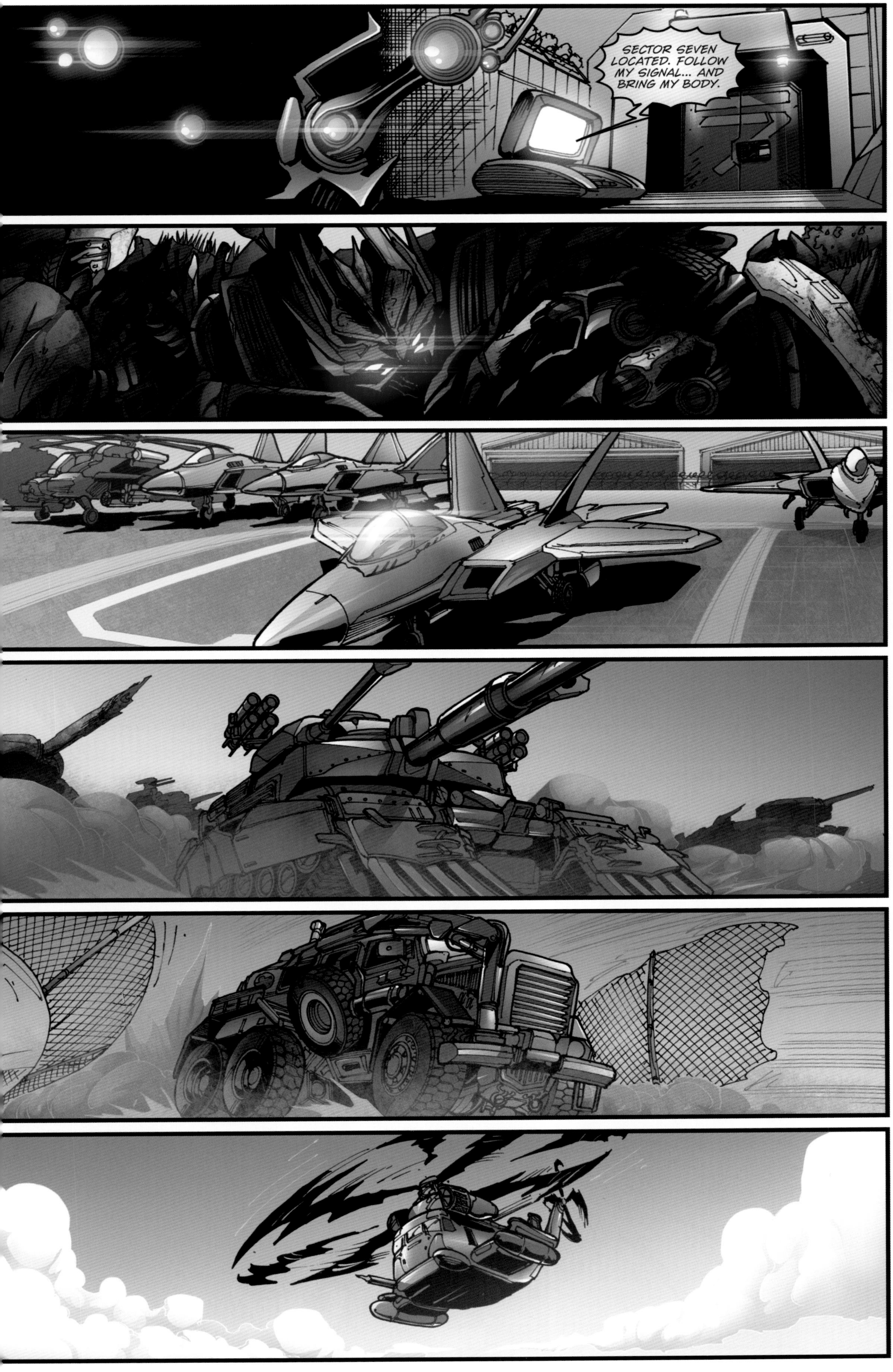
SECTOR SEVEN LOCATED. FOLLOW MY SIGNAL... AND BRING MY BODY.

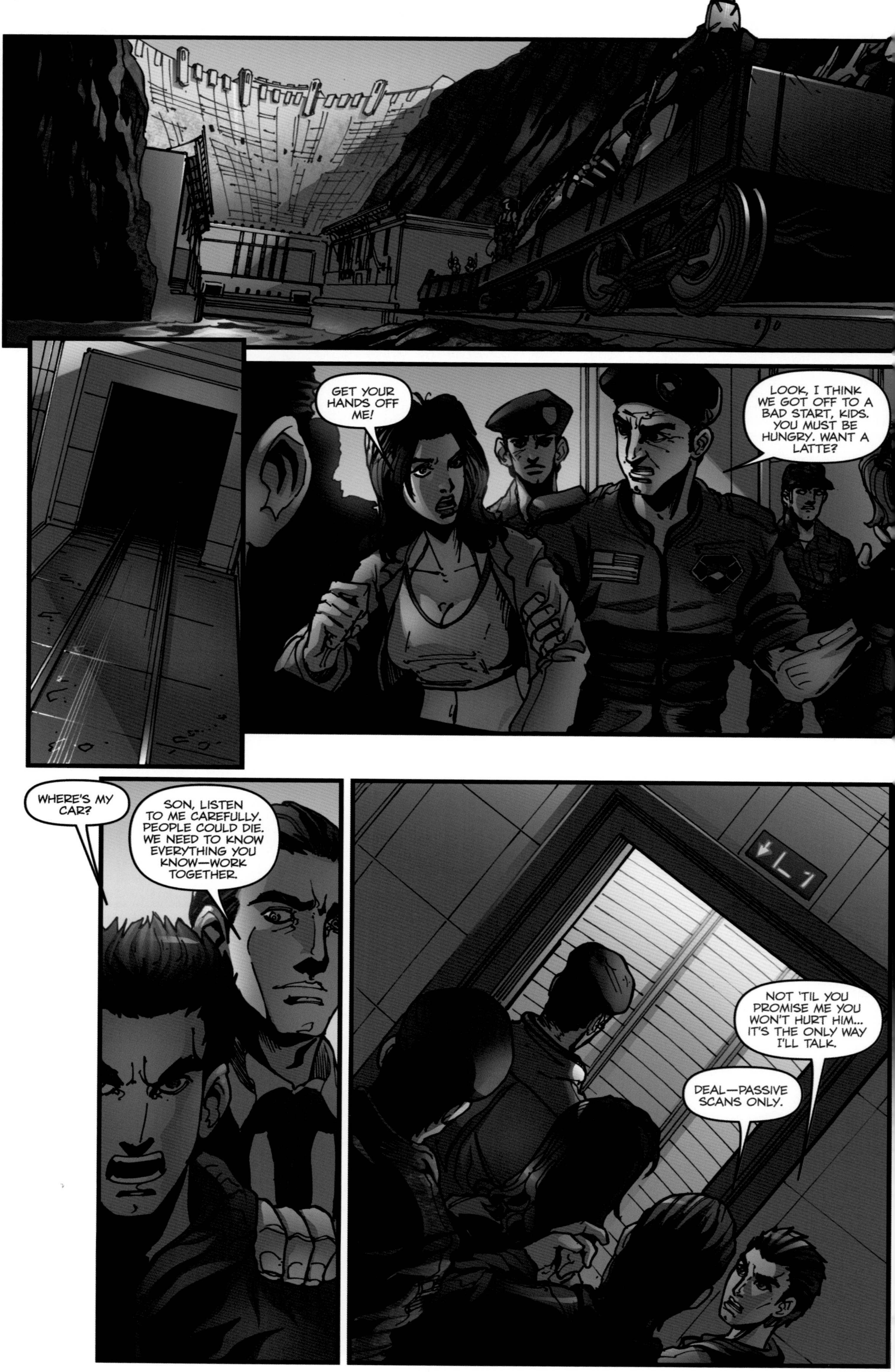
GET YOUR HANDS OFF ME!
LOOK, I THINK WE GOT OFF TO A BAD START, KIDS. YOU MUST BE HUNGRY. WANT A LATTE?
WHERE'S MY CAR?
SON, LISTEN TO ME CAREFULLY. PEOPLE COULD DIE. WE NEED TO KNOW EVERYTHING YOU KNOW—WORK TOGETHER.
NOT 'TIL YOU PROMISE ME YOU WON'T HURT HIM... IT'S THE ONLY WAY I'LL TALK.
DEAL—PASSIVE SCANS ONLY.

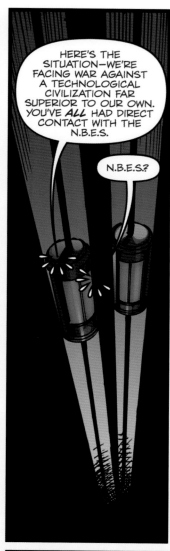

HERE'S THE SITUATION—WE'RE FACING WAR AGAINST A TECHNOLOGICAL CIVILIZATION FAR SUPERIOR TO OUR OWN. YOU'VE ALL HAD DIRECT CONTACT WITH THE N.B.E.S.

N.B.E.S.?

NON-BIOLOGICAL EXTRA-TERRESTRIALS. TRY AND KEEP UP WITH THE ACRONYMS.

THEY'RE CALLED TRANSFORMERS.

THEY TOLD YOU THAT?

THEY TOLD ME A LOT. WE'RE TIGHT.

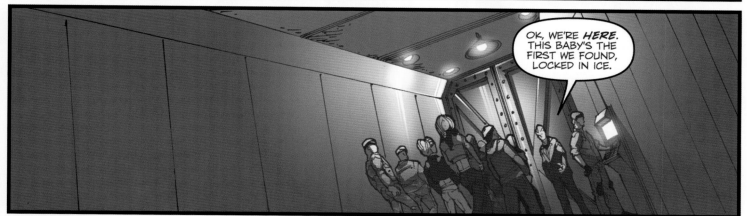

OK, WE'RE HERE. THIS BABY'S THE FIRST WE FOUND, LOCKED IN ICE.

DON'T FORGET TO BREATHE.

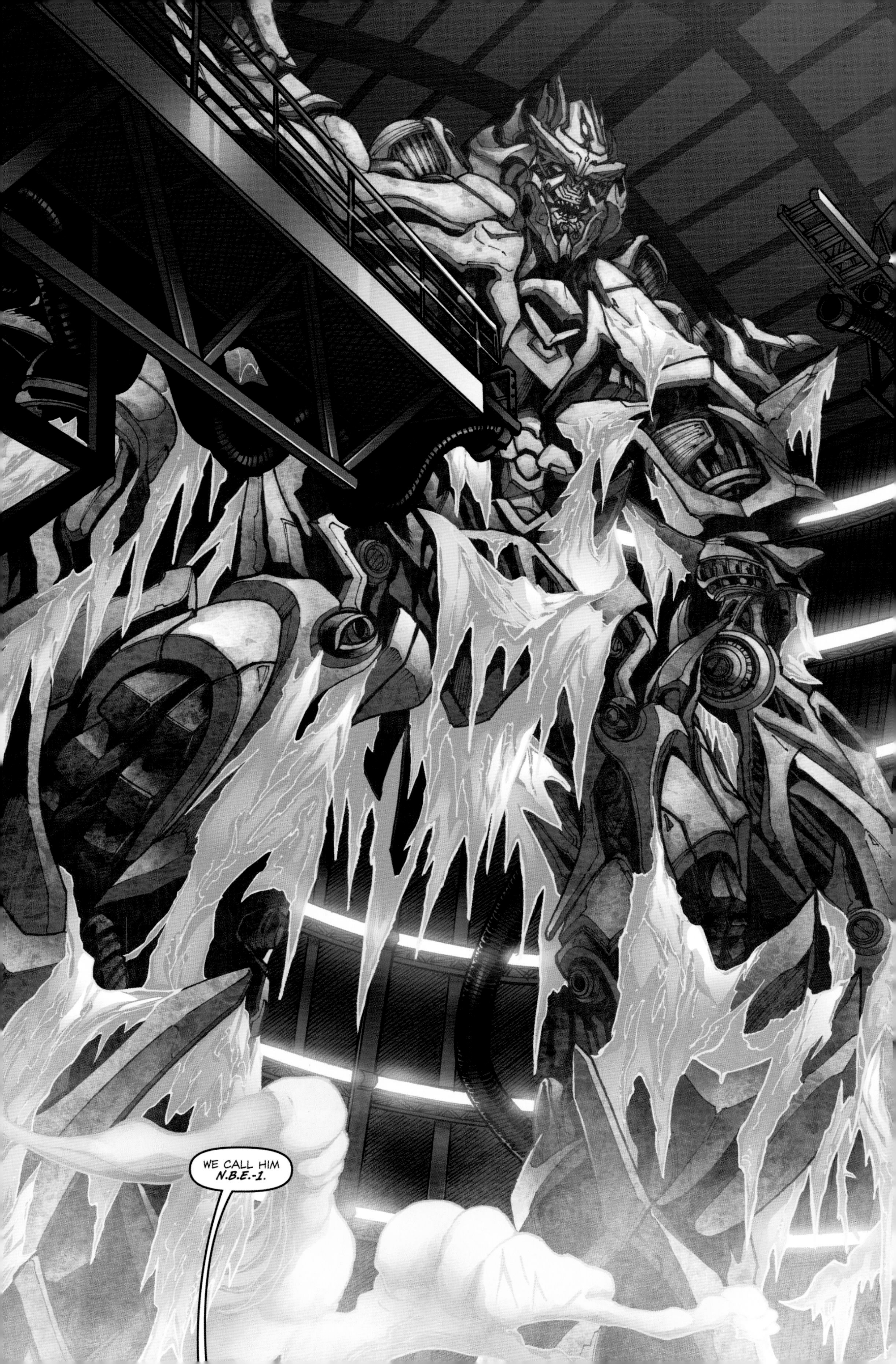
WE CALL HIM N.B.E.-1.

NO, SIR. THAT IS *MEGATRON*— LEADER OF THE *DECEPTICONS!*

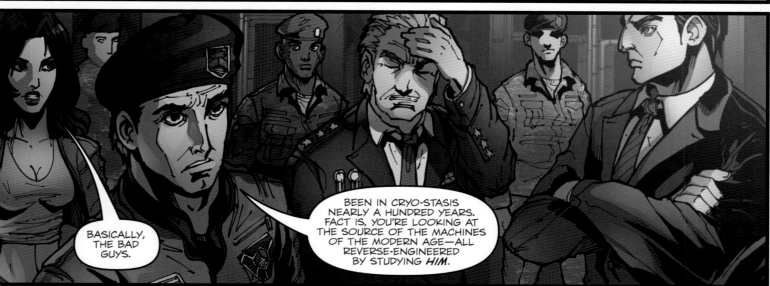

BASICALLY, THE BAD GUYS.

BEEN IN CRYO-STASIS NEARLY A HUNDRED YEARS. FACT IS, YOU'RE LOOKING AT THE SOURCE OF THE MACHINES OF THE MODERN AGE—ALL REVERSE-ENGINEERED BY STUDYING *HIM.*

BUT WHY ARE THEY HERE? WHY EARTH?

THE *ALLSPARK.* MEGATRON WANTS IT TO TRANSFORM ALL OUR TECHNOLOGY AND TAKE OVER THE UNIVERSE.

WAIT...

YOU *KNOW* WHERE IT IS!

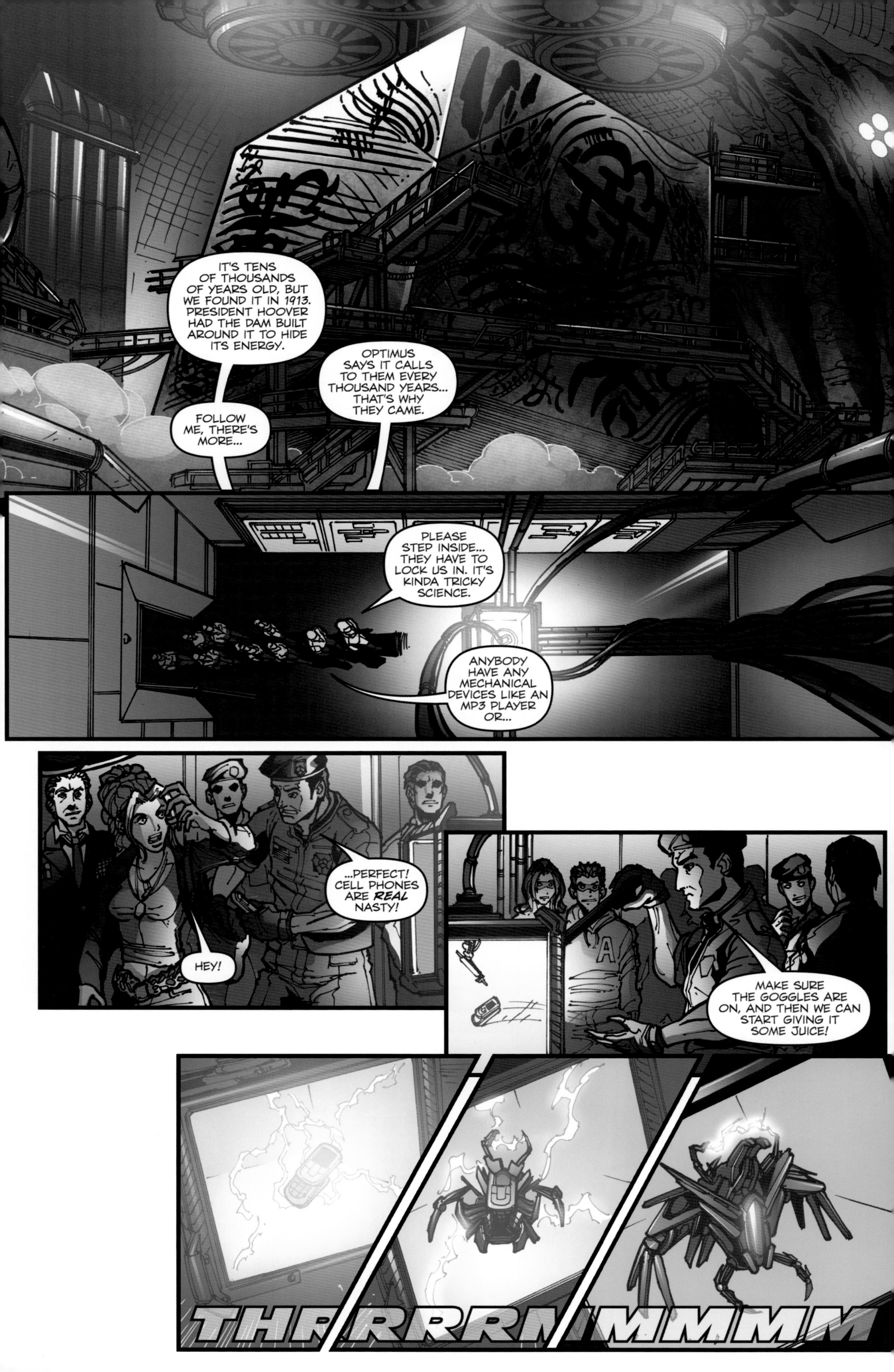
IT'S TENS OF THOUSANDS OF YEARS OLD, BUT WE FOUND IT IN 1913. PRESIDENT HOOVER HAD THE DAM BUILT AROUND IT TO HIDE ITS ENERGY.
OPTIMUS SAYS IT CALLS TO THEM EVERY THOUSAND YEARS... THAT'S WHY THEY CAME.
FOLLOW ME, THERE'S MORE...
PLEASE STEP INSIDE... THEY HAVE TO LOCK US IN. IT'S KINDA TRICKY SCIENCE.
ANYBODY HAVE ANY MECHANICAL DEVICES LIKE AN MP3 PLAYER OR...
...PERFECT! CELL PHONES ARE **REAL** NASTY!
HEY!
MAKE SURE THE GOGGLES ARE ON, AND THEN WE CAN START GIVING IT SOME JUICE!
THRRRRMMMMMM

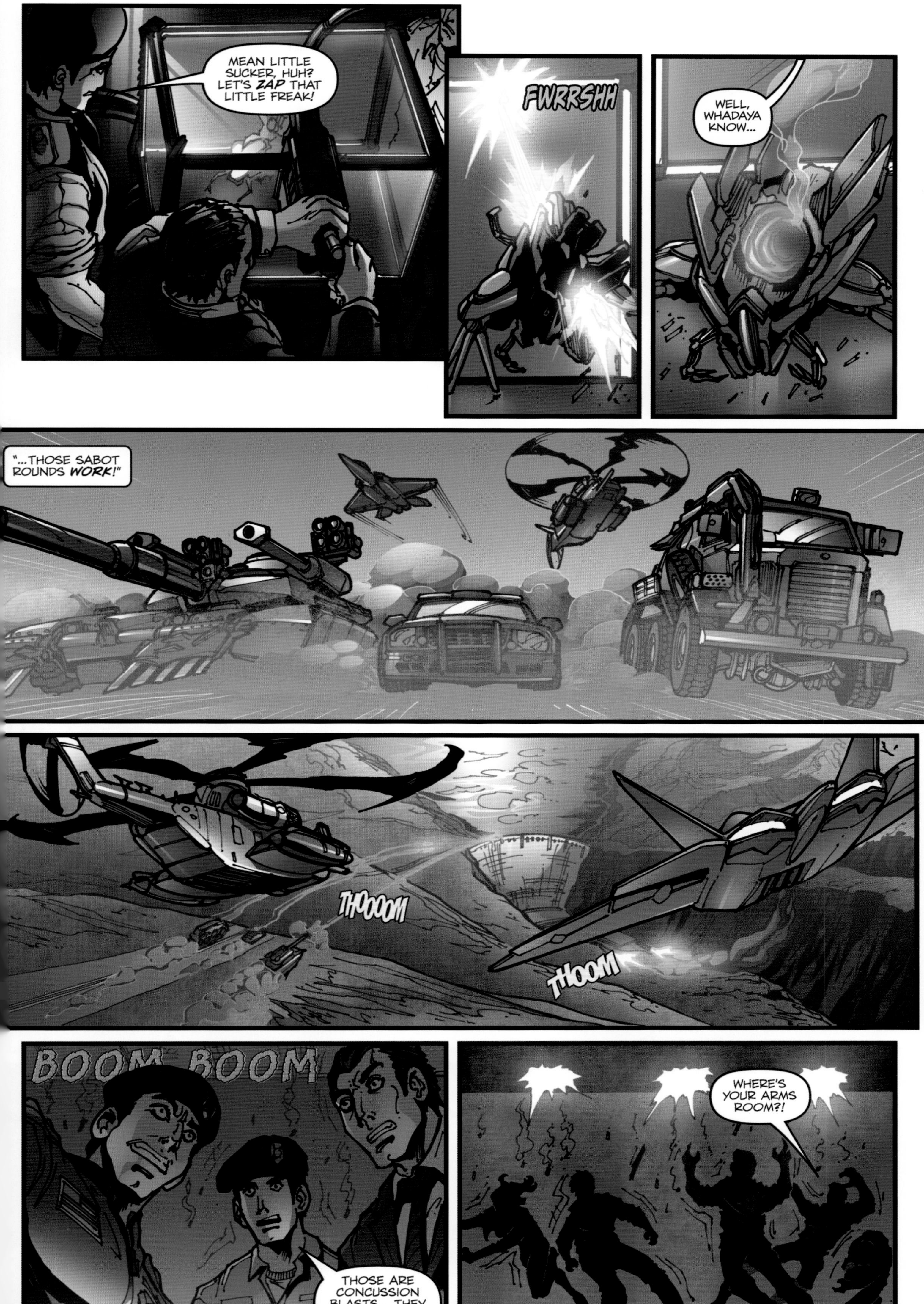
MEAN LITTLE SUCKER, HUH? LET'S ZAP THAT LITTLE FREAK!
FWRRSHH
WELL, WHADAYA KNOW...
"...THOSE SABOT ROUNDS WORK!"
THOOOOM
THOOM
BOOM BOOM
THOSE ARE CONCUSSION BLASTS... THEY KNOW IT'S HERE!
WHERE'S YOUR ARMS ROOM?!

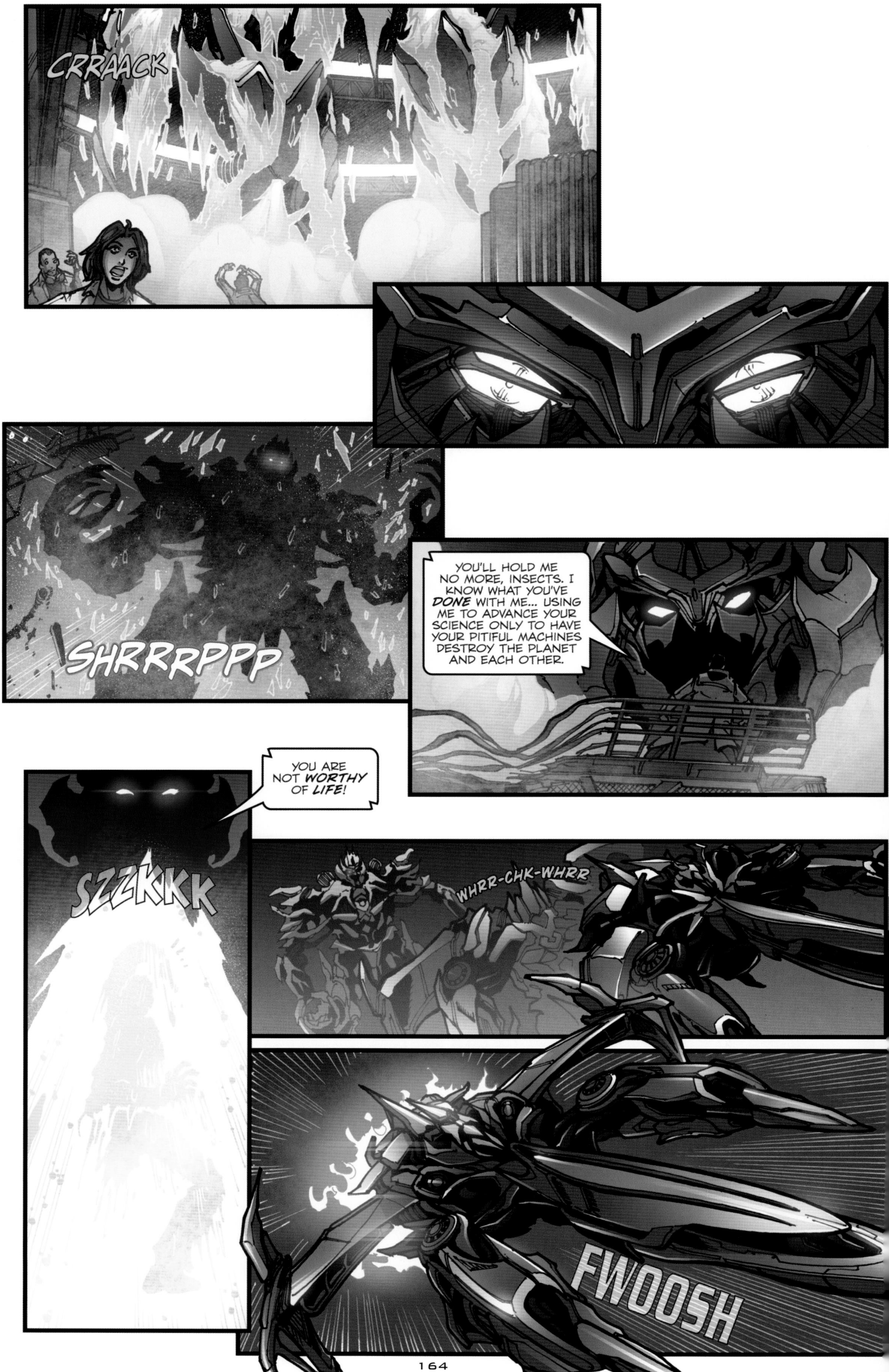
CRRAACK
SHRRRPPP
YOU'LL HOLD ME NO MORE, INSECTS. I KNOW WHAT YOU'VE DONE WITH ME... USING ME TO ADVANCE YOUR SCIENCE ONLY TO HAVE YOUR PITIFUL MACHINES DESTROY THE PLANET AND EACH OTHER.
YOU ARE NOT WORTHY OF LIFE!
SZZKKK
WHRR-CHK-WHRR
FWOOSH

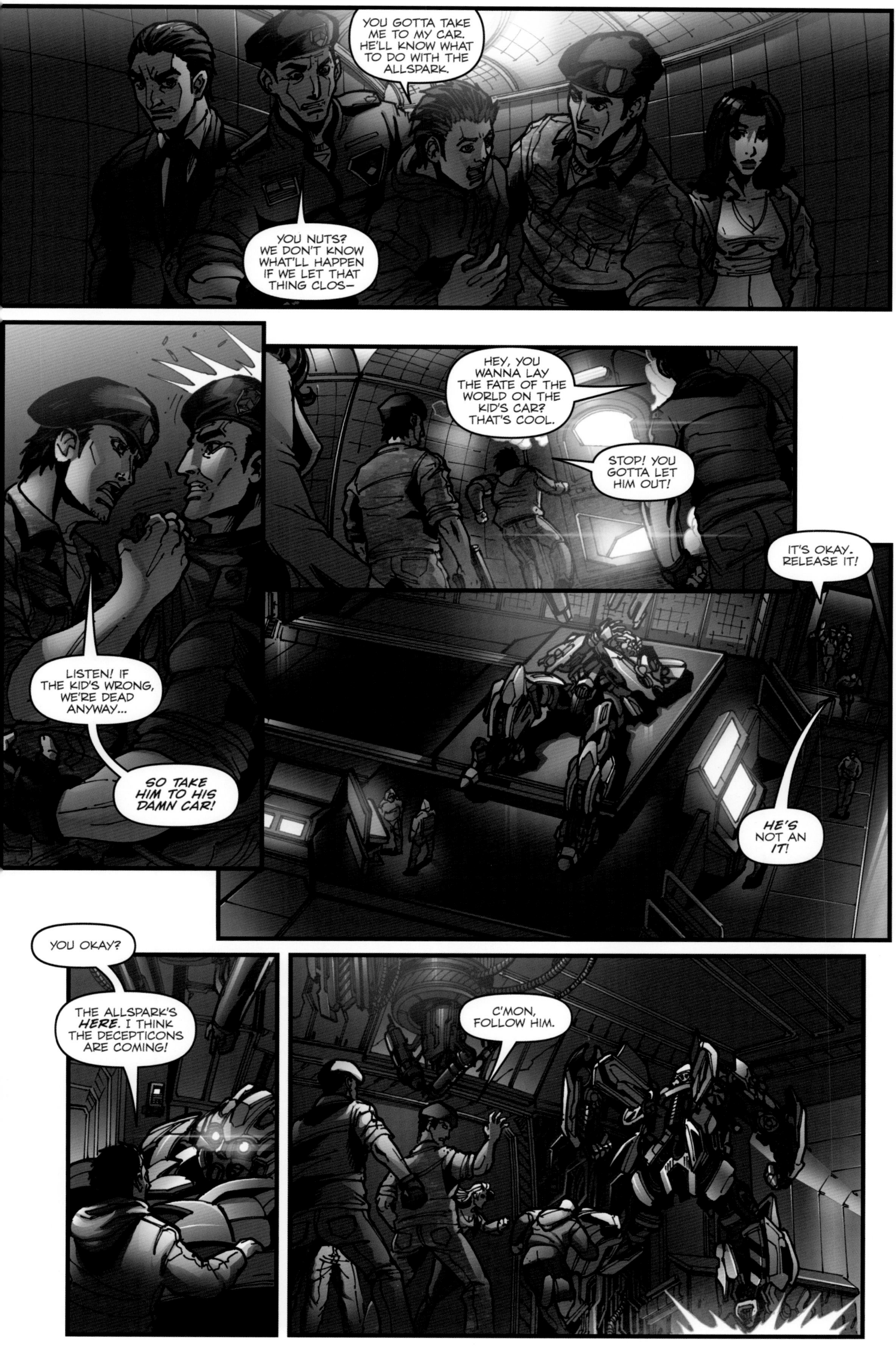
YOU GOTTA TAKE ME TO MY CAR. HE'LL KNOW WHAT TO DO WITH THE ALLSPARK.
YOU NUTS? WE DON'T KNOW WHAT'LL HAPPEN IF WE LET THAT THING CLOS–
HEY, YOU WANNA LAY THE FATE OF THE WORLD ON THE KID'S CAR? THAT'S COOL.
STOP! YOU GOTTA LET HIM OUT!
LISTEN! IF THE KID'S WRONG, WE'RE DEAD ANYWAY...
SO TAKE HIM TO HIS DAMN CAR!
IT'S OKAY. RELEASE IT!
HE'S NOT AN IT!
YOU OKAY?
THE ALLSPARK'S HERE. I THINK THE DECEPTICONS ARE COMING!
C'MON, FOLLOW HIM.

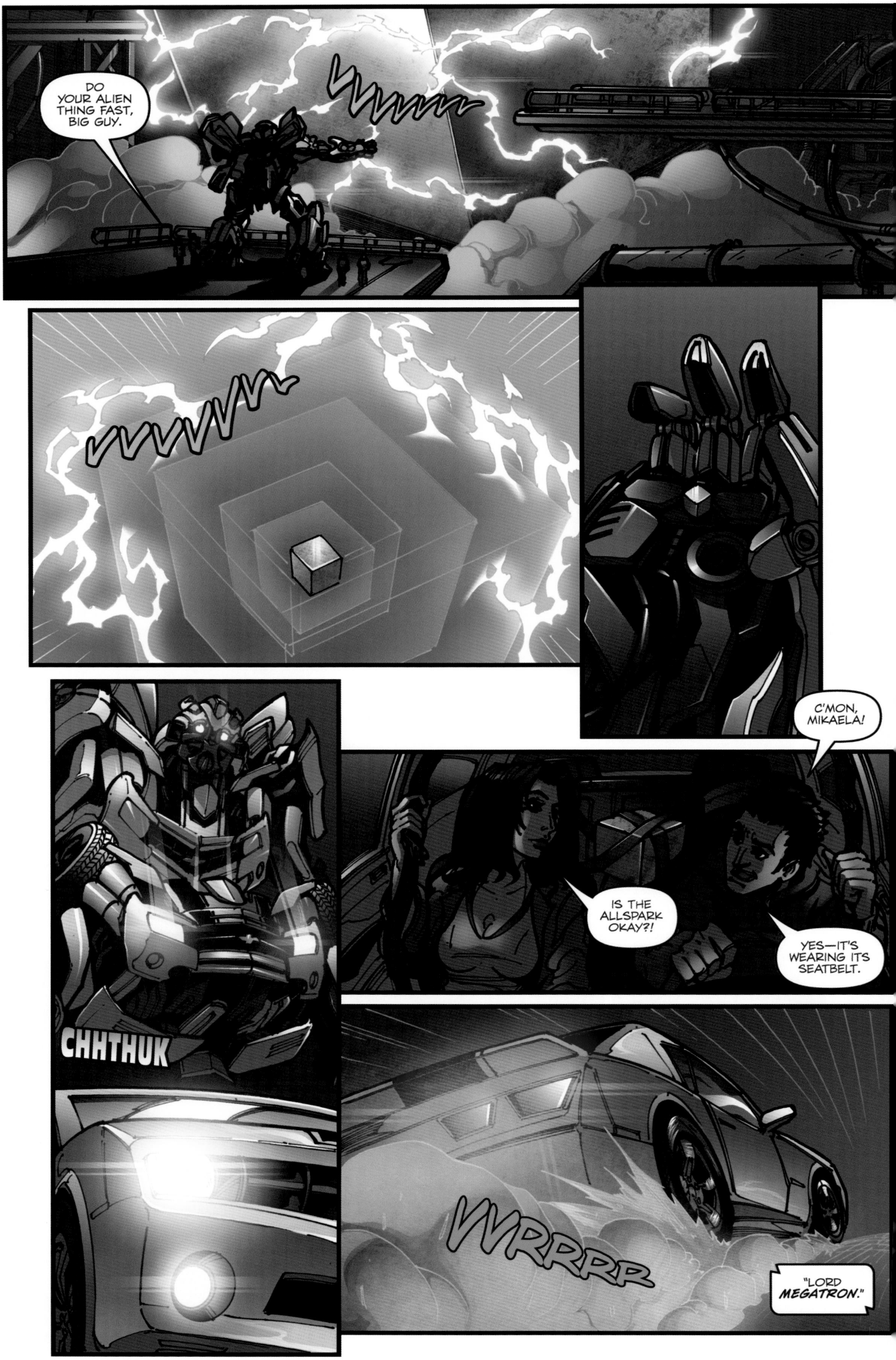

DO YOUR ALIEN THING FAST, BIG GUY.
VVVVVVVV
VVVVVVVV
CHHTHUK
C'MON, MIKAELA!
IS THE ALLSPARK OKAY?!
YES—IT'S WEARING ITS SEATBELT.
VVRRRR
"LORD MEGATRON."

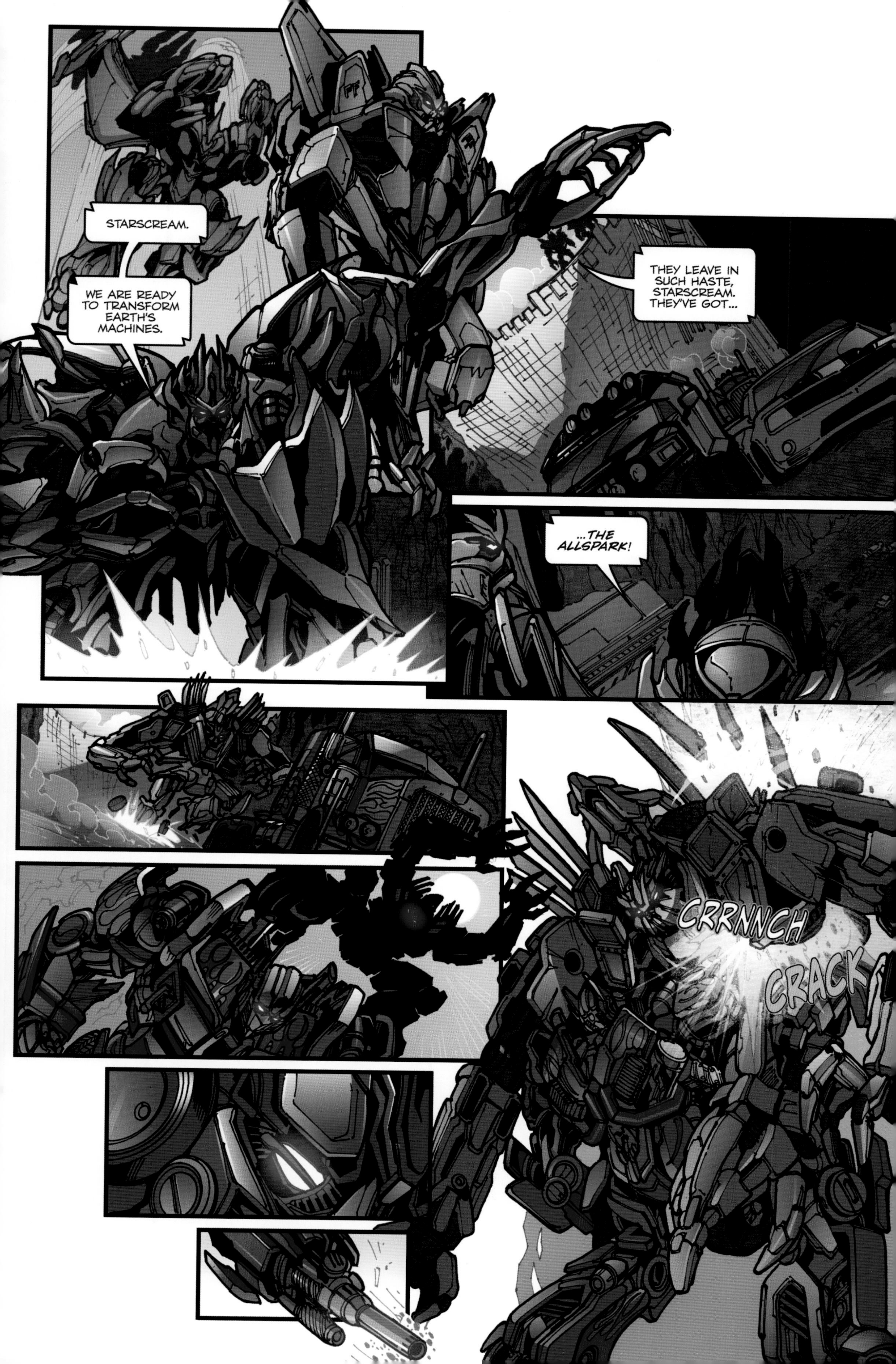
STARSCREAM.
WE ARE READY TO TRANSFORM EARTH'S MACHINES.
THEY LEAVE IN SUCH HASTE, STARSCREAM. THEY'VE GOT...
...THE ALLSPARK!
CRRNNCH
CRACK

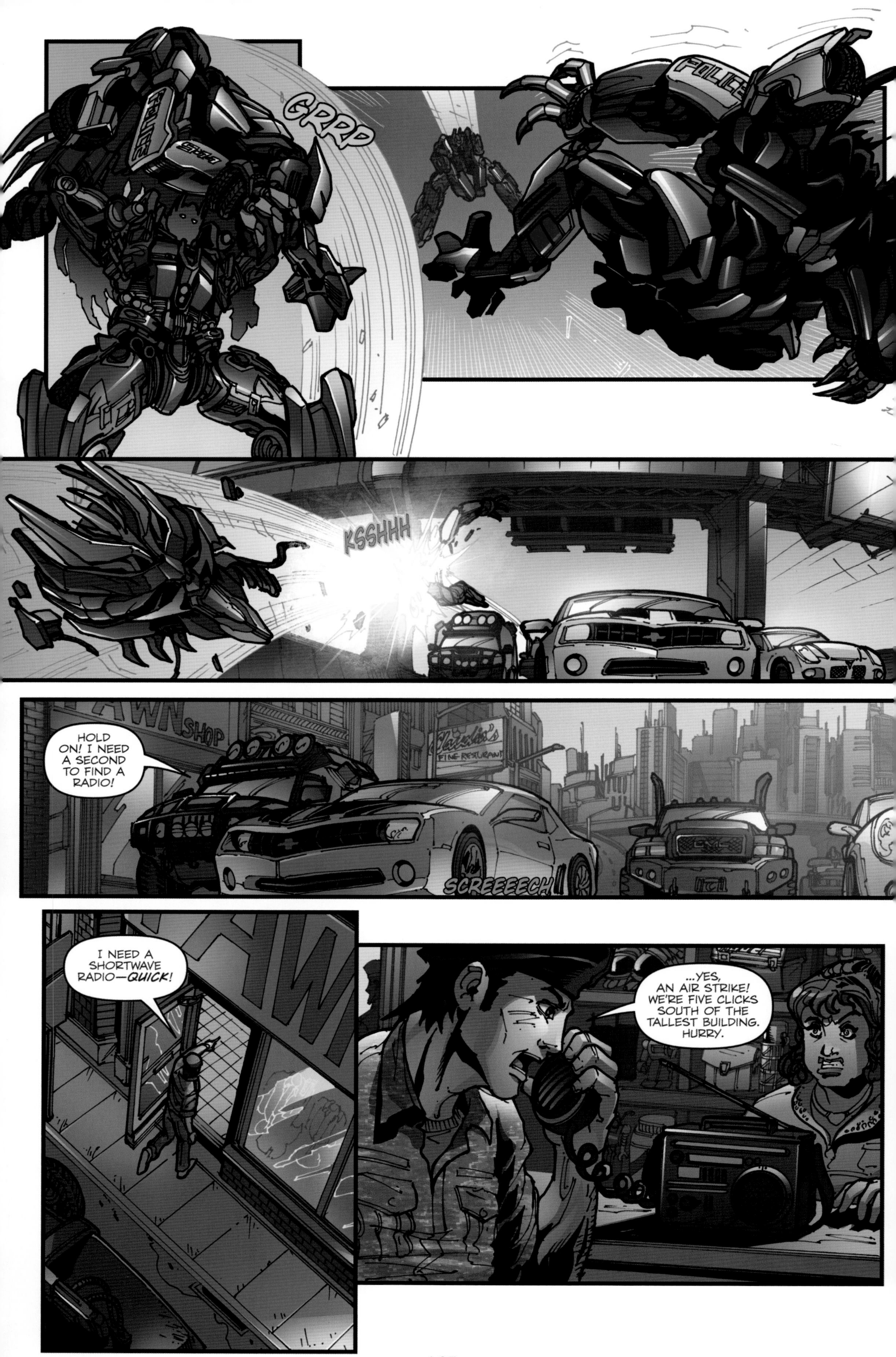
GRRP
KSSHHH
HOLD ON! I NEED A SECOND TO FIND A RADIO!
SHOP
FINE RESTURANT
SCREEEEECH
I NEED A SHORTWAVE RADIO—*QUICK*!
...YES, AN AIR STRIKE! WE'RE FIVE CLICKS SOUTH OF THE TALLEST BUILDING. HURRY.

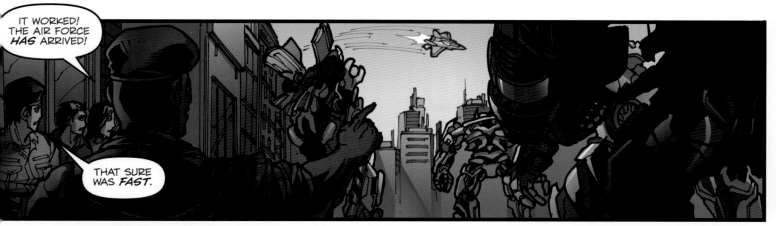

IT WORKED! THE AIR FORCE *HAS* ARRIVED!

THAT SURE WAS *FAST.*

SOMETHING'S NOT RIGHT...

FLANKING POSITIONS!

THOOOOM

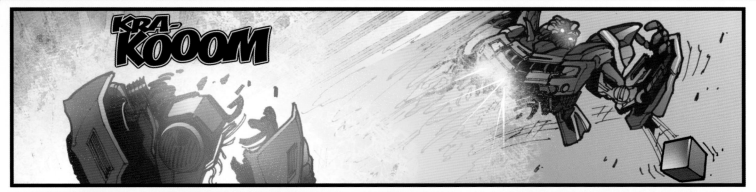

KRA-KOOOM

BUMBLEBEE...

169

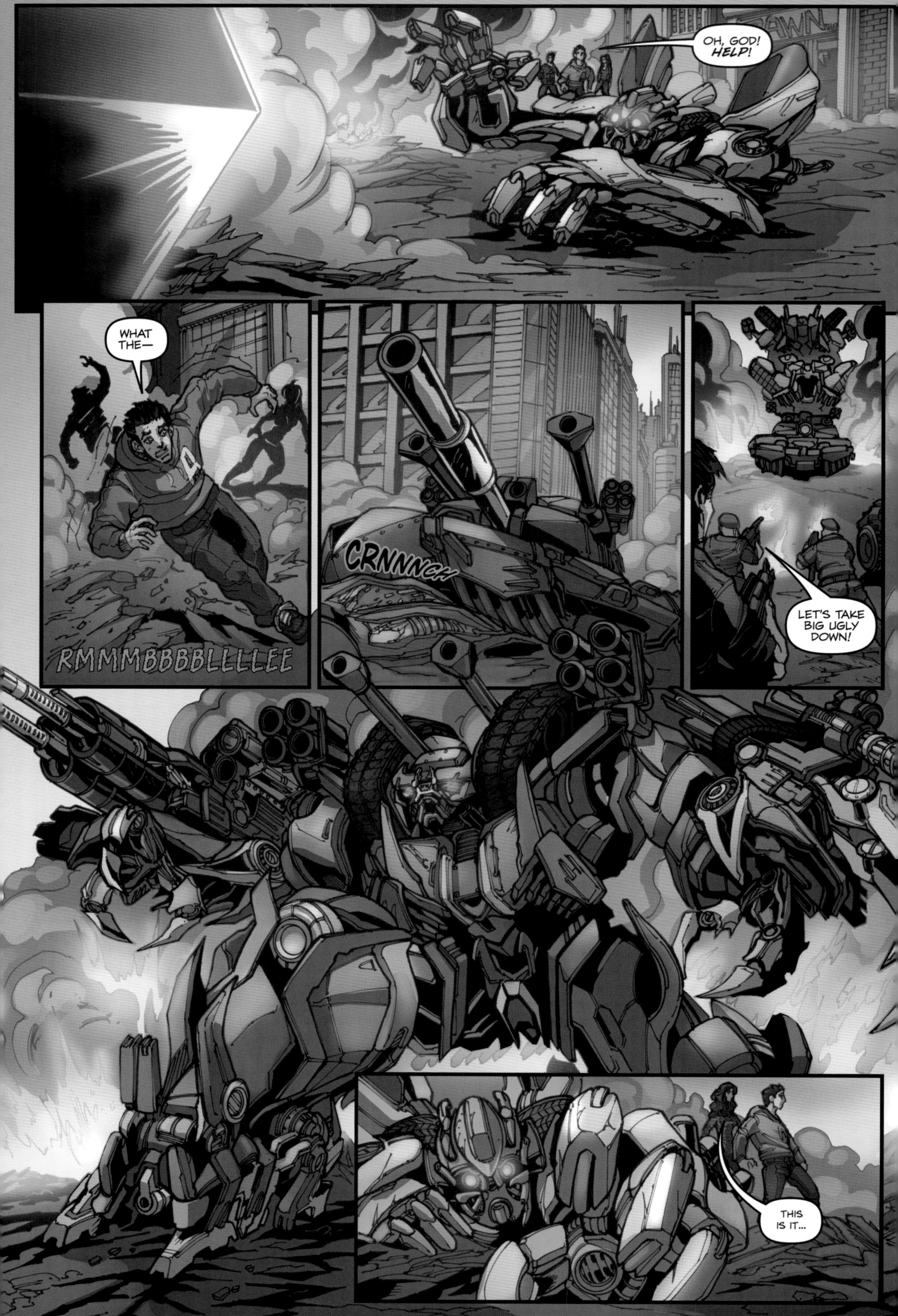
PAWN
OH, GOD! HELP!
WHAT THE—
RMMMBBBBLLLLEE
CRNNNCH
LET'S TAKE BIG UGLY DOWN!
THIS IS IT...

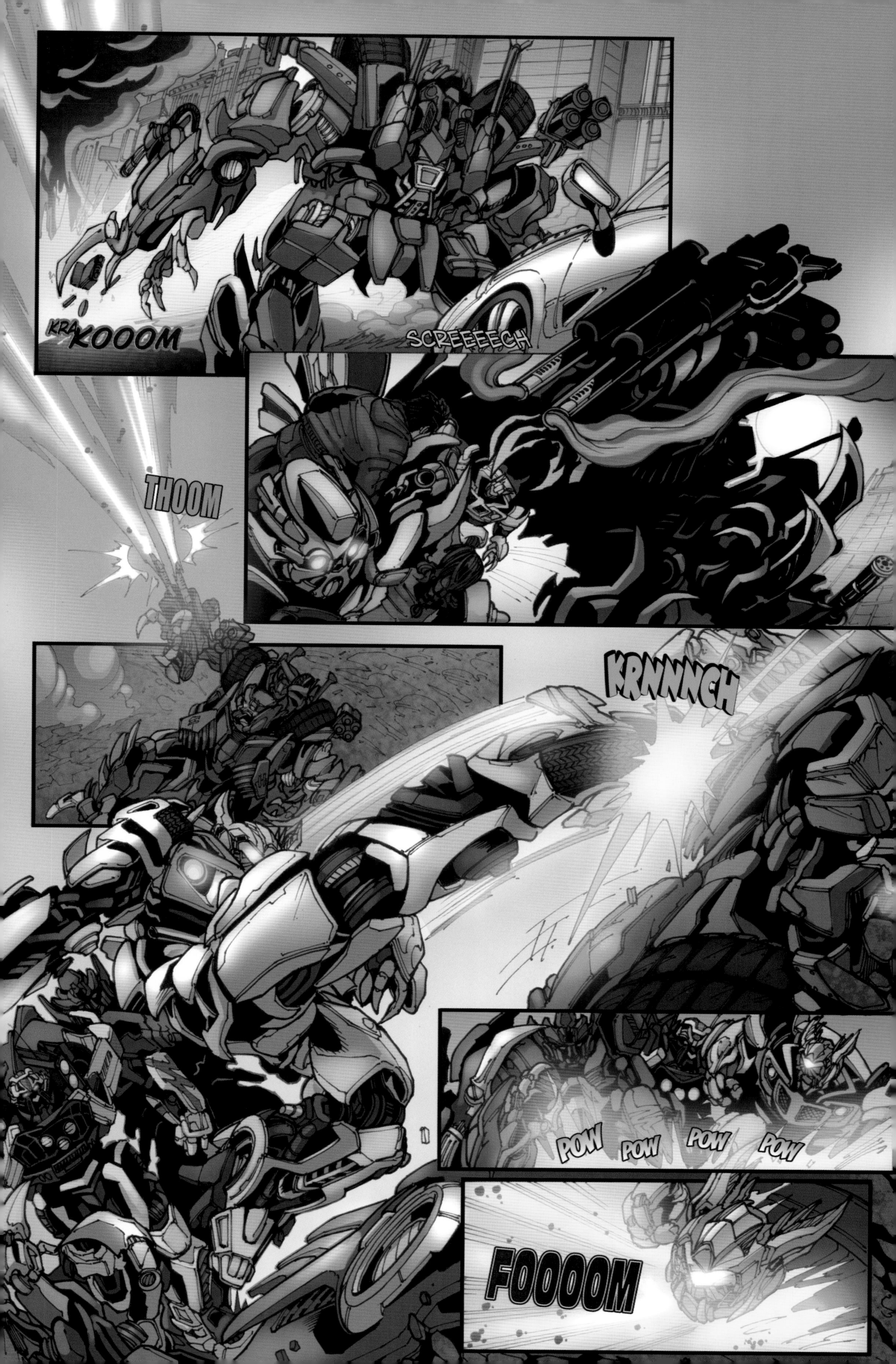
KRAKOOOM
SCREEEEECH
THOOM
KRNNNCH
POW POW POW POW
FOOOOM

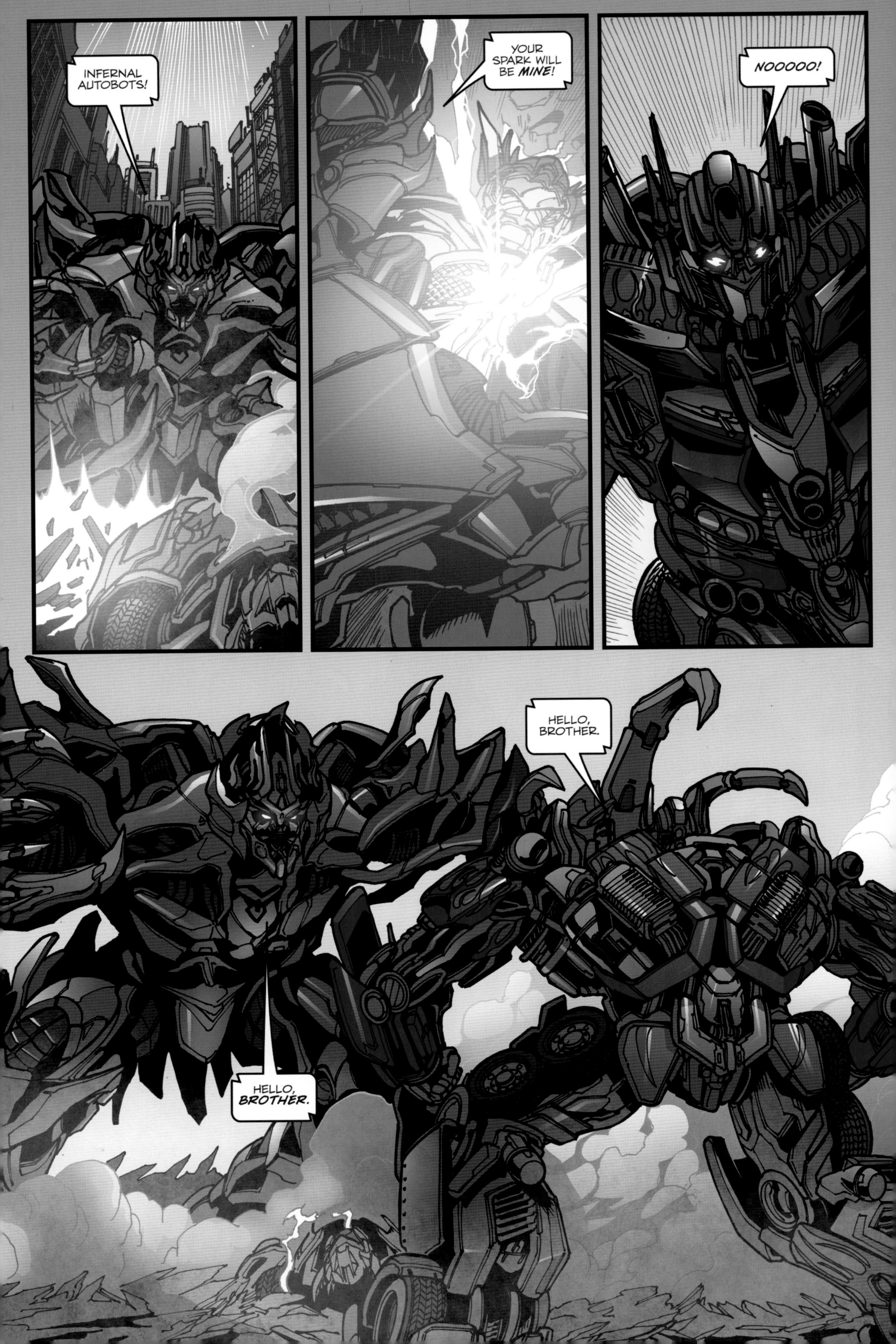
INFERNAL AUTOBOTS!
YOUR SPARK WILL BE *MINE*!
NOOOOO!
HELLO, BROTHER.
HELLO, *BROTHER*.

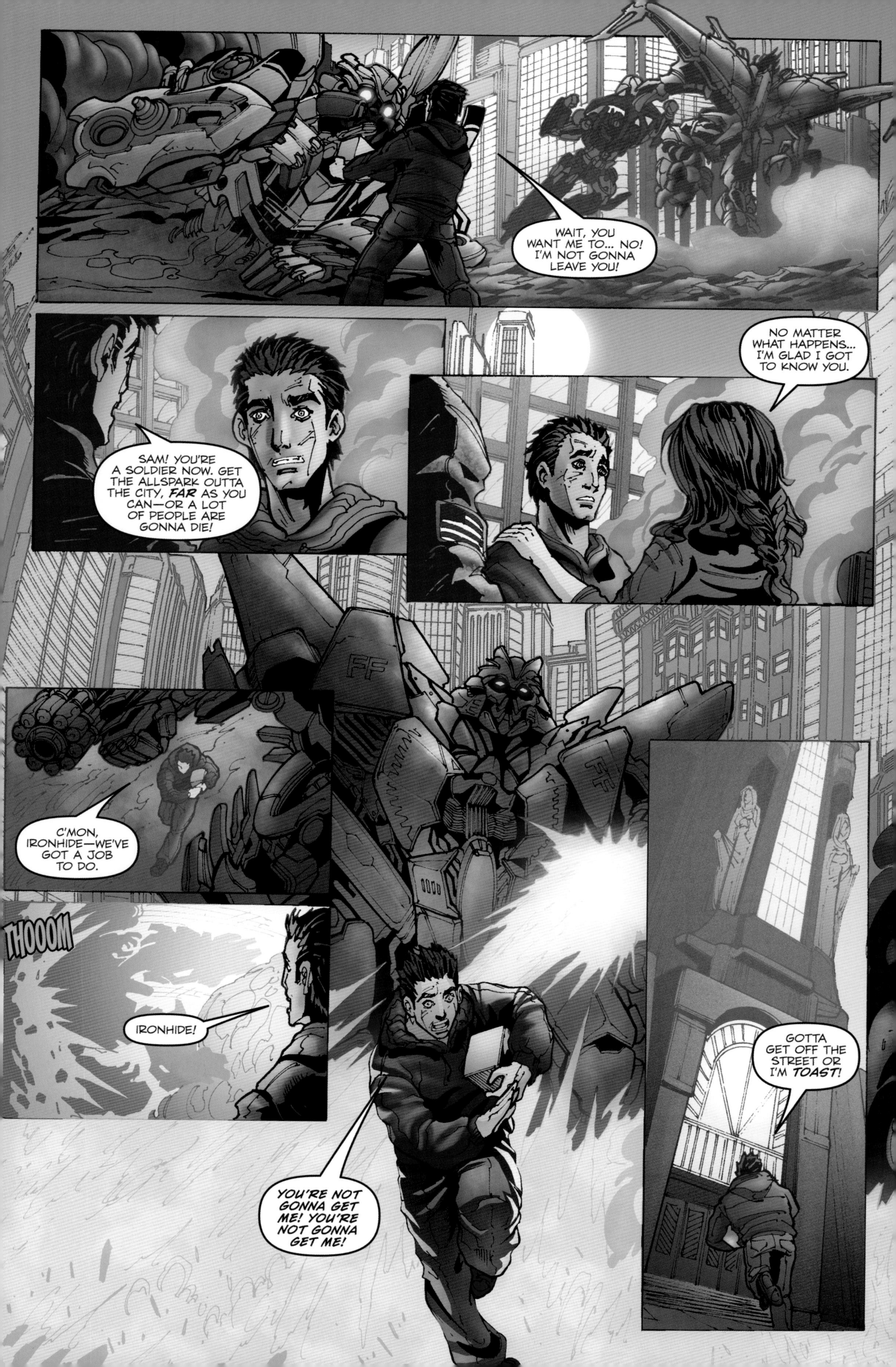
WAIT, YOU WANT ME TO... NO! I'M NOT GONNA LEAVE YOU!
SAM! YOU'RE A SOLDIER NOW. GET THE ALLSPARK OUTTA THE CITY, FAR AS YOU CAN—OR A LOT OF PEOPLE ARE GONNA DIE!
NO MATTER WHAT HAPPENS... I'M GLAD I GOT TO KNOW YOU.
C'MON, IRONHIDE—WE'VE GOT A JOB TO DO.
THOOOM
IRONHIDE!
YOU'RE NOT GONNA GET ME! YOU'RE NOT GONNA GET ME!
GOTTA GET OFF THE STREET OR I'M TOAST!

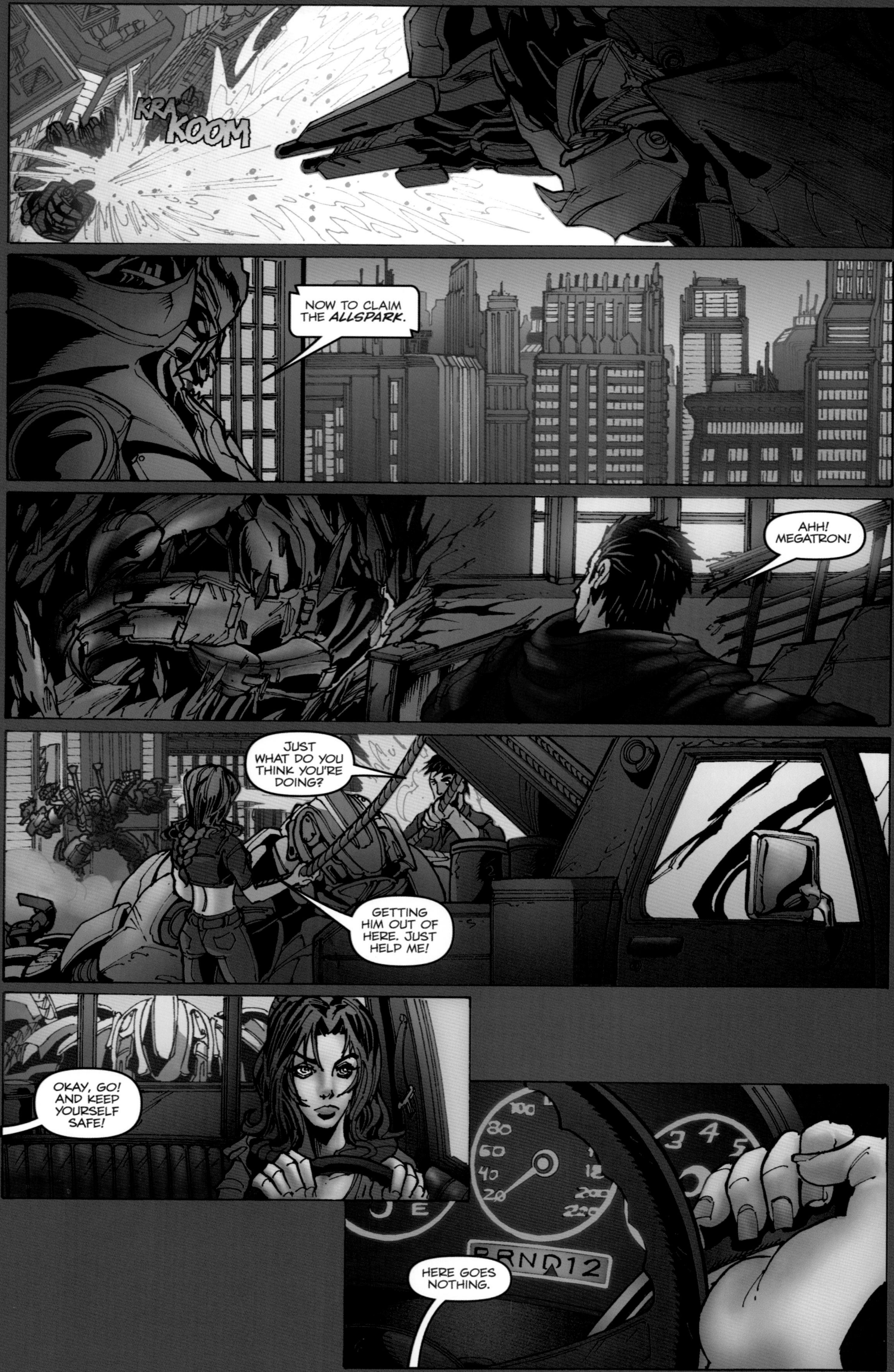
KRA-KOOM
NOW TO CLAIM THE ALLSPARK.
AHH! MEGATRON!
JUST WHAT DO YOU THINK YOU'RE DOING?
GETTING HIM OUT OF HERE. JUST HELP ME!
OKAY, GO! AND KEEP YOURSELF SAFE!
HERE GOES NOTHING.

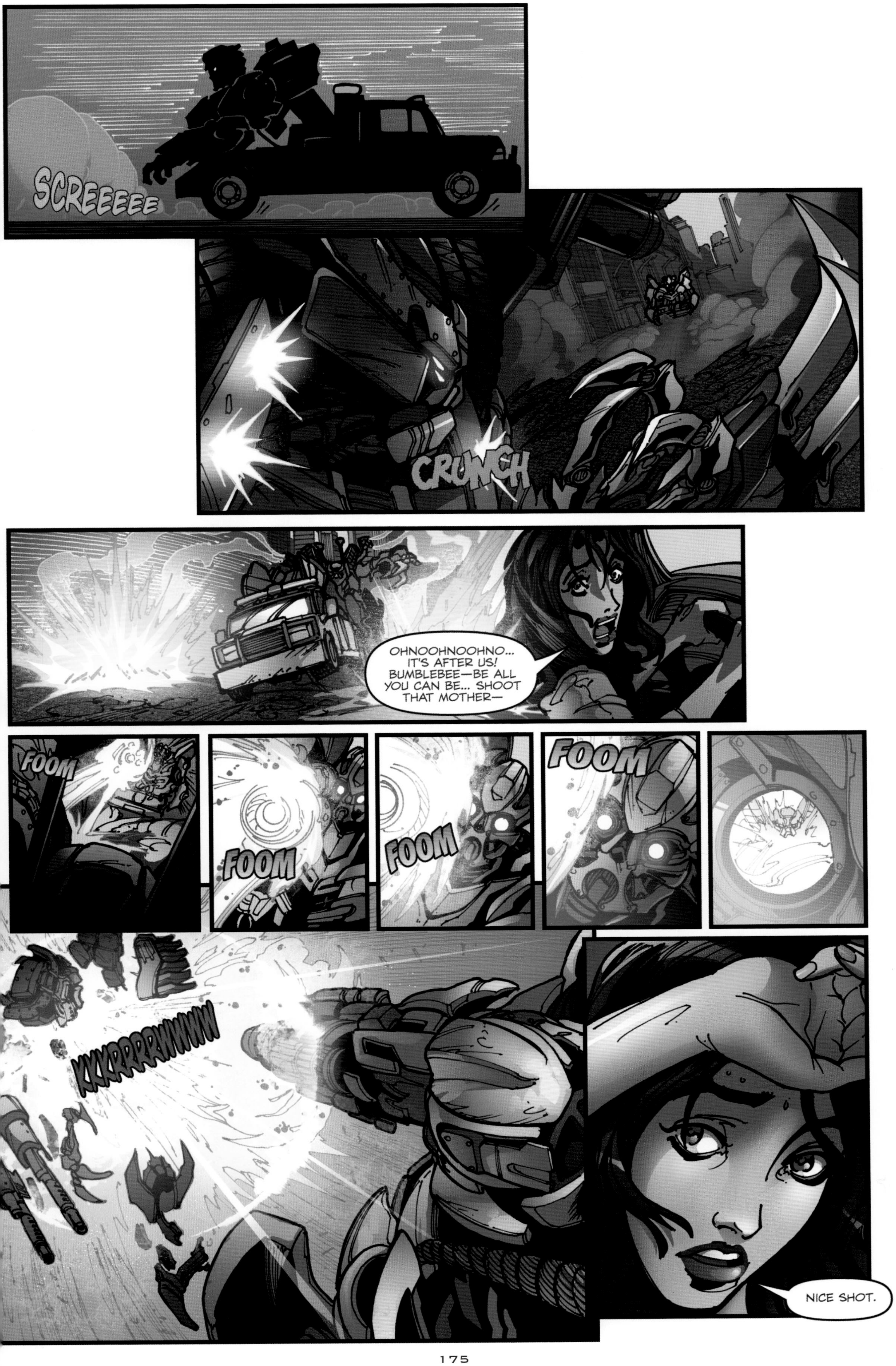
SCREEEEEE
CRUNCH
OHNOOHNOOHNO... IT'S AFTER US! BUMBLEBEE—BE ALL YOU CAN BE... SHOOT THAT MOTHER—
FOOM
FOOM
FOOM
FOOM
KKKRRRRWWWW
NICE SHOT.

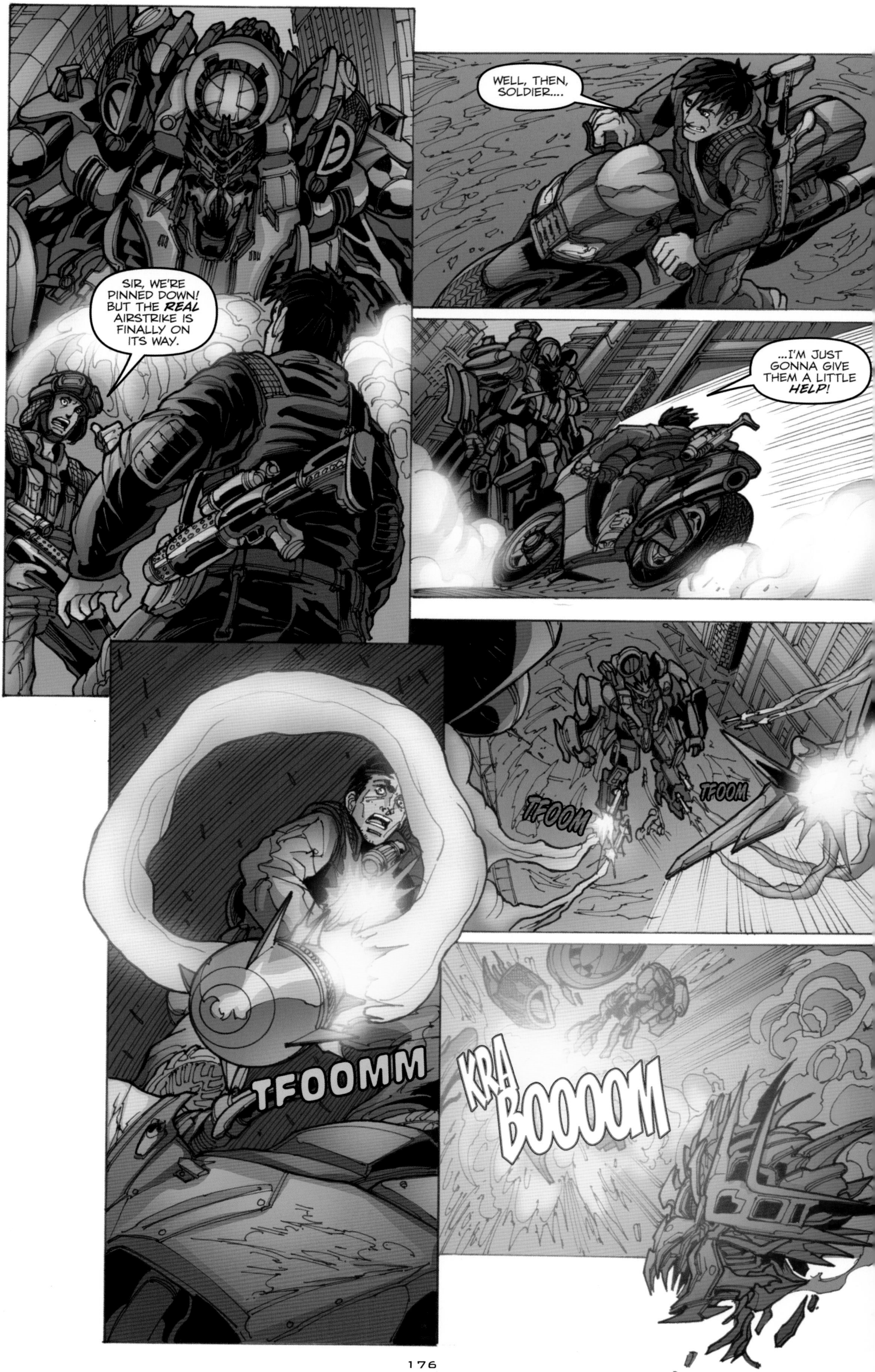
SIR, WE'RE PINNED DOWN! BUT THE REAL AIRSTRIKE IS FINALLY ON ITS WAY.
WELL, THEN, SOLDIER....
...I'M JUST GONNA GIVE THEM A LITTLE HELP!
TFOOMM
TFOOM
TFOOM
KRA BOOOOM

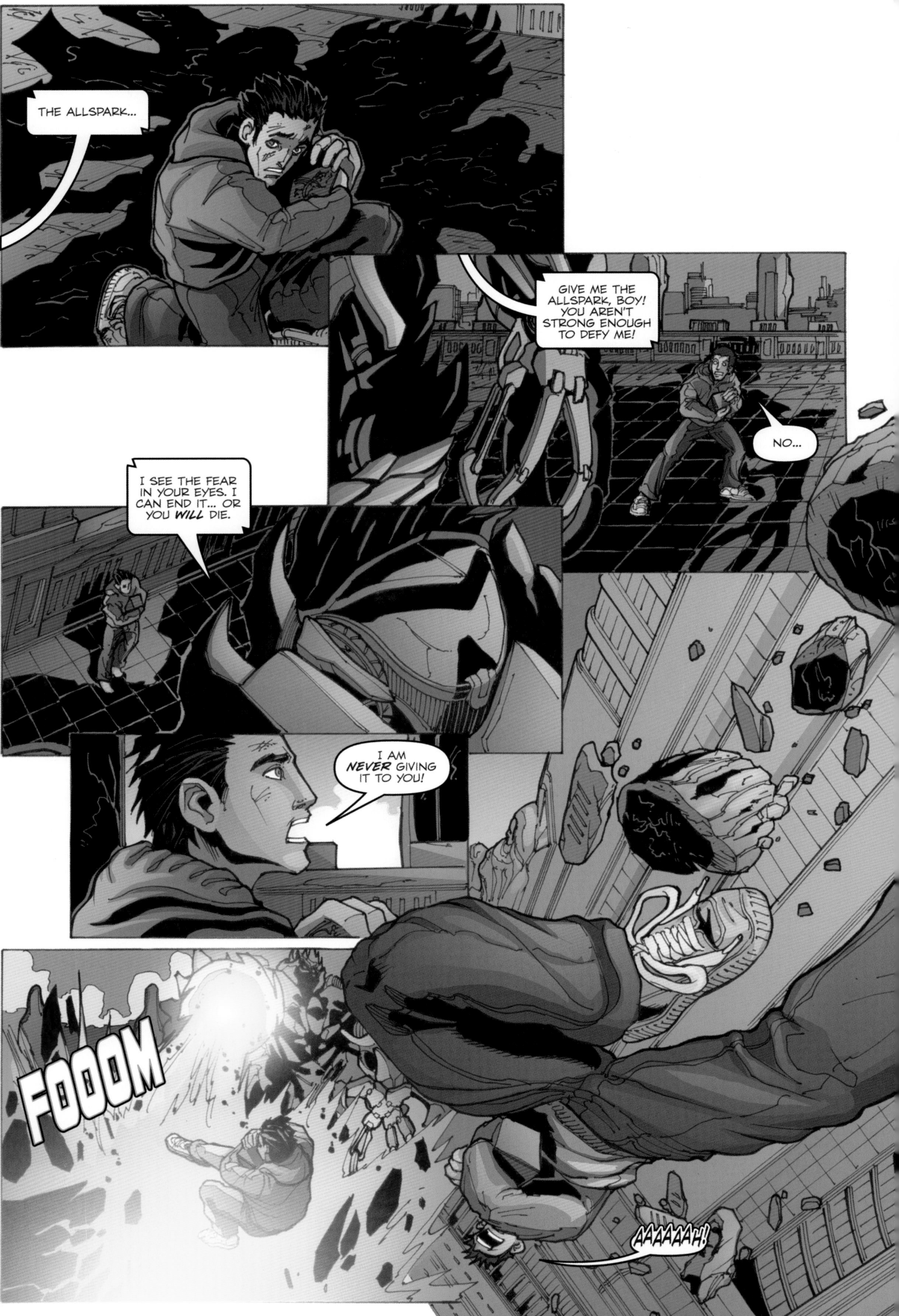
THE ALLSPARK...
GIVE ME THE ALLSPARK, BOY! YOU AREN'T STRONG ENOUGH TO DEFY ME!
NO...
I SEE THE FEAR IN YOUR EYES. I CAN END IT... OR YOU WILL DIE.
I AM NEVER GIVING IT TO YOU!
FOOOM
AAAAAAH!

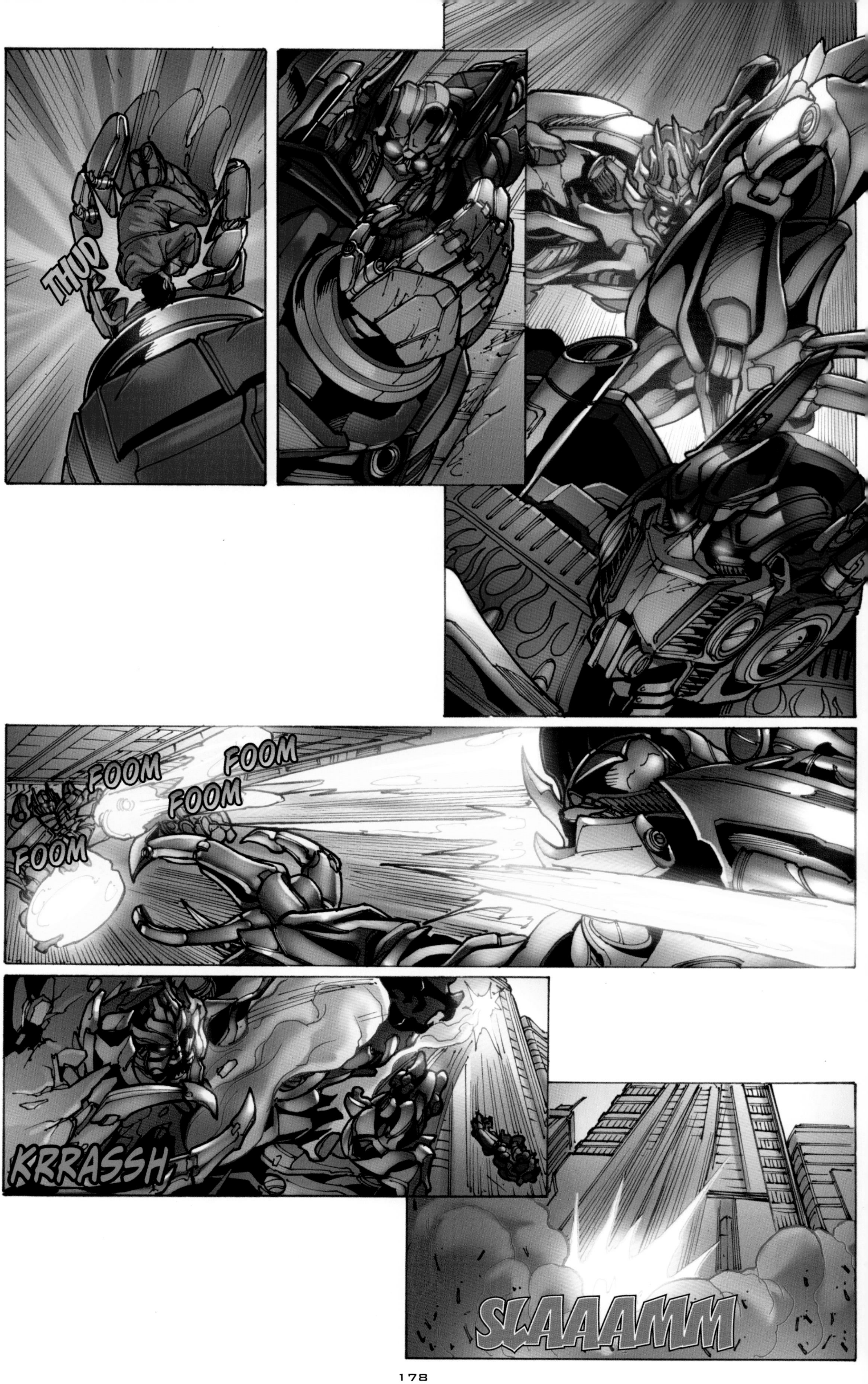
THUD
FOOM
FOOM
FOOM
FOOM
KRRASSH
SLAAAAMM

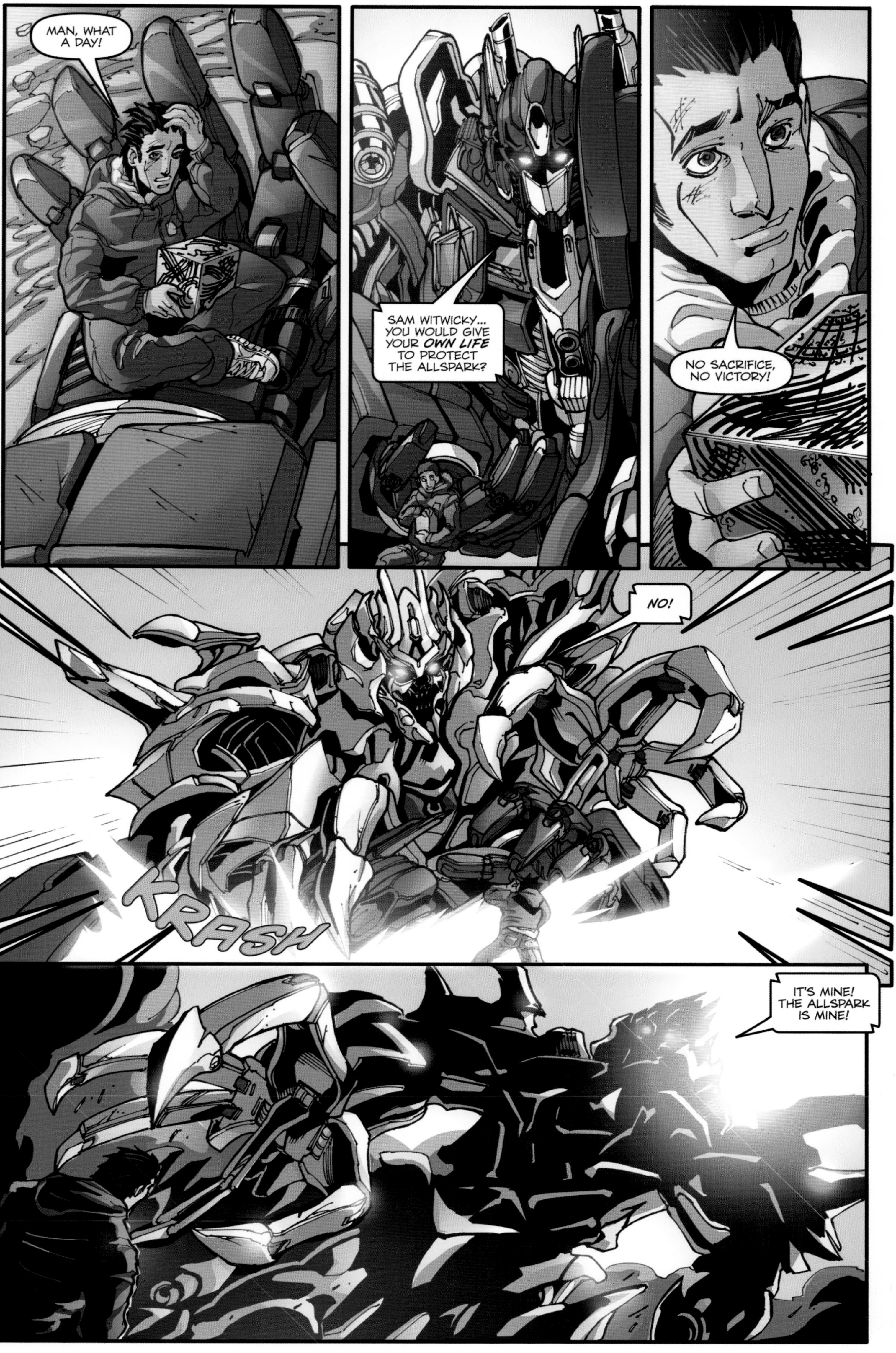
MAN, WHAT A DAY!
SAM WITWICKY... YOU WOULD GIVE YOUR OWN LIFE TO PROTECT THE ALLSPARK?
NO SACRIFICE, NO VICTORY!
NO!
KRASH
IT'S MINE! THE ALLSPARK IS MINE!

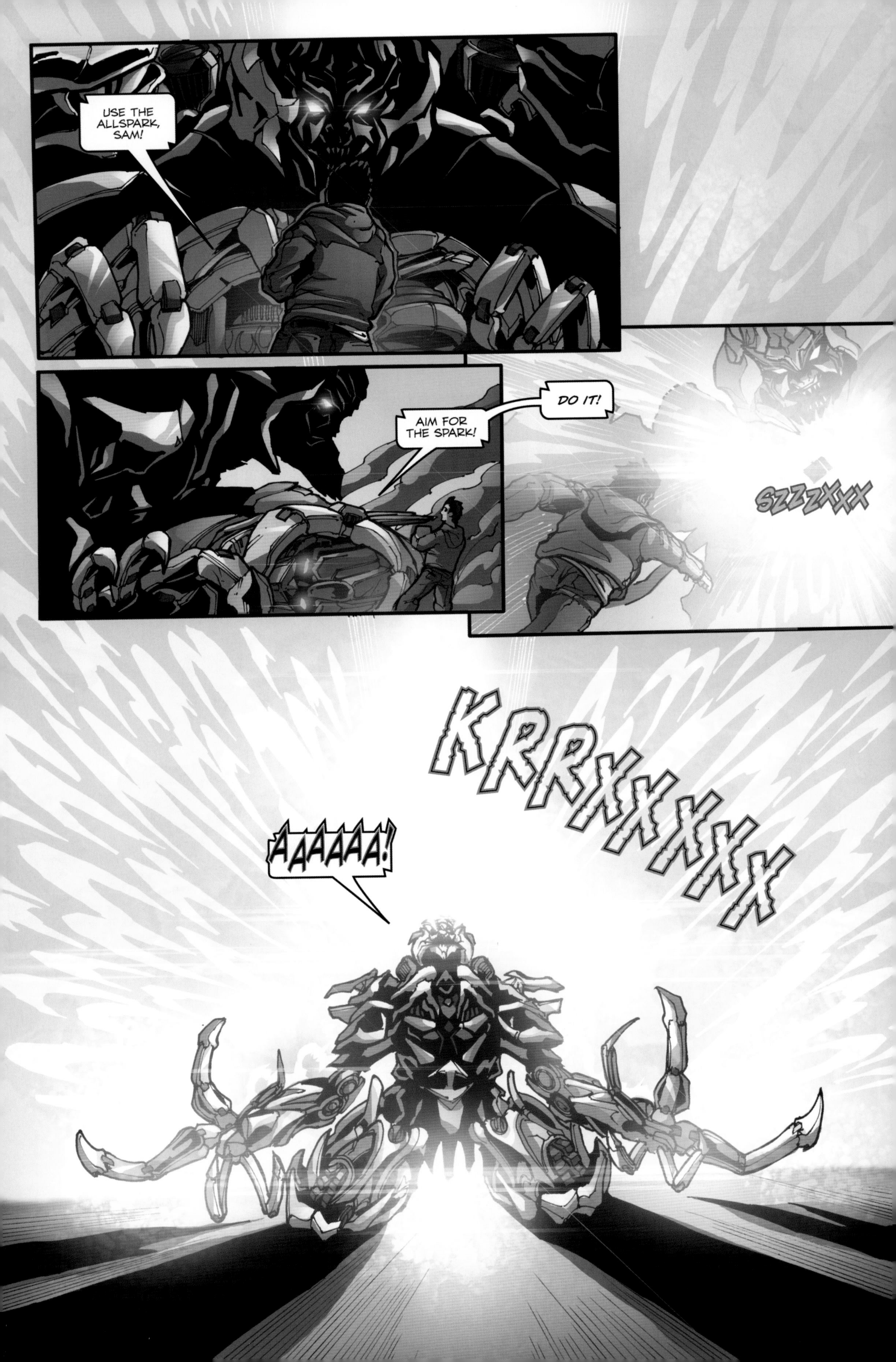

USE THE ALLSPARK, SAM!
AIM FOR THE SPARK!
DO IT!
SZZZXXX
KRRXXXXX
AAAAAA!

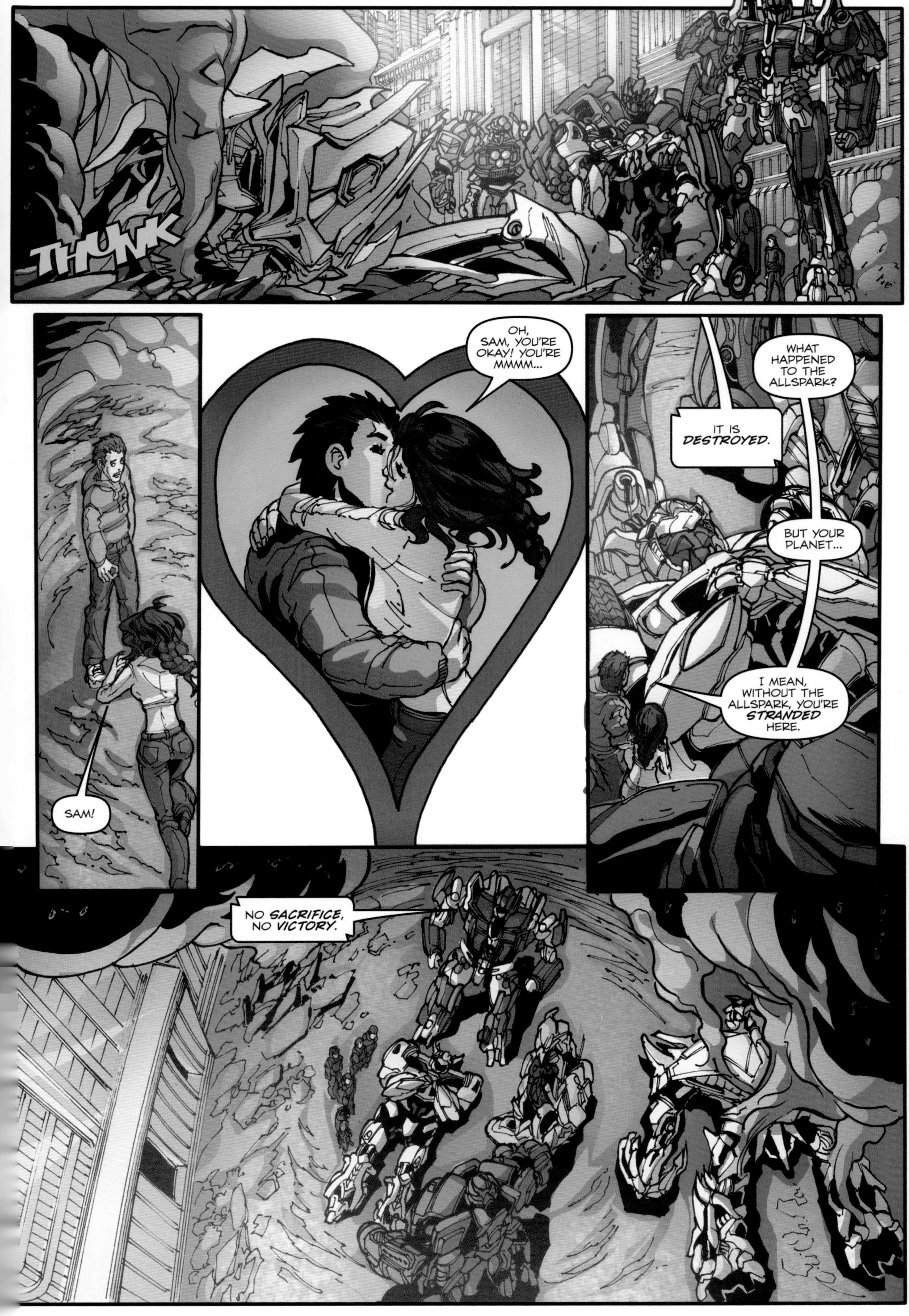
THUNK
SAM!
OH, SAM, YOU'RE OKAY! YOU'RE MMMM...
WHAT HAPPENED TO THE ALLSPARK?
IT IS DESTROYED.
BUT YOUR PLANET...
I MEAN, WITHOUT THE ALLSPARK, YOU'RE STRANDED HERE.
NO SACRIFICE, NO VICTORY.

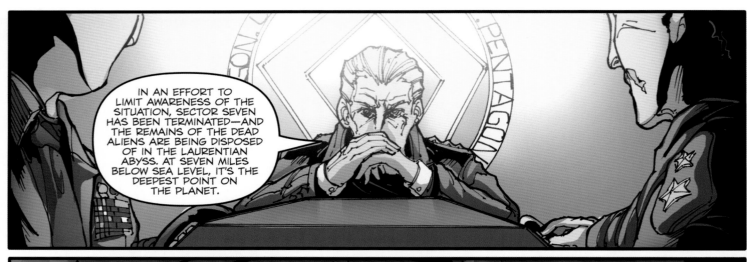

IN AN EFFORT TO LIMIT AWARENESS OF THE SITUATION, SECTOR SEVEN HAS BEEN TERMINATED—AND THE REMAINS OF THE DEAD ALIENS ARE BEING DISPOSED OF IN THE LAURENTIAN ABYSS. AT SEVEN MILES BELOW SEA LEVEL, IT'S THE DEEPEST POINT ON THE PLANET.

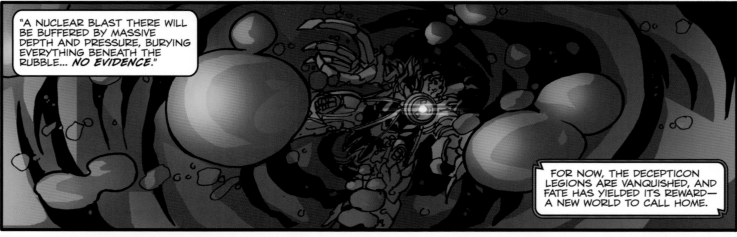

"A NUCLEAR BLAST THERE WILL BE BUFFERED BY MASSIVE DEPTH AND PRESSURE, BURYING EVERYTHING BENEATH THE RUBBLE... *NO EVIDENCE.*"

FOR NOW, THE DECEPTICON LEGIONS ARE VANQUISHED, AND FATE HAS YIELDED ITS REWARD— A NEW WORLD TO CALL HOME.

WE LIVE AMONG ITS PEOPLE NOW, HIDING IN PLAIN SIGHT... BUT WATCHING OVER THEM IN SECRET. WAITING. PROTECTING.

I HAVE WITNESSED THEIR CAPACITY FOR COURAGE. AND THOUGH WE ARE WORLDS APART, LIKE US, THERE'S *MORE TO THEM THAN MEETS THE EYE.*

I AM OPTIMUS PRIME, AND I SEND THIS MESSAGE TO ANY SURVIVING AUTOBOTS TAKING REFUGE AMONG THE STARS. YOU ARE NOT ALONE.

WE ARE HERE. WE ARE WAITING.

END.

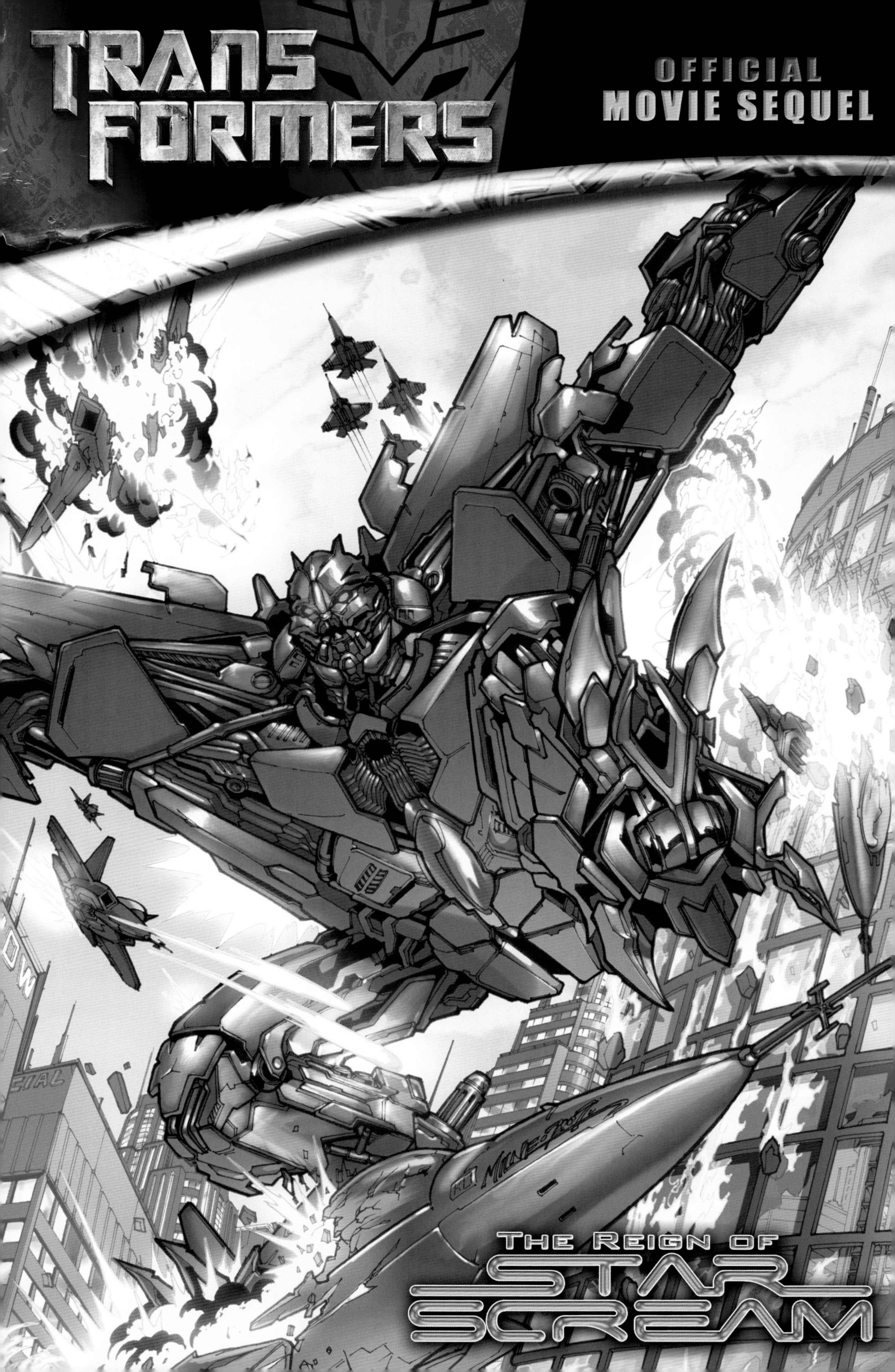
TRANSFORMERS
OFFICIAL
MOVIE SEQUEL
THE REIGN OF
STAR
SCREAM

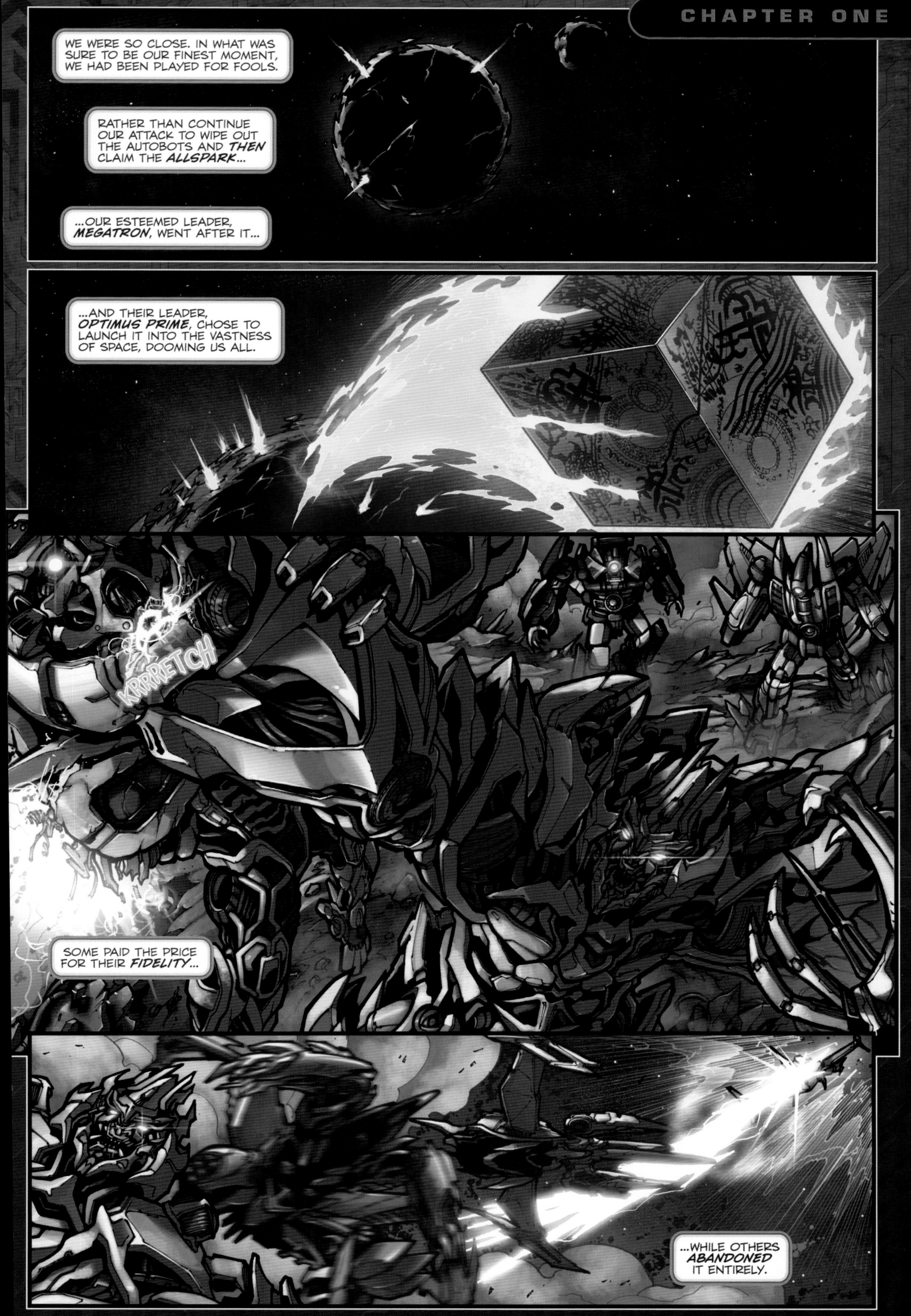
WE WERE SO CLOSE. IN WHAT WAS SURE TO BE OUR FINEST MOMENT, WE HAD BEEN PLAYED FOR FOOLS.
RATHER THAN CONTINUE OUR ATTACK TO WIPE OUT THE AUTOBOTS AND *THEN* CLAIM THE *ALLSPARK*...
...OUR ESTEEMED LEADER, *MEGATRON*, WENT AFTER IT...
...AND THEIR LEADER, *OPTIMUS PRIME*, CHOSE TO LAUNCH IT INTO THE VASTNESS OF SPACE, DOOMING US ALL.
KRRRETCH
SOME PAID THE PRICE FOR THEIR *FIDELITY*...
...WHILE OTHERS *ABANDONED* IT ENTIRELY.

LORD MEGATRON, WHERE ARE YOU GOING?

PRIME INTENDS TO KEEP THE ALLSPARK FROM ME—FROM US—BUT SIMPLY SENDING IT INTO ORBIT WILL NOT BE ENOUGH.

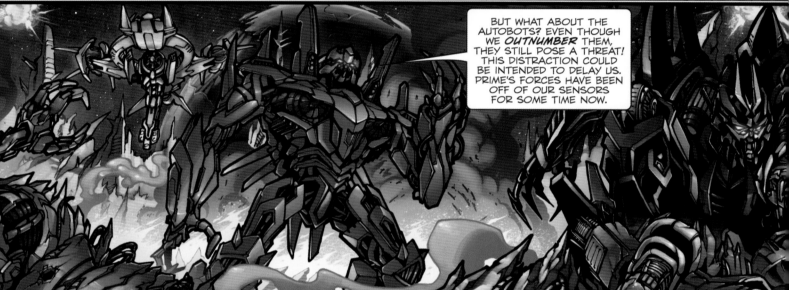

BUT WHAT ABOUT THE AUTOBOTS? EVEN THOUGH WE *OUTNUMBER* THEM, THEY STILL POSE A THREAT! THIS DISTRACTION COULD BE INTENDED TO DELAY US. PRIME'S FORCES HAVE BEEN OFF OF OUR SENSORS FOR SOME TIME NOW.

STARSCREAM, YOU IDIOT... WITHOUT THE ALLSPARK, PRIME IS FINISHED—DEFEATED! SOON I SHALL HAVE THE CUBE...

...AND YOU SHALL HAVE HIM AND HIS FOLLOWERS. *NONE* ARE TO SURVIVE. WHEN I RETURN WITH THE ALLSPARK, CYBERTRON WILL BE MINE—*OURS*.

"DO NOT *FAIL* ME, STARSCREAM."

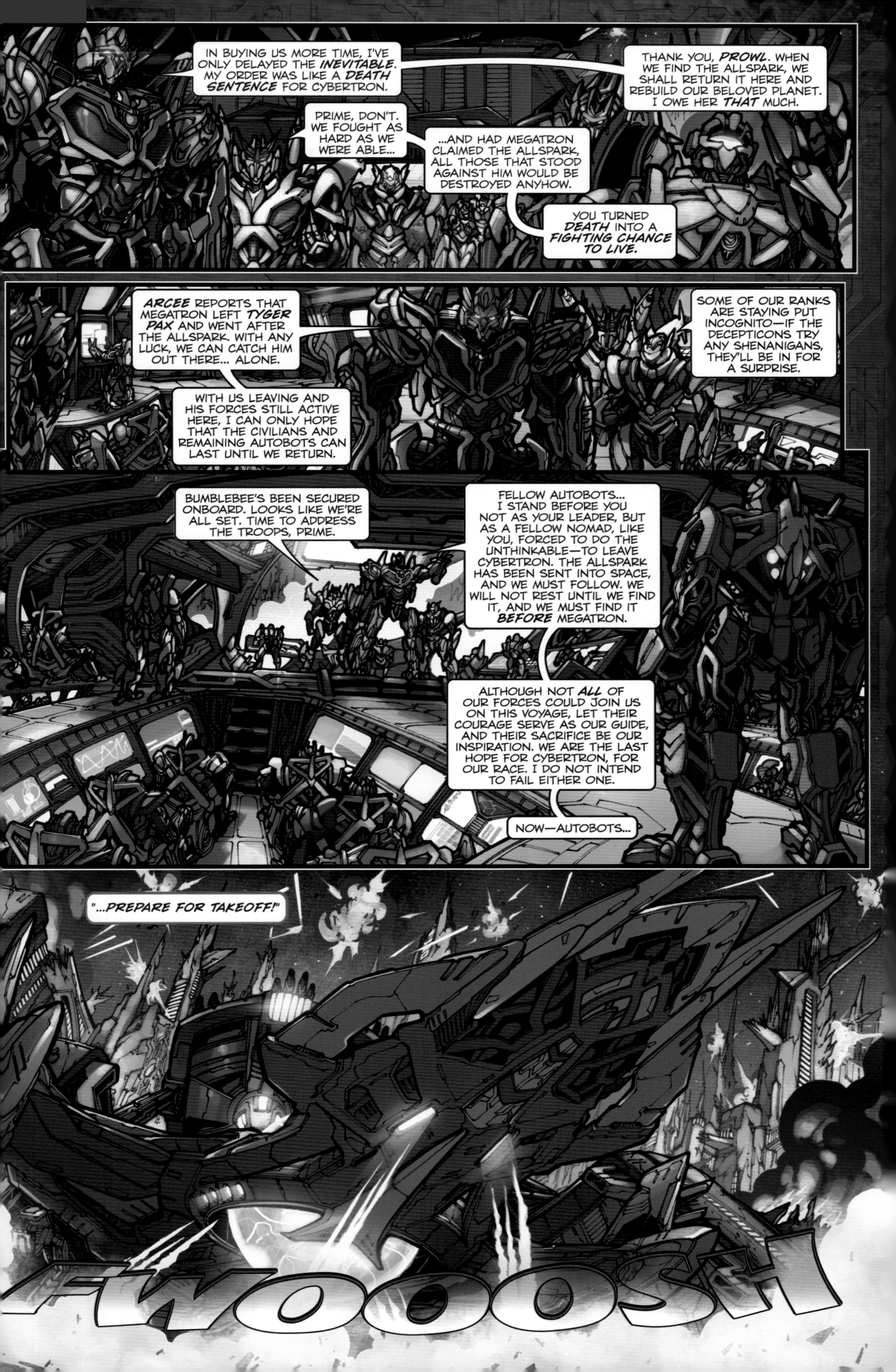
IN BUYING US MORE TIME, I'VE ONLY DELAYED THE INEVITABLE. MY ORDER WAS LIKE A DEATH SENTENCE FOR CYBERTRON.
PRIME, DON'T. WE FOUGHT AS HARD AS WE WERE ABLE...
...AND HAD MEGATRON CLAIMED THE ALLSPARK, ALL THOSE THAT STOOD AGAINST HIM WOULD BE DESTROYED ANYHOW.
YOU TURNED DEATH INTO A FIGHTING CHANCE TO LIVE.
THANK YOU, PROWL. WHEN WE FIND THE ALLSPARK, WE SHALL RETURN IT HERE AND REBUILD OUR BELOVED PLANET. I OWE HER THAT MUCH.
ARCEE REPORTS THAT MEGATRON LEFT TYGER PAX AND WENT AFTER THE ALLSPARK. WITH ANY LUCK, WE CAN CATCH HIM OUT THERE... ALONE.
WITH US LEAVING AND HIS FORCES STILL ACTIVE HERE, I CAN ONLY HOPE THAT THE CIVILIANS AND REMAINING AUTOBOTS CAN LAST UNTIL WE RETURN.
SOME OF OUR RANKS ARE STAYING PUT INCOGNITO—IF THE DECEPTICONS TRY ANY SHENANIGANS, THEY'LL BE IN FOR A SURPRISE.
BUMBLEBEE'S BEEN SECURED ONBOARD. LOOKS LIKE WE'RE ALL SET. TIME TO ADDRESS THE TROOPS, PRIME.
FELLOW AUTOBOTS... I STAND BEFORE YOU NOT AS YOUR LEADER, BUT AS A FELLOW NOMAD, LIKE YOU, FORCED TO DO THE UNTHINKABLE—TO LEAVE CYBERTRON. THE ALLSPARK HAS BEEN SENT INTO SPACE, AND WE MUST FOLLOW. WE WILL NOT REST UNTIL WE FIND IT, AND WE MUST FIND IT BEFORE MEGATRON.
ALTHOUGH NOT ALL OF OUR FORCES COULD JOIN US ON THIS VOYAGE, LET THEIR COURAGE SERVE AS OUR GUIDE, AND THEIR SACRIFICE BE OUR INSPIRATION. WE ARE THE LAST HOPE FOR CYBERTRON, FOR OUR RACE. I DO NOT INTEND TO FAIL EITHER ONE.
NOW—AUTOBOTS...
"...PREPARE FOR TAKEOFF!"
FWOOOSH

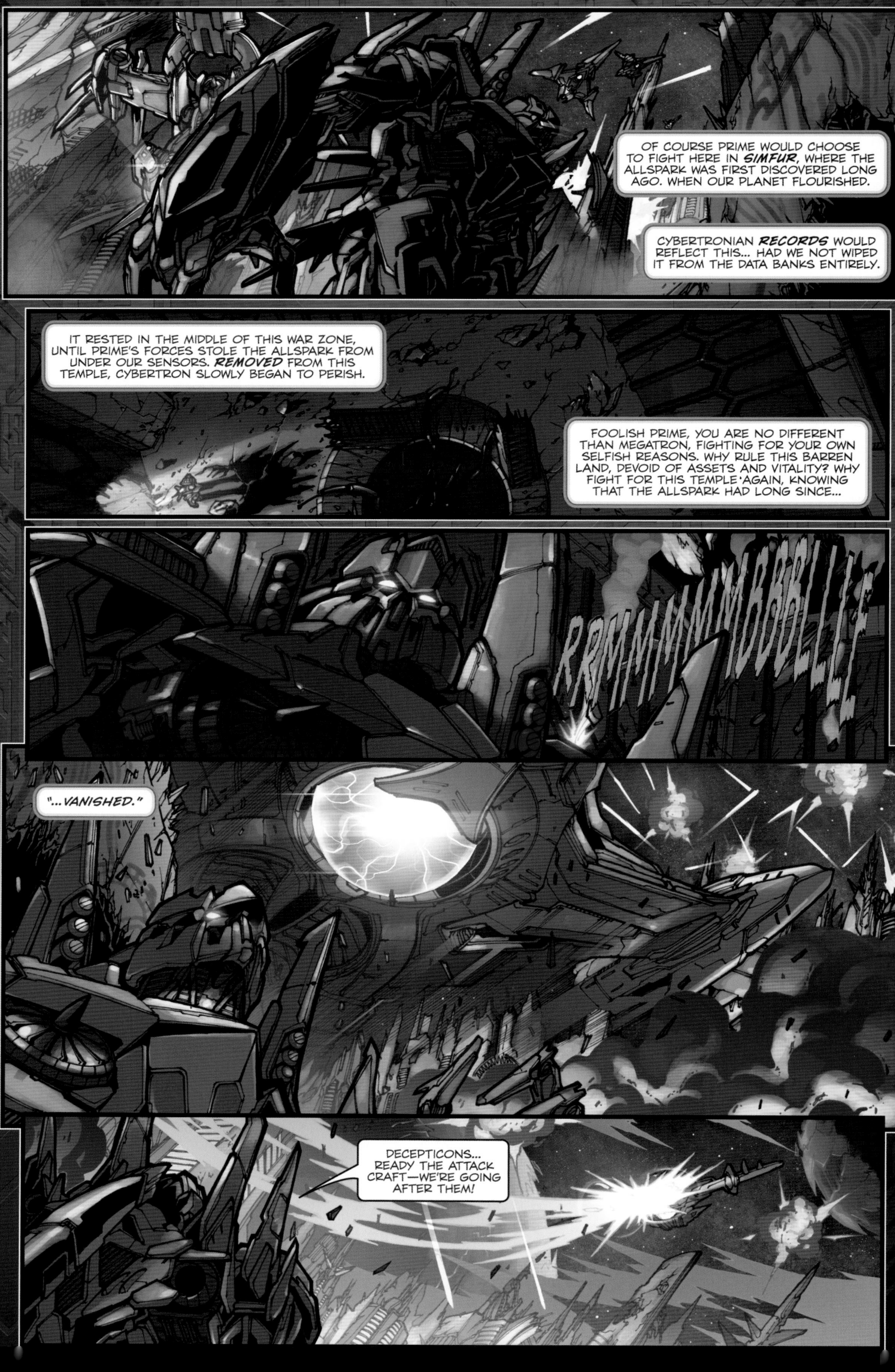

OF COURSE PRIME WOULD CHOOSE TO FIGHT HERE IN SIMFUR, WHERE THE ALLSPARK WAS FIRST DISCOVERED LONG AGO. WHEN OUR PLANET FLOURISHED.
CYBERTRONIAN RECORDS WOULD REFLECT THIS... HAD WE NOT WIPED IT FROM THE DATA BANKS ENTIRELY.
IT RESTED IN THE MIDDLE OF THIS WAR ZONE, UNTIL PRIME'S FORCES STOLE THE ALLSPARK FROM UNDER OUR SENSORS. REMOVED FROM THIS TEMPLE, CYBERTRON SLOWLY BEGAN TO PERISH.
FOOLISH PRIME, YOU ARE NO DIFFERENT THAN MEGATRON, FIGHTING FOR YOUR OWN SELFISH REASONS. WHY RULE THIS BARREN LAND, DEVOID OF ASSETS AND VITALITY? WHY FIGHT FOR THIS TEMPLE AGAIN, KNOWING THAT THE ALLSPARK HAD LONG SINCE...
RRMMMMMBBLLE
"...VANISHED."
DECEPTICONS... READY THE ATTACK CRAFT—WE'RE GOING AFTER THEM!

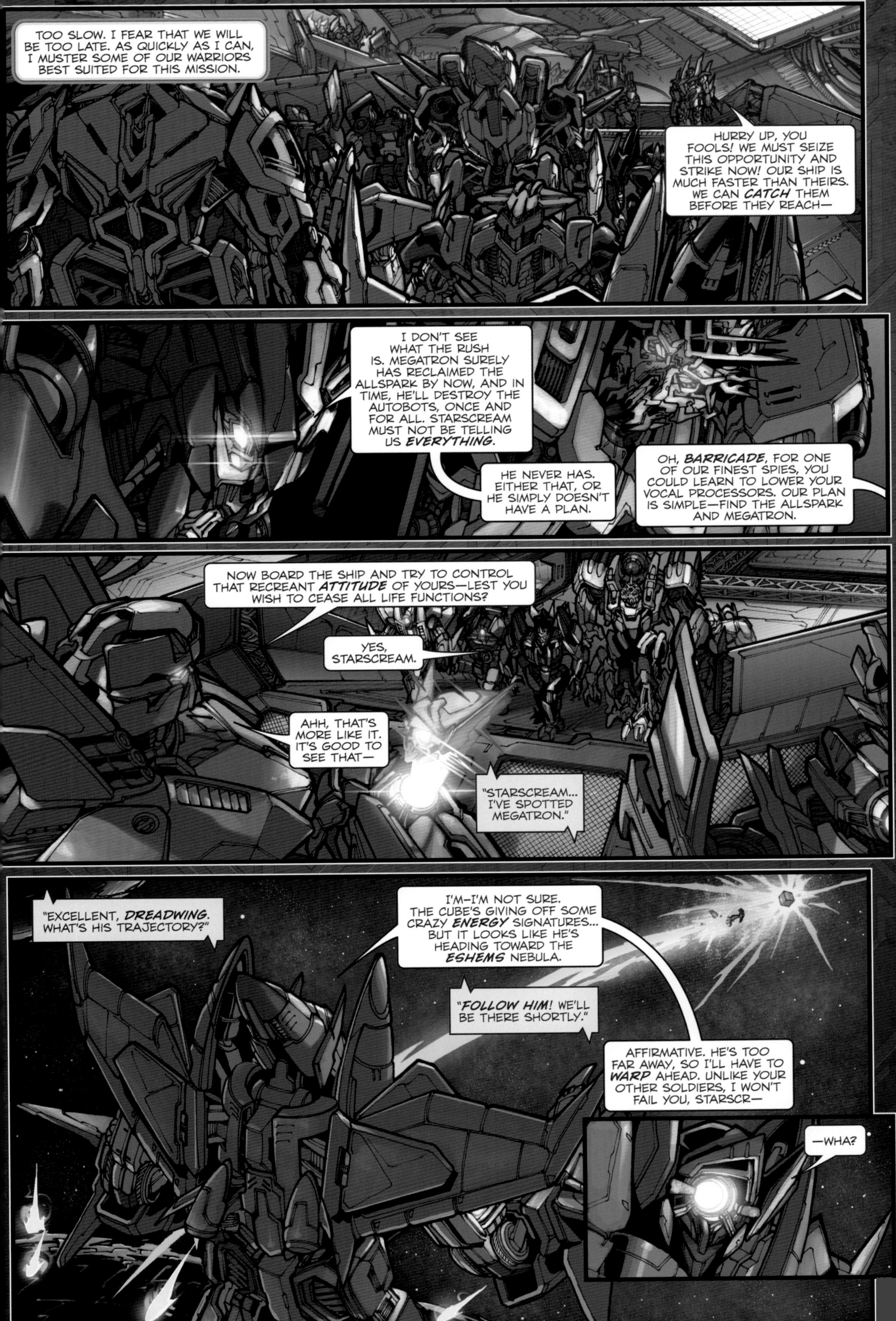
TOO SLOW. I FEAR THAT WE WILL BE TOO LATE. AS QUICKLY AS I CAN, I MUSTER SOME OF OUR WARRIORS BEST SUITED FOR THIS MISSION.
HURRY UP, YOU FOOLS! WE MUST SEIZE THIS OPPORTUNITY AND STRIKE NOW! OUR SHIP IS MUCH FASTER THAN THEIRS. WE CAN CATCH THEM BEFORE THEY REACH—
I DON'T SEE WHAT THE RUSH IS. MEGATRON SURELY HAS RECLAIMED THE ALLSPARK BY NOW, AND IN TIME, HE'LL DESTROY THE AUTOBOTS, ONCE AND FOR ALL. STARSCREAM MUST NOT BE TELLING US EVERYTHING.
HE NEVER HAS. EITHER THAT, OR HE SIMPLY DOESN'T HAVE A PLAN.
OH, BARRICADE, FOR ONE OF OUR FINEST SPIES, YOU COULD LEARN TO LOWER YOUR VOCAL PROCESSORS. OUR PLAN IS SIMPLE—FIND THE ALLSPARK AND MEGATRON.
NOW BOARD THE SHIP AND TRY TO CONTROL THAT RECREANT ATTITUDE OF YOURS—LEST YOU WISH TO CEASE ALL LIFE FUNCTIONS?
YES, STARSCREAM.
AHH, THAT'S MORE LIKE IT. IT'S GOOD TO SEE THAT—
"STARSCREAM... I'VE SPOTTED MEGATRON."
"EXCELLENT, DREADWING. WHAT'S HIS TRAJECTORY?"
I'M—I'M NOT SURE. THE CUBE'S GIVING OFF SOME CRAZY ENERGY SIGNATURES... BUT IT LOOKS LIKE HE'S HEADING TOWARD THE ESHEMS NEBULA.
"FOLLOW HIM! WE'LL BE THERE SHORTLY."
AFFIRMATIVE. HE'S TOO FAR AWAY, SO I'LL HAVE TO WARP AHEAD. UNLIKE YOUR OTHER SOLDIERS, I WON'T FAIL YOU, STARSCR—
—WHA?

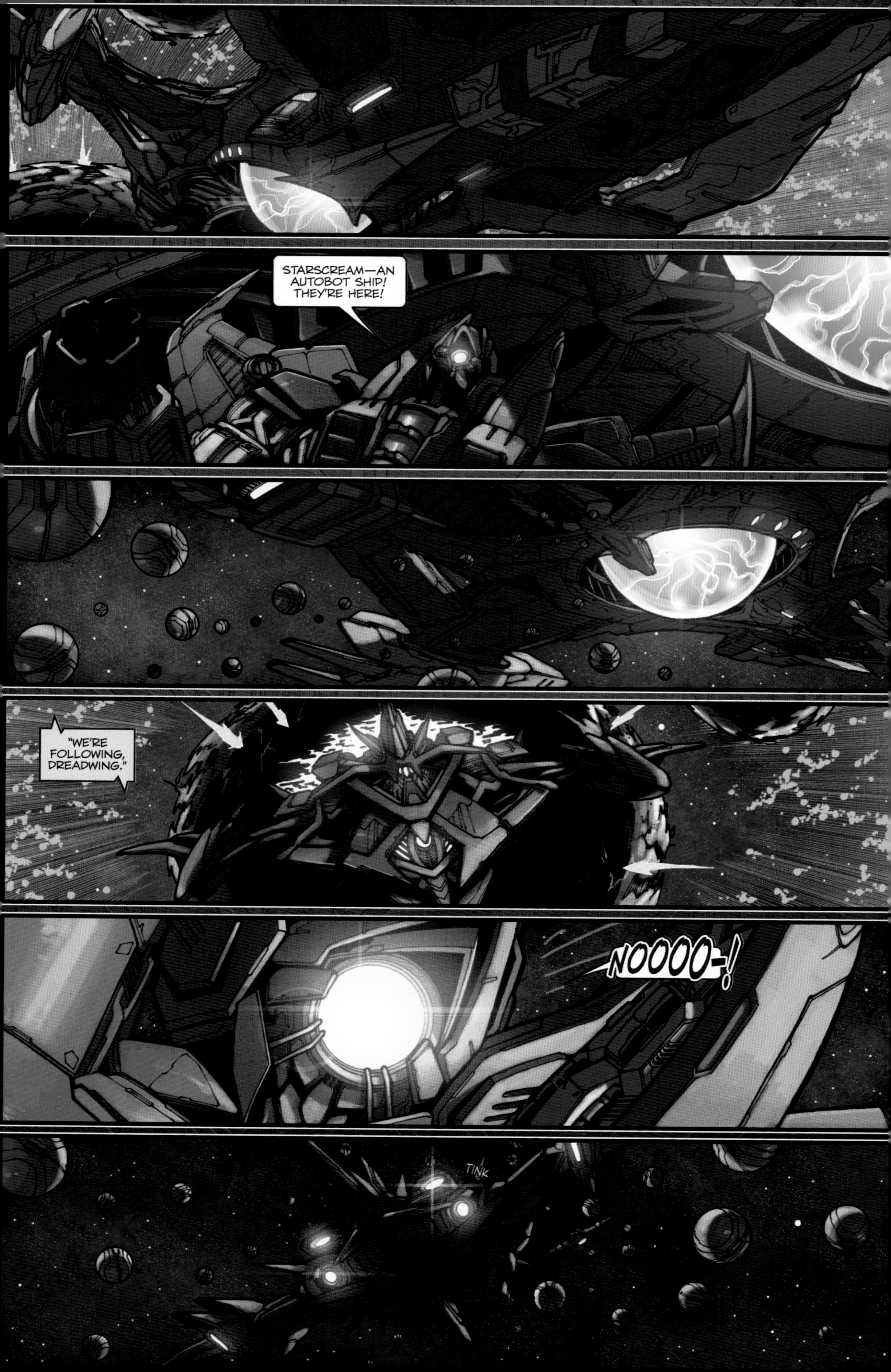
STARSCREAM—AN AUTOBOT SHIP! THEY'RE HERE!
"WE'RE FOLLOWING, DREADWING."
NOOOO--!
TINK

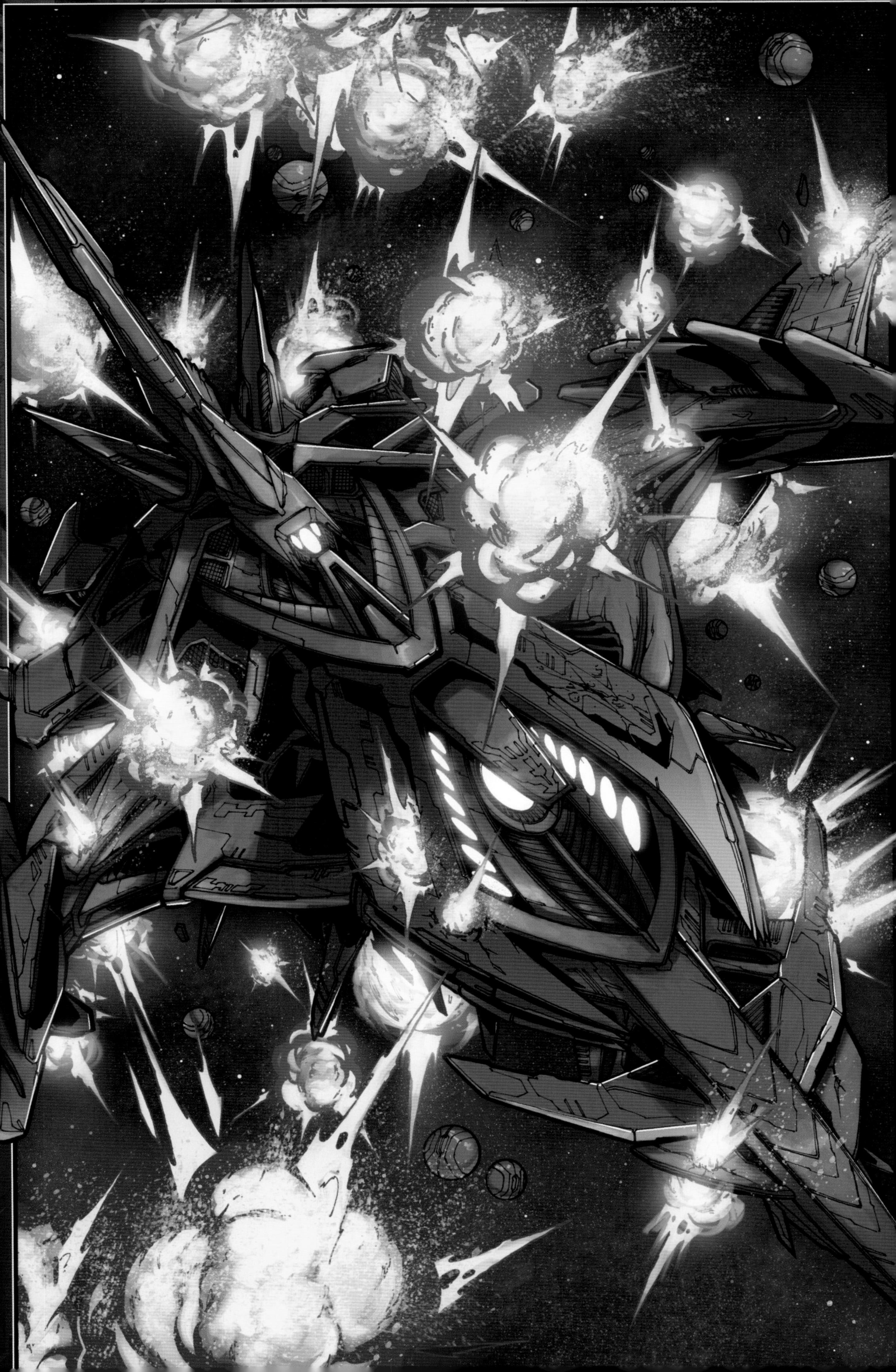

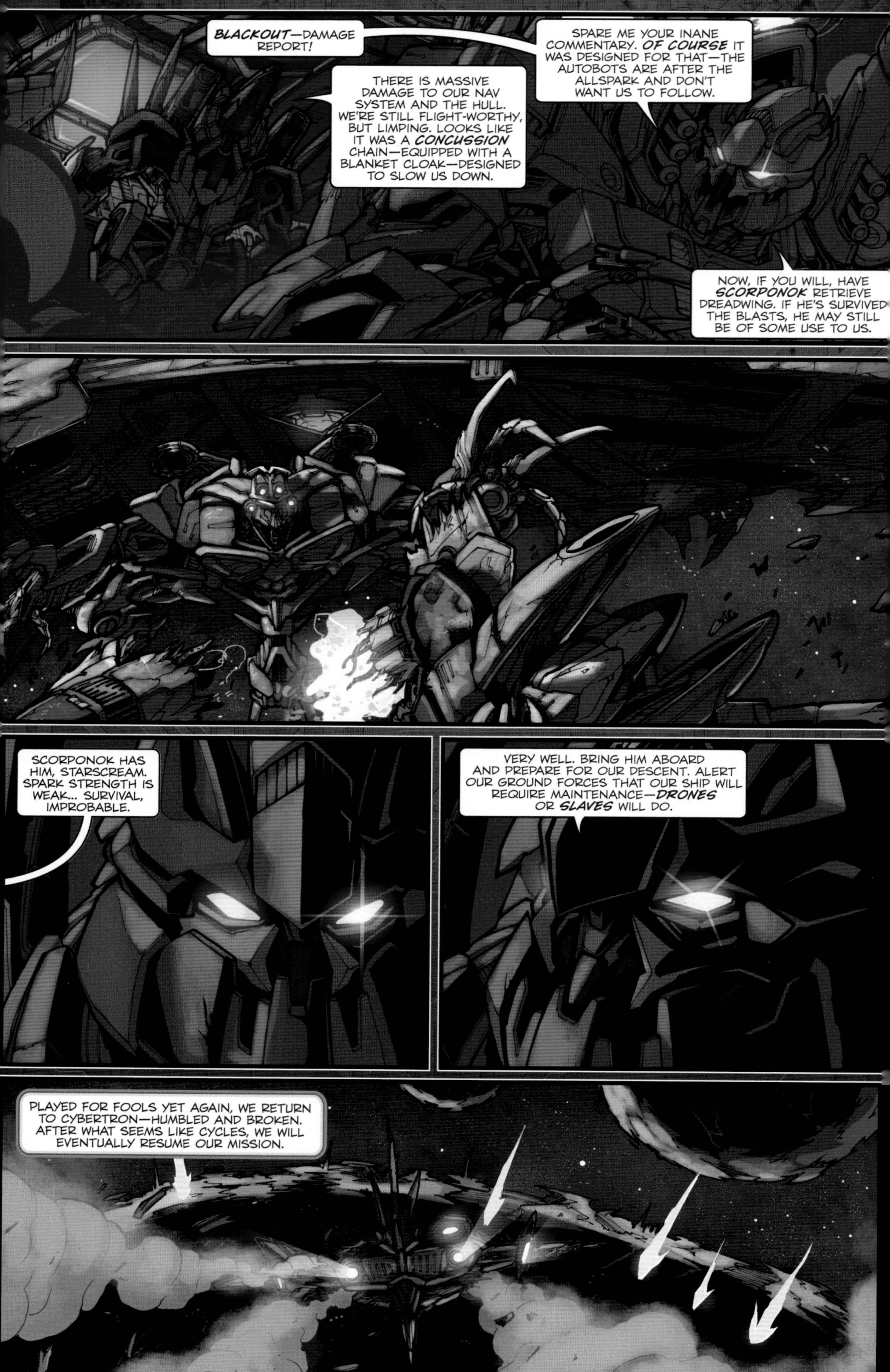

BLACKOUT—DAMAGE REPORT!
THERE IS MASSIVE DAMAGE TO OUR NAV SYSTEM AND THE HULL. WE'RE STILL FLIGHT-WORTHY, BUT LIMPING. LOOKS LIKE IT WAS A CONCUSSION CHAIN—EQUIPPED WITH A BLANKET CLOAK—DESIGNED TO SLOW US DOWN.
SPARE ME YOUR INANE COMMENTARY. OF COURSE IT WAS DESIGNED FOR THAT—THE AUTOBOTS ARE AFTER THE ALLSPARK AND DON'T WANT US TO FOLLOW.
NOW, IF YOU WILL, HAVE SCORPONOK RETRIEVE DREADWING. IF HE'S SURVIVED THE BLASTS, HE MAY STILL BE OF SOME USE TO US.
SCORPONOK HAS HIM, STARSCREAM. SPARK STRENGTH IS WEAK... SURVIVAL, IMPROBABLE.
VERY WELL. BRING HIM ABOARD AND PREPARE FOR OUR DESCENT. ALERT OUR GROUND FORCES THAT OUR SHIP WILL REQUIRE MAINTENANCE—DRONES OR SLAVES WILL DO.
PLAYED FOR FOOLS YET AGAIN, WE RETURN TO CYBERTRON—HUMBLED AND BROKEN. AFTER WHAT SEEMS LIKE CYCLES, WE WILL EVENTUALLY RESUME OUR MISSION.

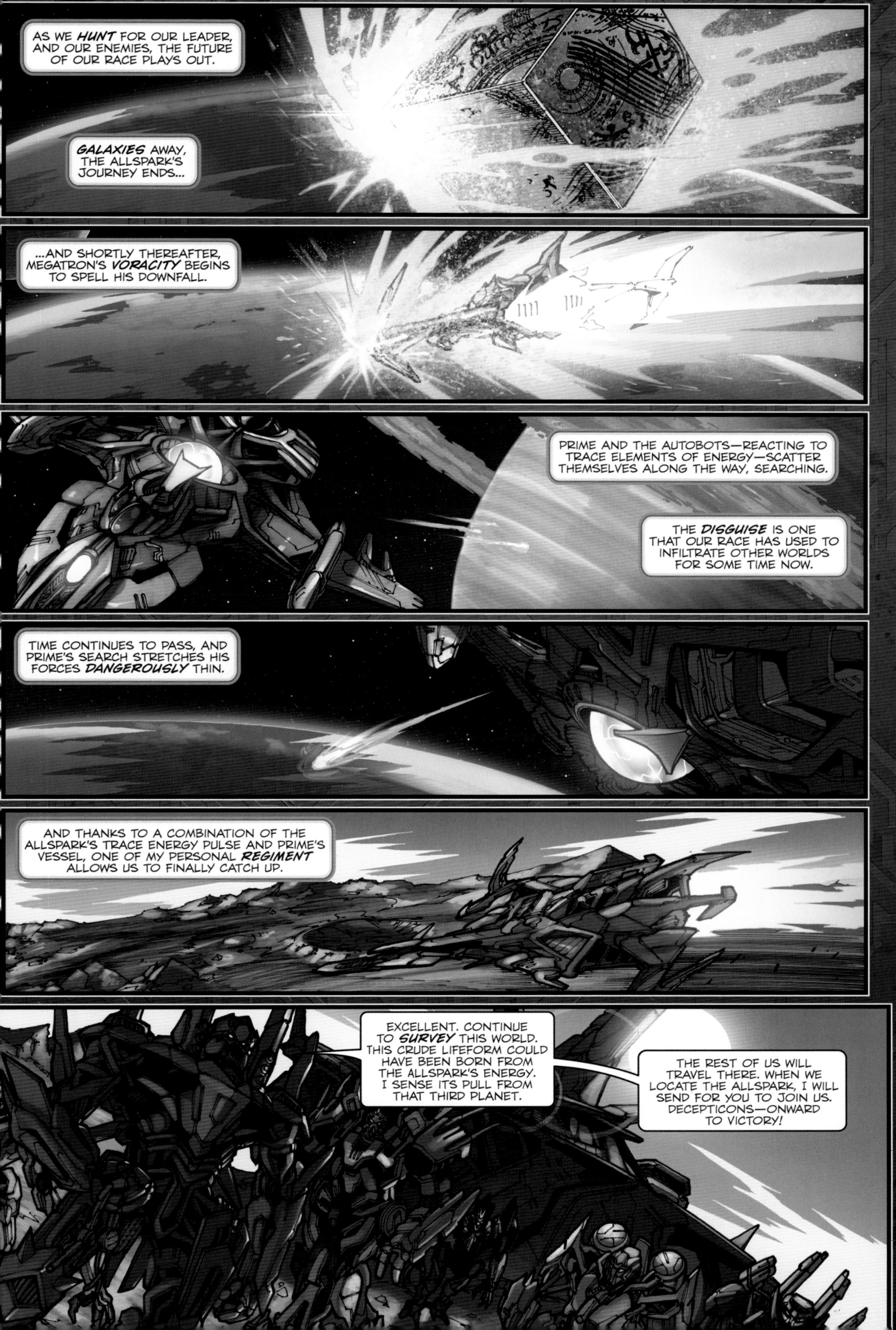

AS WE HUNT FOR OUR LEADER, AND OUR ENEMIES, THE FUTURE OF OUR RACE PLAYS OUT.
GALAXIES AWAY, THE ALLSPARK'S JOURNEY ENDS...
...AND SHORTLY THEREAFTER, MEGATRON'S VORACITY BEGINS TO SPELL HIS DOWNFALL.
PRIME AND THE AUTOBOTS—REACTING TO TRACE ELEMENTS OF ENERGY—SCATTER THEMSELVES ALONG THE WAY, SEARCHING.
THE DISGUISE IS ONE THAT OUR RACE HAS USED TO INFILTRATE OTHER WORLDS FOR SOME TIME NOW.
TIME CONTINUES TO PASS, AND PRIME'S SEARCH STRETCHES HIS FORCES DANGEROUSLY THIN.
AND THANKS TO A COMBINATION OF THE ALLSPARK'S TRACE ENERGY PULSE AND PRIME'S VESSEL, ONE OF MY PERSONAL REGIMENT ALLOWS US TO FINALLY CATCH UP.
EXCELLENT. CONTINUE TO SURVEY THIS WORLD. THIS CRUDE LIFEFORM COULD HAVE BEEN BORN FROM THE ALLSPARK'S ENERGY. I SENSE ITS PULL FROM THAT THIRD PLANET.
THE REST OF US WILL TRAVEL THERE. WHEN WE LOCATE THE ALLSPARK, I WILL SEND FOR YOU TO JOIN US. DECEPTICONS—ONWARD TO VICTORY!

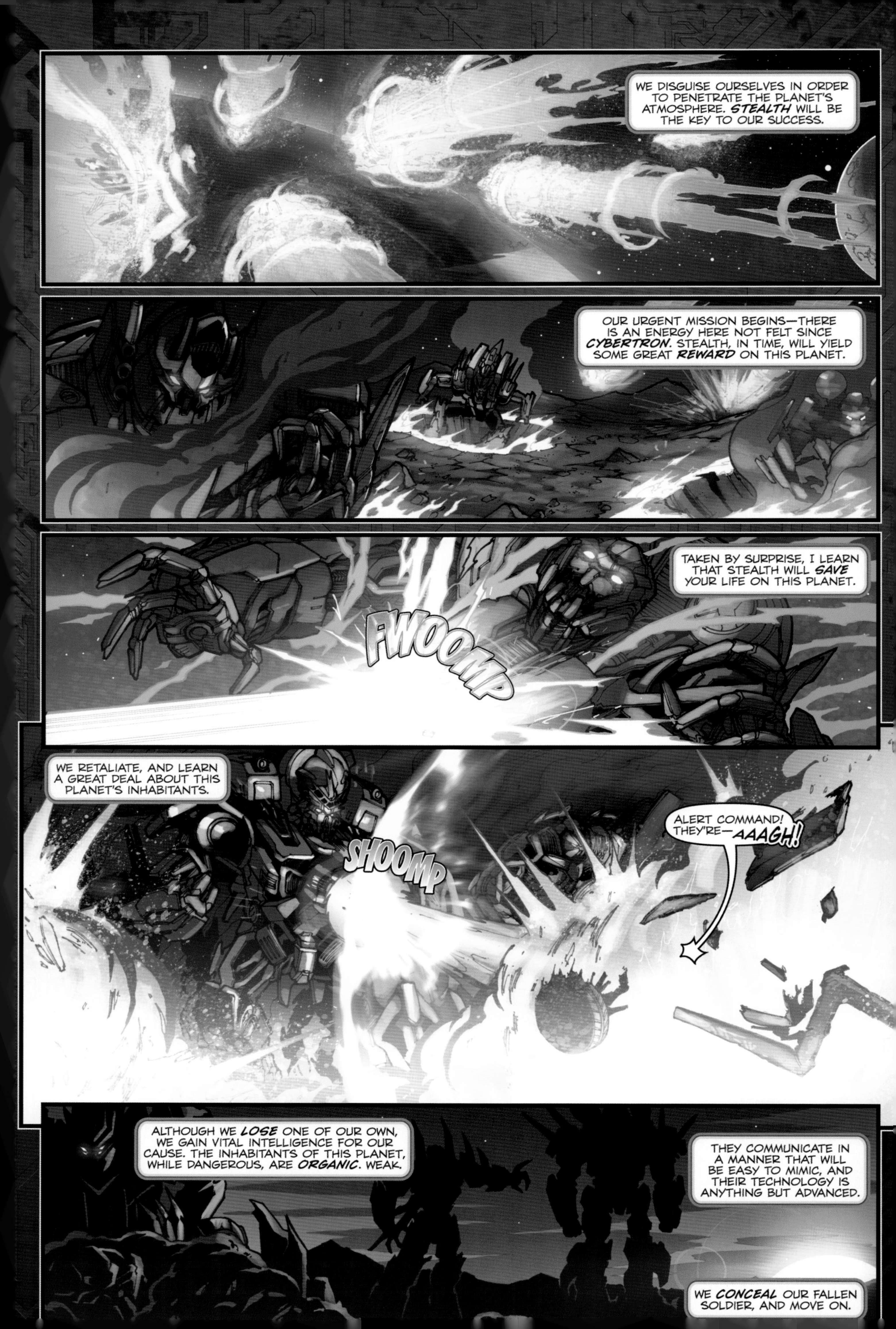
WE DISGUISE OURSELVES IN ORDER TO PENETRATE THE PLANET'S ATMOSPHERE. STEALTH WILL BE THE KEY TO OUR SUCCESS.
OUR URGENT MISSION BEGINS—THERE IS AN ENERGY HERE NOT FELT SINCE CYBERTRON. STEALTH, IN TIME, WILL YIELD SOME GREAT REWARD ON THIS PLANET.
TAKEN BY SURPRISE, I LEARN THAT STEALTH WILL SAVE YOUR LIFE ON THIS PLANET.
FWOOMP
WE RETALIATE, AND LEARN A GREAT DEAL ABOUT THIS PLANET'S INHABITANTS.
SHOOMP
ALERT COMMAND! THEY'RE—AAAGH!
ALTHOUGH WE LOSE ONE OF OUR OWN, WE GAIN VITAL INTELLIGENCE FOR OUR CAUSE. THE INHABITANTS OF THIS PLANET, WHILE DANGEROUS, ARE ORGANIC. WEAK.
THEY COMMUNICATE IN A MANNER THAT WILL BE EASY TO MIMIC, AND THEIR TECHNOLOGY IS ANYTHING BUT ADVANCED.
WE CONCEAL OUR FALLEN SOLDIER, AND MOVE ON.

TAKING THEIR VEHICLE FORMS GIVES US THE PERFECT DISGUISE.

SOME CHOOSE ALTERNATE FORMS—AND BARELY LIVE TO SEE ANOTHER CYCLE...

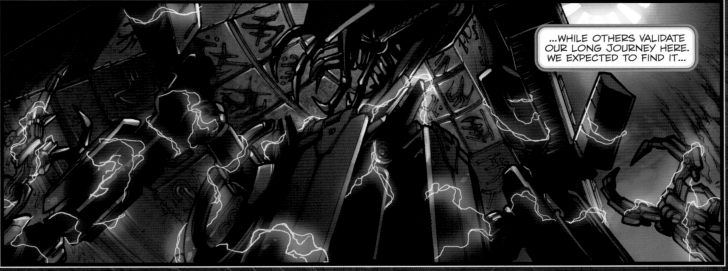

...WHILE OTHERS VALIDATE OUR LONG JOURNEY HERE. WE EXPECTED TO FIND IT...

...BUT FINDING *HIM* THERE WAS STAGGERING.

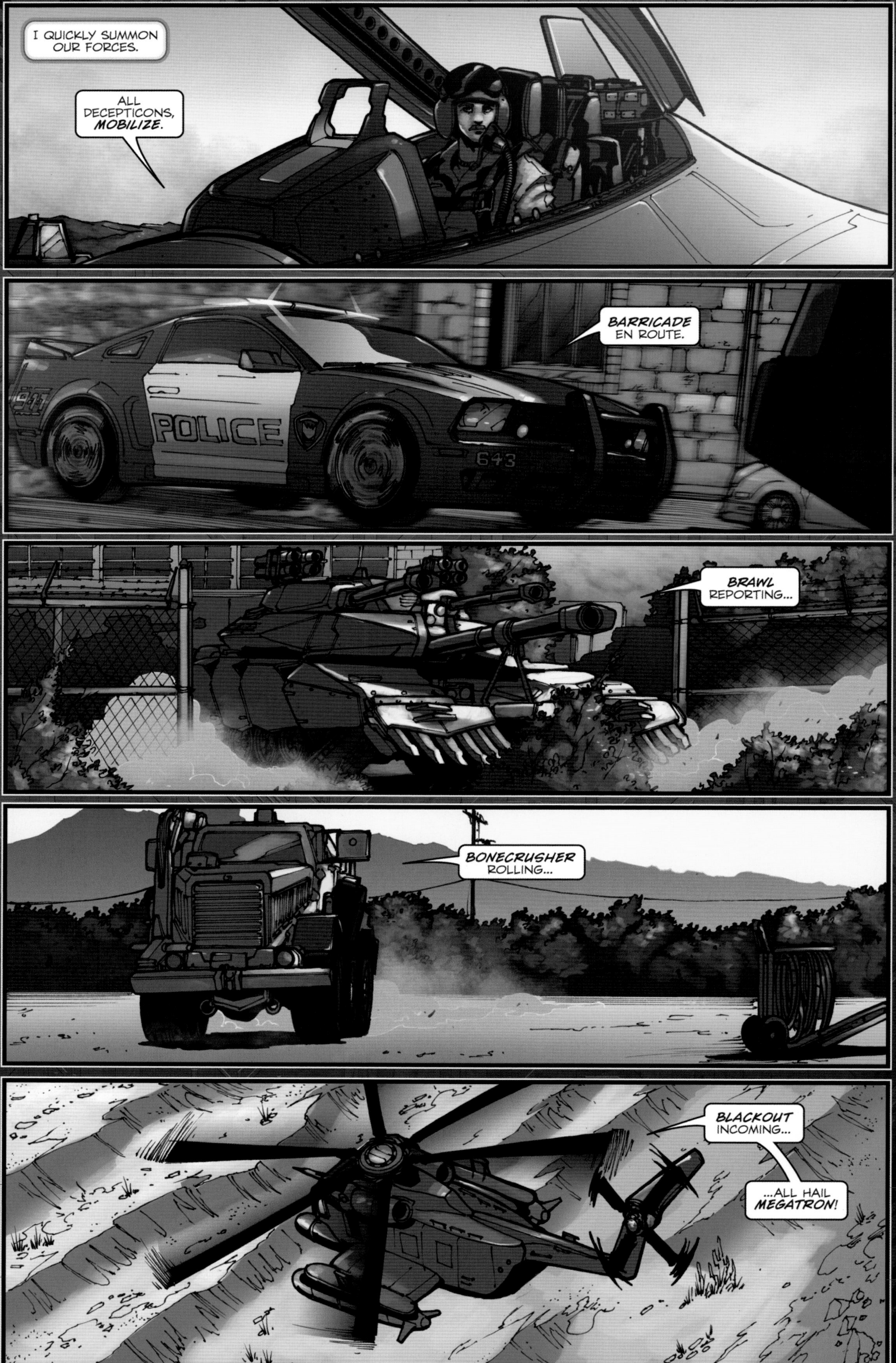
I QUICKLY SUMMON OUR FORCES.
ALL DECEPTICONS, *MOBILIZE*.
POLICE
643
BARRICADE EN ROUTE.
BRAWL REPORTING...
BONECRUSHER ROLLING...
BLACKOUT INCOMING...
...ALL HAIL *MEGATRON*!

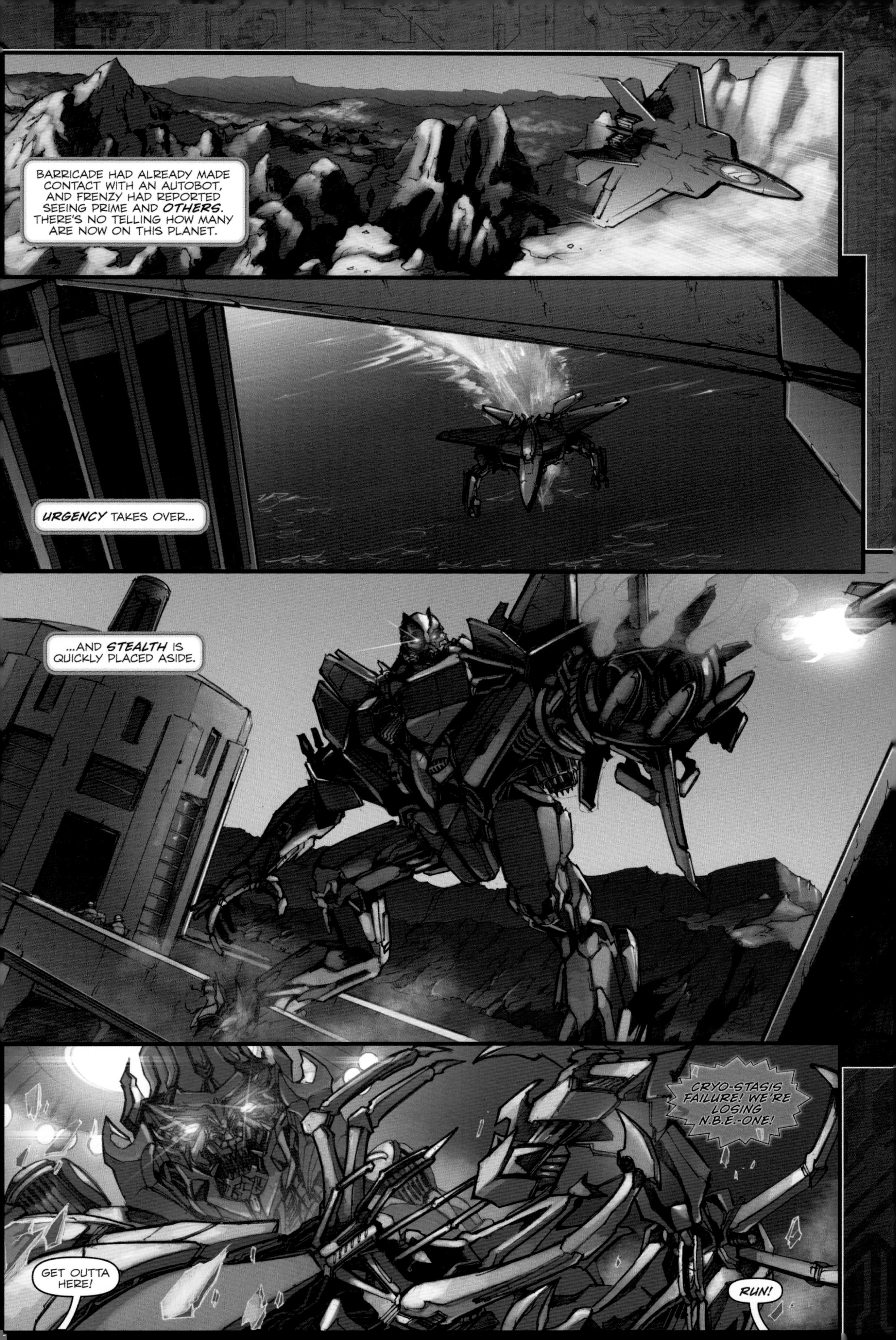
BARRICADE HAD ALREADY MADE CONTACT WITH AN AUTOBOT, AND FRENZY HAD REPORTED SEEING PRIME AND *OTHERS*. THERE'S NO TELLING HOW MANY ARE NOW ON THIS PLANET.
URGENCY TAKES OVER...
...AND *STEALTH* IS QUICKLY PLACED ASIDE.
CRYO-STASIS FAILURE! WE'RE LOSING N.B.E.-ONE!
GET OUTTA HERE!
RUN!

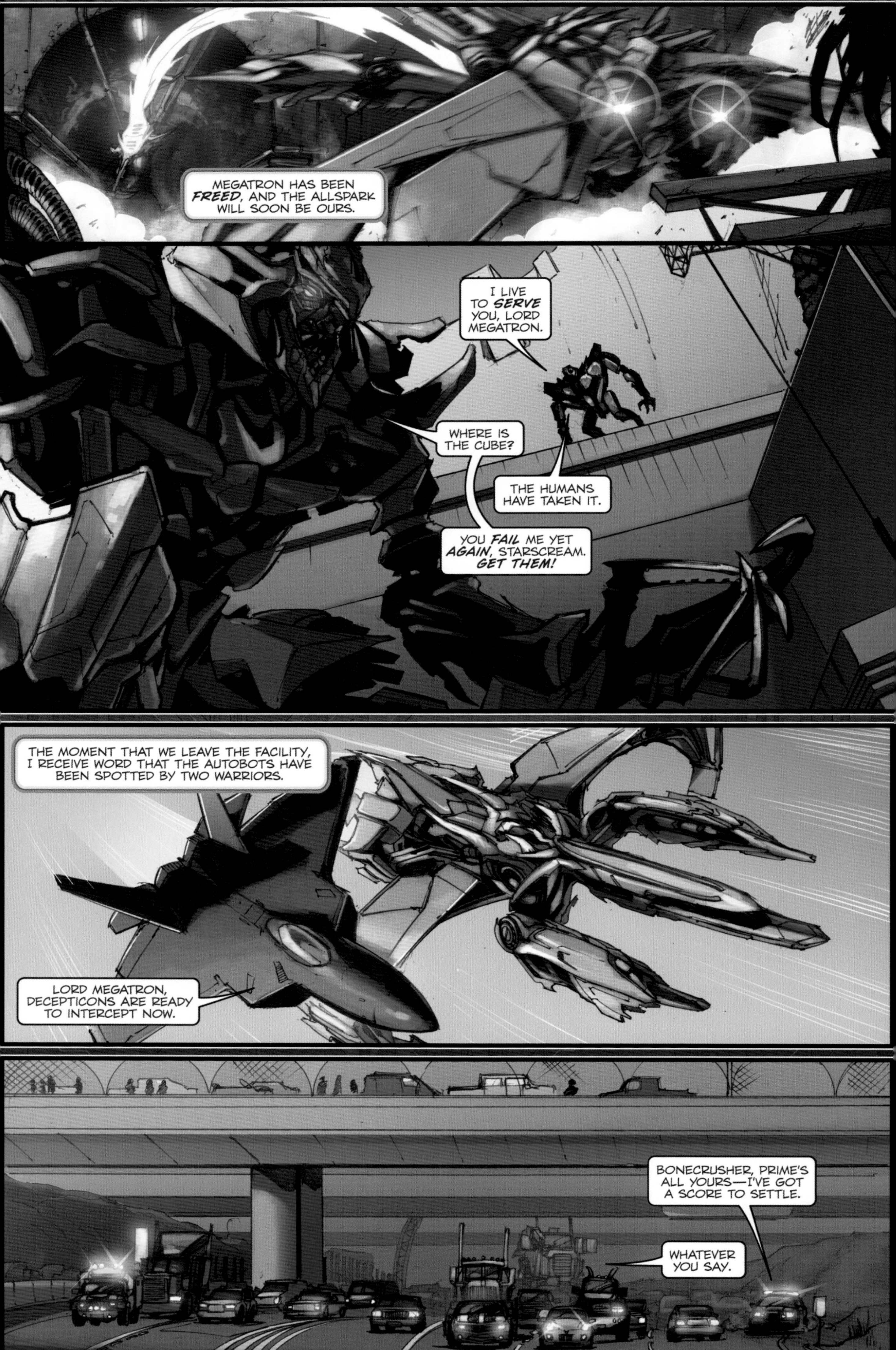
MEGATRON HAS BEEN FREED, AND THE ALLSPARK WILL SOON BE OURS.
I LIVE TO SERVE YOU, LORD MEGATRON.
WHERE IS THE CUBE?
THE HUMANS HAVE TAKEN IT.
YOU FAIL ME YET AGAIN, STARSCREAM. GET THEM!
THE MOMENT THAT WE LEAVE THE FACILITY, I RECEIVE WORD THAT THE AUTOBOTS HAVE BEEN SPOTTED BY TWO WARRIORS.
LORD MEGATRON, DECEPTICONS ARE READY TO INTERCEPT NOW.
BONECRUSHER, PRIME'S ALL YOURS—I'VE GOT A SCORE TO SETTLE.
WHATEVER YOU SAY.

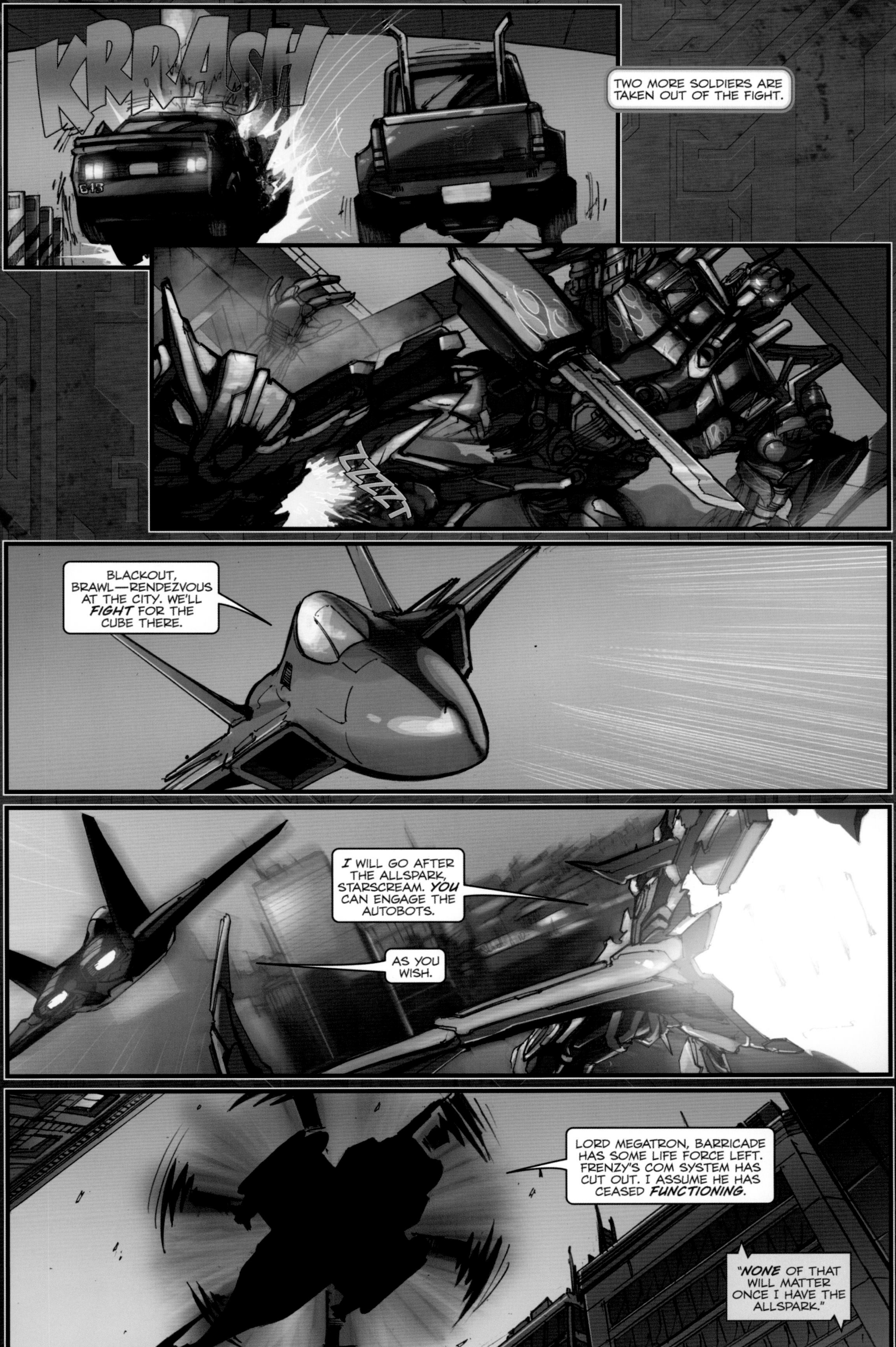
KRRASH
TWO MORE SOLDIERS ARE TAKEN OUT OF THE FIGHT.
ZZZZT
BLACKOUT, BRAWL—RENDEZVOUS AT THE CITY. WE'LL FIGHT FOR THE CUBE THERE.
I WILL GO AFTER THE ALLSPARK, STARSCREAM. YOU CAN ENGAGE THE AUTOBOTS.
AS YOU WISH.
LORD MEGATRON, BARRICADE HAS SOME LIFE FORCE LEFT. FRENZY'S COM SYSTEM HAS CUT OUT. I ASSUME HE HAS CEASED FUNCTIONING.
"NONE OF THAT WILL MATTER ONCE I HAVE THE ALLSPARK."

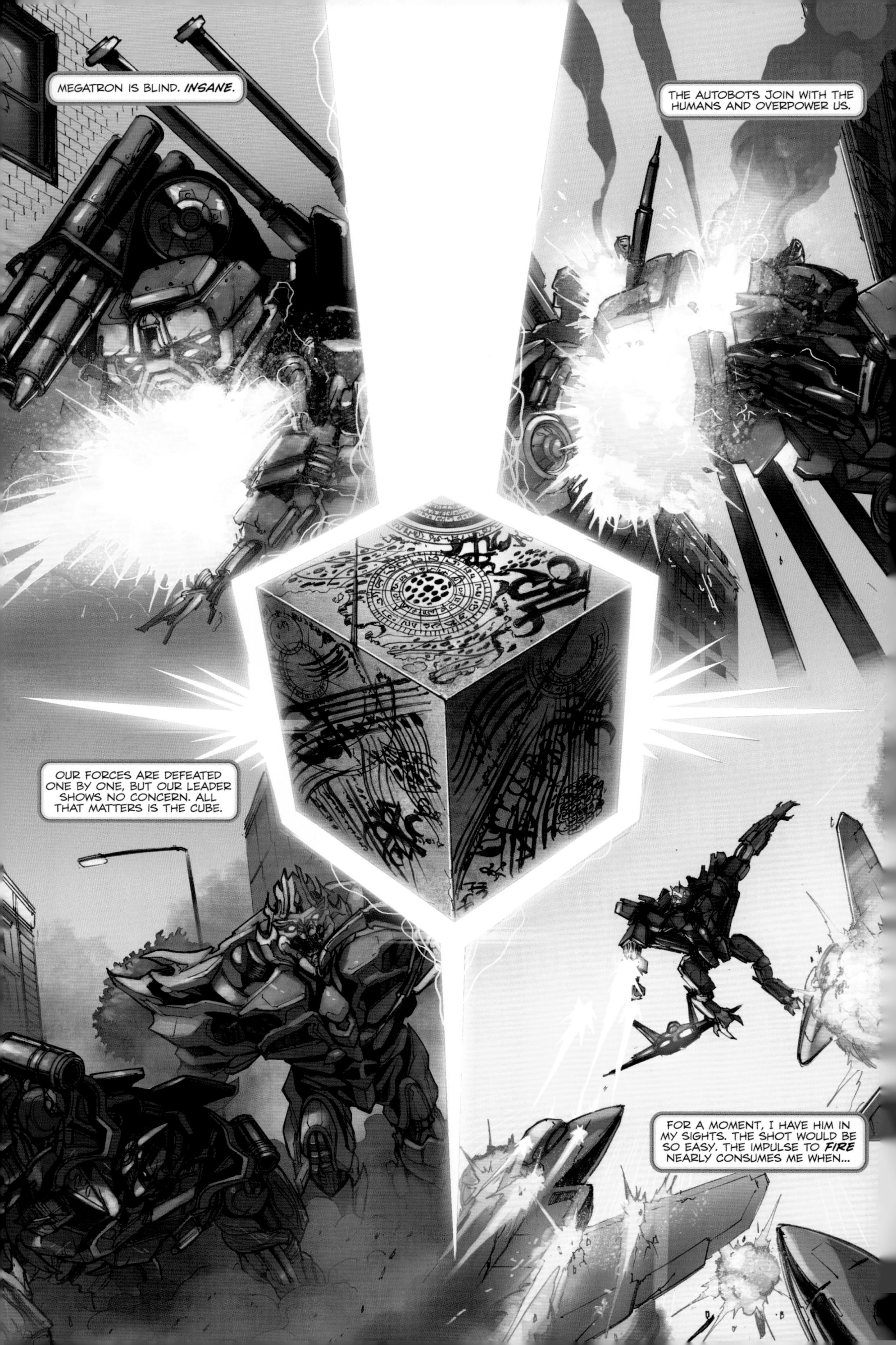
MEGATRON IS BLIND. *INSANE.*
THE AUTOBOTS JOIN WITH THE HUMANS AND OVERPOWER US.
OUR FORCES ARE DEFEATED ONE BY ONE, BUT OUR LEADER SHOWS NO CONCERN. ALL THAT MATTERS IS THE CUBE.
FOR A MOMENT, I HAVE HIM IN MY SIGHTS. THE SHOT WOULD BE SO EASY. THE IMPULSE TO *FIRE* NEARLY CONSUMES ME WHEN...

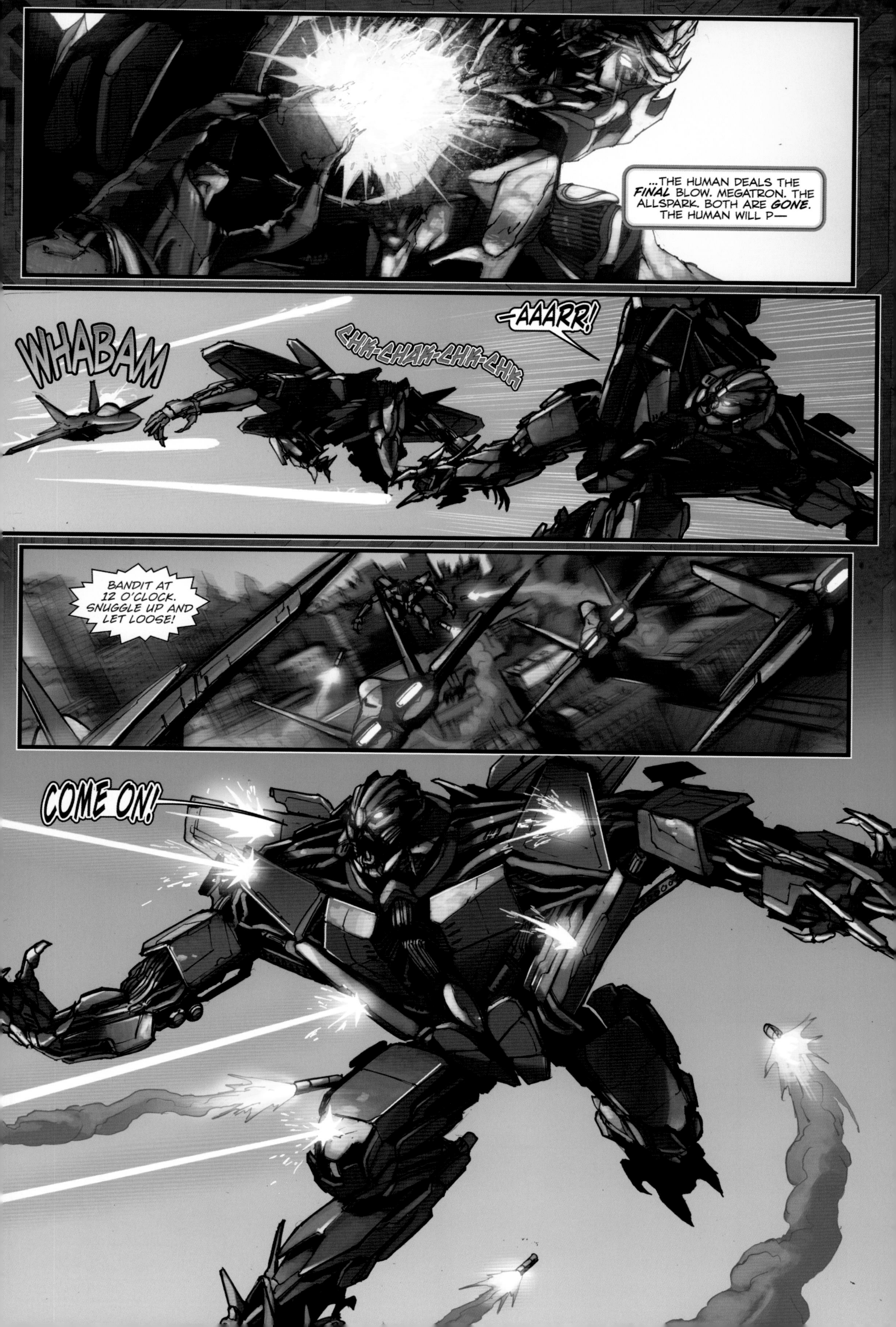
...THE HUMAN DEALS THE FINAL BLOW. MEGATRON. THE ALLSPARK. BOTH ARE GONE. THE HUMAN WILL P—
WHABAM
CHK-CHAK-CHK-CHK
—AAARR!
BANDIT AT 12 O'CLOCK. SNUGGLE UP AND LET LOOSE!
COME ON!

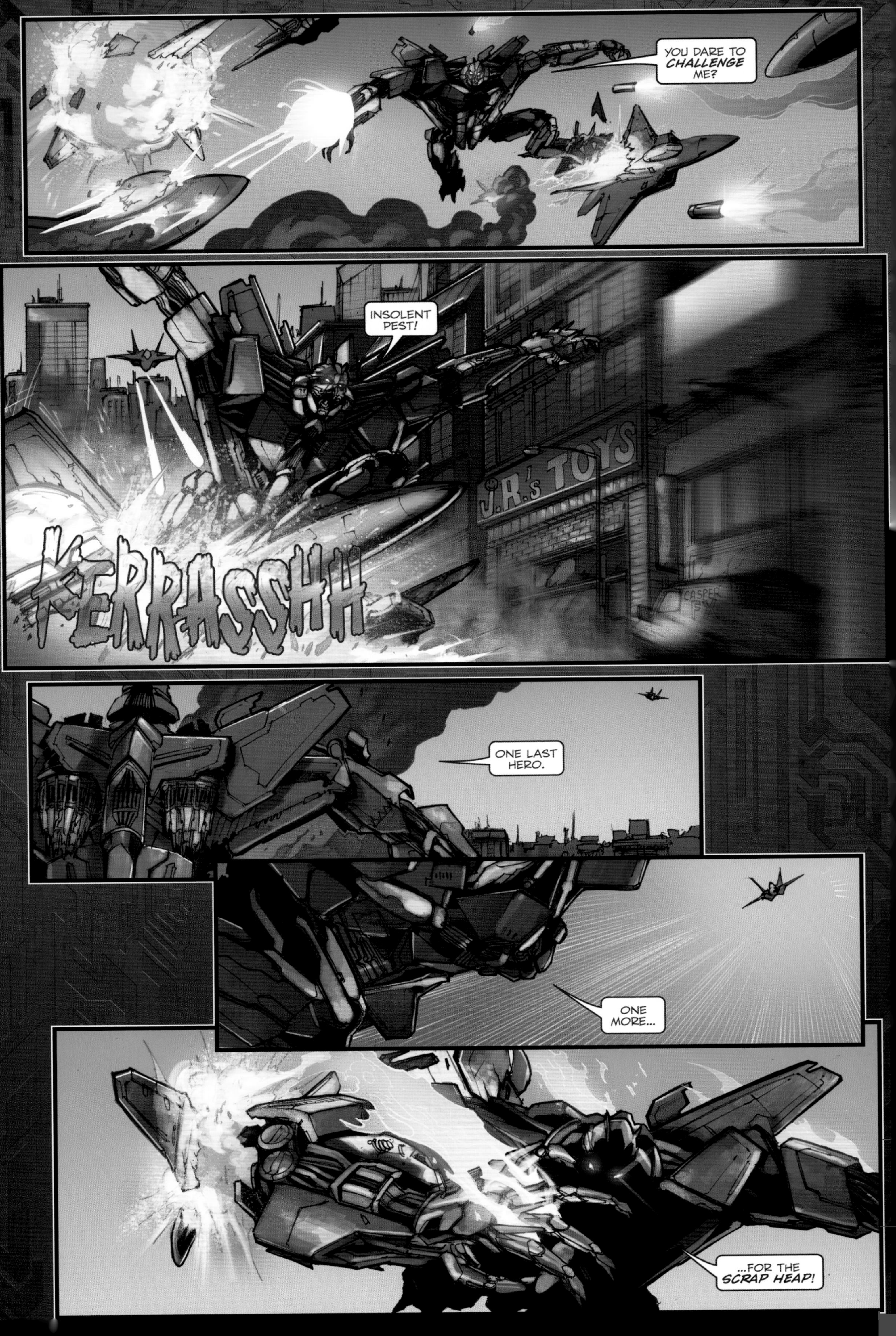
YOU DARE TO CHALLENGE ME?
INSOLENT PEST!
KERRASSHH
J.R.'s TOYS
ONE LAST HERO.
ONE MORE...
...FOR THE SCRAP HEAP!

I'D LOVE TO STAY AND EXACT MY *REVENGE*, BUT I FEAR THAT I MAY BE THE LAST DECEPTICON ON THIS PLANET.

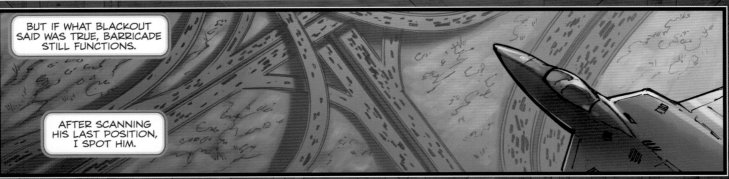

BUT IF WHAT BLACKOUT SAID WAS TRUE, BARRICADE STILL FUNCTIONS.

AFTER SCANNING HIS LAST POSITION, I SPOT HIM.

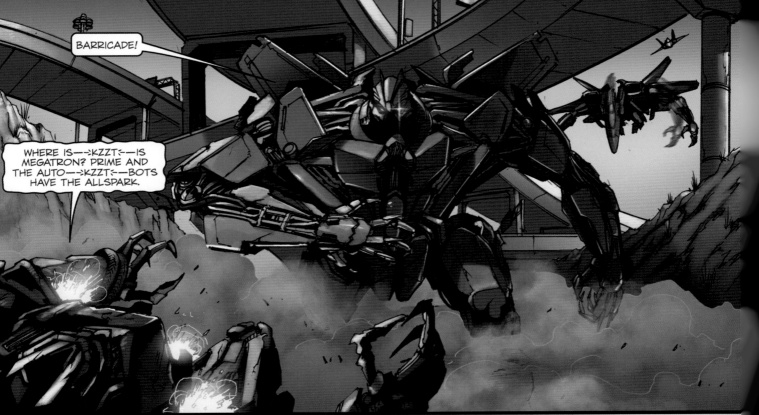

BARRICADE!

WHERE IS—⇥KZZT⇤—IS MEGATRON? PRIME AND THE AUTO—⇥KZZT⇤—BOTS HAVE THE ALLSPARK.

YES, I KNOW. WHEN CAN I CONSIDER YOU FUNCTIONAL?

SHORTLY. MY ENERGON LEV—⇥KZZT⇤—LEVELS ARE RECHARGING.

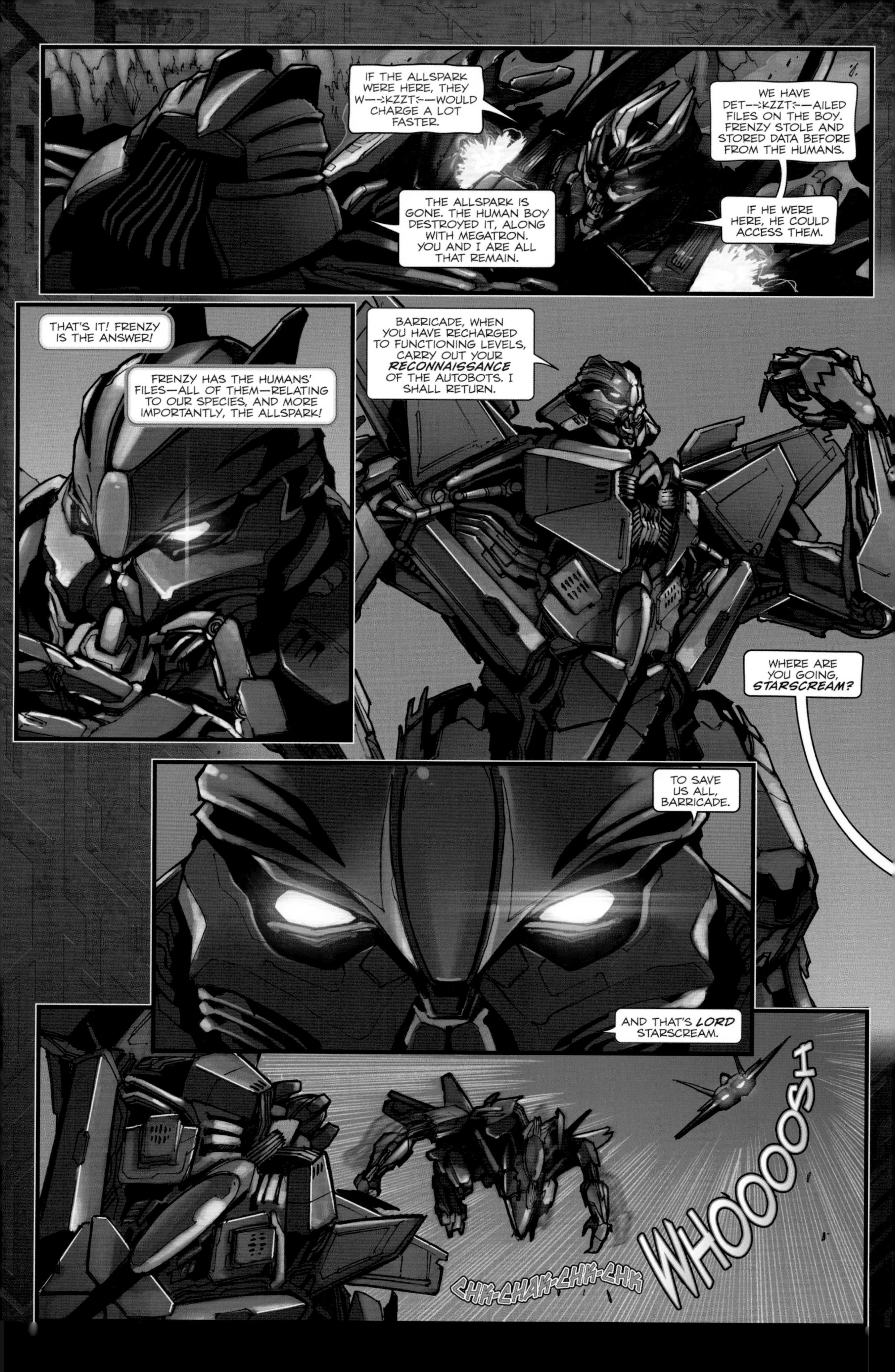

IF THE ALLSPARK WERE HERE, THEY W—KZZT—WOULD CHARGE A LOT FASTER.
THE ALLSPARK IS GONE. THE HUMAN BOY DESTROYED IT, ALONG WITH MEGATRON. YOU AND I ARE ALL THAT REMAIN.
WE HAVE DET—KZZT—AILED FILES ON THE BOY. FRENZY STOLE AND STORED DATA BEFORE FROM THE HUMANS.
IF HE WERE HERE, HE COULD ACCESS THEM.
THAT'S IT! FRENZY IS THE ANSWER!
FRENZY HAS THE HUMANS' FILES—ALL OF THEM—RELATING TO OUR SPECIES, AND MORE IMPORTANTLY, THE ALLSPARK!
BARRICADE, WHEN YOU HAVE RECHARGED TO FUNCTIONING LEVELS, CARRY OUT YOUR ***RECONNAISSANCE*** OF THE AUTOBOTS. I SHALL RETURN.
WHERE ARE YOU GOING, ***STARSCREAM?***
TO SAVE US ALL, BARRICADE.
AND THAT'S ***LORD*** STARSCREAM.
CHK-CHAK-CHK-CHK
WHOOOOSH

I DID NOT FAIL *YOU*, MEGATRON... YOU FAILED *US*.

YOU ARE *DEAD* NOW, AND PRIME HAS NOTHING AS WELL. HEH, SOME LEADERS.

OUR SPECIES HELPED WIPE OUT THE RECORDS OF THE ALLSPARK, AND A HUMAN DESTROYED IT ENTIRELY.

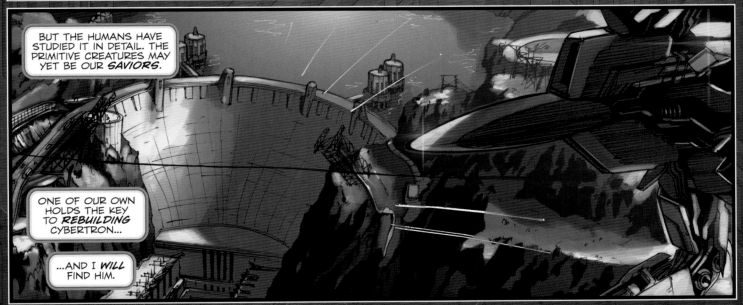

BUT THE HUMANS HAVE STUDIED IT IN DETAIL. THE PRIMITIVE CREATURES MAY YET BE OUR *SAVIORS*.

ONE OF OUR OWN HOLDS THE KEY TO *REBUILDING* CYBERTRON...

...AND I *WILL* FIND HIM.

BELOW, MY NEW *ENEMIES* HAVE GATHERED.

I HAVE NO FEAR, ONLY *AMBITION*. BESIDES...

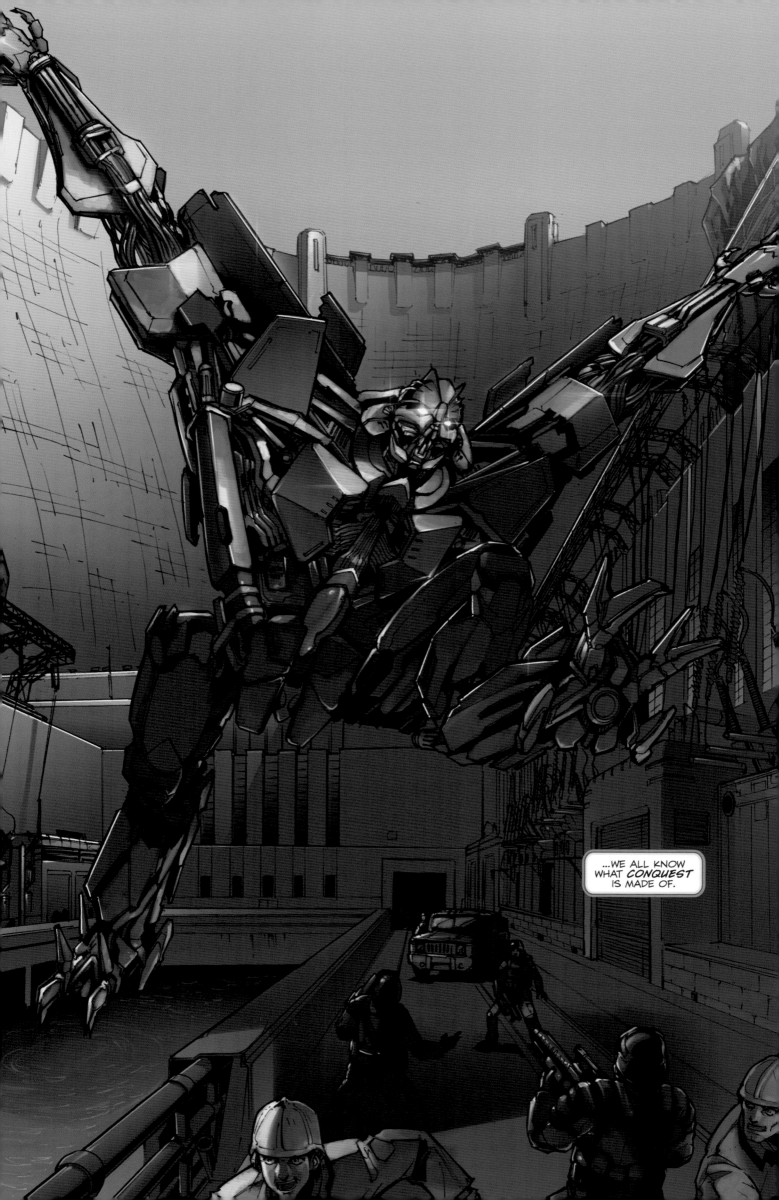

...WE ALL KNOW WHAT CONQUEST IS MADE OF.

CHAPTER TWO

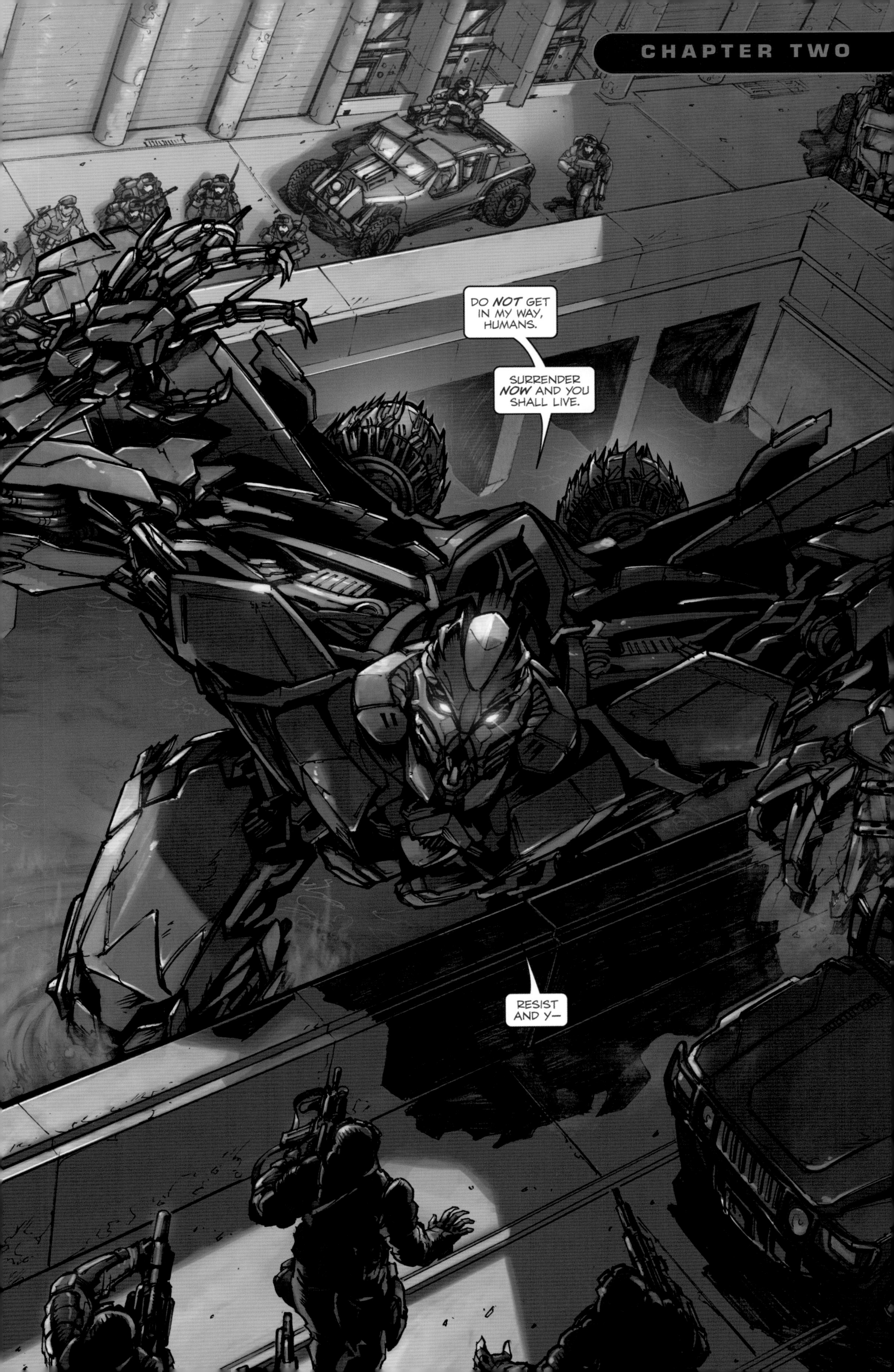

DO *NOT* GET IN MY WAY, HUMANS.
SURRENDER *NOW* AND YOU SHALL LIVE.
RESIST AND Y—

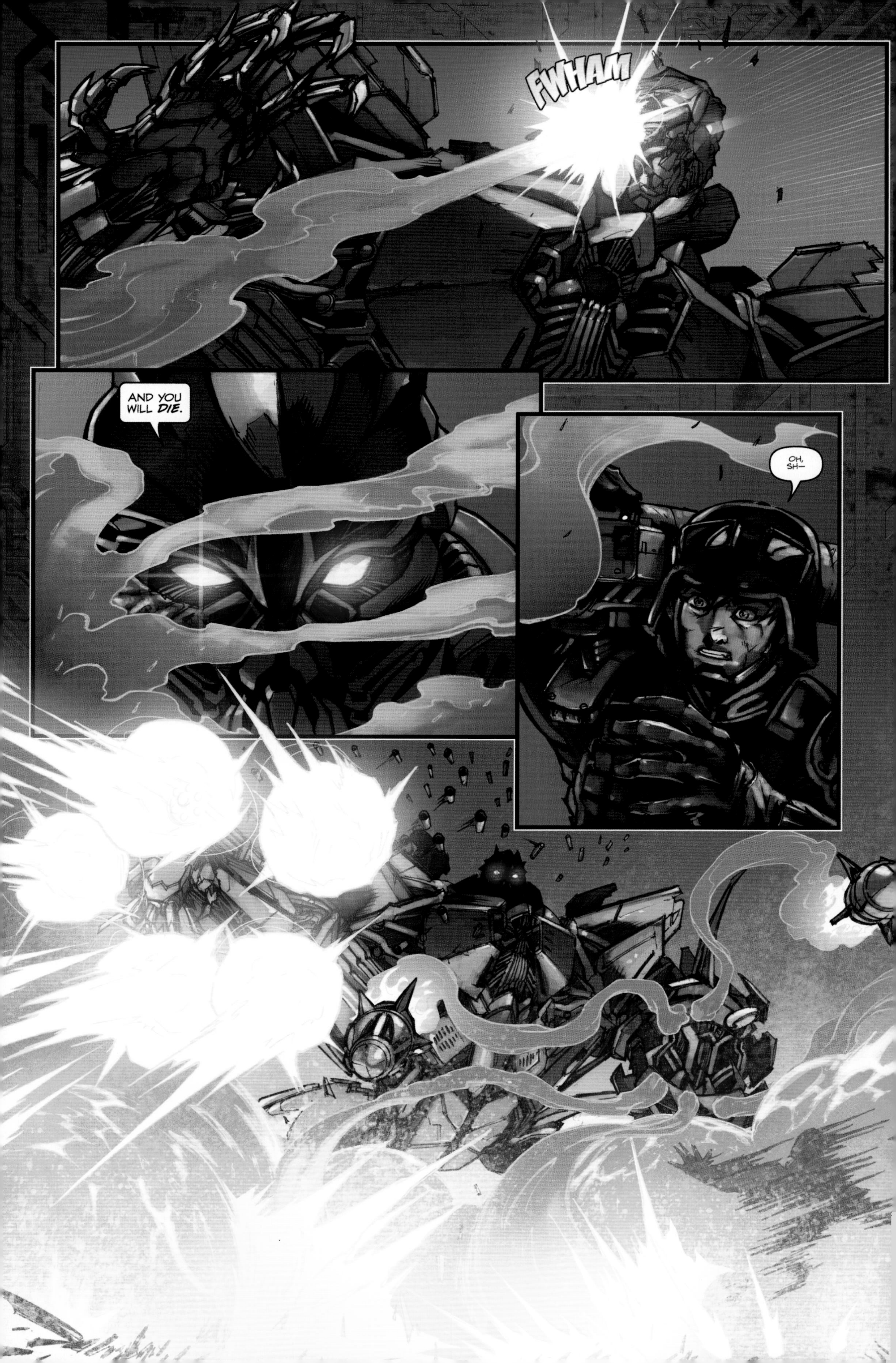
FWHAM
AND YOU WILL DIE.
OH, SH—

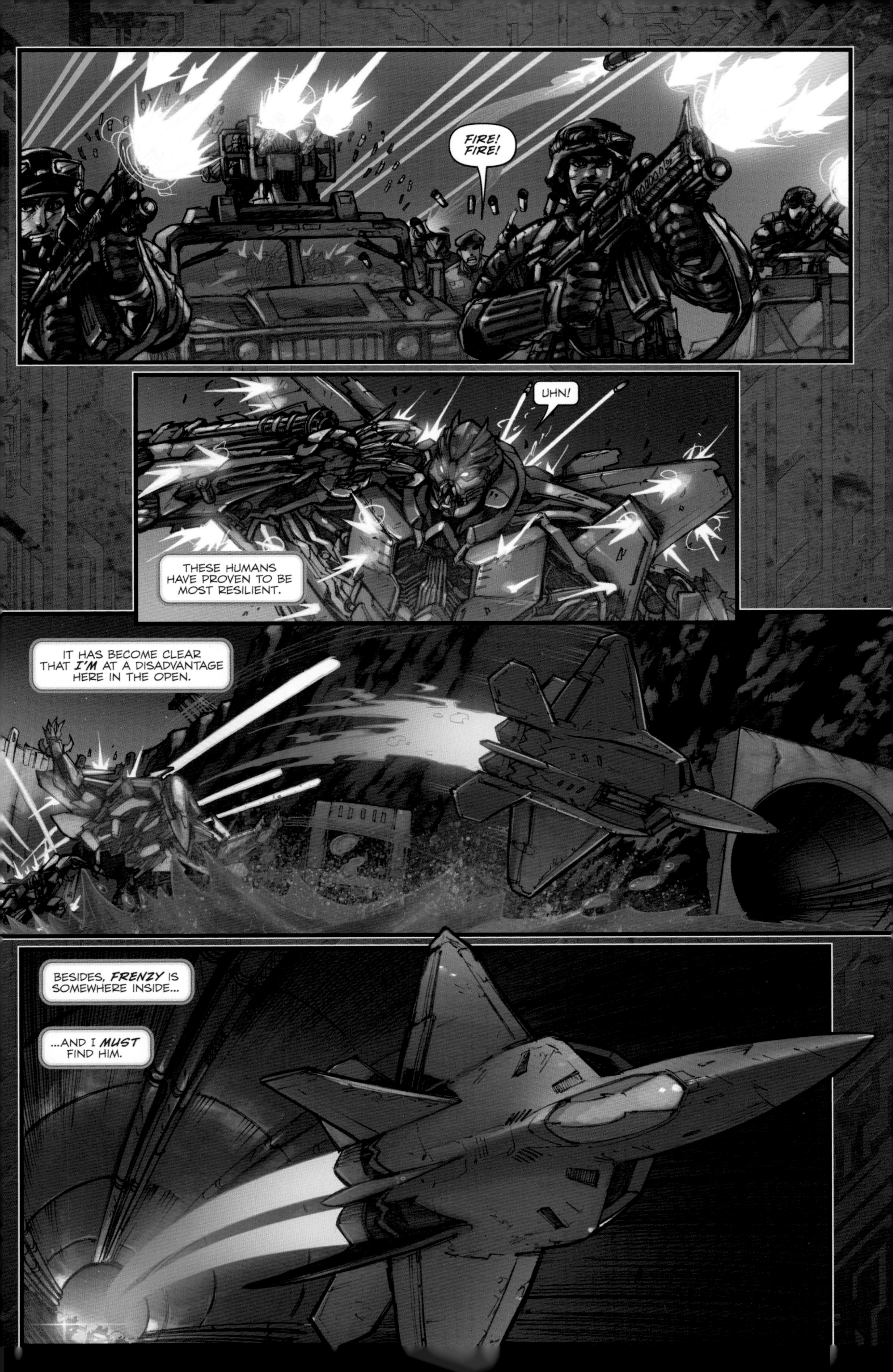
FIRE! FIRE!
UHN!
THESE HUMANS HAVE PROVEN TO BE MOST RESILIENT.
IT HAS BECOME CLEAR THAT I'M AT A DISADVANTAGE HERE IN THE OPEN.
BESIDES, FRENZY IS SOMEWHERE INSIDE...
...AND I MUST FIND HIM.

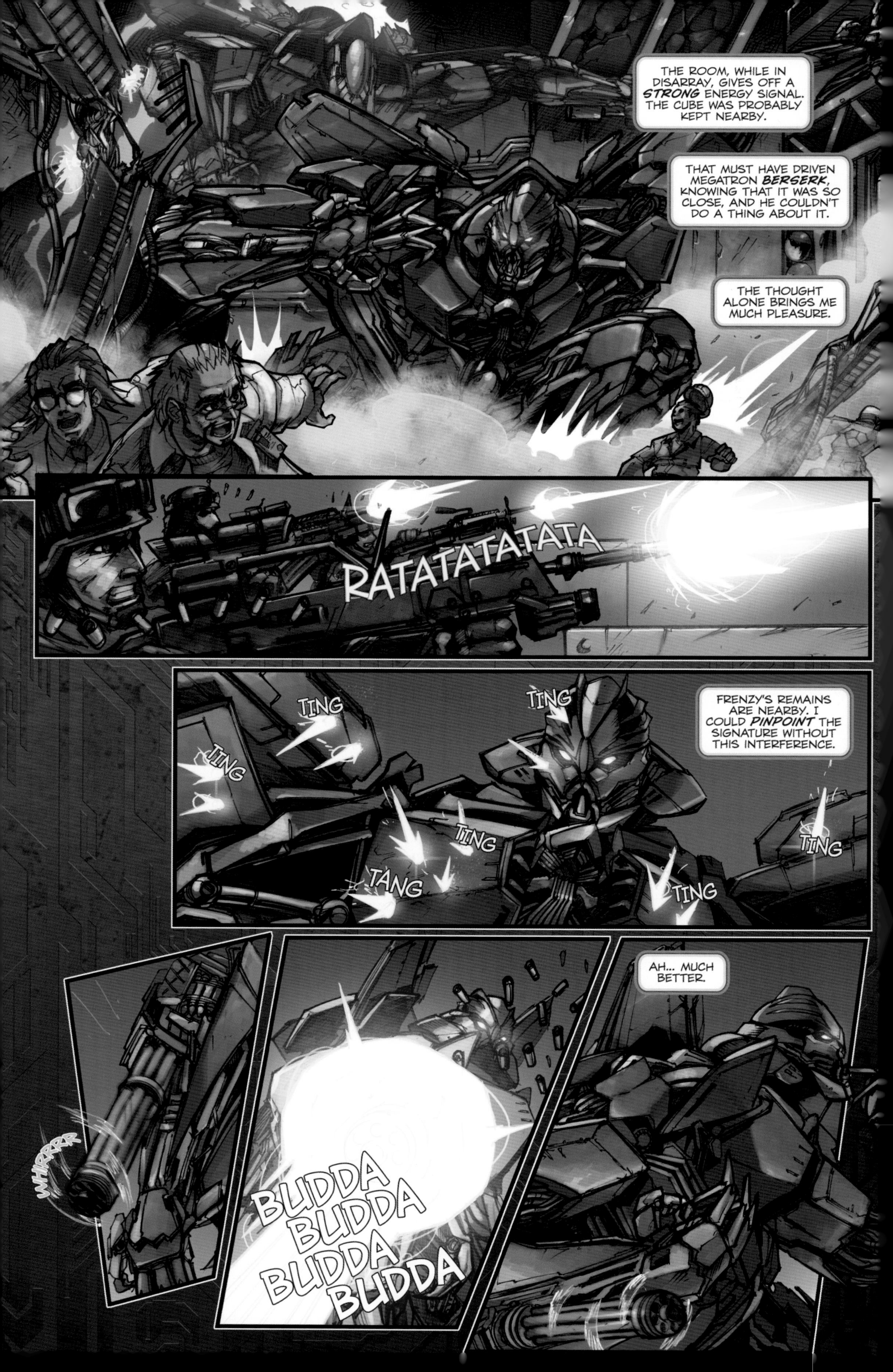
THE ROOM, WHILE IN DISARRAY, GIVES OFF A STRONG ENERGY SIGNAL. THE CUBE WAS PROBABLY KEPT NEARBY.
THAT MUST HAVE DRIVEN MEGATRON BERSERK, KNOWING THAT IT WAS SO CLOSE, AND HE COULDN'T DO A THING ABOUT IT.
THE THOUGHT ALONE BRINGS ME MUCH PLEASURE.
RATATATATATA
TING
TING
TING
FRENZY'S REMAINS ARE NEARBY. I COULD PINPOINT THE SIGNATURE WITHOUT THIS INTERFERENCE.
TING
TING
TANG
TING
WHIRRRR
BUDDA BUDDA BUDDA BUDDA
AH... MUCH BETTER.

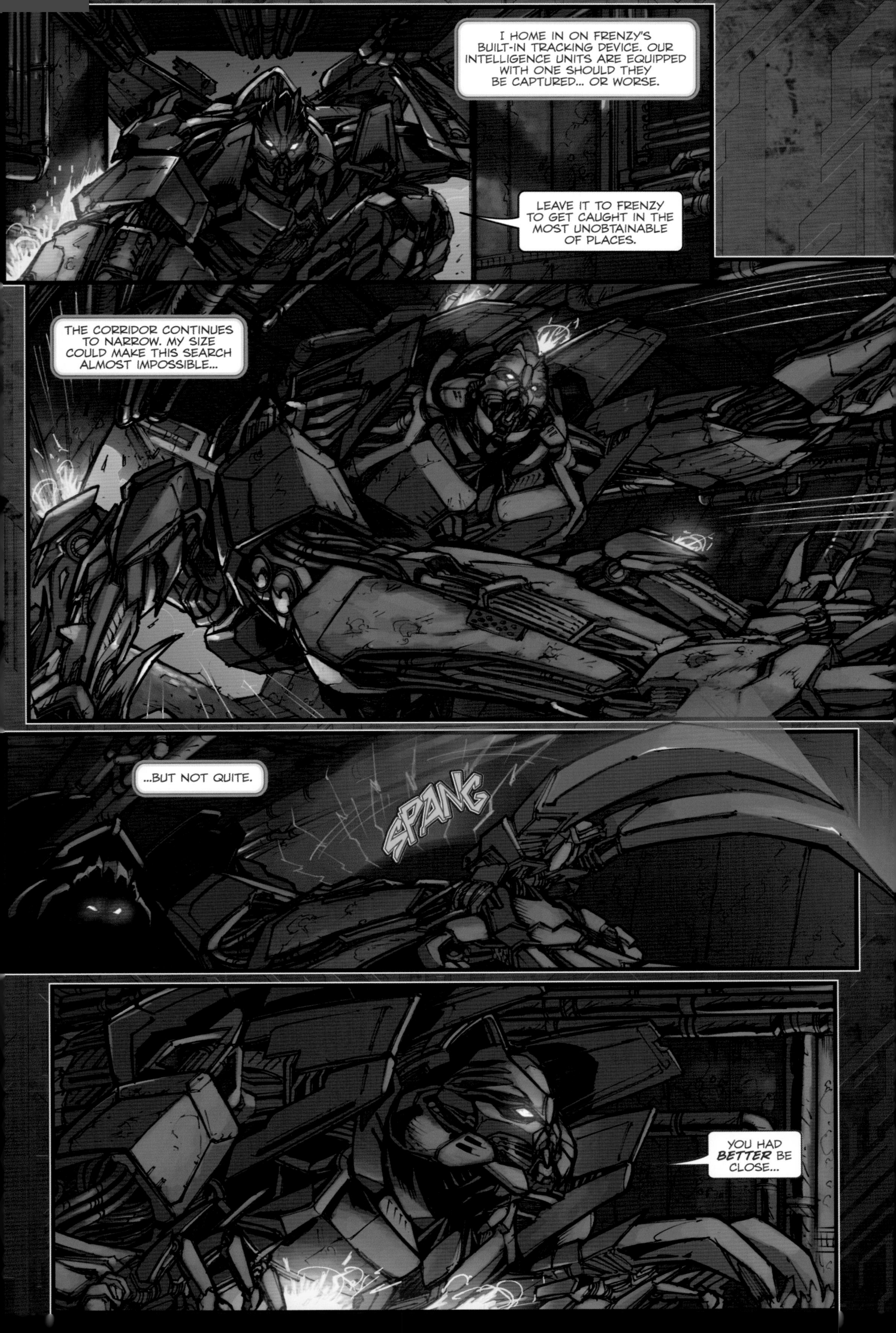
I HOME IN ON FRENZY'S BUILT-IN TRACKING DEVICE. OUR INTELLIGENCE UNITS ARE EQUIPPED WITH ONE SHOULD THEY BE CAPTURED... OR WORSE.
LEAVE IT TO FRENZY TO GET CAUGHT IN THE MOST UNOBTAINABLE OF PLACES.
THE CORRIDOR CONTINUES TO NARROW. MY SIZE COULD MAKE THIS SEARCH ALMOST IMPOSSIBLE...
...BUT NOT QUITE.
SPANG
YOU HAD **BETTER** BE CLOSE...

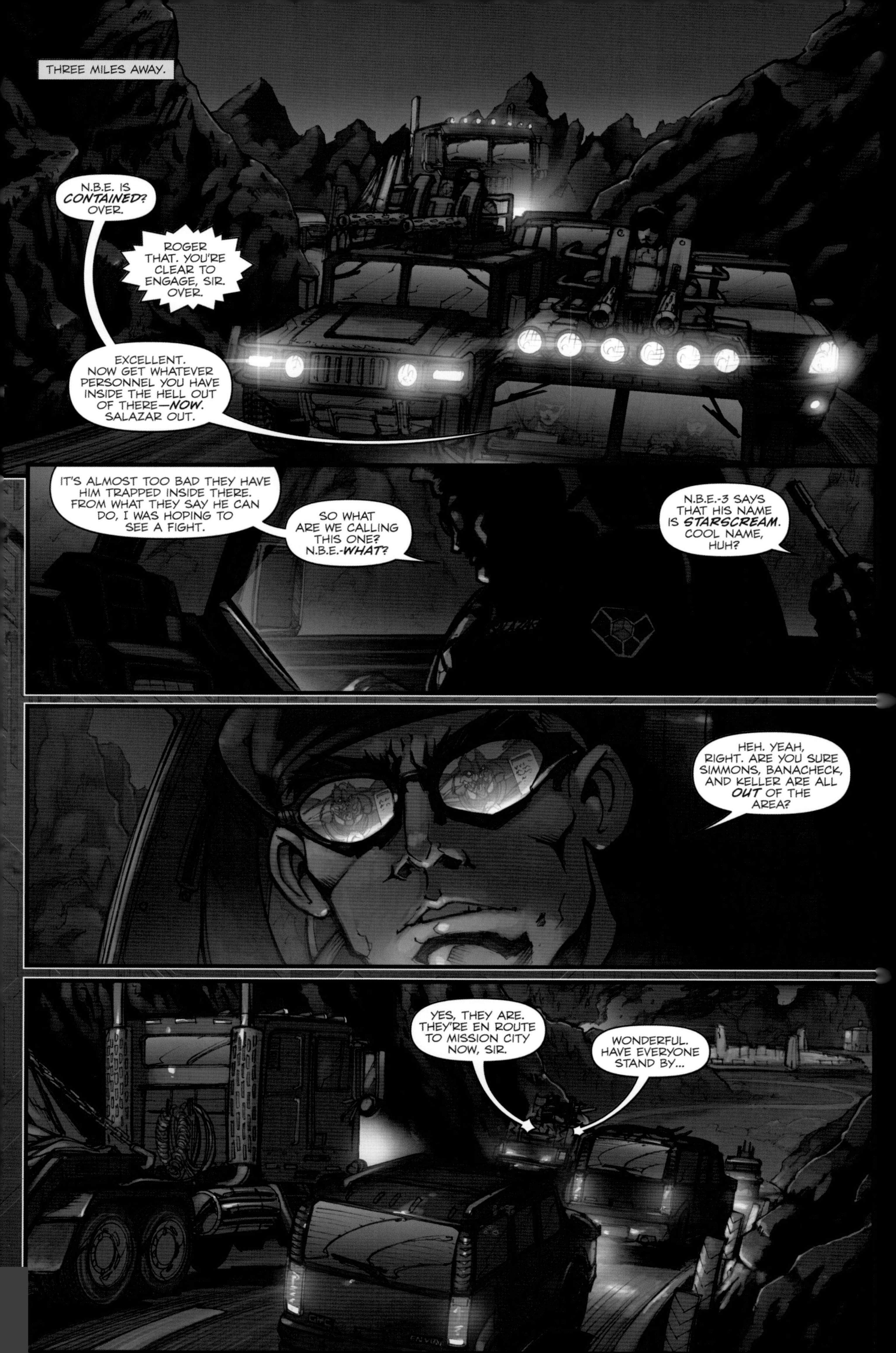
THREE MILES AWAY.
N.B.E. IS *CONTAINED?* OVER.
ROGER THAT. YOU'RE CLEAR TO ENGAGE, SIR. OVER.
EXCELLENT. NOW GET WHATEVER PERSONNEL YOU HAVE INSIDE THE HELL OUT OF THERE—*NOW*. SALAZAR OUT.
IT'S ALMOST TOO BAD THEY HAVE HIM TRAPPED INSIDE THERE. FROM WHAT THEY SAY HE CAN DO, I WAS HOPING TO SEE A FIGHT.
SO WHAT ARE WE CALLING THIS ONE? N.B.E.-*WHAT?*
N.B.E.-3 SAYS THAT HIS NAME IS *STARSCREAM*. COOL NAME, HUH?
HEH. YEAH, RIGHT. ARE YOU SURE SIMMONS, BANACHECK, AND KELLER ARE ALL *OUT* OF THE AREA?
YES, THEY ARE. THEY'RE EN ROUTE TO MISSION CITY NOW, SIR.
WONDERFUL. HAVE EVERYONE STAND BY...

"...WE'RE ALMOST THERE."

JUST SHORT OF MY GOAL.

I SENSE FRENZY—OR WHAT REMAINS OF HIM—JUST BEYOND THE DOORS AHEAD.

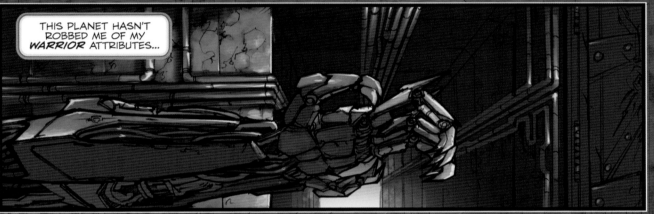

THIS PLANET HASN'T ROBBED ME OF MY *WARRIOR* ATTRIBUTES...

SKRRTCH

...OR OF OUR SPECIES' INHERENT ABILITY TO *ADAPT.*

FSSHH

WHAM

–GASP–

WHAT THE—

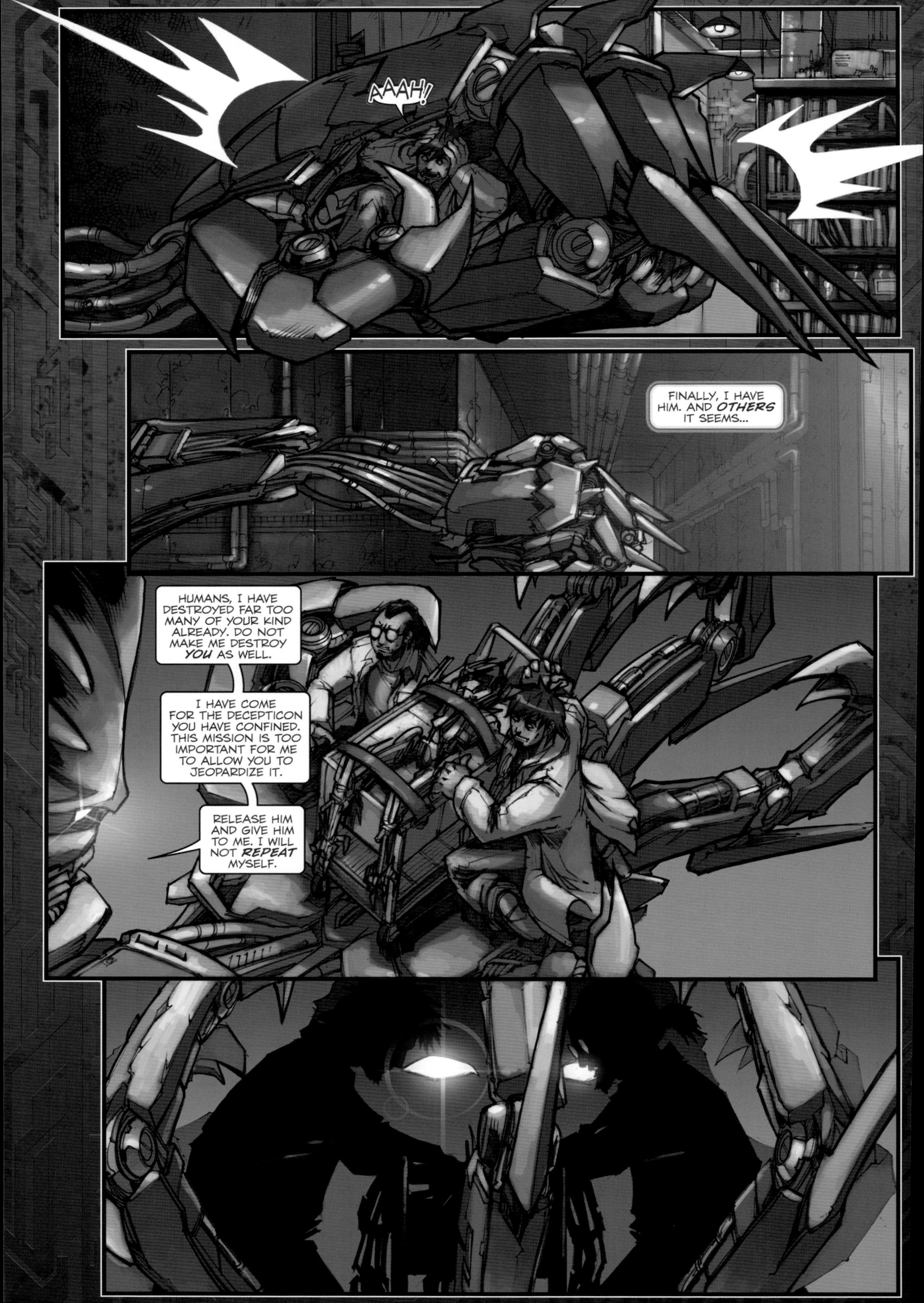
AAAH!
FINALLY, I HAVE HIM. AND *OTHERS* IT SEEMS...
HUMANS, I HAVE DESTROYED FAR TOO MANY OF YOUR KIND ALREADY. DO NOT MAKE ME DESTROY *YOU* AS WELL.
I HAVE COME FOR THE DECEPTICON YOU HAVE CONFINED. THIS MISSION IS TOO IMPORTANT FOR ME TO ALLOW YOU TO JEOPARDIZE IT.
RELEASE HIM AND GIVE HIM TO ME. I WILL NOT *REPEAT* MYSELF.

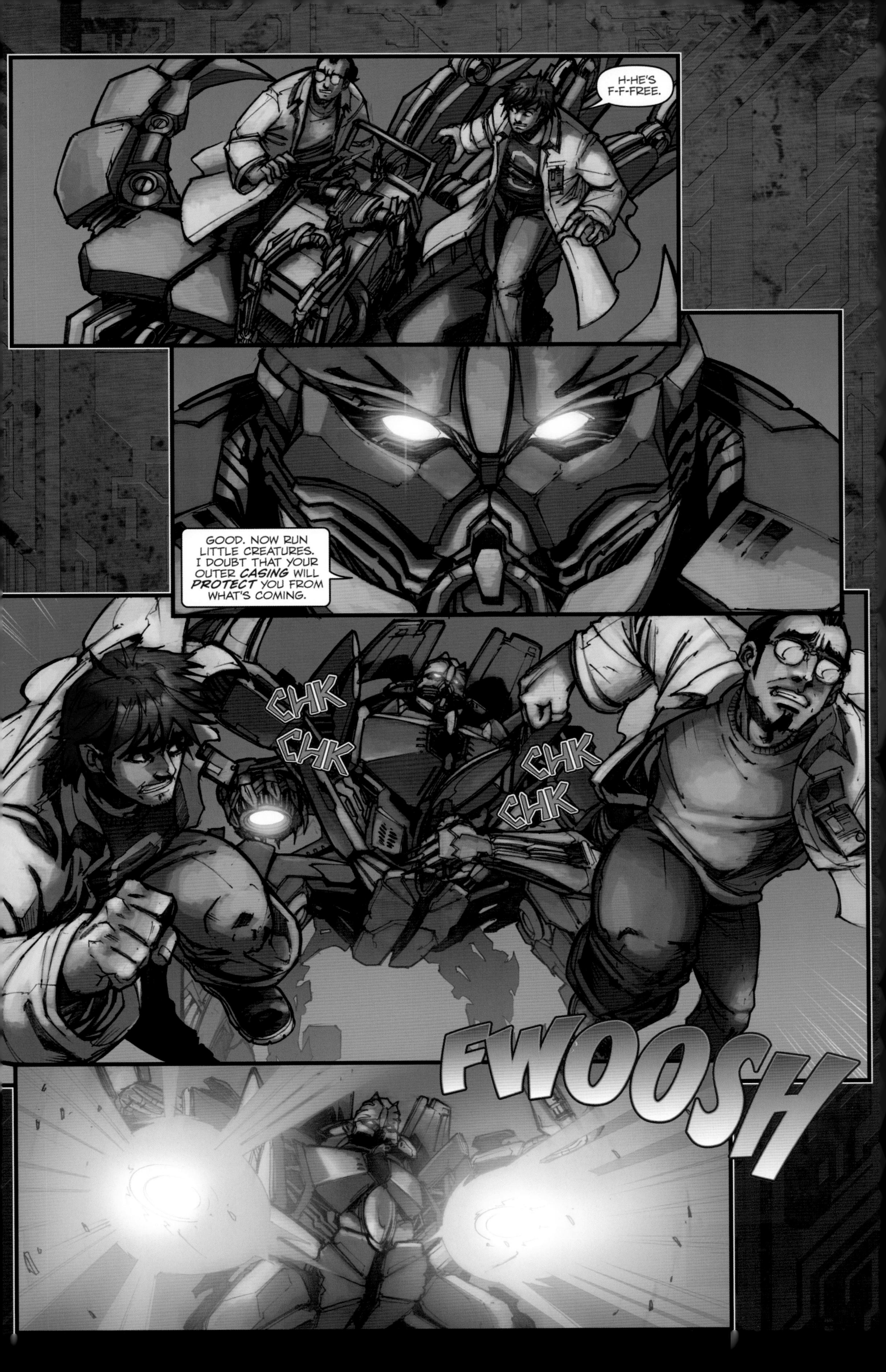
H-HE'S F-F-FREE.
GOOD. NOW RUN LITTLE CREATURES. I DOUBT THAT YOUR OUTER CASING WILL PROTECT YOU FROM WHAT'S COMING.
CHK CHK
CHK CHK
FWOOSH

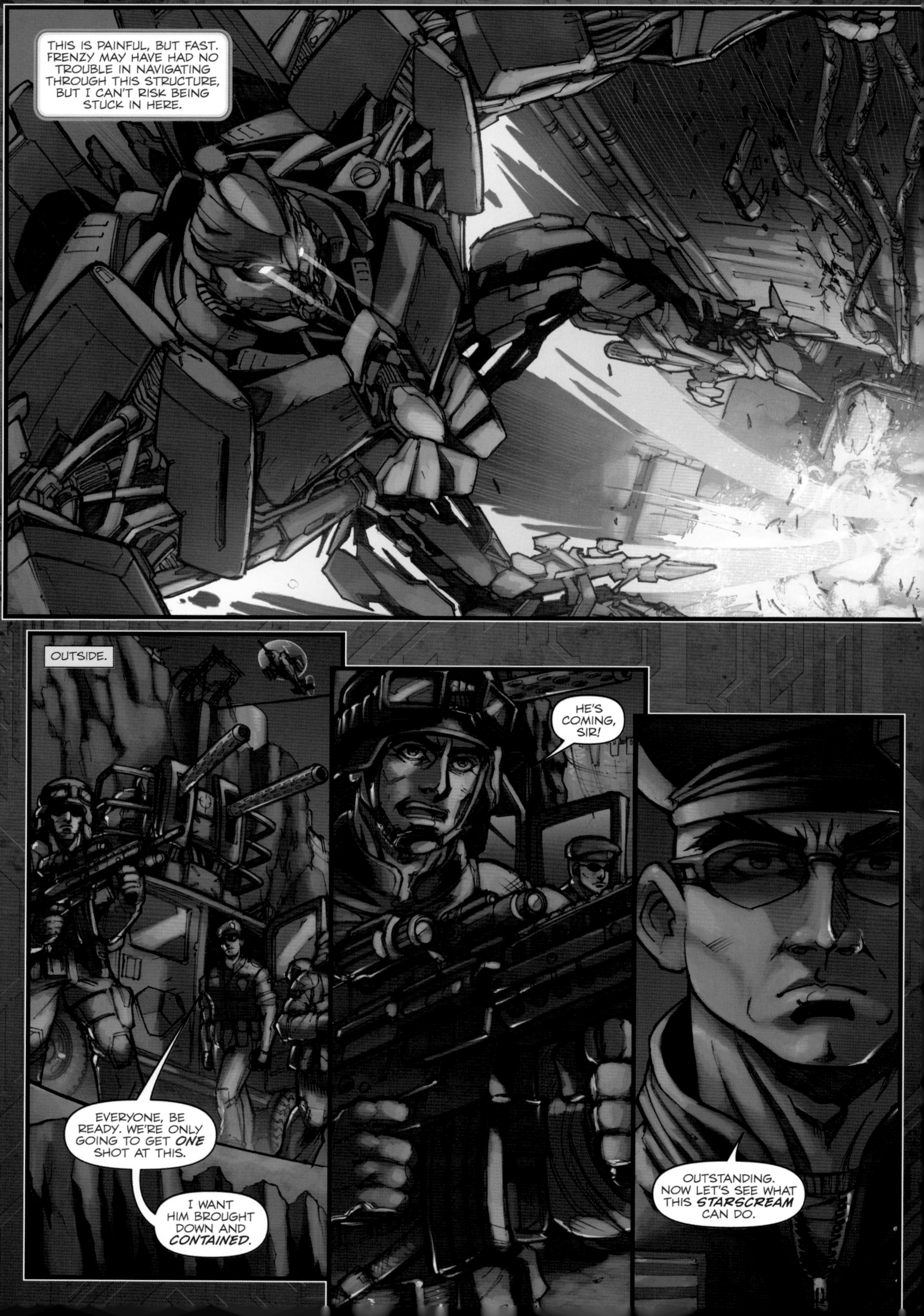
THIS IS PAINFUL, BUT FAST. FRENZY MAY HAVE HAD NO TROUBLE IN NAVIGATING THROUGH THIS STRUCTURE, BUT I CAN'T RISK BEING STUCK IN HERE.
OUTSIDE.
EVERYONE, BE READY. WE'RE ONLY GOING TO GET ***ONE*** SHOT AT THIS.
I WANT HIM BROUGHT DOWN AND ***CONTAINED***.
HE'S COMING, SIR!
OUTSTANDING. NOW LET'S SEE WHAT THIS ***STARSCREAM*** CAN DO.

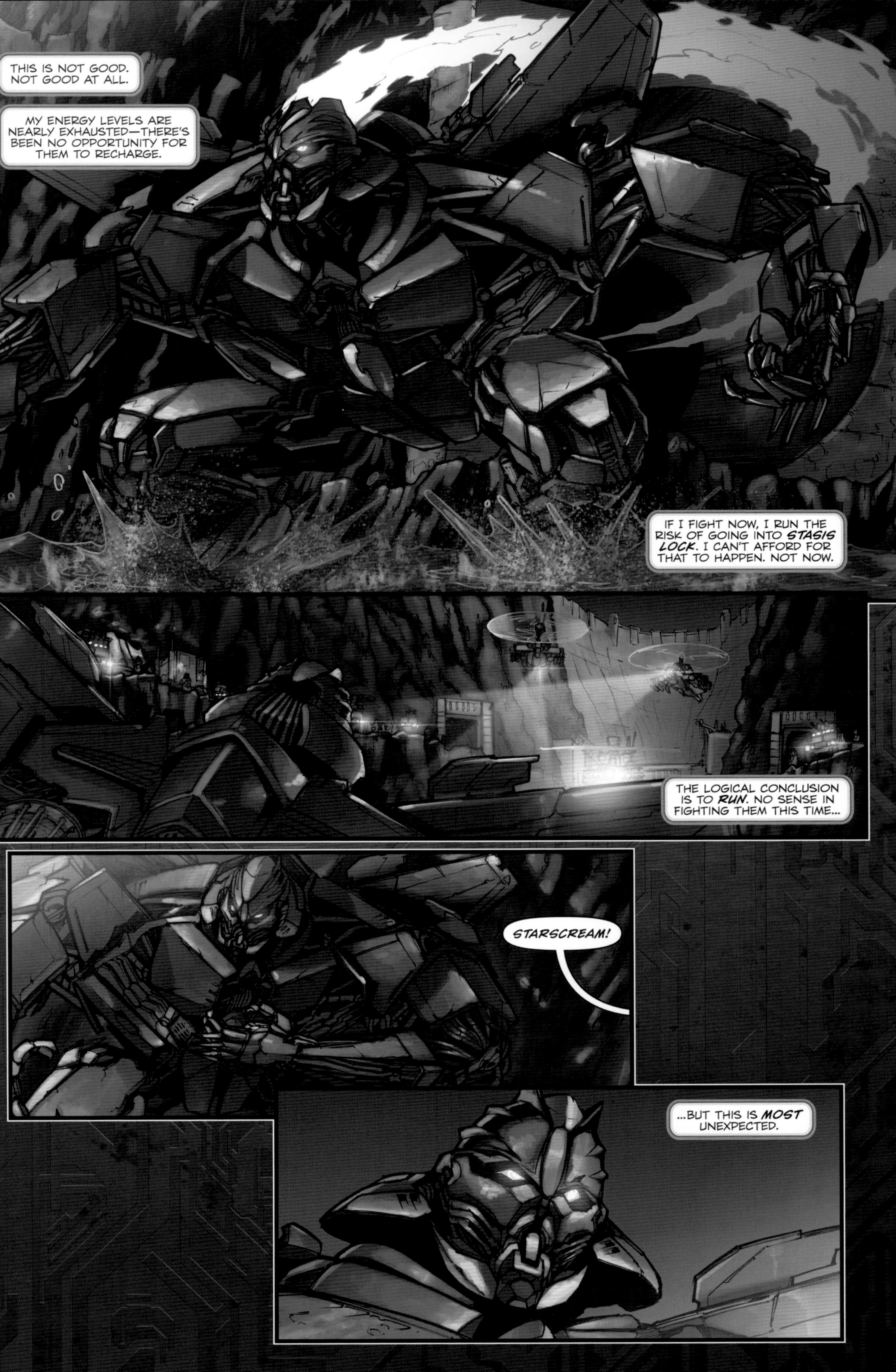
THIS IS NOT GOOD. NOT GOOD AT ALL.
MY ENERGY LEVELS ARE NEARLY EXHAUSTED—THERE'S BEEN NO OPPORTUNITY FOR THEM TO RECHARGE.
IF I FIGHT NOW, I RUN THE RISK OF GOING INTO STASIS LOCK. I CAN'T AFFORD FOR THAT TO HAPPEN. NOT NOW.
THE LOGICAL CONCLUSION IS TO RUN. NO SENSE IN FIGHTING THEM THIS TIME...
STARSCREAM!
...BUT THIS IS MOST UNEXPECTED.

STARSCREAM! I AM AGENT SALAZAR WITH SECTOR SEVEN. WE DON'T WISH TO HARM YOU, SO DON'T MAKE ANY *SUDDEN* MOVES AND YOU'LL BE JUST FINE.

THINK HE UNDERSTANDS?

UH, I WOULD SAY PROBABLY *NOT*.

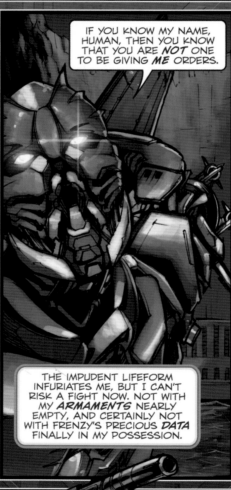

IF YOU KNOW MY NAME, HUMAN, THEN YOU KNOW THAT YOU ARE *NOT* ONE TO BE GIVING *ME* ORDERS.

THE IMPUDENT LIFEFORM INFURIATES ME, BUT I CAN'T RISK A FIGHT NOW. NOT WITH MY *ARMAMENTS* NEARLY EMPTY, AND CERTAINLY NOT WITH FRENZY'S PRECIOUS *DATA* FINALLY IN MY POSSESSION.

HE'S NOT GOING TO COOPERATE...

...RELEASE *L.M.-1!*

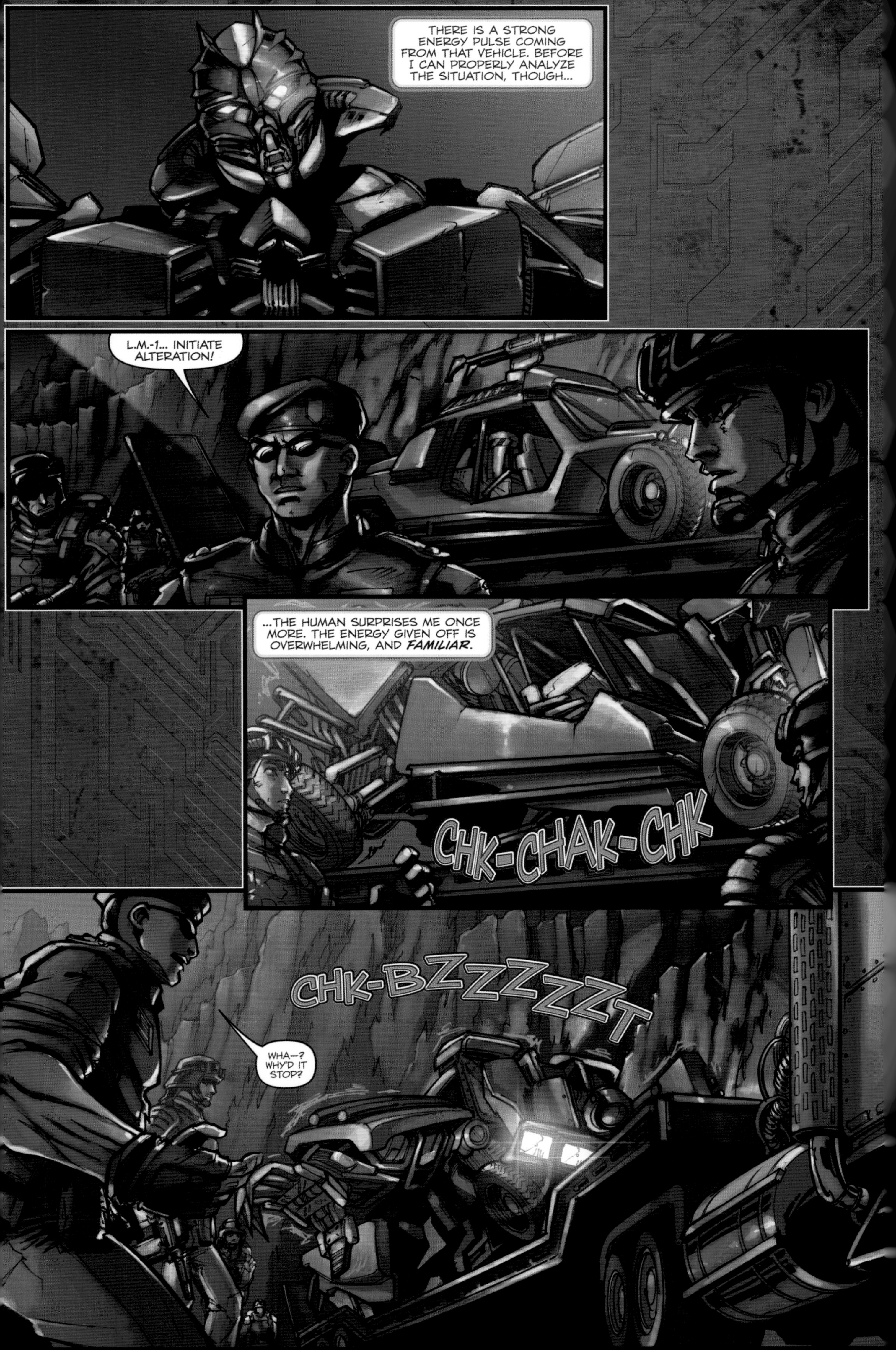
THERE IS A STRONG ENERGY PULSE COMING FROM THAT VEHICLE. BEFORE I CAN PROPERLY ANALYZE THE SITUATION, THOUGH...
L.M.-1... INITIATE ALTERATION!
...THE HUMAN SURPRISES ME ONCE MORE. THE ENERGY GIVEN OFF IS OVERWHELMING, AND FAMILIAR.
CHK-CHAK-CHK
CHK-BZZZZZZT
WHA—? WHY'D IT STOP?

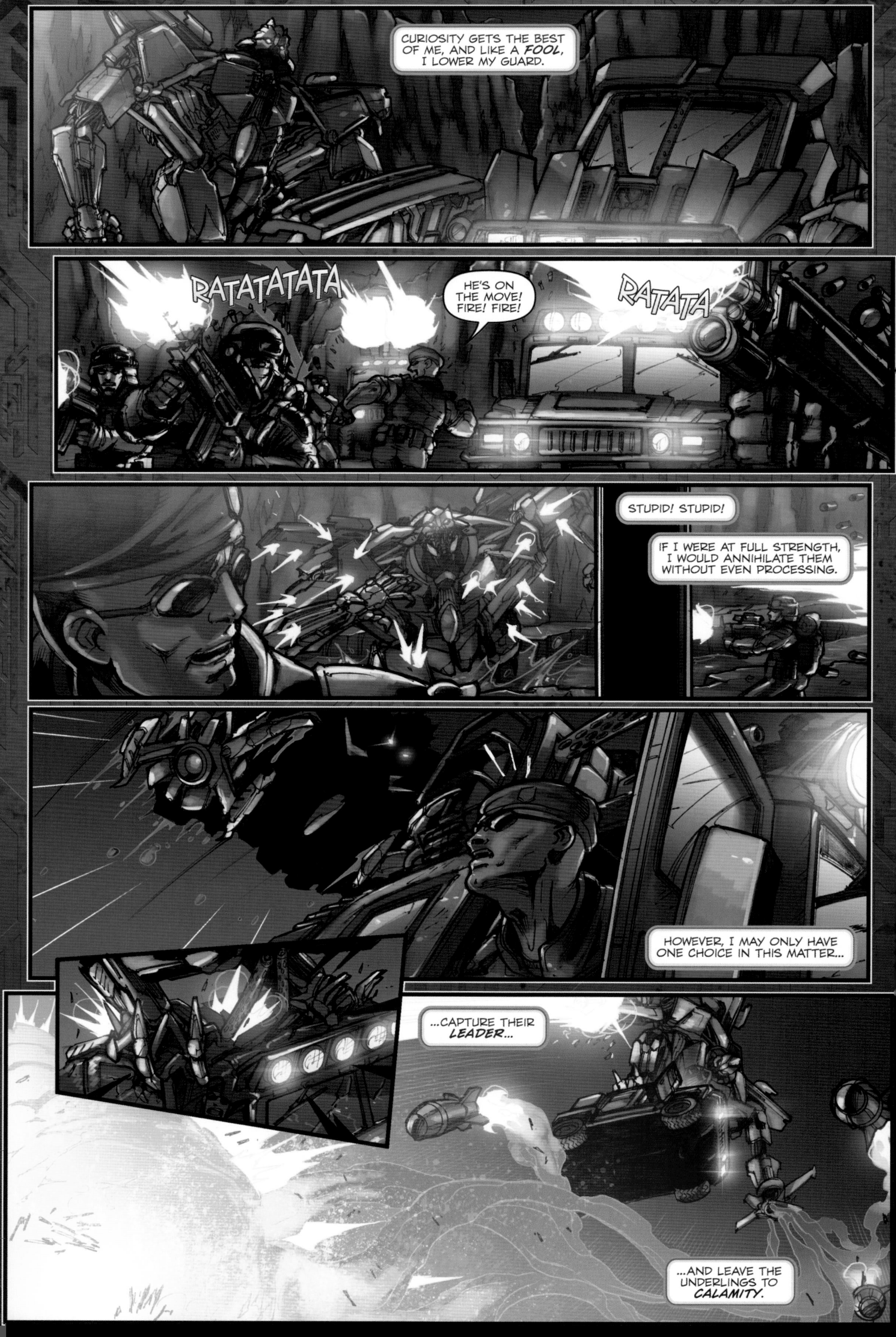
CURIOSITY GETS THE BEST OF ME, AND LIKE A *FOOL*, I LOWER MY GUARD.
RATATATATA
HE'S ON THE MOVE! FIRE! FIRE!
RATATA
STUPID! STUPID!
IF I WERE AT FULL STRENGTH, I WOULD ANNIHILATE THEM WITHOUT EVEN PROCESSING.
HOWEVER, I MAY ONLY HAVE ONE CHOICE IN THIS MATTER...
...CAPTURE THEIR *LEADER*...
...AND LEAVE THE UNDERLINGS TO *CALAMITY*.

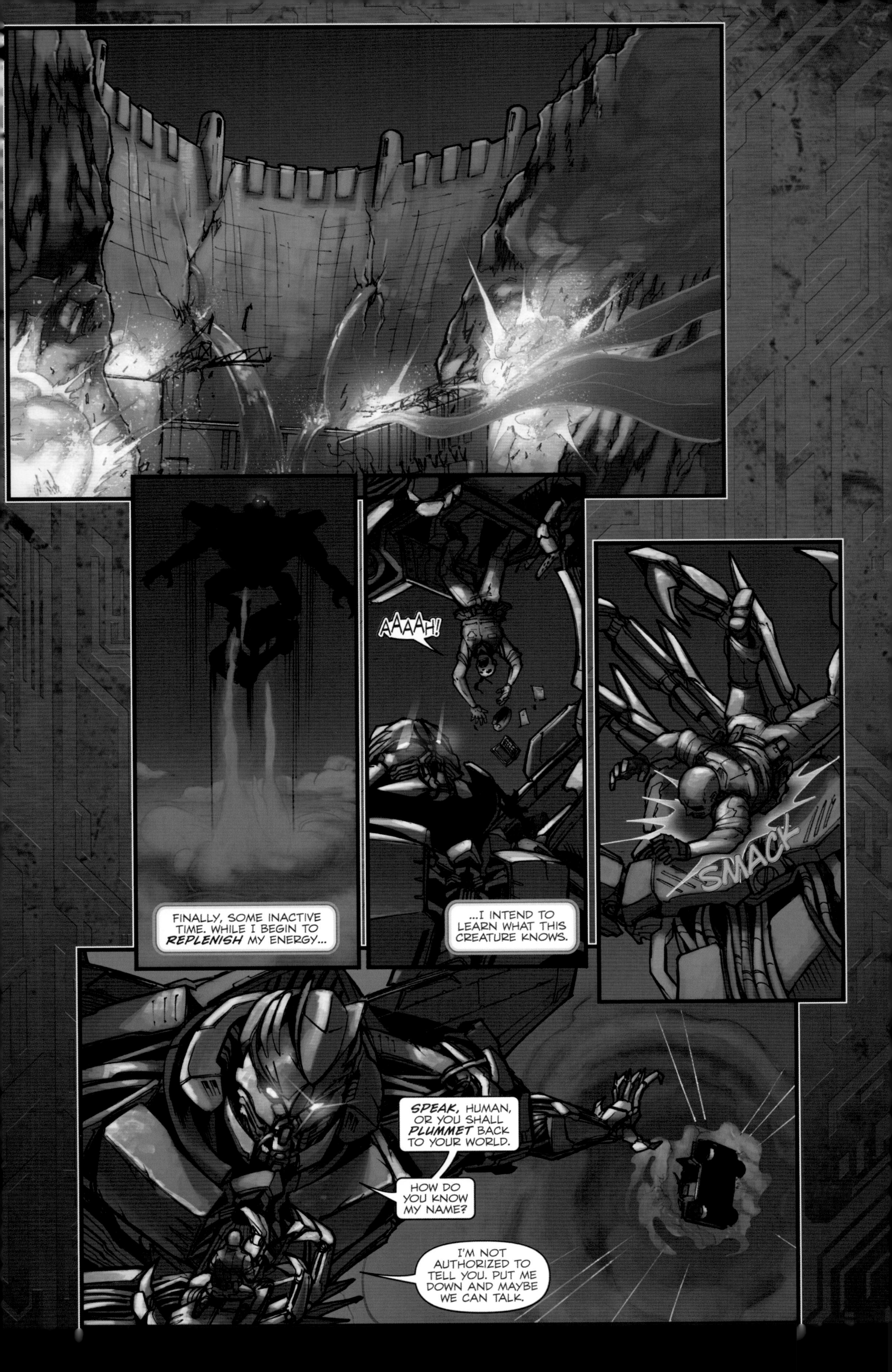

AAAAH!
FINALLY, SOME INACTIVE TIME. WHILE I BEGIN TO REPLENISH MY ENERGY...
...I INTEND TO LEARN WHAT THIS CREATURE KNOWS.
SMACK
SPEAK, HUMAN, OR YOU SHALL PLUMMET BACK TO YOUR WORLD.
HOW DO YOU KNOW MY NAME?
I'M NOT AUTHORIZED TO TELL YOU. PUT ME DOWN AND MAYBE WE CAN TALK.

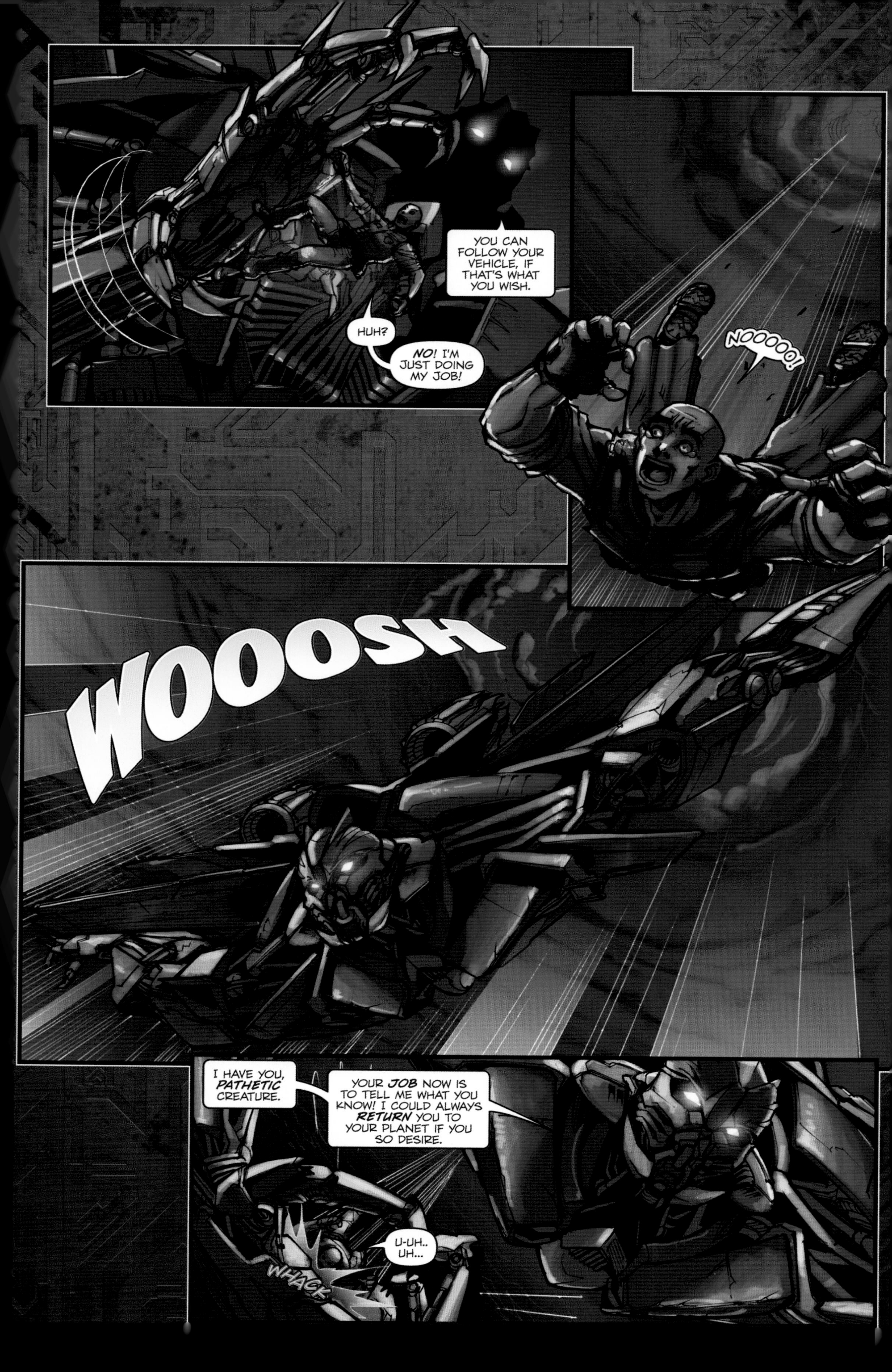

YOU CAN FOLLOW YOUR VEHICLE, IF THAT'S WHAT YOU WISH.
HUH?
NO! I'M JUST DOING MY JOB!
NOOOOO!
WOOOSH
I HAVE YOU, PATHETIC CREATURE.
YOUR JOB NOW IS TO TELL ME WHAT YOU KNOW! I COULD ALWAYS RETURN YOU TO YOUR PLANET IF YOU SO DESIRE.
U-UH.. UH...
WHACK

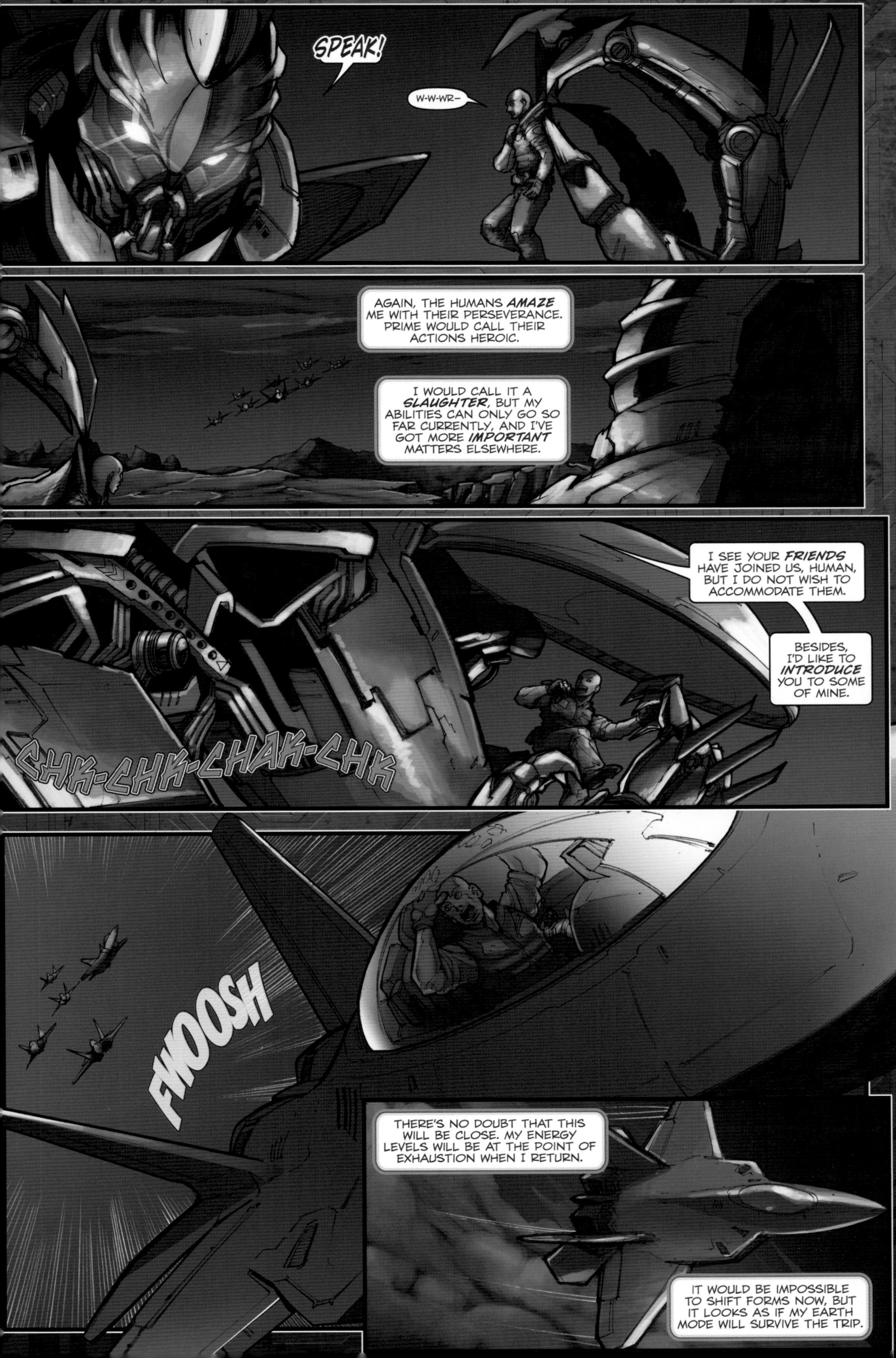

SPEAK!
W-W-WR–
AGAIN, THE HUMANS AMAZE ME WITH THEIR PERSEVERANCE. PRIME WOULD CALL THEIR ACTIONS HEROIC.
I WOULD CALL IT A SLAUGHTER, BUT MY ABILITIES CAN ONLY GO SO FAR CURRENTLY, AND I'VE GOT MORE IMPORTANT MATTERS ELSEWHERE.
I SEE YOUR FRIENDS HAVE JOINED US, HUMAN, BUT I DO NOT WISH TO ACCOMMODATE THEM.
BESIDES, I'D LIKE TO INTRODUCE YOU TO SOME OF MINE.
CHK-CHK-CHAK-CHK
FWOOSH
THERE'S NO DOUBT THAT THIS WILL BE CLOSE. MY ENERGY LEVELS WILL BE AT THE POINT OF EXHAUSTION WHEN I RETURN.
IT WOULD BE IMPOSSIBLE TO SHIFT FORMS NOW, BUT IT LOOKS AS IF MY EARTH MODE WILL SURVIVE THE TRIP.

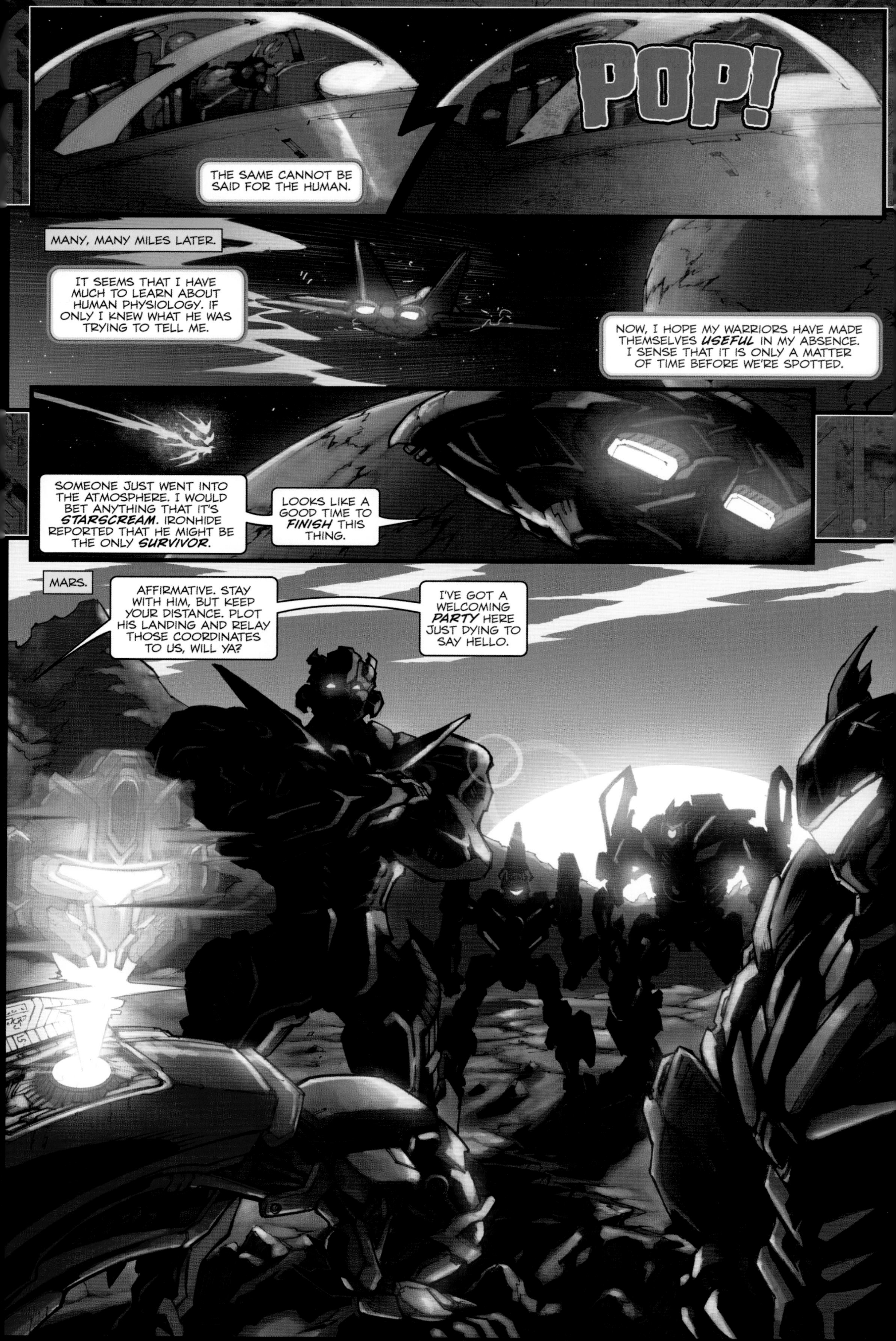

POP!
THE SAME CANNOT BE SAID FOR THE HUMAN.
MANY, MANY MILES LATER.
IT SEEMS THAT I HAVE MUCH TO LEARN ABOUT HUMAN PHYSIOLOGY. IF ONLY I KNEW WHAT HE WAS TRYING TO TELL ME.
NOW, I HOPE MY WARRIORS HAVE MADE THEMSELVES USEFUL IN MY ABSENCE. I SENSE THAT IT IS ONLY A MATTER OF TIME BEFORE WE'RE SPOTTED.
SOMEONE JUST WENT INTO THE ATMOSPHERE. I WOULD BET ANYTHING THAT IT'S STARSCREAM. IRONHIDE REPORTED THAT HE MIGHT BE THE ONLY SURVIVOR.
LOOKS LIKE A GOOD TIME TO FINISH THIS THING.
MARS.
AFFIRMATIVE. STAY WITH HIM, BUT KEEP YOUR DISTANCE. PLOT HIS LANDING AND RELAY THOSE COORDINATES TO US, WILL YA?
I'VE GOT A WELCOMING PARTY HERE JUST DYING TO SAY HELLO.

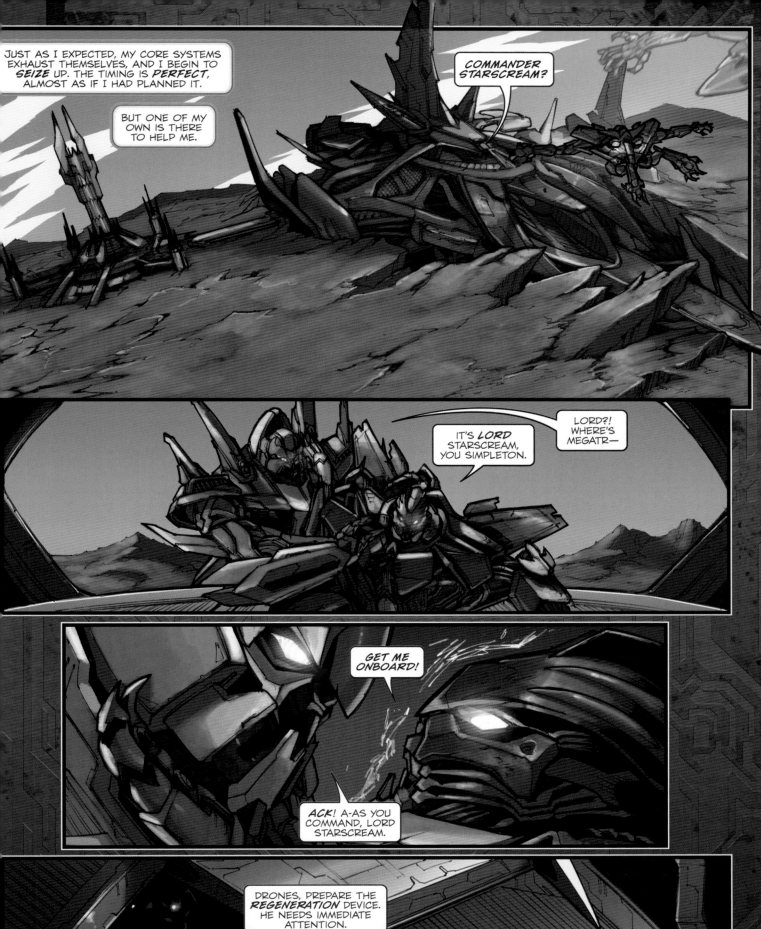

JUST AS I EXPECTED, MY CORE SYSTEMS EXHAUST THEMSELVES, AND I BEGIN TO *SEIZE* UP. THE TIMING IS *PERFECT*, ALMOST AS IF I HAD PLANNED IT.

BUT ONE OF MY OWN IS THERE TO HELP ME.

COMMANDER STARSCREAM?

LORD?! WHERE'S MEGATR—

IT'S *LORD* STARSCREAM, YOU SIMPLETON.

GET ME ONBOARD!

ACK! A-AS YOU COMMAND, LORD STARSCREAM.

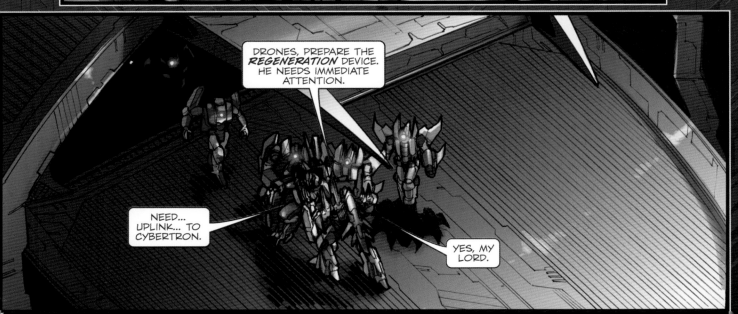

DRONES, PREPARE THE *REGENERATION* DEVICE. HE NEEDS IMMEDIATE ATTENTION.

NEED... UPLINK... TO CYBERTRON.

YES, MY LORD.

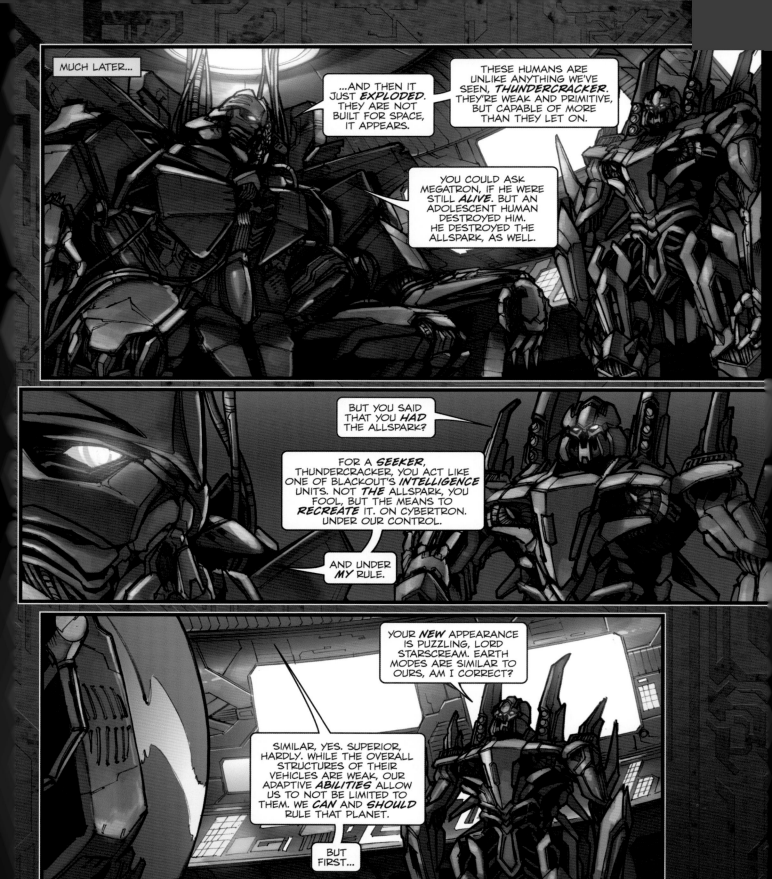

MUCH LATER...

...AND THEN IT JUST *EXPLODED*. THEY ARE NOT BUILT FOR SPACE, IT APPEARS.

THESE HUMANS ARE UNLIKE ANYTHING WE'VE SEEN, *THUNDERCRACKER*. THEY'RE WEAK AND PRIMITIVE, BUT CAPABLE OF MORE THAN THEY LET ON.

YOU COULD ASK MEGATRON, IF HE WERE STILL *ALIVE*. BUT AN ADOLESCENT HUMAN DESTROYED HIM. HE DESTROYED THE ALLSPARK, AS WELL.

BUT YOU SAID THAT YOU *HAD* THE ALLSPARK?

FOR A *SEEKER*, THUNDERCRACKER, YOU ACT LIKE ONE OF BLACKOUT'S *INTELLIGENCE* UNITS. NOT *THE* ALLSPARK, YOU FOOL, BUT THE MEANS TO *RECREATE* IT. ON CYBERTRON. UNDER OUR CONTROL.

AND UNDER *MY* RULE.

YOUR *NEW* APPEARANCE IS PUZZLING, LORD STARSCREAM. EARTH MODES ARE SIMILAR TO OURS, AM I CORRECT?

SIMILAR, YES. SUPERIOR, HARDLY. WHILE THE OVERALL STRUCTURES OF THEIR VEHICLES ARE WEAK, OUR ADAPTIVE *ABILITIES* ALLOW US TO NOT BE LIMITED TO THEM. WE *CAN* AND *SHOULD* RULE THAT PLANET.

BUT FIRST...

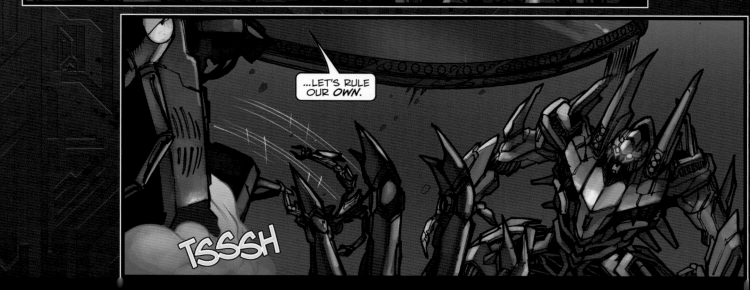

...LET'S RULE OUR *OWN*.

TSSSH

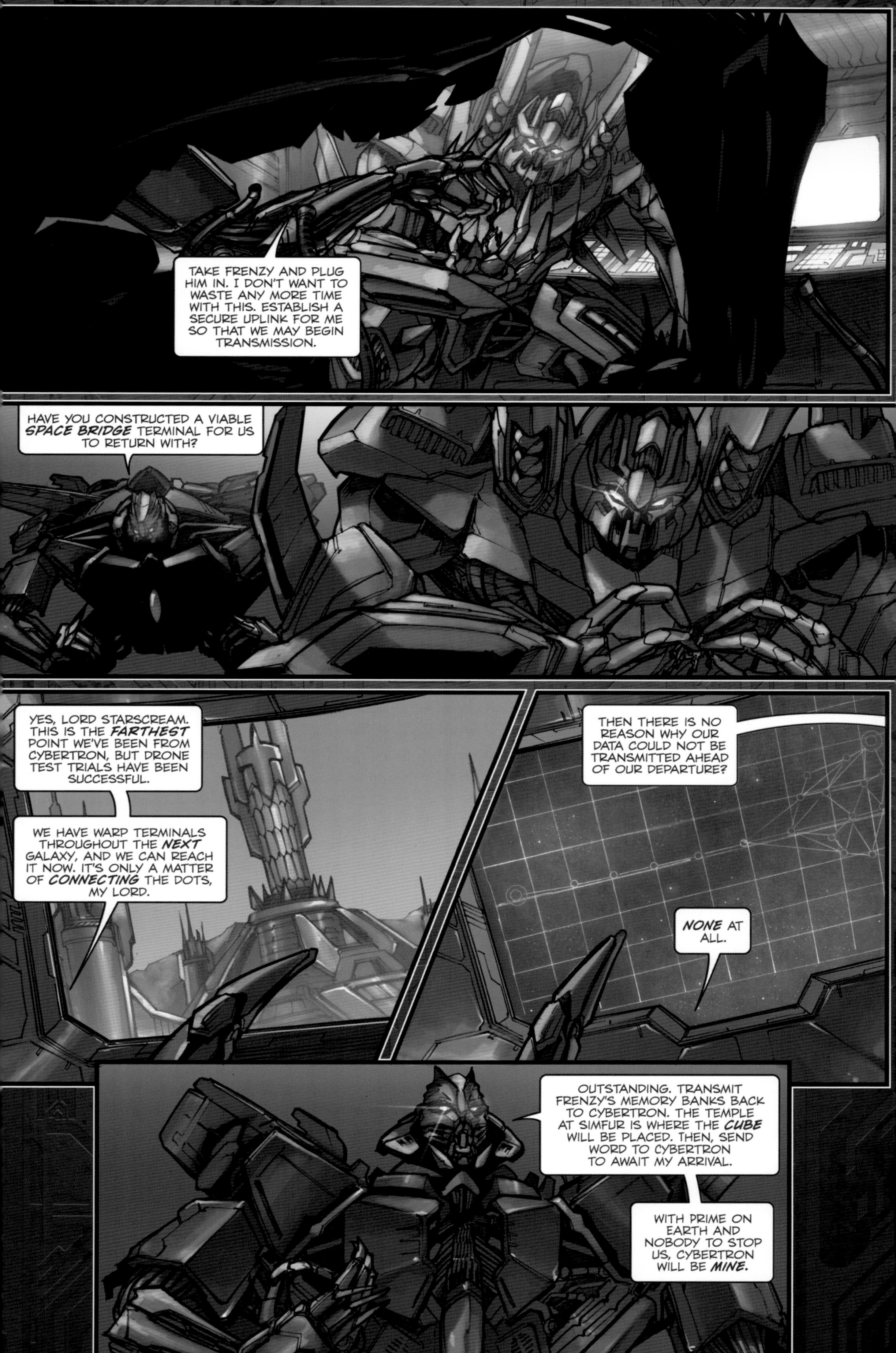

TAKE FRENZY AND PLUG HIM IN. I DON'T WANT TO WASTE ANY MORE TIME WITH THIS. ESTABLISH A SECURE UPLINK FOR ME SO THAT WE MAY BEGIN TRANSMISSION.
HAVE YOU CONSTRUCTED A VIABLE SPACE BRIDGE TERMINAL FOR US TO RETURN WITH?
YES, LORD STARSCREAM. THIS IS THE FARTHEST POINT WE'VE BEEN FROM CYBERTRON, BUT DRONE TEST TRIALS HAVE BEEN SUCCESSFUL.
WE HAVE WARP TERMINALS THROUGHOUT THE NEXT GALAXY, AND WE CAN REACH IT NOW. IT'S ONLY A MATTER OF CONNECTING THE DOTS, MY LORD.
THEN THERE IS NO REASON WHY OUR DATA COULD NOT BE TRANSMITTED AHEAD OF OUR DEPARTURE?
NONE AT ALL.
OUTSTANDING. TRANSMIT FRENZY'S MEMORY BANKS BACK TO CYBERTRON. THE TEMPLE AT SIMFUR IS WHERE THE CUBE WILL BE PLACED. THEN, SEND WORD TO CYBERTRON TO AWAIT MY ARRIVAL.
WITH PRIME ON EARTH AND NOBODY TO STOP US, CYBERTRON WILL BE MINE.

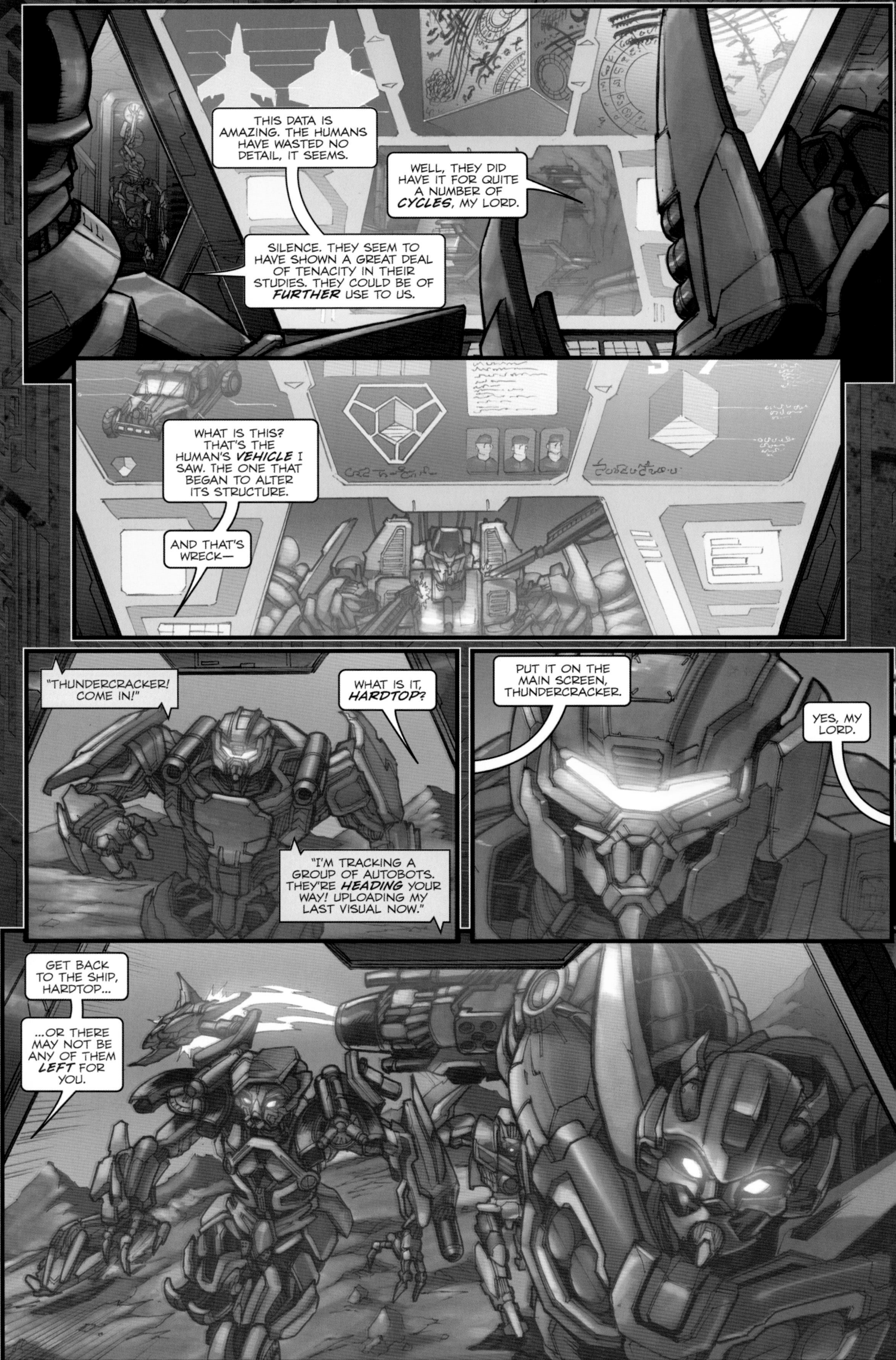
THIS DATA IS AMAZING. THE HUMANS HAVE WASTED NO DETAIL, IT SEEMS.
WELL, THEY DID HAVE IT FOR QUITE A NUMBER OF CYCLES, MY LORD.
SILENCE. THEY SEEM TO HAVE SHOWN A GREAT DEAL OF TENACITY IN THEIR STUDIES. THEY COULD BE OF FURTHER USE TO US.
WHAT IS THIS? THAT'S THE HUMAN'S VEHICLE I SAW. THE ONE THAT BEGAN TO ALTER ITS STRUCTURE.
AND THAT'S WRECK—
"THUNDERCRACKER! COME IN!"
WHAT IS IT, HARDTOP?
"I'M TRACKING A GROUP OF AUTOBOTS. THEY'RE HEADING YOUR WAY! UPLOADING MY LAST VISUAL NOW."
PUT IT ON THE MAIN SCREEN, THUNDERCRACKER.
YES, MY LORD.
GET BACK TO THE SHIP, HARDTOP...
...OR THERE MAY NOT BE ANY OF THEM LEFT FOR YOU.

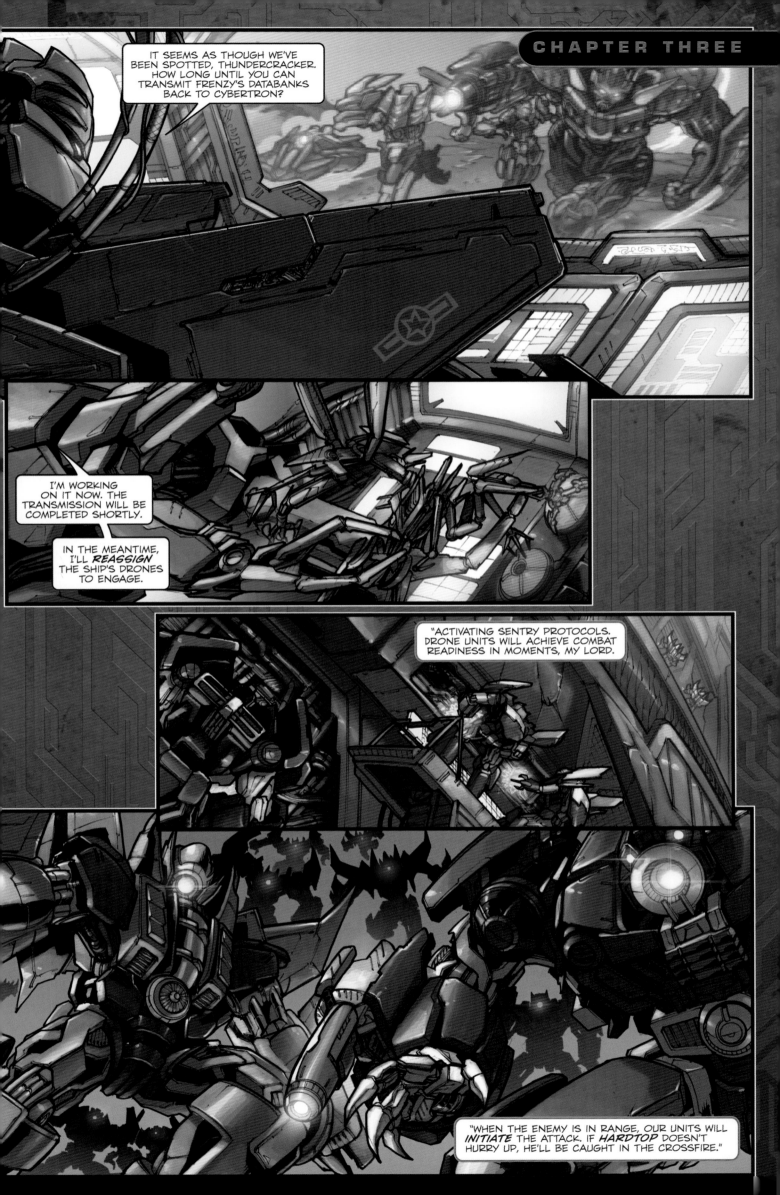

IT SEEMS AS THOUGH WE'VE BEEN SPOTTED, THUNDERCRACKER. HOW LONG UNTIL YOU CAN TRANSMIT FRENZY'S DATABANKS BACK TO CYBERTRON?

I'M WORKING ON IT NOW. THE TRANSMISSION WILL BE COMPLETED SHORTLY.

IN THE MEANTIME, I'LL *REASSIGN* THE SHIP'S DRONES TO ENGAGE.

"ACTIVATING SENTRY PROTOCOLS. DRONE UNITS WILL ACHIEVE COMBAT READINESS IN MOMENTS, MY LORD.

"WHEN THE ENEMY IS IN RANGE, OUR UNITS WILL *INITIATE* THE ATTACK. IF *HARDTOP* DOESN'T HURRY UP, HE'LL BE CAUGHT IN THE CROSSFIRE."

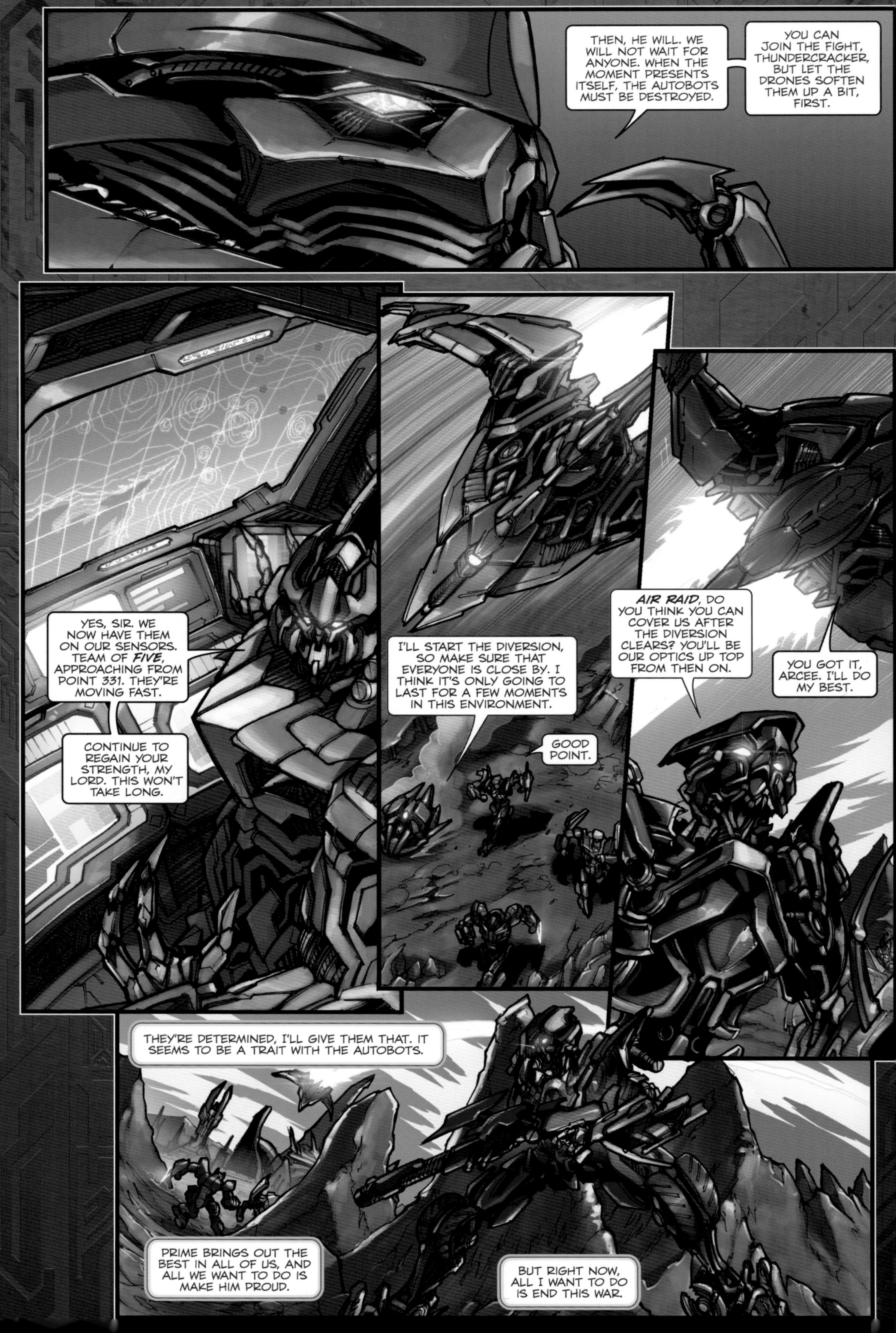
THEN, HE WILL. WE WILL NOT WAIT FOR ANYONE. WHEN THE MOMENT PRESENTS ITSELF, THE AUTOBOTS MUST BE DESTROYED.
YOU CAN JOIN THE FIGHT, THUNDERCRACKER, BUT LET THE DRONES SOFTEN THEM UP A BIT, FIRST.
YES, SIR. WE NOW HAVE THEM ON OUR SENSORS. TEAM OF *FIVE*, APPROACHING FROM POINT 331. THEY'RE MOVING FAST.
CONTINUE TO REGAIN YOUR STRENGTH, MY LORD. THIS WON'T TAKE LONG.
I'LL START THE DIVERSION, SO MAKE SURE THAT EVERYONE IS CLOSE BY. I THINK IT'S ONLY GOING TO LAST FOR A FEW MOMENTS IN THIS ENVIRONMENT.
GOOD POINT.
AIR RAID, DO YOU THINK YOU CAN COVER US AFTER THE DIVERSION CLEARS? YOU'LL BE OUR OPTICS UP TOP FROM THEN ON.
YOU GOT IT, ARCEE. I'LL DO MY BEST.
THEY'RE DETERMINED, I'LL GIVE THEM THAT. IT SEEMS TO BE A TRAIT WITH THE AUTOBOTS.
PRIME BRINGS OUT THE BEST IN ALL OF US, AND ALL WE WANT TO DO IS MAKE HIM PROUD.
BUT RIGHT NOW, ALL I WANT TO DO IS END THIS WAR.

I'M PICKING UP DECEPTICON UNITS STRAIGHT AHEAD. LOOKS LIKE STARSCREAM MIGHT NOT BE ALONE.
SMOKESCREEN, YOU READY TO LAY DOWN THE *COVER* FOR US?
FOOSH
FOOSH
FOOSH
ALWAYS READY. STAND BY FOR CLOUD ACTIVATION.
FOOSH
FOOSH
ZZZK
ZZZK
ION CLOUD *DEPLOYED*. TIME TO MOVE IN, GUYS... THEY CAN'T DETECT US AT THE MOMENT.

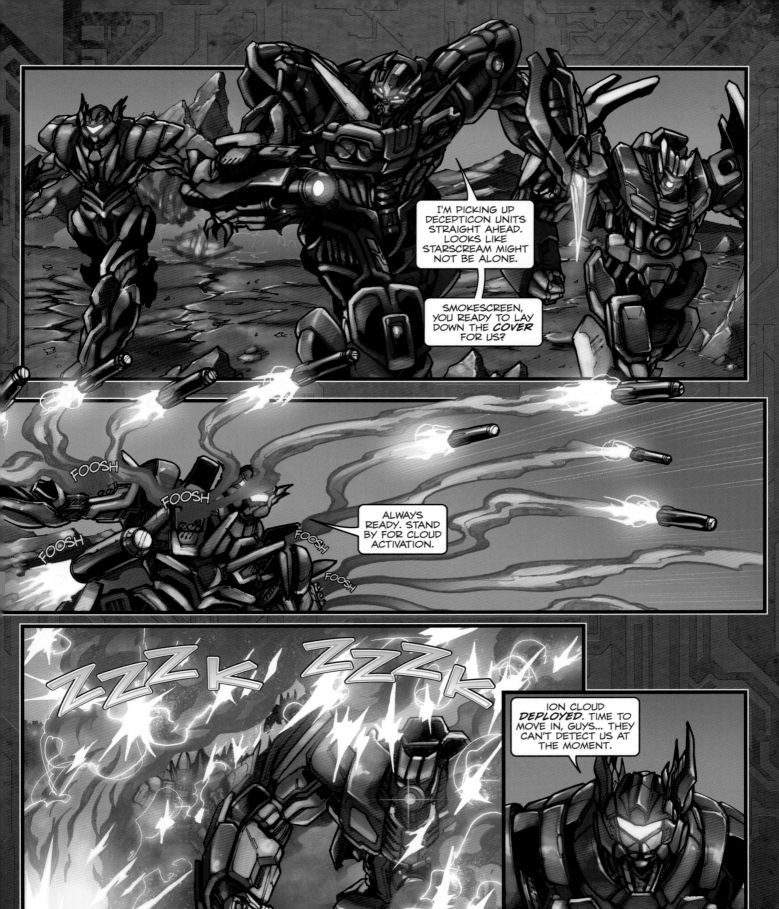

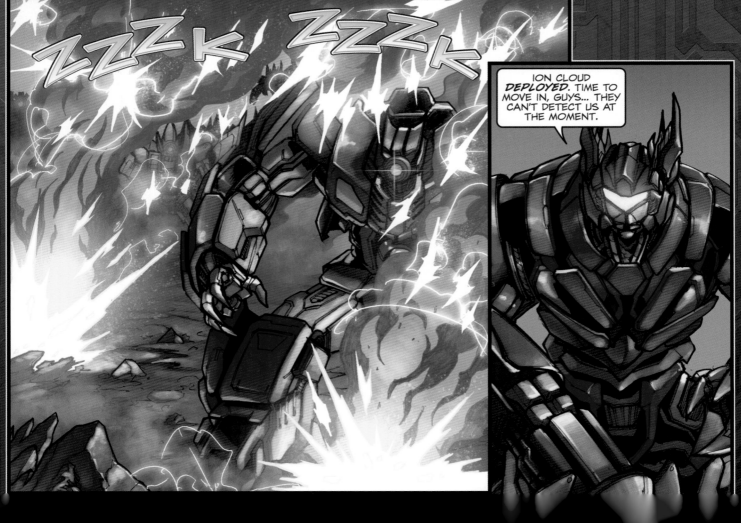

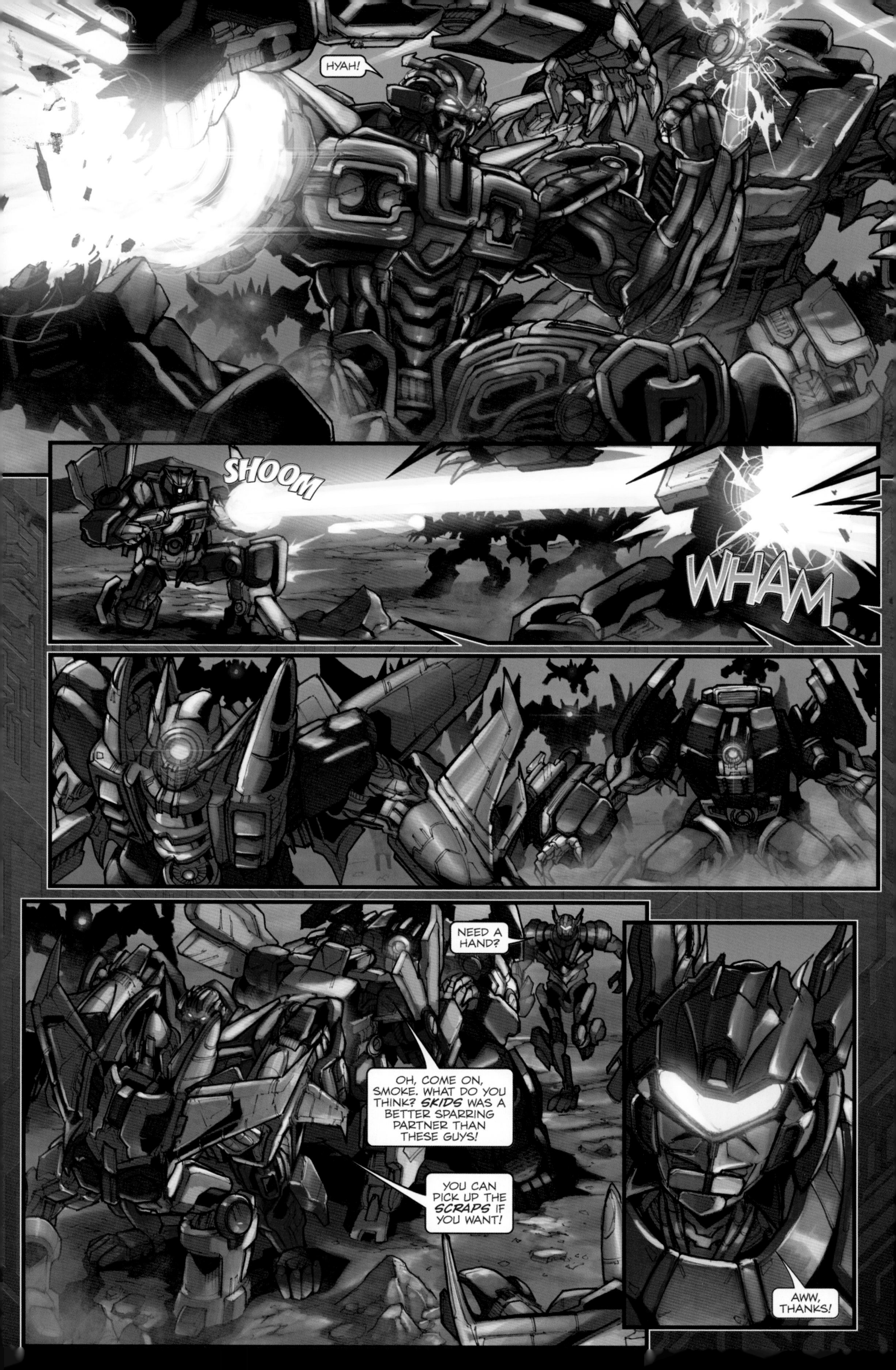
HYAH!
SHOOM
WHAM
NEED A HAND?
OH, COME ON, SMOKE. WHAT DO YOU THINK? SKIDS WAS A BETTER SPARRING PARTNER THAN THESE GUYS!
YOU CAN PICK UP THE SCRAPS IF YOU WANT!
AWW, THANKS!

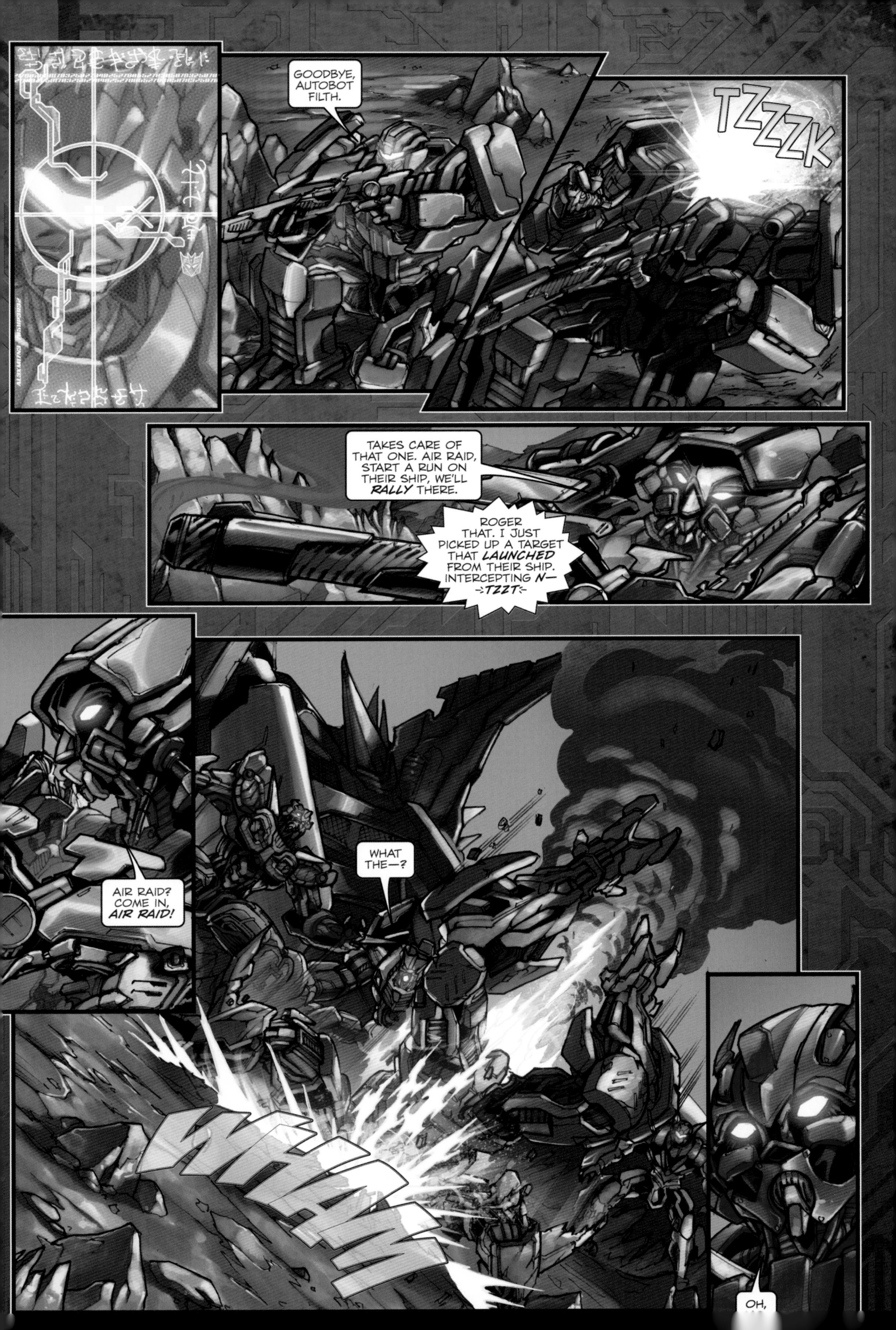
GOODBYE, AUTOBOT FILTH.
TZZZK
TAKES CARE OF THAT ONE. AIR RAID, START A RUN ON THEIR SHIP, WE'LL *RALLY* THERE.
ROGER THAT. I JUST PICKED UP A TARGET THAT *LAUNCHED* FROM THEIR SHIP. INTERCEPTING N— *-TZZT-*
AIR RAID? COME IN, *AIR RAID!*
WHAT THE—?
WHAM
OH,

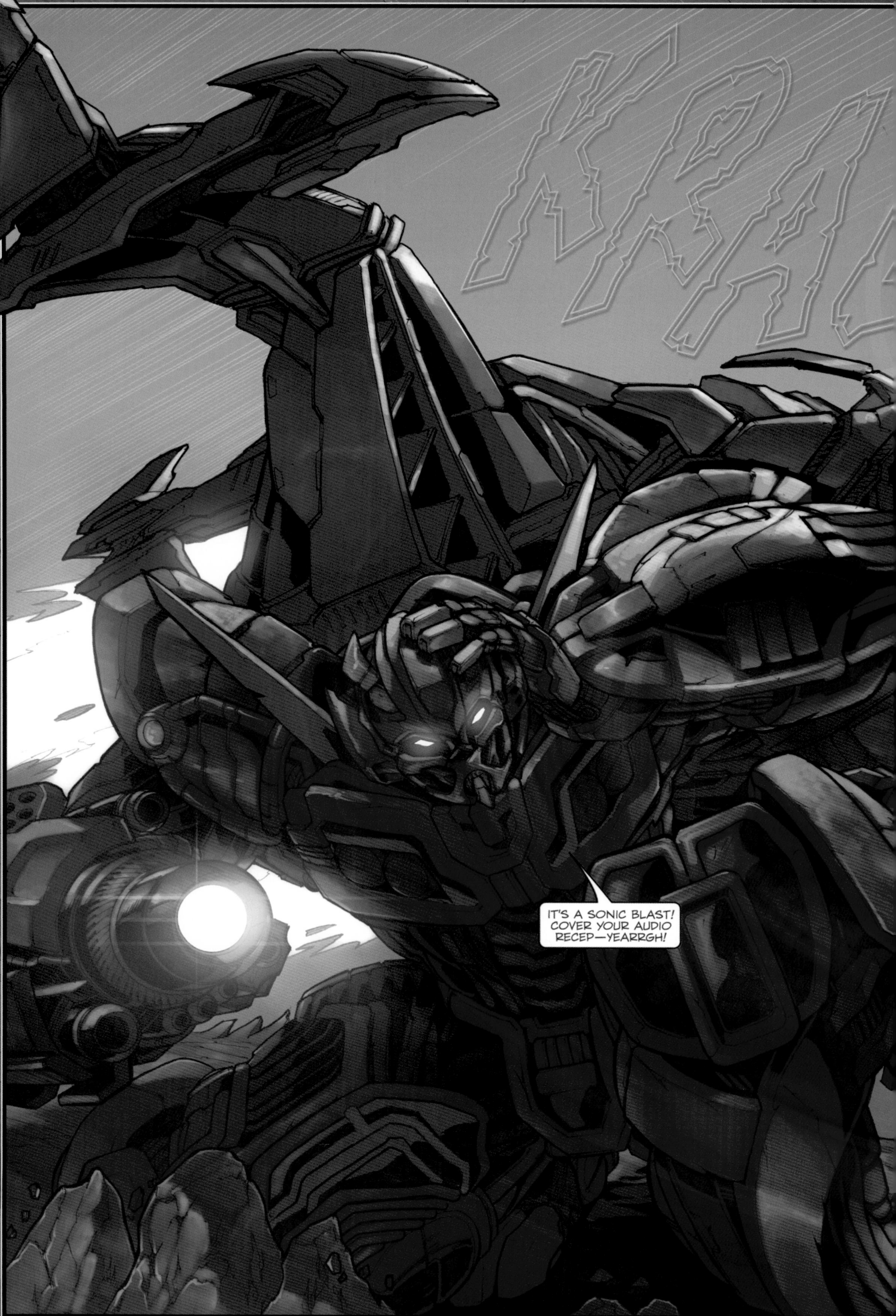
IT'S A SONIC BLAST! COVER YOUR AUDIO RECEP—YEARRGH!

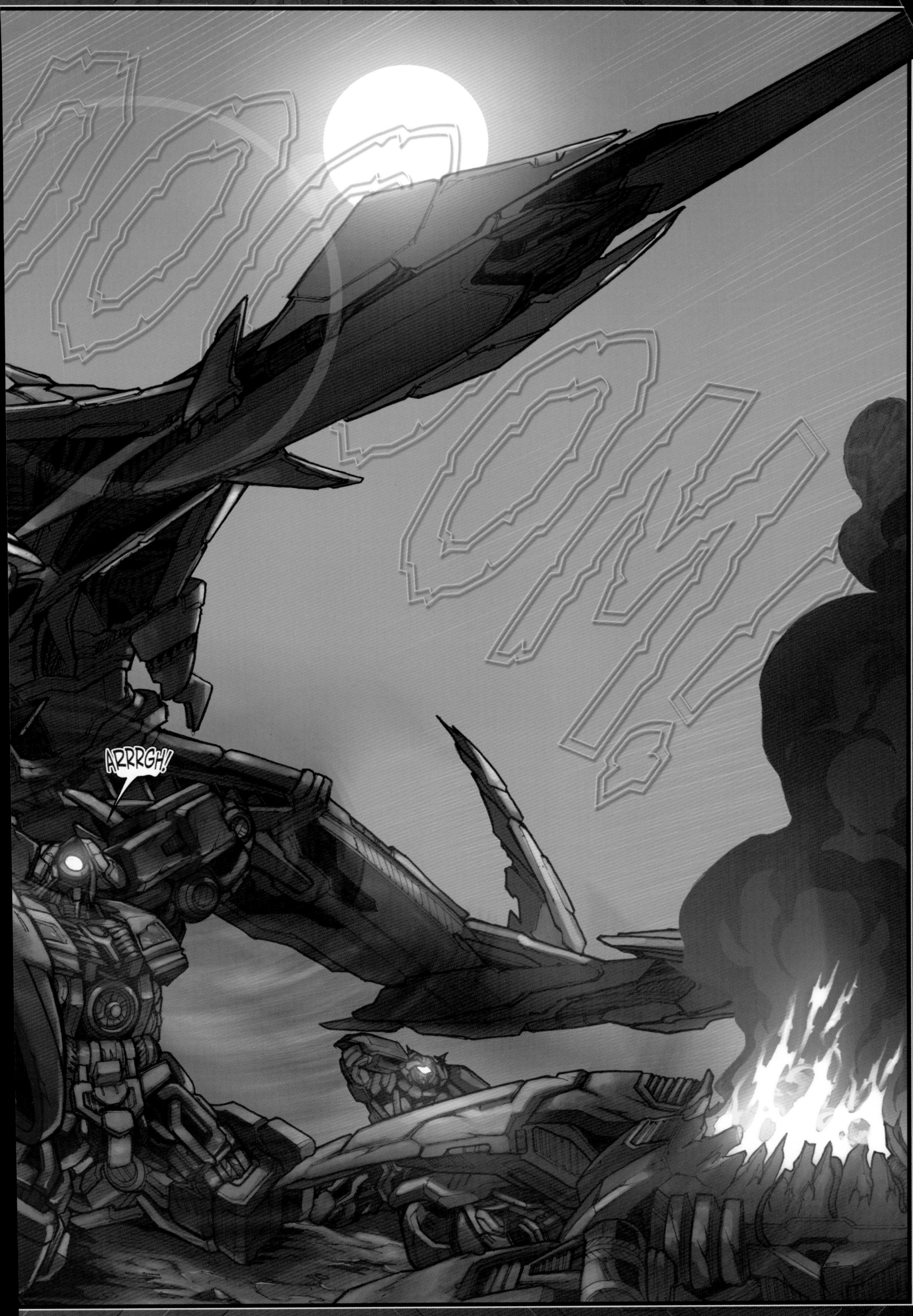
ARRRGH!

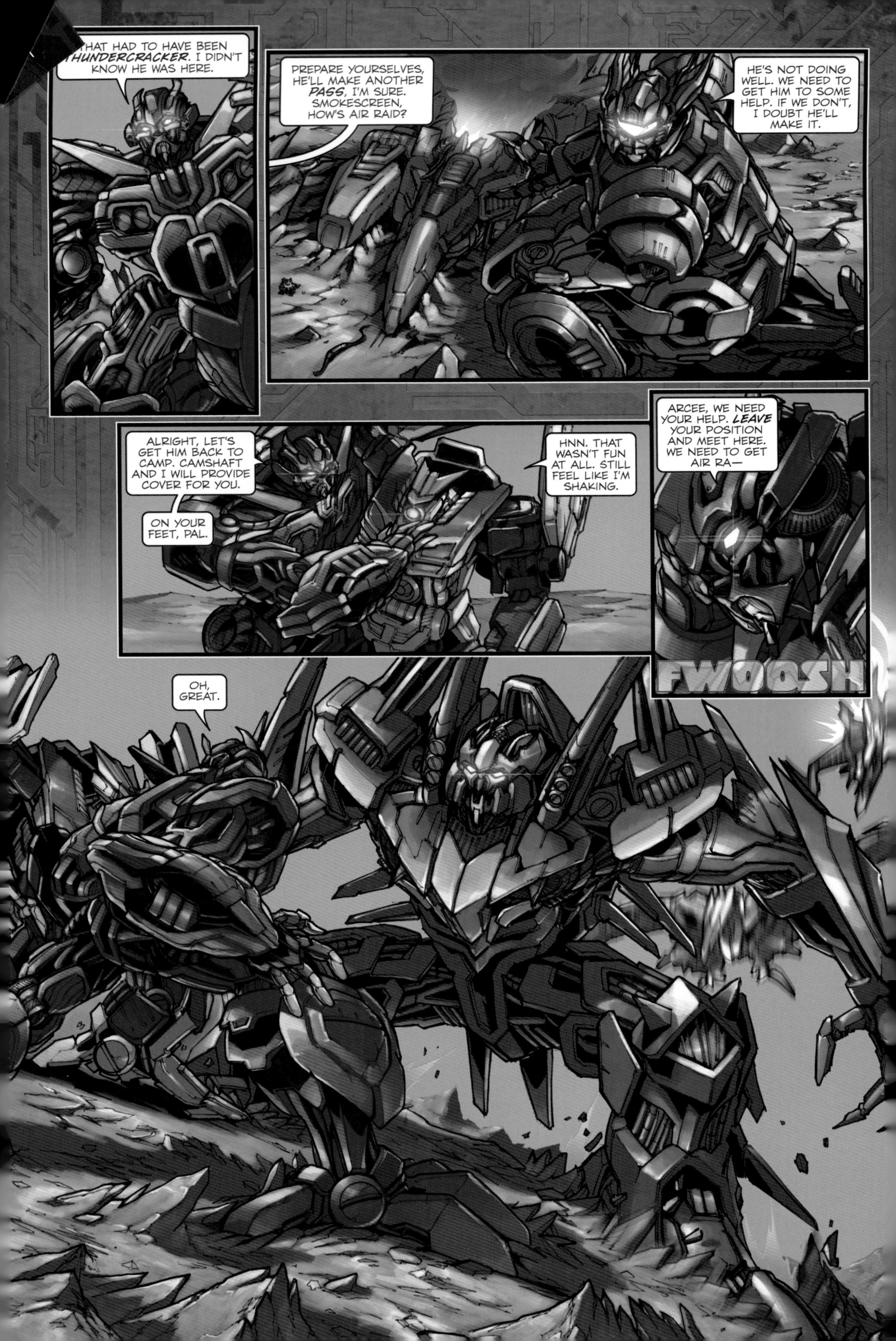
THAT HAD TO HAVE BEEN THUNDERCRACKER. I DIDN'T KNOW HE WAS HERE.
PREPARE YOURSELVES, HE'LL MAKE ANOTHER PASS, I'M SURE. SMOKESCREEN, HOW'S AIR RAID?
HE'S NOT DOING WELL. WE NEED TO GET HIM TO SOME HELP. IF WE DON'T, I DOUBT HE'LL MAKE IT.
ALRIGHT, LET'S GET HIM BACK TO CAMP. CAMSHAFT AND I WILL PROVIDE COVER FOR YOU.
ON YOUR FEET, PAL.
HNN. THAT WASN'T FUN AT ALL. STILL FEEL LIKE I'M SHAKING.
ARCEE, WE NEED YOUR HELP. LEAVE YOUR POSITION AND MEET HERE. WE NEED TO GET AIR RA—
FWOOSH
OH, GREAT.

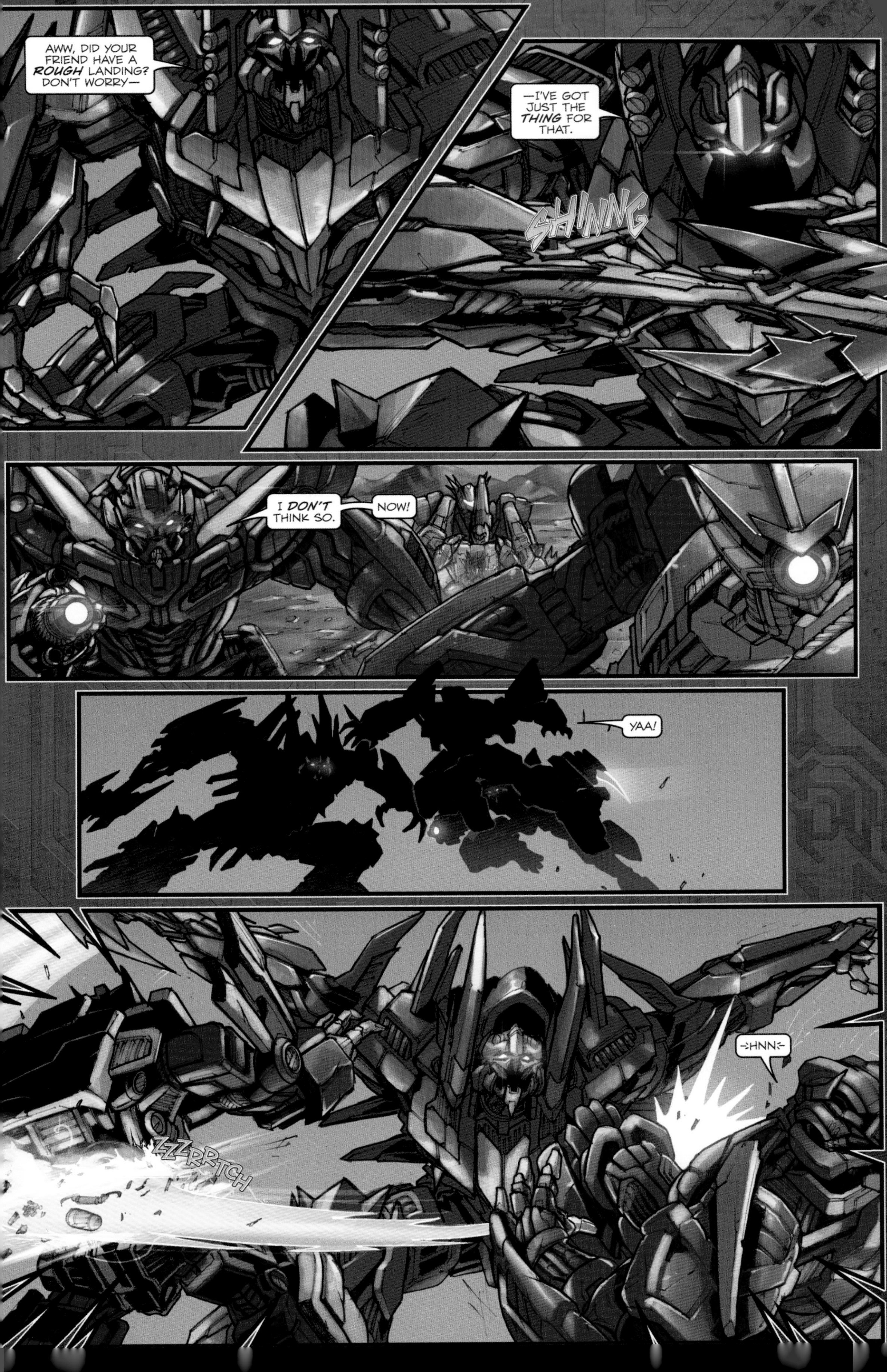
AWW, DID YOUR FRIEND HAVE A ROUGH LANDING? DON'T WORRY—
—I'VE GOT JUST THE THING FOR THAT.
SHING
I DON'T THINK SO.
NOW!
YAA!
ZZZRRTCH
-HNN-

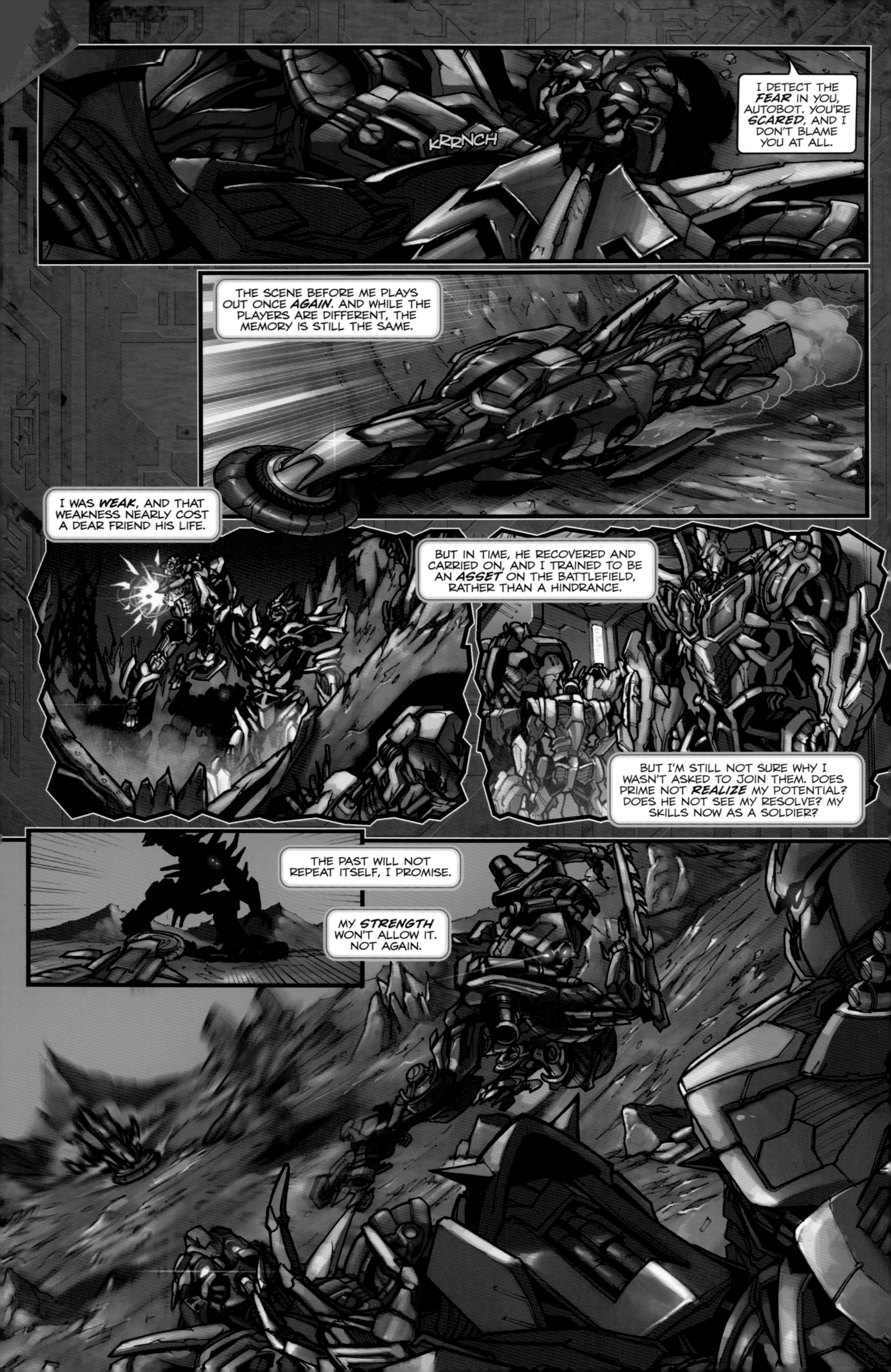
I DETECT THE FEAR IN YOU, AUTOBOT. YOU'RE SCARED, AND I DON'T BLAME YOU AT ALL.
KRRNCH
THE SCENE BEFORE ME PLAYS OUT ONCE AGAIN. AND WHILE THE PLAYERS ARE DIFFERENT, THE MEMORY IS STILL THE SAME.
I WAS WEAK, AND THAT WEAKNESS NEARLY COST A DEAR FRIEND HIS LIFE.
BUT IN TIME, HE RECOVERED AND CARRIED ON, AND I TRAINED TO BE AN ASSET ON THE BATTLEFIELD, RATHER THAN A HINDRANCE.
BUT I'M STILL NOT SURE WHY I WASN'T ASKED TO JOIN THEM. DOES PRIME NOT REALIZE MY POTENTIAL? DOES HE NOT SEE MY RESOLVE? MY SKILLS NOW AS A SOLDIER?
THE PAST WILL NOT REPEAT ITSELF, I PROMISE.
MY STRENGTH WON'T ALLOW IT. NOT AGAIN.

THANKS, ARCEE. NOW LET'S TAKE HIM DOWN.

VIP

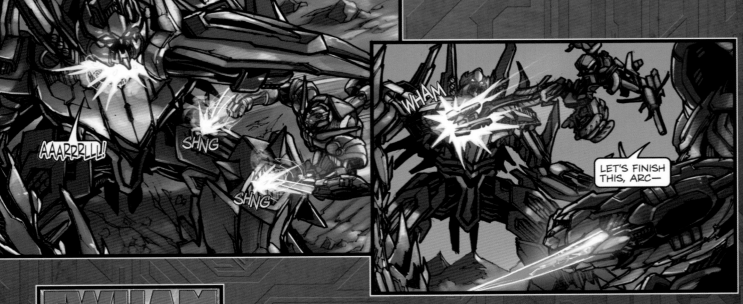

AAARRRLLL!

SHNG

SHNG

WHAM

LET'S FINISH THIS, ARC—

FWHAM

—AACK!

FOR A TIME, I THOUGHT OF THUNDERCRACKER AS A WORTHY SECOND TO MY COMMAND.

THAT THOUGHT HAS NOW *VANISHED.*

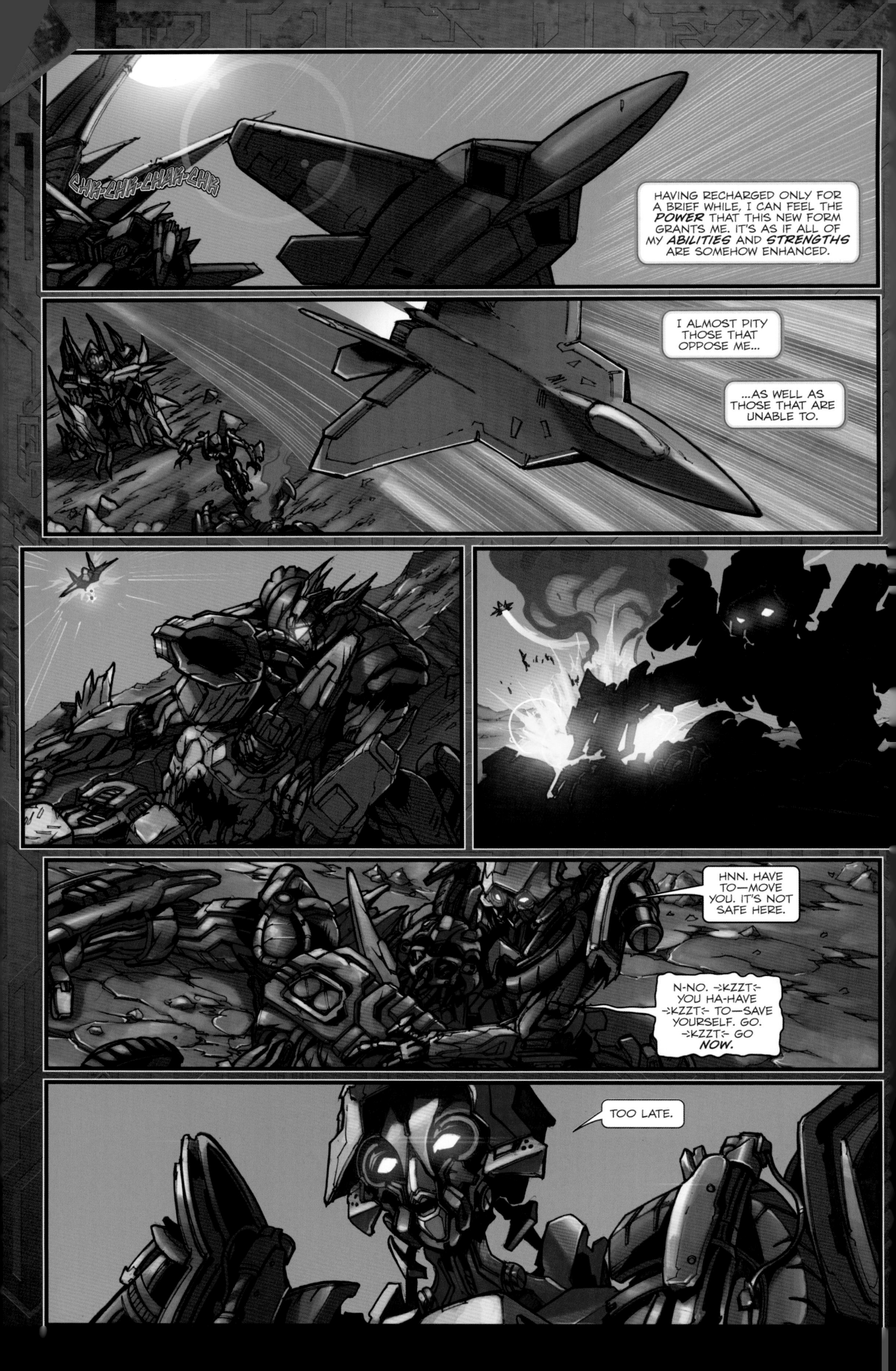
CHK-CHK-CHAK-CHK
HAVING RECHARGED ONLY FOR A BRIEF WHILE, I CAN FEEL THE **POWER** THAT THIS NEW FORM GRANTS ME. IT'S AS IF ALL OF MY ***ABILITIES*** AND ***STRENGTHS*** ARE SOMEHOW ENHANCED.
I ALMOST PITY THOSE THAT OPPOSE ME...
...AS WELL AS THOSE THAT ARE UNABLE TO.
HNN. HAVE TO—MOVE YOU. IT'S NOT SAFE HERE.
N-NO. -KZZT- YOU HA-HAVE -KZZT- TO—SAVE YOURSELF. GO. -KZZT- GO ***NOW.***
TOO LATE.

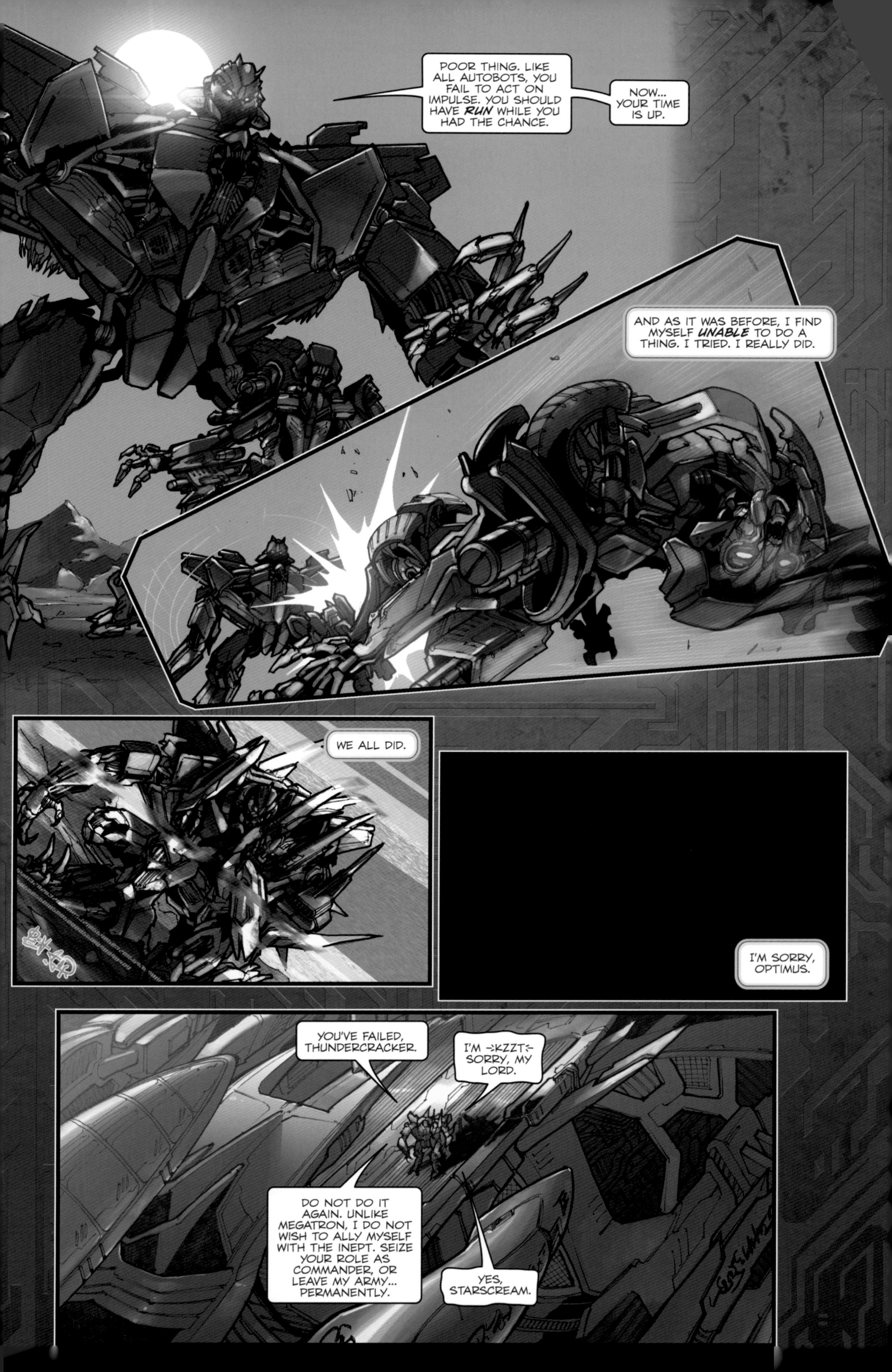
POOR THING. LIKE ALL AUTOBOTS, YOU FAIL TO ACT ON IMPULSE. YOU SHOULD HAVE RUN WHILE YOU HAD THE CHANCE.
NOW... YOUR TIME IS UP.
AND AS IT WAS BEFORE, I FIND MYSELF UNABLE TO DO A THING. I TRIED. I REALLY DID.
WE ALL DID.
I'M SORRY, OPTIMUS.
YOU'VE FAILED, THUNDERCRACKER.
I'M -KZZT- SORRY, MY LORD.
DO NOT DO IT AGAIN. UNLIKE MEGATRON, I DO NOT WISH TO ALLY MYSELF WITH THE INEPT. SEIZE YOUR ROLE AS COMMANDER, OR LEAVE MY ARMY... PERMANENTLY.
YES, STARSCREAM.

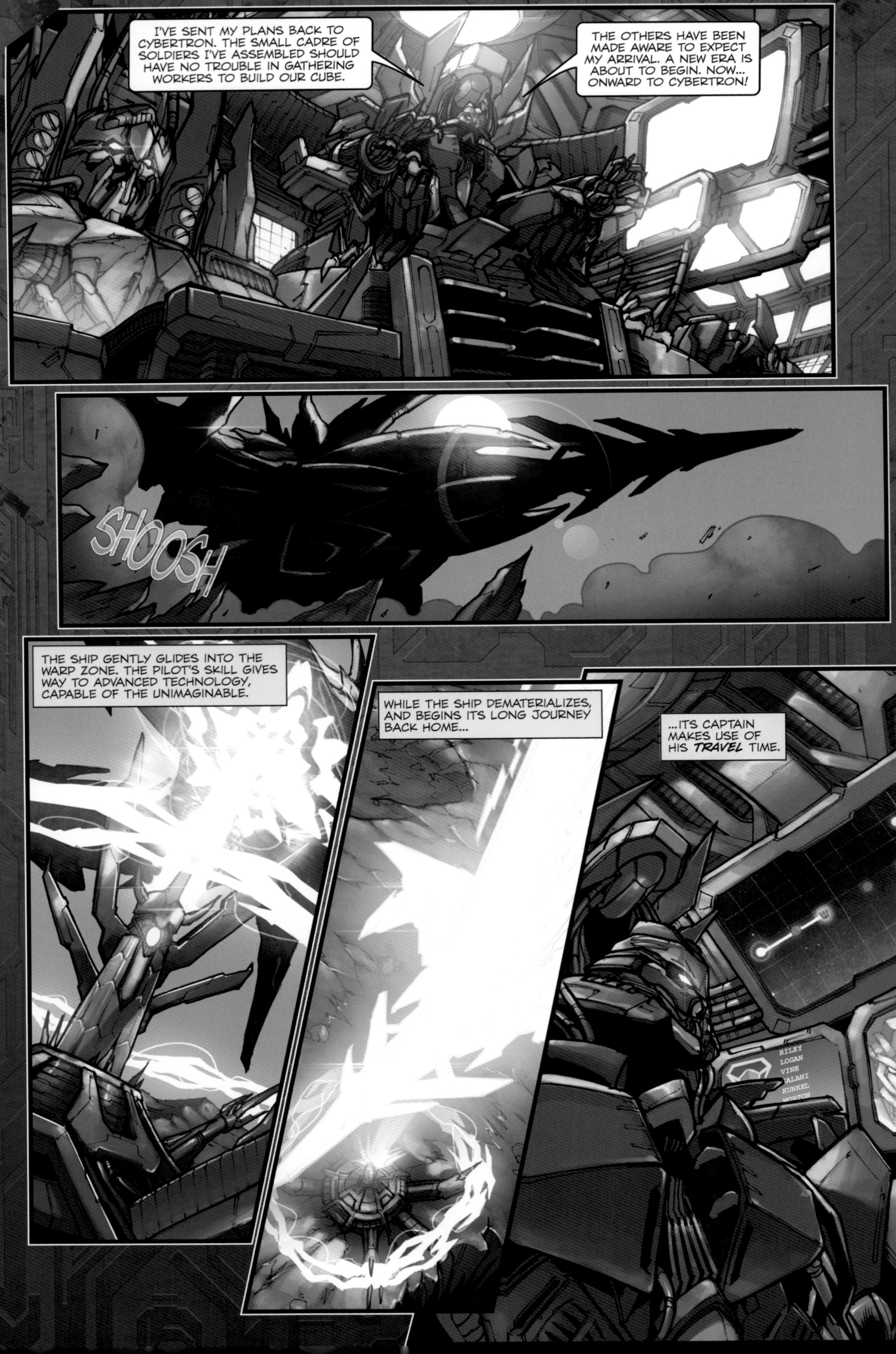
I'VE SENT MY PLANS BACK TO CYBERTRON. THE SMALL CADRE OF SOLDIERS I'VE ASSEMBLED SHOULD HAVE NO TROUBLE IN GATHERING WORKERS TO BUILD OUR CUBE.
THE OTHERS HAVE BEEN MADE AWARE TO EXPECT MY ARRIVAL. A NEW ERA IS ABOUT TO BEGIN. NOW... ONWARD TO CYBERTRON!
SHOOSH
THE SHIP GENTLY GLIDES INTO THE WARP ZONE. THE PILOT'S SKILL GIVES WAY TO ADVANCED TECHNOLOGY, CAPABLE OF THE UNIMAGINABLE.
WHILE THE SHIP DEMATERIALIZES, AND BEGINS ITS LONG JOURNEY BACK HOME...
...ITS CAPTAIN MAKES USE OF HIS *TRAVEL* TIME.
RILEY
LOGAN
VINE
KUNKEL

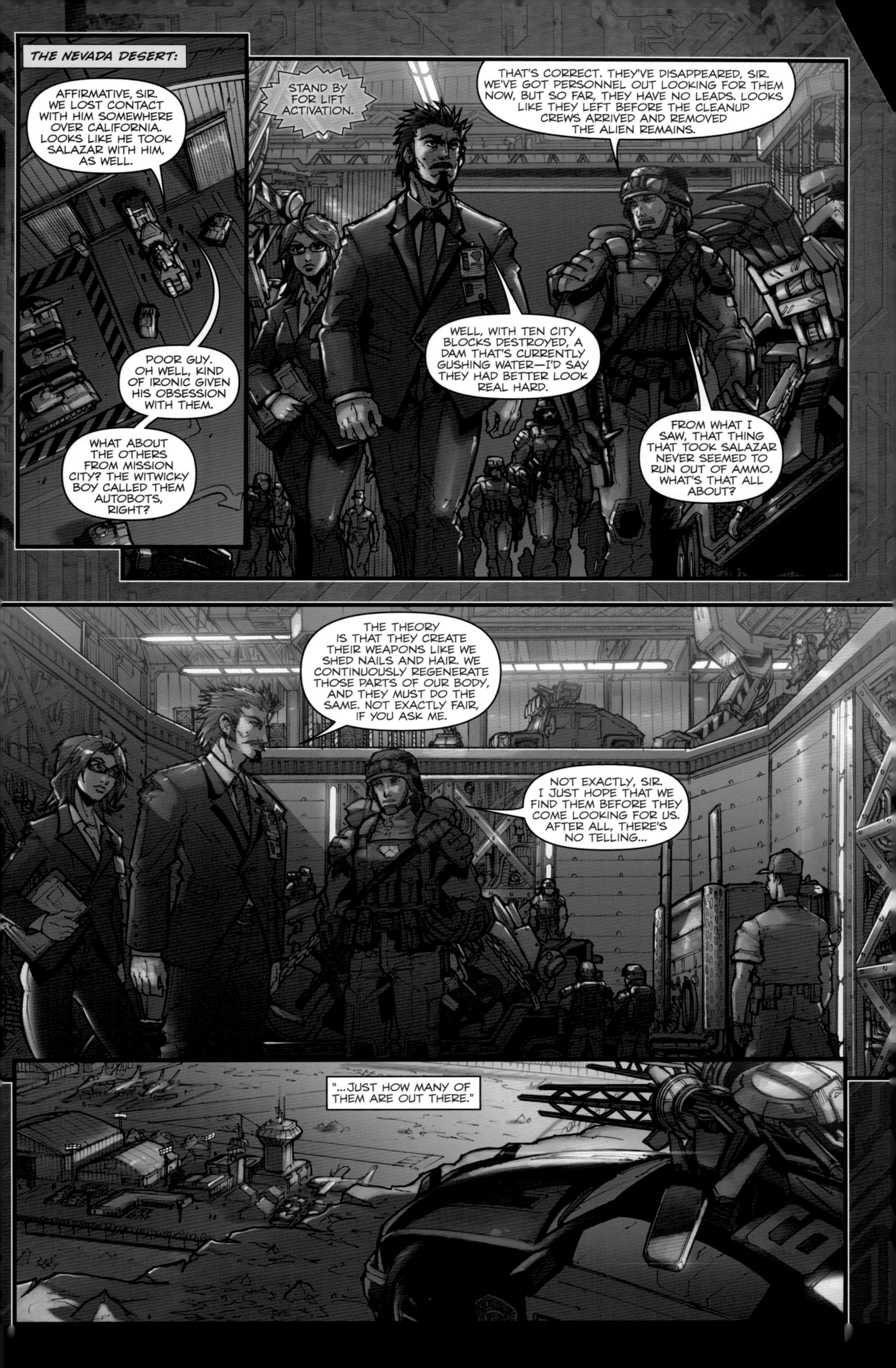
THE NEVADA DESERT:
AFFIRMATIVE, SIR. WE LOST CONTACT WITH HIM SOMEWHERE OVER CALIFORNIA. LOOKS LIKE HE TOOK SALAZAR WITH HIM, AS WELL.
POOR GUY. OH WELL, KIND OF IRONIC GIVEN HIS OBSESSION WITH THEM.
WHAT ABOUT THE OTHERS FROM MISSION CITY? THE WITWICKY BOY CALLED THEM AUTOBOTS, RIGHT?
STAND BY FOR LIFT ACTIVATION.
THAT'S CORRECT. THEY'VE DISAPPEARED, SIR. WE'VE GOT PERSONNEL OUT LOOKING FOR THEM NOW, BUT SO FAR, THEY HAVE NO LEADS. LOOKS LIKE THEY LEFT BEFORE THE CLEANUP CREWS ARRIVED AND REMOVED THE ALIEN REMAINS.
WELL, WITH TEN CITY BLOCKS DESTROYED, A DAM THAT'S CURRENTLY GUSHING WATER—I'D SAY THEY HAD BETTER LOOK REAL HARD.
FROM WHAT I SAW, THAT THING THAT TOOK SALAZAR NEVER SEEMED TO RUN OUT OF AMMO. WHAT'S THAT ALL ABOUT?
THE THEORY IS THAT THEY CREATE THEIR WEAPONS LIKE WE SHED NAILS AND HAIR. WE CONTINUOUSLY REGENERATE THOSE PARTS OF OUR BODY, AND THEY MUST DO THE SAME. NOT EXACTLY FAIR, IF YOU ASK ME.
NOT EXACTLY, SIR. I JUST HOPE THAT WE FIND THEM BEFORE THEY COME LOOKING FOR US. AFTER ALL, THERE'S NO TELLING...
"...JUST HOW MANY OF THEM ARE OUT THERE."

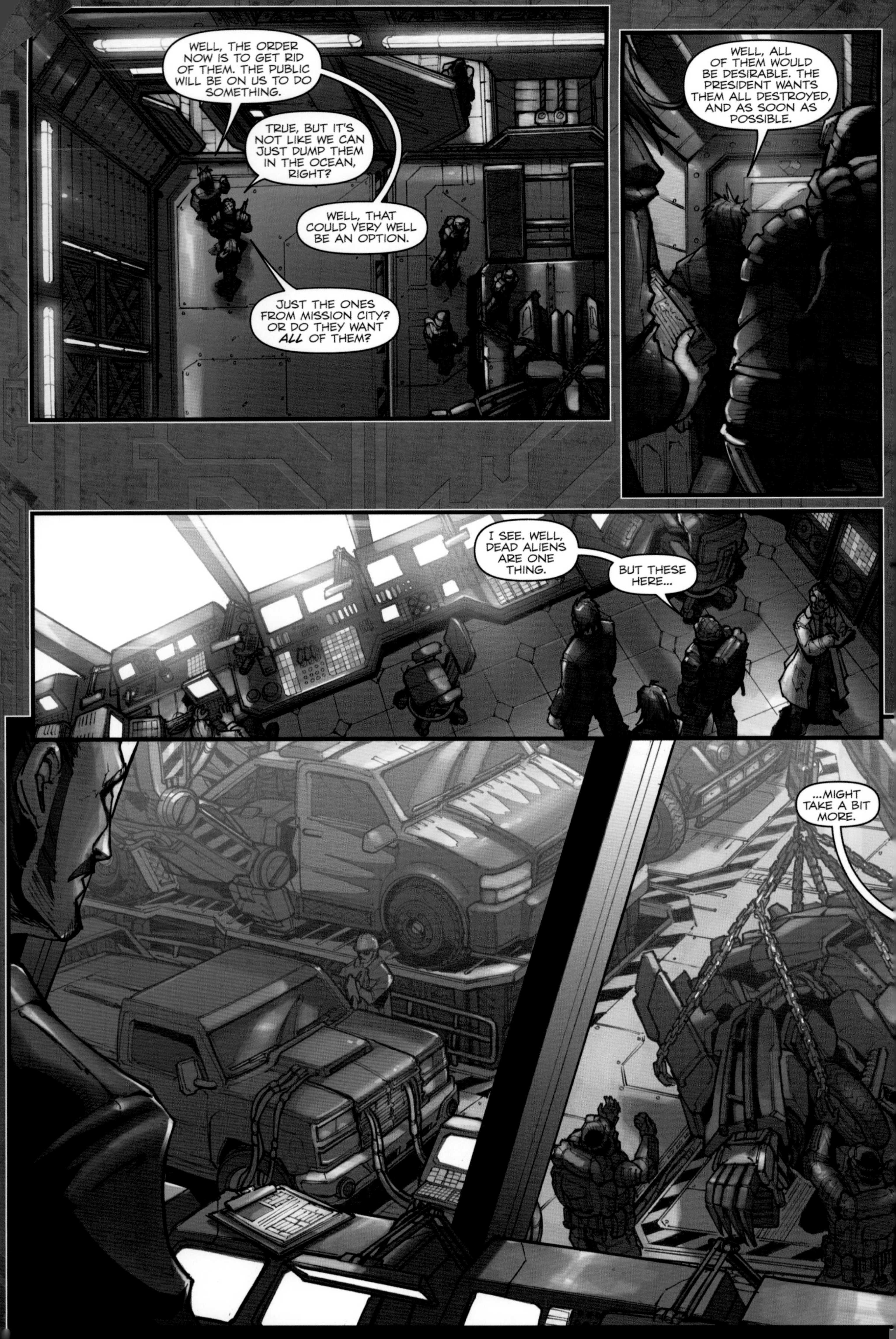
WELL, THE ORDER NOW IS TO GET RID OF THEM. THE PUBLIC WILL BE ON US TO DO SOMETHING.
TRUE, BUT IT'S NOT LIKE WE CAN JUST DUMP THEM IN THE OCEAN, RIGHT?
WELL, THAT COULD VERY WELL BE AN OPTION.
JUST THE ONES FROM MISSION CITY? OR DO THEY WANT *ALL* OF THEM?
WELL, ALL OF THEM WOULD BE DESIRABLE. THE PRESIDENT WANTS THEM ALL DESTROYED, AND AS SOON AS POSSIBLE.
I SEE. WELL, DEAD ALIENS ARE ONE THING.
BUT THESE HERE...
...MIGHT TAKE A BIT MORE.

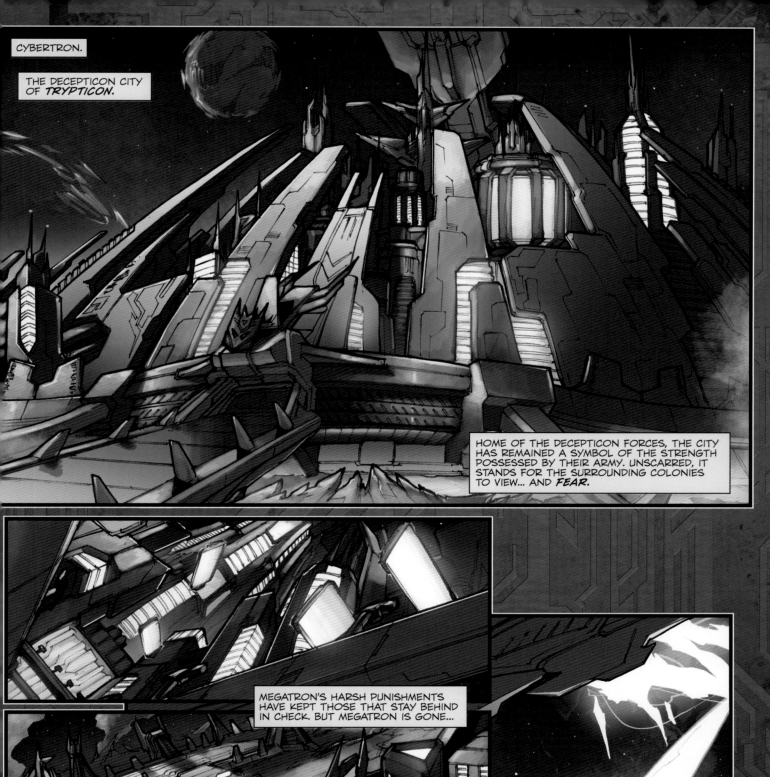

CYBERTRON.

THE DECEPTICON CITY OF *TRYPTICON*.

HOME OF THE DECEPTICON FORCES, THE CITY HAS REMAINED A SYMBOL OF THE STRENGTH POSSESSED BY THEIR ARMY. UNSCARRED, IT STANDS FOR THE SURROUNDING COLONIES TO VIEW... AND *FEAR*.

MEGATRON'S HARSH PUNISHMENTS HAVE KEPT THOSE THAT STAY BEHIND IN CHECK. BUT MEGATRON IS GONE...

...AND A NEW LEADER HAS JUST RETURNED HOME.

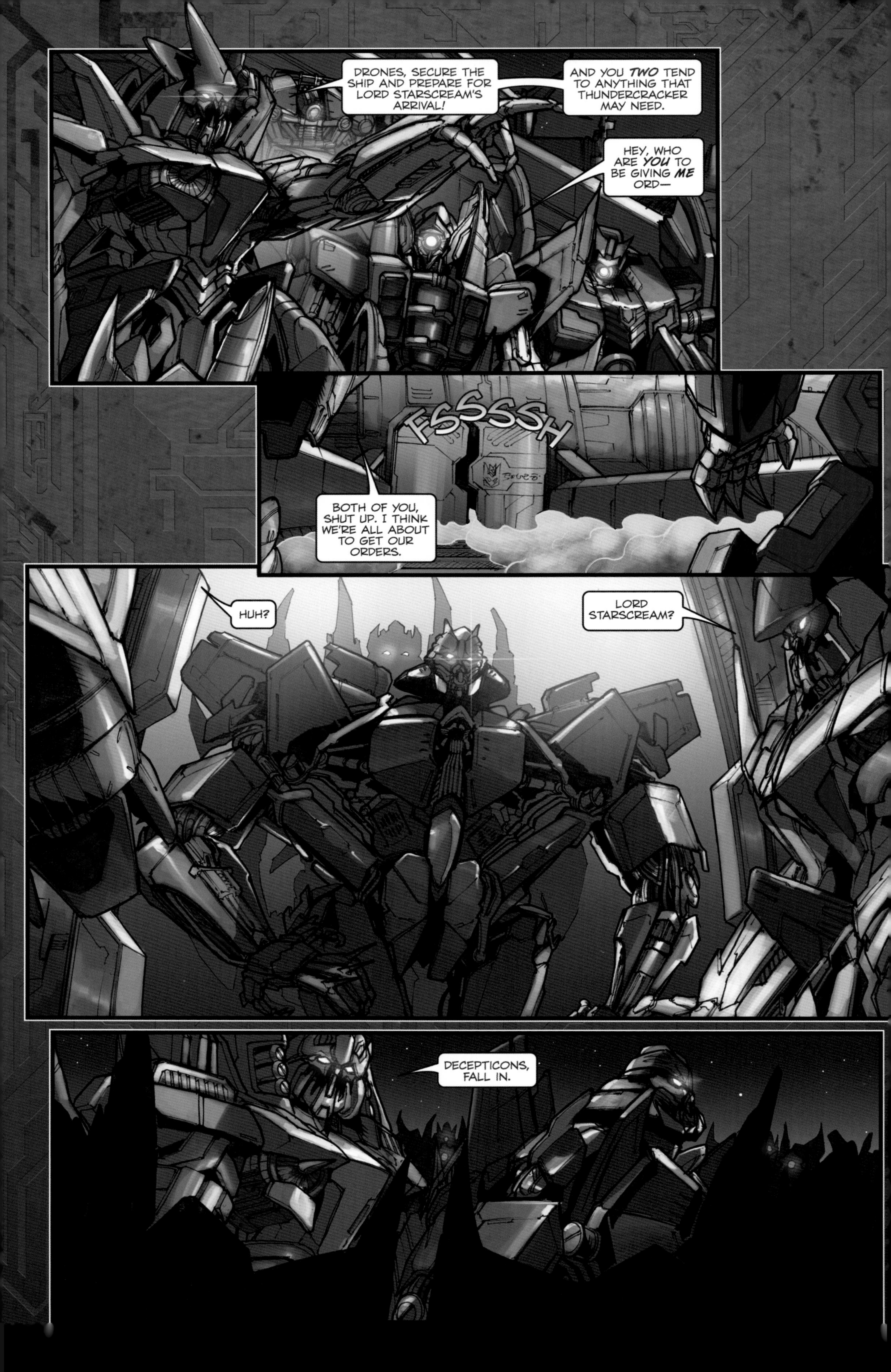
DRONES, SECURE THE SHIP AND PREPARE FOR LORD STARSCREAM'S ARRIVAL!
AND YOU TWO TEND TO ANYTHING THAT THUNDERCRACKER MAY NEED.
HEY, WHO ARE YOU TO BE GIVING ME ORD—
FSSSSH
BOTH OF YOU, SHUT UP. I THINK WE'RE ALL ABOUT TO GET OUR ORDERS.
HUH?
LORD STARSCREAM?
DECEPTICONS, FALL IN.

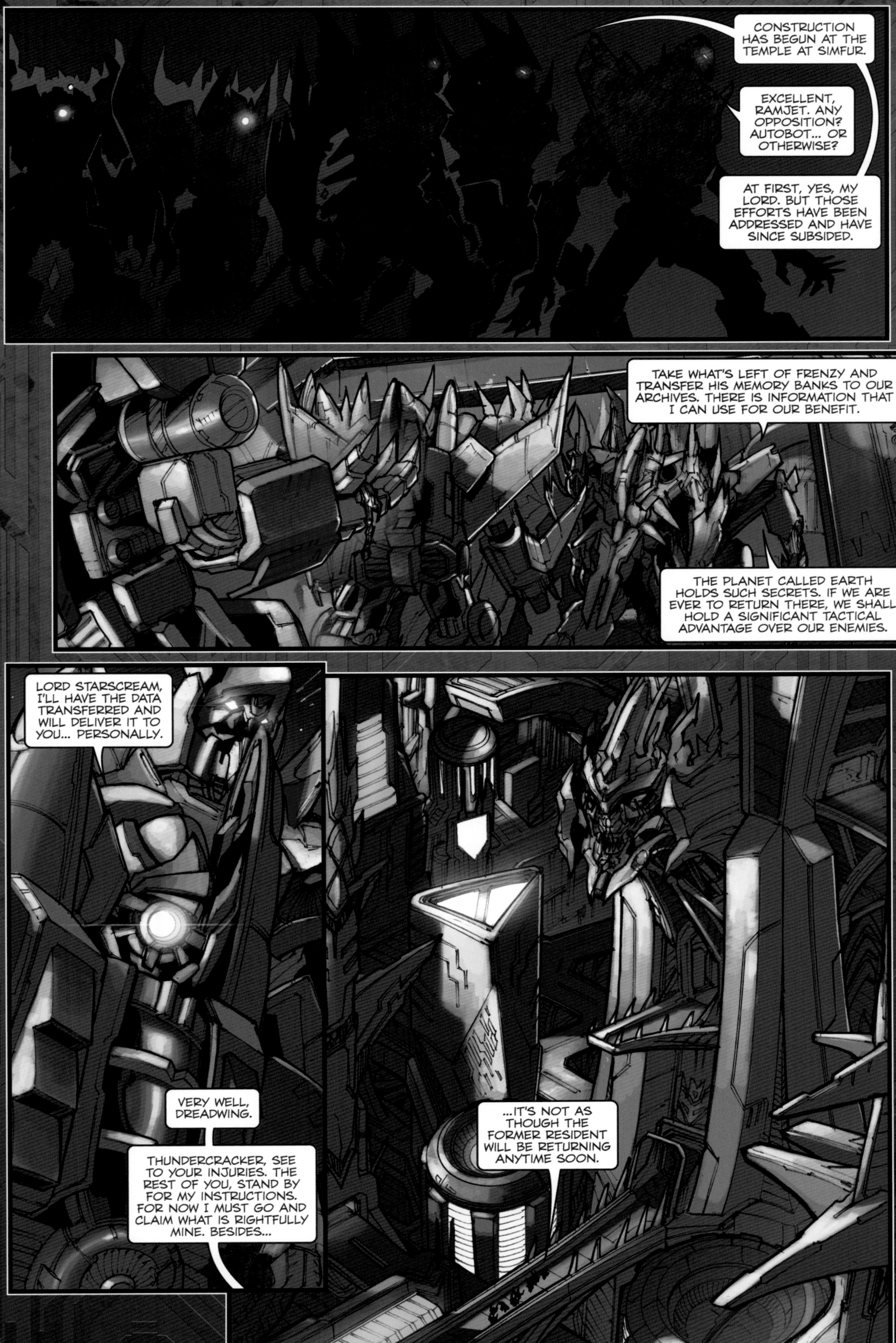
CONSTRUCTION HAS BEGUN AT THE TEMPLE AT SIMFUR.
EXCELLENT, RAMJET. ANY OPPOSITION? AUTOBOT... OR OTHERWISE?
AT FIRST, YES, MY LORD. BUT THOSE EFFORTS HAVE BEEN ADDRESSED AND HAVE SINCE SUBSIDED.
TAKE WHAT'S LEFT OF FRENZY AND TRANSFER HIS MEMORY BANKS TO OUR ARCHIVES. THERE IS INFORMATION THAT I CAN USE FOR OUR BENEFIT.
THE PLANET CALLED EARTH HOLDS SUCH SECRETS. IF WE ARE EVER TO RETURN THERE, WE SHALL HOLD A SIGNIFICANT TACTICAL ADVANTAGE OVER OUR ENEMIES.
LORD STARSCREAM, I'LL HAVE THE DATA TRANSFERRED AND WILL DELIVER IT TO YOU... PERSONALLY.
VERY WELL, DREADWING.
THUNDERCRACKER, SEE TO YOUR INJURIES. THE REST OF YOU, STAND BY FOR MY INSTRUCTIONS. FOR NOW I MUST GO AND CLAIM WHAT IS RIGHTFULLY MINE. BESIDES...
...IT'S NOT AS THOUGH THE FORMER RESIDENT WILL BE RETURNING ANYTIME SOON.

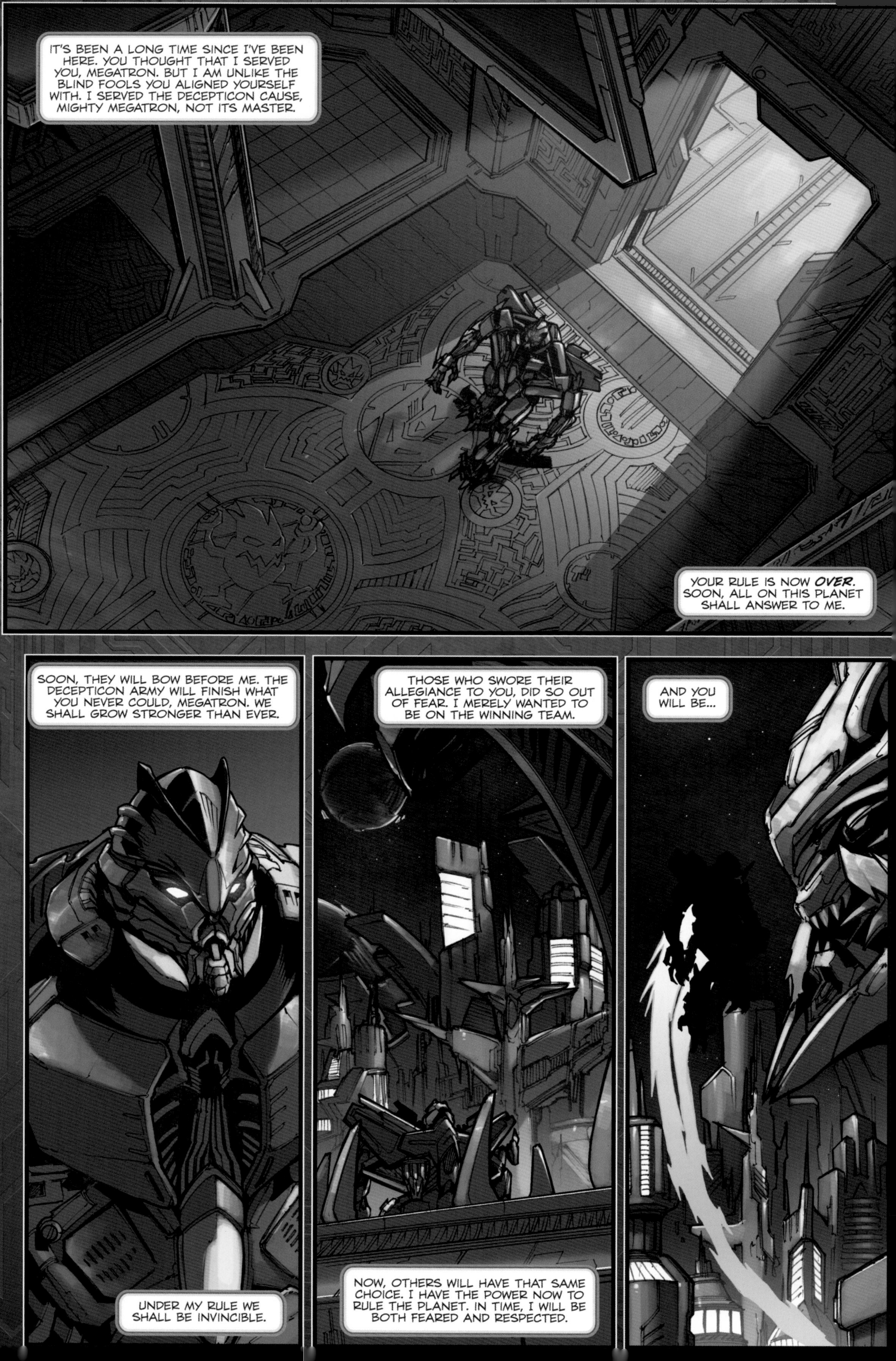
IT'S BEEN A LONG TIME SINCE I'VE BEEN HERE. YOU THOUGHT THAT I SERVED YOU, MEGATRON. BUT I AM UNLIKE THE BLIND FOOLS YOU ALIGNED YOURSELF WITH. I SERVED THE DECEPTICON CAUSE, MIGHTY MEGATRON, NOT ITS MASTER.
YOUR RULE IS NOW *OVER*. SOON, ALL ON THIS PLANET SHALL ANSWER TO ME.
SOON, THEY WILL BOW BEFORE ME. THE DECEPTICON ARMY WILL FINISH WHAT YOU NEVER COULD, MEGATRON. WE SHALL GROW STRONGER THAN EVER.
UNDER MY RULE WE SHALL BE INVINCIBLE.
THOSE WHO SWORE THEIR ALLEGIANCE TO YOU, DID SO OUT OF FEAR. I MERELY WANTED TO BE ON THE WINNING TEAM.
NOW, OTHERS WILL HAVE THAT SAME CHOICE. I HAVE THE POWER NOW TO RULE THE PLANET. IN TIME, I WILL BE BOTH FEARED AND RESPECTED.
AND YOU WILL BE...

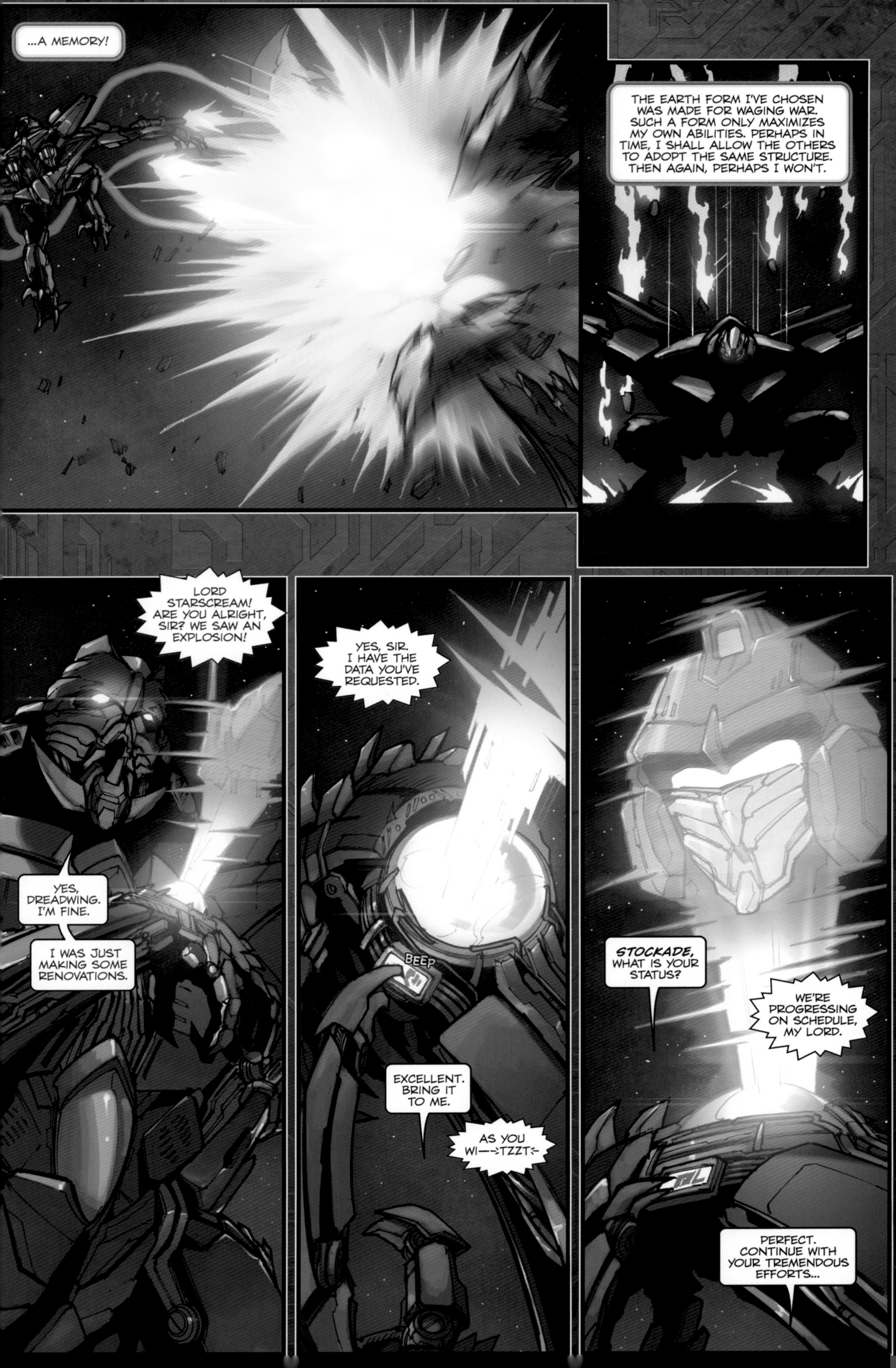
...A MEMORY!
THE EARTH FORM I'VE CHOSEN WAS MADE FOR WAGING WAR. SUCH A FORM ONLY MAXIMIZES MY OWN ABILITIES. PERHAPS IN TIME, I SHALL ALLOW THE OTHERS TO ADOPT THE SAME STRUCTURE. THEN AGAIN, PERHAPS I WON'T.
LORD STARSCREAM! ARE YOU ALRIGHT, SIR? WE SAW AN EXPLOSION!
YES, DREADWING. I'M FINE.
I WAS JUST MAKING SOME RENOVATIONS.
BEEP
YES, SIR. I HAVE THE DATA YOU'VE REQUESTED.
EXCELLENT. BRING IT TO ME.
AS YOU WI—TZZT
STOCKADE, WHAT IS YOUR STATUS?
WE'RE PROGRESSING ON SCHEDULE, MY LORD.
PERFECT. CONTINUE WITH YOUR TREMENDOUS EFFORTS...

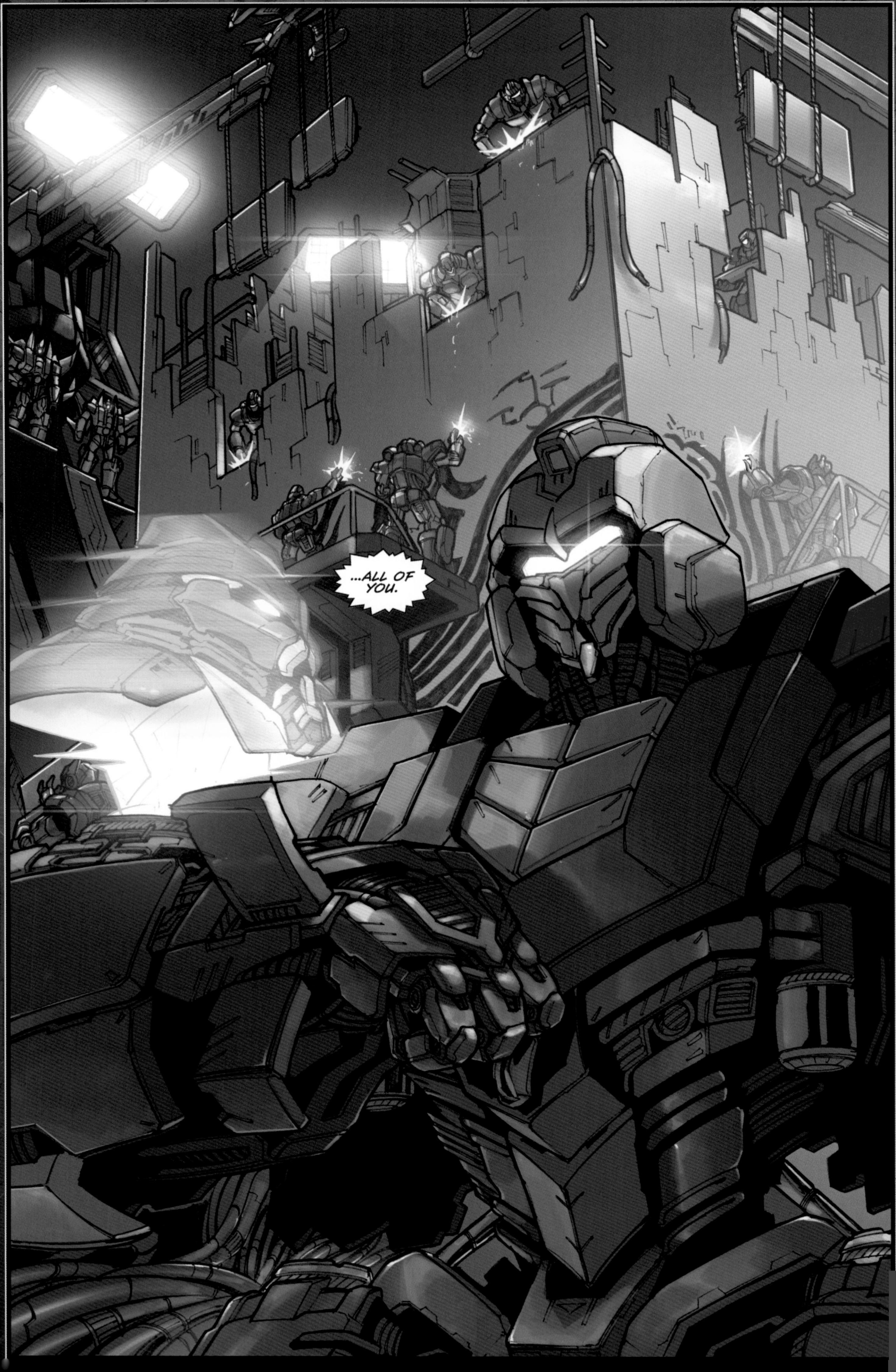
...ALL OF YOU.

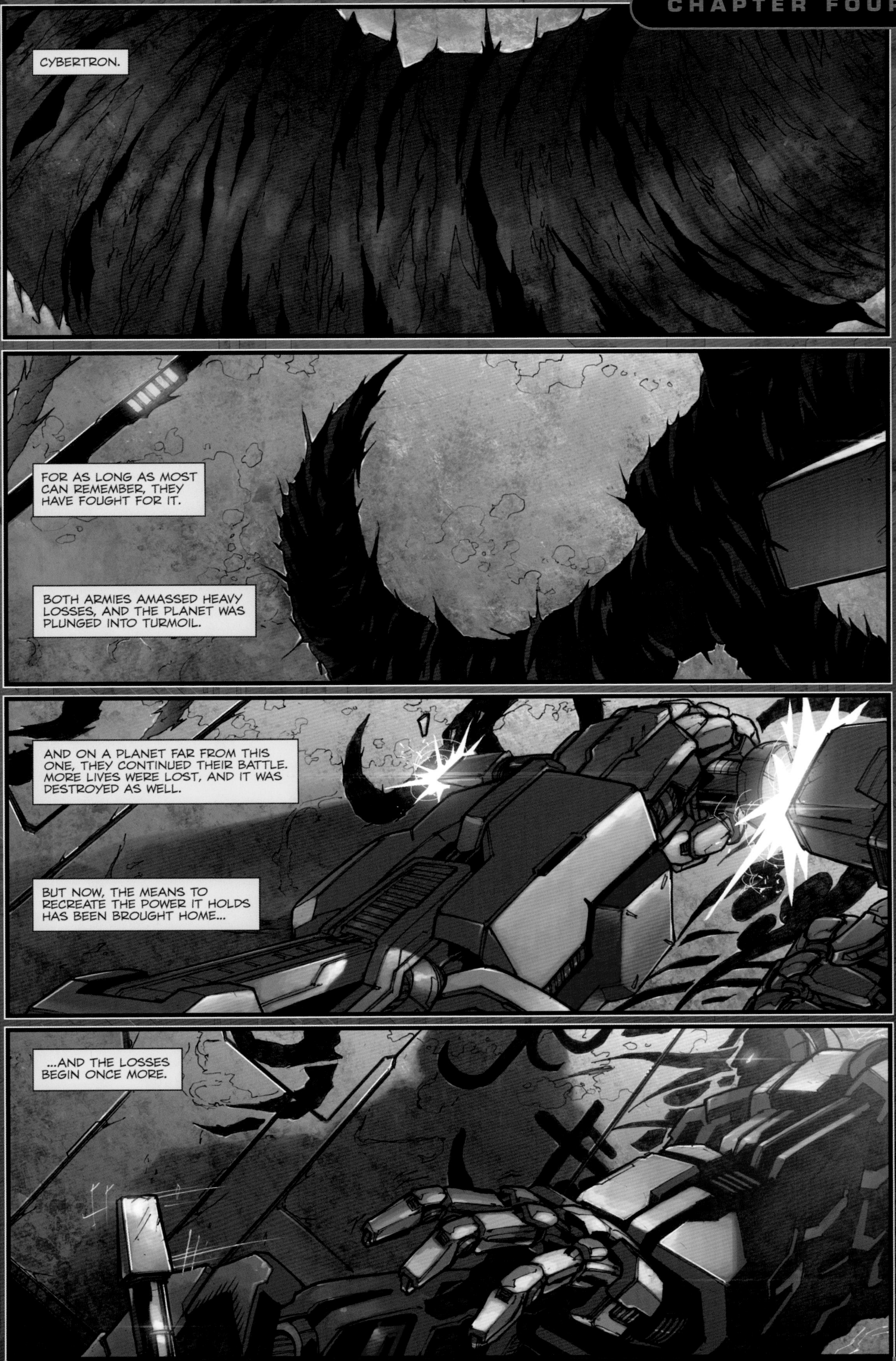
CYBERTRON.
FOR AS LONG AS MOST CAN REMEMBER, THEY HAVE FOUGHT FOR IT.
BOTH ARMIES AMASSED HEAVY LOSSES, AND THE PLANET WAS PLUNGED INTO TURMOIL.
AND ON A PLANET FAR FROM THIS ONE, THEY CONTINUED THEIR BATTLE. MORE LIVES WERE LOST, AND IT WAS DESTROYED AS WELL.
BUT NOW, THE MEANS TO RECREATE THE POWER IT HOLDS HAS BEEN BROUGHT HOME...
...AND THE LOSSES BEGIN ONCE MORE.

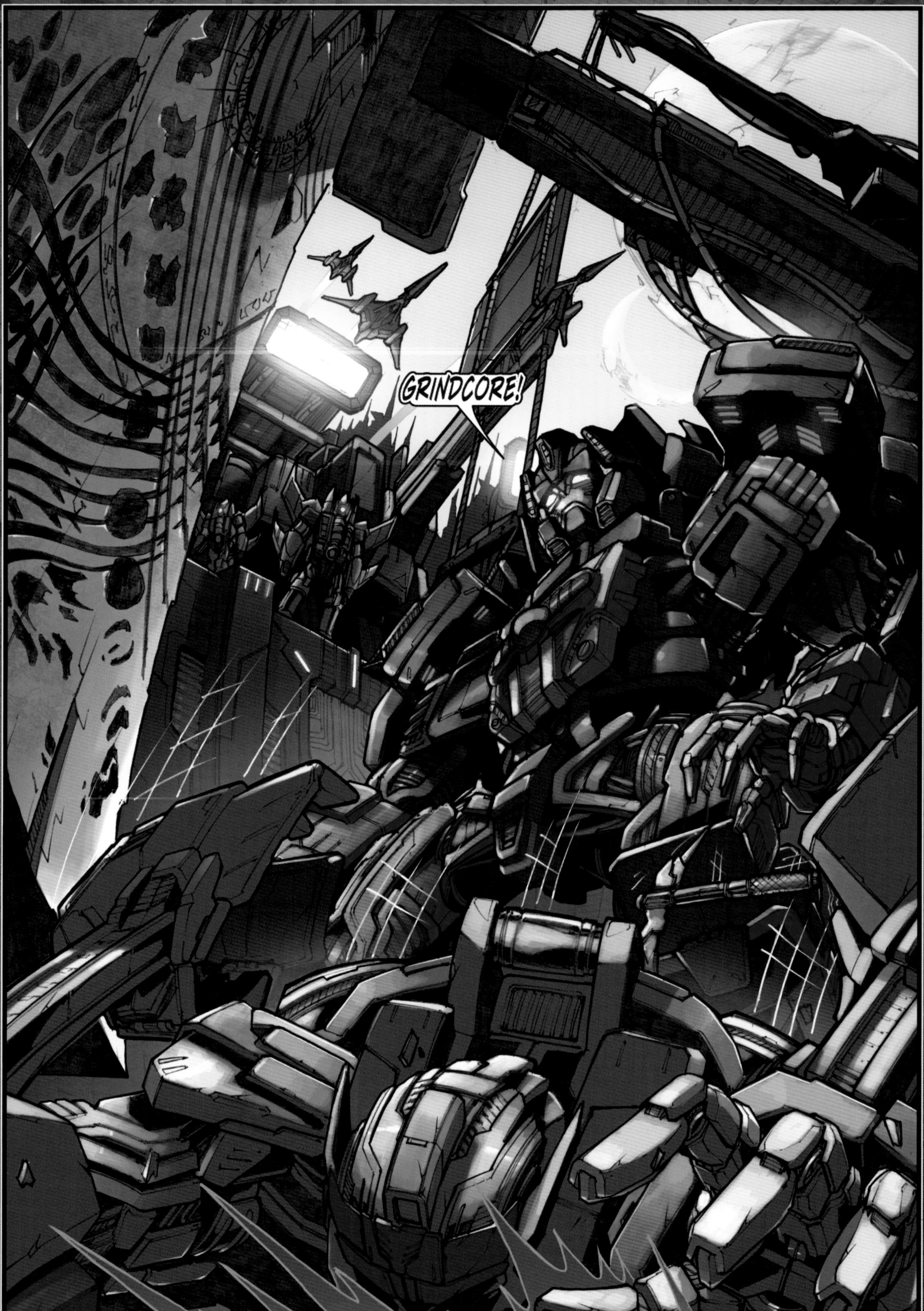
GRINDCORE!

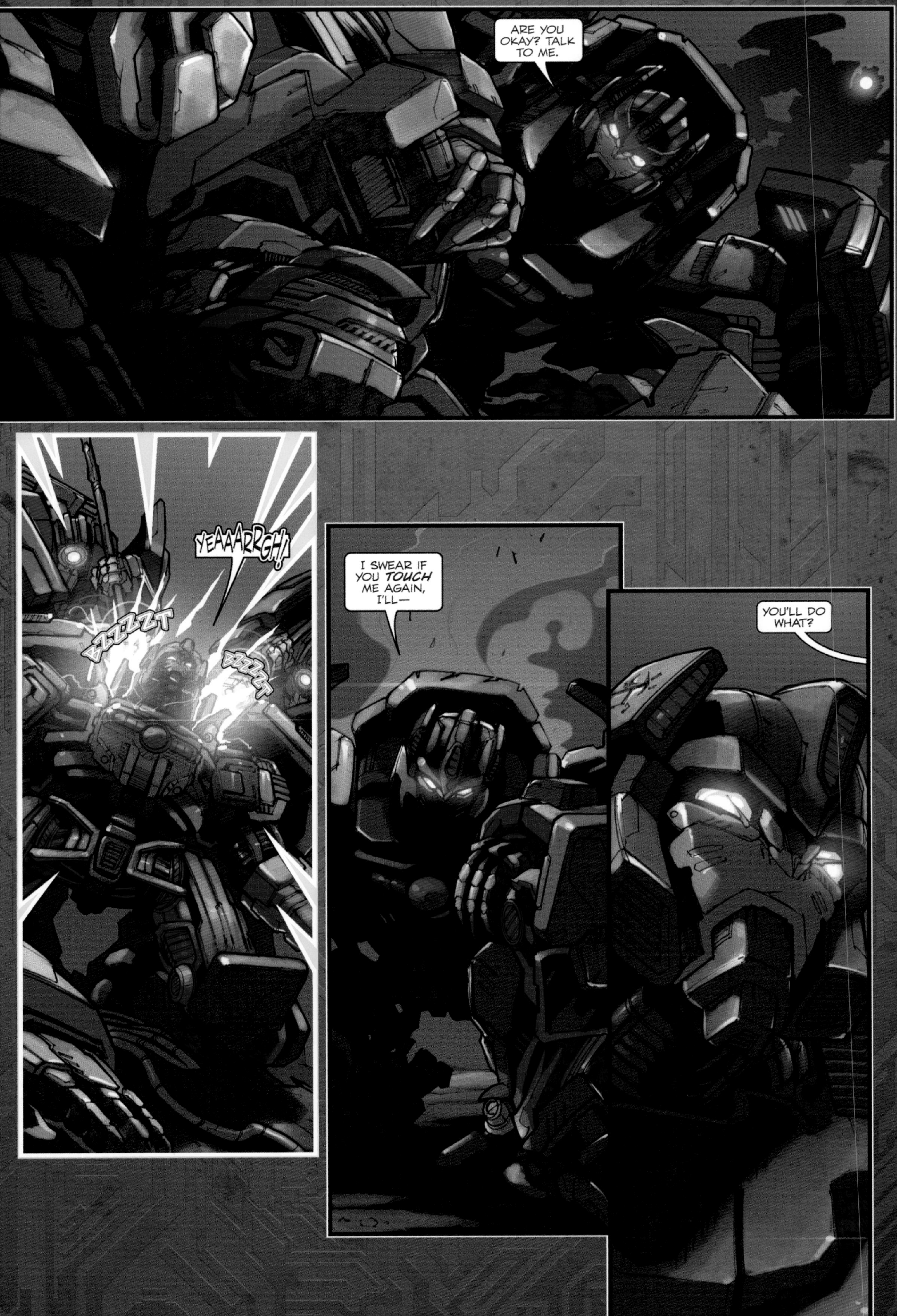
ARE YOU OKAY? TALK TO ME.
YEAAARRGH!
BZZZZT
BZZZZT
I SWEAR IF YOU *TOUCH* ME AGAIN, I'LL—
YOU'LL DO WHAT?

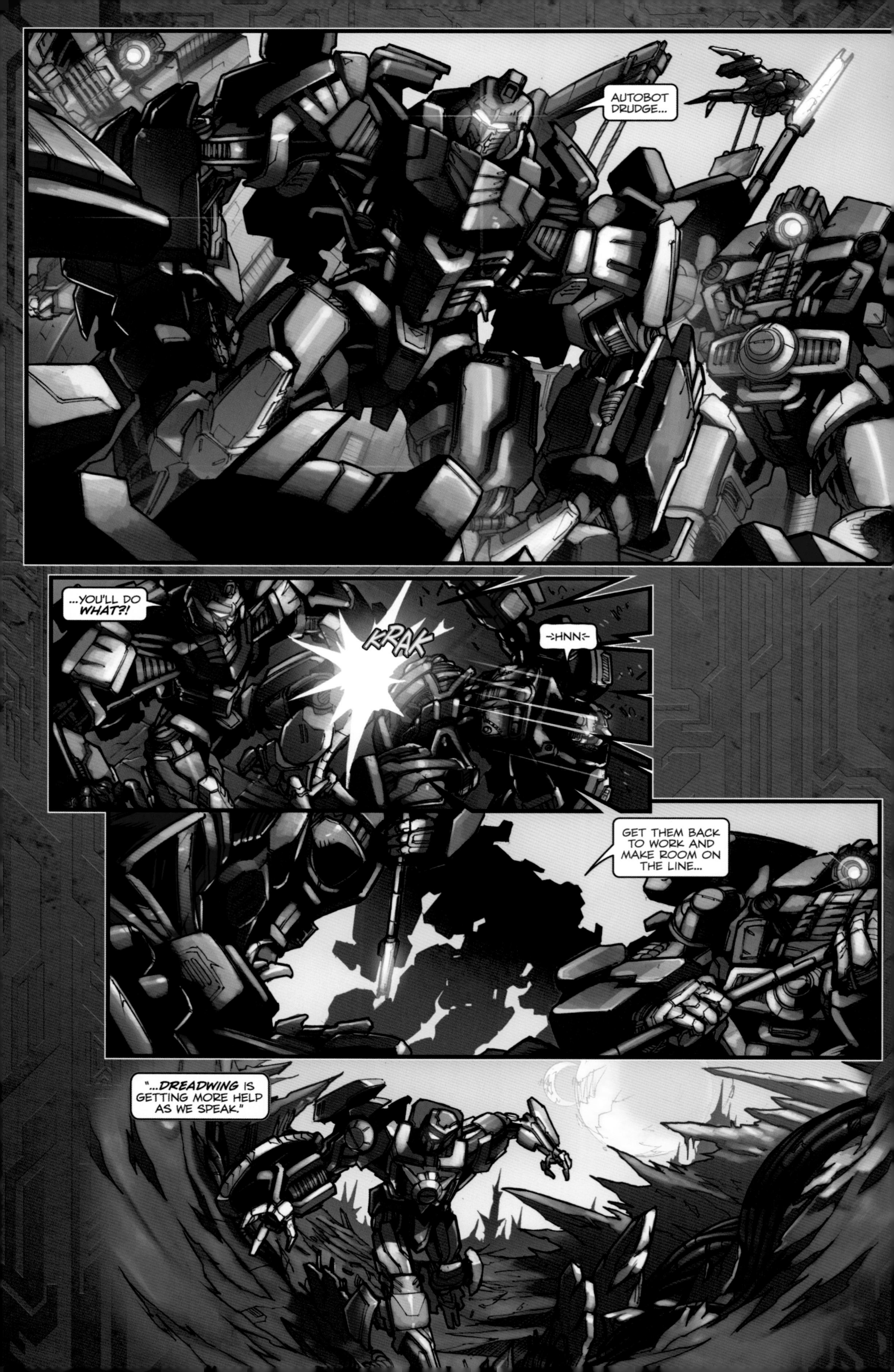

AUTOBOT DRUDGE...
...YOU'LL DO WHAT?!
KRAK
-HNN-
GET THEM BACK TO WORK AND MAKE ROOM ON THE LINE...
"...DREADWING IS GETTING MORE HELP AS WE SPEAK."

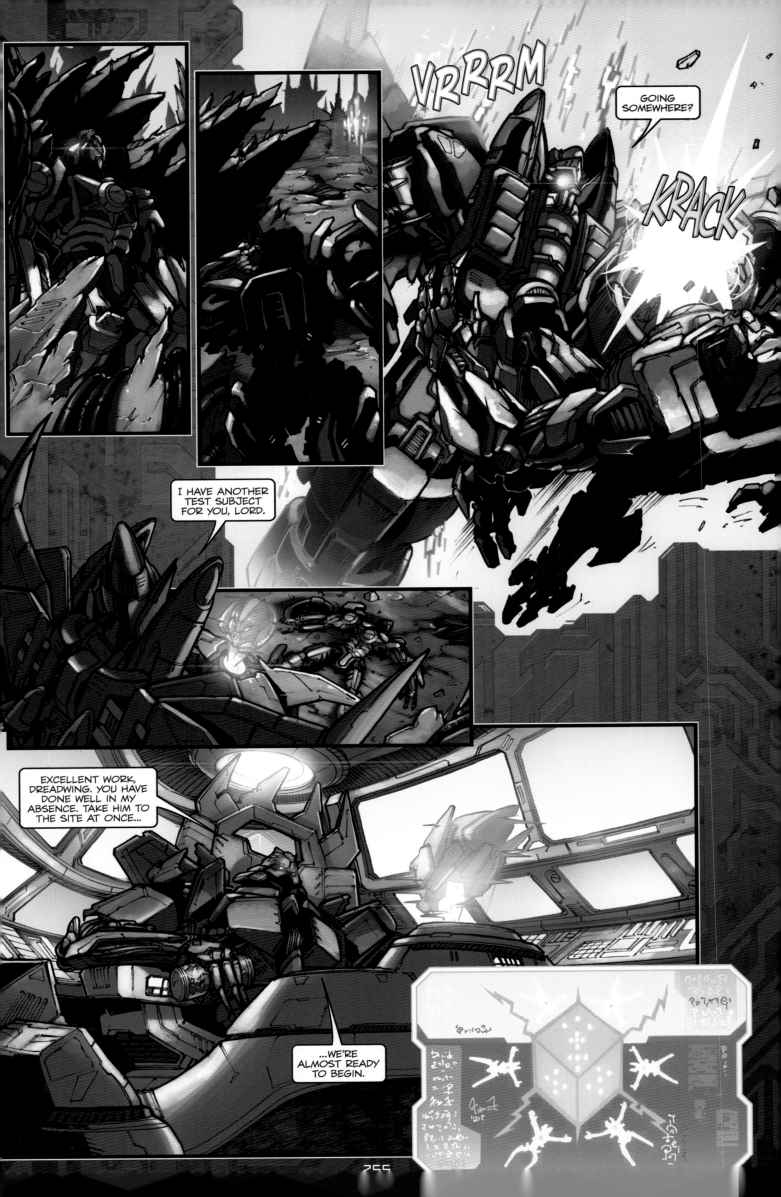

GOING SOMEWHERE?

VRRRM

KRACK

I HAVE ANOTHER TEST SUBJECT FOR YOU, LORD.

EXCELLENT WORK, DREADWING. YOU HAVE DONE WELL IN MY ABSENCE. TAKE HIM TO THE SITE AT ONCE...

...WE'RE ALMOST READY TO BEGIN.

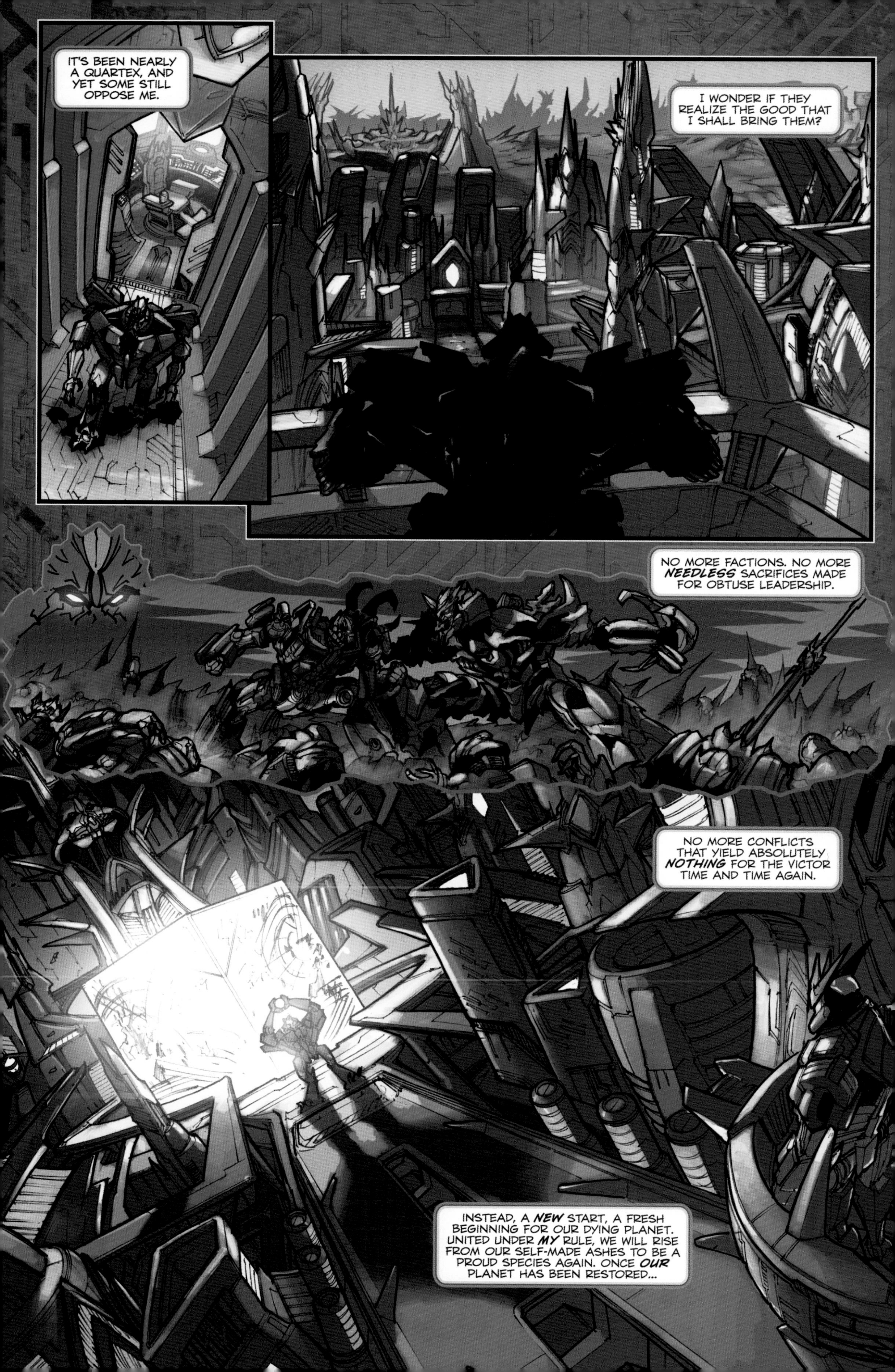
IT'S BEEN NEARLY A QUARTEX, AND YET SOME STILL OPPOSE ME.
I WONDER IF THEY REALIZE THE GOOD THAT I SHALL BRING THEM?
NO MORE FACTIONS. NO MORE NEEDLESS SACRIFICES MADE FOR OBTUSE LEADERSHIP.
NO MORE CONFLICTS THAT YIELD ABSOLUTELY NOTHING FOR THE VICTOR TIME AND TIME AGAIN.
INSTEAD, A NEW START, A FRESH BEGINNING FOR OUR DYING PLANET. UNITED UNDER MY RULE, WE WILL RISE FROM OUR SELF-MADE ASHES TO BE A PROUD SPECIES AGAIN. ONCE OUR PLANET HAS BEEN RESTORED...

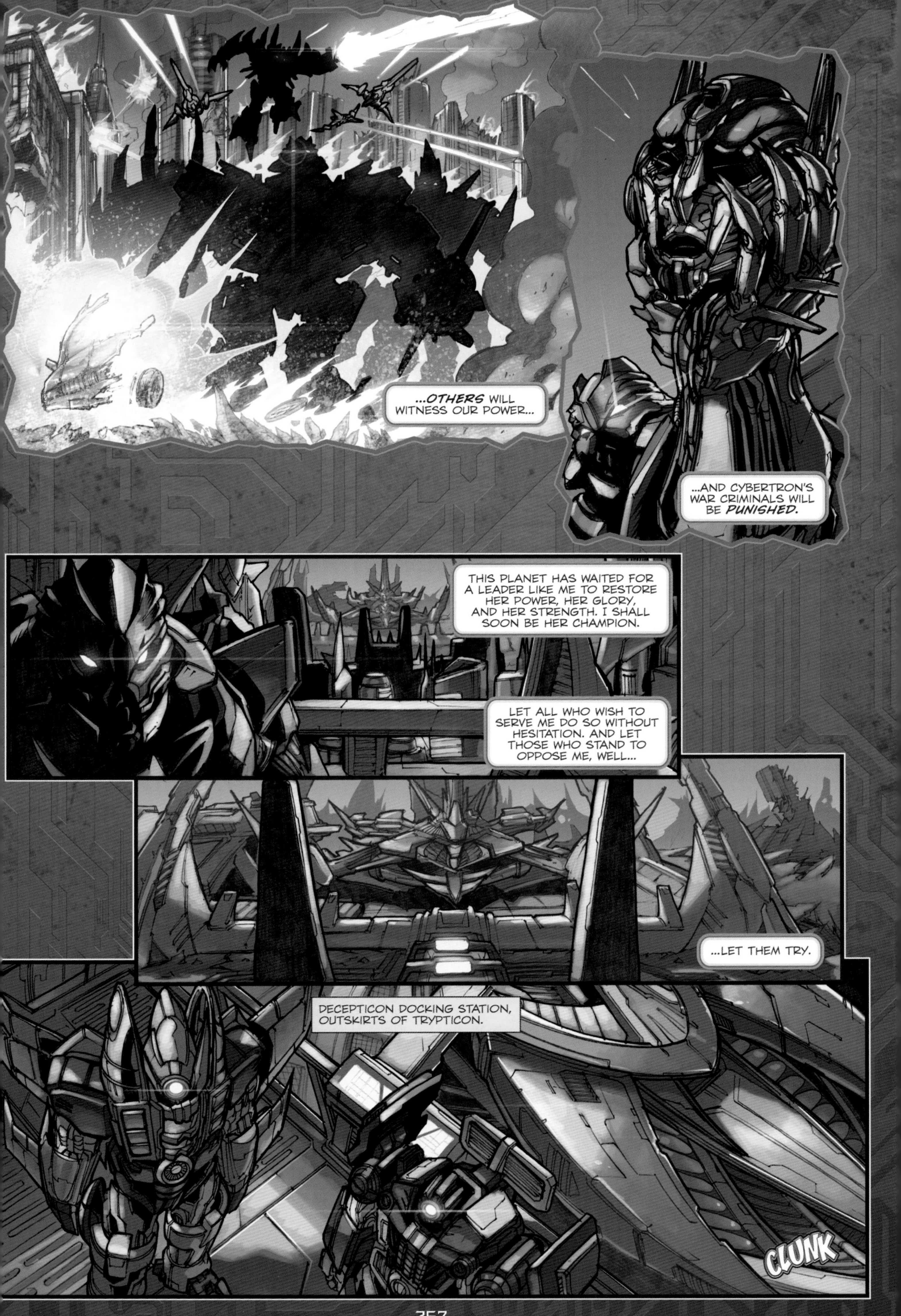
...OTHERS WILL WITNESS OUR POWER...
...AND CYBERTRON'S WAR CRIMINALS WILL BE PUNISHED.
THIS PLANET HAS WAITED FOR A LEADER LIKE ME TO RESTORE HER POWER, HER GLORY, AND HER STRENGTH. I SHALL SOON BE HER CHAMPION.
LET ALL WHO WISH TO SERVE ME DO SO WITHOUT HESITATION. AND LET THOSE WHO STAND TO OPPOSE ME, WELL...
...LET THEM TRY.
DECEPTICON DOCKING STATION, OUTSKIRTS OF TRYPTICON.
CLUNK

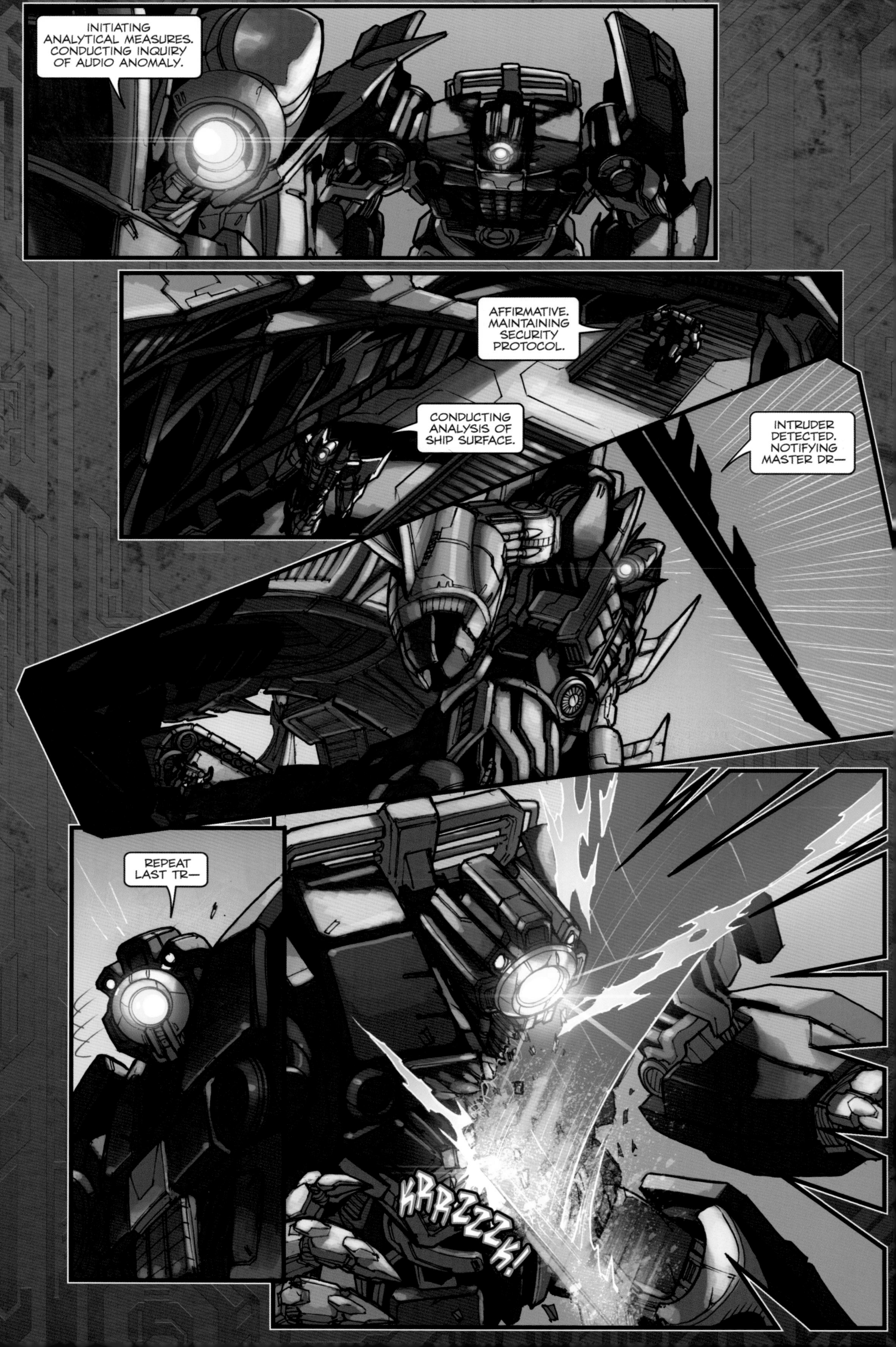
INITIATING ANALYTICAL MEASURES. CONDUCTING INQUIRY OF AUDIO ANOMALY.
AFFIRMATIVE. MAINTAINING SECURITY PROTOCOL.
CONDUCTING ANALYSIS OF SHIP SURFACE.
INTRUDER DETECTED. NOTIFYING MASTER DR—
REPEAT LAST TR—
KRRZZZK!

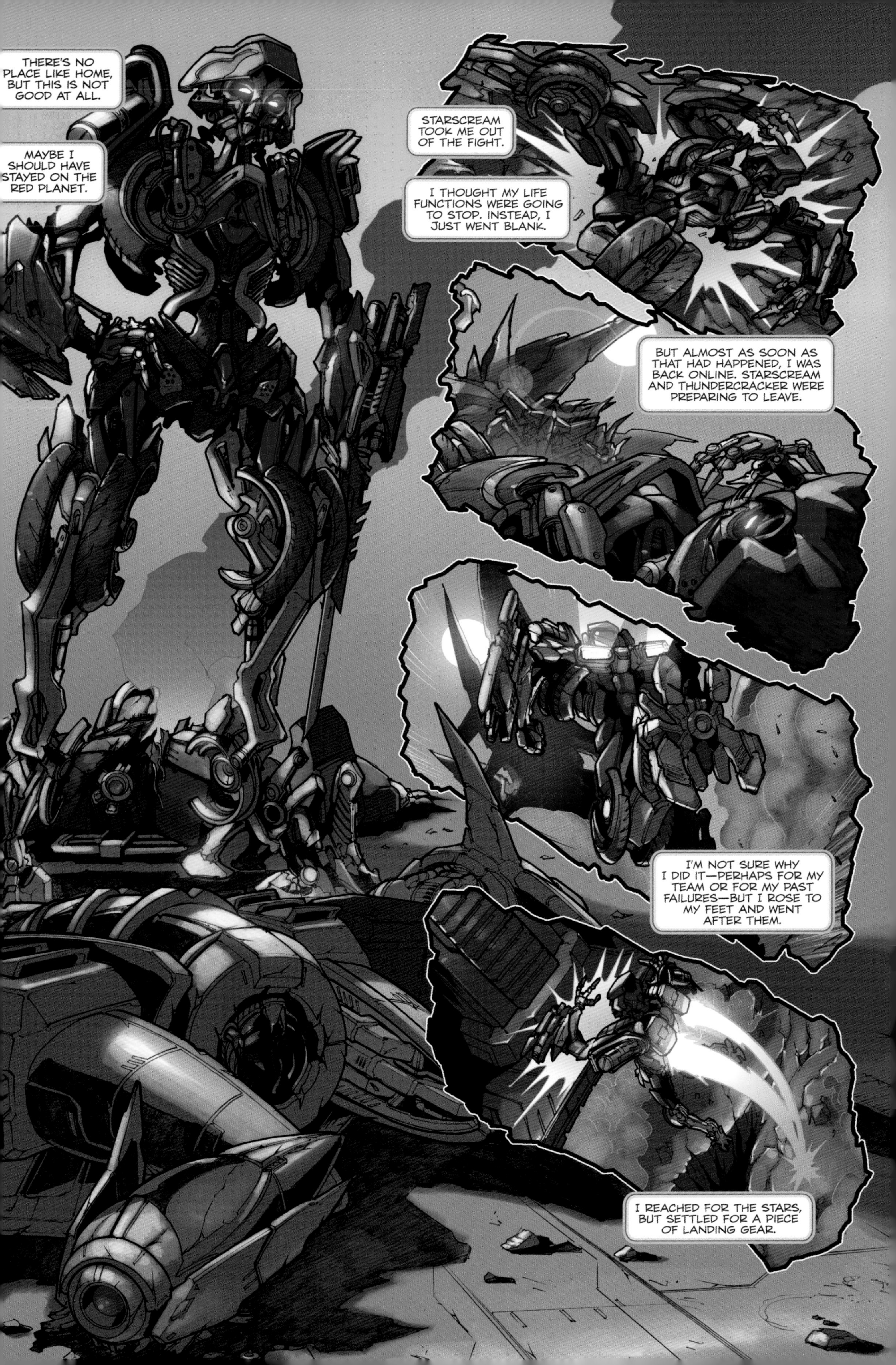
THERE'S NO PLACE LIKE HOME, BUT THIS IS NOT GOOD AT ALL.
MAYBE I SHOULD HAVE STAYED ON THE RED PLANET.
STARSCREAM TOOK ME OUT OF THE FIGHT.
I THOUGHT MY LIFE FUNCTIONS WERE GOING TO STOP. INSTEAD, I JUST WENT BLANK.
BUT ALMOST AS SOON AS THAT HAD HAPPENED, I WAS BACK ONLINE. STARSCREAM AND THUNDERCRACKER WERE PREPARING TO LEAVE.
I'M NOT SURE WHY I DID IT—PERHAPS FOR MY TEAM OR FOR MY PAST FAILURES—BUT I ROSE TO MY FEET AND WENT AFTER THEM.
I REACHED FOR THE STARS, BUT SETTLED FOR A PIECE OF LANDING GEAR.

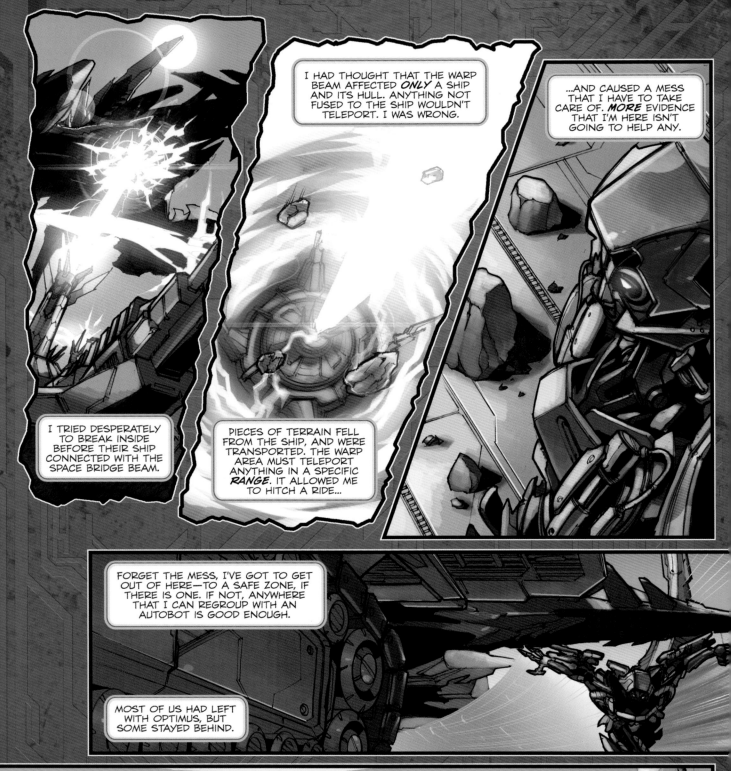

I HAD THOUGHT THAT THE WARP BEAM AFFECTED *ONLY* A SHIP AND ITS HULL. ANYTHING NOT FUSED TO THE SHIP WOULDN'T TELEPORT. I WAS WRONG.

...AND CAUSED A MESS THAT I HAVE TO TAKE CARE OF. *MORE* EVIDENCE THAT I'M HERE ISN'T GOING TO HELP ANY.

I TRIED DESPERATELY TO BREAK INSIDE BEFORE THEIR SHIP CONNECTED WITH THE SPACE BRIDGE BEAM.

PIECES OF TERRAIN FELL FROM THE SHIP, AND WERE TRANSPORTED. THE WARP AREA MUST TELEPORT ANYTHING IN A SPECIFIC *RANGE.* IT ALLOWED ME TO HITCH A RIDE...

FORGET THE MESS, I'VE GOT TO GET OUT OF HERE—TO A SAFE ZONE, IF THERE IS ONE. IF NOT, ANYWHERE THAT I CAN REGROUP WITH AN AUTOBOT IS GOOD ENOUGH.

MOST OF US HAD LEFT WITH OPTIMUS, BUT SOME STAYED BEHIND.

I HOPE THAT I CAN FIND THEM.

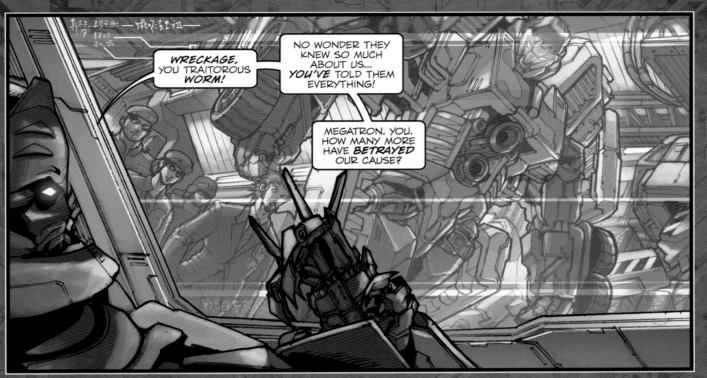

WRECKAGE, YOU TRAITOROUS *WORM!*

NO WONDER THEY KNEW SO MUCH ABOUT US... *YOU'VE* TOLD THEM EVERYTHING!

MEGATRON. YOU. HOW MANY MORE HAVE *BETRAYED* OUR CAUSE?

LORD STARSCREAM, I HAVE RETURNED.

SO YOU HAVE, DREADWING. IS THE *CUBE* FINALLY READY?

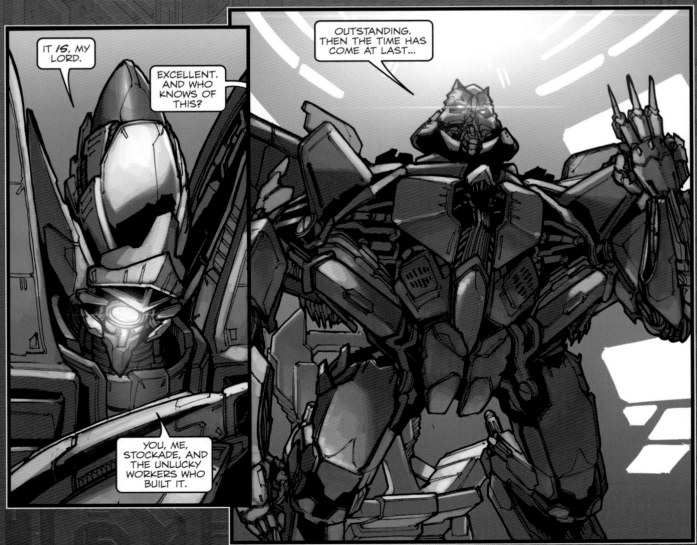

IT *IS,* MY LORD.

EXCELLENT. AND WHO KNOWS OF THIS?

OUTSTANDING. THEN THE TIME HAS COME AT LAST...

YOU, ME, STOCKADE, AND THE UNLUCKY WORKERS WHO BUILT IT.

261

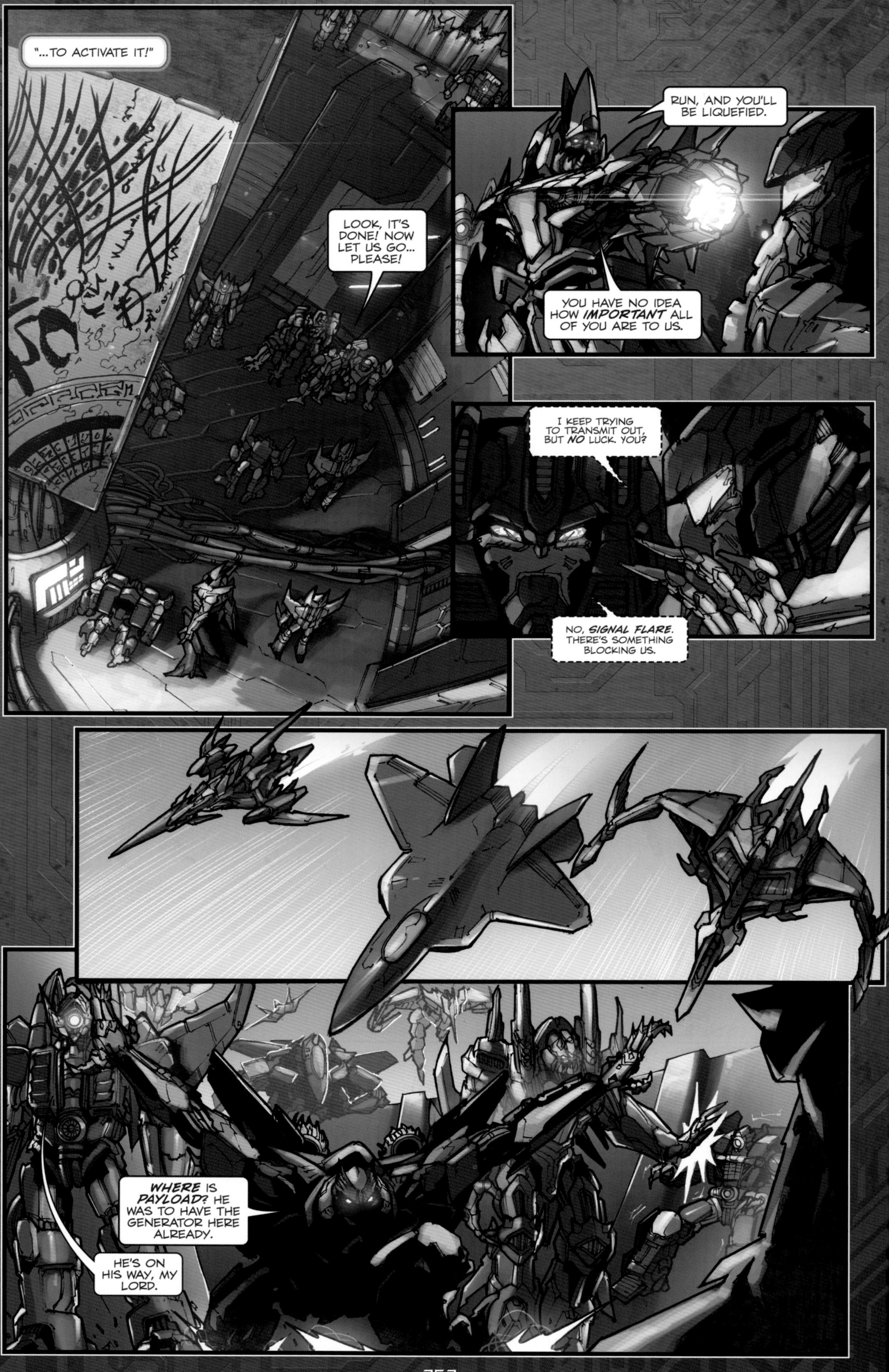
"...TO ACTIVATE IT!"
LOOK, IT'S DONE! NOW LET US GO... PLEASE!
RUN, AND YOU'LL BE LIQUEFIED.
YOU HAVE NO IDEA HOW IMPORTANT ALL OF YOU ARE TO US.
I KEEP TRYING TO TRANSMIT OUT, BUT NO LUCK. YOU?
NO, SIGNAL FLARE. THERE'S SOMETHING BLOCKING US.
WHERE IS PAYLOAD? HE WAS TO HAVE THE GENERATOR HERE ALREADY.
HE'S ON HIS WAY, MY LORD.

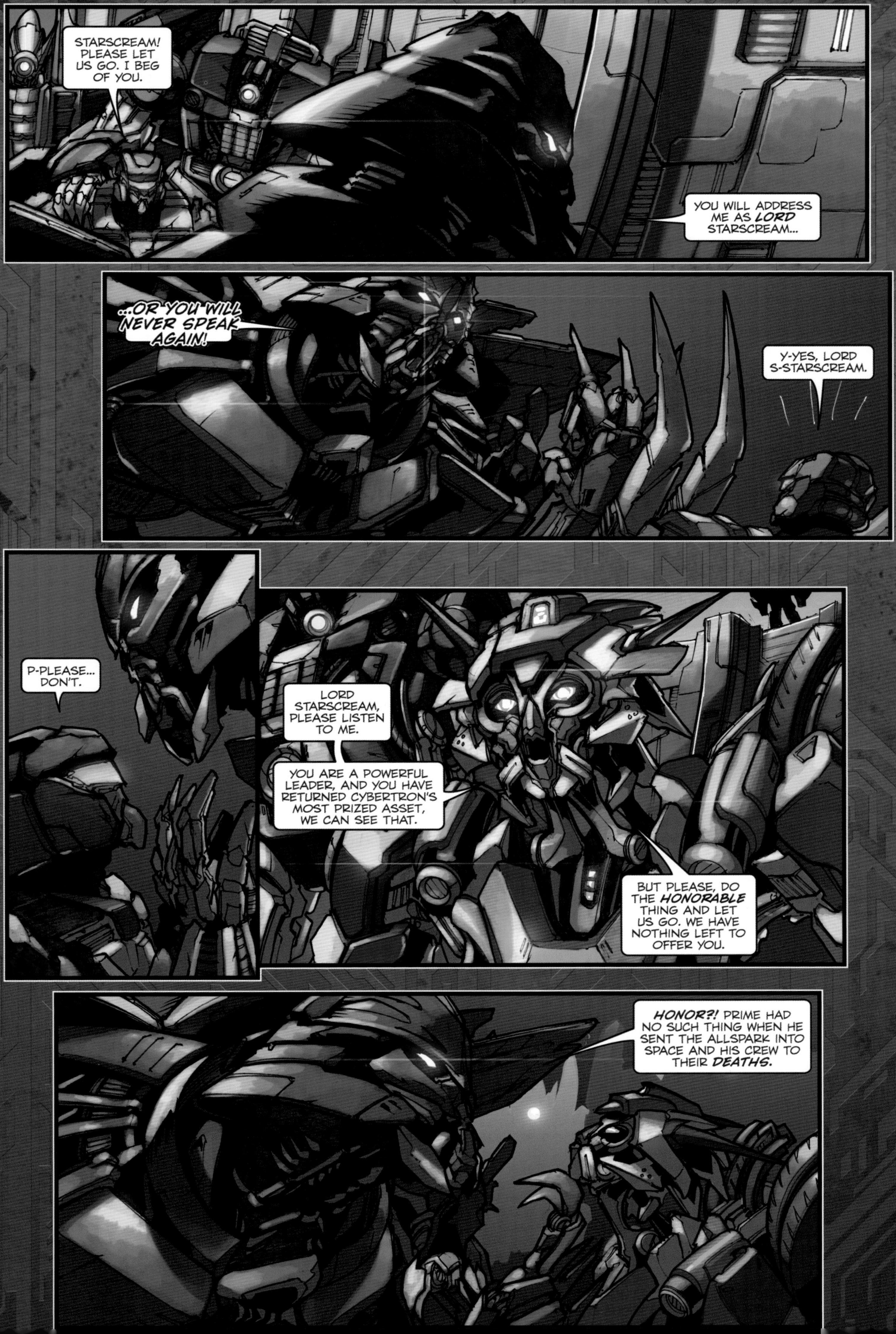
STARSCREAM! PLEASE LET US GO. I BEG OF YOU.
YOU WILL ADDRESS ME AS LORD STARSCREAM...
...OR YOU WILL NEVER SPEAK AGAIN!
Y-YES, LORD S-STARSCREAM.
P-PLEASE... DON'T.
LORD STARSCREAM, PLEASE LISTEN TO ME.
YOU ARE A POWERFUL LEADER, AND YOU HAVE RETURNED CYBERTRON'S MOST PRIZED ASSET, WE CAN SEE THAT.
BUT PLEASE, DO THE HONORABLE THING AND LET US GO. WE HAVE NOTHING LEFT TO OFFER YOU.
HONOR?! PRIME HAD NO SUCH THING WHEN HE SENT THE ALLSPARK INTO SPACE AND HIS CREW TO THEIR DEATHS.

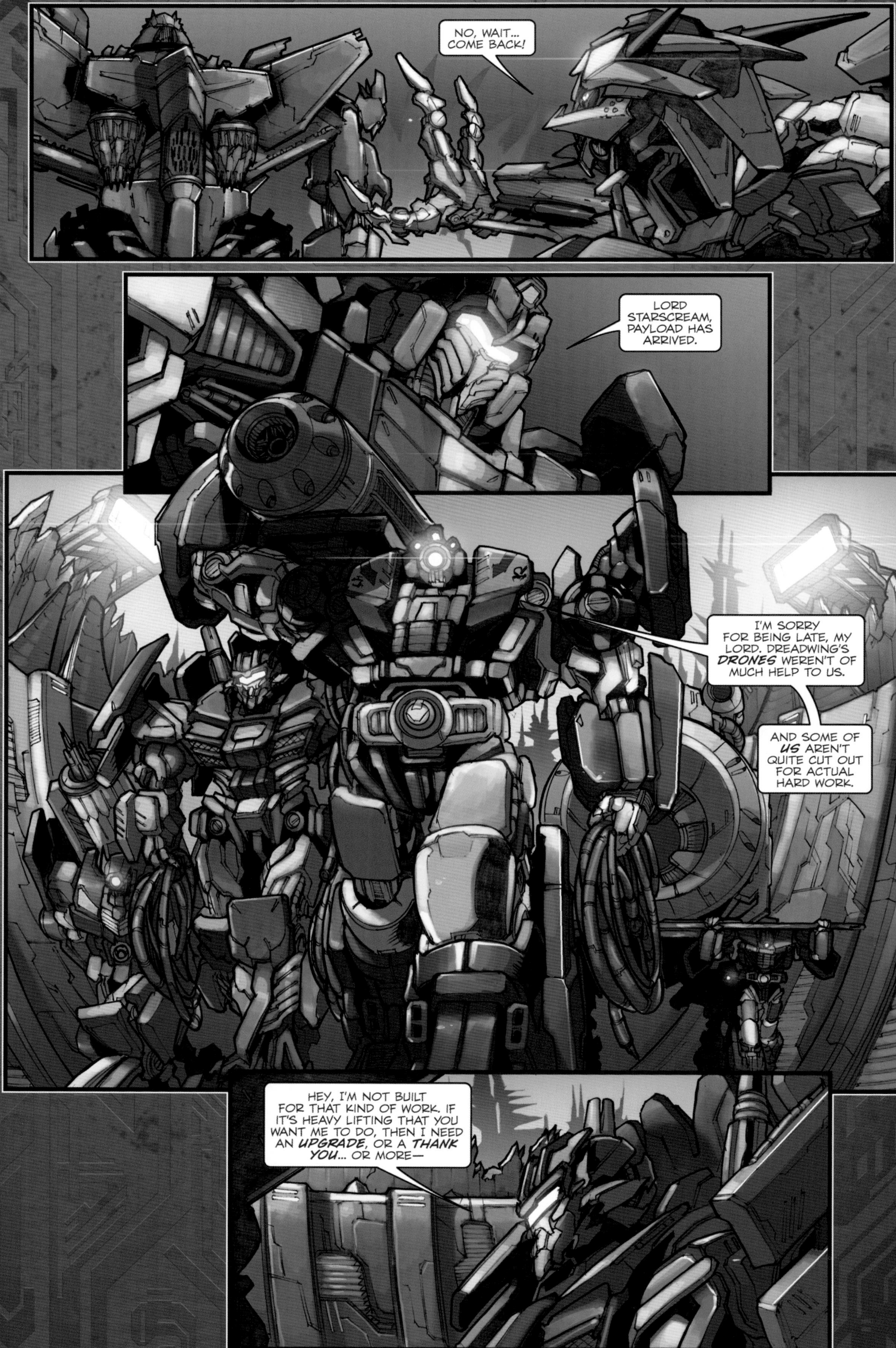

NO, WAIT... COME BACK!
LORD STARSCREAM, PAYLOAD HAS ARRIVED.
I'M SORRY FOR BEING LATE, MY LORD. DREADWING'S *DRONES* WEREN'T OF MUCH HELP TO US.
AND SOME OF *US* AREN'T QUITE CUT OUT FOR ACTUAL HARD WORK.
HEY, I'M NOT BUILT FOR THAT KIND OF WORK. IF IT'S HEAVY LIFTING THAT YOU WANT ME TO DO, THEN I NEED AN *UPGRADE*, OR A *THANK YOU*... OR MORE—

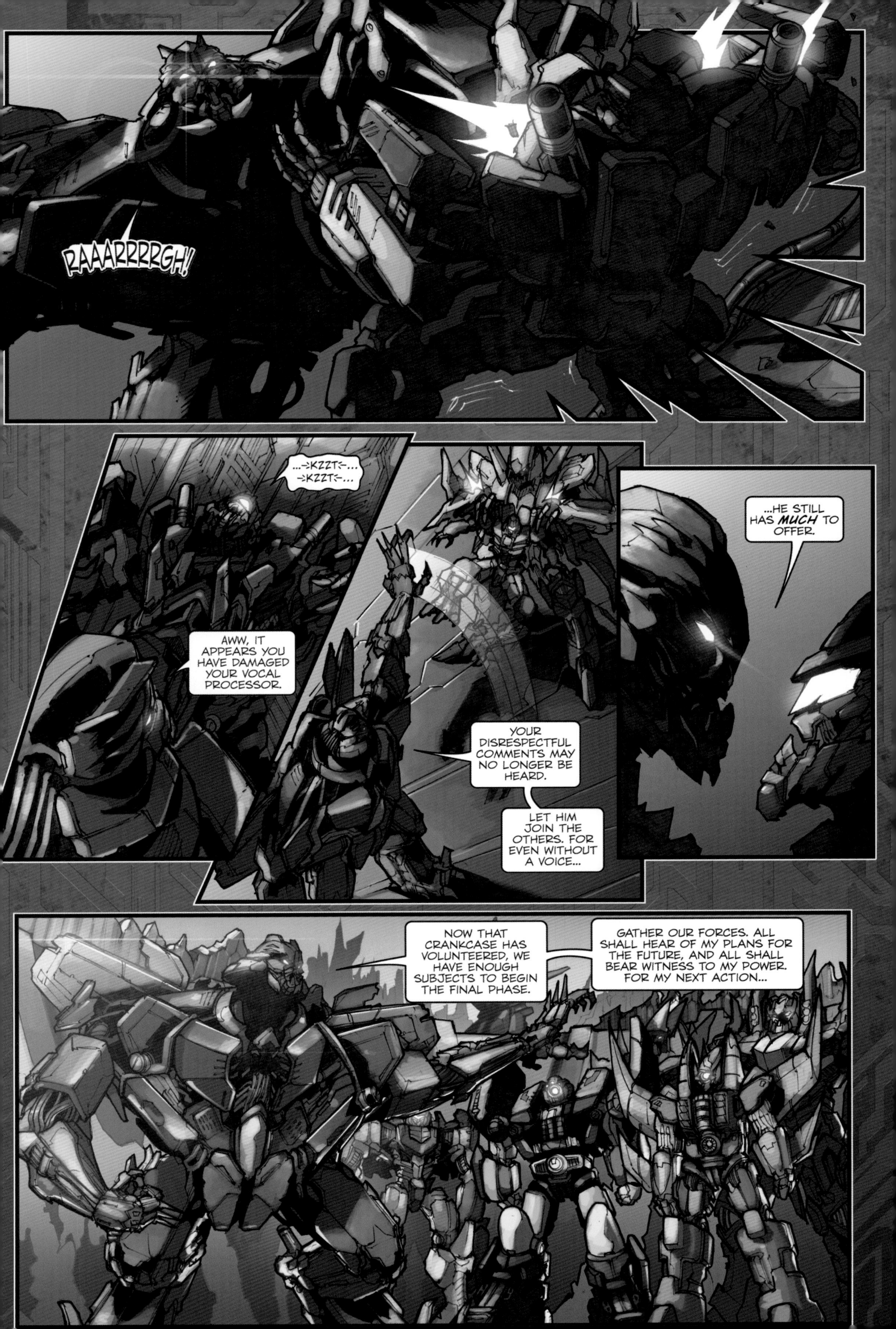
RAAARRRRGH!
...-KZZT-...
-KZZT-...
AWW, IT APPEARS YOU HAVE DAMAGED YOUR VOCAL PROCESSOR.
YOUR DISRESPECTFUL COMMENTS MAY NO LONGER BE HEARD.
LET HIM JOIN THE OTHERS. FOR EVEN WITHOUT A VOICE...
...HE STILL HAS MUCH TO OFFER.
NOW THAT CRANKCASE HAS VOLUNTEERED, WE HAVE ENOUGH SUBJECTS TO BEGIN THE FINAL PHASE.
GATHER OUR FORCES. ALL SHALL HEAR OF MY PLANS FOR THE FUTURE, AND ALL SHALL BEAR WITNESS TO MY POWER. FOR MY NEXT ACTION...

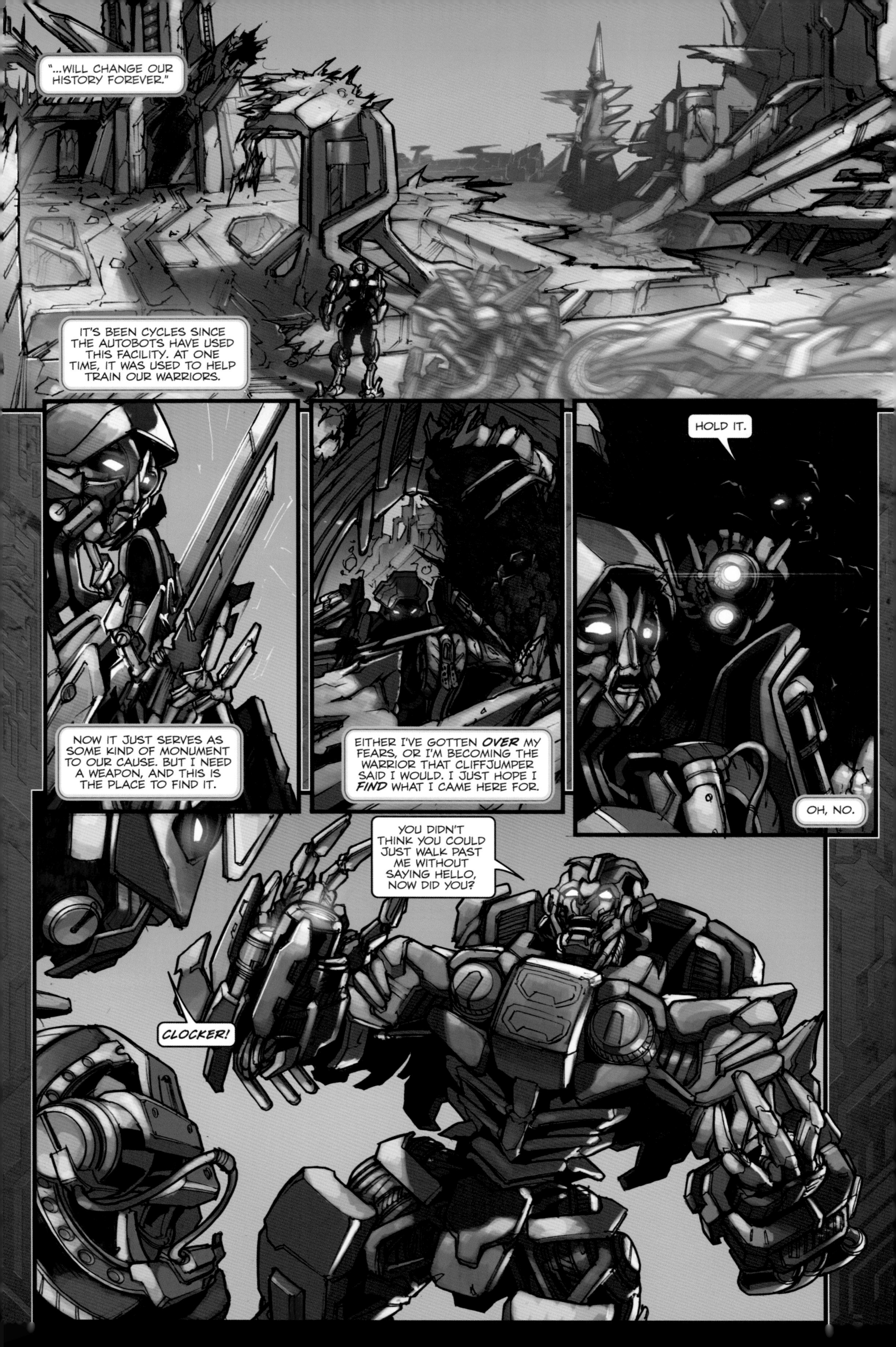
"...WILL CHANGE OUR HISTORY FOREVER."
IT'S BEEN CYCLES SINCE THE AUTOBOTS HAVE USED THIS FACILITY. AT ONE TIME, IT WAS USED TO HELP TRAIN OUR WARRIORS.
NOW IT JUST SERVES AS SOME KIND OF MONUMENT TO OUR CAUSE. BUT I NEED A WEAPON, AND THIS IS THE PLACE TO FIND IT.
EITHER I'VE GOTTEN OVER MY FEARS, OR I'M BECOMING THE WARRIOR THAT CLIFFJUMPER SAID I WOULD. I JUST HOPE I FIND WHAT I CAME HERE FOR.
HOLD IT.
OH, NO.
YOU DIDN'T THINK YOU COULD JUST WALK PAST ME WITHOUT SAYING HELLO, NOW DID YOU?
CLOCKER!

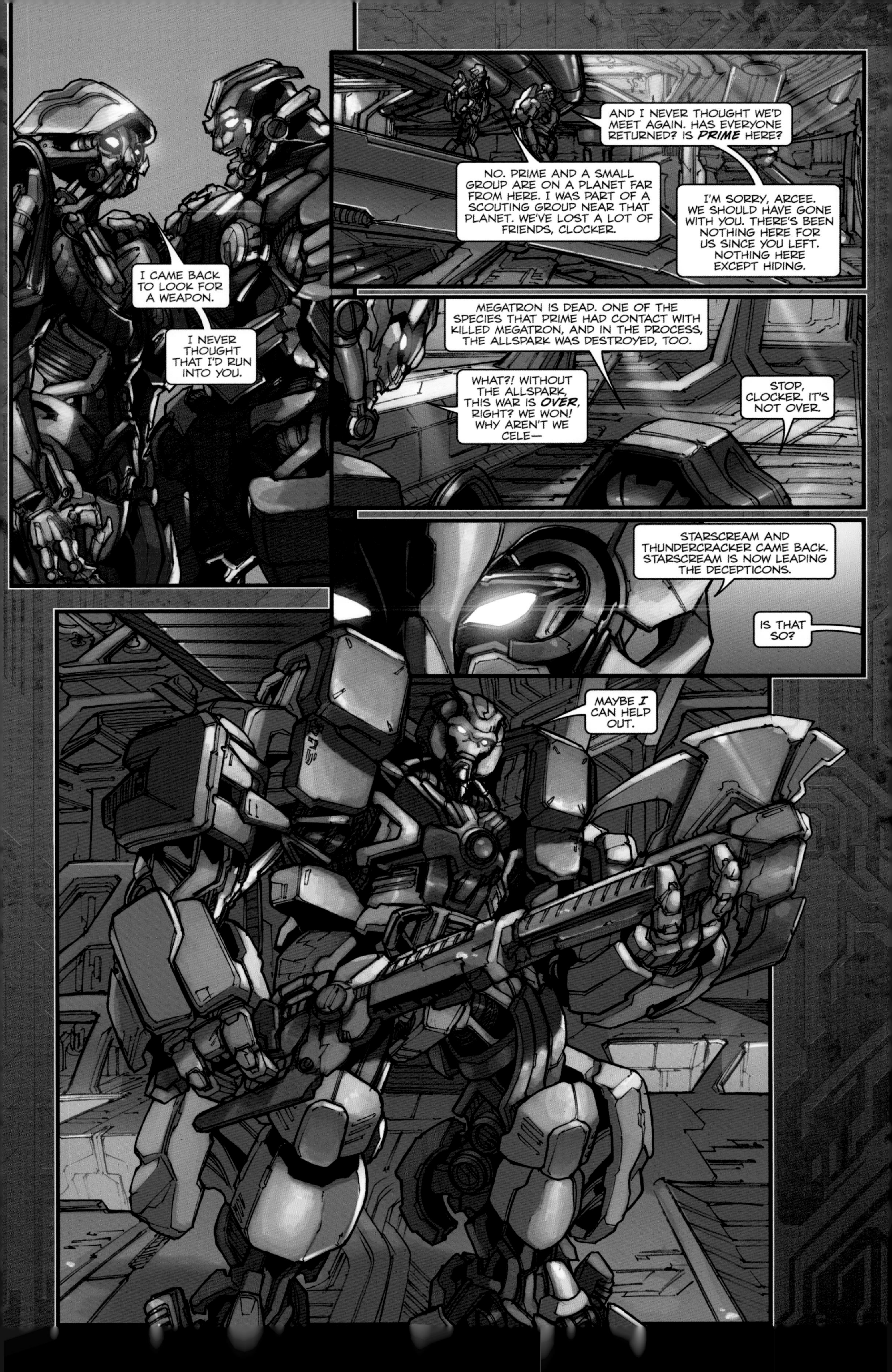
I CAME BACK TO LOOK FOR A WEAPON.
I NEVER THOUGHT THAT I'D RUN INTO YOU.
AND I NEVER THOUGHT WE'D MEET AGAIN. HAS EVERYONE RETURNED? IS *PRIME* HERE?
NO. PRIME AND A SMALL GROUP ARE ON A PLANET FAR FROM HERE. I WAS PART OF A SCOUTING GROUP NEAR THAT PLANET. WE'VE LOST A LOT OF FRIENDS, CLOCKER.
I'M SORRY, ARCEE. WE SHOULD HAVE GONE WITH YOU. THERE'S BEEN NOTHING HERE FOR US SINCE YOU LEFT. NOTHING HERE EXCEPT HIDING.
MEGATRON IS DEAD. ONE OF THE SPECIES THAT PRIME HAD CONTACT WITH KILLED MEGATRON, AND IN THE PROCESS, THE ALLSPARK WAS DESTROYED, TOO.
WHAT?! WITHOUT THE ALLSPARK, THIS WAR IS *OVER*, RIGHT? WE WON! WHY AREN'T WE CELE—
STOP, CLOCKER. IT'S NOT OVER.
STARSCREAM AND THUNDERCRACKER CAME BACK. STARSCREAM IS NOW LEADING THE DECEPTICONS.
IS THAT SO?
MAYBE *I* CAN HELP OUT.

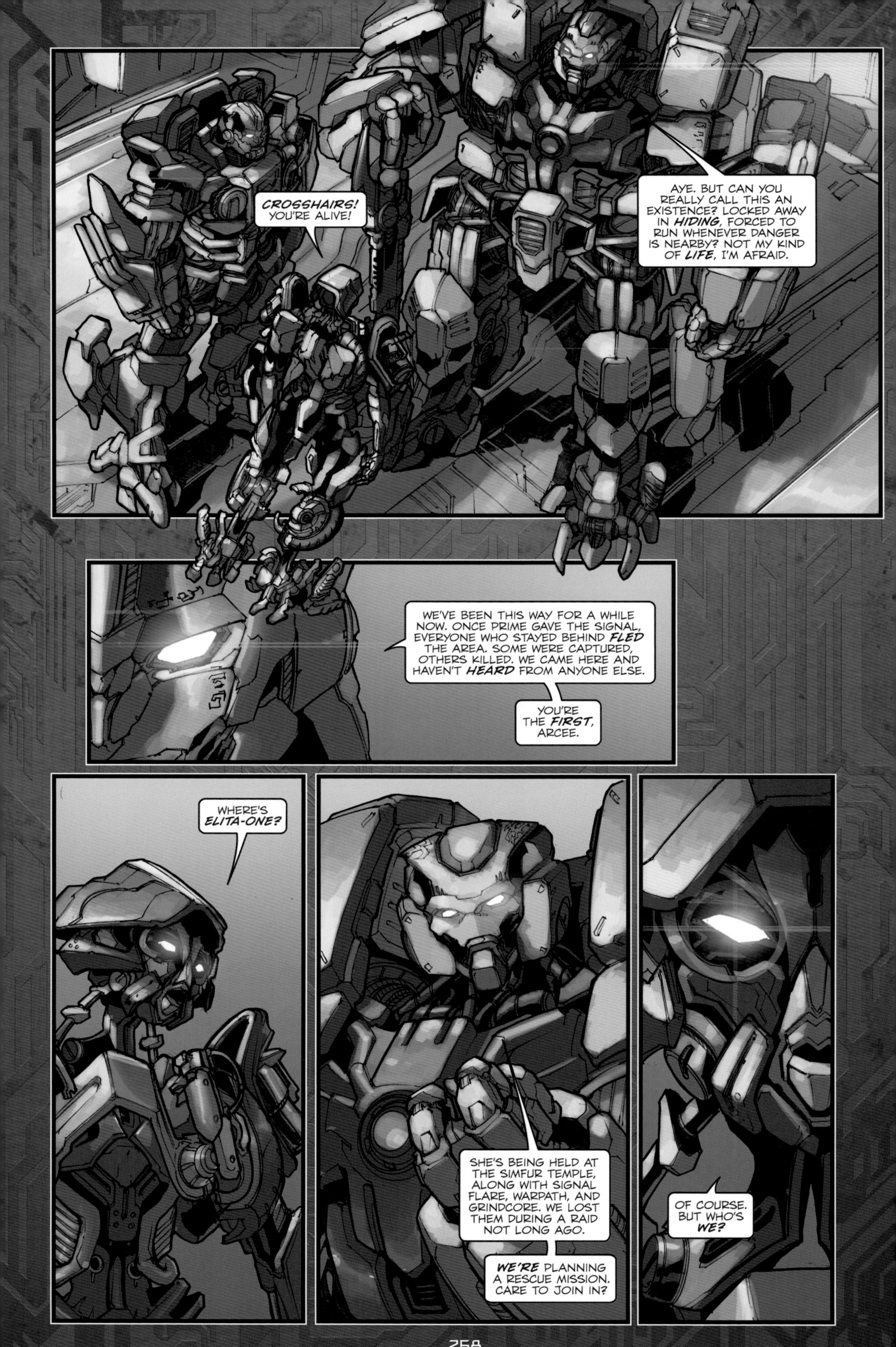

CROSSHAIRS! YOU'RE ALIVE!
AYE. BUT CAN YOU REALLY CALL THIS AN EXISTENCE? LOCKED AWAY IN HIDING, FORCED TO RUN WHENEVER DANGER IS NEARBY? NOT MY KIND OF LIFE, I'M AFRAID.
WE'VE BEEN THIS WAY FOR A WHILE NOW. ONCE PRIME GAVE THE SIGNAL, EVERYONE WHO STAYED BEHIND FLED THE AREA. SOME WERE CAPTURED, OTHERS KILLED. WE CAME HERE AND HAVEN'T HEARD FROM ANYONE ELSE.
YOU'RE THE FIRST, ARCEE.
WHERE'S ELITA-ONE?
SHE'S BEING HELD AT THE SIMFUR TEMPLE, ALONG WITH SIGNAL FLARE, WARPATH, AND GRINDCORE. WE LOST THEM DURING A RAID NOT LONG AGO.
WE'RE PLANNING A RESCUE MISSION. CARE TO JOIN IN?
OF COURSE. BUT WHO'S WE?

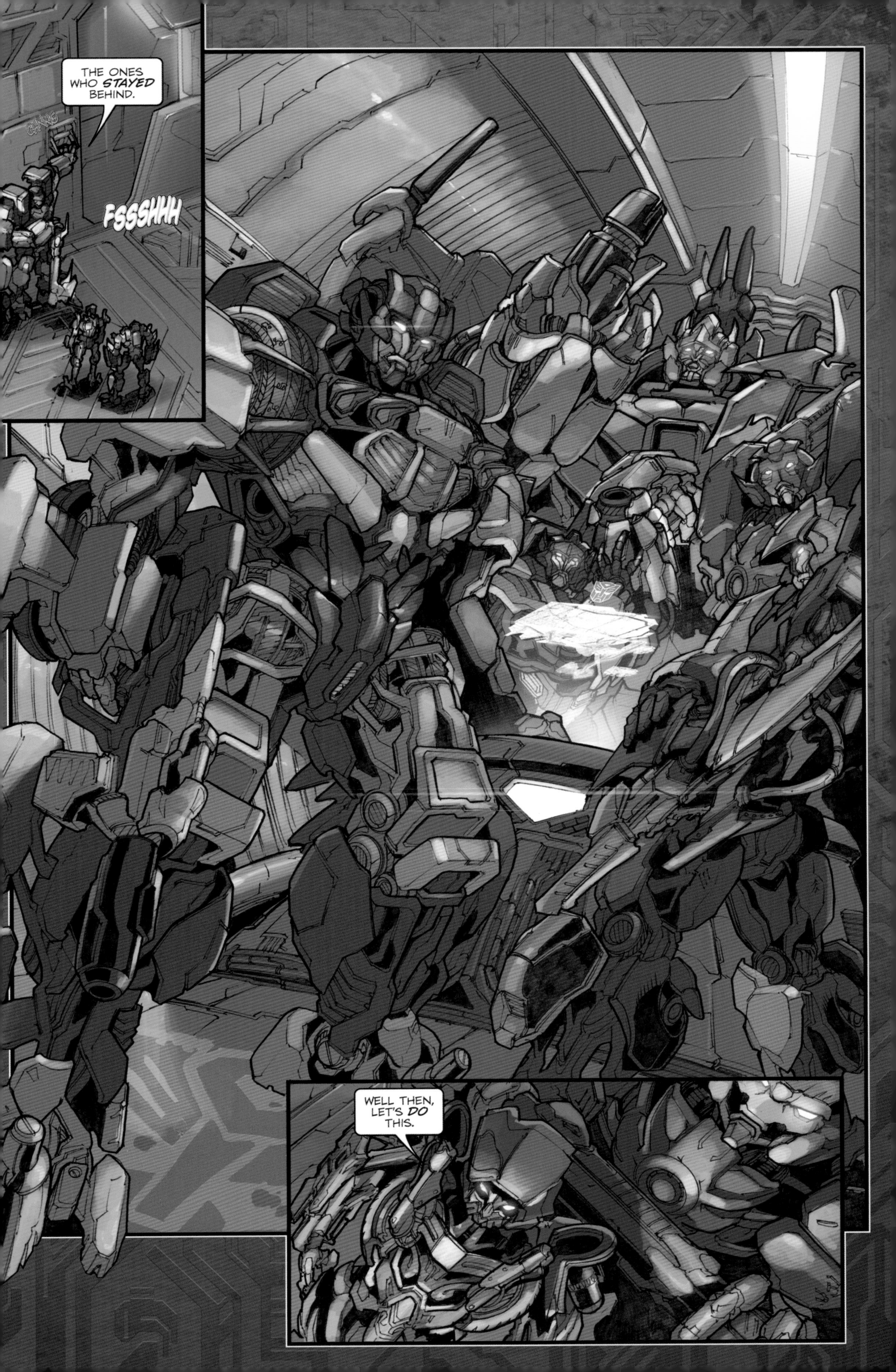
THE ONES WHO STAYED BEHIND.
CHNNG
FSSSHHH
WELL THEN, LET'S DO THIS.

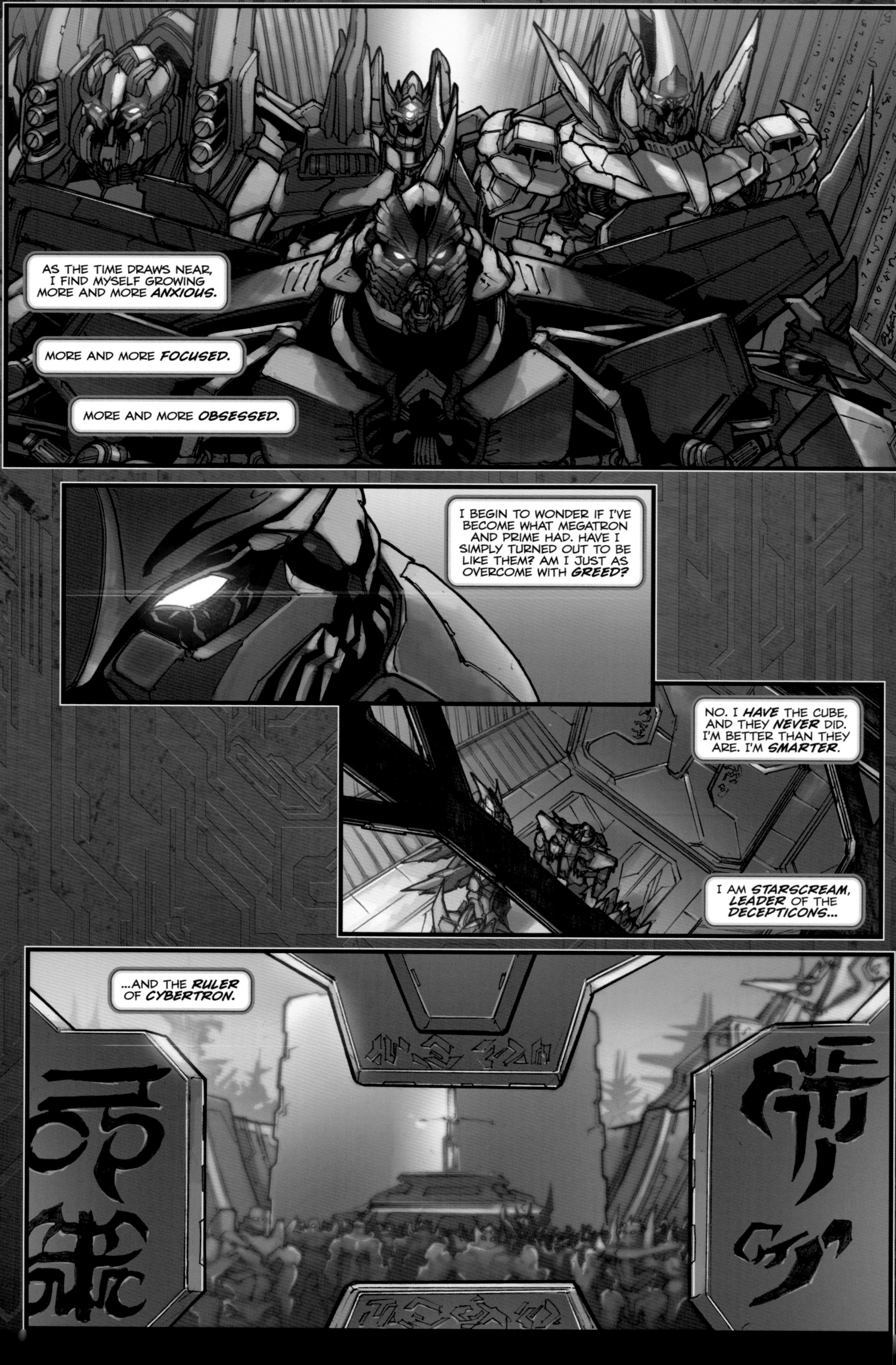
AS THE TIME DRAWS NEAR, I FIND MYSELF GROWING MORE AND MORE ANXIOUS.
MORE AND MORE FOCUSED.
MORE AND MORE OBSESSED.
I BEGIN TO WONDER IF I'VE BECOME WHAT MEGATRON AND PRIME HAD. HAVE I SIMPLY TURNED OUT TO BE LIKE THEM? AM I JUST AS OVERCOME WITH GREED?
NO. I HAVE THE CUBE, AND THEY NEVER DID. I'M BETTER THAN THEY ARE. I'M SMARTER.
I AM STARSCREAM, LEADER OF THE DECEPTICONS...
...AND THE RULER OF CYBERTRON.

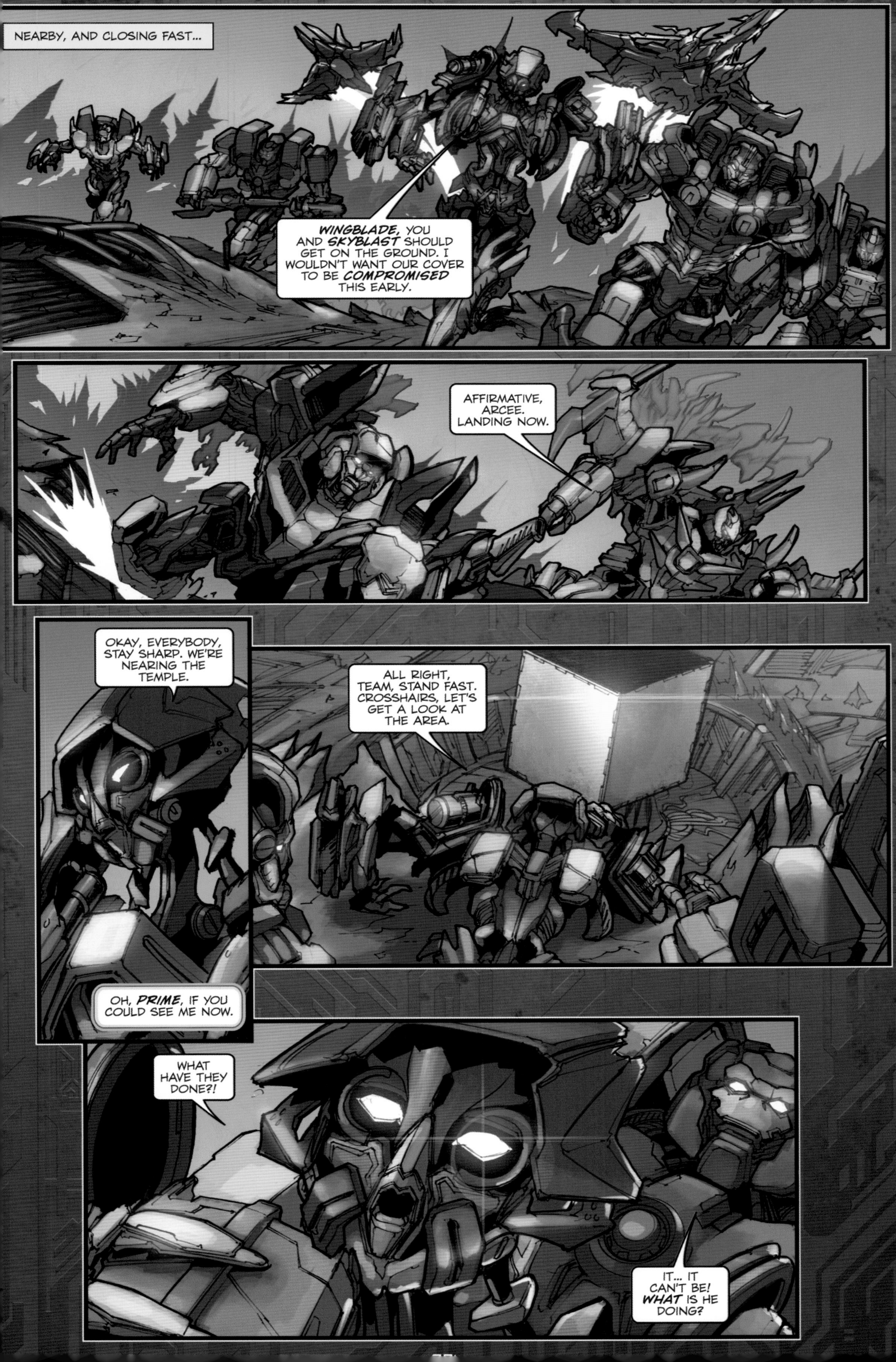
NEARBY, AND CLOSING FAST...
WINGBLADE, YOU AND SKYBLAST SHOULD GET ON THE GROUND. I WOULDN'T WANT OUR COVER TO BE COMPROMISED THIS EARLY.
AFFIRMATIVE, ARCEE. LANDING NOW.
OKAY, EVERYBODY, STAY SHARP. WE'RE NEARING THE TEMPLE.
OH, PRIME, IF YOU COULD SEE ME NOW.
ALL RIGHT, TEAM, STAND FAST. CROSSHAIRS, LET'S GET A LOOK AT THE AREA.
WHAT HAVE THEY DONE?!
IT... IT CAN'T BE! WHAT IS HE DOING?

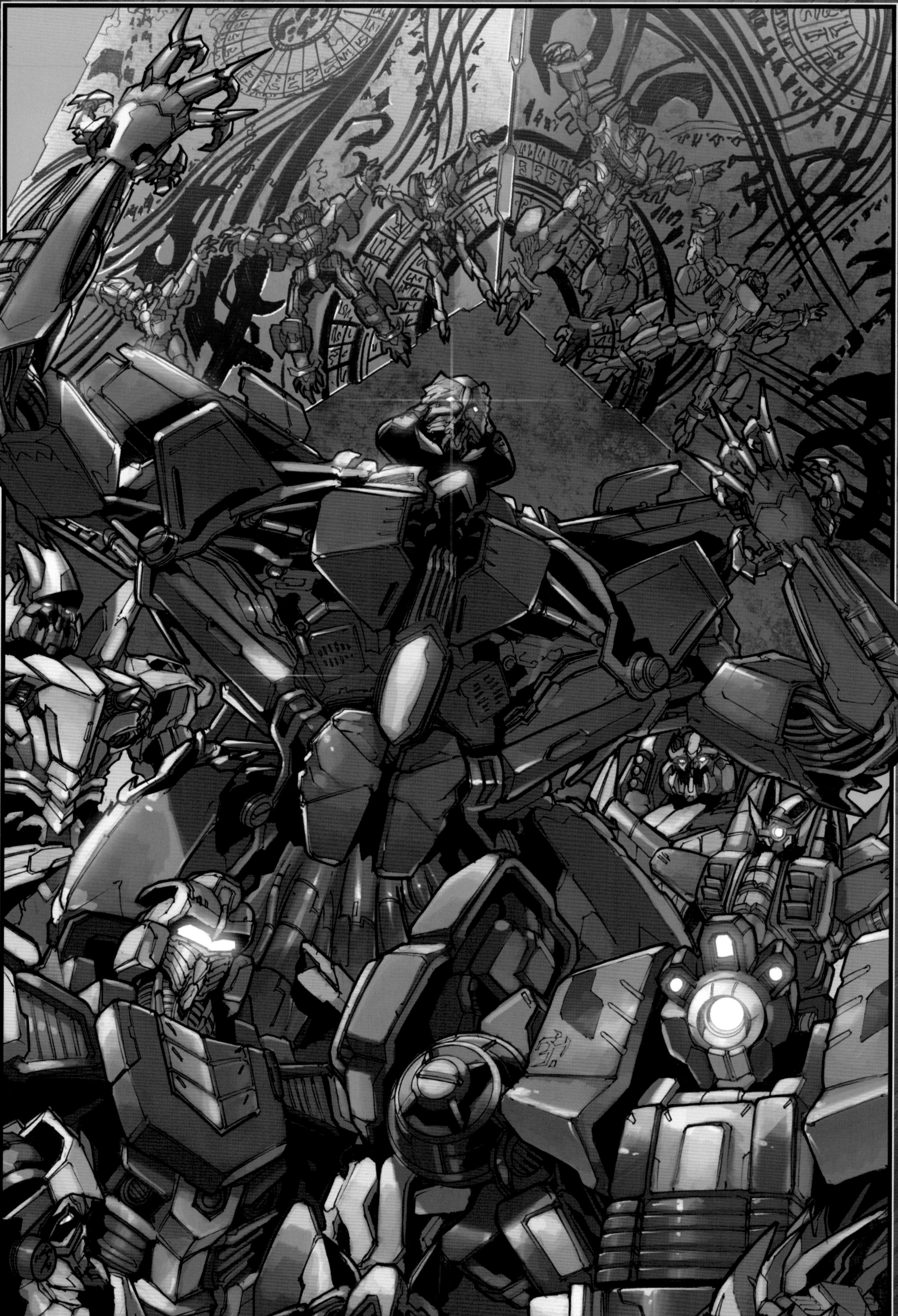

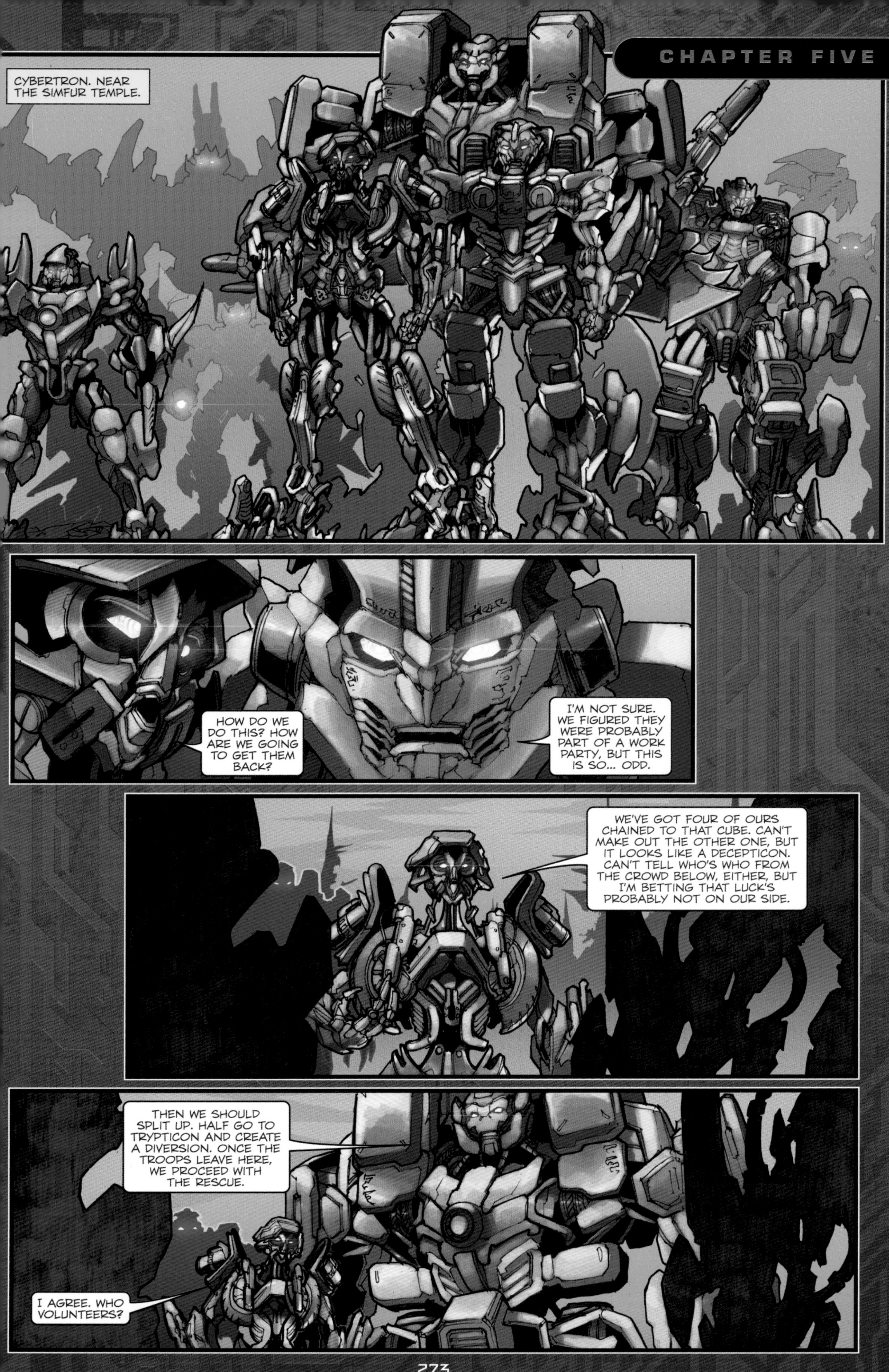
CYBERTRON. NEAR THE SIMFUR TEMPLE.
HOW DO WE DO THIS? HOW ARE WE GOING TO GET THEM BACK?
I'M NOT SURE. WE FIGURED THEY WERE PROBABLY PART OF A WORK PARTY, BUT THIS IS SO... ODD.
WE'VE GOT FOUR OF OURS CHAINED TO THAT CUBE. CAN'T MAKE OUT THE OTHER ONE, BUT IT LOOKS LIKE A DECEPTICON. CAN'T TELL WHO'S WHO FROM THE CROWD BELOW, EITHER, BUT I'M BETTING THAT LUCK'S PROBABLY NOT ON OUR SIDE.
THEN WE SHOULD SPLIT UP. HALF GO TO TRYPTICON AND CREATE A DIVERSION. ONCE THE TROOPS LEAVE HERE, WE PROCEED WITH THE RESCUE.
I AGREE. WHO VOLUNTEERS?

CAN'T WAIT TO GET SOME PAYBACK. COUNT ME IN.
YOU COULD PROBABLY USE SOME SPEED, BIG GUY. I'M WITH STRONGARM.
PROBABLY WOULDN'T HURT TO HAVE SOME AIR SUPPORT. ALL RIGHT, LET'S DO THIS.
OKAY, WINGBLADE, WE'LL WAIT FOR YOUR SIGNAL, AND WHEN THERE'S A CLEARING HERE, WE'LL MOVE IN.
CROSSHAIRS AND I CAN SECURE THE AREA, YOU CAN PROVIDE SNIPER SUPPORT WITH SKYBLAST.
ROGER THAT, ARMORHIDE.
FOR CYBERTRON... FOR OUR FUTURE.
GOOD LUCK, FRIENDS.

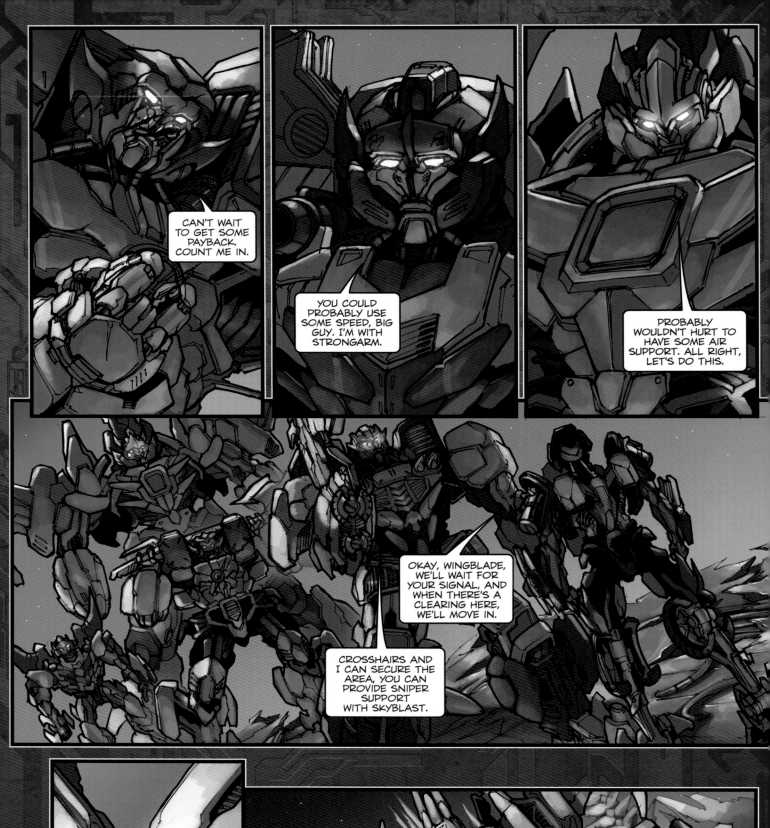

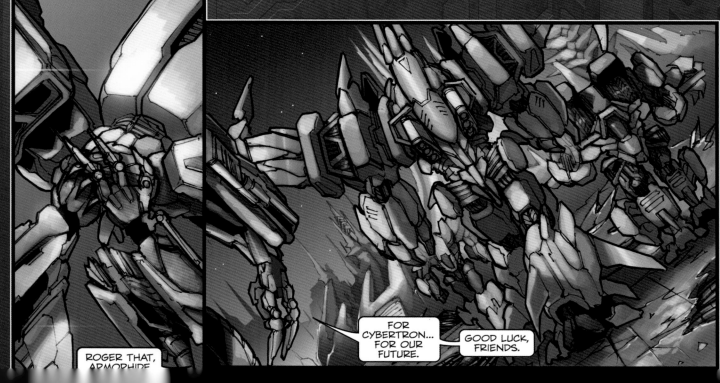

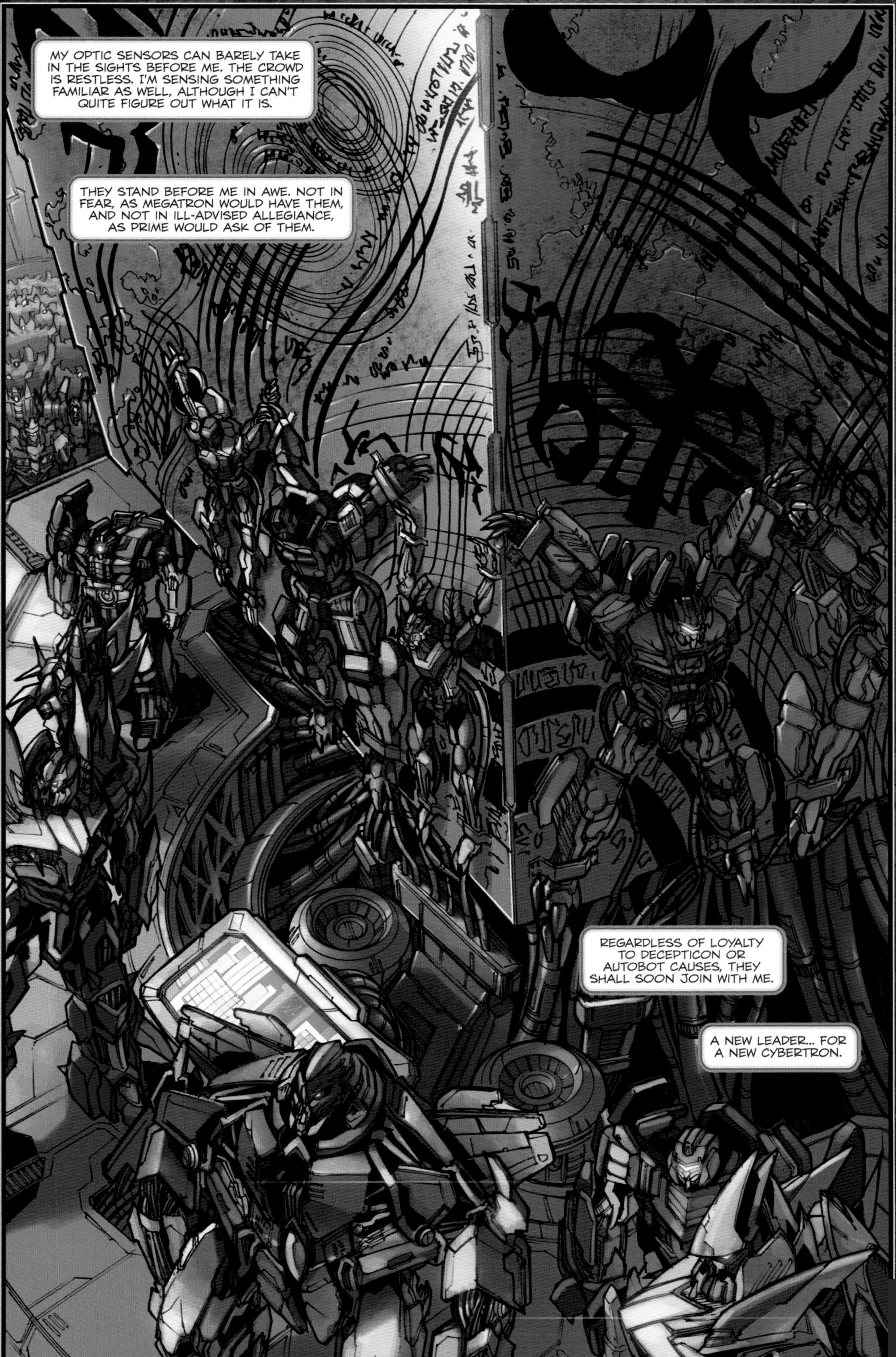
MY OPTIC SENSORS CAN BARELY TAKE IN THE SIGHTS BEFORE ME. THE CROWD IS RESTLESS. I'M SENSING SOMETHING FAMILIAR AS WELL, ALTHOUGH I CAN'T QUITE FIGURE OUT WHAT IT IS.
THEY STAND BEFORE ME IN AWE. NOT IN FEAR, AS MEGATRON WOULD HAVE THEM, AND NOT IN ILL-ADVISED ALLEGIANCE, AS PRIME WOULD ASK OF THEM.
REGARDLESS OF LOYALTY TO DECEPTICON OR AUTOBOT CAUSES, THEY SHALL SOON JOIN WITH ME.
A NEW LEADER... FOR A NEW CYBERTRON.

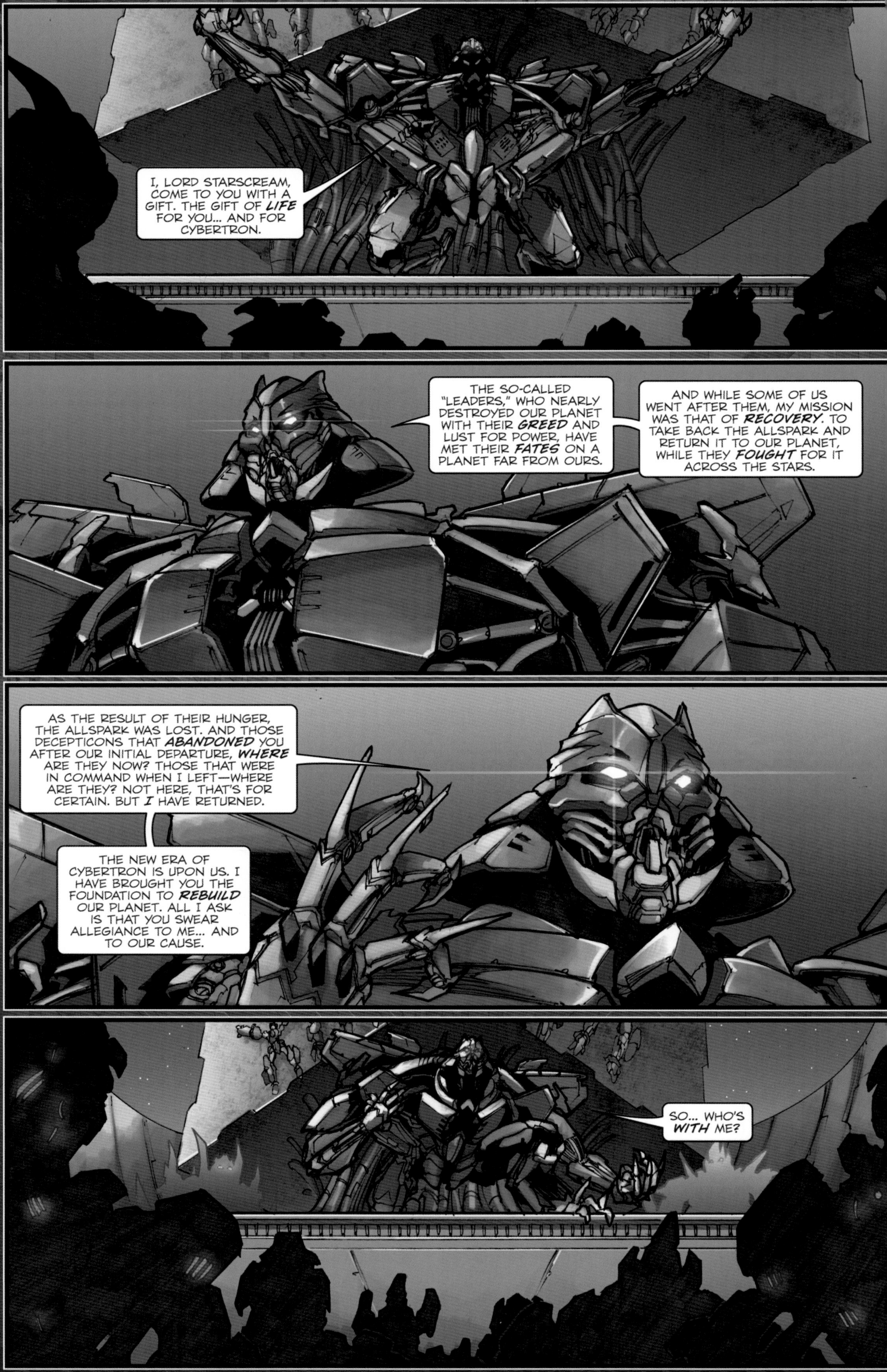
I, LORD STARSCREAM, COME TO YOU WITH A GIFT. THE GIFT OF LIFE FOR YOU... AND FOR CYBERTRON.
THE SO-CALLED "LEADERS," WHO NEARLY DESTROYED OUR PLANET WITH THEIR GREED AND LUST FOR POWER, HAVE MET THEIR FATES ON A PLANET FAR FROM OURS.
AND WHILE SOME OF US WENT AFTER THEM, MY MISSION WAS THAT OF RECOVERY. TO TAKE BACK THE ALLSPARK AND RETURN IT TO OUR PLANET, WHILE THEY FOUGHT FOR IT ACROSS THE STARS.
AS THE RESULT OF THEIR HUNGER, THE ALLSPARK WAS LOST. AND THOSE DECEPTICONS THAT ABANDONED YOU AFTER OUR INITIAL DEPARTURE, WHERE ARE THEY NOW? THOSE THAT WERE IN COMMAND WHEN I LEFT—WHERE ARE THEY? NOT HERE, THAT'S FOR CERTAIN. BUT I HAVE RETURNED.
THE NEW ERA OF CYBERTRON IS UPON US. I HAVE BROUGHT YOU THE FOUNDATION TO REBUILD OUR PLANET. ALL I ASK IS THAT YOU SWEAR ALLEGIANCE TO ME... AND TO OUR CAUSE.
SO... WHO'S WITH ME?

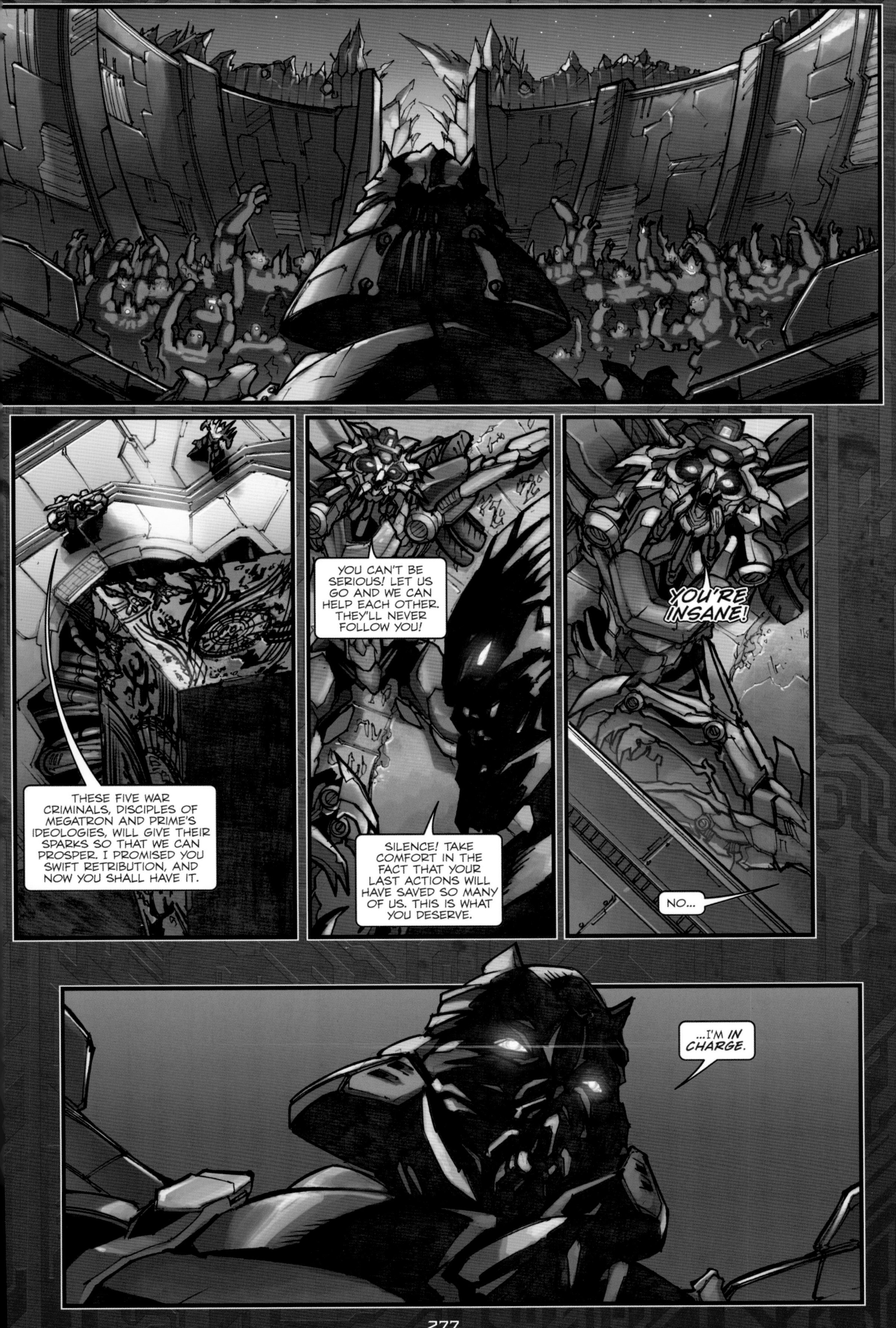
THESE FIVE WAR CRIMINALS, DISCIPLES OF MEGATRON AND PRIME'S IDEOLOGIES, WILL GIVE THEIR SPARKS SO THAT WE CAN PROSPER. I PROMISED YOU SWIFT RETRIBUTION, AND NOW YOU SHALL HAVE IT.
YOU CAN'T BE SERIOUS! LET US GO AND WE CAN HELP EACH OTHER. THEY'LL NEVER FOLLOW YOU!
SILENCE! TAKE COMFORT IN THE FACT THAT YOUR LAST ACTIONS WILL HAVE SAVED SO MANY OF US. THIS IS WHAT YOU DESERVE.
YOU'RE INSANE!
NO...
...I'M IN CHARGE.

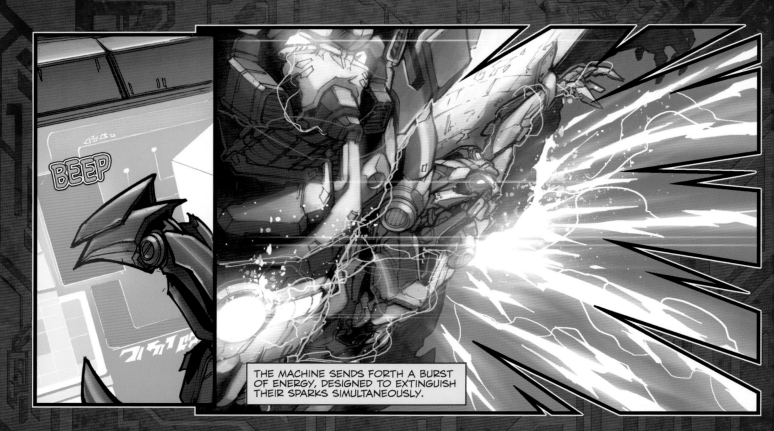

BEEP

THE MACHINE SENDS FORTH A BURST OF ENERGY, DESIGNED TO EXTINGUISH THEIR SPARKS SIMULTANEOUSLY.

FSSH

FSSH

WHEN THEIR LIVES HAVE PASSED, AND THEIR SPARK CORES RETIRE...

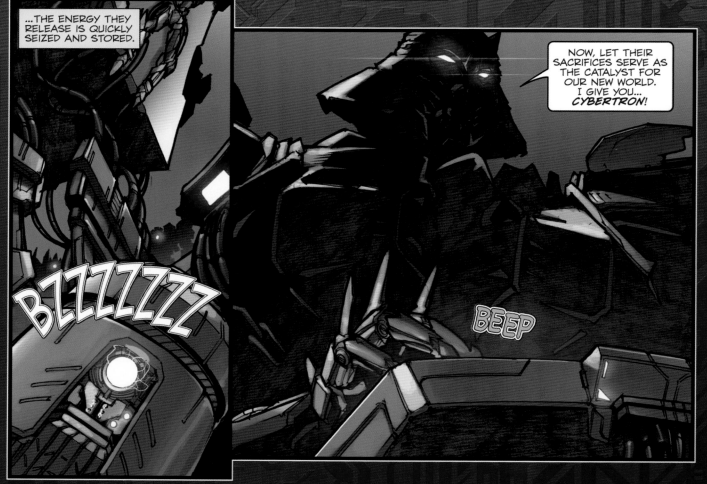

...THE ENERGY THEY RELEASE IS QUICKLY SEIZED AND STORED.

NOW, LET THEIR SACRIFICES SERVE AS THE CATALYST FOR OUR NEW WORLD. I GIVE YOU... CYBERTRON!

BZZZZZZZ

BEEP

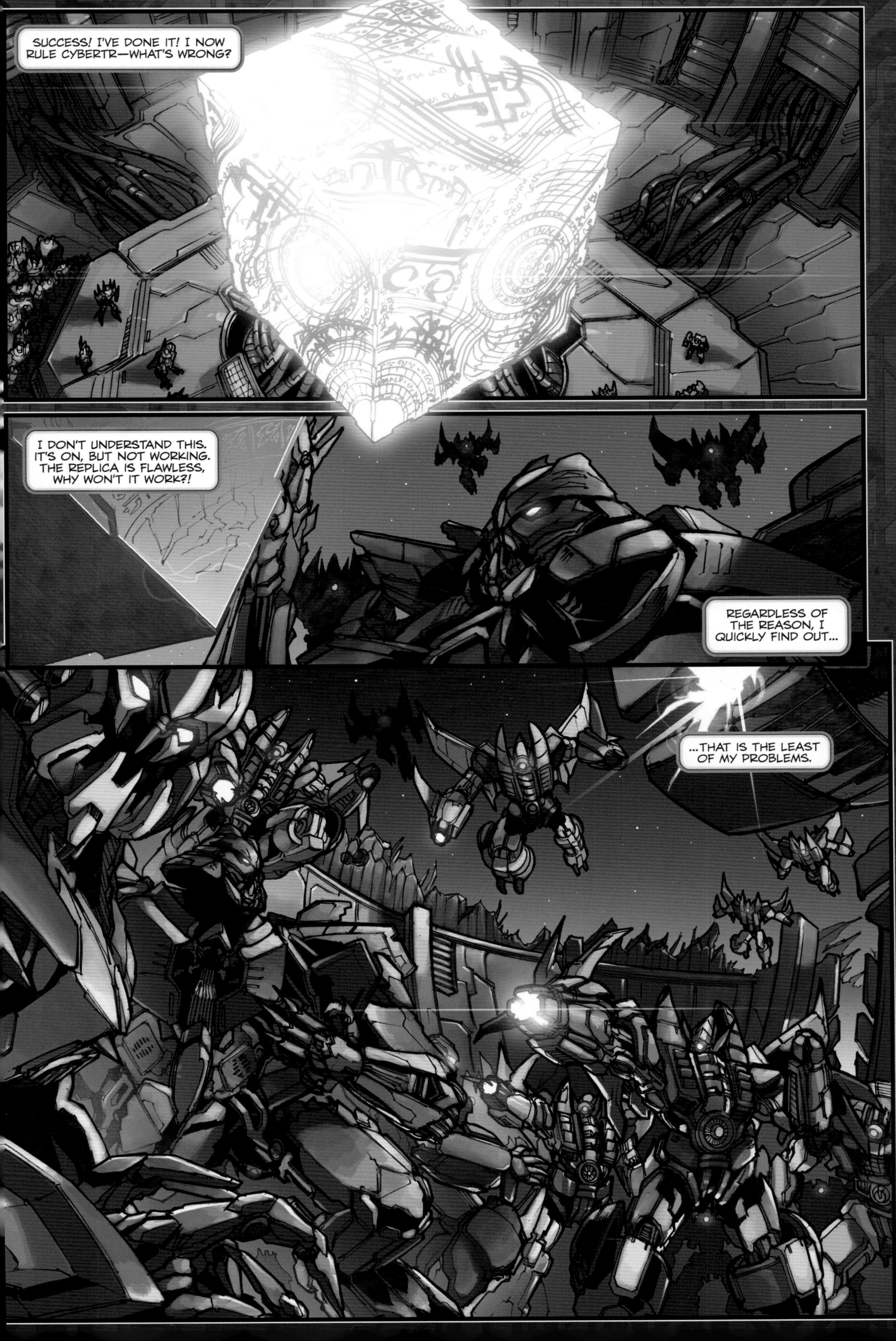
SUCCESS! I'VE DONE IT! I NOW RULE CYBERTR—WHAT'S WRONG?
I DON'T UNDERSTAND THIS. IT'S ON, BUT NOT WORKING. THE REPLICA IS FLAWLESS, WHY WON'T IT WORK?!
REGARDLESS OF THE REASON, I QUICKLY FIND OUT...
...THAT IS THE LEAST OF MY PROBLEMS.

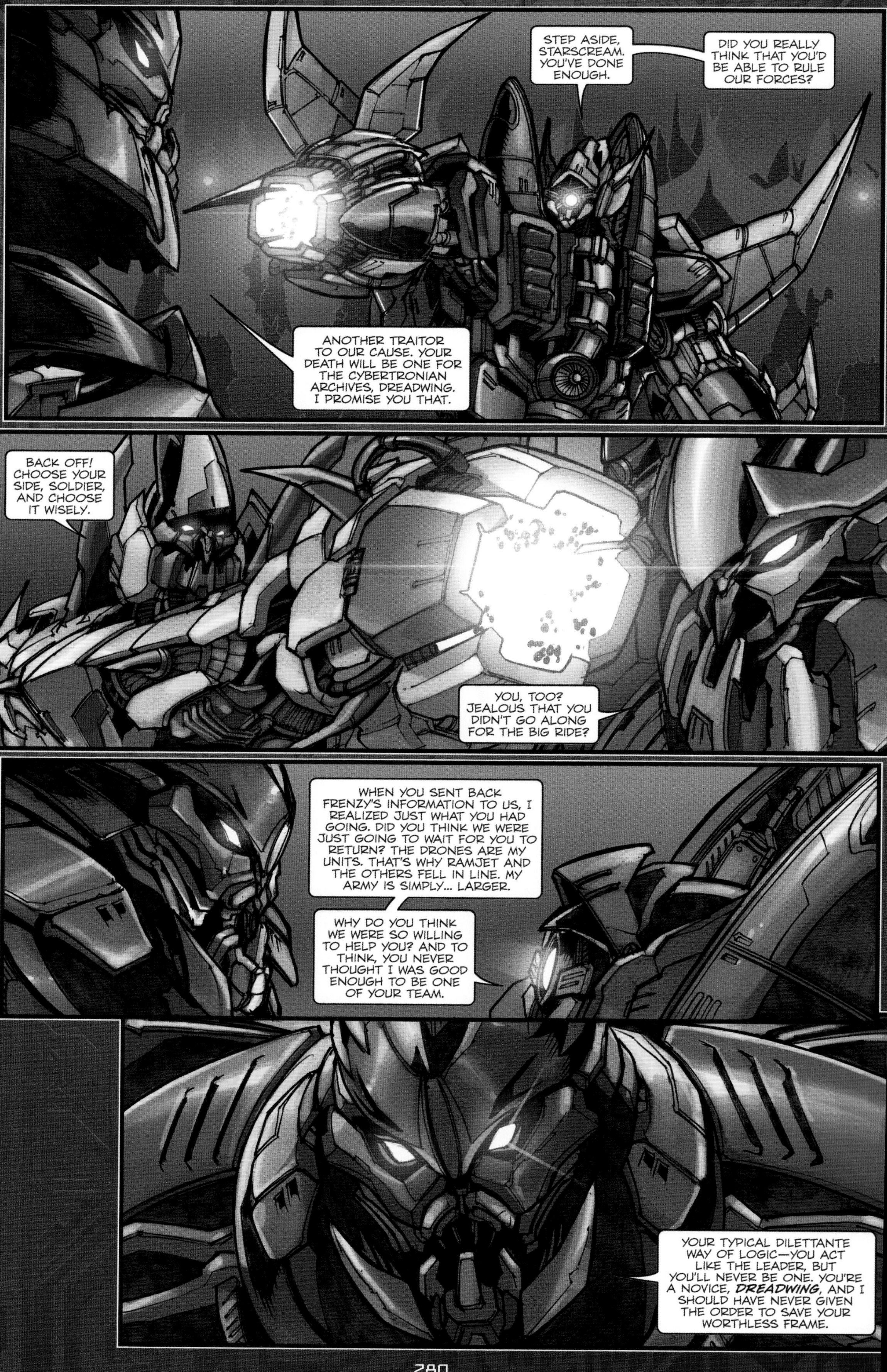

STEP ASIDE, STARSCREAM. YOU'VE DONE ENOUGH.
DID YOU REALLY THINK THAT YOU'D BE ABLE TO RULE OUR FORCES?
ANOTHER TRAITOR TO OUR CAUSE. YOUR DEATH WILL BE ONE FOR THE CYBERTRONIAN ARCHIVES, DREADWING. I PROMISE YOU THAT.
BACK OFF! CHOOSE YOUR SIDE, SOLDIER, AND CHOOSE IT WISELY.
YOU, TOO? JEALOUS THAT YOU DIDN'T GO ALONG FOR THE BIG RIDE?
WHEN YOU SENT BACK FRENZY'S INFORMATION TO US, I REALIZED JUST WHAT YOU HAD GOING. DID YOU THINK WE WERE JUST GOING TO WAIT FOR YOU TO RETURN? THE DRONES ARE MY UNITS. THAT'S WHY RAMJET AND THE OTHERS FELL IN LINE. MY ARMY IS SIMPLY... LARGER.
WHY DO YOU THINK WE WERE SO WILLING TO HELP YOU? AND TO THINK, YOU NEVER THOUGHT I WAS GOOD ENOUGH TO BE ONE OF YOUR TEAM.
YOUR TYPICAL DILETTANTE WAY OF LOGIC—YOU ACT LIKE THE LEADER, BUT YOU'LL NEVER BE ONE. YOU'RE A NOVICE, ***DREADWING***, AND I SHOULD HAVE NEVER GIVEN THE ORDER TO SAVE YOUR WORTHLESS FRAME.

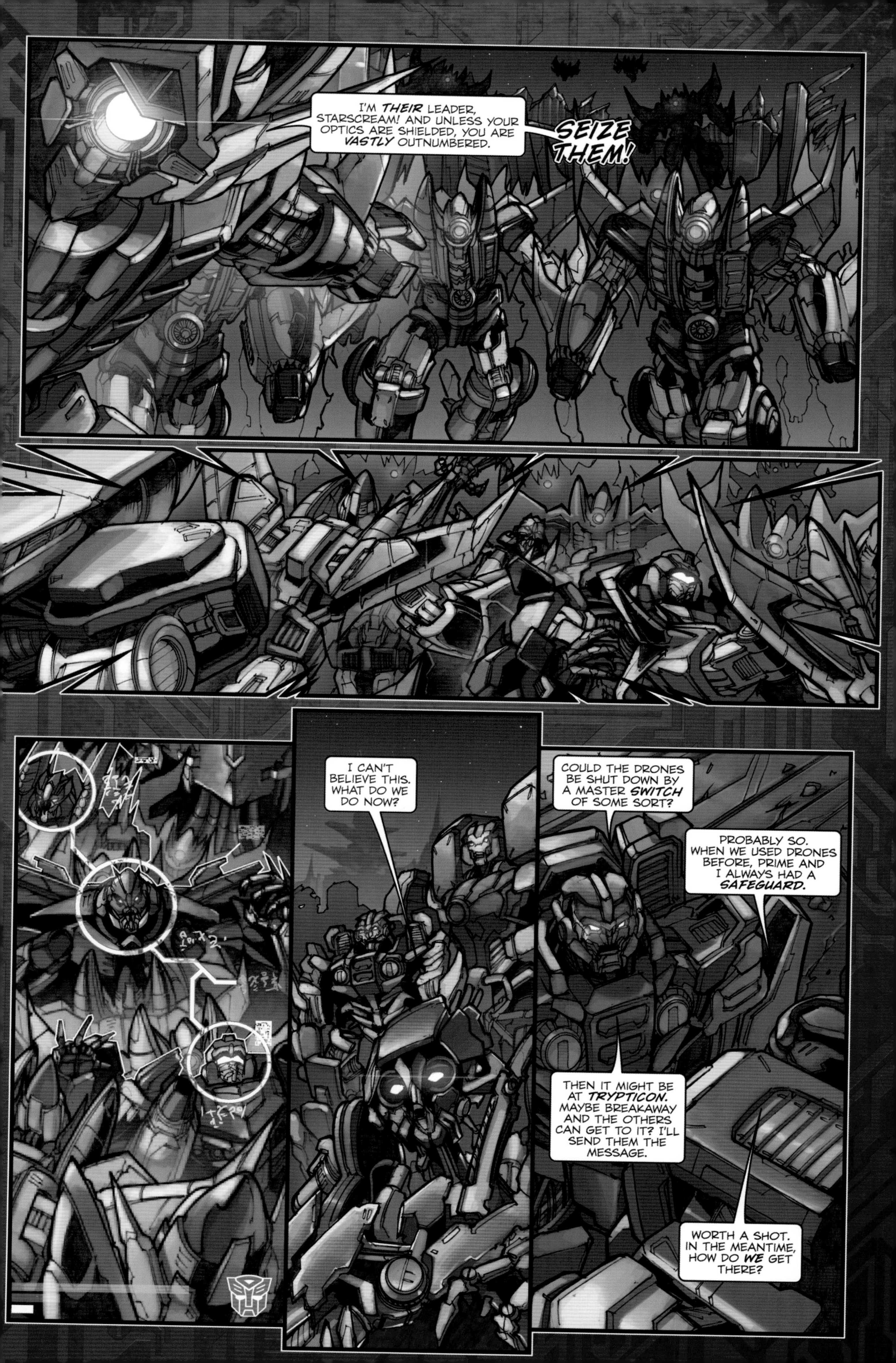

I'M THEIR LEADER, STARSCREAM! AND UNLESS YOUR OPTICS ARE SHIELDED, YOU ARE VASTLY OUTNUMBERED.
SEIZE THEM!
I CAN'T BELIEVE THIS. WHAT DO WE DO NOW?
COULD THE DRONES BE SHUT DOWN BY A MASTER SWITCH OF SOME SORT?
PROBABLY SO. WHEN WE USED DRONES BEFORE, PRIME AND I ALWAYS HAD A SAFEGUARD.
THEN IT MIGHT BE AT TRYPTICON. MAYBE BREAKAWAY AND THE OTHERS CAN GET TO IT? I'LL SEND THEM THE MESSAGE.
WORTH A SHOT. IN THE MEANTIME, HOW DO WE GET THERE?

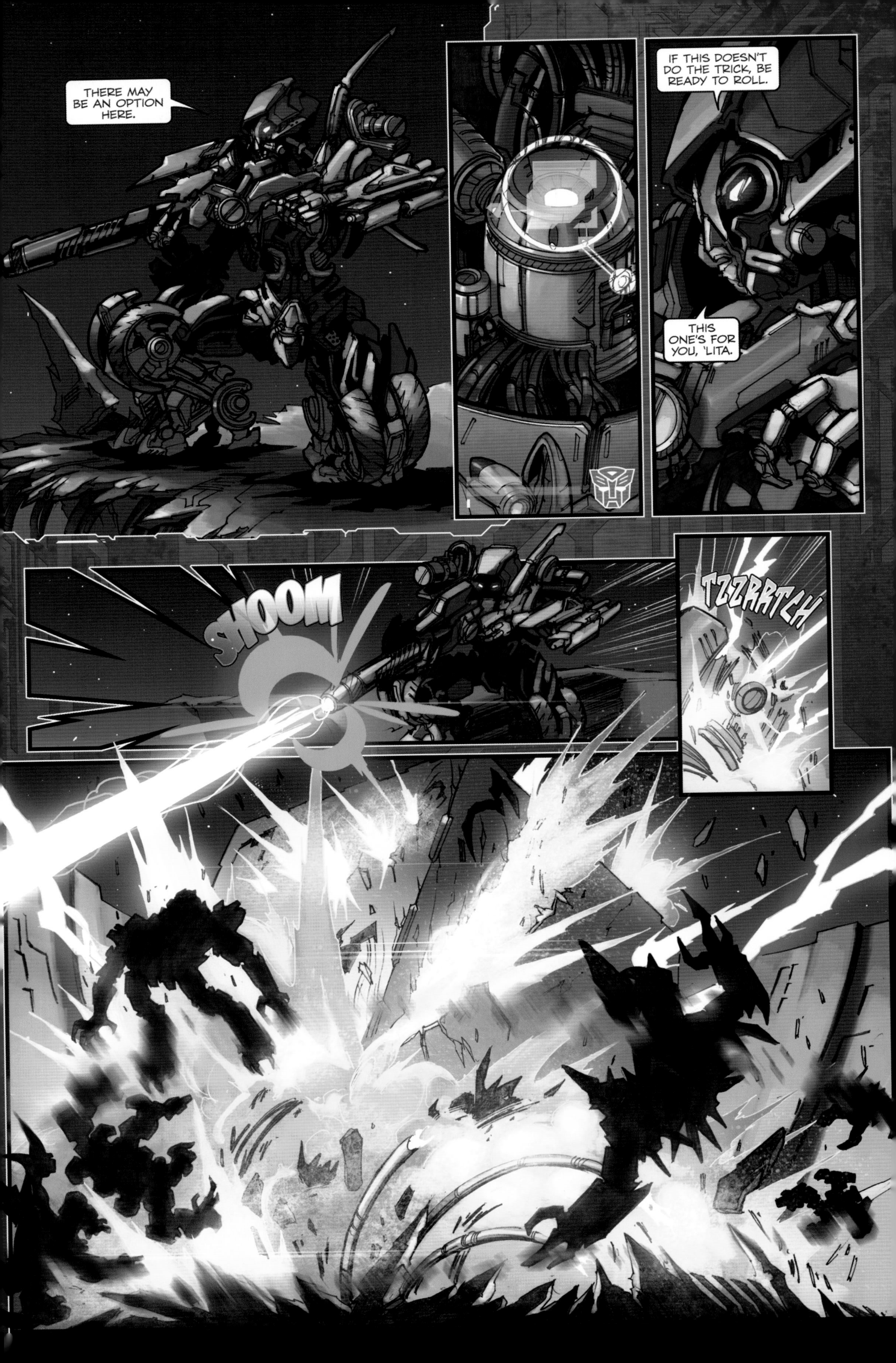
THERE MAY BE AN OPTION HERE.
IF THIS DOESN'T DO THE TRICK, BE READY TO ROLL.
THIS ONE'S FOR YOU, 'LITA.
SHOOM
TZZRRRTCH

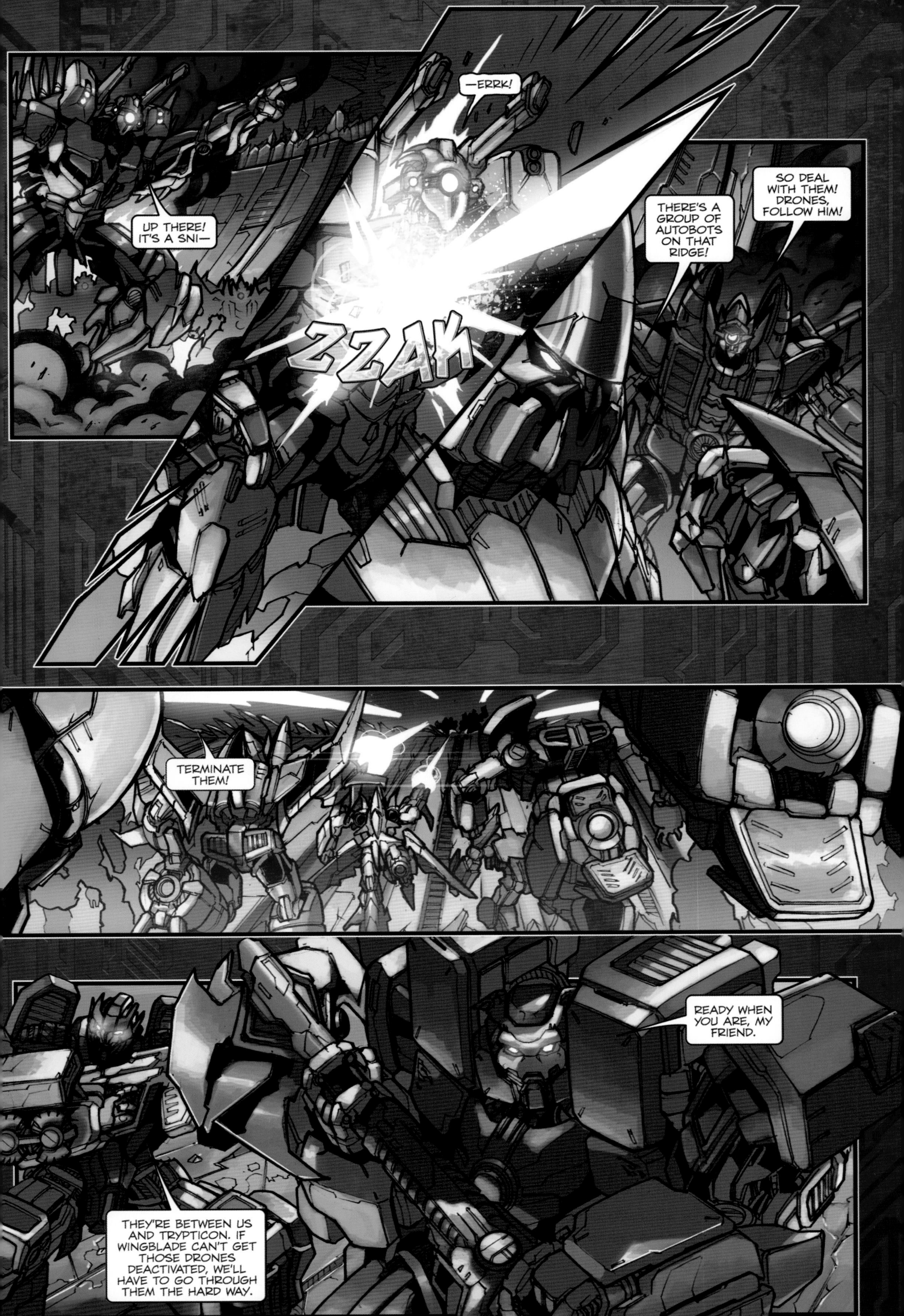
UP THERE! IT'S A SNI—
—ERRK!
ZZAK
THERE'S A GROUP OF AUTOBOTS ON THAT RIDGE!
SO DEAL WITH THEM! DRONES, FOLLOW HIM!
TERMINATE THEM!
READY WHEN YOU ARE, MY FRIEND.
THEY'RE BETWEEN US AND TRYPTICON. IF WINGBLADE CAN'T GET THOSE DRONES DEACTIVATED, WE'LL HAVE TO GO THROUGH THEM THE HARD WAY.

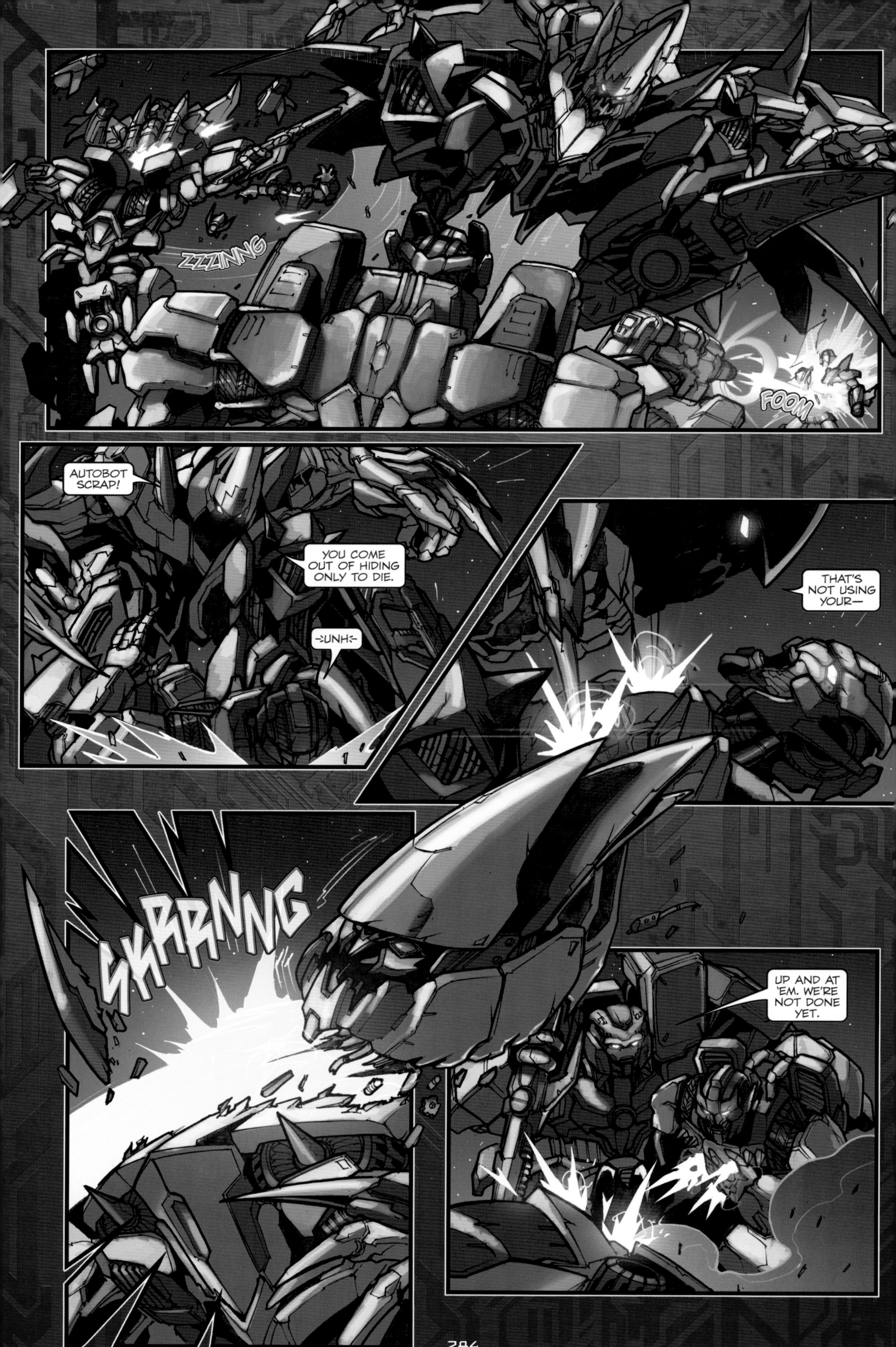
ZZZINNG
FOOM
AUTOBOT SCRAP!
YOU COME OUT OF HIDING ONLY TO DIE.
-UNH-
THAT'S NOT USING YOUR—
SKRRNNG
UP AND AT 'EM. WE'RE NOT DONE YET.

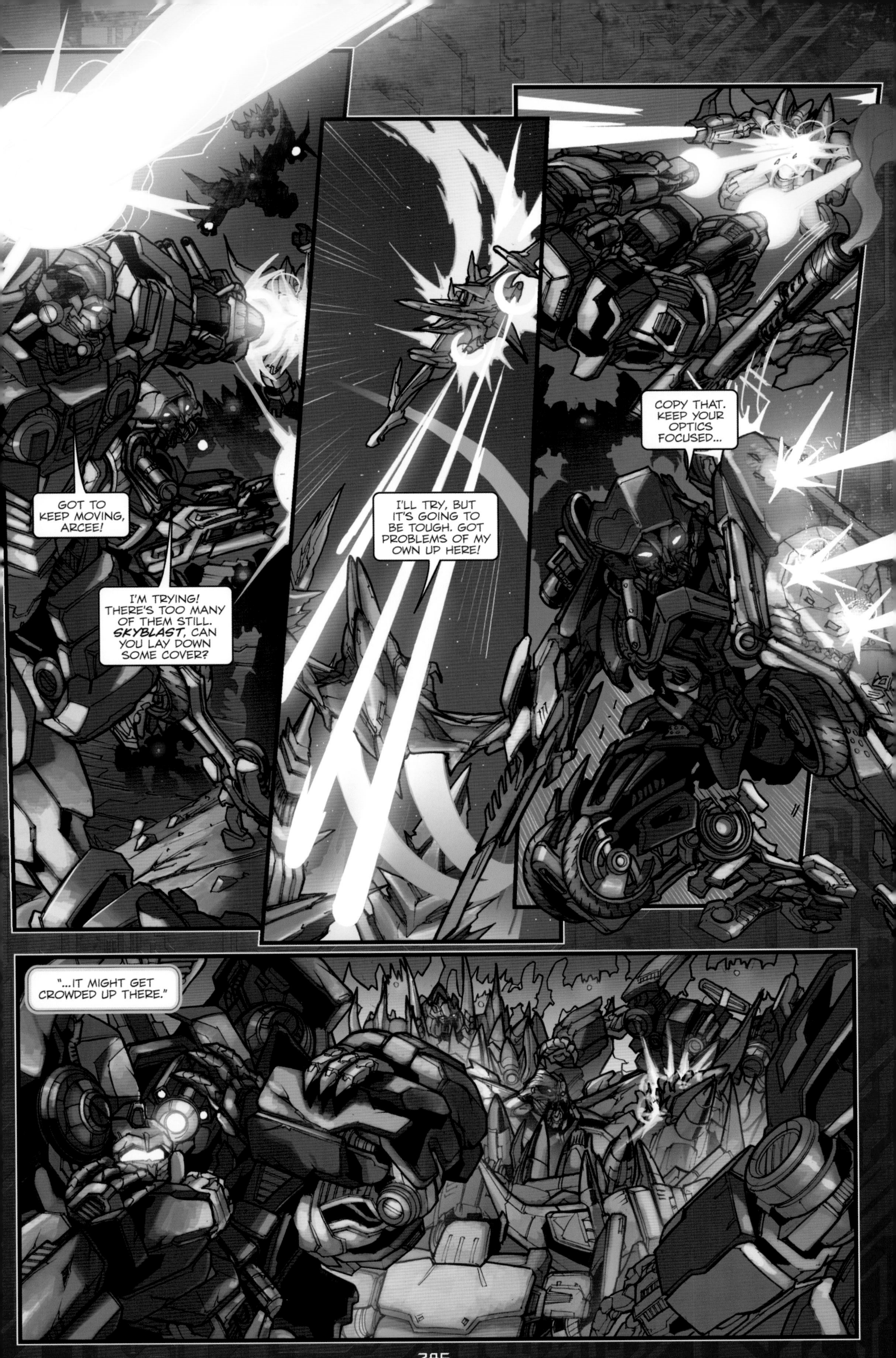
GOT TO KEEP MOVING, ARCEE!
I'M TRYING! THERE'S TOO MANY OF THEM STILL. SKYBLAST, CAN YOU LAY DOWN SOME COVER?
I'LL TRY, BUT IT'S GOING TO BE TOUGH. GOT PROBLEMS OF MY OWN UP HERE!
COPY THAT. KEEP YOUR OPTICS FOCUSED...
"...IT MIGHT GET CROWDED UP THERE."

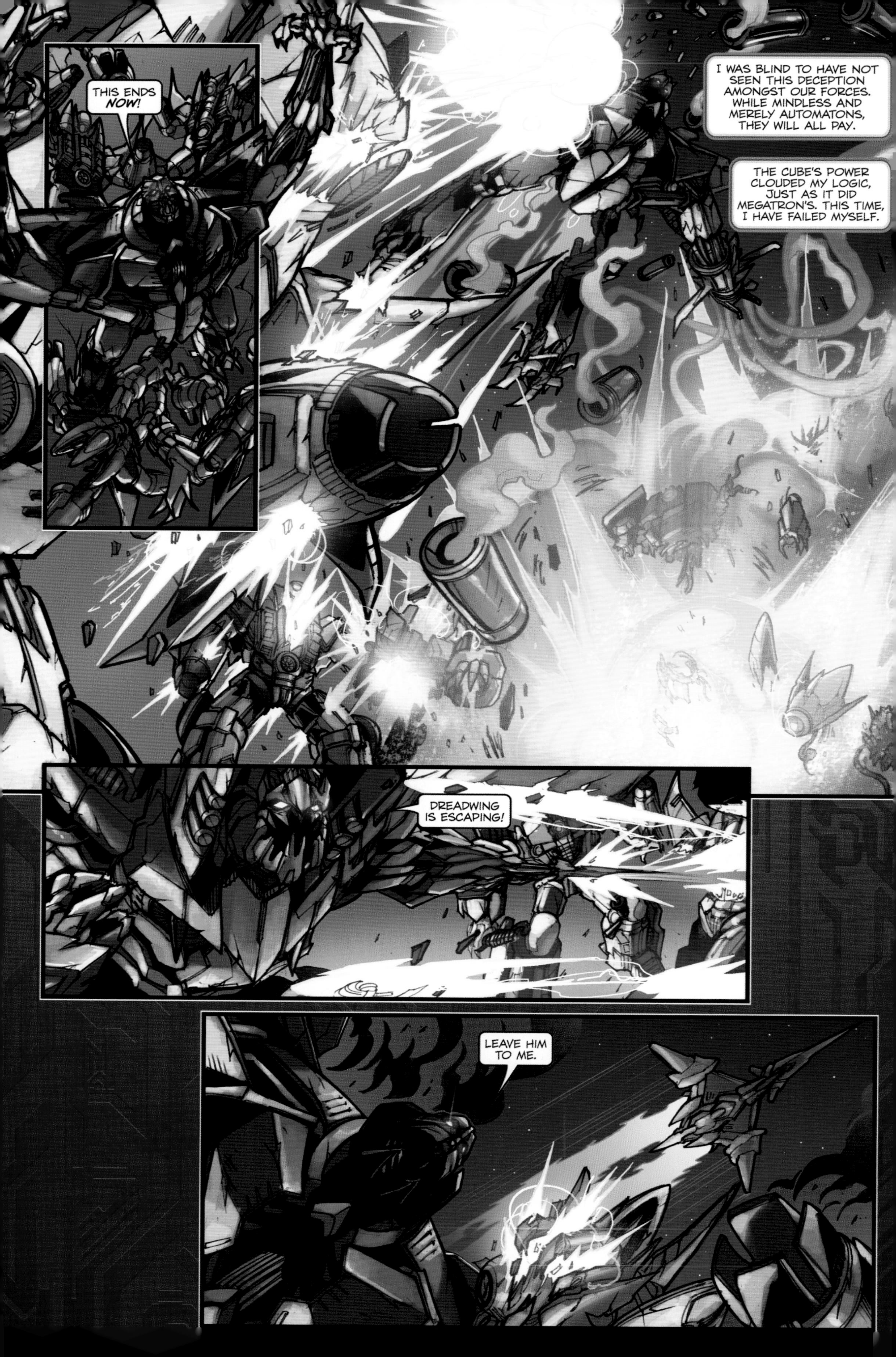
THIS ENDS *NOW*!
I WAS BLIND TO HAVE NOT SEEN THIS DECEPTION AMONGST OUR FORCES. WHILE MINDLESS AND MERELY AUTOMATONS, THEY WILL ALL PAY.
THE CUBE'S POWER CLOUDED MY LOGIC, JUST AS IT DID MEGATRON'S. THIS TIME, I HAVE FAILED MYSELF.
DREADWING IS ESCAPING!
LEAVE HIM TO ME.

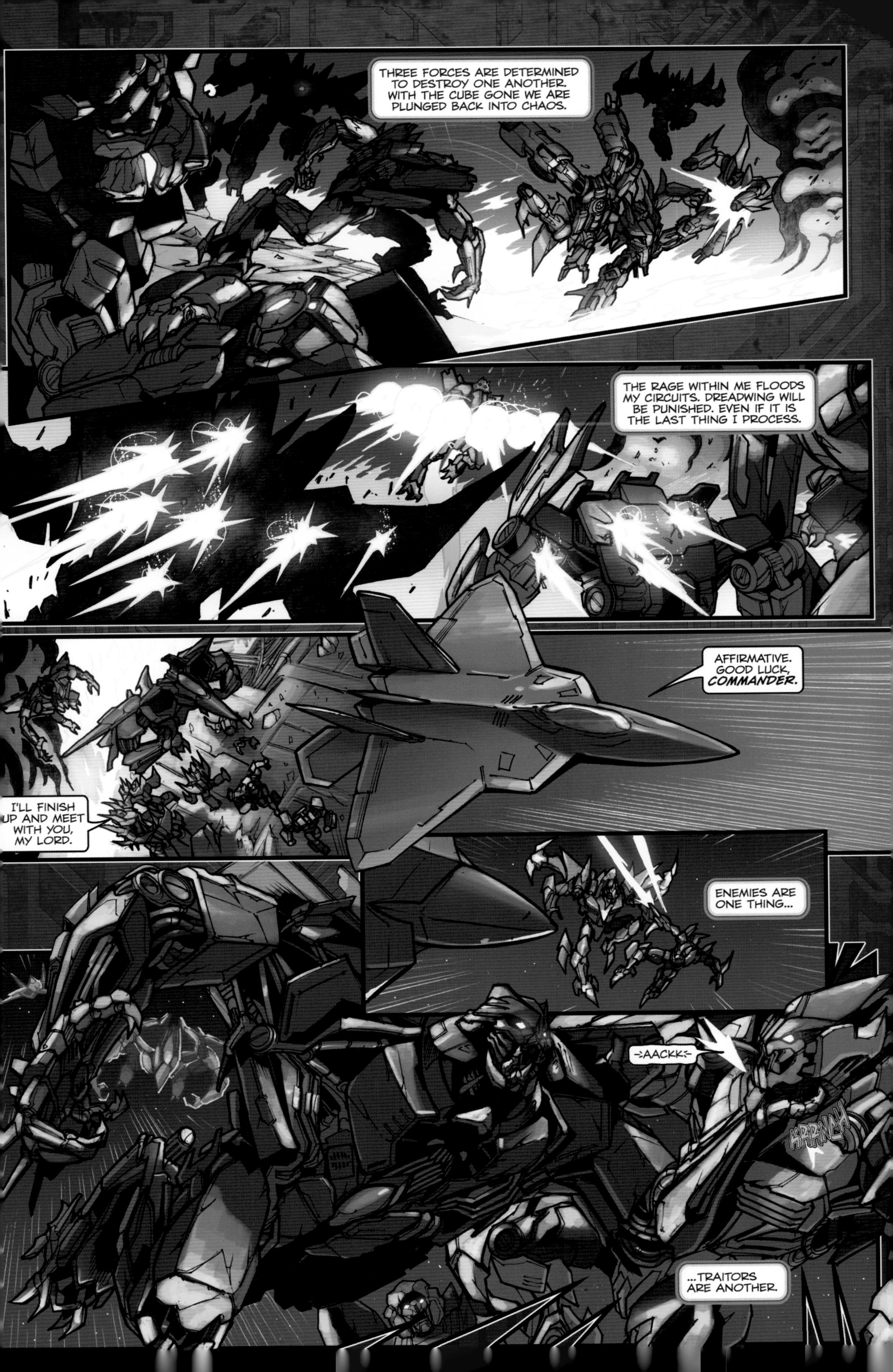

THREE FORCES ARE DETERMINED TO DESTROY ONE ANOTHER. WITH THE CUBE GONE WE ARE PLUNGED BACK INTO CHAOS.
THE RAGE WITHIN ME FLOODS MY CIRCUITS. DREADWING WILL BE PUNISHED. EVEN IF IT IS THE LAST THING I PROCESS.
I'LL FINISH UP AND MEET WITH YOU, MY LORD.
AFFIRMATIVE. GOOD LUCK, COMMANDER.
ENEMIES ARE ONE THING...
AACKK
KRRANCH
...TRAITORS ARE ANOTHER.

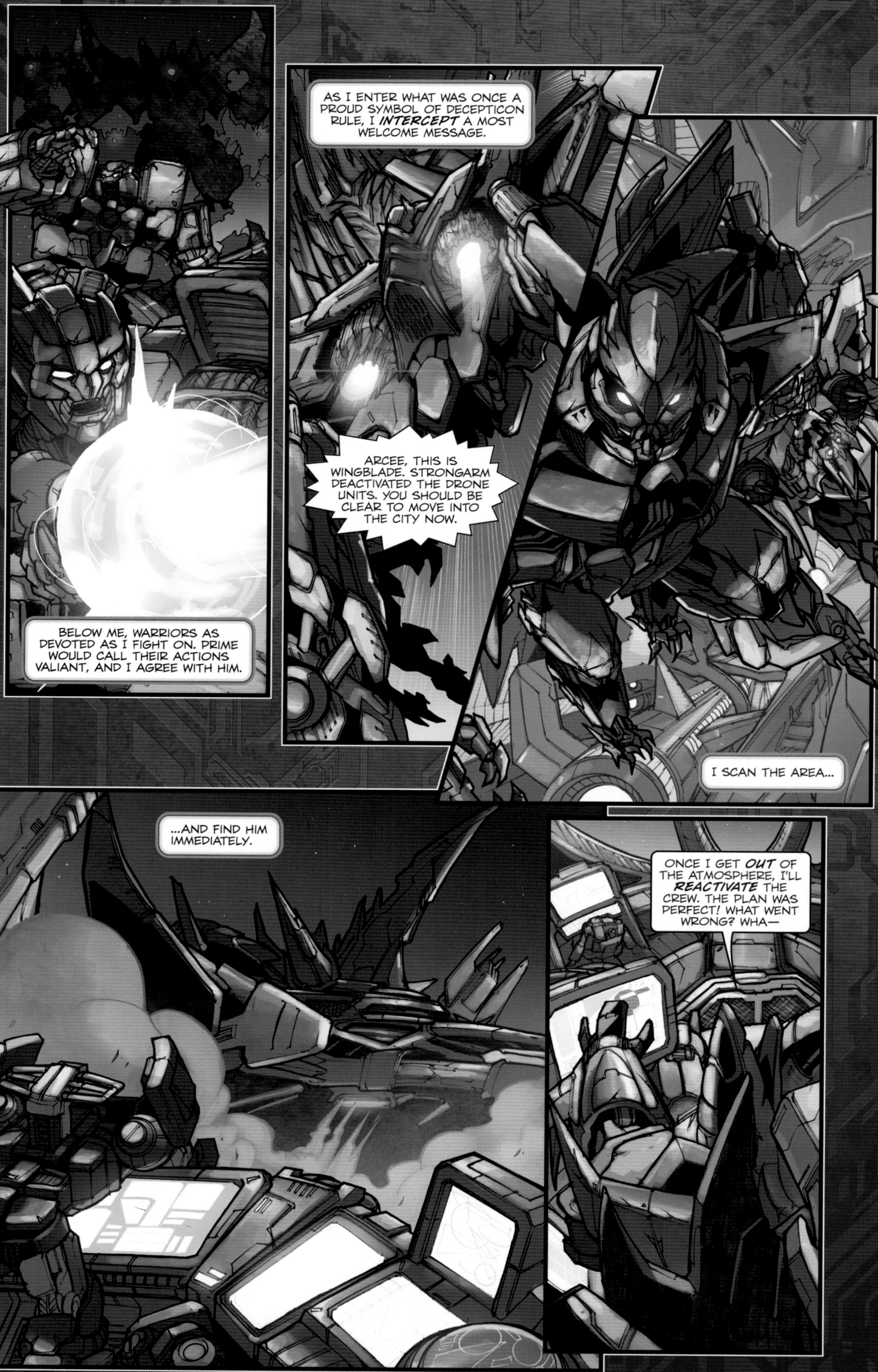

BELOW ME, WARRIORS AS DEVOTED AS I FIGHT ON. PRIME WOULD CALL THEIR ACTIONS VALIANT, AND I AGREE WITH HIM.
AS I ENTER WHAT WAS ONCE A PROUD SYMBOL OF DECEPTICON RULE, I *INTERCEPT* A MOST WELCOME MESSAGE.
ARCEE, THIS IS WINGBLADE. STRONGARM DEACTIVATED THE DRONE UNITS. YOU SHOULD BE CLEAR TO MOVE INTO THE CITY NOW.
I SCAN THE AREA...
...AND FIND HIM IMMEDIATELY.
ONCE I GET *OUT* OF THE ATMOSPHERE, I'LL *REACTIVATE* THE CREW. THE PLAN WAS PERFECT! WHAT WENT WRONG? WHA—

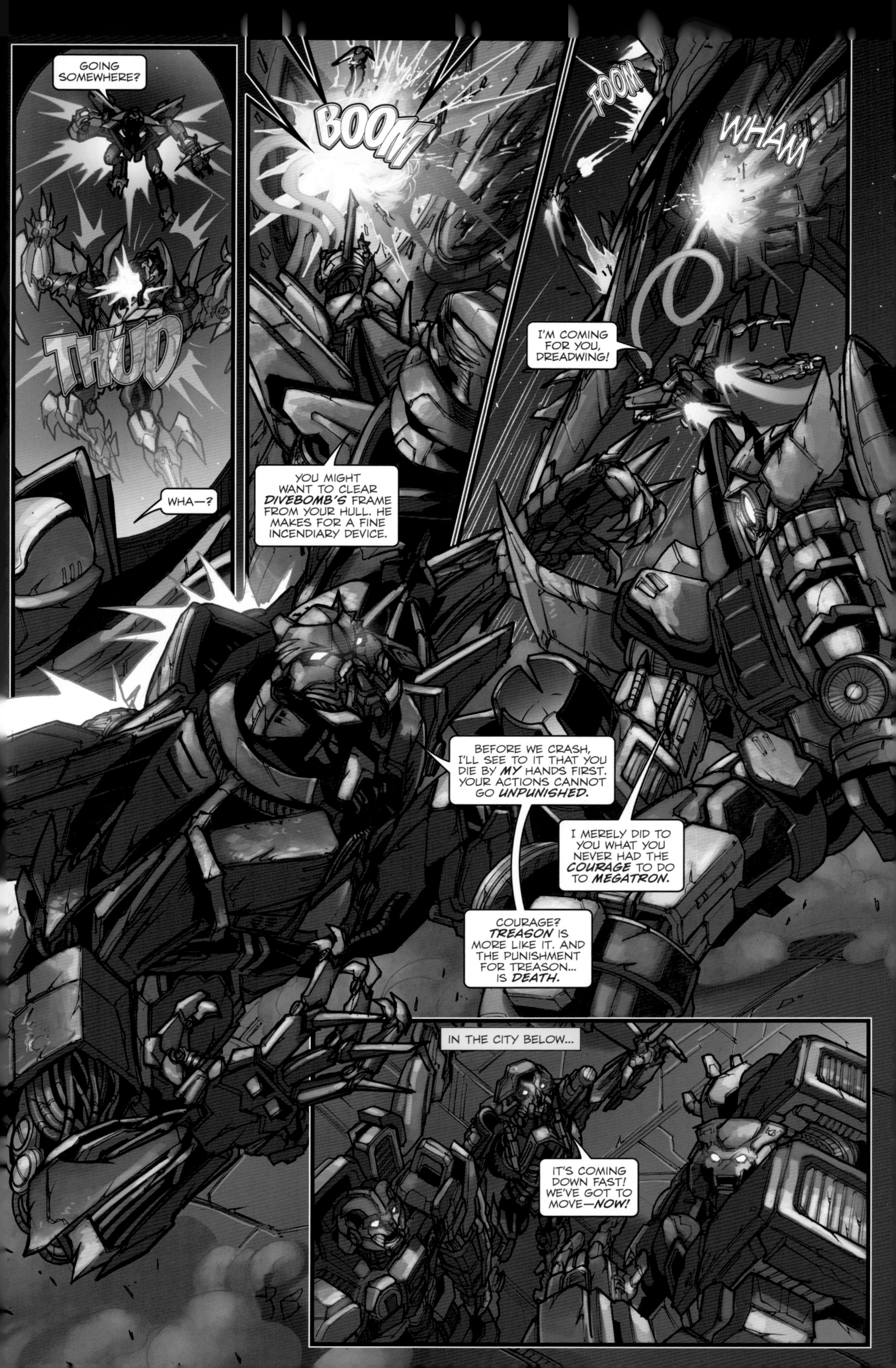
GOING SOMEWHERE?
THUD
WHA—?
BOOM
YOU MIGHT WANT TO CLEAR DIVEBOMB'S FRAME FROM YOUR HULL. HE MAKES FOR A FINE INCENDIARY DEVICE.
FOOM
WHAM
I'M COMING FOR YOU, DREADWING!
BEFORE WE CRASH, I'LL SEE TO IT THAT YOU DIE BY MY HANDS FIRST. YOUR ACTIONS CANNOT GO UNPUNISHED.
I MERELY DID TO YOU WHAT YOU NEVER HAD THE COURAGE TO DO TO MEGATRON.
COURAGE? TREASON IS MORE LIKE IT. AND THE PUNISHMENT FOR TREASON... IS DEATH.
IN THE CITY BELOW...
IT'S COMING DOWN FAST! WE'VE GOT TO MOVE—NOW!

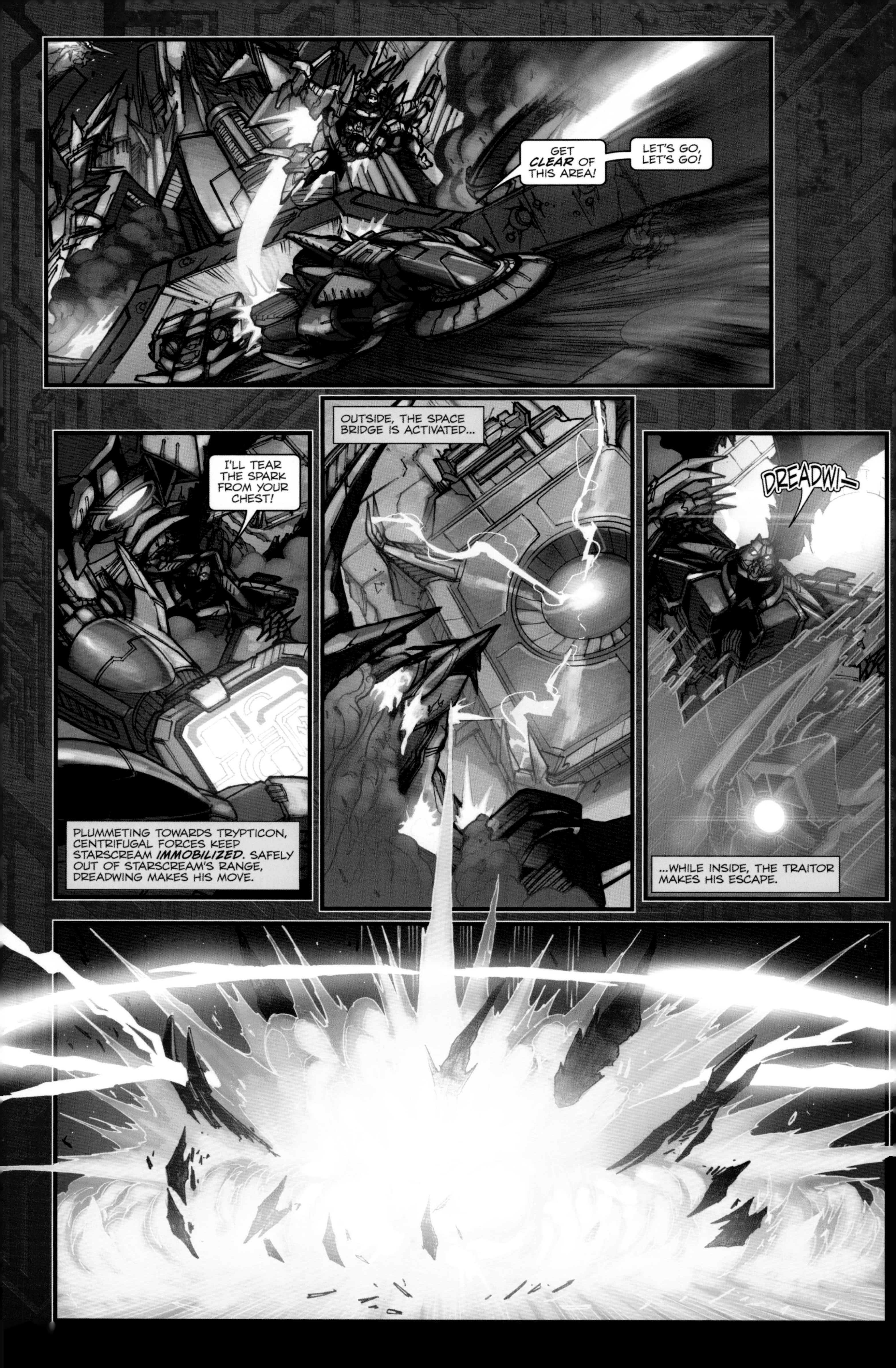
GET CLEAR OF THIS AREA!
LET'S GO, LET'S GO!
I'LL TEAR THE SPARK FROM YOUR CHEST!
PLUMMETING TOWARDS TRYPTICON, CENTRIFUGAL FORCES KEEP STARSCREAM IMMOBILIZED. SAFELY OUT OF STARSCREAM'S RANGE, DREADWING MAKES HIS MOVE.
OUTSIDE, THE SPACE BRIDGE IS ACTIVATED...
DREADWI—
...WHILE INSIDE, THE TRAITOR MAKES HIS ESCAPE.

THE BURNING SKY ENGULFS THE CITY, THEN IS QUICKLY ABSORBED... A BRIEF, DESTRUCTIVE FLASH, AND THEN IT IS GONE.

TRYPTICON—ONCE MAJESTIC AND IMPOSING—LIES IN RUINS. SMOLDERING AND BROKEN, THE DECEPTICON CITY IS NO MORE.

THIS COULD BE THE TURNING POINT WE NEED IN THIS WAR.

BUT IF STARSCREAM SURVIVED, HE'S STILL A THREAT. AND I HAVE TO FIND HIM.

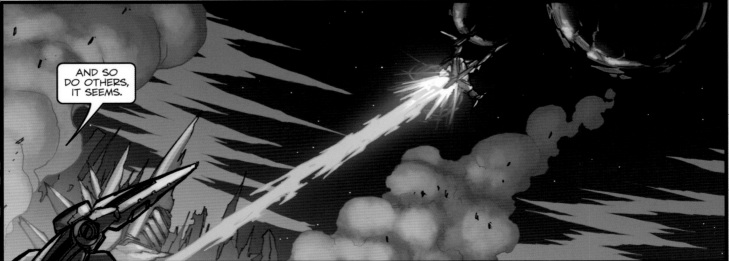

AND SO DO OTHERS, IT SEEMS.

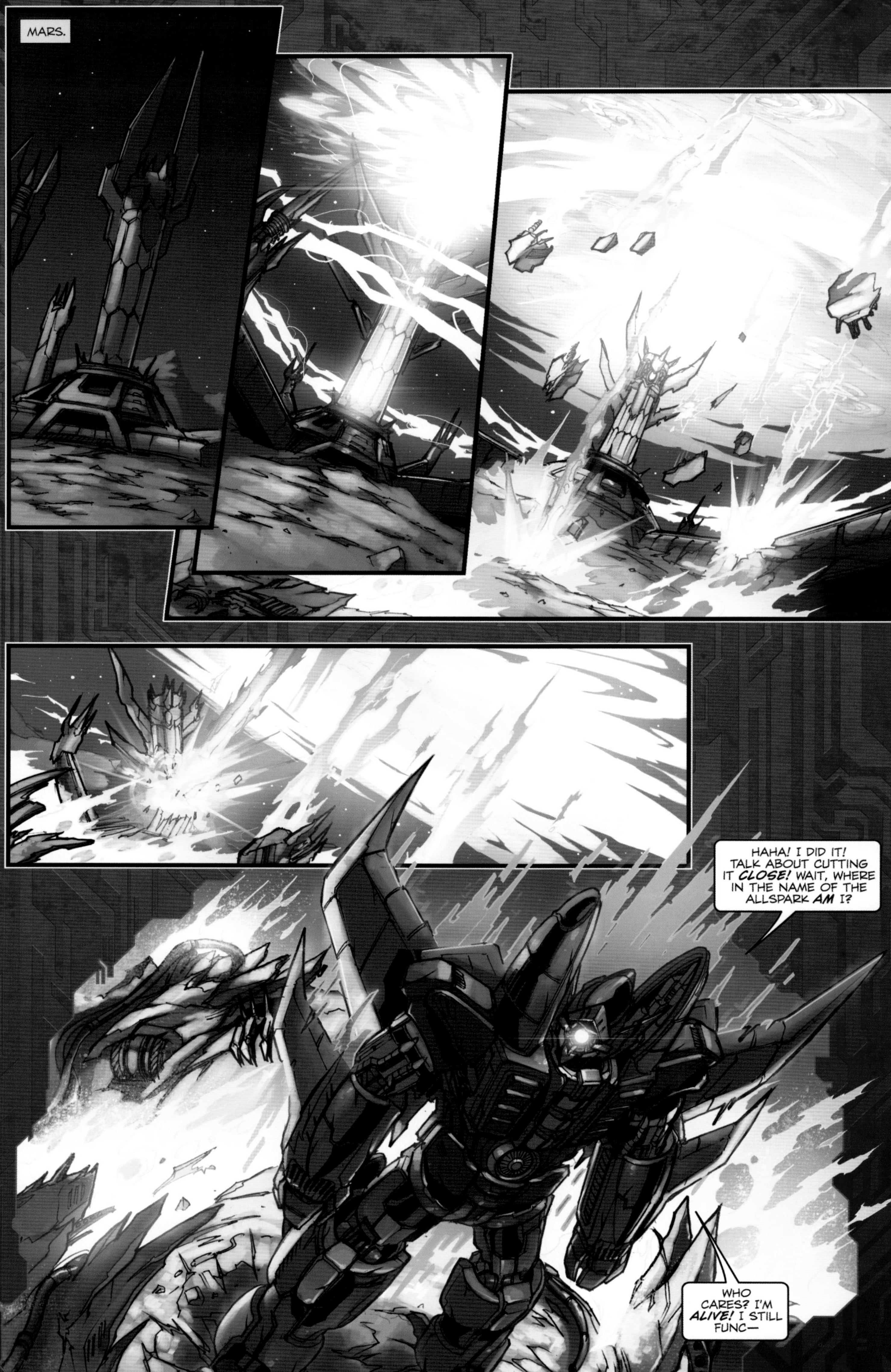
MARS.
HAHA! I DID IT! TALK ABOUT CUTTING IT CLOSE! WAIT, WHERE IN THE NAME OF THE ALLSPARK AM I?
WHO CARES? I'M ALIVE! I STILL FUNC—

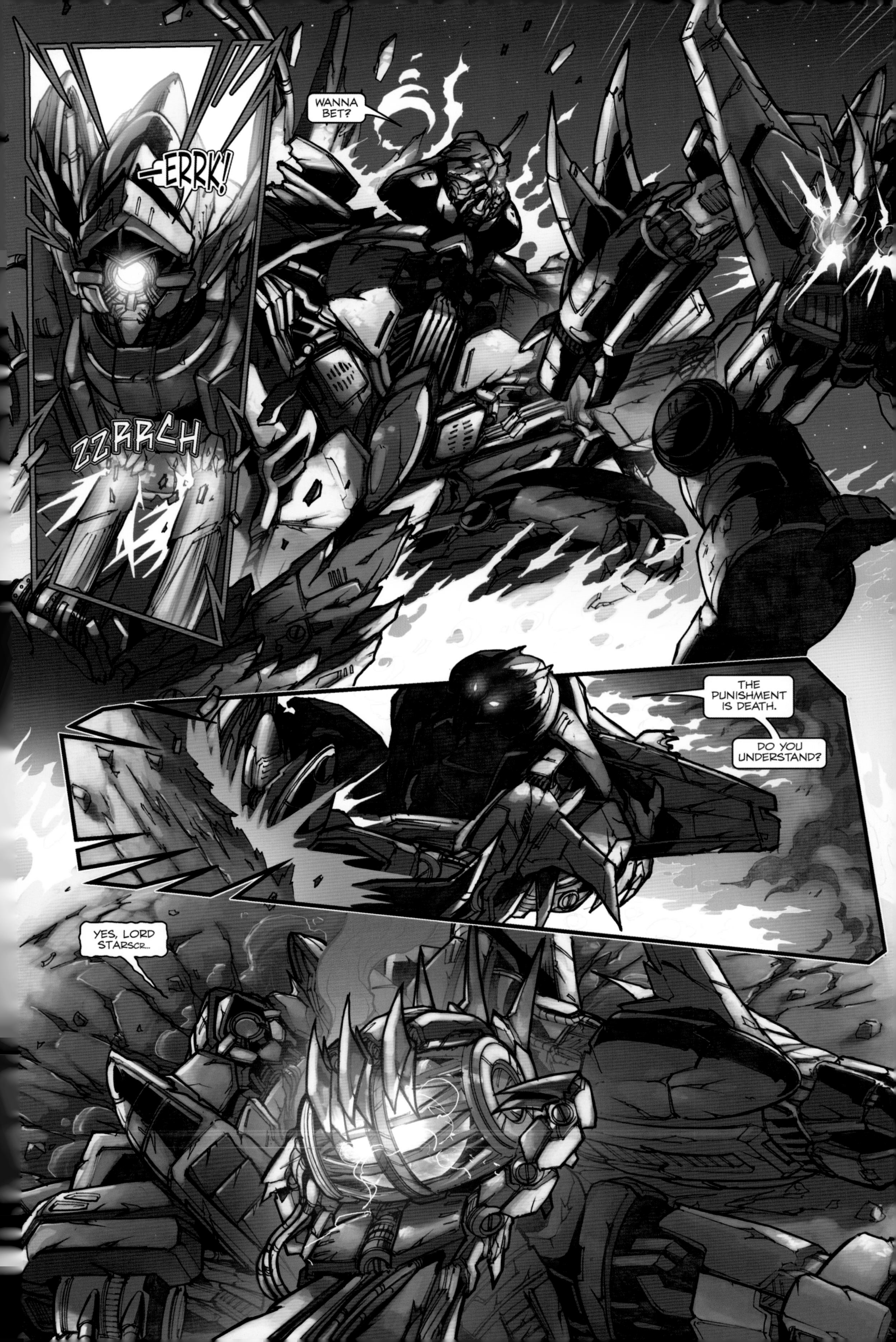

WANNA BET?
—ERRK!
ZZRRRCH
THE PUNISHMENT IS DEATH.
DO YOU UNDERSTAND?
YES, LORD STARSCR...

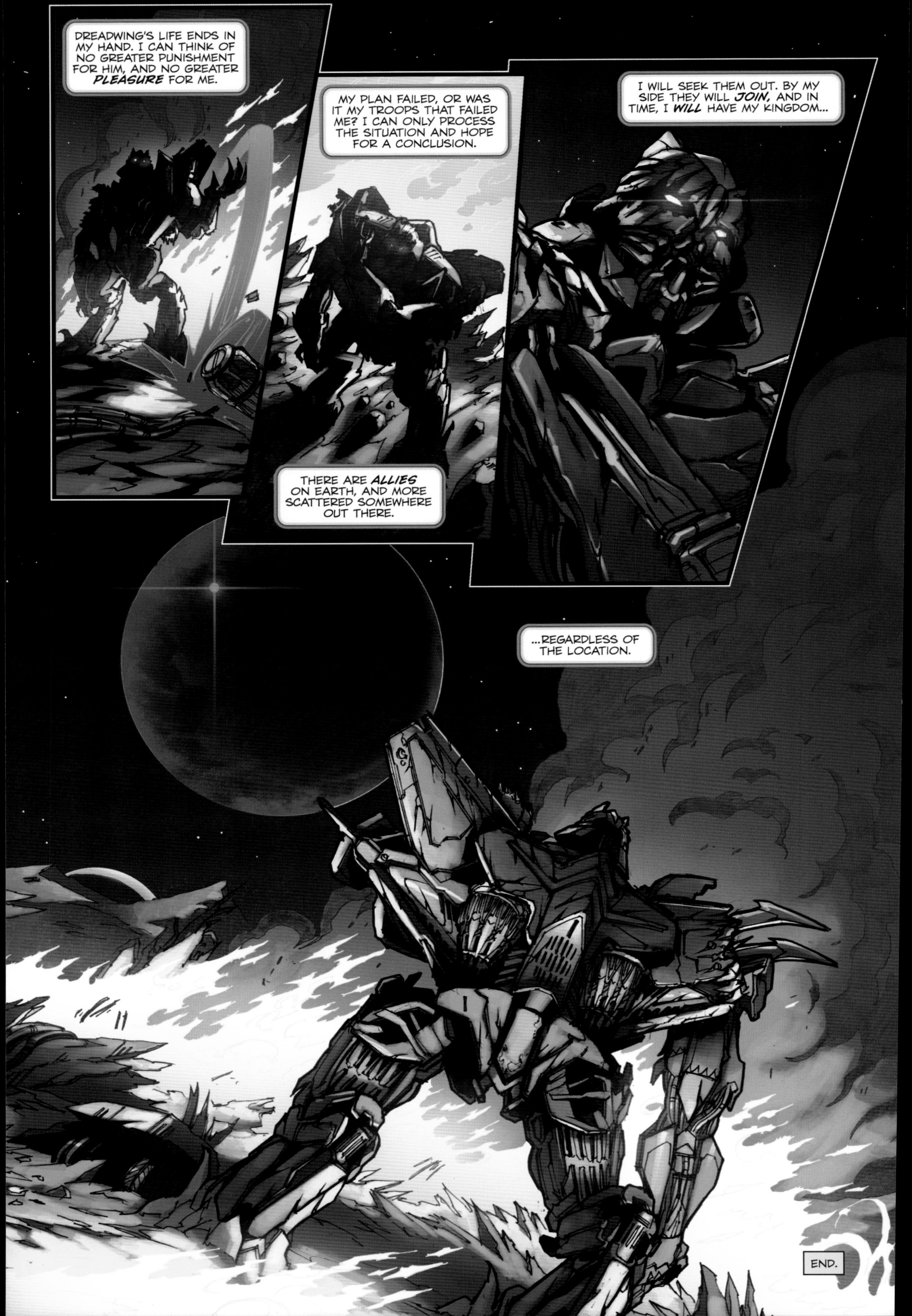
DREADWING'S LIFE ENDS IN MY HAND. I CAN THINK OF NO GREATER PUNISHMENT FOR HIM, AND NO GREATER PLEASURE FOR ME.
MY PLAN FAILED, OR WAS IT MY TROOPS THAT FAILED ME? I CAN ONLY PROCESS THE SITUATION AND HOPE FOR A CONCLUSION.
THERE ARE ALLIES ON EARTH, AND MORE SCATTERED SOMEWHERE OUT THERE.
I WILL SEEK THEM OUT. BY MY SIDE THEY WILL JOIN, AND IN TIME, I WILL HAVE MY KINGDOM...
...REGARDLESS OF THE LOCATION.
END.

ART GALLERY

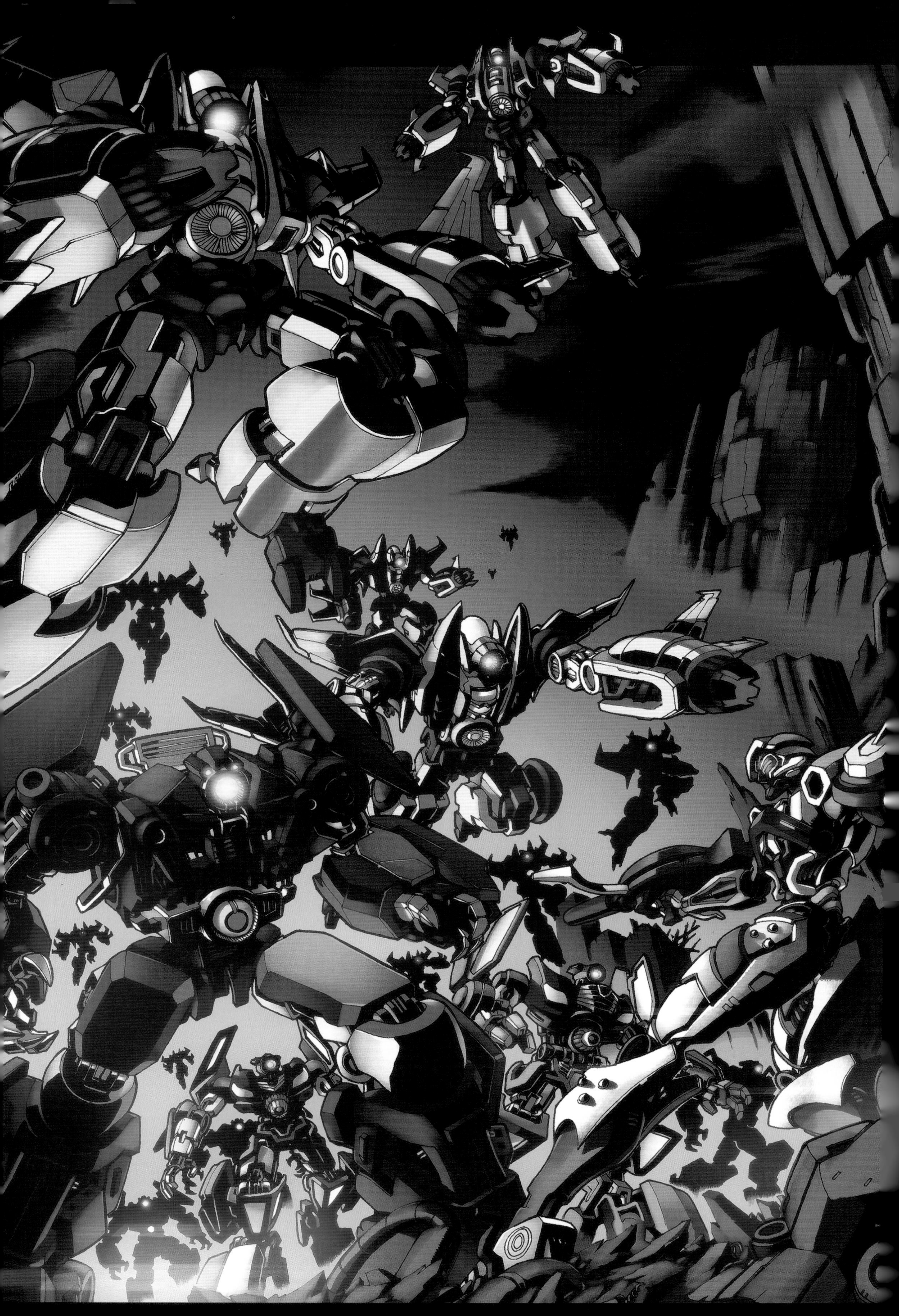

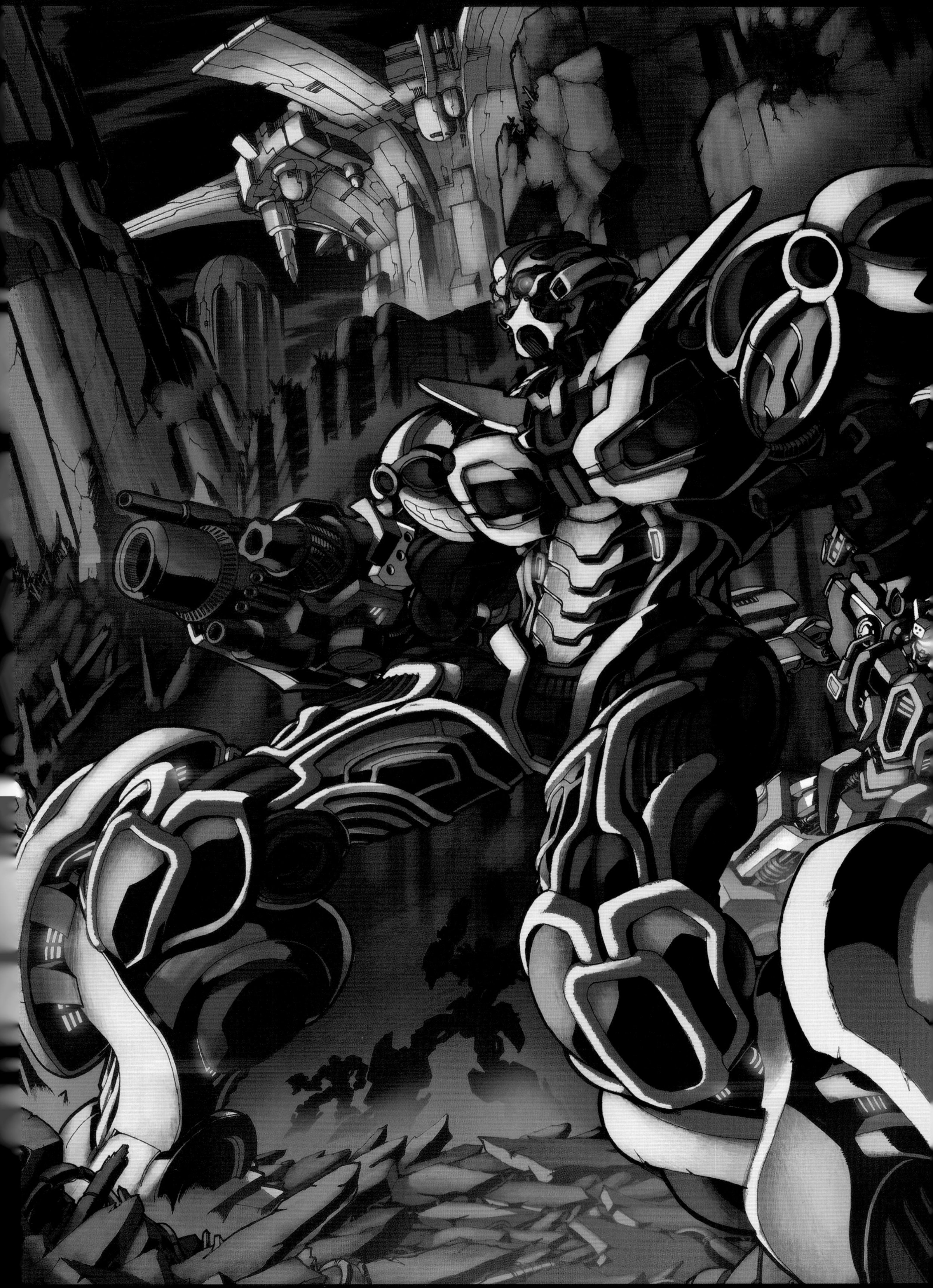

Art by Don Figueroa • Colors by Josh Burcham

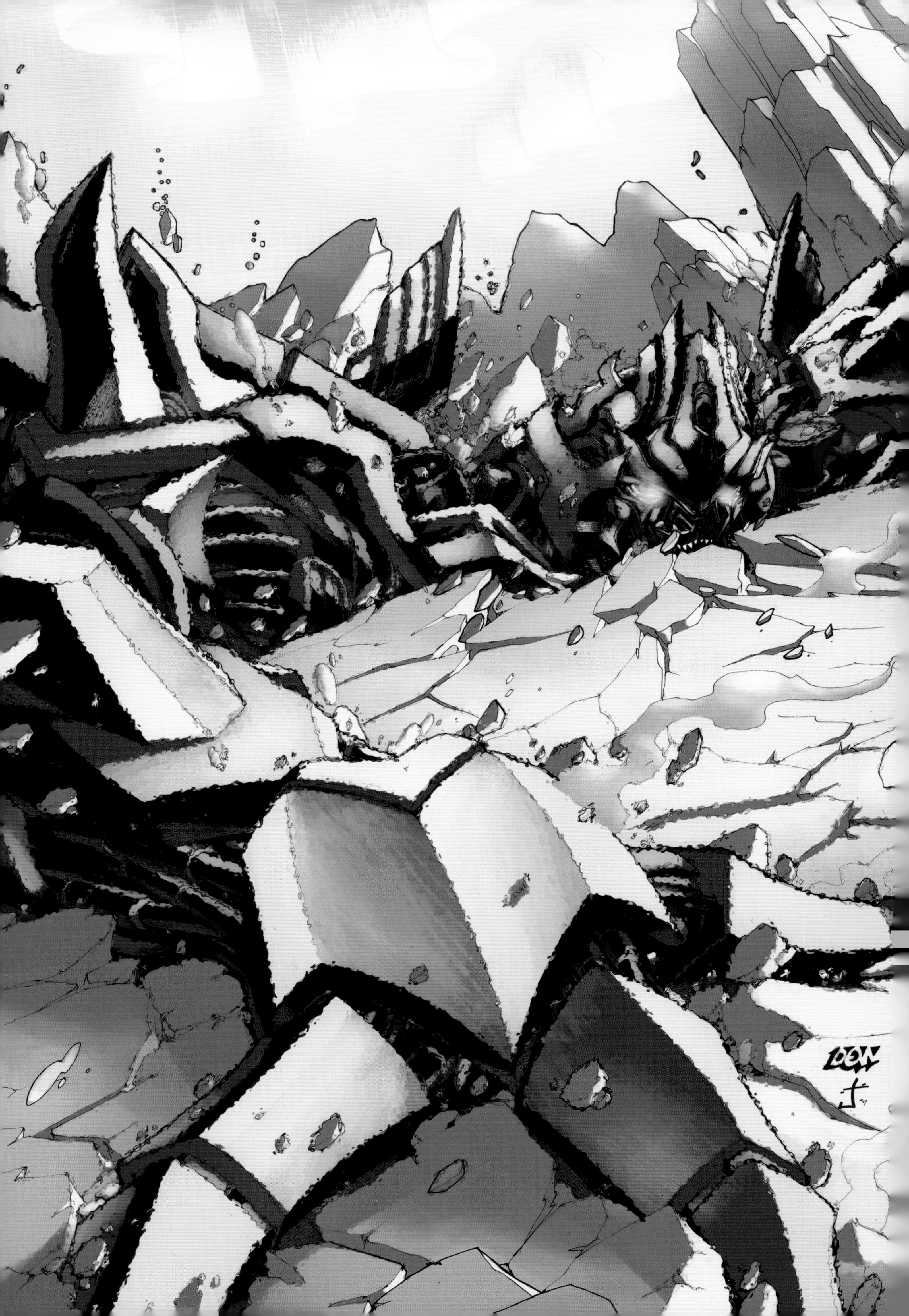

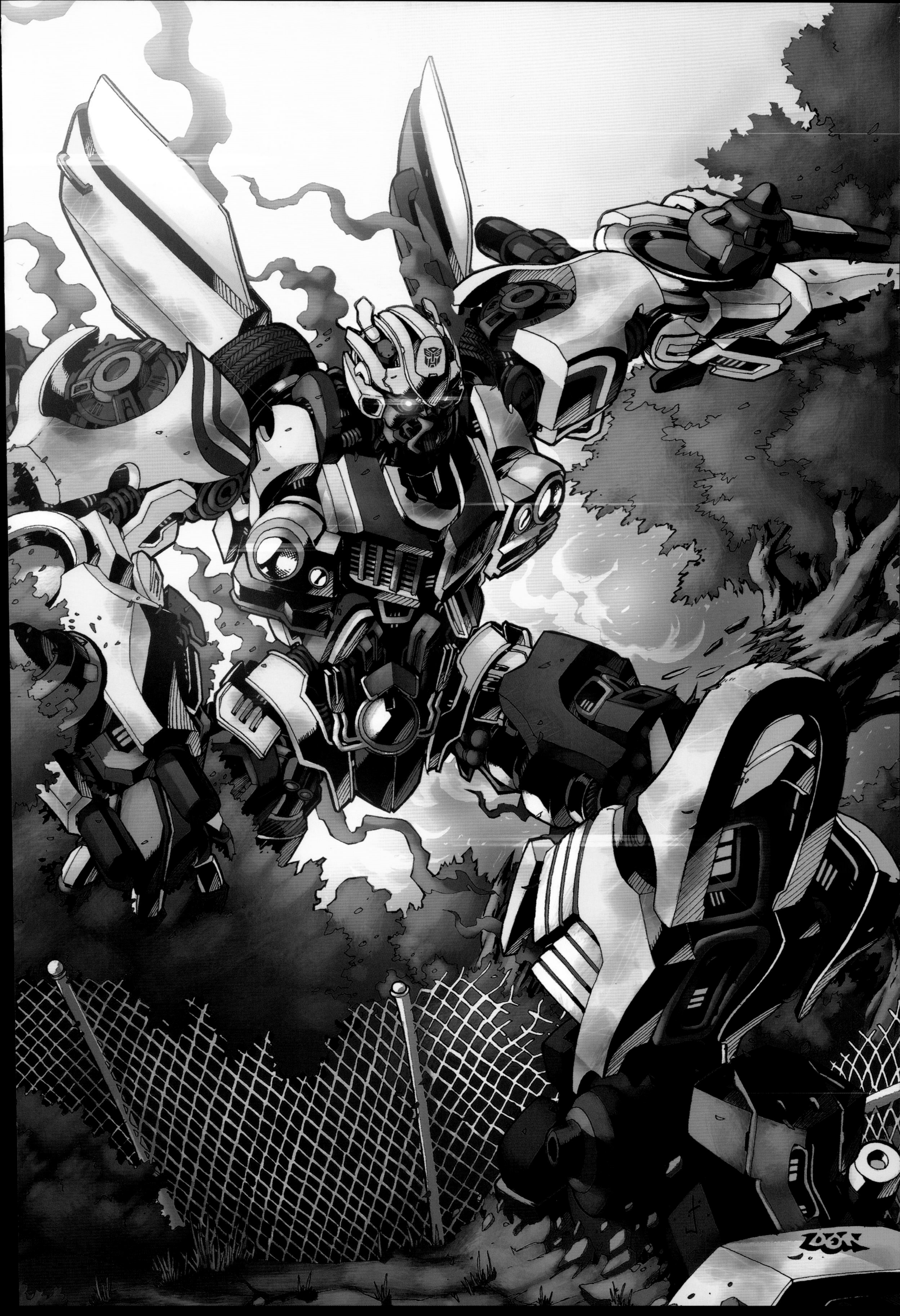
DON

Art by Don Figueroa • Colors by Josh Burcham

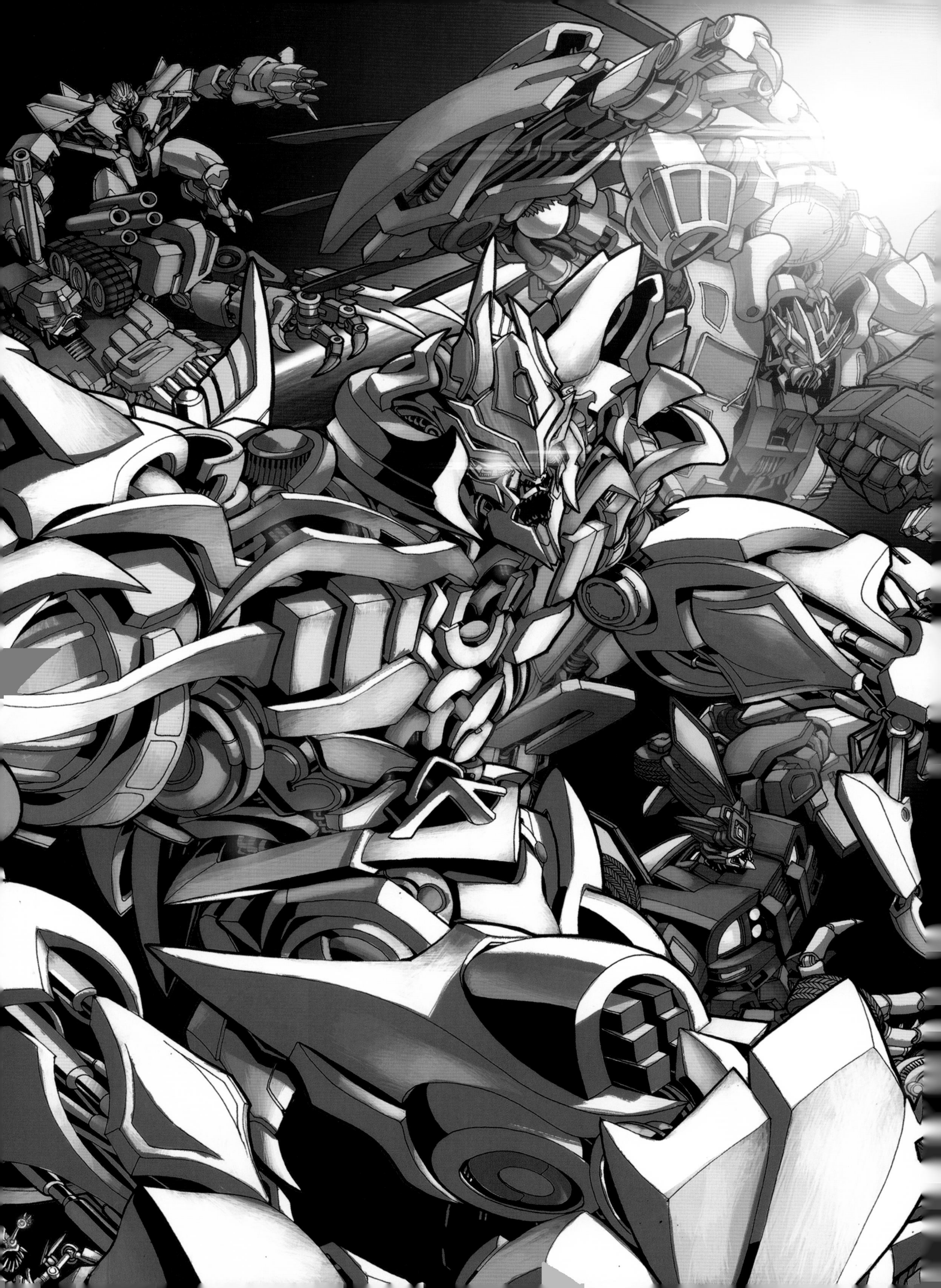

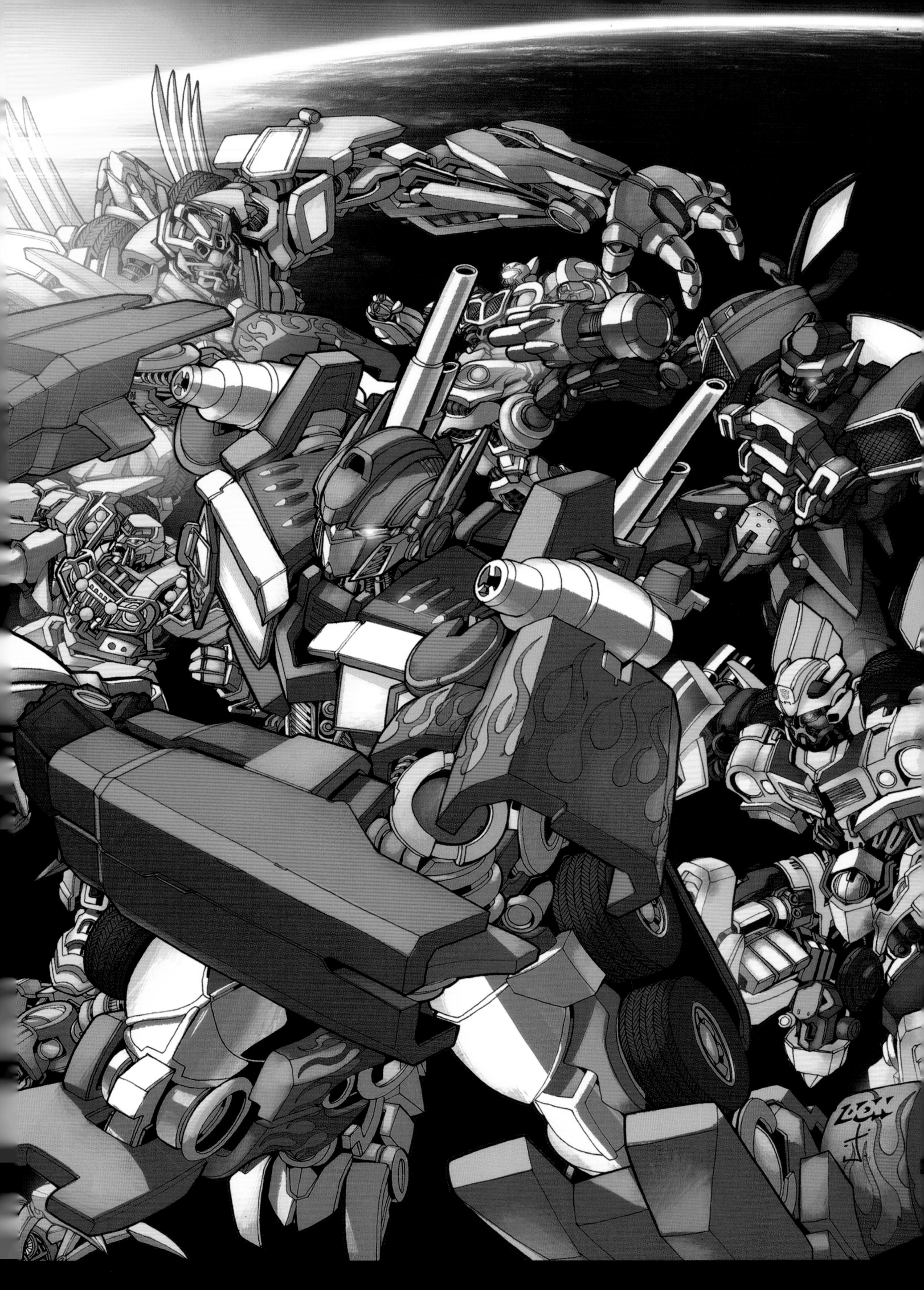

Art by Don Figueroa • Colors by Josh Burcham

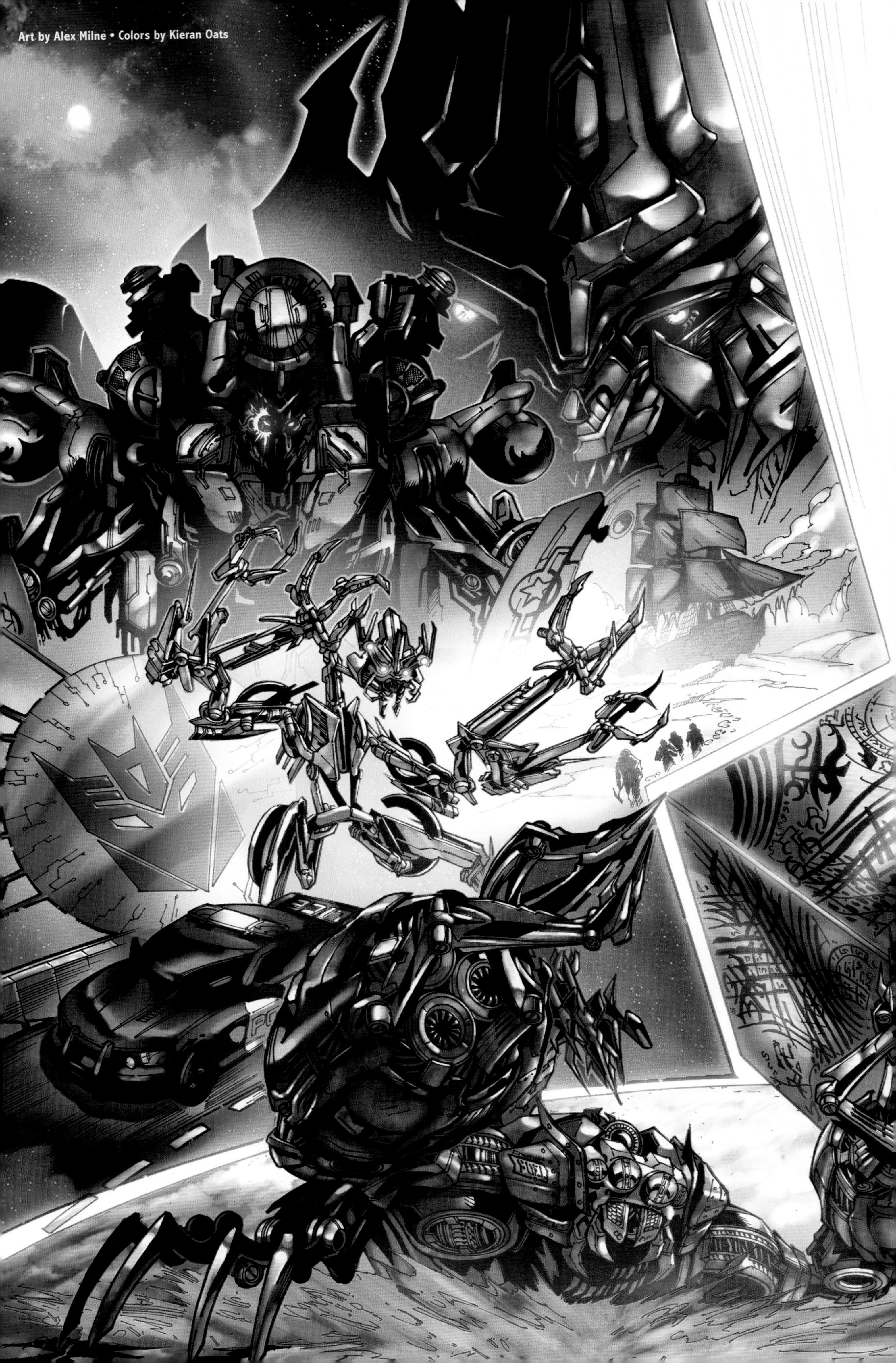

Art by Alex Milne • Colors by Kieran Oats

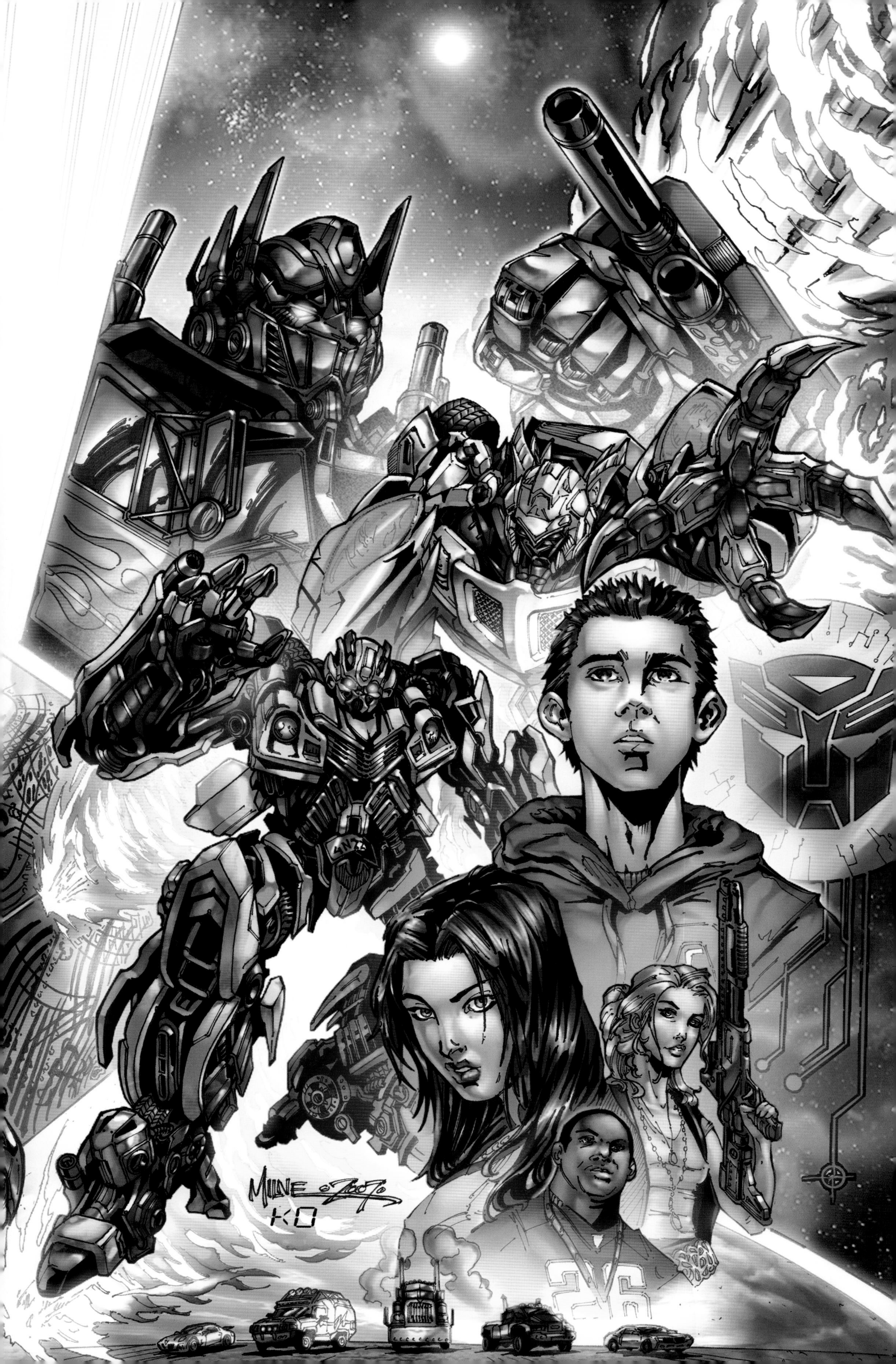
MILNE ©2007
KO

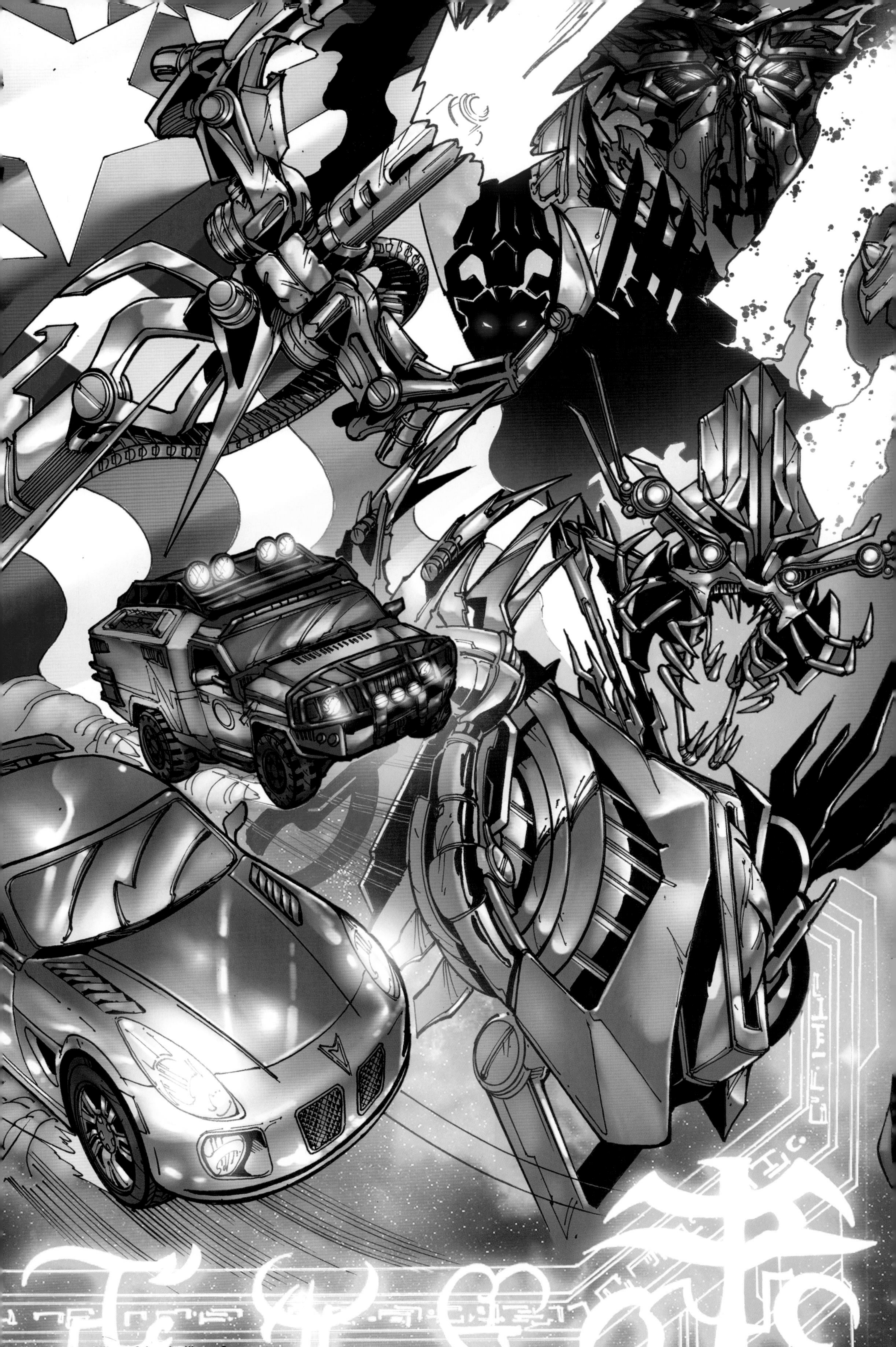

Art by Alex Milne • Colors by Kieran Oats

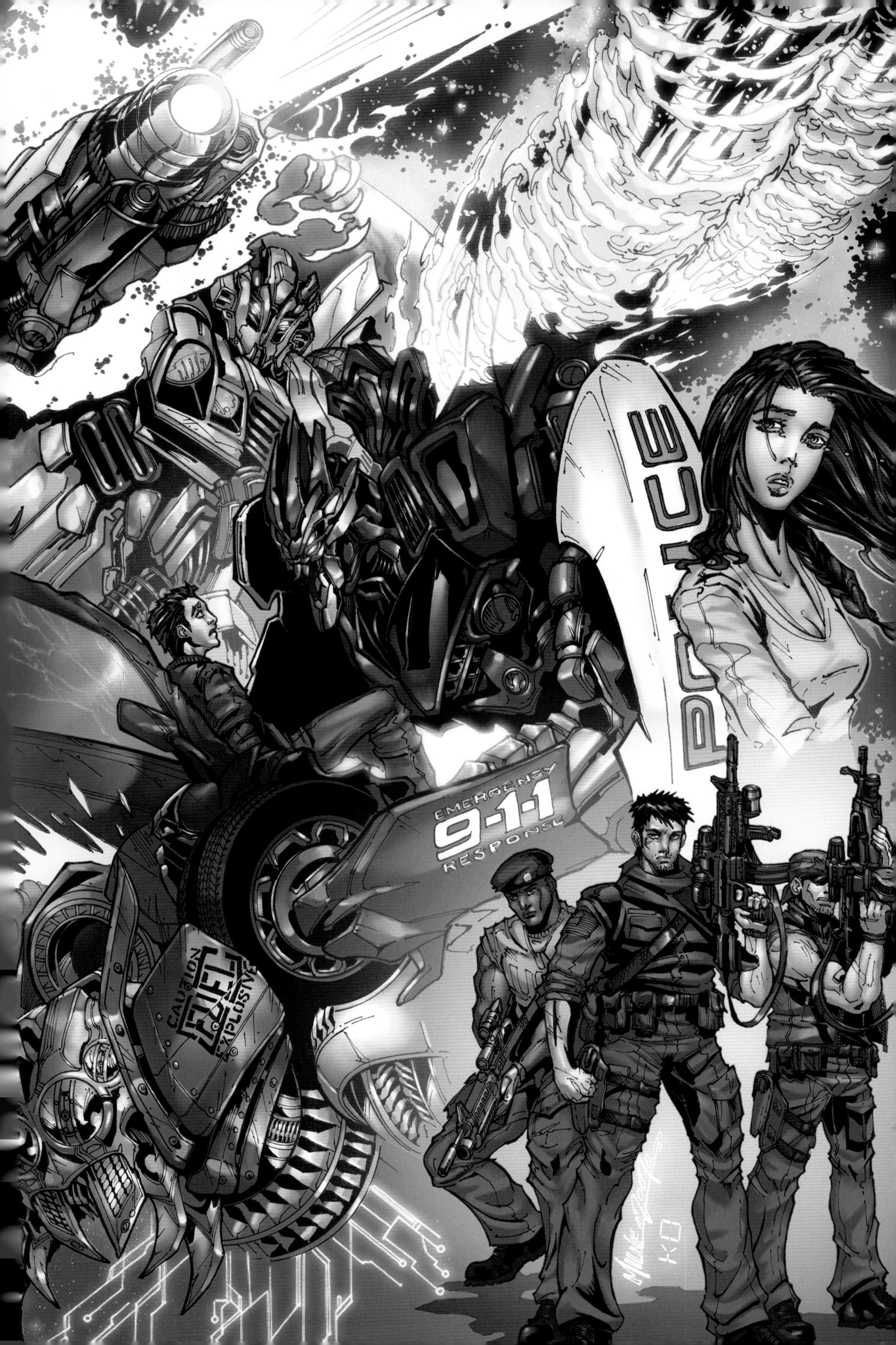
POLICE
EMERGENCY
9-1-1
RESPONSE
CAUTION
FUEL
EXPLOSIVE

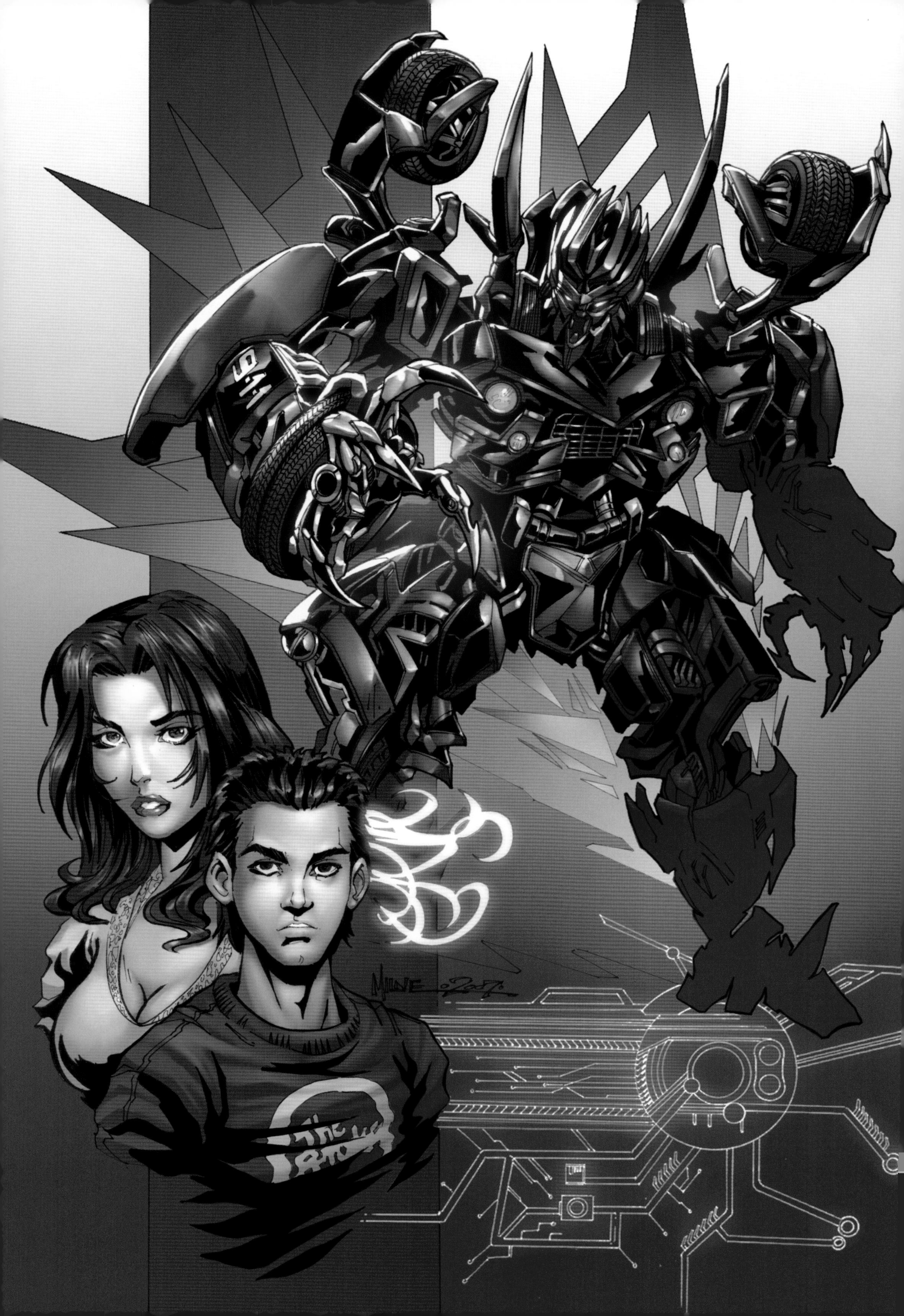

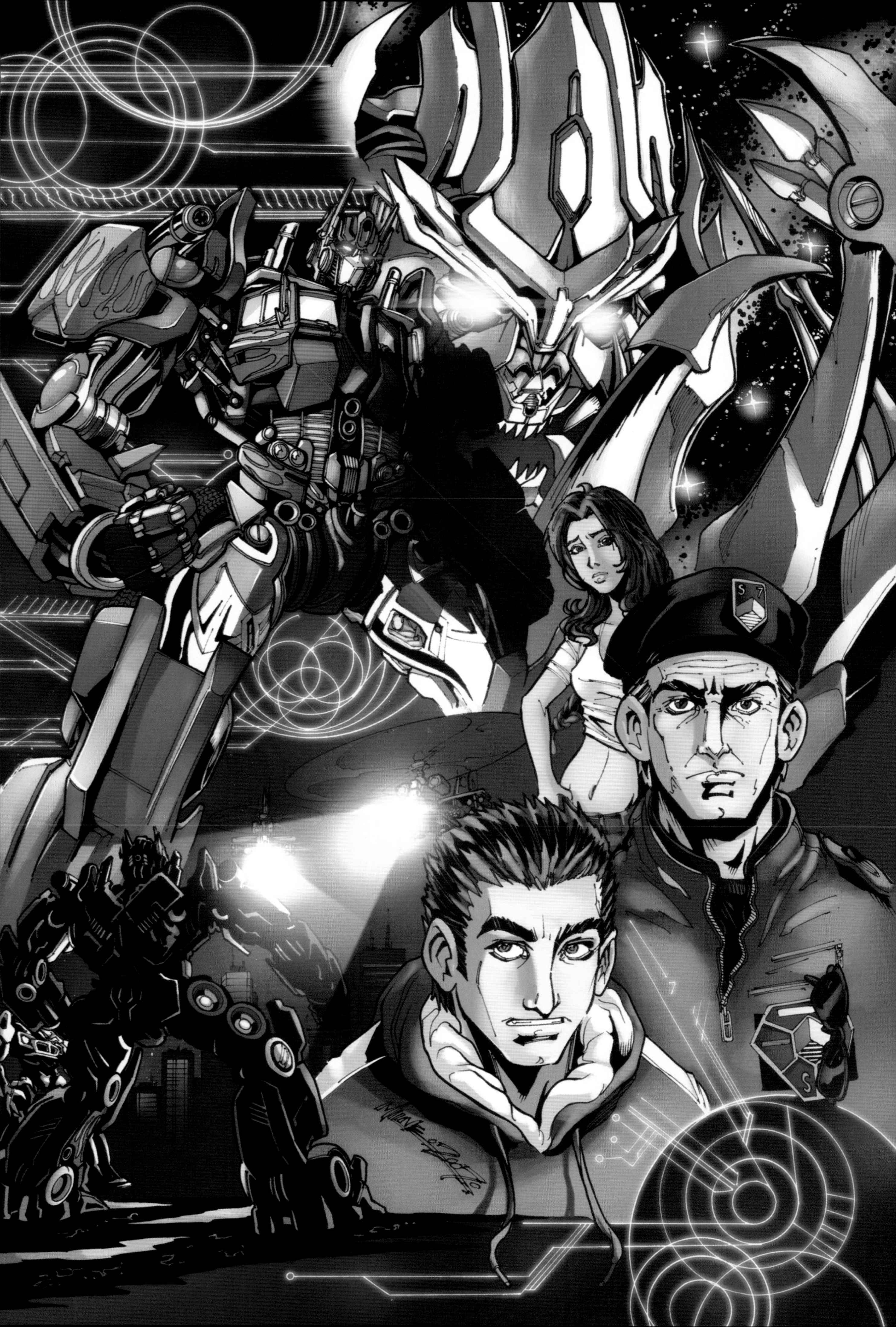

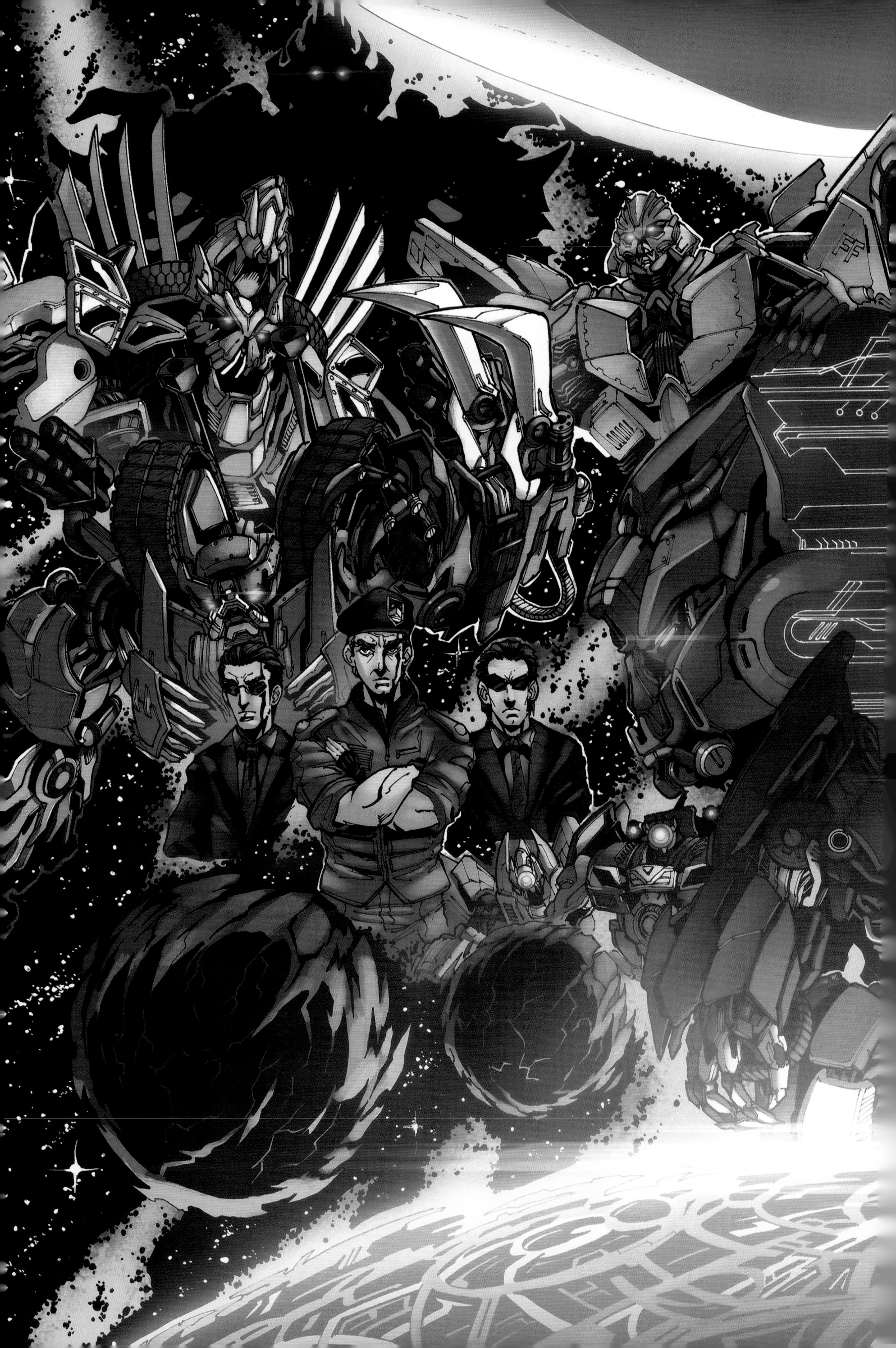

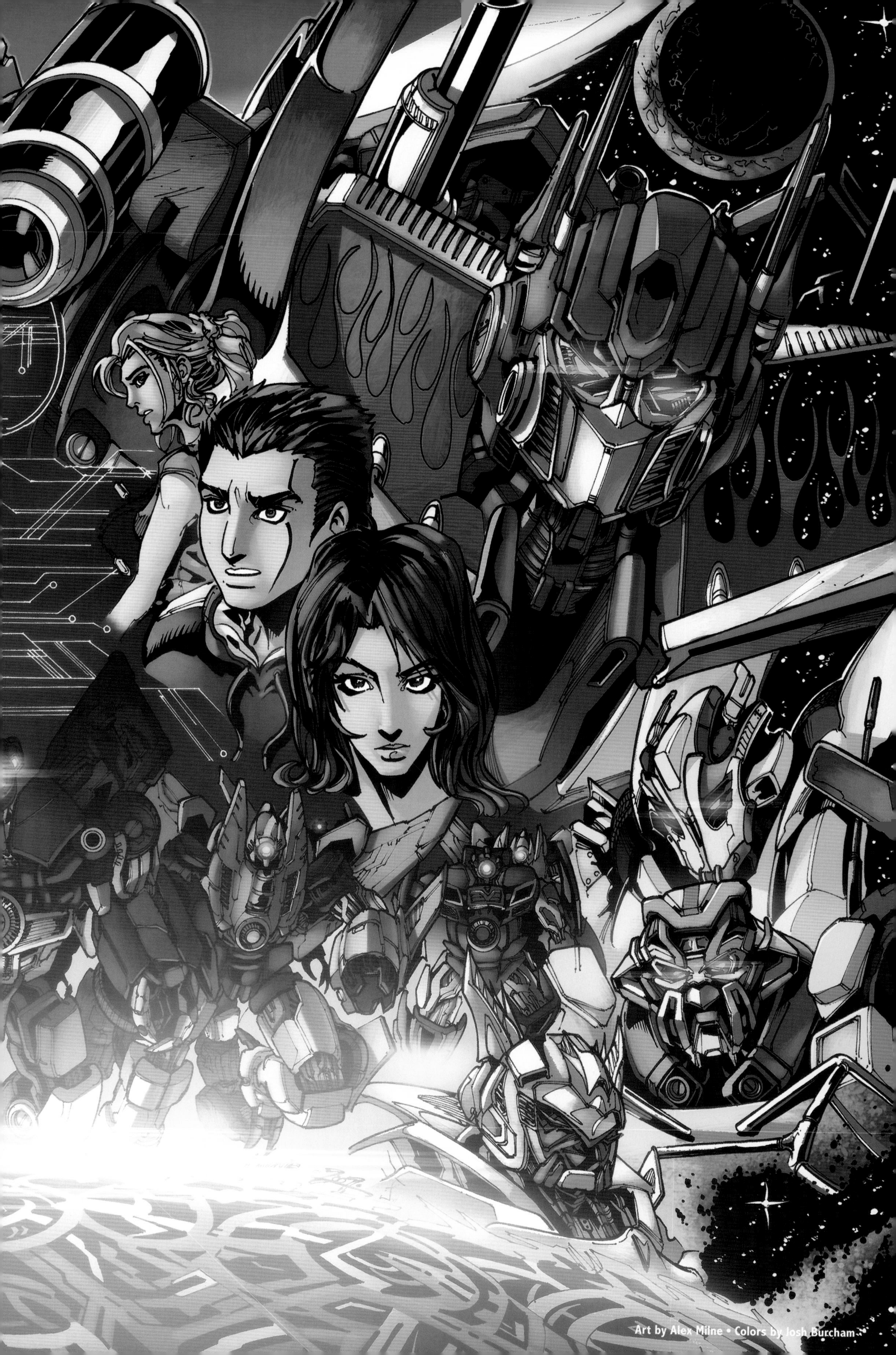
Art by Alex Milne • Colors by Josh Burcham

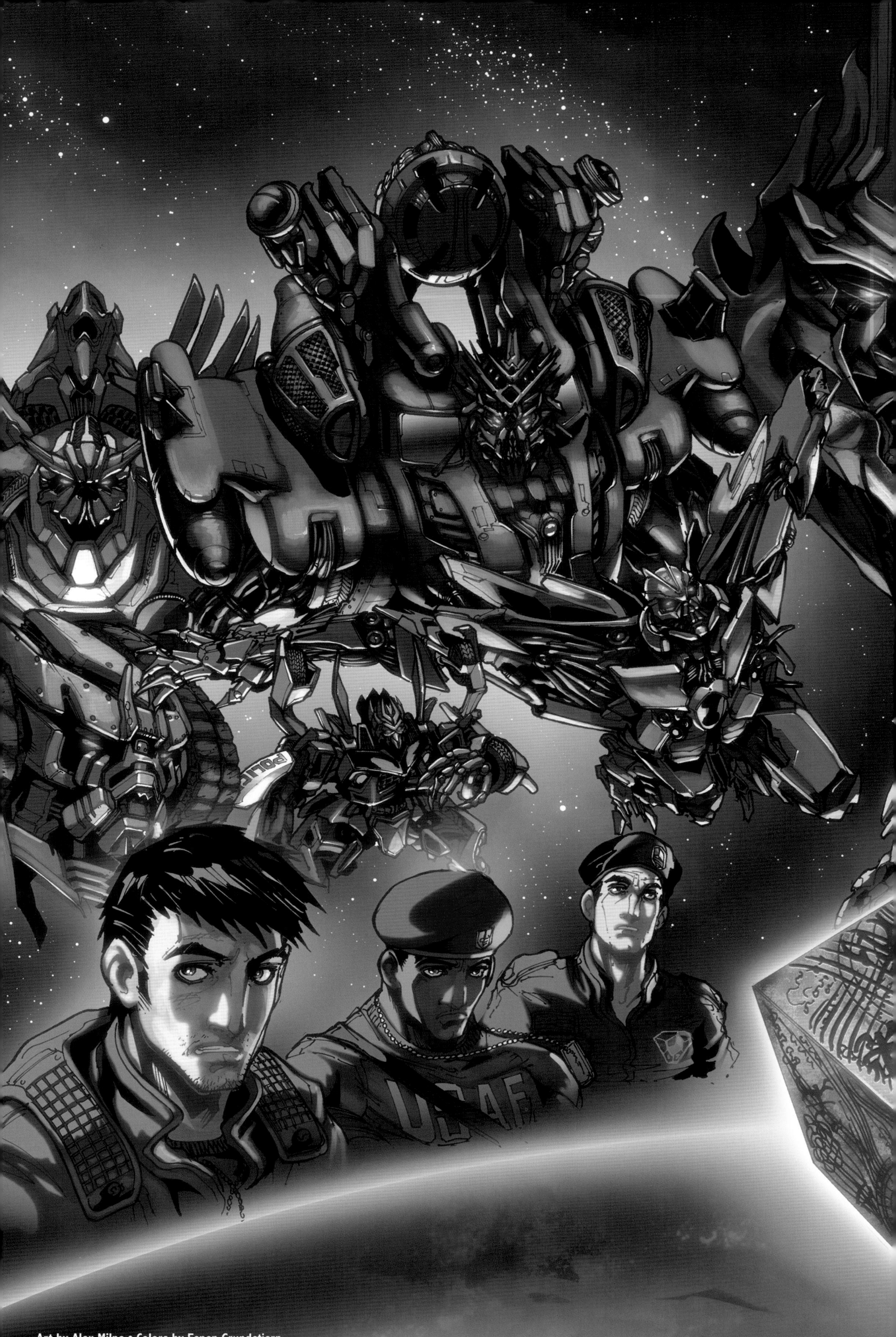

Art by Alex Milne • Colors by Espen Grundetjern

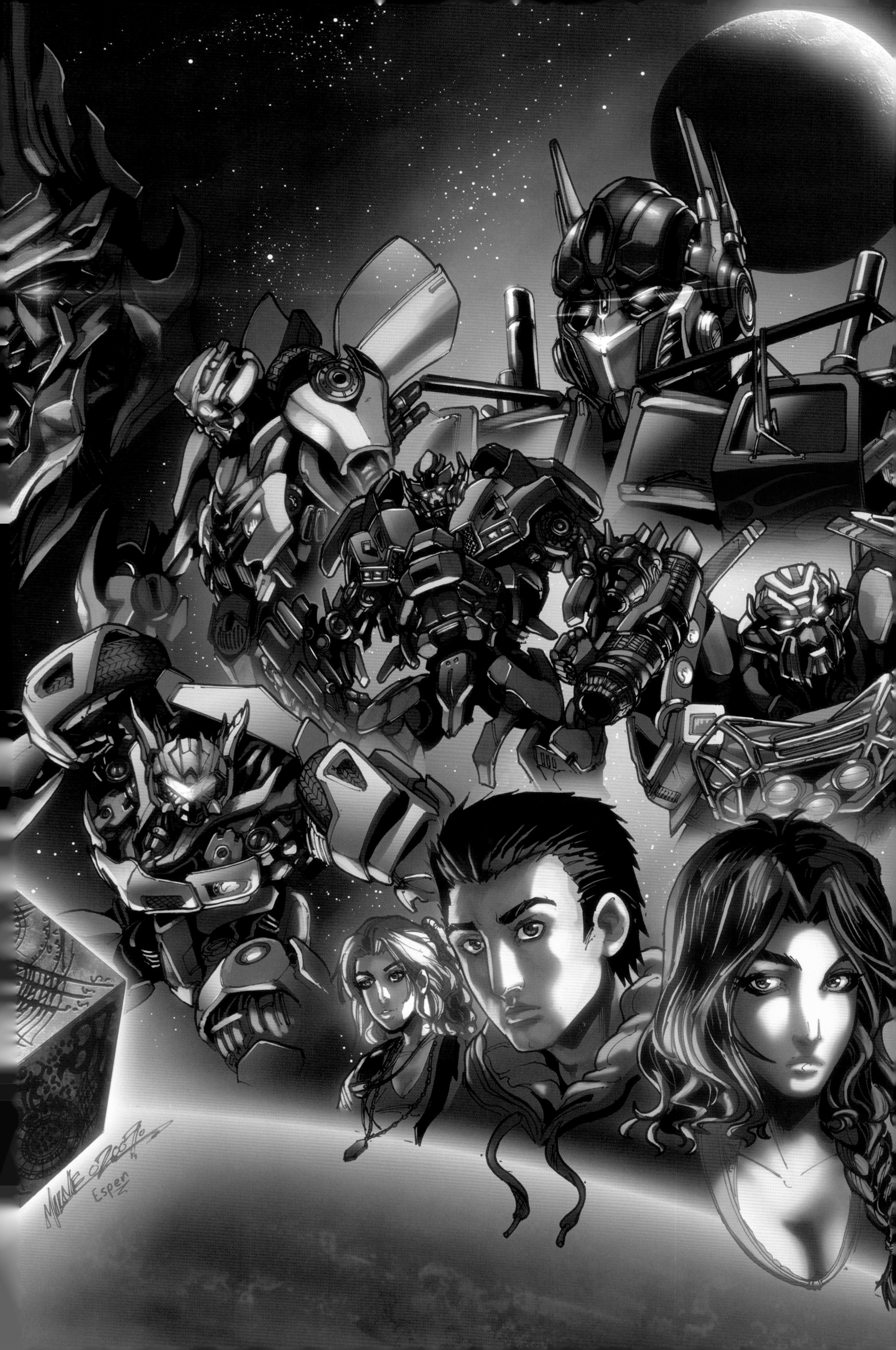
Espen

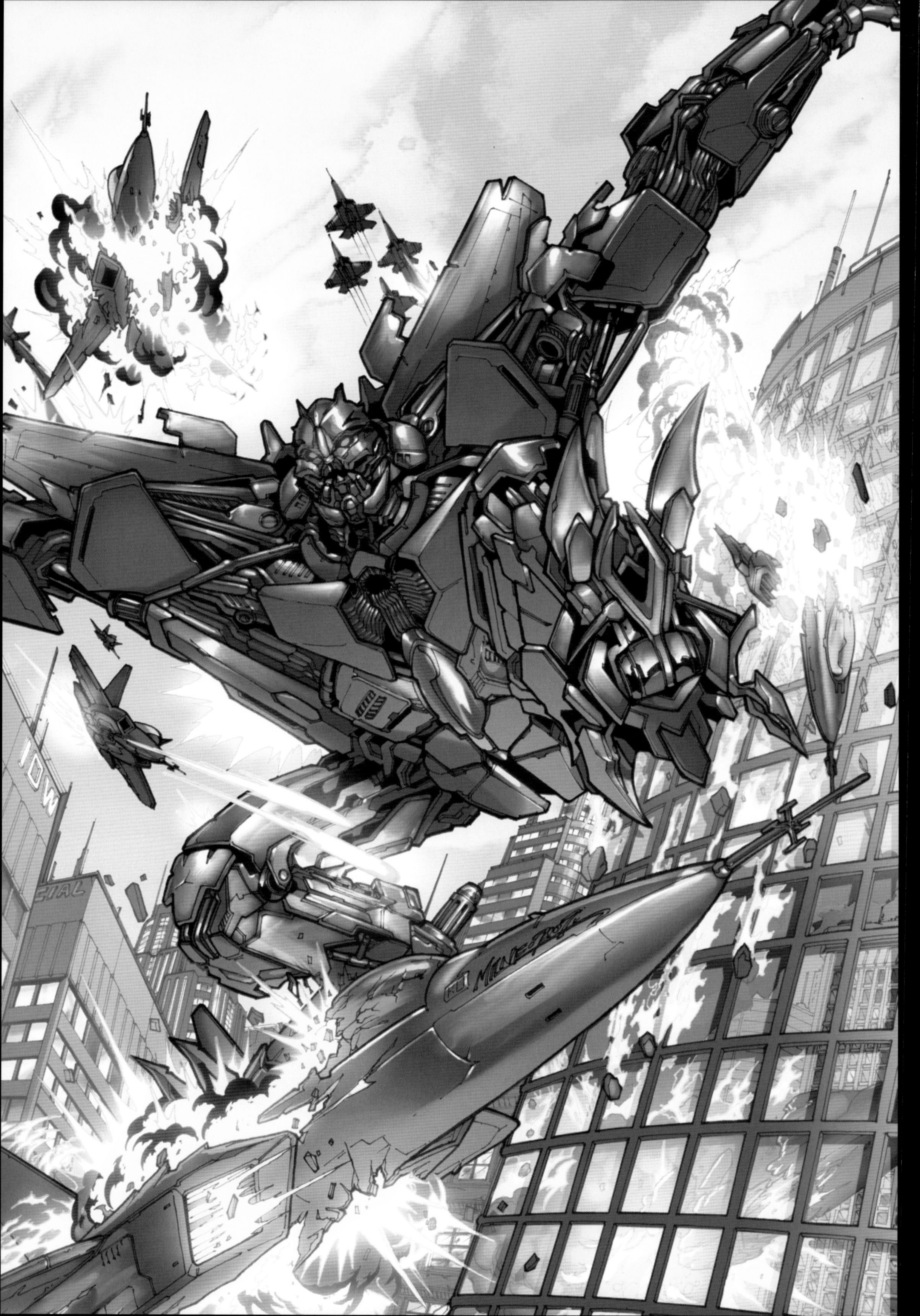
IDW
CIAL

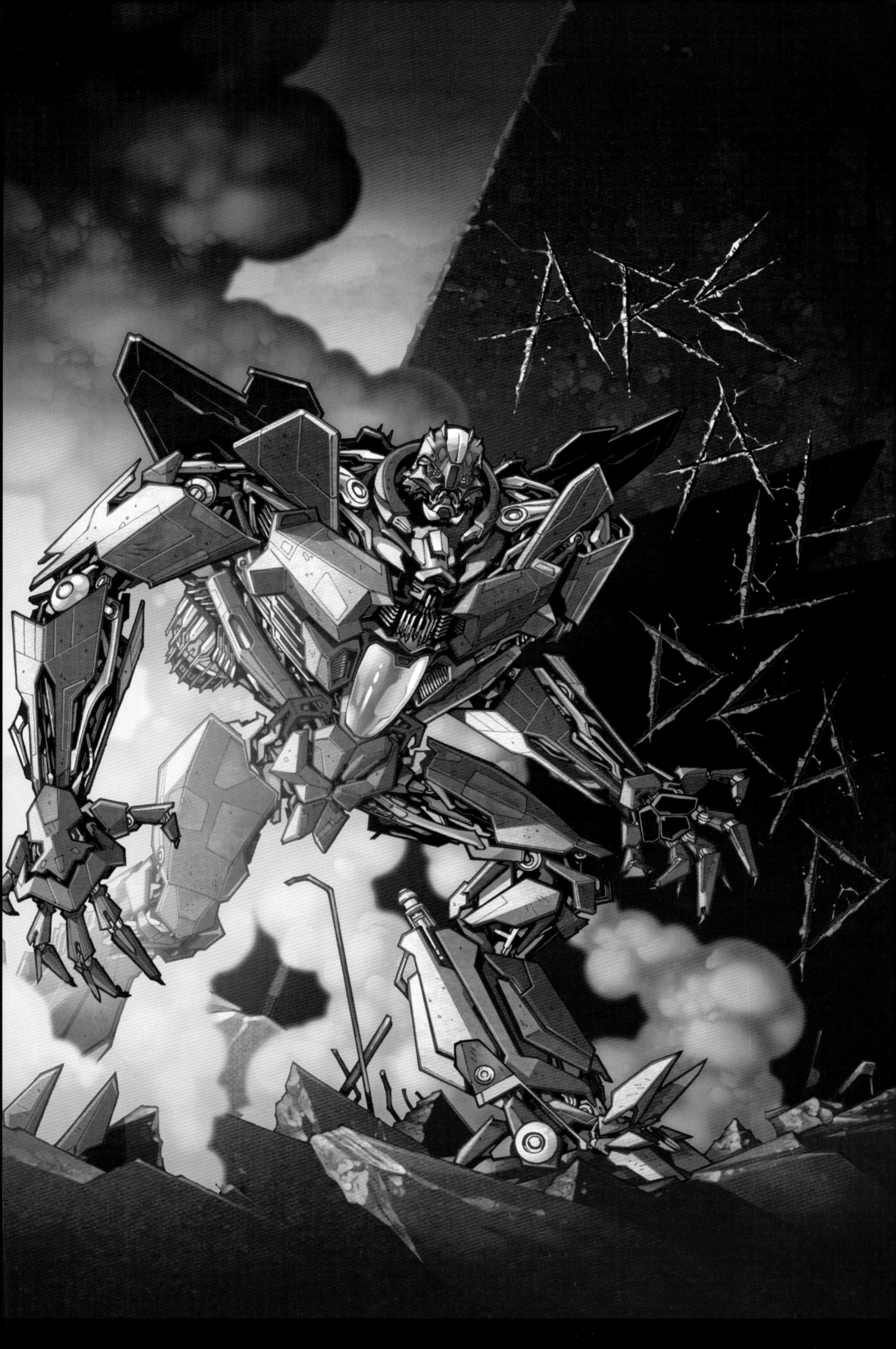
ARE
ALL
DEAD

Art and Colors by Gabriel Rodriguez after Mark Bri

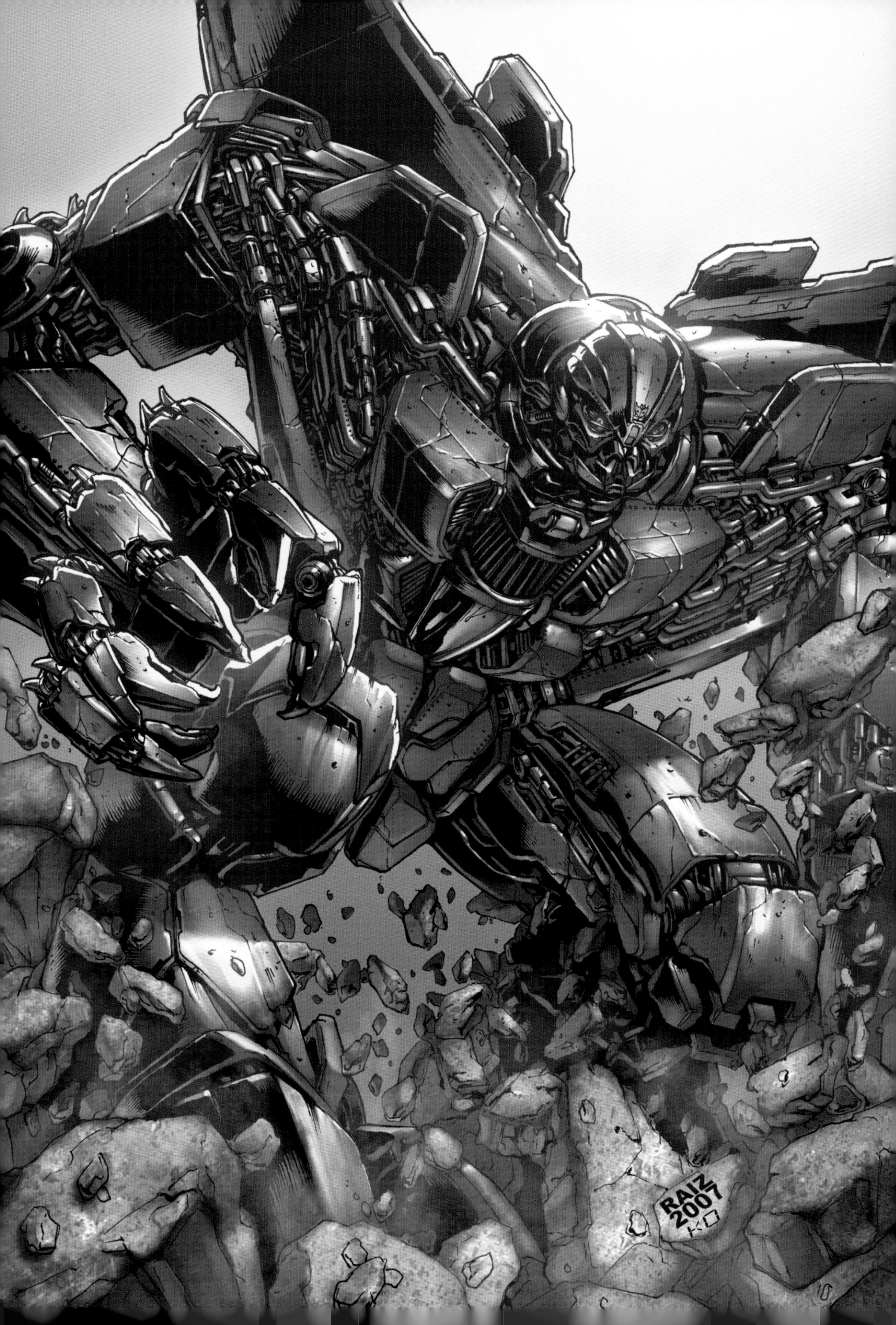
RAIZ
2007

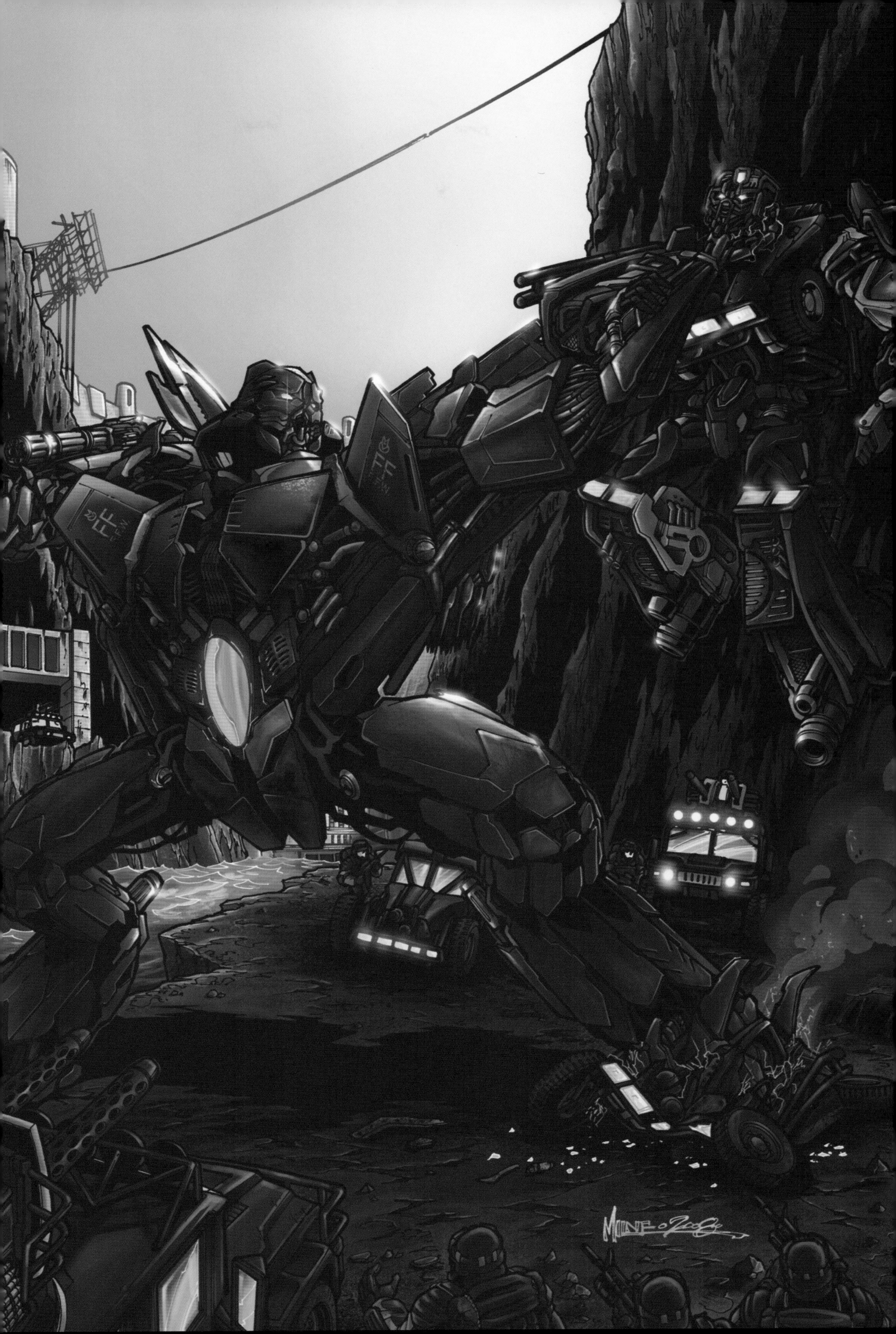
FF
FF

Art and Colors by Alex Mil

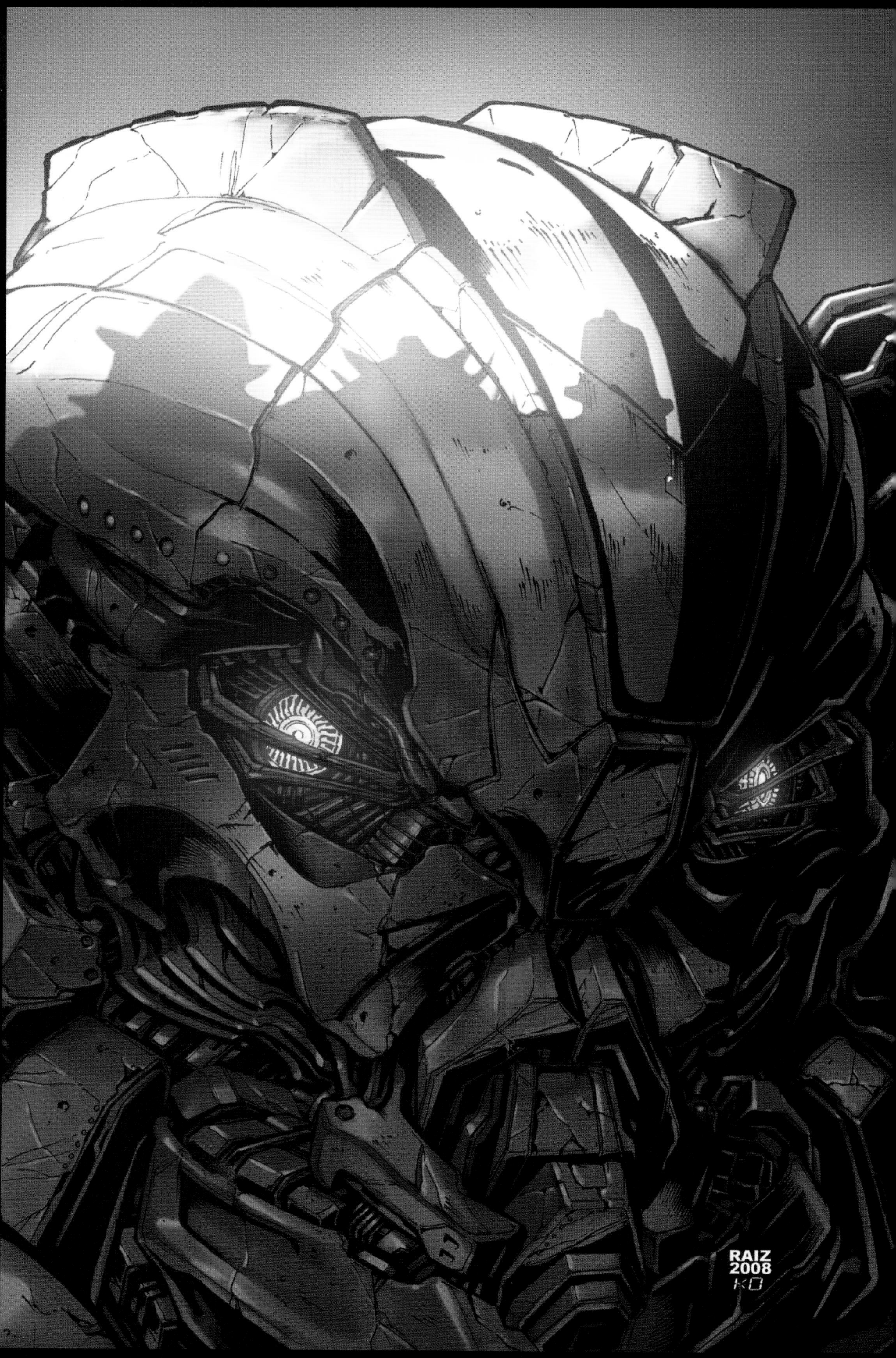
RAIZ
2008
KO

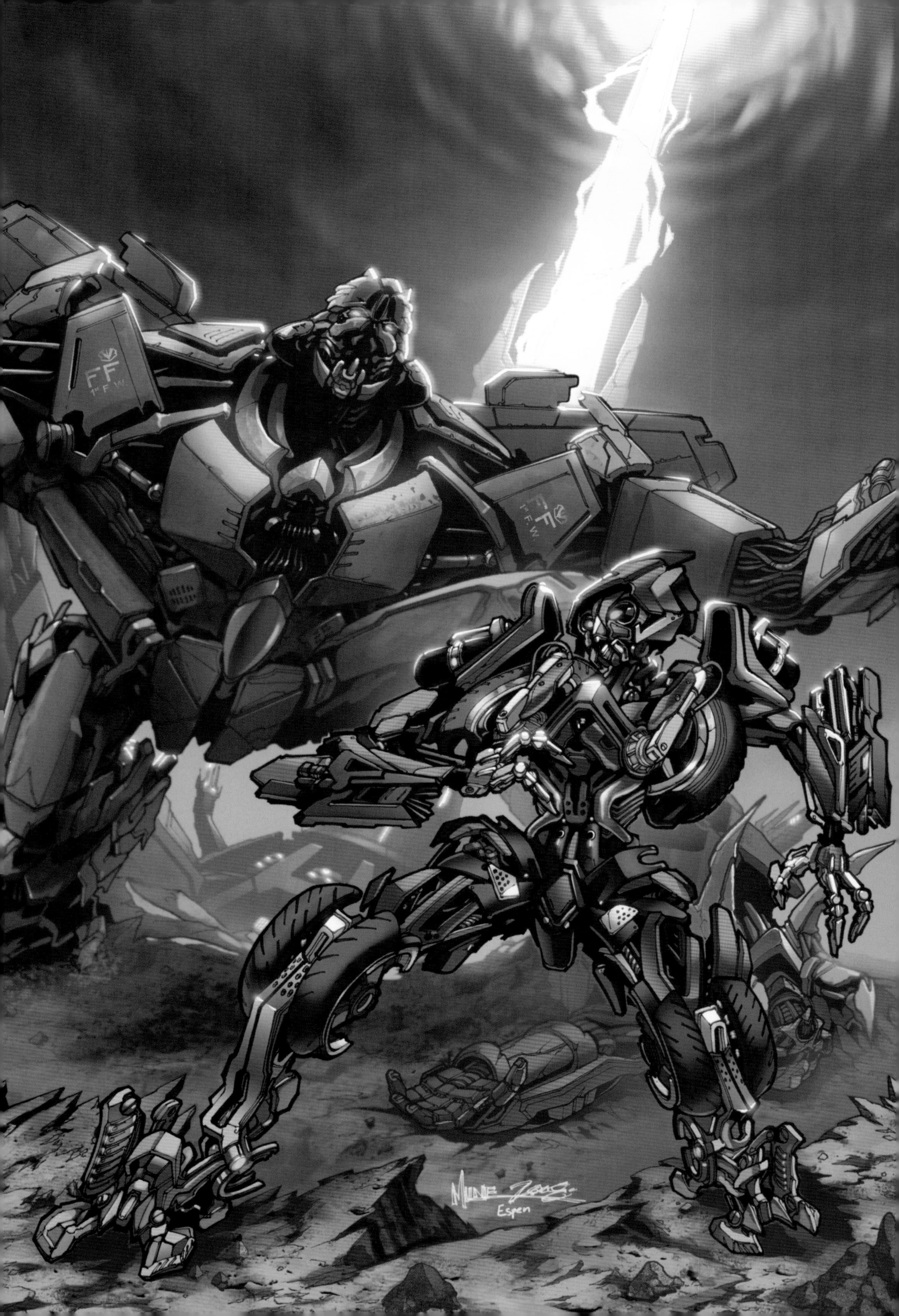
FF
1st F.W.
Espen

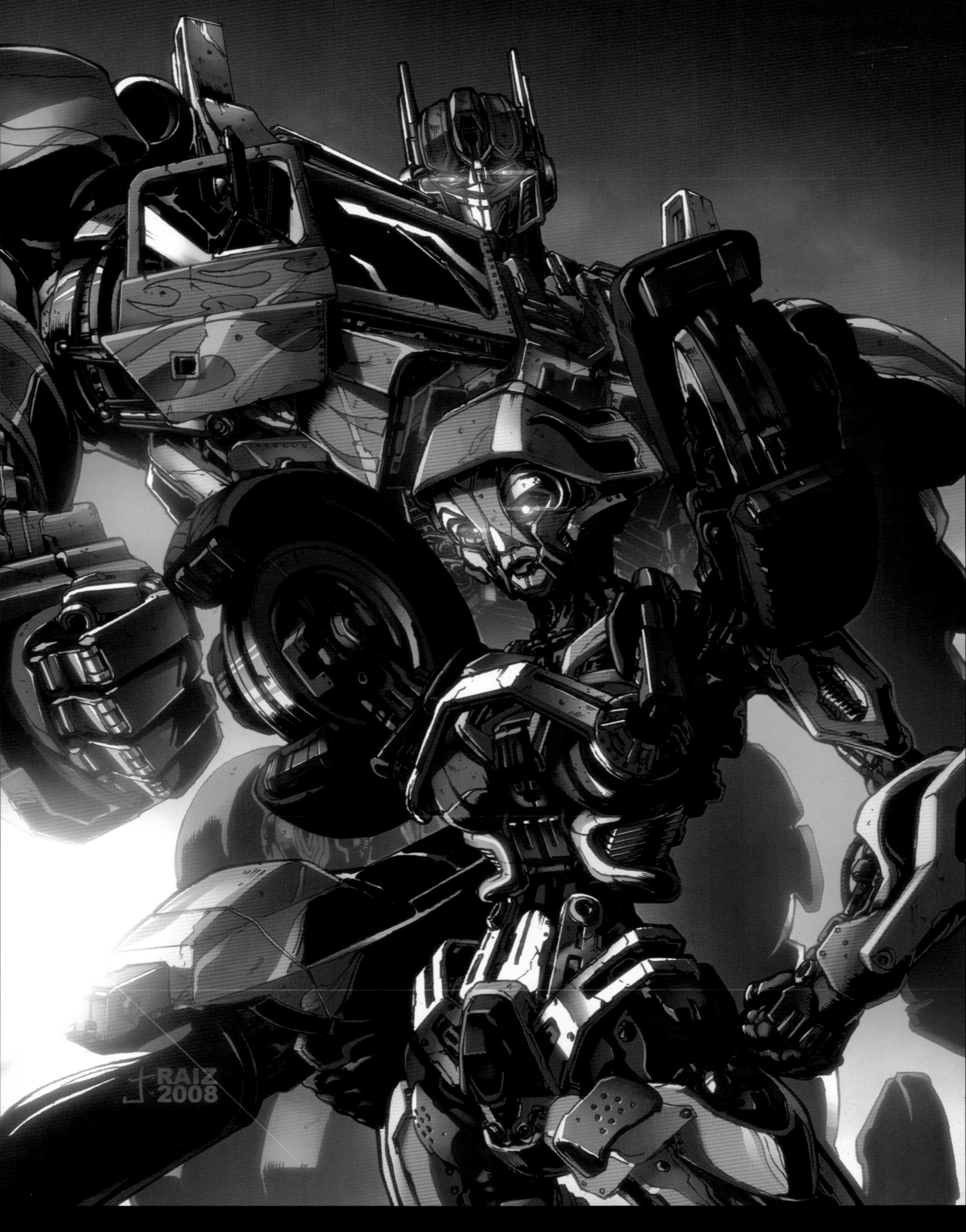
RAIZ
2008

Art by James Raiz • Colors by Josh Burcham

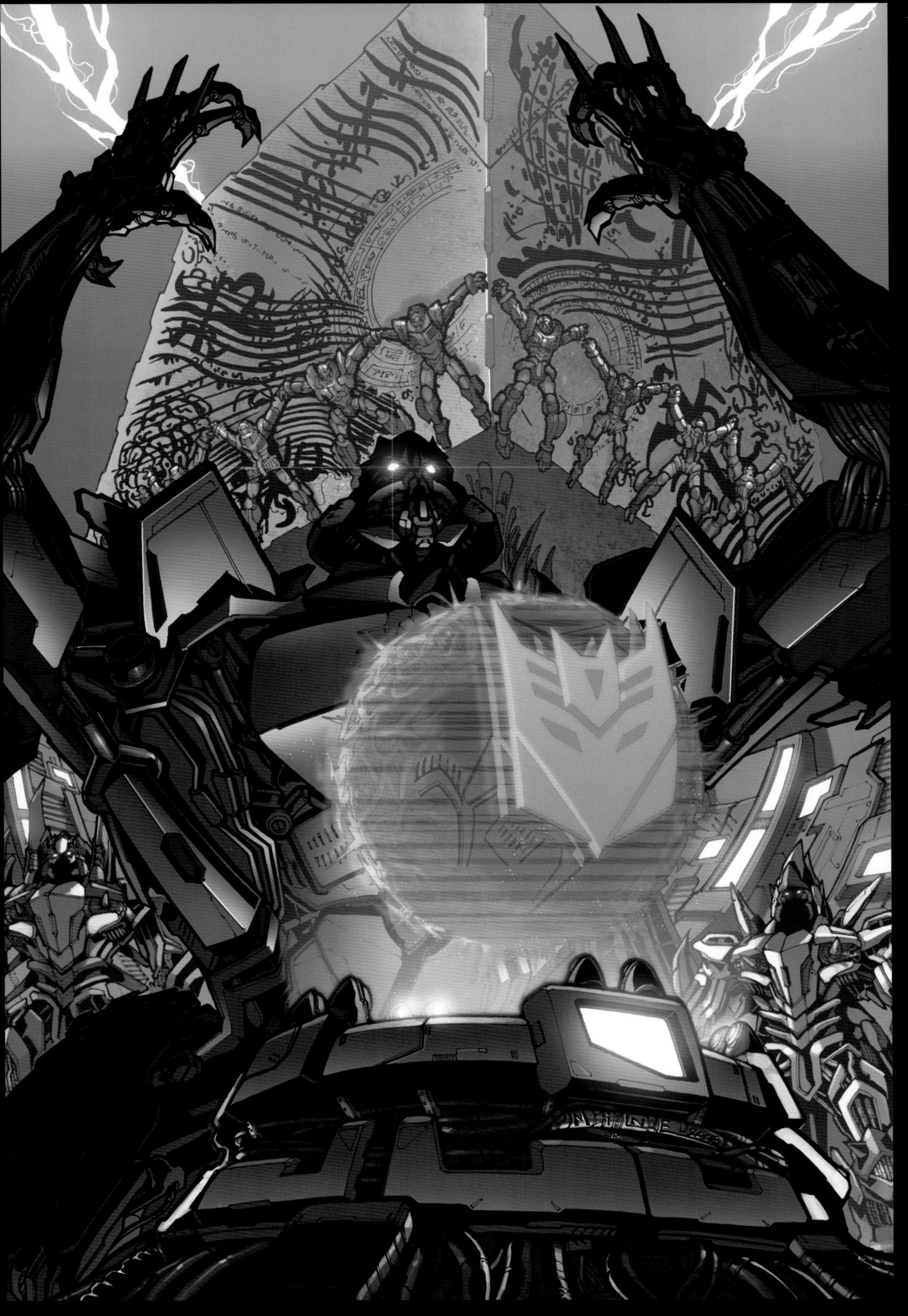

Art by Alex Milne • Colors by Josh Perez

Art by Alex Milne • Colors by Espen Grundetjern

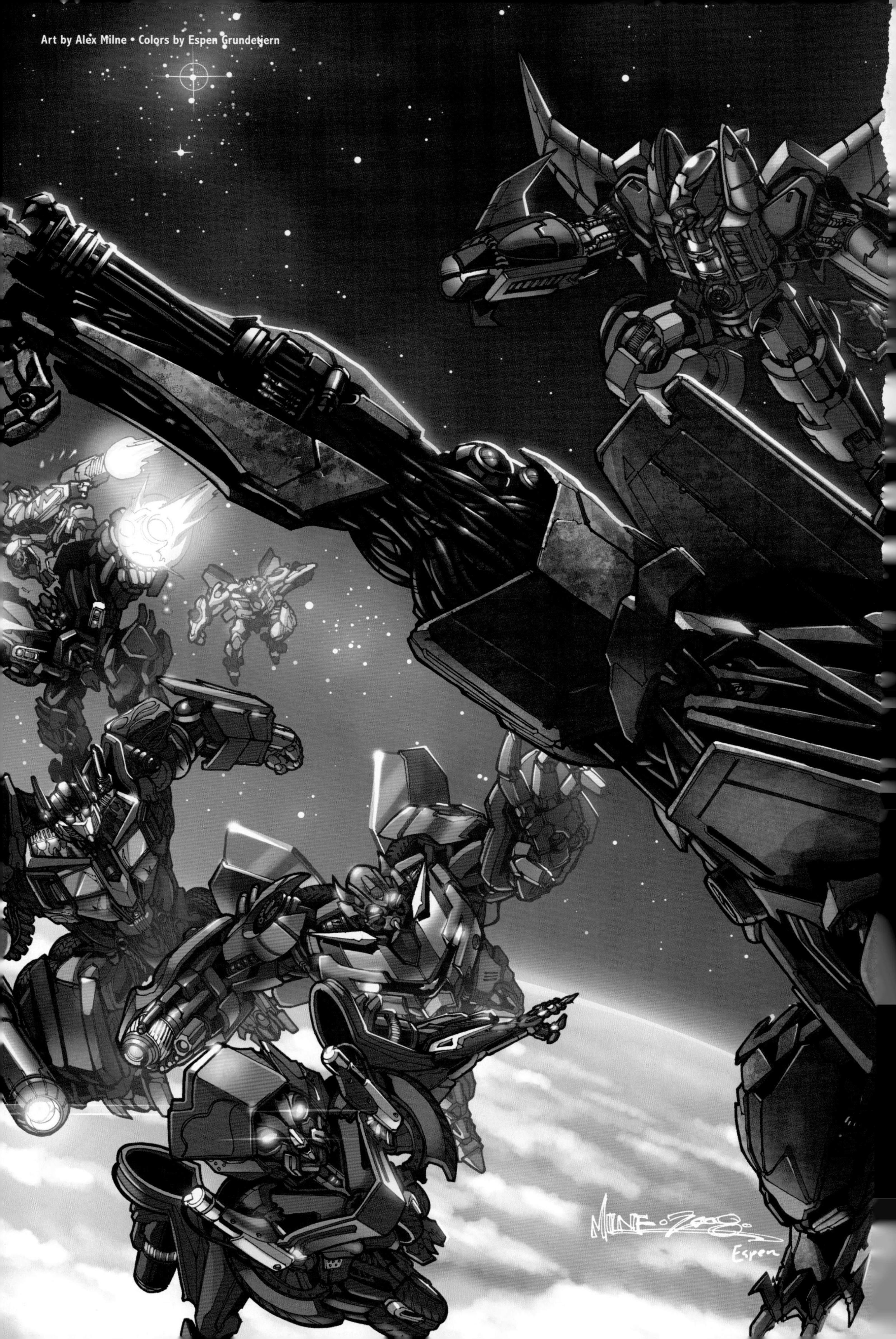
Espen

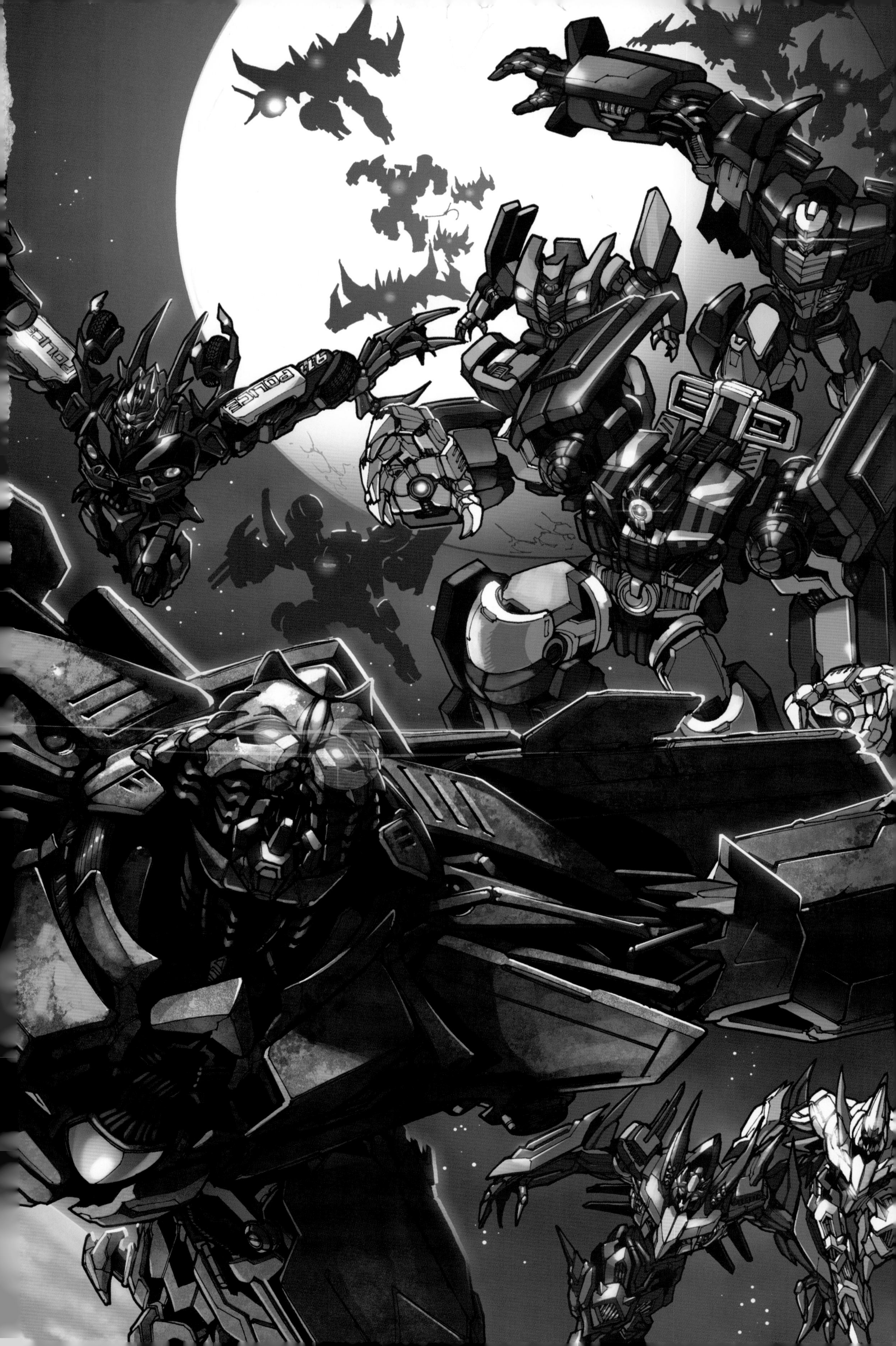
POLICE
POLICE

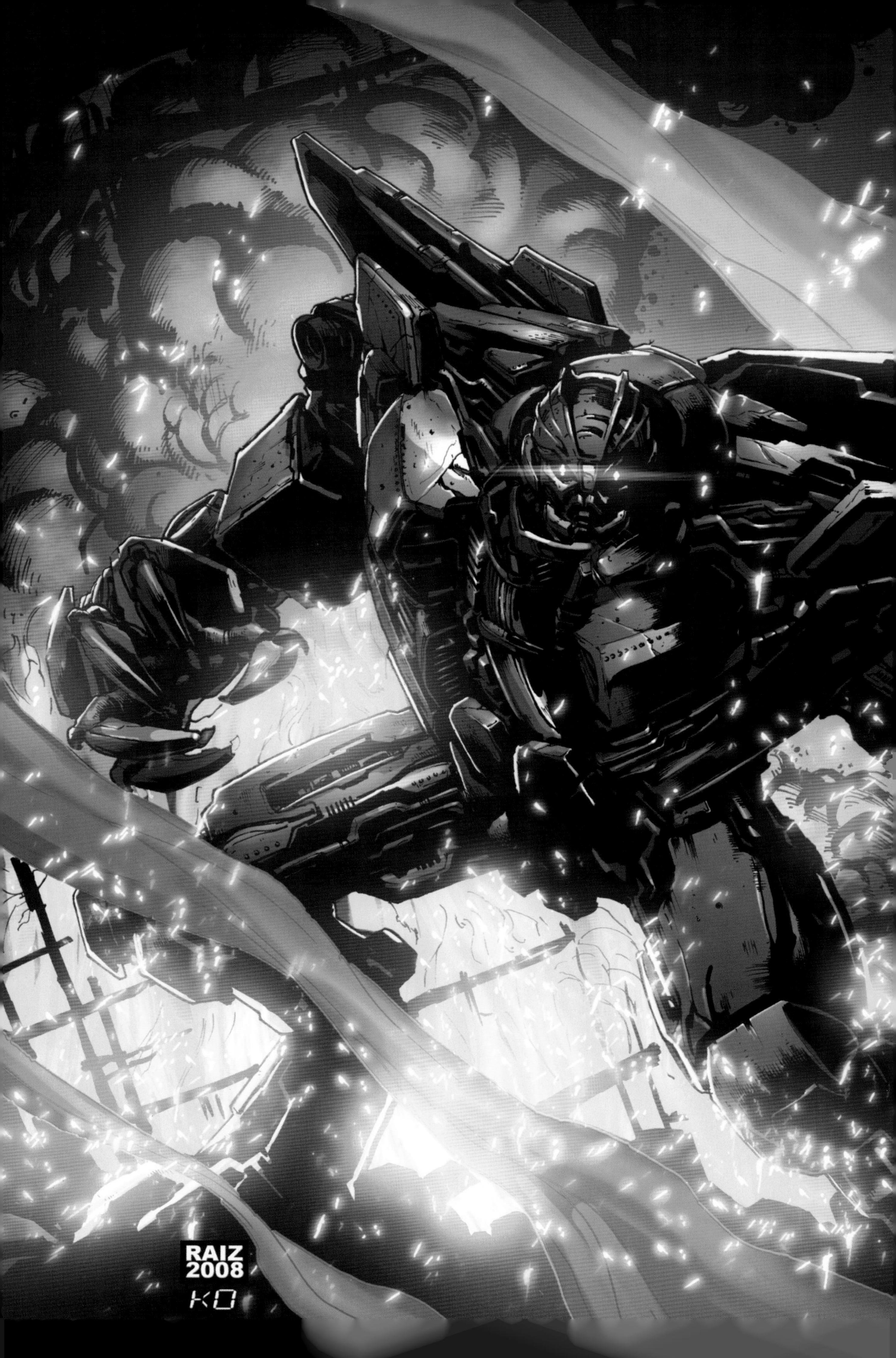
RAIZ
2008
KO